All the Cardinal's Men and a Few Good Nuns

A Hospital Story

by Ted Druhot

Author's Note: This is a work of fiction. All chacters and events portrayed in this novel are fictitious or used fictitiously

The contents of this work, including, but not limited to, the accuracy of events, people, and places depicted; opinions expressed; permission to use previously published materials included; and any advice given or actions advocated are solely the responsibility of the author, who assumes all liability for said work and indemnifies the publisher against any claims stemming from publication of the work.

Dorrance Publishing Co
585 Alpha Drive
Suite 103
Pittsburgh, PA 15238
Visit our website at www.dorrancebookstore.com

ISBN: 978-1-4809-5501-1
eISBN: 978-1-4809-5478-6

This story is dedicated to those who care for others, not for profit but to relieve pain and suffering.

INTRODUCTION

For over two centuries nearly ninety-five percent of hospitals in the United States were owned and operated by religious organizations, i.e. Baptist, Lutheran, Jewish, Presbyterian, Catholic, to name a few. Caring for the sick and injured was considered a ministry. The hospitals operated as charities dependent upon donations and some reimbursement from the patients. A gradual change began in the 1930's as prepaid hospital and physician insurance gained popularity. By the 1950's Insurance plans became a popular source of reimbursement for medical services. By the 1960's most patients had some form of medical coverage. In 1965 Medicare and Medicaid were initiated and the United States Government became the primary payer for health Services. Hospitals became profitable. The trend began to accelerate as the National Affordable Health Care program was initiated 2008.

As hospitals became solvent, they used their capital gains to expand their capacity and services to additional tertiary levels. The quality of care was on a rapid increase. The growing fiscal prominence of hospitals caught the interest of entrepreneurs who either bought the Church hospitals or developed their own proprietary hospitals. The resulting conversion of the healing ministry to an industry caused many religious organizations to reduce their involvement or withdraw from the hospital ministry.

This is a fictitious story about a hospital, religious sponsors, proprietors, and people caught in the confusion of change from hospital ministry to medical industry as it began to peak in the late 1990's.

The story also includes fictitious characters who participate in a society punctuated by a drug culture suggesting the advent of a revised healing ministry.

Part One

Chapter One

The little man in the expensive suit parked the midnight blue Mercedes in the small parking lot at the end of the circle drive marking the entrance to the Cardinal's Residence. The Chancery, Seminary, and Library buildings spread around the wooded rolling campus opposite the Residence all looked deserted. The Seminary was only partially used when classes were in session because of the steady declining enrollment. The rest of the central campus of the Boston Catholic Archdiocese seemed to be standing at ease waiting for orders. It would be at least a week before the busy offices and agencies of the Archdiocese would be in full swing. The new Cardinal had been installed in office last week and the many celebrations marking the event were only completed a few days ago. It was at the Installation Ceremony in the great Cathedral of the Immaculate Conception in downtown Boston that Kevin Hardly, First Leading Knight of the Order of the Knights of the Holy Cross, had been advised by Bishop Hanks, Auxiliary Bishop and Vicar General of the Archdiocese, that Francis Cardinal McMahon requested a meeting at their earliest convenience to discuss serious fiscal matters regarding the Church's healing ministry. Kevin Hardly was proud to be of service to his Church and the Cardinal. He had served the recently deceased Cardinal Riley as the First Knight for several years. Hardly was sworn to be a Knight of the Church—sworn on his mother's grave.

The Beacon Street Campus of the St. James Seminary that also served as the main administrative complex for the large Catholic Archdiocese of Boston was in full bloom with manicured lawns and large oaks casting refreshing shade from the penetrating brightness of the sun. Kevin breathed the cool air as he walked to the entrance of the Cardinal's Residence. Once there he paused to straighten his tie before ringing the ornate bell. The door opened suddenly and Bishop Hanks beckoned him to enter. Hanks was also anxious to make a good impression on his new boss by making sure that Hardly was in place and waiting at the appointed time. He was quick to point that out to Kevin in his first statement.

"Ah, Mr. Hardly, we are right on time. I expect His Eminence will join us shortly. Did you bring the information?"

Kevin nodded as he patted the brief case under his arm. "Yes, Bishop, I have all the data regarding St. Anslem's. I'm sorry that I had not brought this here before but Cardinal Riley, bless his departed soul, never asked for a report. We will certainly miss him. May he rest in peace? Cardinal McMahon seems very nice but very different, don't you think?"

Bishop Hanks was not about to discuss the relative merits or demerits of Cardinals past or present. He simply gave Kevin a bland look and gestured for him to sit on the old English wooden bench next to the conference room door.

Kevin took the hint and tried to change the subject. "Bishop, I hope you don't mind if I take some time today to brief His Eminence on the work of the Knights of the Holy Cross. The Knights were highly regarded by Cardinal Riley."

Bishop Hanks was quick to respond. "Kevin, His Eminence has a complete file on the Knights and their good work. He is well aware that you are the First Leading Knight and I'm sure he will ask you for a briefing in time. Today he is interested in the institutional healing ministry and particularly the fiscal status of St. Anslem's Hospital. I explained to him that you and your bank have served the Archdiocese well. He expects you to give us your suggestions and assistance on reversing the potentially scandalous bankrupt condition of the hospital. Are you prepared for that?"

Hardly began to open his briefcase when the conference room door popped open. A tall well-built man in his mid-fifties dressed in black slacks and short sleeved collared white shirt stood briefly in the doorway and then without saying a word, waved Hanks and Hardly into the room. Cardinal McMahon was in excellent physical condition. His six-foot-two-inch frame was tanned and muscular. Only the gray hair betrayed his age. Otherwise, he could easily be mistaken for an athlete. His appointment as Cardinal Archbishop of Boston was well received by the faithful. McMahon was almost a native son. He was born and raised in Falmouth on Cape Cod by middle-class parents who managed to send him to Harvard where he studied the performing arts. After graduation he discovered his vocation and entered St. James Seminary. Following ordination, he volunteered to be a Chaplain in the Marine Corps. Twenty-five years later he retired as a Brigadier General and head of the Chaplain Services for the entire United States Armed Forces. Following his military retirement, he served as Director of the National Shrine in Washington where he learned the fine art of Church politics. From there he was appointed Bishop of the Diocese of Scranton, PA, where he perfected the art of Church administration. It was a foregone conclusion that he was destined to lead a principal Diocese and be a Cardinal Prince of the Church. He waited in Scranton for the opportunity. Boston was the first opening and McMahon moved up in the ranks.

Graciously he greeted Kevin Hardly and invited him to sit down at the long hand-carved wooden conference table. Bishop Hanks in true servant fashion moved to serve coffee from the tray behind the Cardinal. The Cardinal acknowledged the cup of coffee that Bishop Hanks put before him. After Kevin had been served, the Cardinal motioned for the Bishop to take a chair. Hanks moved promptly and the Cardinal began the conversation. He got right to the point.

"Mr. Hardly, I am aware that The Hardly Security and Trust Bank have served the Archdiocese for many years. You, your parents, and your grandparents have generously contributed to the support of the Church. It is on this basis that I have asked you here to help me as I begin my assignment in this Archdiocese. From all the information that has been provided me so far by Bishop Hanks and the Chancellor it seems that we are in deep trouble."

The thought of admitting to the Cardinal that the Archdiocese had fiscal trouble was very discomforting to Kevin Hardly. He felt that it was his personal responsibility to maintain fiscal stability since all the Archdiocesan funds including St. Anslem's treasury had been entrusted to his bank. In truth, the problem had been the result of the deceased Cardinal Riley. John Cardinal Riley, a Prince of the old Church, who led the Boston Catholic Archdiocese for nearly thirty years. During that time he expanded the teaching, charity, and healing ministries of the Church to serve the entire Diocese especially the poor and disadvantaged. In Robin Hood style, he extracted funds from wealthy parishes and services to create and support ministerial programs that had not a prayer of fiscal success. Deeply religious, he led his flock with great affection for the members of the Mystical Body of Christ. His charity was evidenced by his determination to preserve the teaching and healing ministries in the very poor neighborhoods of his Archdiocese. At the time of his death the financial condition of the Archdiocese of Boston was deplorable. His successor, Francis Cardinal McMahon, had been appointed with specific instructions from the Holy See to solve the fiscal problems of the Archdiocese and avoid the scandal of bankruptcy. Prominent in that regard was the prospect of financial failure of St. Anslem's Hospital.

The Hardly Security and Trust Bank with Kevin Hardly as Chairman of the Board and Chief Executive Officer, was the primary bank for the Archdiocese and the hospital. Acting upon the advice of Bishop Hanks, the Cardinal invited Kevin Hardly to meet with him to plan for the return of fiscal security to the Archdiocese. St. Anslem's Hospital was the most prominent of the Archdiocesan services and as such became the focus of public scrutiny. The hospital sat on the highest ground in Brighton Center overlooking the semi blighted commercial area of taverns, beauty parlors, ethnic food stores, and video stores. An antiquated precinct station of the Boston Police Department sat a block away on the opposite side of the street. Next to the Police Station was the Knights of Columbus Hall directly across from the Masonic Lodge. The Elks Lodge was on the corner. Churches of various denominations dotted the landscape a block west of Cambridge Avenue, the main street of the community. Trolley tracks still ran down the middle of Cambridge although the wires had long been removed. Originally, the trolley served to link Brighton with the North End and South Boston where the population originated. In modern times the famous Boston MTA replaced the trolley although the nearest station was several blocks from the hospital and Brighton Center. Those who ventured out of the original ghettos and migrated west to Brighton built the churches and supported the hospital. Their offspring eventually moved to the affluent suburbs and were replaced in Brighton within the past twenty years by an influx of Vietnamese and Russian Jews. Absentee landlords bought many of the original triple-deckers and converted them into apartment houses for student housing and low income rentals. Hospitals and Churches exempt from taxes were then viewed by the property owners as elements of cost because of their tax-exempt status. The landlords opposed expansion of the institution's services. The hospital fought back, arguing that it was a valuable institution in the provision of health services, now recognized as the leading industry in Boston. Alienation between the hospital and its neighbors was typical of the age. Not only was the Cardinal interested in fiscal security for this Catholic institution, he was interested in restoring it as a friend of the community as well.

Aside from the community attitude, St. Anslem's held fast to its original Church affiliation. It was the only remaining hospital in Boston to be operated under direct Church control. Others made reference to their religious origination within their name but had moved to a corporate mode apart from Church sponsorship. It was difficult for St. Anslem's to make such a departure since the Code of Canon Law within the Catholic Church prohibited alienation of Church property and therefore prevented a separation of the ministries to lay control. Consequently, St. Anslem's faced the difficult task of functioning in a secular medical environment that presented countless ethical challenges, Regardless, the Cardinal Archbishop of the Boston Catholic Archdiocese was resolute that the healing ministry would be conducted by and through St. Anslem's Hospital.

Kevin Hardly thought briefly about how his warnings to Cardinal Riley had been brushed aside with the admonition that "God will provide." Kevin had faith and did believe a miracle would bring the money necessary for the Church to continue its mission. Now a new Cardinal dispelled that myth and asked him to bring forth the miracle from his knowledge of business and finance. Kevin opened his brief case and spread several of St. Anslem's recent operating reports on the long table as he spoke.

"Your Eminence, as you will note from these financial reports of the current year, St. Anslem's is losing money each month at an increasing rate. Revenue is experiencing a slight decline while expenses are rapidly increasing. Mr. O'Shea, my executive vice-president and controller, is very confident that with the right management the hospital could reverse the situation. It is his suggestion, and I agree, that the hospital should have new leadership and governance. We propose that a lay businessman be installed as the chief executive of the hospital and that a Board of Trustees comprised of Catholic businessmen be established."

St. A's, as it was affectionately called by the residents and interns, was a teaching hospital far removed from the geographic center of the medical academic centers on Longwood Avenue. The hospital began in South Boston over a century ago through the initiative of three poor Irish spinsters who walked the streets caring for the poor and bringing them to their home for care. When the Bishop of the time learned of the work of these fine ladies, he arranged to buy them a more appropriate place on the outskirts of the City in the Brighton neighborhood. The ladies fit well into the desire of the Bishop to form a healing ministry. A year later the house was formally dedicated as St. Anslem's Hospital and the three ladies were organized into an order of Nuns known as the Poor Sisters of Charity of Boston following the rule of Elizabeth Ann Seton and the dictate of the Bishop, A century later the small house on the top of the hill grew into a very large tan brick-and-glass institution resembling a spaceship overlooking Brighton from the heights. Its many buildings of modem design dominated the landscape and cast the small neighborhood into comparative blight.

Under the direction of the Sisters, St. Anslem's became the heart of the community. Its compassion and charity were revered by patients, employees, nurses and physicians. Many young ladies were trained as nurses by the Sisters and from that experience several accepted the vows of religious life. The St. Anslem's School of Nursing was a special quality of the hospital and eventually became the foundation for the neighboring Boston College School of Nursing. Additionally, the physicians who sought the opportunity to serve the Brighton community were well trained practitioners who in time created a teaching service affiliated with Tuffs University School of Medicine. A Research Center for Cardiac Disease was established in the 1960's that brought St. Anslem's into the big time with the downtown hospitals. Full-time faculty crowded the halls and cafeteria. Residents pushed into the required conferences. Administrators pondered the plight of sophisticated data processing. New buildings replaced old. Bonds were issued. Fund campaigns were conducted. The Sisters watched, wondered, and worried about their advancing age and declining numbers, but continued to look for ways to serve the poor.

The physicians, on the other hand, continually looked for ways to better serve the patient. They pressed for advanced state of the art technology. Specialists were recruited to administer the new discovered miraculous cures. Special Nursing Units were created within new and remodeled buildings that housed the equipment and gave office to the specialists. Nurses and technicians also became specialized in intensive care of medical, surgical, and other critically ill patients. Intensive care units (ICU's) of several varieties absorbed a significant part of the hospital and provided the greater part of the revenue as well as momentum for the institution's spiraling costs.

Bishop Hank's mouth popped wide open when he heard Kevin's suggestion for lay control of the hospital. He knew that the dear departed, Cardinal Riley, was spinning in his fresh grave. He was about to express his opposition to the idea when he saw Cardinal McMahon give a slight positive nod. Then the Bishop opted for a different tact.

"Kevin, your suggestion is unexpected but well intended I'm sure. It seems that His Eminence will want to give it time as he reviews the total integration of the laity into the various ministries of the Archdiocese. Is money available that we could use in the meantime to shore up the hospital?"

Cardinal McMahon was a man of action. He was not interested in a detailed study of lay ministries. He was anxious to plug the leaks and stop the ship from sinking. He gave Bishop Hanks a quick disapproving glance and then turned his view to Hardly. "Mr. Hardly, what you suggest is that good business management will repair the situation. I believe that to be so. Do you have suggestions on who we could get to volunteer to serve on the hospital's Board?"

Hardly pulled another sheet of paper from his briefcase. It was on the bank's best bond and carried the name of Thomas O'Shea under the banner on the letterhead. O'Shea had told Hardly to expect this question when they discussed the meeting. O'Shea had also prepped Hardly that St. Anslem's Hospital was overdrawn in its operating account and several months delinquent on its mortgage payments. O'Shea further explained to his boss that St. Anslem's Hospital generated over two hundred million dollars in revenue each year. The accelerator effect of that amount of business through Boston Security was delicious.

Hardly handed the paper to the Cardinal and explained, "Your Eminence, in order to support our suggestion, Mr. O'Shea prepared this list for me to give to you if you were interested. It contains three names with their background in addition to my own who are Knights of the Holy Cross and proven loyal to the Church. The four of us could be on the Board with you as the Chairman and Bishop Hanks as Vice Chair. That would give us five people. I have a few other names that have been suggested if you would like to increase the Board."

Cardinal McMahon took the list from Kevin. He reached in his shirt pocket and pulled out his tri-focal glasses that with some embarrassment he pushed on his head. After focusing the glasses and moving the paper in view of the proper lens he began to study the list. Bishop Hanks glared at Hardly. He resented the layman, regardless of his prominence, pushing the laity into a position of control without at least informing the Bishop's office in advance. Bishop Hanks felt he had been betrayed. As the Cardinal scanned the paper, Bishop Hanks decided to pout.

The first name on the list was Kevin Hardly. The Cardinal was already acquainted with some of Kevin's background. The recommended appointees to St. Anslem's Board were wealthy Catholics that had penetrated the Protestant-controlled commerce of the greater Boston community. Catholic wealth had registered its strength over the past thirty years and was demonstrated by the vast amount of Archdiocese real estate in Boston. Certainly, the most prominent on the list was the very wealthy Kevin Hardly. Mr. Hardly, benefited from his grandfather's seafaring interest that evolved into one of the world's largest shipping fleets in the 19th century, coupled with his father's combined import and export business. The Hardly family, of which Kevin was now the patriarch, was repudiated to be one of the wealthiest families in New England. He was very prominent as well in political affairs especially the Democratic Party. President Kennedy had appointed him to a special commission to investigate the trade imbalance and President Carter had appointed Hardly chairman of a special Presidential commission to investigate waste in purchasing practices of the Department of Defense. The resulting Hardly Commission Report had given Mr. Kevin Hardly international acclaim that he flaunted on every occasion. Kevin Hardly was perpetually inebriated with his own exuberance. A power broker well positioned, he was convinced that he would command the wealth of the Church to benefit God with a return better than the Dow. His immortality was assured by his staunch support of the Church which he also reasoned gave him a license to modify specific moral practices in the interest of profit.

Remarkably, Kevin Hardly was not an offspring of Catholic tradition. The Hardly clan, staunch Protestants from Scotland, was one of Boston's first families arriving on the legendary ship, Mary and John, from England in 1632. This gallant ship managed to traverse the tricky currents of Massachusetts Bay and landed on the shore of a hospitable area that the settlers named Dorchester. The Puritan tradition of hard work and thrift carried the family through the next two centuries with compounding wealth and prominence.

However, Kevin Hardly's grandfather in his youth committed an unpardonable sin that seriously offended their Protestant heritage. He fell in love and married an Irish-Catholic lass from South Boston. Kevin's grandfather was disowned by the family so he took his portion of the family's wealth and started the Catholic branch of the Hardly clan. Kevin's grandmother became determined that her descendants would be strong in their Catholic faith and defenders of the Church. The two factions of the Hardly clan from the time of the unforgivable marriage shared only the hate of religious differences. Both sides continued to prosper and eventually became major competitors in business, finance, politics, and religion. Although they shared the same ancestors there was absolutely no love lost between their Protestant and Catholic descendants.

The second name on the list was that of the author of the recommendations, Mr. Thomas O'Shea. Cardinal McMahon was not previously aware of Mr. O'Shea although the O'Shea name was well known throughout the Archdiocese. He was the son of poor Irish immigrants who gained respectability by serving on the Boston Police Department, attending Catholic schools, and joining the Knights of Columbus. Thomas extended the ambition of the O'Shea clan by becoming the first of the family to earn a college degree and then a master's degree in finance both from Boston College. He began working in the mail room of The Hardly Security and Trust Bank when he was a senior in high school. Eventually he became a clerk in the trust department, passed the CPA exam, promoted to Internal Auditor, then to Vice President, and ultimately Treasurer—the first Irish Catholic to be admitted to the executive structure of Boston's leading financial institution. Needless to say, his friendship with Kevin Hardly established during their undergraduate days at Boston College also contributed to his ascension at the bank.

Richard Folley, M.D., was next on the list. In addition to being the Chairman of medicine and medical staff power broker, he was also O'Shea's son-in-law. Cardinal McMahon was very much aware of the great doctor. Dr. Folley had been Cardinal Riley's personal physician. Before his death, Riley had the opportunity to discuss the transition of the Archdiocese with then Bishop McMahon of Scranton, PA. Riley had sworn Folley to secrecy when his unannounced successor, Bishop McMahon, came to Boston for an orientation visit. McMahon met with Folley and discussed Riley's care. McMahon began administering the Archdiocese several months before Riley's death. Folley knew who was in charge and he managed to keep it secret.

The last name on the list was that of Charles Patello. Mr. Patello was an investment banker, broker, and member of the Board of Hardly Security and Trust Bank. Little was known about Mr. Patello in Church circles. Charlie did not court the clergy as Hardly did. Yet, Patello was known as a generous man who made sizable contributions to activities and charities of the Archdiocese. Bishop Hanks knew the name but he didn't know the man. Just the same he was a proven supporter of the Church and friend of Kevin Hardly.

Charles Patello was always a man destined for success. Raised on Boston's North End, he learned the fine art of integrating business ventures to his personal benefit from the knee of his favorite uncle, Big Frank Patello, who eventually became head of the largest juice operation in the Northeast known in the legitimate world as National Associated Investors of New York City. Through Uncle Frank's support, Patello became the owner of a successful investment firm in Boston that specialized in financing small businesses. He also became a prominent partner in Uncle's operations in New England although that part of his business was never publicly disclosed. In addition, and as a result of his careful cultivation of his college association with Hardly and O'Shea, he became a Boardmember of the Hardly Security and Trust. What was not known was that the relationship between Hardly, O'Shea and Patello began at Boston College during exam week of their junior year. The poor O'Shea sought out the very rich Hardly because it was known to O'Shea that both of them were destined to flunk their Ethics course. O'Shea explained to Hardly that he knew Charlie Patello had acquired an advance copy of the examination that Patello was willing to share for negotiated consideration. Hardly bought himself and O'Shea into the proposition and as a consequence each earned a passing grade in Ethics. From that point on Hardly saw to it that O'Shea and Patello were always positioned to support his goals and ambitions.

Cardinal McMahon turned to the second page of Hardly's list of recommended hospital Boardmembers. This page was actually a letter written to Hardly by Patello that thanked him for being recommended to the Cardinal. In addition, the letter contained two names that Charlie asked Kevin to bring to the Cardinal's attention. The first was Mr. Mark Meehan, CEO of Action Waste Management Company. The second name was Mr. Phil Mondi, Manager of Patriot Courier Service. The letter was written in haste by Patello. He was taken off guard when Kevin Hardly informed him that the Cardinal would be contacting him to be a member of the St. Anslem's Board. Patello agreed to serve and then called his uncle, Big Frank Patello, to discuss the prospects of such a venture.

Big Frank Patello was quick to recognize the potential of getting into the hospital treasury. He was uncertain how to develop the opportunity, but advised his nephew to gain as much influence as possible while the matter was researched. Big Frank also suggested that Philip Mondi, owner of Patriot Transport and Courier Service, the front organization for Patello's drug-dealing business in Boston and Mark Meheen, a young graduate from Notre Dame and Harvard Business School who was making it big as the CEO of Action Waste Management, another of Patello's public service skimming ventures, be added to the St. Anslem's Board. Meehan and Mondi were to serve as additional eyes and ears for an opportunity for National Associated Investors.

Charlie Patello had called Hardly and convinced him to add both Meheen and Mondi, good Catholic businessmen, to the list. O'Shea refused to add them to his recommendations, so Patello sent his own list that Hardly included in his report to the Cardinal.

After completing his review of the letters, Cardinal McMahon passed them to Bishop Hanks. While Hanks scanned the names, Cardinal McMahon responded to Hardly, "Mr. Hardly, assuming that these men are all good Catholics and active in their parishes, I will accept them on the St. Anslem's lay Board. Now there are some others that need to be included. Bishop Hanks, of course, will be on the Board but as my personal representative since I will have honorary chairman status. You, Sir, will serve as Chairman of the Board. May I suggest that your Mr. O'Shea be vice-chairman? Perhaps Mr. Patello could be Secretary. In addition to Dr. Folley, Mr. Meehan, and Mr. Mondi, I believe it proper that the religious leader of the Poor Sisters of Charity also serve on the Board. I know you want to remove them from the operation but I believe their one hundred years of sponsoring and administering the hospital mandates their continued participation. Don't you agree?"

Hardly was not prepared for the question. He made a quick glance at Bishop Hanks who chose to look at the ceiling. Hardly was on his own. Carefully, he began a shaky reply. "Of course, Your Eminence, we want the Sisters to continue to serve the patients with the love and kindness that they have given for so long. Having a Sister on the Board will be good for us and good for her, I'm sure."

The Cardinal smiled at the response. Bishop Hanks glanced back at the letters.

Kevin fidgeted. Sweat was very visible on his forehead. Somewhere a clock chimed and the Cardinal looked at his watch.

"Well, gentlemen, unfortunately we have to cut this short. I have a few other details to contend with this afternoon. Can we say that we agree on the hospital's board? Tell me, Bishop, do the recommended members seem to be in good standing with the Church?"

Hanks knew that he had to agree. A Church politician at his best, he managed a political response. "Your Eminence, I have no information that any of the candidates are less than active Catholics. Mr. Hardly has recommended them so they must be acceptable."

Hardly saw an opportunity to make a pitch for the Knights. "Your Eminence, you will be pleased to know that all of the gentlemen are members with advanced rank in the Knights of the Holy Cross. Since Bishop Hanks is also a Knight it seems that the Board is made up completely of the Order. I guess the Sister would be an exception since she doesn't qualify to be a knight and since she isn't married to a Knight she doesn't qualify to be a Lady. We really don't need a Lady—just a Nun. That shouldn't make a difference. We have yet to discuss the hospital's CEO. I believe that a Knight should do that as well. Your Eminence, all the Knights are reviewed by the Chancery before they are installed in the Order. Our files are current and complete. You can be certain that a Knight is a practicing Catholic in good standing."

The Cardinal looked at Kevin as if to say that enough had been said. Bishop Hanks thought too much had been said and was having a difficult time controlling his contempt. Cardinal McMahon recognized the Bishop's body language.

It was time to bring the Bishop into the game and make him own the decision. "Bishop Hanks, I thank you and Mr. Hardly for these recommendations. In time, we will see the benefit of new leadership at the hospital. For the immediate future, we will inform the members of their appointment to the hospital Board. Please send them the appointment letter. But before any of the letters are sent please meet with Sister Elizabeth, I believe that she is the religious leader of the Poor Sisters, and inform her of this reorganization. She will need to explain it to the Sisters at the hospital."

Suddenly Bishop Hanks came back to life. He had just been given the proverbial dirty end of the stick. He needed to counter. "Your Eminence, what about the reserve powers, Canon Law requires us to control the Board."

The Cardinal had gotten out of his chair and was at the door when the Bishop brought up the Reserved Powers. He turned slowly and glared at the Bishop. "Bishop, I expect that you will see to it that the Code of Canon Law is properly applied. Nothing that we have done here this afternoon was intended to absent that. Do you understand? I expect you to represent me and the Church in the conduct of the Board so you are the authority of the Church in by behalf."

"I understand Your Eminence, but the Chief Executive Officer has always been appointed by the Cardinal. Will you appoint the layman as well?"

The Cardinal's response was brief. "Yes, Bishop, I will." Then he walked out of the conference room without saying another word.

Kevin Hardly was uncertain about what had happened. He had been called to the Cardinal's Residence by Bishop Hanks at the Cardinal's request to discuss the financial status of St. Anslem's Hospital. The conversation centered on the appointment of a lay Board that the Cardinal accepted. Now his friend, Bishop Hanks was apparently upset over the outcome. Kevin wanted to know why. "Bishop, I think we had a good meeting although I'm not sure. Are you disturbed with the appointment of the Board?"

The Bishop was pensive. "Kevin, you are a married man of many years. I've not had the pleasure of marital bliss. I opted for Holy Orders because I felt the calling of Christ's Church. My new boss accepted your recommendation and left me with the task of telling the Sisters that they are out and you are in. Kevin, my good man, I may be celibate but I fully understand that hell hath no fury like a woman scorned. You can be sure that His Eminence knows that even better than me. That's why I have the task. The Holy Spirit will need to guide me through this. I wonder if I'm up to it. Pray for me, Kevin."

The Motherhouse of the Poor Sisters of Charity sat on twenty acres of valuable land on the top of the same hill that St. Anslem's Hospital was located. The Sisters' Motherhouse was very controversial in the community because it was rumored at one time that the hospital was going to tear down the ancient buildings and develop the area into low rent condos. The community, to counter such a possibility, attempted to have the Buildings registered as a National Historic Site. The Poor Sisters of Charity supported the proposal but the Archdiocese, as owners, strongly opposed the Historic Registry claiming that is was confiscation of Church property and a violation of the principle of separation of Church and State. In the end the Church lost and the Motherhouse was entered on the list of National Historic Sites in the Boston area.

Prominent in the decision was a letter to the Historical Commission from Sister Elizabeth, religious leader of the Poor Sisters of Charity, stating that the Sisters would be proud to have their building and their history established permanently in the history of Boston and the United States. Other letters and testimony from the lawyers of the Archdiocese had no impact. After the decision had been made, Bishop Hanks gave Sister Elizabeth a non-spiritual talking to that evolved into a shouting match about who was boss. Now the good Bishop was again given the task of talking to the tough little Nun who didn't take any of his guff.

In addition to the subtle conflict of running a hospital to serve the patient and creating a good payer mix, the good Sisters experienced the not so subtle conflict of serving God in a male-dominated Church that saw them as hand maidens to the tasks of the ministries. The many changes within the conduct of the Church that resulted from Vatican II seemed to enhance their frustration as the Sisters adjusted to the modern world and struggled for position in the modern Church. St. Anslem's Hospital, even after the Reform by Vatican II and the subsequent revisions to the Code of Canon Law, remained the property of the Cardinal Archbishop of Boston and his Holy Roman Catholic Church. Sister Elizabeth resented the subordination of her religious Community and herself as the religious leader within the spiritual and temporal affairs of the Church. She had made this very clear to the Bishop.

It seemed reasonable to Bishop Hanks that the Sisters would welcome the opportunity to reduce their governing responsibility and yield to the lay Board. The Sisters were declining in number. They had less than one hundred and twenty-five members and their average age was seventy-five. The only Sister still functioning in a full-time position was the hospital's CEO, Sister Celest. Otherwise, the elderly Sisters volunteered in the hospital's Pastoral Care Department and served as hostesses and greeters in Admitting and Reception.

Kevin Hardly and the Bishop felt they performed a valuable service in those functions. Bolstered by this logic the Bishop arrived at the Convent door two weeks after being dispatched by the Cardinal, somewhat confident that his mission might not be as traumatic as he originally expected

Sister Elizabeth received the Bishop with great courtesy. The obligatory coffee and cookies were in place on the coffee table in the Convent reception room. Sister preferred to meet in the comfortable room with its padded chairs and couch rather than her convent office that only had a desk and a few ancient wooden chairs. The Bishop had been in the conference room before and knew what to expect. The two exchanged pleasantries, sipped coffee, talked about the weather, and munched cookies.

After a half-hour, Sister Elizabeth prompted the purpose of the meeting. "Bishop, I'm sure that you were sent here on a mission. Let's get on with it. What, pray tell, is His Eminence up to?"

The good Bishop was somewhat blindsided by Sister's sudden thrust to the point. He emptied his coffee cup and reached for the last cookie. "Sister, His Eminence asked me to convey to you his deep appreciation for your dedication to the healing ministry. You have carried the burden of caring for the ill for over a hundred years. He wishes to offer you some relief and assistance."

Sister Elizabeth felt the chill. Relief and Assistance meant that the Sisters were being ousted from the hospital and put on the retirement shelf. She had expected it but was determined that the Poor Sisters would not be canned while she was their religious leader. "Bishop, we appreciate the Cardinal's concern. Please inform him that we are able to continue serving the poor, ill, and injured. There is no need to give us relief and assistance when so much is needed in his parishes. We can continue as we are."

Hanks had to get the message delivered. The coffee had fired him up, his temper was hot, and his bladder was about to burst. "Sister, let me be direct. His Eminence has decided that the Sisters will be replaced in the Governance of the hospital by a group of lay Catholic businessmen. You and I will represent the Church. Sister Celest will be replaced by a person with a business background who will be charged with straightening out the hospital. We don't have to discuss this. The Cardinal expects the change to happen immediately."

The response from Sister Elizabeth was just as direct. "Hanks, you can tell the Cardinal that if he wants to kick the Sisters out then he should do it himself rather than send his boy. We aren't going to give anything up and

Sister Celest will stay as the hospital administrator. That's it. Don't let the door hit you on the way out."

She had done it again. The tough Nun had bounced the Bishop out the Convent door with a strong message for his boss. He delivered the message in the same words that Sr. Elizabeth had used. The Cardinal listened to the report and without hesitation picked up the phone and dialed the Convent. He was put through to Sr. Elizabeth who was expecting the call. However, instead of being summoned to the throne for a dose of discipline, the Cardinal announced to Sister that he was coming to see her to discuss the St. Anslem's changes. When they met, the Cardinal carefully explained that the use of businessmen in governance was an attempt to secure the hospital as an instrument for the continuation of the ministry in the future. He allowed that as long as the Sisters were able they could continue to be a part of hospital's governance and administration providing that the Sister appointed to the post was qualified.

Cardinal McMahon left the Convent with Sister Elizabeth's support for the reorganization of the hospital's Board. In return for her support, Cardinal McMahon agreed to allow Sister Celest to continue as the hospital administrator as long as a lay businessman could be employed as an Executive Vice President and chief operating officer. Executive Officers as second in command were common in military organization.

Sister Elizabeth didn't think this change was significant enough to merit an in-depth explanation to Sister Celest. She would let the new Chairman of the Board handle that. The Sister and the Cardinal had a deal.

Sister Celest was a qualified hospital executive. Her twenty years of experience in hospital administration was backed by a master's degree from the Harvard School of Public Health, a master's degree in nursing from Regis College, and a bachelor degree in nursing from Boston College. She had inspired St. Anslem's to fulfill its mission by opening several storefront clinics in Dorchester, Roxbury, and Chelsea that used considerable resources thus contributing to the expanding deficit of the hospital.

The medical staff, particularly the Department of Medicine, complained bitterly about the apparent waste of money when priorities demanded that teaching and research personnel be increased and better compensated. Doctor Richard Folley produced an extensive slide presentation at the meeting of the entire medical staff documenting the many benefits and profits available to the hospital by adding two cardiac catheterization laboratories, expanding the cardiac care intensive care unit, and employing three additional cardiologists and one more cardiac surgeon.

Folley made his presentation again at the first meeting of the newly reconstituted St. Anslem's Board meeting that met in executive session without Sister Celest. The Board voted to close the clinics with Sister Elizabeth casting the only descending ballot. Cardinal McMahon was recorded as absent and excused. They also voted to build the cath. labs, raise faculty salaries, and hire the recommended physicians. In executive session the Board appointed Hardly, O'Shea, and Patello as an executive committee authorized to recruit, select, and employ an executive vice president for St. Anslem's Hospital. The Terrific Trinity consisting of Hardly, O'Shea, and Patello felt they were in substantial control. They were determined that the Catholic nature of the hospital would be conducted always as a credit to the healing ministry of the Cardinal who they fully recognized as the boss of the Archdiocese.

It seemed reasonable to Kevin Hardly that the Executive Committee of St. Anslem's Board of trustees consisting of himself, O'Shea and Patello would seek first of all a Catholic gentleman dedicated to the propagation of the faith to assume the Executive Vice President position at their Hospital. Finding a person with qualification was no problem. Within the Order of the Knights of the Holy Cross that Kevin Hardly commanded as the Leading Knight, there was unquestionably a defender of the faith who would ride forward to the challenge given by the Cardinal. However, that loyal Knight must be a trustworthy person who would attain the goal of fiscal stability and avoid public scandal. The trinity discussed the matter at lunch and concluded that Knight Joseph Bauman was the man for the job. Bauman was a democrat and recently retired as an Inspector in charge of Vice for the Boston Police Department. He had been installed in the Knights by Hardly with expectation that he would be Boston's top cop.

However, the unpredictability of the Boston voters had placed a non-believer in the mayor's office thus putting Bauman's ascension on permanent hold. The portly appearance of Bauman coupled with his red nose and ever present grin seemed appropriate nonetheless for the hospital position. The good officer had graduated from the Boston Police Academy with honors thirty five years ago. Otherwise, his education was supplemented by occasional night classes in law enforcement and continuing education at the school of hard knocks on Boston's South Side. A natural ability to compromise law, politics, and personal financial need into an accommodating personality led him through the ranks of Boston's Finest to a top job in the department.

Since his retirement, he had been waiting for the call to again serve humanity.

Bauman was elated when Hardly informed him of his new charge. The compensation was double his former salary as a Police Inspector. His experience in hospitals was limited to a three-day stay riding the sheets while the "pagan clowns in white at a downtown medical center" pondered his suspected ulcer. By virtue of this experience, he made critical observations from a horizontal perspective that he was certain would complement his proven leadership skills.

Bishop Hanks pushed the appointment letter into the Cardinal's hands as the Cardinal was about to board a plane for Rome. The Cardinal, grateful that the executive committee had found a qualified person, immediately signed the letter. Banks asked Hardly to inform Sister Elizabeth of Bauman's appointment so she could inform Sister Celest. Sister Elizabeth told Hardly that it was his duty to inform Sister Celest since he was Chairman of the Board. Hardly agreed. A few days later he took Bauman by the hand as they entered Sister Celest's office. He gently placed that hand in Sister Celest's hand and explained that this was a joining of their efforts to forward the healing and spiritual mission of St. Anslem's. They sat in Sister's comfortable but sparsely furnished office while Hardly explained that the role of the Sister was to represent compassion and caring while the role of administration was to deal with the hard realities of business.

Sister Celest, as President, Hardly explained, "Would have the assignment of seeing that the Sisters would continue to be present and that the patient was comfortable." Bauman would "run the hospital" and report to Hardly and the Board of directors.

"Of course, Sister will keep her office," Hardly added with emphasis. He then asked Sister Celest if she could "arrange for a suitable office for Mr. Bauman and see that he was well received by the members of the staff." Having given Sister her charge, he released their hands and looked at Sister for a reply.

Sister Celest, for the first time in her many years as a religious, was overcome with uncontrollable anger. The decision of the lay Board to close the clinics was about all she could take. Now she was presented with the crowing blow to her dignity as a nurse, administrator, and a religious. She could hardly speak and managed to avoid shedding tears. Instead she seemed to be pondering the matter as she looked at the ceiling of her office. After a long pause, Sister smiled at Mr. Bauman and slowly turned her head to gaze into Hardly's eyes. The sunlight from the window in back of Sister Celest was directly in Hardly's face causing him to squint deceptively and blink frequently. Celest recognized his sincerity and his innocence cloaked in ignorance. Hardly actually thought he was doing a service to her and the hospital. In true charity, the good Sister thanked them for their good intentions. She carefully avoided accepting or even implying that Hardly and his man of wisdom were reasonable assistance to the hospital. With great tact she managed to escort them out the door realizing that she could not get them out of her life.

When Sister Celest was sure that Hardly and Bauman had cleared the front door, she called Sister Elizabeth and in words uncommon to a religious explained to Elizabeth where she could "park this damn job." Sister Elizabeth, after a long and heated conversation, eventually convinced Sister Celest that punching out Hardly and "his damn fat-faced friend" was not a proper course. Celest wouldn't let go. She pushed Sister Elizabeth to fight the Bauman appointment by organizing a protest march by the Sisters to the Cardinal's Residence.

Sister Elizabeth had her hands full when Sister Celest was mad. Celest had been an outspoken rebel throughout her religious life. Elizabeth thought it time to remind her of that "Celest, a march on the Cardinal's mansion would not work. First of all we don't have that many Sisters that can walk that far. Second, the Cardinal is in Rome and won't be back for a month. I don't think we could stay out in his yard that long. More importantly, the people of Brighton are not sympathetic to your long walks. That trip you made to Selma in the sixties was one thing but marching with the Gay and Lesbian Coalition in the St. Patrick's Day Parade in South Boston was something else. No, my dear, we are not going to protest this thing with one of your favorite walks for freedom!"

Sister Celest went from red hot to white heat when Sr. Elizabeth mentioned the Gay and Lesbian March. Now she began to shout," Elizabeth, damn it, you gave me permission to be in that march. We agreed that it was a case of public discrimination that required our involvement as a matter of social justice. You can't hold that against me."

"Permission might be somewhat of an overstatement, Cecile. You told me you were going to march in the parade. I had no idea that you would be carrying a sign espousing Gay Rights. I'm sure that little escapade is well instilled in the memory of the fine Irish clergy that dominate our Diocese. My suggestion is that we find another way to deal with Mr. Bauman other than public protest. Do you understand?"

Sister Celest remembered the many hate letters that she had received after her participation in the St. Patrick's Day Parade had made the evening television news. She knew that Sr. Elizabeth was right. A public demonstration would possibly make things worse. Together the two agreed to conspire for the eventual crash of Joe Bauman and the restoration of the healing ministries' preferred option of caring for the poor.

Bauman began his career in hospital administration one week after his introduction to Sister Celest. She complied with Mr. Hardly's request and converted a reception room opposite the chapel into an attractive office. Several get acquainted sessions were held in the hospital's cafeteria so the employees could meet and greet the new executive. Bauman was received with courtesy for the most part. An exception was the environmental service department employees who expressed resentment over the hiring of another executive instead of adding service workers. Bauman promised the housekeepers a complete review of the matter and charged the director of human resources to satisfy the "Troops" within the week. *This administration stuff was a breeze for a seasoned street fighter*, he thought. Otherwise, what Bauman didn't understand about the hospital was covered up by his friend and ally Dr. Folley who became the power behind the throne. Gradually, Folley's power became evident and an informal structure formed around the Chairman of Medicine. Bauman walked the halls as he once walked the streets as a policeman greeting the public, shaking hands, and admonishing staff for improper dress or conduct.

Sister Celest fully anticipated that Dr. Folley would be in control. She knew that she could not stop his power play. Alternatively, she set her sights on Mr. Bauman with the objective in mind to "stick it in the ear of a male chauvinist Cardinal and his male-dominated Church." One good shot was all she wanted and then it was off to the Sisters' Retirement House of Prayer on Cape Cod. Sister Elizabeth had already given her permission. The Sisters at the hospital had agreed as well.

The Reception Room opposite the Chapel entrance that served as Bauman's office was originally a store room and actually part of the Sisters Convent. It was windowless and very small. Heating pipes running along the ceiling made a constant hissing sound. They also made the room unbearably hot unless the door was constantly left open.

The Convent was contained within the hospital on the east wing of the first floor adjacent to the main entrance lobby. Most of the Sisters had opted to live in small homes in the community or had moved to the spacious Motherhouse on the hill. Consequently, the hospital's convent was nearly empty except for a few Sisters who had chosen to remain and take care of the Sisters admitted to the infirmary.

Bauman's office/reception room was always seen as a part of the Chapel. On that same floor was the Sisters' infirmary where the Order's sick Sisters were treated. When a Sister passed away her funeral was held in the east wing Chapel. The Reception room that Bauman occupied had always had been used for the wake. A special team of Sisters from the Motherhouse was permanently assigned to make arrangements and conduct the Sisters' funerals. All of the protocols and procedures had been preapproved by the Master of Ceremonies for the Cardinal who frequently attended the wake and funeral Mass. No person or power on earth could change a pre-approved protocol or procedure.

So it was on a Wednesday afternoon two weeks after Bauman began his distinguished career that he was in his office having a chat with a very attractive young lady who had applied to be the hospital's food and nutrition director. Suddenly three Sisters pushed a casket containing a deceased member of the Order through the open door. They positioned the casket on the wall opposite Bauman's desk, placed two kneelers beside the casket and left, followed in short order by the attractive young lady who decided to withdraw her application.

Bauman knew that this was nothing Folley could handle so he placed a call to Hardly. Hardly remembered that he had charged Sr. Celest with finding an office for Bauman. A call to Sister Celest revealed that the Convent Reception Room was the only available space since the new cardiologists and surgeons had occupied the only remaining offices in the hospital. Hardly next placed a call to Bishop Hanks to see about changing the reception room. Bishop Hanks was sympathetic but explained that he had no control over these kinds of things. The Cardinal's Master of Ceremonies was the sole source of authority, other than the Cardinal himself, in these matters. Furthermore,

Bishop Hanks explained that the Master of Ceremonies was "an independent little cuss" that only listened to the Cardinal. Banks ended the conversation by informing Hardly that "The Cardinal was out of the country for at least another month and the matter will have to wait his return."

While waiting for the Cardinal's return three more Sisters gained their eternal reward. Bauman became a basket case not knowing when the deceased would appear before him. He began having nightmares. His lack of sleep caused him to doze while sitting in the lobby waiting for the funerals to begin. One afternoon the hospital's director of maintenance told him about a plan that Sister Celest had designed several years ago to remodel the spacious chapel and build a new reception room in the Chapel proper. Bauman was overjoyed. At his request the maintenance director called the hospital's architect who still had the remodeling plans on file. Without even looking at the plans or asking the price Bauman authorized the job. Three days later Bauman put a chain and padlock on the Chapel door in order to prepare it for remodeling. That night a construction crew cut a hole in the Lobby wall for the new entrance to the Chapel. However, the new entrance was boarded up waiting for door frames and the old entrance was still locked when the Sisters assembled for Mass the next morning.

A lock on the Chapel door was beyond Sister Celest's most extreme expectations of Bauman's stupidity. At most, she had expected him to lock the Sisters out of his office and that way force a confrontation between the Cardinal's fair haired boys and his gofer master of ceremonies. She had the early cooperation of the Sisters and benefited from the loyalty of her maintenance director in setting him up. But locking the Chapel was an invasion of the Sanctuary unequaled since the Turks' heathen acts caused the Crusades.

The war started within minutes after Father Curley, Pastor of St. Gabriel's Parish across the street from St. Anslem's, arrived to say the seven o'clock Mass for the Sisters and the staunch Catholic members of the hospital's night shift. They were gathered in the corridor confused and bewildered when Curley came on the scene. Sister Celest was among the assembled faithful. Carefully, she explained to the angry Father Curley that she was omitted from the decision loop but with his support she would ask the maintenance man to pry open the Chapel door. Curley gave her the necessary support and after Mass placed a heated angry call to the Cardinal's secretary reporting that the lay administration of St. Anslem's, for whatever reason, had decided to deny the Sacraments to the Sisters, staff and patients of the largest and most prominent Catholic hospital in the archdiocese. While the secretary was frantically attempting to locate the Cardinal, Father Curley was contacting every cleric in God's kingdom to report that St. Anslem's Hospital under lay control was no longer Catholic.

It took five hours for the Cardinal to receive the message to call his office. He delayed responding until there was a break in the Council of Bishops meeting that he was attending in Dallas. By that time his entire flock of ordained men were ranting at the Chancery. There was no room for mediation—only reparation. The Cardinal took the first flight back to Boston and within an hour after landing at Logan airport had convened an executive session of St. Anslem's Board of Trustees, of which he was the honorary chairman, and keeper of the reserved powers. The most significant reserved power was the appointment of the hospital's executive and the Cardinal felt he also had the power of disappointment. Sr. Elizabeth reminded him that the hospital's chief executive was Sr. Celest and that he had permitted the terrific trinity to select the executive vice president His Eminence caught the drift and knew that he had been had. With careful terms he requested that Sr. Celest be remembered for her many years of dedicated service to St. Anslem's and to the healing ministry. Sister Elizabeth mentioned that Sr. Celest was looking forward to her retirement at the Sisters House of Prayer.

The Cardinal then emphatically suggested to Mr. Hardly that Mr. Bauman be provided a warm handshake as he left the hospital with the reminder that he would always be remembered in the prayers of the faithful. As a concluding point His Eminence decreed that St. Anslem's Hospital would be administered by an experienced, professional Catholic healthcare Executive of the kind that he had heard about at the Council of Bishops meeting in a session conducted by the Catholic Health Association.

The Cardinal realized that the good Nuns were determined to make his life miserable. He also recognized that the terrific trinity was his Achilles heel but he desperately needed their financial strength. The solution, he reasoned, would be to insert a buffer between them and his office that they could both love and hate. This would require an innocent well-intentioned, good-natured, loving, strong, intelligent, educated person who understood Church politics and teaching. If such a person could be found and if such a person, once found, became corrupted by faction on or off the Board, then His Eminence would simply apply his reserved powers and look for another boy. In his mind, he stressed the word "boy." He calculated that the new boy would have to be from a distant land and therefore, viewed as an expert divorced of hospital politics.

Hardly left the Chancery and went to Bauman's office to give him his warm handshake. He didn't intend to mention the prayers of the faithful. When he arrived, a wake was in process. In response to Kevin's inquiry the Sister in attendance suggested that "Himself" usually drank lunch at the Emerald Tap. As he entered the comforting surroundings of the Emerald, Kevin spotted the former Police Inspector of Vice turned Hospital Executive Vice President seated at the long ornate bar in the dark recesses of the large room taking another taste. Kevin slid onto the next barstool and ordered Irish double and neat.

Bauman felt the presence of the Leading Knight but offered no sign of recognition. He simply gazed into his small glass of whiskey that reflected a distorted image of Hardly.

Without a greeting, Hardly began to speak to him. "Joseph, my friend, when you were but a mere lad at St. Patrick's, don't you remember the good Sisters telling you that you never were to fuck with the Chapel?"

Bauman didn't look up. He took a short sip of his whiskey before he replied, "I do, Kevin. I do indeed. But I don't think they'd be saying it in just that way which is why I forgot, I suppose. Are you to tell me that I'm to pick up my time?"

Hardly gave an affirmative nod into the mirror visible to Bauman. "That I am, Joseph, and as one good Knight to another, hear me when I say that it will be a short time until we find a more suitable place for a man with your talent."

Bauman was a man of faith who trusted friendship. He was confident that Kevin would soon have him reinstated in a prominent position. Kevin was not as confident but was loyal to his brother Knight. He would try. With a pat on the back he wished Joseph the best of the day and signaled the bartender to put his drink on Joe's tab. Then he slipped off the barstool and left for his plush corporate office with the satisfaction of knowing that he had completed another task for his Church.

Chapter Two

The entire Bauman affair extended over six months. There were an additional few months of healing while the Cardinal pondered a way to recruit a new hospital chief executive officer. In the interim Sister Celest remained in office under the careful eye of Sister Elizabeth. The Terrific Trinity of Hardly, O'Shea, and Patello, walked in the shadows using Doctor Folley as their agent. Folley became an adept medical politician using his power base wisely to build an empire that would prevail regardless of the chief executive be he or she religious or lay. All of the employed faculty physicians regardless of department or specialty were in some manner beholding to Dr. Folley's informal control of the budget. The community-based private practice physicians used Folley to reserve special rooms and surgery times and Folley in turn used the private practitioners to expand his political base. Through his connection with Patello, he became a regular at political dinners, cocktail parties, and even wedding receptions. He eventually became the personal and confidential physician to leading State representatives and senators whose medical record contents bought Folley their unlisted telephone numbers and a first name relationship. There wasn't a door that Doctor Folley couldn't open or an arm he couldn't twist. He reached the summit when Francis Cardinal McMahon asked Doctor Richard Folley to advise him about his chronic hypertension, weight gain, and nutrition problems.

Cardinal McMahon recognized the need to expedite the selection of the hospital's chief executive officer. He sought the counsel of the Washington office of the Council of Bishops who in turn sought counsel from the Catholic

Health Association who recommended their immediate past chairman of the Board, Mr. Joseph Durant. Joseph Durant was well known in Catholic Health Care. He was a professional administrator who for some unknown reason had only been employed in Catholic hospitals. His career extended over four decades and three different positions in three large mid-western cities. The Archbishop Cardinal of Chicago knew Durant well as an Executive at the Daughters of Charity Hospital. He advised Cardinal McMahon that Mr. Durant would be a fine Catholic to administer St. Anslem's Hospital. Acting on the good advice, Cardinal McMahon directed Bishop Hanks to retain an executive search firm to contact Mr. Durant and recruit his services. The Cardinal also appointed Bishop Hanks to chair a search committee that would recommend Mr. Durant to him as the new hospital CEO. Other members of the search committee included Sister Elizabeth, Dr. Richard Folley and Mr. Thomas O'Shea.

The search firm selected by Bishop Hanks was deliriously happy to charge a big fee to recruit a single candidate pre-selected by the client. Durant had no idea that he had been pre-selected. The head hunters promoted the job with the idea that many qualified applicants were fighting for the position. Durant put on a pretty face, shined his shoes, and went for it. His background check was squeaky clean. His interviews with the search committee were flawless except for the time spent with Mr. O'Shea. O'Shea regarded Durant as a carpet bagger. He resented Durant's statement that mission was the first consideration over margin. He later informed Hardly that Durant was a male nun and therefore no different than Sr. Celest. At the second and final meeting of the search committee O'Shea protested Durant's selection and refused to allow a unanimous recommendation to the Cardinal. Folley provided some consolation to O'Shea by reminding him that Dr. Folley was the real authority at Sr. Anslem's and would "control the clod from the mid-west."

The search firm represented the Archdiocese and the trustees in negotiating the employment agreement with Durant. O'Shea contemptuously noted that the $250,000 salary was more than twice the amount paid to Bauman. The termination clause provided eighteen months' continuation of salary and benefits, except for cause, which most certainly would include putting a lock on the chapel door. All expenses of moving the Durant family from their comfortable three-bedroom ranch in Waukegan to a four-bedroom colonial in Hingham was paid by St. Anslem's. Again, O'Shea protested by pointing out that selection of a local candidate would have avoided this outrageous expense. The Cardinal confided to Bishop Hanks that the salary and benefits were far more than he had expected. He wondered if the amount would be the cause of scandal if the public media exposed it in view of the hospital's fiscal plight. Bishop Hanks offered no consolation. The employment agreement was signed and Joseph Durant became the chief executive officer of St. Anslem's Hospital.

Kevin Hardly was on a world tour as a guest of the State Department during the month that the St. Anslem's search committee was doing its work. Consequently, Joseph Durant was installed as the CEO by O'Shea in his capacity as vice-chairman. The fanfare was reserved for Durant and more directed to Sr. Celest's retirement. The *Boston Globe*, in an editorial, took delight in bashing the Cardinal and the Catholic Church as a male-dominated bastion while praising Sr. Celest as a heroine of modern time. Durant was completely overlooked by the media as was typical of St. Anslem's in a City overcrowded with major and numerous world famous medical centers. It was five weeks later before Hardly met Durant. That first meeting left Durant wondering if he had made a fatal mistake.

Joe Durant knelt in a slouched way as he reflected on his first months as St. Anslem's CEO. Somehow in the back of his mind he heard the words "Lord Jesus Christ, you said to your apostles; I leave you peace, my peace I give you. Look not on our sins but on the faith of your Church, and grant us the peace and unity of your kingdom, where you live for ever and ever." The familiar words spoken by the Priest and the responding "Amen" by the assembled worshipers brought Durant back to paying attention to the Mass. He heard the Priest say, "The peace of the Lord be with you always." He responded with the congregation, "And also with you."

Durant was mentally engrossed in the circumstances that had pressurized the hospital's Board as he and his wife sat in a side aisle pew at St. Francis by the Sea Catholic Church in Hingham, a quiet suburban New England town where he settled after being recruited to St. Anslem's from Illinois. The small Church was less than half occupied on this warm Sunday morning as the elderly Priest noticeably struggled through the liturgy. The most solemn part of the Mass brought Joseph Durant out of his contemplations of temporal matters to the realization that, according to the teachings of the Church, the Body and Blood of Jesus Christ was about to become present, transformed from bread and wine. Joseph was baptized a Catholic a few weeks after his birth and had been educated in the teachings of the Church by the Sisters of the Holy Cross through elementary and high school followed by a Jesuit undergraduate and graduate education at Xavier University; He was comfortable in his religion and practiced it faithfully but not scrupulously. The Jesuits had convinced him that faith and morality were matters of personal moral convictions supported by the teachings of the Church. He concluded early in his Jesuit years that religious regimentation and dictate was for the benefit of the uneducated who required procedure to establish belief. Attention to his personal spiritual wellbeing was conducted without intellectual conflict as he ignored the confusion of the faithful brought about by modifications in Church practice. He sometimes pondered the inconsistency of the Church Hierarchy in moral dictates from diocese to diocese but as a Catholic hospital administrator of nearly thirty five years he had come to realize that the Church was, above all else, human. Those human qualities were the focus of the healing ministry.

Durant had been deep in thought about the many problems of St. Anslem's Hospital when the words of the Eucharist recalled his spiritual attention. In less than forty-eight hours the Board of Trustees was scheduled to meet and hear, among other things, a report by the finance committee that St. Anslem's operating result for the past month was in severe deficit, as it had been for the past ten months. Gallant attempts by Rod Weaver, St. A's Vice President for Finance, to explain the deficit as a consequence of market reorganization had failed to convince, much less satisfy, the Finance Committee consisting of Thomas O'Shea and Dr. Folley. Their reaction was to shoot the messenger. After the last finance committee meeting O'Shea told Durant that Weaver had to go. Durant attempted to explain the injustice of that to Mr. O'Shea only to be advised that if Weaver stayed, the CEO would go. He then appealed to the O'Shea's sympathy pointing out that Weaver was forty-seven years old with two children in grammar school, one in high school and one in her second year at Boston College. To relocate at this time in his life would be extremely traumatic for his family. O'Shea was unmoved.

As the Priest gave the final blessing Joe was again pondering St. Anslem's. He had learned about the hospital's corporate history from Sister Celest during the two months that she stayed on after his appointment to help with the transition. She respected Joseph as a professional and he appreciated her dedication to the religious community and the ministry. In contrast to Bauman, Sister recognized that Durant was a sincere professional administrator who understood charity and compassion for the poor and under served as primary to the healing ministry. Durant realized that Sister Celest had attempted to equate modem technical medical expertise with the hospital's mission. He respected her for the attempt and became determined to expand the mission as she had done. When time came for Sister to formally retire she did so with the assurance that Joe Durant would direct St. Anslem's as the Poor Sisters of Charity had intended. Sister Celest and Joe Durant were good friends.

The hospital continued to experience hard times in spite of the pseudo expertise of the reconstituted Board of Trustees. Within the halls and units of the hospital there was continuous bickering over the demands by administrators to reduce spending. Folley acted as the consummate politician in soothing the ruffled feathers of the many prima donnas who paraded into his office seeking special exemption and favors at the expense of their colleagues. Doctor Ronald Anderson, M.D., Ph.D., Director of St. Anslem's Hospital's Chemical Addiction Program, referred to as SACAP, was a specialist of a different breed. He was a primary care physician boarded in Internal Medicine who had great compassion for the addicted and chronically ill. Anderson was a passionate Catholic who had deep appreciation and loyalty to the Church, the Cardinal, and the Sisters. The slightly built somewhat lanky man remained focused on his patients and tried to be oblivious to the changing patterns of health delivery. However, the fiscal pressures put upon him by administration frequently spirited his temper causing an outburst of profanity directed at the source of agitation. He began his day at 7 A.M. with the usual review of the administrative junk scattered on his cluttered desk. Pressure to reduce staffing in the face of increasing census in the program seemed ludicrous. Cutbacks in reimbursement by the State Department of Public Aid had almost destroyed the program last year and now the encroachment of managed care practices by the insurance companies were threatening to finish the job. Administration had put increasing pressure on his boss, Doctor Richard Folley, Chairman of St. Anslem's Department of Medicine to either dump the program or find a way to make it profitable. To make matters worse the Budget Director was scheduled to meet with him to question him about over spending in last month's supply expenses.

Anderson had built the substance abuse program from the ground up in times when money was plentiful thanks to the generosity of cost based reimbursement structured in the original Medicare and Medicaid programs. In his mind so-called healthcare reform was detrimental to the Nation's health. He was about to launch into one of his early morning tirades about the Fascist plot to destroy the practice of good medicine when his secretary mercifully informed him that his lead patient counselor, Bob Markley, was holding on line one. Anderson immediately changed his mood as he answered the phone. "Bob—what's happening? Don't ask for more because administration won't give us anything but grief. What's on your mind?"

Markley was the most respected member of Anderson's staff. He was a recovering alcoholic and one of Anderson's success stories who didn't fear the old man's bark or bite. He held his mentor in high regard. After a brief pause and an audible deep breath, he managed to reply, "And a cheery good morning to you, Dr. Anderson. I take it from your warm greeting that all goes well. Perhaps you could digress from your routine aggressive behavior for a while to consider a clinical matter. You do remember patientcare—if not I could take this matter to Doctor Folley who I'm sure would give me the immediate assistance of the senior resident."

Mentioning Dr. Folley was a quick jab to Anderson's ego. Folley was the hospital's Chief of Medicine and leading medical politician. Anderson was Folley's senior but had declined the opportunity to lead the Department of Medicine in deference to Folley. Anderson respected Folley as an administrator, teacher and physician but despised his political techniques that he thought were unbecoming to the physician's image.

Somewhat irritated, he fired back, "Markley, you have made my day. The VP for finance is looking to roll some heads out of the salary lines and you just volunteered. Maybe I should take that bit of news to Folley with whatever else you have banging on that pickled brain of yours."

Markley sensed that Anderson was running a bit hot so he switched to a more tactful approach. "Sorry, Doctor. I need your advice and professional help with a client. His name is Jay Marquart, who has been in the program for only a week. He managed to clear the first hurdle and now some things are entering into the mix that are explosive and I mean with a big bang. The chart is on its way to your office. I'd appreciate it if you would review it, especially the social history, and then set a time when we can discuss it. Please take very careful note of the incident report clipped to the back of the record. It has not been sent to Risk Management yet so you can judge how far this thing needs to travel. I'll fill you in on all the gory details after you review the chart."

Anderson was delighted to be inserted into clinical matters. He was personally convinced that was where a physician was supposed to be instead of wasting clinical skills arguing about the need to justify every penny lost or found. He couldn't understand the young residents who openly announced their intent to be public health administrators or worse yet, hospital administrators. "Why go to medical school and study science to be custodian of the farm" was his constant lament. He was about to work himself into another emotional fit when his faithful secretary politely placed Jay Marquart's medical record on the desk.

Anderson sat back in his comfortable desk chair. He pushed aside the administrative clutter and placed the medical record in its metal cover on the desk in front of him. He switched on the desk lamp and began a close inspection of the record as if he was the attending physician. The record was complete up to the time of the patient's last encounter with his counselor. The many blood and urine lab tests recorded a steady decline in the adverse chemical substance levels of an abuser. Anderson noted with disgust that the test results were not available when the patient came for his counseling sessions. This forced the attending physician to fly blind in assisting the counselor in prescribing the course of treatment. Anderson damned the pathologist for her inefficiency and the hospital CEO for his continual cutback of lab technicians. He made a mental note to make this an issue at the next meeting of the medical staff Quality Assurance Committee.

The admitting notes recorded that Jay Marquart checked into the SACAP unit of St. Anslem's Hospital in response to and at the direction of the Employee Assistance Program of Action Waste Management Company. In fact, the EAP Director drove Jay to the hospital after Jay had gone into a severe depression at a staff meeting. Anderson's curiosity began to peak as he scanned the clinical data. His professional research in the field of substance abuse supported his contention that inherited physiological qualities of a potential addict required an environmental trigger usually related to emotional stress coupled with depression. The cure often required medication to supplant an absent chemical in the patient's blood that erased the addictive urge for the so-called recreational drugs. As a young Ph.D. pharmacologist and researcher at Tuft's University School of Medicine he wanted to expand his theories to the test. His professional curiosity heightened and he eventually enrolled in the School of Medicine to earn his M.D. and board certification in internal medicine. He joined the St. Anslem's Medical Staff following his residency and gradually over the years promoted his theories about the treatment of substance abuse. The Sisters were captivated by his dedication and with the support of the physicians gave him some unused space, formally the Sisters' Infirmary, to be developed into the St. Anslem's Substance Abuse Program.

Jay Marquart's medical record contained social history notes entered by various counselors doing the admitting evaluation. They all concluded that Jay's quasi voluntary admission into the program was the beginning of a long overdue turn around in his thirty-six years. Typically, Marquart denied his problem but after several sessions took the first step and admitted his dependency. His motivation was based on his resolve not to lose shared custody of his five year old daughter, Kirstie. She was the focus of his adult life and the only reason he held for living. Anderson was becoming increasingly disturbed that the notes seemed to avoid pinpointing the trigger of the patient's emotional collapse. He remembered Bob Markley's request that he take careful note of the social history to be followed by an in-depth discussion of the case. He also remembered Bob informing him about an incident report attached to the chart. The incident report was clipped to the back of the metal chart cover. Anderson pulled it off and placed it aside. He intended to review it after he completed reviewing all the clinical data.

Unfortunately the social history in the medical record was only a sketch of Jay's current life. It detailed his family, job, income, and interests but failed to reveal the evolution of his addiction that began as an adolescent determined to lead his life as a free spirit. His natural intelligence and average athletic ability were set aside for the good times with his buddies who invented ways to bypass the rules at Brighton High School. Marquart set a record at the High School for breaking more rules than anyone else in history. The revised student handbook published after his graduation was referred to by the exhausted faculty as the Marquart Manual of Mischief

Jay loved life and he was extremely loyal to his family and friends. He always came home for birthdays and holidays and then would disappear after dinner. He would hug his mother with true affection before leaving the house. Anyone who offended his brothers or sisters or the family dog would find Jay in their face ready to do combat. Anyone who Jay considered a friend had his full loyalty and access to his last joint. He would defend his shiftless friends to his parents who constantly pleaded with him to hang out with a better class.

As Jay was quick to love, he was also quick to hate. His temper tantrums as a baby seemed to carry forward through his teens and into his young adult years. When he became angry he became violent as well. Scars from his street encounters were apparent on his face and arms. On two occasions his parents were called to the hospital where Jay was treated for a concussion and then released. Aside from being happy go lucky, free-wheeling, and occasionally violent he somehow managed to avoid being charged of any form of crime.

Jay's high school academic record would not have qualified him for admission to Harvard. This was not a matter of great concern. In fact, Jay, was not interested in advanced studies of any kind except what he might learn partying and hanging out. Funds for his various adventures were scarce since Dad announced that Jay had reached a point of finding a means of supporting himself. Jay's first job out of high school was driving a Senior Citizen Van for a nursing home. He loved the job and he loved helping the old folks. The men would tell Jay stories about fishing, hunting, and drinking that convinced Jay that the life in the wild was the true course of happiness. Unfortunately, the money that he earned from Senior Citizens was not adequate for him to support his increasing habits so he followed his compassionate instincts to St. Anslem's Hospital where he was first employed as a janitor and eventually became trained as a cardiac technician by a Nun who adopted Jay as a project.

Jay Marquart married Cecile Kelly when they were both twenty and ironically employees at St. Anslem's. Jay was a technician in the Cardiac Catheterization Laboratory and Cecile a licensed practical nurse in the Medical Intensive Care Unit. Their marriage lasted twelve painful years during which time they drank booze, smoked pot, and sniffed cocaine for recreation and socialization. Jay's efficiency eventually became hampered by a perpetual hangover that, combined with a companion state of depression, led him away from gainful employment and for lack of a better option into taking classes at the University of Massachusetts in Boston. His parents, pleased at his apparent effort to improve himself, picked up most of the tab.

Cecile contributed to the effort by continuing to work at St. Anslem's and, in addition, entered the associate degree program for registered nursing at Bunker Hill College. After three years of questionable social existence they both graduated. Jay, with a degree in political science, became a slave of the political bosses in Boston. This eventually led to his employment at Action Waste Management. Cecile passed her Massachusetts State Nursing

Boards and was elevated to registered nurse in St. Anslem's Medical Intensive Care Unit.

Cecile's life had been a constant struggle since her father abandoned her and her mother when she was ten. The petite, feisty, five-foot Irish lass accepted her fate and companion poverty with the resolve to control her adult life free of domination from any direction. Her marriage to Jay was more for convenience and economy than affection and companionship. Jay was acquainted with the people on the street and supplied her with the good times and obligatory high of their youth. Now she held the respected status of a professional nurse and resolved to be excellent. As she became established in her nursing profession she became less dependent on the particulars of her relationship with Jay. Within a year after her graduation from Bunker Hill she knew that her marriage was no longer of benefit.

Kristie was an accident of fate following the usual weekend binge. Sex was never enjoyable for Cecile. She responded without emotion to Jay's passionate begging and ignored him most of the time. It was a tremendous shock when she discovered her pregnancy. They had been married eight years and over that time had gradually moved into different worlds. Now the threat seemed real that a child could merge their relationship into a traditional family. Furthermore, Cecile feared that as a mother she could possibly be subordinated to the role of a domestic. In her mind this meant the loss of all that she had accomplished in her quest for professional status. Her Catholic upbringing never offered her the thought of terminating the pregnancy. Instead she became determined to dominate her child and eliminate the involvement of the father.

Jay was elated over the prospect of becoming a father. He had the benefit of a stable family background that included three brothers and two sisters. The warmth of family gatherings at Thanksgiving and Christmas would become more appealing as their baby entered the extended family with new cousins, brothers, and sisters-in-law. Jay remembered these same good times as a boy and recalled as well how he had rejected the family circle for the attraction of a joint, cheap wine, and hanging out with his buddies. He was the one who had the use of Mom's car to roam the streets looking for the connection and then using a motel for a rousing party. While still in high school he also tried his hand as a delivery boy for local drug dealers but found it not to his benefit when his dad found the unpaid for stash in the garage and threw it in the garbage can. Somehow Jay convinced his supplier that the loss of the stash, while tragic, was not of great consequence since he had talked his father out of reporting the matter to the police and, worse yet, the school authorities. The supplier had accepted Jay's foggy reasoning without breaking either of his legs but as punishment the delivery concession was transferred to Jay's best friend, Brian, who was well recognized as the main mule for both the senior and junior high schools in Brighton.

Actually, Jay had been sleeping off a jag when Dad decided to clean the garage and found the stash. Dad was pondering his find when the garbage truck pulled into the driveway. As the garbage man was wrestling with the family trash Dad handed him the stash and asked him to dispose of it. The environmental attendant was immediately responsive. Subsequently the Marquart household had the benefit of extraordinary attention by an array of City Sanitation Employees who made frequent and unscheduled checks on the trash accumulation in the Marquart garage

Cecile's pregnancy was uneventful but very uncomfortable. As she approached term it was apparent that a cesarean delivery was required. Kristie was born without complications but Cecile became determined that Kristie would be her one and only child. She would have the best education and formation for her child which certainty required divorce from a father who lacked social foundation, direction, and ambition. It would take time to reorganize her life to maintain her career advancement, accommodate the seemingly limitless requirements of her baby, and maneuver herself to the desired status of a single parent. In the interim she would see that Jay became disciplined in his conduct and correct in taking care of the child. She began by volunteering for as much overtime and extra duty as the hospital could offer in order to maximize her income.

She also made sure that she and Jay had separate bank accounts so their respective contributions to the family income were well recorded. Jay's various endeavors such as fishing, hunting, smoking, drinking and gambling were financed by his own earnings except for the times that she went along.

Jay's life was one of constant instability but that was the way he liked it. Following graduation from UMass he attempted to find a position that would provide him with a moderate sense of dignity that he reasoned a college graduate should have. He purposefully steered away from anything to do with healthcare especially St. Anslem's Hospital. His degree in political science and persuasive personality led him to the Democratic Party Headquarters where he offered to assist office seekers in campaigns.

At first, he was strictly a volunteer, but eventually he gained the confidence of a few people on the first level who recommended him to a few of people on the middle level who asked permission of a few people on the top level who authorized a few patronized bucks to provide Jay a small salary, provided he kicked back a piece to the Party's Widows and Orphans Fund. Jay accepted the draw as part of the cost of doing business. He also accepted the rigors of long hours, endless meetings, standing on corners holding campaign signs, and brown nosing as the price he had to pay for the good times at campaign parties with lots of good booze. His daughter, Kristie, put a new perspective to his life, however, and Jay found himself wheeling and dealing within the Party's power base for a real job. Eventually he was able to convince a power broker from the North End to sponsor him on the patronage role for an entry job with the Massachusetts Department of Environmental Services.

Jay, at first, enjoyed his life as a low-level bureaucrat. The flexible hours allowed by the State accommodated his night time sorties for the party bosses. He found that he was in great demand to attend to seemingly endless details of real or imagined office seekers. Occasionally his sponsor would ask Jay to do a few minor tasks apparently not related to the work of the Democratic Party. Jay presumed the tasks were benefits of being a party boss so he delivered the packages, picked up the envelopes, washed the car, and mowed the lawn. Eventually the good times began to wear thin and he began looking for improved status. His sponsor, Mr. Charles Patello, was reluctant to consider promoting him up the patronage ladder and instead advised Jay to seek an opportunity in the private sector.

Mr. Patello was an investment banker of sorts who was well acquainted with expanding companies. Jay was appreciative of Mr. Patello's assistance but sought to find his own opportunities. He responded to a notice on the public bulletin board in the cafeteria that announced several openings with a State grant supported private company called Action Waste Management. Jay had reviewed several parts of their grant request and had the honor of presenting the Action proposal to the Grant Committee. While it was a minor role in the process of obtaining State favor, Jay was certain that the Action executives who were at his presentation would remember his efforts and be attracted to bringing him on board.

As he had hoped he was well received by Action's personnel clerk who, after an hour and a half, moved Jay on to meet Ken Ryan, Supervisor of the Quality Control Section of Action's waste recycling program. Jay's knowledge of waste recycling was nearly perfect. Ryan offered him the position on the spot. Following the required two-week notice Jay left the world of politics and patronage for a career in private enterprise—or so he thought.

Ryan was only five years older than Jay, in his second marriage, had a great sense of humor, and seemed tolerant if not understanding of Jay's difficulties in adjusting from the loose working requirements of the State to the precise timeclock practice of good business. In fact, Ryan had started as a State employee, like Jay, in the department of Environmental Services. He stayed less than a year until the opportunity in industry came through. An executive of Action approached him after a legislative hearing on recycling where Mr. Ryan had been a key witness for the Representatives proposing mandatory recycling for all municipalities by the year 2000. He accepted the offer to head the Quality control section of Action on the spot. That was five years ago and while he was still in the same position his salary had doubled. On two occasions he had received a generous bonus for assisting the implementation of the Action Recycling System in Foxboro and Braintree. A fact he was quick to point out to Jay. Otherwise, Ryan had not been subjected to the political scutt work of ward healing and patronage.

Jay enjoyed the status of a real job. He responded to his duties with genuine effort and sincerity. Cecile, while favorably impressed with his demeanor, remained critical of his slothful attitude at household duties. She prepared a list of tasks for him to accomplish each day after work with the understanding that they would be completed before she left the hospital at the end of her twelve-hour shift. Little Kristie was to be picked up each day by Jay on his way home from work at Cecil's parents. As Kristie grew older Jay would take her to the zoo or for a late afternoon walk in the park. Their bonding grew in spite of Cecile's objective to remove Jay from the family.

Kristie was four years old when her mother's nagging finally broke Jay down. He was at the point of violence on several occasions but backed away due to the good advice of his boss and friend, Ryan. However, Ryan also advised Jay that he was bringing his troubles to work too often. Jay knew that a solution had to be found. He thought of moving out of their small house but again Ryan suggested that he should avoid any action that would appear as an act of abandonment. Jay compensated for his misery by playing softball and bowling with his old high school buddies that included Brian. Brian shared his pot with Jay as they compared tales of misery about women, jobs, and get rich quick schemes.

Cecile refused to let Brian in their house and threatened to have him arrested if he came into the neighborhood. Jay, always loyal to his friends, countered with the announcement that the house was his as much as it was hers and that Brian could visit any time he wanted. Cecile explained to Jay that she had made the down payment, qualified for the mortgage, made the monthly payments and paid the taxes out of her bank account. It was all documented and available for review by lawyers, judges, or J. Christ if necessary. She was ready for the contest of a divorce. Jay knew that divorce was the only possible answer and was opting for a no contest settlement until the question of child custody came up. Cecile was determined that she would have exclusive custody of Kristie and Jay would be forever removed from both her and Kristie's life. She was certain that the divorce settlement would uphold her position that Jay was unsuitable as a father.

Cecile's confidence in winning her way in the divorce was well founded. Jay's support of the family was indeed minimal. He contributed little to the necessary wherewithal of the economic household unit. He could offer little evidence to the contrary.

Aside from his all-too-frequent consumption of booze and pot he had somehow been able to keep his reputation intact. He did have a job and above all else he demonstrated true love and affection for Kristie that could be proven. Jay was determined that the one person in his life for whom he cared the most would not be taken from him. There was one weakness that he was certain Cecile would exploit in forcing a settlement to her liking. Jay was broke and could not afford a complicated and costly legal battle. He knew that Cecile had the upper hand when it came to the money. His attempts to offset Cecil's determined child custody with total concession on all matters of property were accepted by her without compromise. Cecile sensed total victory and filed for divorce.

Throughout his adult life, Jay had wanted to be independent. He, nevertheless, was sensitive about his parents, brothers and sisters. They in turn always stood by him in time of crises. The Marquarts were a strong family anchored in love. Over the four years since Kristie's birth she had become a true member of the Marquart clan and held status equal to any other member.

It was inconceivable that she would be separated from the family and her father by the cunning aspirations of her mother who had never gained the complete acceptance of Jay's sisters. Jay entered the initial steps of the divorce process with his usual air of independence and was blindsided by Cecile's lawyer who made a forceful demand for custody of Kristie.

Jay entered into a deep state of depression and, as he had done on many occasions in his developing years, called his sister, Martha, who in addition to being Kristie's aunt, was a lawyer. Martha recognized Jay's call to arms. The family circle was convened with Dad and Mom fronting the necessary cash to carry the day. Martha amassed her professional chits that brought the firm's leading divorce attorney forward to represent Jay in all proceedings. She backed the legal team with her own pro-bono efforts. What followed was an ugly brawl that ended with the Court granting joint custody of Kristie. Her time with each parent was to be mutually determined. Jay was obligated to pay the usual amount of child support to Cecile with whom Kristie would reside. Cecile contended throughout the proceedings that Jay's conduct was unfitting as a parent. The Court took careful notice of her contentions and warned Jay that any inappropriate conduct including failure to pay child support could result in loss of joint custody. It was also noted that Jay would be responsible to provide Kristie with an appropriate safe environment during the times that she was in his care.

Jay came out of the divorce as he had gone into it-flat broke. He was grateful for the help that Martha had provided even though he thought the efforts of the firm's super divorce attorney should have "slammed dunked Cecile into the shitter." He let Martha know that her Law Firm could use better help which resulted into a brother and sister shouting match not unlike their teen age years. He was free of Cecile's nagging and had the occasional opportunity to be a real loving father. He was also free of a place to live. He had a monthly check to write for child support. His ten-year old Jeep needed a valve job and his fishing license had expired. Other than these few minor problems he was a new man. He picked up the phone and gave his old buddy, Brian, a call.

Finding a place to live was a real problem for a man of very limited means. A house or an apartment was prohibitive until Jay could recover from the divorce. As a temporary measure, he arranged to sleep on the sofa in Brian's dingy studio pad in Chelsea. In addition to his many other remarkable qualities Brian was also a slob. The apartment was decorated with an assortment of trash that would have required an all-out effort by Action Waste Management to correct. Jay knew that he could not bring Kristie to Brian's pad. He also suspected that if Ken Ryan knew an employee of Action was living in such squalor he would see his job on the line. On the positive side, he was Brian's guest at no charge. He reunited with some of his old contacts in the Party and started earning a few bucks on the side doing the routine delivery jobs. He also had the eerie feeling that Cecile was watching his every move. To keep her off the trail he would take Kirstie to visit Aunt Marie or Uncle Mike or Grandma on her weekends with Dad. Aunt Martha would usually appear at the family homestead during Kristie's visit and take the opportunity to remind Jay of the terms of the divorce. She told him about a livable shack in Waltham that she had recently repossessed for a client. It was available and affordable on Jay's meager income provided he would attend to a disciplined budget. Mom came across with the security deposit and the first month's rent. Martha prepared the lease. Jay told Martha to mind her own business and moved to the shack in Waltham.

The town of Waltham was a few miles west of Boston. It sprang to life after World War Two when the need for housing the returning servicemen resulted in the town tripling its size with acres of two-bedroom prefab houses. Waltham became the first blue collar bedroom community in New England. Jay's drive to work was around a half-hour depending on traffic. His living conditions were definitely Spartan, however. He had no furniture except for a bed that was used by Kristie on weekends and Jay on week nights. He stood in the small kitchen to cook and eat except when Kristie visited. Then they had a picnic in the empty living room sitting Indian fashion on the floor. The plumbing was a sometimes thing and the old oil furnace just managed to keep the pipes from freezing in the winter. If there was any redeeming qualities about the place it was his neighbor who taught Jay how to maintain his old Jeep and do a lot of the home repairs that the landlord ignored. Again the family pitched in and gradually Jay collected modest furnishings including a used color TV that Kristie adored.

Jay realized that he was heading for trouble when Cecile arrived on a cold February evening to collect Kristie and found her sitting in the middle of the living room in her snowsuit playing fish with her Daddy. The temperature in the shack was slightly above fifty degrees and Kristie had a cold. Cecile, on the other hand, was definitely hot under the collar and proceeded to put Jay's feet to the fire. Jay called Martha who put him in touch with an out of firm attorney who successfully carried Jay through the resulting court appearances. It was apparent that Jay would have to find suitable housing if he was to counter future challenges to joint custody.

By the end of the first year following the divorce Jay had managed to pocket the down stroke on a small three-bedroom ranch in good condition just a few blocks away from his shack. Martha maneuvered him out of his lease and used her connections to get him a mortgage that He felt was a rip-off. He was now a homeowner in a respectable neighborhood that had working sewers, inside plumbing, and electric lights. His career as a quality control technician at Action Waste Management was apparently secure evidenced by a satisfactory evaluation and a six percent raise. His life was improving in spite of all the "crap" he had to crawl through to keep that "bitch off his back." Now he began to plan a counterattack. By next year he intended to turn the tables and take full custody of Kristie. Ken Ryan said it was possible. Ken didn't have any kids when he went through his divorce but his attorney said it was possible. The attorney offered to represent Jay when the time was right. Jay also had overcome his total acquired distrust of the female persuasion and began to have an occasional date.

Jay enjoyed his freedom, his times with Kristie, his frequent hunting and fishing trips, his job at Action, and partying. Brian had become his constant companion. They would meet every night after work for a few pops that frequently extended into "all-nighters." Brian's career in the parcel delivery business had expanded to include a whole new line. He offered to introduce Jay to the business. Jay declined the offer but did agree to sample the products from time to time. Brian also introduced Jay to a young lady whose husband had been in the business until an unfortunate sale to an undercover agent put the man on extended leave. Alice had a daughter that she dearly loved and in her best interest gave testimony under protection about her husband's business affairs. This led to his conviction and eventually his parole. It also led to their divorce coupled with a bout with the Internal Revenue Service and Bankruptcy Court. Needless to say, Alice was flat broke when she met Jay and it was love at first sight. She moved in, lasted three months, and abruptly moved out, contending that Jay had more affection for his fishing pole than her. Jay did not contest the issue except to offer the excuse that the similar appearance of Alice and his fishing pole caused the problem. He once again vowed that women were no damn good.

A few weeks after the Alice Fishing Pole incident, Jay and Brian were positioned in the Waltham Tap and Keg when Jay spotted a familiar face among the five o'clock boozers. Her name was Susan Testa. Susan had been a regular participant at the high school pot parties that seemed to have been in another century. Jay had never gotten to know Susan in those days and he now had the urge to make up for lost time. After a rather clumsy approach he took the direct route and asked if she remembered him as the one and only good looking guy in the class. Susan remembered him but not so much for his good looks as his constant burnt-out expression which seemed to her to be a lasting quality.

It was obvious that the two understood one another and had a lot in common. After a prolonged courtship of three months they were married by a justice of the peace on the Boston Commons at three in the afternoon. The hour was perfect for passersby to view the proceedings and extend best wishes. Jay's buddy Brian and his boss Ken Ryan were also present along with his Sister, Martha. After the ceremony, the entire party went to dinner at Mama Roses in the North End. Once again Jay was a married man.

Susan was small like Cecile but her Italian ancestry was accented with coal black hair and fiery eyes that were occasionally clear. She moved into Jay's house and brought with her several rooms of furniture, cooking utensils, linens, a washer and dryer, and two sons, ages eight and four, from a previous marriage. Jay now had a real house with a real family that included three kids and a good cook, His life seemed complete. Susan was no nag. She shared Jay's love for children, family, fishing, hunting and partying. They knew a lot of the same people and enjoyed the same culture.

Susan's former husband, an employee of Patriot Transportion and Courier Service, was Brian's boss. Eddie the Enforcer, as he was known, had the task of collecting accounts receivable from delinquent customers. It was common knowledge that his habit of practicing his technique on Susan a couple times a week led to their breakup. Contrary to Jay, Susan's first husband apparently had no love or interest in his kids. He had gladly adhered to the restraining order served on him after he gave her the last bashing. Susan also shared Jay's attitude that the mother should attend to the proper raising of the children in the home and not be employed full-time away from the children. Jay was determined to be the sole support of his family.

Contrary to Jay's hopes, Cecile had not abandoned her quest for sole custody of Kristie. Over the years since their divorce she had also learned that a single parent offered little confidence to a judge in matters of custody when the other parent presented the prospect of a stable family environment. This created a matter of great concern. Cecile detested the thought of marriage. She especially hated the idea of a sexual relationship of a permanent nature. A one night stand now and then was more than adequate to solve occasional biological urges. Her social life had presented several such opportunities that were satisfying but marginally enjoyable. However, one Friday evening at a nursing staff TGIF party she was introduced by a nursing buddy to a good-looking cop from the Brighton precinct. He not only was good looking but was a true gentleman who didn't try to score on the first try. Cecile decided to pursue the relationship and since the officers from the Brighton precinct ate lunch in St. Anslem's cafeteria it was easy to meet at lunch and get better acquainted. After three weeks of a steady diet of salad and yogurt, Cecile popped the question and asked if he wanted to modify their lunch breaks into a more extended relationship. The good policeman took the hint and offered to have dinner at Cecile's house that very evening.

Their first nocturnal affair was a shocking but satisfying experience for Cecile and Officer Michael O'Sullivan. Contrary to Cecil's expectations of a rocking night in the sack, she was exposed to a person of sincere good nature with honorable intentions who explained that he occasionally enjoyed the alternate lifestyle. He confessed that his association with Cecile was to cover his opposite life while his superiors considered his application for undercover assignment to Narcotics Division of the Boston PD. Cecile also let it be known that she was looking for a front to recover her kid. After extensive analysis by both parties they mutually agreed to a working relationship within a formal marriage. The event took place a month later when the former Mrs. John Marquart, RN, became Mrs. Cecile O'Sullivan, RN, wife of Officer Michael O'Sullivan—Boston Police Department—recently assigned to Narcotics.

Dr. Anderson learned little of Jay's history from reading the medical record. It simply mentioned that Jay had admitted to habitual heavy use of intoxicating substances and that he had been on a weekend binge prior to his collapse at his workplace, Action Waste Management. Markley's notes described Jay's violent behavior. The course of treatment was routine. The patient's background was typical of a user who was capable of being helped.

Anderson liked what he saw. Markley had found another prospect.

The Chief Executive Office of St. Anslem's Hospital had no idea that there had been an incident in the SACAP involving Patient, Jay Marquart. Such matters rarely, if ever, required the attention of the hospital's chief executive. More appropriately, Joe Durant, St. Anslem's chief executive, consistently thought about the institution's occupancy, staffing, quality and fiscal wellbeing. Operational problems were handled by the extensive chain of command that blended physicians directing departments of medical specialists with vice presidents administering nursing, business affairs, hotel services such as food, housekeeping, engineering, and the like. Frequently the various medical disciplines conflicted with each other or more often with the lay administrative activities. Durant felt that he served more as a referee in these struggles. He tried to administer the institution to the benefit of the patient and the goals of the hospital established by the Board of Trustees. The inconsistency of patient care and corporate goals that had occurred in recent times seemed to put him in an impossible position but as a seasoned professional he was confident that he could better any challenge.

Chapter Three

Charlie Patello at first gave little thought to St. Anslem's Hospital. He placated Hardly at the Board meetings by appearing to be interested in the loose discussion. Otherwise, he thought that Folley's wining about the hospital's administration was pure crap. He, Meehan and Mondi had plenty of other things to worry about in addition to finding a way to bring St. Anslem's into their web. Mondi's distribution and sale of cocaine to Boston's rich and famous under the cover of National Associated Investors, was rapidly expanding and needed more outlets. Meehan's Action Waste Management Company was not as established. It was riding the crest of a new wave industry that required a great amount of political lubrication to be supplied by Patello if the right people could be bought. Patello was totally absorbed in doing the undercover work for the benefit of the firm. If successful, National Associated Investors through Action Waste Management would add another major revenue source to its grand list of money laundering and skimming operations. At a casual dinner one evening Patello and Meehan hit on an idea to combine Action's future with the hospital. The combination of the two could be the entree that Big Frank Patello had asked them to develop.

Waste management in the Boston area and in most towns and cities in the State was provided by the municipal administration. By convincing the politicians that it was to their personal benefit to privatize the service, Action Waste Management could get the market base it was seeking. Typically, hospitals created large waste disposal problems for the municipalities because of the infectious nature on their waste material. This gave Action an angle. Promote hospital waste as a municipal problem and then ride to the rescue on a white horse of a private company dedicated to save the day.

Initially, tax increases were tolerated by the voters but soon became a burden for political incumbents trying to stay in office. Party bosses on both sides of the aisle warned the administration that other forms of revenue for water reclamation and waste control had to be found. The next alternative was an increase in utility rates particularly water and sewer services. Eventually the naive users became sensitive to the highest water rates in the United States and strongly challenged, once again, the concept of taxation without representation. Massachusetts Governor Dukar's handlers sensed that the cost of the Water Reclamation Project could not only sink their man's chances of reelection but forever end his political career. Dukar was the property of the Republican Party and the Party was the supported in no small part by big money from big business. It was essential to maintain control of the State administration in the heavily populated Northeastern United States. However, the reaction of the public to taxes and water rates provided an opportunity for the NAI syndicate to initiate the project called Privatization. Patello and Meehan knew that NAI's experiences in other States proved that the public, given the right motivation, would demand that waste management be placed in the hands of competent private companies that would guarantee a cleaner, safer environment. Dukar they reasoned would want to be the named author and hero of the privatization program. Big Frank had schooled his nephew, Charlie Patello, early in life that the first step in any good business venture is to create the demand.

That demand was initiated by an angry mother, compensated by Patello, who summoned the *Boston Globe* Investigation Team to Squantum Beach in North Quincy. The beach had been closed to swimmers for several years because of the water pollution but it still was a popular place for sunbathing, jogging and family recreation. The caller's voice went beyond angry to violent as she described how her three-year-old had found and began playing with a syringe with needle that apparently washed onto the beach. She claimed the place was littered with trash that contained bloody bandages, toilet paper, and other items that she couldn't identify. Within minutes Boston's number-one newspaper had its crack Investigative Team with photographer on the scene. The next edition carried the story on page one with a four-column photo of the trash. The banner story detailed the incompetent procedures that area hospitals used in collecting and bagging trash. It concentrated on the disposal of the trash by City Sanitation Service that indiscriminately threw the trash bags on open trucks and carted the debris to barges that supposedly dumped the material miles offshore. Other area newspapers, not to be out done by their Big City competitor, ran front page stories with focus on the infectious waste that contributed to the rapid spread of AIDS. Television and radio stations throughout New England picked up on the story with syringe and needles spotted on every beach from Maine to New Jersey. In less than a week an irate public was demanding that the Governor mobilize the State's resources to eliminate the threat to public safety.

Mayor Cowan of Boston represented the demands of the citizens to the Governor's office. He pointed out to the governor and the assembled media that the City Sanitation workers were overwhelmed by the enormous task of segregating infectious hospital waste from ordinary trash. To place such a burden on the municipality would require extensive subsidization from the State. He emphasized that significant increase in taxes was not only required but well worth the investment. The Boston Taxpayers Association countered the Mayor's contention that additional taxes were necessary to solve the problem. They pointed out that private companies could be invited to collect and dispose of infectious waste and other debris on a fee for service basis that would place the burden on the producer of the waste thus relieving the taxpayer. The Governor acknowledged the wisdom of the Tax Payers Association and appointed a blue-ribbon commission to formulate a plan for the privatization of waste collection and disposal for Massachusetts' municipalities. The resulting report of the commission titled Infectious Waste Control for Towns and Cities in Massachusetts served as the basis for enabling legislation that established an Office of Waste Management within the State Department of Public Health that, among other things, applied to the Federal Government for block grants to be used to support Towns and Cities in the development of recycling and waste control. The office of Waste Management reviewed all local grant applications and passed them on for final review and recommendation to the former blue ribbon commission now named The Governor's Special Taskforce for Waste Management. Once the Taskforce gave its positive recommendation on a specific grant application it was forwarded to Governor Dukar for final approval. Once a grant was approved by the Governor it was placed in the capable hands of the secretary of Public Health who delegated it to the director of the office of Waste Management who assigned the project to a Regional Coordinator of Waste Management Services who assigned the project to a grant manager who regulated the local implementation through the municipal public health official and the recognized private contractor named in the grant award.

The legislation was initially opposed by the Massachusetts Hospital Association that contended the whole program was politically motivated. The Association attempted unsuccessfully to demonstrate that private companies would charge outrageous fees to hospital thus dramatically increasing the cost of health services. The media destroyed the Hospital Association's arguments with a series of programs and articles about the Boston teaching hospitals' enormous wealth and extreme profits. Faced with the embarrassing truth the Hospital Association retreated to safer grounds and fortified itself against the Governor's promised assault on hospitals' tax exempt status.

Organized Labor took up the fight and denounced the entire privatization program of the Governor as a scam certain to lead to a criminal conviction. The Boston Workers' Guild organized a strong campaign to counter the privatization of waste management that was diminished by editorial sentiment pointing to the advantage of private cost-effective companies that would create jobs and contribute to the tax base of the local community and State. The fact that none of the companies named in the grant applications approved by the Governor had Union contracts was somehow overlooked by the media in spite of Union commentary and editorial reply.

Somewhat as the last resort, the Boston Workers' Guild organized a massive rally to be held on the Capitol steps to protest the signing of the legislation by Governor Dukar. They had convinced the Massachusetts Hospital Association to cosponsor the rally. The gathering was large by usual protest standards and equally unruly. The steps of the Golden Domed State Capitol Building were packed with demonstrators. The crowd overflowed into the street and onto Boston Commons where tourists mingled with the protesters. The bright, warm sunny afternoon gave the affair a festive mood. Many openly drank beer and sang. The local media had a field day filming staged fist fights between hecklers and angels of mercy in white uniforms. Hospital CEOs stood side by side Union leadership and angrily denounced the private control of waste management. Statements issued by hospital administrators were cheered by hospital employees and Union members. The excitement grew to a fever pitch and came to an explosive climax when Bob Muldoon, President of the

Boston Workers' Guild came to the podium. He waxed eloquent about the solidarity of the Guild and the unyielding opposition to the privatization of waste management. Then to the sudden dismay and surprise of the hospital officials he announced a City wide strike of organized hospitals in the Boston area if the Hospital Association endorsed the signing of contracts with private waste management companies. He also pledged that any Union hospital that signed a waste management agreement on its own would be faced with a strike vote post haste.

Dukar took special note of the furor in the local Boston media and silently prayed that it would blow over. He had been well advised that the Union might try a grandstand play with a strike threat. He had also been advised by the attorney general that a strike of this kind was illegal and could be dissolved by injunction. Muldoon was also well aware of the legal status of the threat. He knew and fully expected any strike that occurred not to be sanctioned by the Union. Muldoon also knew a big threat made big news that would draw national attention. As he had hoped all the wire services and networks filled their nightly news with scenes from the latest edition of the Boston Tea Party. Muldoon had bigger fish to fry and now the skillet was hot and ready.

Number One Park Ave in New York City is a very tall prestigious building located a block south of Grand Central Station. The name has no relationship to the building's location on Park Avenue. It simply represents the wealth and influence of the developers and the way of doing business in New York. A significant amount of money found its way into the hands of the NYC zoning and planning commission that, in turn, rewarded the developer for improving the image of the City with its grand edifice. The true address of One Park Ave is classified information held by the United States Post Office that delivers mail routinely throughout Manhattan by building name and area code.

The occupants of the thirty-fifth floor at One Park Ave, National Associated Investors, had little concern about the building's name. NAI's purpose was to build new and highly profitable business ventures for its wealthy stockholders. Mario Capizzi, President of NAI, had initiated the formation of Park Environmental Inc., a subsidiary of NAI, two years earlier following the passage of the Federal Environmental Protection Act. Capizzi had convinced the

Board of NIA that public demand for waste management and the motivation for States to use available Federal funds to establish waste management standards by and through the use of private enterprise offered excellent profit potential, respectability, possible tax advantages, and opportunities for cash investors to launder income from other sources. Big Frank Patello, NAI's chairman and head of the Patello family formerly of Brooklyn and recently Providence, Rhode Island, accepted Capizzi's recommendation and, with unanimous consent of NAI's board of trustees, funded the formation and operation of Park Environmental Inc.

Capizzi as Chairman of Park Environmental Inc. and President of National Associated Investors, selected Anthony Marone as President of Park. Marone built Park into a prominent national consulting firm on environmental and waste management practices that offered quality, inexpensive advice to State legislators and governors on acquisition and use of Federal grants for waste management in addition to making the obligatory contributions to election campaigns. Park also became recognized as the foremost consulting firm to private investors and entrepreneurs interested in the formation and operation of Waste Management Companies. Using the resources of NAI, Park invested in each of the Companies that it helped to initiate. NAI found working capital loans from local banks and investment companies for their various waste management ventures. Park, because of its particular method of financing, was able to guarantee cost/price advantage to its companies. Park also provided an exclusive franchise. As a consequence, there was little competition that favorably compared to Park's services.

Marone, following Capizzi's direction, used the national organizational structure established by NAI to access local markets. This well-established organization, staffed with well-connected prominent individuals, provided Park instant success. The New England Region was based in Boston and therefore would best be initiated in Massachusetts. Rhode Island was an alternate consideration because of Patello's banking influence but was dismissed due to a sudden and unexpected defection that caused a prominent publicized disruption in the savings and loan business. NAI's man in Boston was Charles Patello. Uncle Frank had enjoyed bouncing little Charlie on his knee when he was a toddler and now enjoyed contributing to his success as a member of the family. Little Charlie responded to his uncle's kindness by ushering NAI into many profitable ventures in the New England region.

A particular benefit that Patello brought into the NAI ventures in Boston was his close connection with the Irish gang that controlled an estimated one third of the area's wealth including the City of Boston's municipal spending and the spending of the Boston Catholic Archdiocese. Charlie had convinced Uncle Frank many years ago that two Irish kids he had met at Boston College could be compromised for future use, One, Kevin Hardly, came equipped with lots of money, family influence, and little brains—the other, Tom O'Shea, had lots of ambition, no money, and few morals. It seemed to be a perfect combination that only required two hundred dollars to bribe an ethics professor for an advance copy of the final exam. Uncle Frank gave Charlie the money to swing the deal. Charlie pulled it off and returned the two hundred with fifty bucks splitting a hundred-dollar profit down the middle. Big Frank Patello knew at that time that his Sister's youngest son was destined to be his successor and head of the largest operation east of Chicago.

The remaining two-thirds of Boston's wealth seemed problematic to Charles Patello and the interest of National Associated Investors. The Puritan Ethic of avoiding association with Papists and non-Christians created a block that Patello tried vainly to overcome. He also recognized that the WASP strength was based on the unfortunate split in the Hardly family. He decided that a frontal attempt to penetrate the WASP fortification against Catholics and non-Christians was destined to failure. On the other hand, the WASPs were nearly desperate to stop the Irish from controlling key elected posts at Federal and State level. He suspected that a covert action supporting a political WASP candidate might give the NAI a foot in the door. The Governor was a true WASP that offered the NAI the opportunity it was looking for by making him the hero of the Massachusetts' Waste Management Program.

The Governor was also a true politician that recognized the power of organization. He knew that the Mayor of Boston was the strongest opposition to his reelection. The Waste Management issue could give the Governor a powerful base to overcome any threat to reelection.

Patello found his way into the WASP fortress through the backdoor of the Boston Tax-Payers Association that was essentially controlled by WASP business interest, the Boston Chamber of Commerce, and the Republican Party. His offer to the TPA was to use his lobbing strength to support the Governor's Waste Management legislation, to provide campaign contributions anonymously in support of the Republican Governor and the election of a Republican candidate to the U.S. Senate, to mount a media campaign in Boston that would hang the Mayor out to dry for misuse of campaign funds and to use the combined influence of National Associated Investors to promote Boston as the site for the Olympic Games in the year 2008. In return for his generous support the TPA agreed that the Governor would name Richard Folley, M.D., as a member of the Governor's Special Taskforce on Waste Management, Park Environmental Inc. would be retained by the State as consultants to the office of Waste Management, and Action Waste Management of Boston would be given a grant to initiate privatized waste management programs for the Boston Metropolitan area.

Patello, delighted at his success, reported to Marone at Park's New York office that it was time for Action Waste Management to set up shop. A day later the Capitol steps experienced the rally turned into a brawl by the Boston Workers' Guild causing Patello to remember that a third of Boston's wealth and influence was held by organized labor and virtually uncontrolled.

Patello telephoned Marone and reported the problem with Muldoon. Marone in turn called his contacts with the National Federation who called Muldoon. The Federation subsequently advised Marone to schedule an off the record never happened type meeting with himself, Patello, and Muldoon at an inconspicuous place as soon as possible. Marone called Patello who called Muldoon who arranged the meeting in the back room of Stinger's tavern in Dorchester two blocks from the offices of the Boston Workers' Guild.

Stinger's appeared to be a typical neighborhood tap on a frontage road to Interstate 93. Its small neon sign was barely visible. On top of the two-story frame building was a large lighted billboard that pointed to the Workers Guild Building. The electronic billboard flashed Union slogans and pronounced the strength of organized labor for all traveling the Interstate to see. Inside the tavern was dingy but reasonably clean. Wooden tables and chairs were haphazardly spread around the bar room that also contained an old-fashioned bar with a foot rail and no stools.

Stingers was primarily a standing man's drinking establishment. In back was a fairly large room that seemed to be for the private use of the Workers Guild. Four square tables with padded chairs comprised the furnishings. The bland decor of the dirty painted walls featured the latest advertisements of local breweries. Green shade lights hanging from the ceiling were centered over each table making the atmosphere perfect for poker games. A slide window to the bar commanded the attention of the bartender in service of the room's occupants.

Twenty-four hours after the Capitol Steps Rally, three men gathered in the back room of Stinger's. Muldoon, first to arrive, came alone. When Patello and Marone arrived they correctly recognized that this was not a meeting of record with the Workers' Guild. Muldoon had apparently been waiting at Stingers for a few hours and his speech offered a slight expression of a man who had enjoyed a liquid lunch. Patello introduced Marone and ordered a round of Sam Adams beer.

Muldoon remained seated, nodded an acknowledgment to Marone, and motioned the two visitors to sit. He was cordial and asked Marone about his flight from New York, commented about the weather, damned the government, and got to the point. "Patello, you son of a bitch, you put your stinking deal together without asking me in. You know you can't ignore labor. You also know now that I can bring this whole mess down on your head like a rock I used that two by four on your skull yesterday just to get your attention. You got this thing with waste hauling bagged as far as the City goes but you don't move one truck or get one hospital under contract without me saying so. You need my help and that's worth something. I need a piece for labor and I need a piece for me."

Marone became flushed and it was apparent to Patello that good old Mouldy had just bought himself a long ride on a dark night. He felt that there might be an opportunity to gain more than he gave by bringing Muldoon into the program but only at the operational level. To negotiate to that end he needed to penetrate Muldoon's mind and discover how much information he had about the total operation. He also had to be careful to prevent Marone from reverting to his previous life and dusting Muldoon on the spot.

Patello looked at the aging, small Muldoon and recognized that the Union leader had seen better days. Muldoon hands seemed to shake slightly, his hair was very thin on top, and he needed a shave. Best to try a soft sell, he thought.

"Bob, you are right about my oversight. For that I apologize. You know that I'm kind of inexperienced at these things. I have never been involved with unions and Union contracts."

Muldoon leaned forward to get into Patello's face. "That's an understatement. Why did you let New York call the Federation? It took me over an hour to convince them that this was a local fire fight that didn't need their attention.

Now they think they can muscle in on your national organization, Park, whatever. If they get into this it gets the attention of the U.S. Attorney General and we all lose."

Score one for our side, thought Patello.

Muldoon apparently was unaware that the Workers' Federation through its various pension funds was a heavy investor with National Associated Investors. Marone had contacted the head of the Federation through NAI President Capizzi who made the contact through the secretary of the Federation who held a seat on the NAI Board. The Federation had all the information about Park but, for reasons that were becoming more obvious, decided not to let their information available to Muldoon and the Boston Workers' Guild. It occurred to Patello that the Federation had advised Muldoon that the mess he created was all his to handle.

Patello glanced at Marone who was pouring the balance of his Sam Adams into his glass with a slight smile on his face. This indeed was a local matter. "Look, Bob, the last thing we want is trouble with the Feds. Sure we use influence to get what we want but it is all legal."

This time Muldoon rocked back on the legs of his chair and displayed an air of confidence in place of arrogance. "Legal my ass. Your deal with the TPA to fry Cowan's butt is about as legal as murder one."

Score one for the goons, thought Patello. *He knows about the deal with the TPA because the Workers' Guild has a seat on the Chamber of Commerce that ties in with the TPA. Okay, so now what does he want?*

Muldoon shook his empty bottle at the window to the bar and with expert precision the hefty bartender, who seemed disinterested in the trio, produced another round of Boston's finest. Muldoon poured slowly and seemed to be pondering his next comments. "Charlie, my boy, I'm sure it's no surprise for you to hear that the Workers' Guild was a big contributor to the Mayor's election fund. In addition, most of the Locals in the City kicked in as well. Now you and your egg-sucking Ivy coated swells are going to arrange for the Mayor to be exposed for using campaign funds for personal use. It's also no surprise for you to know that all of the Mayor's big dollar contributors not only knew but encouraged his honor to pocket the cash in return for certain concessions. Of course, that means that you and your people got yours the same way that I and my people got ours. It also means that the Mayor is not going to take the fall without dragging his loyal contributors into the mud. Some might even go to the slam with him. Maybe someone else should take the dive."

The point was getting sharper to Patello. The Workers' Guild was fronting for the Mayor. Actually the Guild was protecting its interest and investment in control of municipal services that included garbage collection and sanitation. Patello guessed that Muldoon would back off if he could somehow maintain control of the same services in the private sector without losing the money invested in City Hall.

"Look, Bob, I explained to the TPA that I had no knowledge about the Mayor's use of his campaign funds. Consequently, I am not in a position to make any accusations. I am only in a position to suggest to certain media representatives that looking under certain rocks might produce some interesting results. Are you concerned that I might finger the Workers' Guild?"

Muldon shot forward in his chair and again leaned into Patello who was sitting with his arms resting on the edge of the table. "You should be careful how you use your finger, Charlie, because you wouldn't wanna get it stuck where it didn't belong. What I'm suggesting is that some other guy like the Commissioner of Public Health who before he got appointed commissioner of Public Health was the Mayor's campaign manager, might be responsible for money being directed to diverse use. This is the same campaign manager who as Commissioner of Public Health has advised the media that the Union local is featherbedding at Boston Hospital. Now it seems to me that if the Commissioner of Public Health resigns because of misuse of funds and if the new Commissioner of Public Health not only happens to be a friend of labor but a strong proponent of waste management, recycling, and whatever else Action Waste Management sells, then we are all better served. You get my drift."

Patello caught the drift. In effect, he was being told to renege on his agreement to fry the Mayor. This would preserve the Mayor as the most likely candidate to unseat the Governor at the next election which was the foundation of the deal cut with the governor. Patello was in a vice. They had finished their third beer and Marone made a swayed but hasty trip to the john. The expedient bartender brought a fourth round. Bob and Charlie sat silently waiting for Marone's return. He was back in a few minutes but Muldoon had a sudden urge to urinate and wandered off. Patello felt the urge but he did not want to be anywhere with Muldoon without Marone. He decided to be patient if his bladder would cooperate. Muldoon returned looking refreshed.

When Muldoon was seated, Patello made another try. "Look, Bob, you and the Guild are the ones with the information about the Commissioner. If someone other than me got to the media with the facts about campaign funds first, then whatever I came up with would be yesterday's news. The Mayor could direct fire as he wants. If he gets a little dirty in the trenches it's the cost of doing business so to speak."

"No good, Charlie, my boy, but it's a nice try." Muldoon seemed to regain control. "You have to understand that if Hizzoner gets just a little dirty in this roust then he won't be credible in naming our man to succeed the commissioner. The Mayor stays clean and your organization provides the soap. You understand?"

For the moment Patello was speechless as he thought about Muldoon's last pitch. He wasn't sure he understood the crafty Union leader but he decided to act like he did. "Robert, my man, it seems to me that what your organization needs is grease not soap. We have plenty of grease to slip your man in regardless of the stuff hanging on the Mayor. Trust me. Look at it this way. We convince the Governor's taskforce on waste management to allow Boston to start its conversion to privatized waste management on a voluntary basis. Then we get the hospitals to switch from City trash pick up to a private company with Union employees and that little dance you did at the Capitol yesterday gets forgotten."

Muldoon heard the offer to gain a sweetheart deal with Action Waste Management. None of Patello's ventures had Union shops so this was a major concession. The temptation to deal was strong but he remembered the call from the Mayor who told him in specific terms that Hizzoner would see him in hell if he failed to get Patello off his back. The Mayor was the common man well respected by the working class. He had used the Unions to advance his political career and eventually became their champion. His continued election success and established acceptance among the poor and lower middle-class gave him power that tended to make his creators, such as the Workers' Guild, his eventual subjects. Muldoon was uncertain if Patello knew that the Mayor had the Guild by the throat. He pondered the question and fixed his eyes on his beer.

Marone noticed the change in Muldoon's body language. The lowered eyes was a definite sign that Patello had scored. Patello saw the change as well but was uncertain if he had closed the deal or simply concluded article one of a longer agreement yet to be determined.

Muldoon's reputation as an expert negotiator was well deserved. His emotional control or lack of same was part of his language in doing business. He moved his hands, eyes, and his butt in the chair as a calculated signal to the other side that he had applied a period to a sentence or started another paragraph in the discussion. Muldoon raised his eyes and fixed them squarely on Patello. Discussion was about to begin on article two.

"You son of a bitch. Where do come off offering me a contract with Action? I can organize that sweatshop in a minute. You got to come up with an idea that gives me something other than the sleeves off your vest. Suppose you use your power base to give our squeaky-clean Mayor a real job like running the Catholic Church. Yeah, that's it—let's see you make him Pope. I hear you got connections all the way up with the Democrats by that lard ass Hardly so get Cowan a plush job like ambassador to Pago Pago. You do that and he don't buck the WASP for Governor. You can push one of your flunkies against Dukar that will guarantee Dukar wins and you look good all way 'round."

Now it was Patello's turn to blink. "Let me make sure I'm reading you, Robert. You think the Mayor will resign and accept a job in the Federal administration if we, you and me, can come up with the right appointment. How do we know that he will stand hitched? As for making him Pope we first have to make him Catholic."

"It's better than jail, Charlie." Muldoon was about to go on a roll. "He stays clean which gives him the chance to come back and kick your ass in the future but we can bury a lot of stuff in the meantime. Besides you get a piece of him in the process. Also, you realize that the President of the City Council will step in as the interim Mayor. Siro is one of your boys, a good Catholic kid from Roslindale that holds a Union card, He didn't go to BC but nobody is perfect. He's democrat—steps in as Mayor, fires Logan, and appoints Mike Megan Commissioner of Health. Logan sees it as part of the transition and disappears. Everybody wins. Logan is a young kid that you can take care of with a job in one of these companies that you juice up. Maybe he can work in Hardly's bank and get a night job teaching at Harvard."

Patello glanced at Morone who had his eyes fixed on Muldoon. "Well, we have several problems with your 'everybody wins plan,' Bob. First of all, we have to wait for the right opening at the Federal level. That could take some time. Second, the Massachusetts Hospital Association will take this on in the media as another excuse for the high cost of healthcare. The public will buy in giving the Attorney General an opening to push for an investigation which puts us back in the soup. Maybe while we are waiting for a place to plant the Mayor you could convince him to sign a City contract with Action to handle the waste from Boston Hospital. That would break the MHA hold on the cost thing when the Mayor points to the savings the hospital will experience by using a private contractor. The Tax Payers Association will want to endorse the Mayor's good wisdom which means they won't pressure me to start dragging him in the mud."

Muldoon adopted a conciliatory position as he moved sideways and sat on one hip. "Charlie, it seems to me that we aren't too far apart. I am in a position to know that the Secretary of Labor will be looking for a prominent elected Democrat to step in as the UnderSecretary of Labor. Of course, the person to be selected has to be a friend of Labor and a known supporter of the President. The National Workers' Federation wants the recommendations of its affiliates on possible nominees. Once the Federation decides on the best possible nominee that person has a lock on the appointment. But just to be sure that the right person gets the job it might pay for a big outfit that has a lot of influence to join up with the Federation, say like National Associated Investors, and work out a deal like we're doing here. When I was talking with the Federation earlier they suggested I mention it. That way the confirmation would sail through, you know."

So much for the local fire fight bullshit, thought Patello.

Marone remained impassive. His expression didn't change. This was top floor stuff that he would carry to Big Frank Patello in a few hours followed in short order by a NAI Board meeting and negotiation that set national policy on such matters. The Federation knew the process. They had been through it on other occasions. There was apparently something else on the national agenda that could be advanced by the relatively insignificant Boston item. Muldoon was obviously the messenger boy. He had accomplished his mission by giving a subtle message to the NAI that a powwow was requested with the big chief. That being done he could move back to the details of the local issue. The ball was squarely in Patello's court who decided to go to the men's room. Marone went along.

The usually neat appearance of the NAI and Park executive seemed ruffled. "Charlie, I think you got what you need from that mick. Let's blow this cookie farm. I can't stand this goddamn tasteless Boston beer. It runs right through me. I'll see Big Frank in the morning after he meets with the Board. If there's anything that we need from here we'll let you know. Old Muldoon is good, damn good. Your Uncle might want you to visit with him about this Cowan stiff. I doubt that Cowan means that much to the Federation. Me thinks the goons got a big deal in the offing that merits our combined interest. We'll see. Meanwhile, you keep Cowan's ass out of the mud. I'll take care of the WASP side but you got to make sure that Hardly doesn't piss off his cousins and get the locals all stirred up. This Commissioner Logan should find a nice job in the private sector. Next month maybe he starts as a vice president with Patriot. I'll arrange it with Mondi. He'll contact this kid and cut him a deal he can't refuse. You check out this Mike Megan guy and see if he can be loyal."

Patello nodded his assent to Marone's comments and the duo returned to the table.

Muldoon had a fresh beer in hand with two more set waiting for his party. The expedient bartender was behind the bar tending to other orders. Marone grimaced at the sight of another Sam Adam's but followed Patello's lead in rendering a gratuitous sign to Muldoon.

Patello picked up the conversation. "Okay, Mouldy, we got your message and Mr. Marone will see that the proper people are advised. A representative from Action Waste Management will be appointed to work out the terms of a labor agreement with the appropriate Local. I'm sure that you can make those arrangements. It's my understanding that Commissioner Logan will accept a position in the private sector within the month. There is no basis to think that the Mayor or anyone in his administration has misused campaign funds. You can be sure that I have no intention at this time to imply anything of the kind to the media. We need assurance from the Mayor that Mr. Megan will be appointed to succeed Commissioner Loan. We also need to meet with Mr. Megan in the next couple of days to discuss the details of the Privatized Voluntary Waste Management Program for Boston. The Mayor will want to announce the new arrangement at Boston Hospital next week. I also believe that our mutual interest can be benefited with a private contractor waste management agreement with a private hospital in the City. Since organized labor and the Catholic Church are so supportive of each other it seems reasonable that St. Anslem's should start at the same time as Boston Hospital. Two Boston hospitals going to private waste management will pull the MHA's string. We may need the help of the City health department to convince the CEO of St.

Anslem's that he needs privatized waste management. You take care of your end and keep in touch with me. Is there, anything that I left out? Oh, yeah, no strikes or slowdowns at the hospitals. You keep the locals cool. Anything else?"

"Just one thing." Muldoon stood and turned toward the door. "When you pay the bar tab make sure that my friend Harry, the bartender, gets a good tip."

Phil Mondi was pleased to receive a phone call from an old friend. He and Tony Marone had been friends and teammates at St. Michael's High in the Bronx. They both attended Fordham but Phil later transferred to Pace. Marone graduated a year ahead of Mondi and began his career in the small business investment racket as an account analyst and collector. He was an immediate success and rewarded with a supervisory position and then his own branch of the business in lower Manhattan. Mondi, after graduation, went to work for Marone. He showed equal promise and with Marone's support in a few years was given the opportunity to manage one of NAI's courier ventures, The Patriot Transportion and Courier Service of Boston. With the consent of NAI, Marone and Mondi diversified Patriot into other services and products beyond the basic transport activities.

Mondi enjoyed talking to his friend. "Tony, my main man, how are you doing and how's that beautiful wife and kid?"

"Just fine, Phil. Things well with you?" Marone seemed to register a rhetorical tone. "I know you're making money because I see the reports. You know money isn't everything. You got to relax. Play more golf. Enjoy life, you know what I mean?"

"Tony, when you start with that relax stuff it means you got some bum that I got to put on the payroll for my own good and yours too. Who is the guy and when does he start?"

Marone seemed genuinely hurt that his friend suspected ulterior motives in the call. "I got to explain, Phil. You know about the waste management thing that Patello's handling? Well, we cut a deal with this Muldoon guy at the Union that we take and stash the Boston Commissioner of Health in a private slot so the goons can put a guy they own in the Commissioner's job. So, I figure that we put the guy in with you so if we need to come back later and hit the goons we got this guy Logan to use as a club. You sort of keep him happy but don't let him get too involved if you know what I mean. Anyway, the goons put in a guy named Megan and he opens the door for us with the hospitals as a starter. We give the Union a contract at Action and let them load up on us a little."

The drift was obvious to Mondi. "You're talking about Michael Logan, Tony. He's a clean-cut kid that the Mayor appointed to the commissioner's job after the last election. We know him because he was active with the Young Democrats. I think his thing is public health work. Got a master's degree from Harvard or BU or something. He probably doesn't know squat about the transport business. He takes a job in this outfit and the press is going to smell a deal somewhere. It makes more sense for him to go into health in the private sector. That way the switch is less obvious and keeps him from being offended by a forced career change. Also, the public sees it as reasonable since the kid really isn't a politician. How about this? We get him a job with the Catholics, say at St. Anslem's Hospital. Patello and I convince Hardly that the hospital's CEO needs a guy to help with quality control or something that a master's degree in public health would want to do. Hell, he could be an assistant to our good friend and fellow hospital trustee, Dr. Richard Folley."

"Phil, I knew there was a reason why I put up with your bullshit all these years. That's a good idea. How do we know the boss at St. Anslem's will buy the idea? You got him wrapped?"

"The top job at St. Anslem's is a wild card, Tony. Hardly tried too early to move in and pissed off the Cardinal and the Nuns. They got a guy in there that is a common pro that tries to do a job. He's got some moxie but I don't think he'd take a wrapper. I think I have a better idea. We get Hardly and Folley to convince the Cardinal that he needs an office in the Chancery for health affairs. This guy Logan, obviously, a good Catholic, gets anointed to the post by the Cardinal and everybody cheers. He can still be an assistant to Folley that way we got a wrapper on him but it's transparent. I like it."

Marone jumped at the suggestion. "Okay, Phil, makes sense except for a few management problems and a few bruised egos. Let's give it a try. You call Patello about our talk and work it out. Get back to me. In the meantime I got to talk to Capizzi about what to do with Mayor Cowan and to make sure we got a tight wrapper on Siro. Speaking about wrappers you ought to see if you can get one on the top guy at the hospital. We might need it."

"Whatever. You stay cool, my friend." Mondi closed the conversation.

Chapter Four

The idea of creating a central office for health within the Archdiocese directed by Mike Logan that could be controlled by National Associated Investors required careful cultivation. Phil Mondi gave the idea to Charlie Patello following the conversation with Marone. Patello knew that he could not advance the idea without opposition from O'Shea and his son-in-law, Dr. Folley. Folley had the clout to kill the plan by simply suggesting to the Cardinal that it was not a good idea. On the other hand, Patello reasoned, Folley could also convince the Cardinal to do it. The only way to get Folley to do that was to somehow make it his idea. Since Folley was best influenced by his father-in-law, Patello decided to plant the seed of wisdom with Hardly who was certain to mention it to O'Shea. O'Shea would probably slip the idea as his own to Folley who would run with it. The scheme worked like a charm.

Three days after Patello had a chat with Hardly about a central Office, Hardly, Patello, O'Shea, and Folley met in Hardly's plush conference room to discuss the sad state of affairs surrounding the Church's healing ministry. Hardly was moved by Folley's representation of the lack of coordination among the Catholic hospitals throughout the Archdiocese. O'Shea was readily convinced that a coordinated administrative structure among the hospitals could produce significant cost reductions. O'Shea envisioned a centralized management structure that, among other things, used a central banking concept. Hardly assigned a member of his planning staff to write a complete proposal for the Office of Health Affairs for the Boston Catholic Archdiocese. He also called the Cardinal's office and asked to have a briefing session with

Cardinal McMahon and Bishop Hanks at the earliest possible date. With their consent, the proposal would be given to St. Anslem's Board of Trustees at their next regular meeting.

O'Shea, at Patello's suggestion, was given the assignment of diverting CEO Durant from any anticipation of the proposal. Durant they reasoned, could convince Sr. Elizabeth that the Office of Health Affairs would be strong enough to force the Sisters completely out. The Sisters, if they opposed the idea, could convince the Cardinal to back down. The tactic was to have the Cardinal announce the plan as a fait accompli'. O'Shea decided that the best defense against any interference from Durant was to take the offense and charge the administration of the hospital with fiscal deterioration and managerial incompetence—a charge easy to make since the hospital had experienced increasing deficits with the advent of managed care plans in the Boston area. Hardly's call to the Chancery was promptly returned by Bishop Hanks who reported that the briefing with the Cardinal was set for the next Tuesday and was to follow his cabinet meeting.

That meant the briefing would at best begin around three in the afternoon when the Cardinal's mood would be very unpredictable. Otherwise, the next available date was in three months, much too far in the future for Patello to hold Action in waiting and the Governor, the Mayor, the Workers' Guild, the media, and the public under control. The terrific trinity plus one had to take a chance.

O'Shea began his campaign immediately after the meeting. He placed a heated call to Rod Weaver, CFO at St. Anslem's, demanding that the monthly financial statements be in his hands within a week following the end of the month. He half listened to Weaver's patient explanation why a minimum of ten days was required for accuracy in the reports and then blasted Weaver for not detailing the reports. His next target was cash. The accounts receivable had increased one percent in the last quarter since Durant had taken over. O'Shea asked Weaver what the CEO had done to cause this. Weaver was at a loss to respond. Then O'Shea wanted to know why the doctors weren't contributing to the building fund. He finished his one sided discussion with the announcement that all of the issues under discussion would be items on the agenda and the Board of Trustees meeting a week from next Tuesday.

Durant was in conference with Weaver when he received a call from a screaming O'Shea. Weaver was attempting to explain to his boss that O'Shea was on a tear. O'Shea confirmed Weaver's warning. Durant could only listen to O'Shea's incoherent screaming. The one-sided conversation lasted fifteen minutes during which time O'Shea called Weaver everything but rational and human. He demanded that Durant can Weaver on the spot. If he refused to dump Weaver, O'Shea promised he would have Durant's "ass out of St. Anslem's in a New York minute." Durant offered to discuss Weaver's competence with the Board but asked that O'Shea be patient and allow for time to make corrections. O'Shea would have none of it. Durant was definitely on the defensive and was tactically removed from control at the forthcoming Board meeting. Mission accomplished.

O'Shea met Hardly and Patello for lunch following his conversation with Durant. He was animated as he explained how he had devoured Durant. His obsession with the kill concerned Patello. Patello suggested that Durant had to be held in office if for no other reason than to maintain order while the plan to justify the Office for Health Affairs fell into place. He asked Hardly to calm O'Shea down. O'Shea was offended and a bit angry at Patello's attitude and offered that Durant was an outsider that didn't matter. Patello remembered that Marone for some reason he had not discussed told Mondi to get a wrapper on Durant. Bouncing him wasn't what Marone had in mind. *This goddamn O'Shea had to calm down*, he thought. Nevertheless, the mind game he worked on Durant was right for now. The more immediate objective was to convince the Cardinal to create the Office of Health Affairs. The proposal had to be protected from Durant and the Sisters for a week until the St. Anslem's Board meeting, In the meantime Patello decided he would have a preliminary meeting with Commissioner Logan.

Commissioner Logan grew up in South Boston and held a strong affection for his native Boston. He had no desire for public office but committed himself to public service with a strong passion. He respected the working man and felt that municipal services should be first devoted to the health and safety of the population, especially the poor. While attending Harvard's School of Public Health he made headlines by constantly hassling the City Department of Health about conditions in the disadvantaged neighborhoods of Boston. When Cowan announced his candidacy for Mayor based on a strong public health and safety platform, Logan became a member of his campaign cabinet and was promised early in the campaign that he would be Cowan's commissioner of Public Health. As Commissioner, he also became the nominal head of Boston

Hospital, who provided care for the majority of the poor from Roxbury, South Boston, and Dorchester. He noticed that the cost of providing sub-standard care was higher than the cost of high quality care provided by private teaching hospitals in Boston which he blamed on Union feather bedding among other things. His passion to do the right thing coupled with a certain political insensitivity caused him to grow in disfavor with the Mayor's political supporters—especially The Boston Workers' Guild. Contrary to statements made by the Mayor and others on the City Council, Logan had not any access to campaign funds or the accounting of the funds. He had a growing uneasiness that he was being set up to take a big fall.

Patello had the Human Resource Director from Hardly Security and Trust give Logan a call at home to inquire about his interest in a position in the private sector. The Human Resource Director told Logan that while he was calling for the bank, the position was with a major client of the bank and one of the largest private providers of health services in Massachusetts. If Logan was at all interested he should get his resume to the caller immediately since the client expected to fill the position within the month and there were many possible candidates. Logan hand carried his resume to the bank the next morning. The HR Director called Patello who told him to tell Logan to expect an interview sometime after Tuesday but within the week.

Patello checked in with Muldoon to let him know that the skids were being greased for Logan's departure from public life. It was time, he suggested, to meet Megan and discuss the voluntary privatization of waste management for Boston. He also arranged for Muldoon to meet with Mark Meehan, the President of Action, so that management and labor could begin negotiations on their collective bargaining agreement, Muldoon and Meehan agreed to meet at the Marriott in Framingham, about fifteen miles west of Boston, for an early breakfast out of sight of the Boston Business Journal reporter who had been shadowing Muldoon since his Capitol steps routine. Muldoon, ever cautious, promised Patello that he would arrange a session with Megan when he was sure Meehan was rightly on the come. Patello had to admire the old labor warrior's guts. The guy was tough and careful.

Muldoon came to the Marriott equipped with a contract that was loaded for bear. The two men met in the spacious lobby and moved quickly to the comfortable restaurant with floor to ceiling windows overlooking the rolling fairways of the hotel's golf course. Meehan had arranged for a table away from the center of the dining room. He also paid to have the surrounding tables kept vacant so the two could talk without being overheard. Muldoon immediately realized that the stage had been well set. To counter the effect, he decided to intimidate Meehan with an opening volley and force a quick conclusion. He was counting on Meehan being afraid of having to report to Patello, and especially Marone, that the deal was not done.

As the two sat down, Muldoon fired the first shot. "Let's cut this short. I haven't got time for any of your bullshit. Here's the contract. Just sign it and we can get back to town."

Meehan took Muldoon's opening blast with the unexpected calm of an experienced negotiator. He carefully avoided picking up or even glancing at the document that Muldoon pushed at him. "Mr. Muldoon, before we get to far involved in details, I suggest we have some breakfast. They have an excellent buffet. Otherwise, you might want to look at the menu. Personally, I'll have the buffet."

Muldoon had experienced this tactic many times before in his long career with the Workers' Guild but he was nearly blown away by Meehan's completely unexpected professionalism. Slightly flushed he followed Meehan to the buffet. He picked at his fruit and bagel while Meehan demonstrated total emotional control as he devoured a heaping plate of scrambled eggs, sausage, bacon, two pancakes, and toast. When the waitress poured the third cup of coffee Meehan went back to the buffet and returned with two sweet rolls and a bran muffin. Muldoon was both amazed and disgusted. He had lost his concentration and the initiative.

Between bites, Meehan began the conversation. "You know, Bob, in addition to having one hell of a buffet this place has the cutest waitresses in New England. I do my best work in these conditions. We seem to have the unique opportunity to come to a mutual understanding without the usual time consuming preliminary activities associated with the collective bargaining process. Let's not screw it up with a lot of irritating demands and counter-demands. We also have to be sure that what we agree on has the Department of Labor's good housekeeping seal of approval. I suggest that we have a standard but fast track election at Action that follows the course of collective bargaining. That way the contract will properly represent the employees' interest and maintain the integrity of process. What I'm prepared to offer you is the opportunity to name an individual of your choice to accept a management position in the sales force at Action. This person will be salaried and on commission based on gross sales on all Action contracts signed after, say, the date of our labor agreement. The offset to this is that I want to name the shop steward that the local appoints. That way everything remains in balance. Now if you think that we can agree on this, I'll have my HR director and lawyer meet with your people tomorrow and start the process. As you told Patello, you can organize our sweatshop in a minute."

Muldoon realized immediately that in his first conversation with Patello he had mentioned a piece of the action. He thought Patello had overlooked it so he was intending to bring it up again when the contract was in place. Now he was being offered a piece up front plain and simple. Commission based on gross sales was open ended. He could take the commission and let the stiff he named to the phony sales job take the salary or whatever piece he thought he should have and pocket the rest Muldoon was caught up in the offer. His mind identified several organizers employed by the Union that could be trusted and happy to take the job. All things considered he had what he wanted.

"Did you say twenty percent commission on the gross, Mark?"

Meehan took another bite, swallowed, and gently touched his lips with his napkin. "I didn't say. I usually pay five percent on the gross."

The counter was exactly what Muldoon had expected. Carefully, he held his emotion. "Fifteen percent is the least I could accept."

Meehan put down his fork and leaned forward on the table. He looked squarely into Muldoon's eyes. The final offer was about to happen. "Cut the shit, Muldoon. We both know that ten percent is the number."

Muldoon didn't say a word. He looked into Meehan's eyes and gave a slight nod.

Meehan extended his hand over the table and Muldoon extended his. They shook hands and the deal was done. They started to leave together but Meehan stopped to pay the check and give a tip with an affectionate pat on the shoulder to the waitress. Muldoon gave a slight wave and left. Meehan walked to the lobby gift shop and bought a roll of Tums that he desperately needed. By the time he got to his BMW he had popped four of the white tablets and was having stomach pains. He laboriously moved under the wheel, started the engine and pushed the speed dial on his telephone for Patello's office. Patello answered the direct line to his desk.

Meehan seemed to belch his greeting when Patello answered, "Charlie, this is Mark. The deal is done. You were right. He jumped at the commission.

He'll get me a sales manager and I'll get him a shop steward. We can wrap this up in the week. I'll have the employees notified about the Union this afternoon. My supervisors will keep it in line."

Patello was pleased. "Okay, Charlie. Good work. Look, on this shop steward thing I recommended a young guy from the State Office of Waste Management to Action some time back. I think he told me that he works in your Quality Control section for Ken Ryan another one of our State alumnus. He might be a good man for shop steward. Name is...ah...let me think...ah, yeah, Jay Marquart. Anyway, he's a good kid that did a lot of mule work for the party. Still helps out now and then. I think you can trust him to do as asked or told, whatever. Check it out."

Meehan felt miserable. He was sure he had ulcers. Quickly he accepted Patello's suggestion. "I know Ken Ryan, Charlie. He's clean and innocent. Best we keep it that way. This Marquart guy I guess is like Ryan. We could make him steward without getting him or Ryan dirty. As long as we have Muldoon on the take the steward only has to tell Ryan and Ryan tells us or vice versa. I'll check it out but I'm inclined to go with Marquart. I'll make sure Ryan keeps Marquart available for the appointment."

Within minutes after completing his call from Meehan, Patello's phone rang again. This time it was Hardly calling to report that the proposal for the Cardinal's Office for Health Affairs was ready for a pre-briefing by the terrific trinity plus one. The bank's planning staff had practically worked around the clock to create logical text, definite recommendations, slides, and graphs that all supported the concept. Hardly suggested that they get a room at the Alleton Club that evening, review the proposal, and have dinner. Patello stated his availability and left it to Hardly to make the arrangements.

More pressing in Patello's mind was the deal with the Workers' Guild and the need to get the Guild in line with the Waste Management program. Anxiously, Patello telephoned Muldoon.

When the Union leader answered, Charlie pressed the point. "Bob, this is Charlie. I understand that you and Mark worked things out. Now I believe that Mr. Logan will be well placed in short order. We should have a conversation with Mr. Megan sometime today or tomorrow."

Muldoon had expected Patello's call. He was prepared for the questions and gave immediate answers. "Right, Charlie. We still have a couple of loose ends. The big piece is the Mayor. I have to get him comfortable about the

WASP before we can get Megan into the Commissioner's job. We need to hear from NAI or the Federation or both if the Mayor has a shot for the Federal post. Let's go with the WASP issue first. Can you get a signal that they're going to back him?"

Patello had been put on the defensive. He needed time to make sure that the pieces would stick together. "I'll get back to you, Bob."

Patello hung up and immediately placed a call to Marone in New York. The secretary explained that Mr. Marone and Mr. Capizzi had left early to drive to Providence for a conference with Mr. Frank Patello. She suggested that he could reach Mr. Marone on his car phone or at Mr. Frank Patello's residence. She offered both telephone numbers to Mr. Patello since his name appeared on the approved list now flashing on her CRT. Patello knew Uncle Frank's unlisted number and had Marone's car phone on his index so he graciously declined the secretary's offer. He knew that the questions he had to ask could not be answered until after Marone and Capizzi had met with Big Frank.

Big Frank had been briefed by Capizzi about the Boston issue. He immediately called the Federation's representative on the NAI Board to ask why the Union had not been direct about whatever was on their mind. The Federation rep was Jim Ebber, a former US Senator from New Jersey who was the choice of Labor only to be unseated after four terms by a professional basketball player. Ebber explained to Big Frank that his knowledge of the Federation's interest in Boston was limited but he could have a special advisor from the Washington Headquarters' come with him to explain the matter. Big Frank suggested that they come to Providence and attend the briefing the next morning with Capizzi and Marone. The meeting was scheduled at Big Frank's estate on millionaires' row in Newport.

By ten o'clock the next morning everyone had arrived, introductions were complete, and coffee with Danish was available. At Big Frank's request Ebber opened the meeting with an explanation about the Federation's unusual method of bringing their interest to the NAI table. The underlying reason was that the Federation was uncertain about its interest in an expanding industry that had exploded on the West Coast and seemed about to impact in Boston. Ebber asked Big Frank if the staff man from Washington could be allowed to explain the matter in more detail. Big Frank nodded his approval.

The consultant began by pointing out that over the past ten years Union negotiators, especially on the West Coast, had been making major concessions in health benefits for their members in contract renewals. Cost conscious employers had abandoned the traditional indemnity plans offered by Blue Cross/Blue Shield for a less expensive form of coverage provided by Health Maintenance Organizations. As the plans became more popular they became more profitable. New companies came into the market, generated profits and were bought out and consolidated into major conglomerates. The key to their fiscal success was enrolling a healthy population, limiting and controlling use of services, and putting the providers at financial risk. Now that the conglomerates were expanding into the national market with their managed care plans it occurred to the Unions that the only way to protect their members in contract negotiations was to have an interest in Health Maintenance Organizations. A direct attempt to form a Union Health Maintenance Organization would face a limited market and limited profits. It was reasoned by the Federation that they should partner with an organization that did not have a direct identity with Labor in the formation of this venture. The consultants also pointed out that a national HMO did not sell as well on the local level as an HMO that looked and smelled like it was home grown.

Patello seemed to be tracking on the presentation but Capizzi and Marone were helplessly lost. Ebber continuously glanced at Big Frank to measure his attitude. When he sensed that Big Frank was becoming frustrated he jumped in. "Mr. Patello, the third-highest topic in the minds of the people these days is healthcare. They rate crime and the economy as one and two. Fourth is the environment. The Federation joined with AARP, the national hospital associations, and many other organizations to bring about a national health reform bill. It got clobbered by the republicans because it was too damn expensive. Many members in the house and the senate were defeated because of their support of the President's health reform proposal. The mood of the nation is to control health cost by local determination. It seems to us that there is an opportunity to form a national syndicate on the same order as Park Environmental that will meet the interest of the people and, I hasten to add, be extremely profitable. You ask why we targeted the Boston area to stake our claim. Please let our consultant explain."

The young consultant put down his cup of coffee, adjusted his glasses, and glanced at his notes. He straightened his tie and made eye contact with Big Frank. "Actually, we hadn't considered Boston as a player in this thing until our conversation with Mr. Marone last week regarding Mr. Muldoon's demonstration at the rally on the Capitol steps. During our conversation, it occurred to us that Boston was well saturated even over saturated with health services that controlled the economy or at least a major piece of the economy. We also had in place through Action, a cover for our investment in health services. What we needed to establish was an arrangement with the Workers' Guild and your local operation that gave us the opportunity to create this new venture.

"We didn't want Muldoon to be fully informed about the program because of his, shall we say, tendency to seek personal gain at the risk of the major objective. Nevertheless, a man of his ambition and limited intellect can be helpful in arranging the preliminary details and doing spade work. I expect that by now you have managed to compromise Mr. Muldoon to your own interest. Following our conversation with Mr. Marone, we contacted Mr. Muldoon who explained that the deal cut by your Mr. Patello with the tax payers association was a threat to labor's interest. Actually, we saw it as rather helpful but we did not want to disillusion Mr. Muldoon. We simply directed him to cut the best deal he could, and in the process, get your attention by bringing up the need to get Mayor Cowan a Federal appointment. The good Mayor has been well supported by us over the years and deserves a place in history where we can keep him in line. You can help by using your influence to protect the Mayor from suffering any public embarrassment while we maneuver his appointment."

Marone quickly glanced at Capizzi and then at Big Frank. He caught a nod from the boss that indicated that he had the floor. "I think it's safe to say that Mr. Muldoon will represent our mutual interest from this point forward. We respect his ability. He was very helpful in bringing your message to our attention. We are in process of establishing a labor contract between Action Waste Management and a Guild local. To further advance our interest we must be assured that the Mayor will be happy with a Federal appointment and not seek an elected post in State government."

Senator Ebber leaned forward on the table and glanced at the three gentlemen opposite him. "We quite frankly are unable to control all of the Mayor's ambitions. He has stated to our political action committee that he would be content with a Federal appointment at a high level. However, our people on the President's staff are reluctant to have the slob too close to the top. He could bolt from the Under-Secretary post and run back to the State. We think that the campaign fund issue needs to be held by us as a trump card. If we have to play it, Muldoon and some of his cronies could take a heavy dive. We would appreciate your help in convincing the Democratic leadership that the Mayor can scrub up to look and act respectable."

Big Frank pushed back his chair and stood up. He walked slowly around the table and glanced out the window at the rolling waves breaking against the rocks. The temperature in the room had been elevated by the sun so he took off his jacket and hung it over his chair. The others in the room followed. It was time for a break.

When the meeting resumed, Big Frank took the floor. "This healthcare business is confusing. Everybody says it's expensive and you say it's profitable. Yet I hear the hospitals hollering for more money. The insurance companies want more money from the employers. Doctors are all rich. The States are closing the nut houses because they can't afford them. This new business, HMO, how's it different so it makes money? I don't understand how we get ours. If we go in then we got to have some vigor to stay in. I didn't hear anything that sounded like a good deal. Or did I miss it?"

The young consultant became energized at Frank's commentary. "Let's begin at the top. Healthcare spending is expected to absorb a third of the nation's gross national product in the next ten years. Where is all that money going to be spent? Almost entirely in the private sector. Who spends the money depends on how the Nation's health policy is formed but it's a good bet that the mood of the Country continues to favor the private sector as both buyer and seller of health services. We expect the interest to center on private providers of healthcare for a minimum of ten years—maybe forever. You form a company that sells healthcare and you form another company that buys healthcare. You take the profits off the top on both sides and let the medical providers worry about the bottom line. You have to be careful that you don't get suckered into giving to much away and losing your service base in the process. That's why we supported a tax based program for the poor. The government would prepay for the poor just like the employer would prepay for the employee. We still skim off the top. To get established you need a service base like a big group of doctors and a hospital in a large population area. You also want to begin in an affluent community so that you don't get overrun with the problem of caring for poor people or old folks."

Big Frank looked to be partially convinced but still carried a confused look. "I don't understand this buyer and seller business. Hospitals and doctors sell and the insurance company buys. How am I going to make out selling doctors services when I ain't a doctor? Those bastards are all independent. So are the hospitals."

The consultant smiled at the question and stood to respond. "That's the point, Mr. Patello. As the buyer you determine how you want to buy the product. Setting specifications on health services for your subscriber clients requires the provider groups to provide care according to your specifications. You control the market by controlling volume and cost. The providers are forced to form an organization or join one that you own. It's called a medical services network. Boston is well positioned to accept the reformed model of health services delivery. In fact, the Boston medical community has been converting to managed care for the past ten years without being aware of the transition. The Boston based medical schools, Harvard, Boston University and Tufts, have extensive medical practice plans for their teaching faculty who are mostly employed and salaried by the hospitals. Almost all of the employed physicians are specialists that control referrals from the primary care physician in private practice. In order to maintain the revenue to the practice plans the medical schools and their affiliated hospitals created their own HMO's several years ago that have successfully competed with Blue Cross and other indemnity programs. The attraction of the patients to the medical centers away from the community hospitals and community-based specialists caused the community docs to form group practices that compete with the university practice plans. Right now, the community doctors and the hospital guys are at each other. It's called a town and gown battle."

Big Frank was looking directly at Capizzi who was totally confused. He changed his glance to Marone who slowly shook his head in confusion. Frank breathed deeply and returned eye contact to the consultant who was now seated. "Okay, I can see that there is big money in healthcare and more is going to be in the pot. I understand that the way we get ours is by taking it off the top. I understand that to do that we got to control both ends. That's all very simple. I don't understand this HMO business and I don't understand this doctor to doctor stuff. That is a big mystery. What is even more confusing is how do we get into the act and how do you figure in?"

The consultant nodded an acknowledgment to Frank. He reached into his pocket and distributed business cards to the three men. He then went to his briefcase and extracted brochures that he placed on the table. "I apologize for not beginning with introductory statements. I thought that perhaps Mr. Ebber might have provided this in advance of our meeting but I now realize that he had no time to send any preliminary information. As you can see on the business card, my name is Tom Callahan and I'm a senior partner with Debur and Tandy. We are a public accounting firm and management consultants specializing in public service industries. Our practice has focused over the past five years on consultation to major users and purchasers of healthcare services. We have been advisors to the Federation for nearly ten years. We hope to become the consultants to the joint venture that results within the Federation in the formation of a national health services network. We are confident that the venture could begin with a strong push in the Boston area and spread rapidly across the country. Through our other clients in several industries we could influence the progress. Debur and Tandy is well positioned."

Young Mr. Callahan had their attention. "Allow me to further explain the Boston opportunity. Boston is saturated with health services that are extremely expensive for employers. The high expense is the direct result of overutilization. The overutilization is caused by the control of the payers by the big providers, teaching hospitals. The payers are on the edge because the providers take all the money that the payers exhort from the employers. Our approach is to force an HMO over the edge and pick it up under Chapter Eleven, Bankruptcy. We appear to be riding to the rescue of the subscribing employers and the unfortunate providers wanting for their accounts receivable as well as anyone bonds or mortgages. Wearing our white hats, we convince the employers that our brand of managed care is the Suitable answer to control the surging costs of healthcare benefits. From the other direction, and with another identity, we convince the community doctors and the community hospitals that by joining our network of providers they can control patient volume and thereby maintain income. Now here's what we have going for us. Boston experiences one thousand hospital patient days per one thousand population per year. In California the number is three hundred fifty days per thousand. That difference gives us a lot of room to make some impressive change. The average cost per hospital stay in Boston is the highest in the country. This tells us that there is a lot of room to skim and still reduce the cost. Obviously, the teaching hospitals have been skimming all along. We just take their piece or a part of it and give the rest back. Meanwhile, we take the referring community physician and put him on incentive to reduce the referrals to the high price specialists. In the interest of their own pocketbook they treat the patient at low cost. The specialists eventually come around and accept a negotiated arrangement on our terms."

Big Frank began to get the drift. "What about the hospitals? They got a ton of money stashed from years of skimming. Why can't they do the same as us since, as you said before, they already control both ends?"

Callahan gave a positive response. "They can do it. And they are in the process of moving into managed care arrangements. But they have to get organized. Right now, the hospitals are scrambling to form their own networks. They are concentrating on merging with community hospitals and overlooking the doctors. We move in by buying up the doctors who make the referrals, the so-called primary care doctor. The hospital utilization rate drops like a rock. They can't cut costs fast enough because of the teaching and research load. Big deficits result and we pick 'em off.

Big Frank nodded his gratitude to Mr. Callahan. He then directed his comments to Ebber. "Senator, my colleagues and I are grateful and pleased with your candid statements and honesty in making known your intentions. I will ask Mr. Capizzi to work with Mr. Callahan in formulating a detailed proposal for the consideration of the NAI board of trustees. I'm confident that the due diligence on the matter will give us good reason to initiate our so-called joint venture. I have not forgotten the matter regarding the Mayor. We will use whatever influence we might have to cause his appointment as the Under Secretary of Labor. You can appreciate I'm sure that in so doing we will be discreet."

After the meeting adjourned, Big Frank advised Capizzi to check out Debur and Tandy, especially Tom Callahan, although he held a sudden attraction to the man's style. He also directed Marone to signal Patello that NAI was with the Federation on the deal with Mayor Cowan. He expected the Union to shoulder the matter with NAI in a supporting role. That's why he stressed the discreet aspect to Senator Ebber. In response to Marone's question regarding filling Patello in on the prospect of getting into the Healthcare business, Big Frank opted to have Patello informed in general but not burden him with scant details until after the NAI board had heard the full proposal from Debur and Tandy. Frank knew well that his nephew would call him direct if he wanted the full scope.

On the drive back to New York, Marone placed a call to Patello. Patello expected the call and was pleased to hear Marone's voice. "Charlie, this is Tony, we are on our way back to New York from a meeting with Big Frank and the Union guys. Thought I'd fill you in."

Patello for some reason got out of his chair and stood glancing out the window. "Good to hear from you, Tony. What's this big deal with the Federation?"

The signal faded on the cellular phone as a truck passed. Tony waited a second before continuing the conversation. "Healthcare, Charlie. They want us in the healthcare business. Anyway, we're going to look at it at NAI next week. Big Frank seems like he wants to go along. Not much I can tell you about it because I'm not too sure I understand it. You want to know more maybe you should call Frank."

Patello understood and respected Marone's requirement to limit details about the meeting. He also appreciated Tony's hint that Uncle Frank wanted to explain the details to him personally. With slight hesitation he asked, "Look, Tony, did anything get resolved about the Mayor?"

"Yeah. Big Frank said we would support the Federation's push to get the Mayor out of Boston. You know I don't think they like the son of a bitch."

Patello thought the comment was an understatement. "Thanks, Tony. That's all I need for now. I have to call Muldoon and tell him to relax. Then I need to see that the labor deal between Action and the Local gets done. We also have to see that Meehan and the hospitals sign a trash deal, not to mention getting this guy Logan onto the Cardinal's staff and this Megan into Logan's former job as Commissioner. And, of course, let's not forget to have the Mayor announce the voluntary privatization of waste management project. So, look, if you want to be in the healthcare racket and want my help maybe you should wait until I get a few irons out of the fire."

Marone gave a slight laugh as part of his goodbye. "We'll be in touch, Charlie. When and if this health thing gets approved you know Big Frank will want you to move it along. Don't work too hard."

Patello moved back to his desk and hung up the phone. Then he sat in his comfortable chair and pondered the conversation just ended. It was very reasonable for NAI to go into the health business especially in Boston. The problem is that one Charles Patello was over extended and not in a very good position to give the matter all the attention it would need. He thought about calling Uncle Frank and suggesting that health be given a stand by status until the waste management thing, the Union, the Mayor, and God knows what else got resolved. Such a call to Uncle Frank would also disclose that Charlie was bending under pressure and maybe not the boy wonder that Frank thought he was. This would be very disappointing to Frank. Charlie would never disappoint Uncle Frank. On second thought it was best to let things happen.

Patello never had a chance to finish his second thought. The private line to his office began to buzz and the light began to flash. An important call was in the offing and it no doubt was Uncle Frank. Charlie pulled up the receiver and rendered a friendly greeting, "Hello, Frank. I knew you would be calling. How are you? I was just about to give you a call."

Frank was not surprised that Charlie had guessed that he was calling. Nothing that Charlie did surprised Frank. Frank simply passed on the greeting and went to his agenda, "Yeah, Charlie. I guess maybe Mario and Tony got to you already about this thing the Federation wants to do with the health business. See, I think it's a good thing but it's not the big thing. We need to shoot for something higher. Don't you think?"

Charlie was perplexed. He had no idea what Frank might be thinking, "Uncle Frank, if you think the health business is where we belong then that's where we'll go. I'm sure that I can bag Hardly, O'Shea, and his idiot son-in-law. Beyond that, you have to tell me what to shoot for. I have no idea what you mean by something bigger."

The big picture was only in Big Frank's mind. Suddenly he realized that his favorite nephew was not on the same wave length, "Sorry, Charlie, I'm running way ahead of you. Here's what I'm thinking. We capture waste management but what we really got is City Hall. That's cool. Now we take over health services through waste management. What we got? We got City Hall and the biggest piece of business in town. What's left? Banks! Boston has no industry. All there is in that town is State Government, City Government, a bunch of hospitals and medical schools, and a lot of Colleges and stuff with the banks sucking up the revenue. We get control of City Hall, the hospitals, and the banks, and we own the town. It's a lot better deal than we got in New York because here we got to share the pie with a lot of other interests. Besides, it ain't safe to walk the streets here at night anymore. My thing is to move our show to Boston where we could run everything. Then I retire and you take over. I can hang out in Newport and help when you need me. How's it sound?"

Patello was standing again and looking out his window. He was almost in shock as he tried to contemplate the scope of Uncle Frank's idea. "Uncle Frank, that's a pretty tall order. It could take years to pull it off"

Before Charlie could finish, Frank interrupted, "No Charlie, it's not such a big deal. You got waste management greased with the Mayor and Union guys. The hospital thing with the Catholics is a hanger. What you got to do is push over this nitwit Hardly and grab his bank. Then we pull in a few more banks and the deal is set. I got faith in you. You can do it. For now it's just you and me who got the idea. I'll spring it on Mario and Tony when you got an angle on the banks. Then we bring NAI along. You got it?"

There was a lot of truth in what the old man said. Patello had thought for some time that Hardly was losing it. He would eventually have to be replaced as the bank's new chief executive. Before the bank's Board of Directors focused on that prospect it might be well to have the Board focus on the prospect of being bigger and richer. Greed was the best tactic.

"Uncle Frank, just off the top of my head, I think what we could do is subtly promote a bank merger between Hardly Security and Cambridge Bank. That would undermine Hardly and his goofy cousins at the same time. While the investors whip it about we could move in and buy up the controlling interests. I'll check it out."

That was the attitude Big Frank was hoping for. His nephew was on the move. "You got it, Charlie. Keep me posted on your progress so I know when to spring it here. You also got to remember that the waste management deal and the hospital thing have to come through so we have a solid base of control. Get the Catholics in line. Nice talking to ya. I gotta go."

That was it. Frank hung up before Charlie had a chance to say goodbye. Charlie now had the big picture. Next to Frank, he was the only one who did.

The Terrific Trinity plus One arrived at the Alleton Club at five in the afternoon. Hardly had reserved a room on the third floor of the stately club that was almost as old as the Hardly family tradition. The Hardly clan had been charter members of the exclusive gentlemen's sanctuary reserved then and now for the ancestors of Boston's Brahmans.

Kevin Hardly had membership by default since Catholics were not easily admitted into membership. For sure had he been subjected to a standard application process his Protestant cousins would have had him black balled. For that reason he kept a low profile in club activities and always paid his bill on time. Inviting his Irish and Italian friends to dine was risky. Using a third floor club room was not only appropriate but guaranteed that the club provided quality service without engendering the wrath of the other members with proper heritage. The room was spacious for at least twenty diners. A small table set for six was squarely set in the middle of the room with the unused tables moved to the inner wall. The extra chairs had been removed and a serve yourself bar had been inconspicuously placed in the corner. At the end of the room opposite the door were two easels with poster boards reversed and waiting. A flip chart was positioned between the easels.

Two staff planners from The Hardly Security and Trust Bank had arrived about an hour before the Terrific Trinity plus one and arranged the room for their presentation. Now satisfied that all was in readiness they initiated proceedings at the self-serve bar. Hardly arrived promptly at five and was served his first martini—extra dry, rocks and a twist—by his subjects who had done their homework. Patello and O'Shea arrived at the same time and rode the elevator to the third floor. O'Shea was cool to Patello and still nursed his anger from their last meeting when Charlie admonished him about his attitude toward Durant. Patello tended not to notice the typical Irish grudge and extended a cordial greeting. When they entered the room Patello mistakenly thought that one of the young planners was the bartender and ordered a Duers and water. The young man seemed pleased to be of service. Patello later apologized for the mistake with his usual charm. O'Shea made a cutting comment about how some people were always in need of help. Patello felt a surge of anger that nearly erupted in a Roman response learned years back in the neighborhood. In his mind he knew that *this Irish son of a bitch was going to get his—but not now.* O'Shea appeared oblivious to Patello's concealed anger and nosily gargled a beer.

The Terrific Trinity and the two planners were on their third round when the magnificent Richard Folley, M.D., was escorted into the room by the club manager. Folley thanked the manager for his courtesy and made a grand gesture to his compatriots ignoring the hired help from the bank. In response to Hardly's invitation, he declined his usual martini opting for an iced tea explaining that he was on call for the department and indeed lives were to depend on his clear thinking. With all on board, thirst amply quenched, Hardly beckoned to a waiter standing just outside the door. It was time to eat.

The extensive menu of the Alleton Club allowed each participant to exercise their knowledge of fine dining. Hardly encouraged exploration of all facets of the menu. He enjoyed playing host and making suggestions to his guests about the quality of his favorite entrees. When the orders were complete, he accepted the wine list and made a prominent French selection. He also directed the waiter to continue to pour the wine throughout the meal—no need to ask if another bottle was required—just make sure that his guests were amply refreshed. An hour and a half later the diners were finishing their desert. Hardly suggested that brandy and a good cigar would be a fitting end to their dining experience. Everyone except Hardly declined the cigar but they all enjoyed the brandy. Hardly allowed the bottle to be left on the bar. The waiter brought coffee and asked if could be of additional service. Hardly signed the chit and thanked the man for his excellent attention to his guests. It was time for the staff planners to give their briefing. Both had poured themselves another double shot of brandy.

Hardly explained to Patello, O'Shea and Folley that the Planning Department at Hardly Security and Trust was staffed with Harvard Business School graduates. Their capability was the envy of the banking industry. It was the Planning Department that first recognized the potential of automated teller machines and gave HSTB a big lead in the retail banking market. It was the HSTB planners that engineered the acquisition of rural banks thus forming a network that was the beginning of the HSTB becoming the largest retailer of banking services in the State and the nation. Following the buildup, he invited Stephen and George, HSTB's crack planning team, to begin the briefing that would justify the formation of the Office of Health Affairs for the Boston Catholic Archdiocese.

The evening had lasted beyond the endurance and sobriety of the HSTB crack planning team. Stephen sat at the end of the table with a silly grin on his face. George was laboriously trying to stand. Having accomplished that feat, he proceeded to knock down the first easel. This was too much for Stephen who broke out into uncontrollable laughter. George brought the easel back to an upright position and acknowledged his partner with a wave of his tie signaling the start of their best Laurel and Hardly imitation.

George spoke the opening line. "Well, this is another fine mess you got us into."

Stephen's facial expression turned to remorse and he began to fidget with his fingers. He seemed to be on the verge of crying. "I'm sorry, George. It's just that I'm not used to speaking in public."

George looked at the executives waiting for the report and then cast a disapproving glance at Stephen. "Well, all right, Stephen, I'll do the talking and you handle the cue cards. Can you do that?"

Stephen hung his head in mock remorse. "I'll try, George. What do you want me to do?"

Now in full command, George spoke with authority. "You just stand next to the easel, Stephen, and when I point with my fingers you take one off. Do you think you can do that?"

Stephen appeared confused with the assignment but moved next to the easel with cue cards in place. George strolled to the center of the room above the dining table and introduced the presentation. "Gentlemen, our assignment was to study the possibility and benefit of establishing an Office of Health Affairs for the Archdiocese. I'm pleased to report to you that an office for this purpose could be of valuable service in assisting the Archdiocese meet the expanding demand for healthcare in the Boston metropolitan area. As I will demonstrate on the charts, the healthcare market in Boston has been on a growth curve for the past ten years."

With a flourish, George gestured to the first easel and looked at Stephen. Stephen grabbed George's hand and proceeded to twist his fingers. George began clubbing Stephen who promptly dropped George's hand. Both convulsed with laughter. The humor was lost on Hardly who looked confused. Folley and O'Shea were angry. Patello concealed a smile, not as a result of these expert planner buffoons, but more at the buildup let down posture of Hardly. George took quick note of Hardly and signaled Stephen that fun time was over. Do the job and hope to be still employed in the morning seemed to register with the crack presenters?

George pointed to the first chart that Stephen had placed into view. "Gentlemen, as you see on this graph, hospital admissions in Boston have increased at ten percent per year for the past ten years. This next chart shows that the admissions at St. Anslem's have increased on average of eight percent over the same period. We can conclude that St. Anslem's is losing market share but closer inspection will reveal that St. Anslem's is benefiting from higher intensity than any other major teaching hospital in the area. This high intensity provides a higher revenue per admission than any other hospital and of course contributes to the bottom line. We are confident that St. Anslem's will continue to expand its tertiary market if it becomes the tertiary referral hospital for the three other Catholic hospitals in the Archdiocese. The coordination of this referral base becomes the major function for the Office of Health Affairs."

The time seemed right for Patello to make his pitch. Carefully, he interrupted the presentation by the crack planning staff by offering support for their conclusions. Then he suggested that the office would require a special type of leadership that was adept at coordinating diverse interests. Finally, he very tactfully mentioned that Michael Logan, the current Commissioner of Health for the City of Boston, was an excellent candidate for the position. Hardly agreed. O'Shea was silent, while Folley seemed to applaud the prospect.

Folley was thinking that the presentation was right on. He needed to find a way to take credit for the thinking. Perhaps he could make a call to Bishop Hanks or the Cardinal and suggest that he was best prepared to direct the office. On the other hand, he didn't want to bump off Logan and in the process, bring Patello down on his back. The matter required some thought.

George resumed his commentary. "In addition to the coordination of in patient tertiary care the office could be a central agency for insurance, personnel administration, benefit coordination, purchasing, and any number of administrative tasks. This centralization would noticeably reduce overhead and, therefore, increase profits. We think in time that the office would become the administrative structure for healthcare and the hospitals in the Archdiocese under a single corporate structure. What we have on the remaining charts are organization diagrams and we have also asked our legal staff to prepare a sample set of articles of incorporation and bylaws that can be used when the hospitals are merged. All of this information is contained in the packets that we have prepared for each of you."

The buzz was beginning to wear off. Stephen was in pain and could feel the prospect of vomiting. George noticed that pale look on his partner's face and said a quick prayer for Stephen's life and recovery. George felt fatigue. He had been at the presentation for only about fifteen minutes including the stand-up comedy routine, but had been under pressure from these "stiffs" for nearly four hours. He had a pounding headache. What he needed was a quick ending that gave these "clowns" what they wanted to hear. He chose to distribute the information packets and abandon any further use of the easels and cue cards. Stephen helped distribute the packets and disappeared to the men's room.

George sat at the table and began to explain the information. "Gentlemen, the information contained in these packets is the result of extensive research of the hospital markets in the Boston area. You will note that page one and two are the same charts previously displayed. On page three we begin with the statistical data that shows the growing prospects of the area hospitals. The continuing increase in revenues measured against expenses showing less increases obviously is represented in growing profits. While the last three years have shown what appears to be a slowing of the occupancy rate we note on page four and five that enrollment in the emerging manage care companies is steadily increasing. This leads us to conclude that the increased enrollment will tend to restart the utilization of the hospitals. The growth period will continue as long as the managed care companies continue to expand. The insurance companies are very supportive of the hospital base. Contracts between the providers and the HMOs are in good order."

Patello noticed that the information contained in the packets was nearly two years old. The poor copies still exposed the Massachusetts Hospital Association logo. Apparently, this crack research team had spent all of a half-hour collating material faxed to them by the MHA. O'Shea seemed uncomfortable as well but could not afford to embarrass HSTB by exposing the shabby material. Instead he decided to explore the depth of Frank's analysis.

He glanced at Patello and at George. "George, your positive report about the prospects of the hospitals is encouraging. However, St. Anslem's is experiencing increasing deficits over the past ten months. Is this in any way indicative of a trend or are we just experiencing poor management?"

George wasn't sure what answer the man from the big office wanted. He opted for the middle road. "I don't have the detail of St. Anslem's operations, Mr. O'Shea, but I would have to guess that the St. Anslem circumstance is unique. My suggestion is that you press management for detailed comparative data. You could just well have a management problem."

Right answer, thought Patello. *The kid just saved his ass by accidentally giving O'Shea more ammunition to blow Durant out of office.*

It was late and Patello decided to end the session. He directed his attention to Kevin Hardly who appeared to be dozing. "Kevin, your staff has made an excellent presentation. I personally believe we have what we need to adequately advise His Eminence about the status of his healthcare ministry. Let's bring this to a close and get ready for the presentation at the Chancery."

Kevin's eyes opened when Patello addressed him. Not sure of what was asked he nodded his concurrence. With that the participants began to leave the room. Stephen had just reentered the room and began to pack the easels and other material. When the executives had left the room he lit a joint and sat down. George sat next to him and shared. Stephen complained bitterly about the senior executives' lack of humor. The "Laurel and Hardy" routine had wowed 'em in graduate school.

The smell of pot saturated the room when the club Manager came in to check the room and turn off the lights. He noticed the glass eyed stare of the young bankers and the particular aroma. This was a serious violation of club rules and seemed to be what Kevin Hardly's cousins were expecting and hoping for. Stephen and George sheepishly picked up their junk and headed for the elevator.

CHAPTER FIVE

The events that brought Jay Marquart under the care of St. Anslem's Chemical Abuse Program began weeks before the incident that now sat in report on Dr. Anderson's desk. Marquart's habitual use of substances that started when he was in high school seemed to him to be occasional use especially on weekends when he "let it all hang out." During the week he would drink a few after work with his buddy Brian and have a few more before and after dinner with his wife, Susan. The weekends, however, were nonstop affairs that included plenty of booze, pot, and if he could afford it, cocaine.

Friday afternoon was Jay's second-favorite time of his second-favorite day. His first favorite time was after Friday afternoon and before Monday morning. Action Waste Management was not a pressure packed company. By Friday morning things started to relax. By Friday afternoon the staff was busy making arrangements for the weekend. Jay Marquart was an expert in arranging the weekend. His routine was to first make sure that his loving wife was in a party mood and that the kids' activities were covered. Susan's oldest son, Benny, was in his first year of Little League. Jay enjoyed watching and coaching Benny. He remembered with pride that as a little leaguer he swung a mean bat. Passing a few tips to young Benny was a real blast. He also had to be sure that he picked up Kristie on time from Cecile's when it was his turn to have her. The "Bitch" gave him no end of grief if he was late. Then it was a call to "Ol' Buddy Brian" to arrange for a party with appropriate sustenance. The partying frequently began with late night fishing followed by sleeping in on Saturday morning. The effects of Friday night were dispatched by three or four hours of doing yardwork or house repairs in the hot sun. By late Saturday afternoon Jay was ready for the next blast. He stoked up the Webber grill around four and waited for Brian and, his "main squeeze," Louise, to appear. Then Jay, Susan, Brian, Louise and the kids would have a fish fry with soda, cold beer, loud music and, after the kids hit the sack, a few sniffs to complete the high that kept going until well after midnight. Sunday was recovery time. A little quality time with the kids sparked by gin and grapefruit usually brought the weekend to a close by midnight. Back to work on Monday gave time to rest up for next Friday.

Step one in the process was to check in with Brian. Brian was running his delivery route for Patriot Courier Service on Friday afternoon, but Jay knew he was available by beeper. He called the operator at Patriot and asked her to page his buddy and have him call Action Waste Management.

Within the hour Brian responded with a call back to Jay's desk. As usual, Brian was upbeat and eager to "get it on." He almost shouted over the phone when Jay answered. "Jay, my main man, how's it look from your end? I'm in good shape if you know what I mean. I got to carry the beeper this weekend but that's no thing. We goin' fishing?"

Jay smiled at Brian's youthful attitude. He leaned back in his desk chair and braced his foot on the edge on the open bottom desk drawer. "Yeah, Brian. Benny's got a game at five so I'll be hung up till about seven by the time we get through the Dairy Queen. You want to meet me at the park. Susan can take the kids. I got Kristie this weekend and I gotta pick her up at four-thirty or else her mother, the Bitch, will have a hemorrhage. Then it's over to the ball park. I'll hook up with the family there. Then after, we can cut out for Hingham. You got a boat?"

Brian took the question as a compliment. He loved to boast about his friend and the boat that he borrowed. "Sure. I always got a boat. My customer says I can use it whenever I want. If he wasn't stoned out of his mind on Fridays he would be a good man to have along. He really knows the spots around the Boston light. We just got to be sure we fill it with gas and clean it out when we bring it back in."

Jay closed his conversation with Brian and checked the clock. Two more hours and he was on the move. He had to call Susan and tell her about the arrangement with Brian. He also had to touch base with buddy and boss Ken Ryan to see if he could get a head start on quitting time. With Ken's support, he could sneak out a half-hour early in order to pick up Kristie.

Ken had disappeared after lunch. Jay suddenly feared that Ken had taken the afternoon off which meant he was stuck on the job until four-thirty. This was definitely bad news. He was not interested in starting the weekend with a shouting match with "dear old Cecile."

Ken Ryan had been called into a staff meeting right after the noon hour. This was unusual for a Friday. Action Waste Management routinely held supervisor meetings on Tuesdays. As it turned out this was a special meeting for the big boss, Mark Meehan, to spark the troops about the big opportunity for the company that would result with the advent of privatized waste management in Boston. He pointed out that while growth of the company had been slow, the boom was near. He stressed the need for longer hours as new contracts were obtained. The topper for the meeting was the introduction of an incentive program that could increase earnings by about twenty-five percent if all projects were on time and under budget. Ryan came back to his desk highly motivated. Jay was waiting for him.

Before Ryan had a chance to take a seat, Jay was posing his question. "Ken, I got to get away at four to pick up my kid at her mother's. Okay?"

Jay's lack of tact irritated Ryan. He looked at Jay with disgust and then gave an abrupt answer. "Jay, you have to make some other arrangements for Kristie. Today is okay, but Mr. Meegan says that we are going to get very busy. No more short shifts. This Boston thing means big bucks for the company and they are going to cut us in. We all need the money, especially you. Start figuring on late hours on Friday's and every day."

Christ, thought Jay, *this is a real bummer*. He lived for the weekends. Freedom and time with Kristie meant more to him than money. He only needed the job to earn money for his child support payments. One missed payment and "that Bitch" would have him in court in a second. He suddenly remembered that Susan and her kids also figured into the deal and his life. He felt trapped. Frustration turned into anger. He felt the urge to pop off to Ken with a blast of profanity but retreated from his anger back to frustration. All he could do was glare at his friend and boss signaling everything he had in mind.

Ken Ryan read Jay like a book. He knew what Jay was thinking. "Jay, don't look at me that way. Keep it cool, buddy. You screw this up and you are back to running junk for the syndicate. That can only lead to big trouble and doing time. You think I'm a pain in the ass? What do you think the mob is when they get their hooks into you?"

Jay's glare suddenly turned into a look of amazement. He had no idea that Ken was aware of his work as a party mule. Especially the times when he was doing special trips. Jay had no direct knowledge what was contained in the packages. He only guessed and now was wondering if Ken was guessing too. His anger returned and he popped off.

"You son of a bitch. Where do you come off with that shit about running junk? You don't know shit, man. I'll carry my load around here and you can stick that syndicate up your ass. You want me on the job, man, I'll stay on the job till hell freezes over. Fuck you."

Abruptly, Jay turned and stormed away from Ken's desk. Ken felt bad about the exchange. He also knew that Jay would leave at four anyway so the sentiments were mostly academic. Jay, on the other hand, was depressed and angry that the weekend had begun with a fight with his boss. He saw this as an omen of bad things to come. At four o'clock he was on his way to Cecile's.

After Cecile had married Officer Michael O'Sullivan of the Boston Police Department, she sold the small house that she and Jay had owned and, with Michael, purchased a larger home in Roslindale. It was located in a middle-class neighborhood on a quiet and peaceful street, a perfect setting for the double income parents of a charming little girl. They were accepted by the neighbors who were proud to have an angel of mercy and one of Boston's finest on the block. Some wondered about the beat-up Jeep that routinely pulled up in front of the house and collected Kristie, Cecile usually walked her to the Jeep so she could bomb Jay with a ritual of do's and don'ts concerning Kristie. Mostly she reminded Jay that the matter of joint custody was subject for review at the slightest indication of his misconduct. Furthermore, as the mother of the child she was the parent expected to protect the child from any inappropriate influences. She told Jay she suspected that he was doing drugs in Kristie's presence and she intended to make that an issue before the judge, given the opportunity.

Jay drank a lot of booze in front of the kids and usually had a buzz, but to the best of his foggy memory he could not remember ever smoking pot or sniffing coke in front of the kids. He was convinced that Cecile was on a fishing expedition. To counter her wrath, he persistently threatened to take her to court to have the support money eliminated based on the fact that Kristie spent more time with him and received most of her life's necessities from his meager income. Somehow, they managed to avoid coming to blows or even shouting so the neighbors could hear. Unfortunately, their sharp exchanges and threats were not out of sight or hearing of a little girl who always looked very sad.

Jay arrived in front of the O'Sullivan household promptly at four-thirty. Kristie waved at him from the front window but did not move toward the door. Obviously, she was waiting for her mother's escort. It took about fifteen minutes for the "Bitch" to open the front door. As Jay was waiting his anger was mounting. He could feel another fight on the way. Good. He was in the mood to tell the "Bitch" off. This whole day had turned sour after his bout with Ken. He opened the car door and stepped out to give Kristie a big hug and in the process, antagonize her mother.

To Jay's surprise the first person out of the door was not Kristie or Cecile, but a guy that looked like Rock Hudson wearing a tight pair of jeans and polo shirt. Jay quickly estimated that he went six three and about two hundred pounds of real man stuff. The giant glared at Jay, gave Cecile a peck on the cheek, and hugged Kristie. After that he sauntered to the Toyota in the driveway, backed into the street, and rode off into the sunset never giving Jay a second look.

Jay held a slight smile on his face as Cecile approached. "That's the new Stud? You got a lot to handle. Think you are up to it?"

Cecile tried not to let Jay's comment upset her. In turn she tried to counter his remark. "And that is the kind of comment that makes you such an endearing person, Jay. Yes, that is my husband. He loves me and he loves Kristie. You need to keep that in mind."

The look in Cecile's eyes signaled to Jay that maybe this marriage wasn't all that it appeared to be. He was envious of the house and the apparent material comfort of their dual income life. But something was strange about the way that dude brushed by him and the way he registered a peck on Cecile. He didn't look too serious about any of it. Rumor had it that Cecile had married a cop. It seemed like a good time to verify the fact.

"What's it like sleeping with a cop? He is a cop, right?"

Cecile was uncomfortable with the conversation and noticed that Kristie was very interested in both the tone and content of the discussion. Kristie had crawled into the back of the Jeep and was leaning on the front seat perched on her elbows. Her blue eyes sparkled at what she thought was a rare peaceful exchange between her parents. Cecile reached into the car and hugged her daughter, brushed back Kristie's golden locks, and returned to the conversation.

"Yes, Jay. Michael is a policeman and well regarded. It's sufficient for you to know that we love one another. Other than that, our lives are none of your business."

What's with all this love shit, thought Jay. She seemed to give a lot of emphasis to the marriage thing. He made a mental note to keep pushing the point and see if over time he could find a crack in her solid front. Just one angle and he would drag her into court and even the score. "Well, it's always a pleasure, Cecile. You pick up Kristie about seven Sunday?"

Cecile shook her head and answered with an authoritative tone. "Jay, I'll pick her up at four on Sunday. We are going to a family get together with some of Michael's friends."

Jay was not about to let Cecile call the shots. "No way. This weekend is with me. You and Muscles can go to the policeman's brawl. Susan can bring Kristie to you on Monday."

"Jay, be reasonable. We are invited to a picnic where children will be present. Why shouldn't my child be with me? She deserves to be with other children." Cecile was now pleading with Jay for some concession.

Jay sensed the opportunity to strike a blow. "She will be with other children. Benny and James are two of the best kids on earth. How do I know who these other brats are? No way. I'll bring her back to you late Sunday night if you are too drunk to pick her up or Susan can bring her to you Monday morning. You make the call. Remember, she is my kid too and we have joint custody—that's joint custody."

Little Kristie took immediate notice of the change in tenor of her parents' conversation. She released her grip and slipped into back seat. Her usual sullen expression returned. Both Cecile and Jay recognized the change. It was time to go.

Cecile gave in. "Jay, we expect to be home by ten Sunday night. You bring Kristie here by ten-thirty."

Jay decided to press his advantage. "That's awful late for a child of her age. What kind of a mother are you? Don't bother to answer. I think I know. Kristie will be here before ten-thirty Sunday night. Just make sure you're here."

That was the departing shot. Jay walked around the Jeep, got behind the wheel and started the engine. As he was pulling away Kristie leaned out the back and gave her mother a cheery wave. Cecile returned the gesture. Jay slammed through the gears leaving Cecile in a cloud of dust. The neighbors noticed and wondered.

Jay had called Susan from work and arranged for her to get Benny and Brother James to the ballpark in time. He expected to be at the game with Kristie well before the first inning. Kristie and James enjoyed playing around the park while Benny played baseball. Susan and Jay took turns keeping an eye on them and pulling them out of mud puddles or sand piles or from under the bleachers or whatever else a four and five-year-old could get into. In spite of his debate with Cecile, Jay sensed he was on schedule to make the first inning. His mood moderated slightly from the downer at work. He thought he had bested the "Bitch" in their last exchange, but he remained irritated at her attempt to pry Kristie away from him on Sunday afternoon. His stomach turned and his mad returned.

The drive from Roslindale back to the Waltham Little League Park was obstructed by the usual Friday afternoon traffic jams. Jay's mood deteriorated at every stoplight. He shouted at slow drivers and gave the finger to a few thousand more. His anger was nearly uncontrollable when he blasted through a yellow light and just missed creaming a baby Benz. The driver looked at Jay through his tinted window from an automatically controlled environment with contempt. Jay looked back and rendered the expected middle finger salute. Kristie followed her Father's example and gave the Benz a final tribute with the same sign. Jay saw Kristie render the salute out of the corner of his eye and at the same time caught the open mouth expression of the Benz driver. The combined emotions of anger, shock and humor twisted Jay into control with a resulting smile that he concealed from Kristie. She was most certainly her father's daughter.

The game was in process when they arrived. Jay's anger climbed another octave but simmered when Susan told him that Benny was scheduled to play the last half of the game. He hadn't missed a thing. He was also pleased to see Sister Martha with Susan. Martha had her camera and was taking a picture of Benny in the dugout. James ran to Kristie as she jumped from the Jeep that Jay parked in a towing zone. The two kids immediately emerged themselves in a dirt mound in back of the bleachers. Jay and Susan climbed to the third row and sat down. Martha joined them. Suddenly Jay felt relaxed. The weekend was officially here. Let the good times begin. He unbuttoned his shirt and leaned back.

Martha needed the relaxation as much as Jay. She was the only woman attorney in a firm of forty. She had made partner in nearly record time but she suspected her advancement, while deserved, was salted by a degree of tokenism. Since becoming a partner, the pressure to better her male counterparts was immense. Competition for clients and billings within the firm was cutthroat. Her colleagues were determined not to be outclassed by a woman. She, in turn, found it necessary to double her efforts in order to prevent the male animal from burying her professional presence. Her usual practice on Friday night was to frequent the bar a block from the office and exchange war stories with attorneys from the neighboring firms. This often led to referrals and sometimes a date. In either event, it was an extension of business and not complete relaxation. This Friday she left the office earlier than usual in order to pick up her sister in law Susan, Ben and James, and take them to The Waltham Little League Park where she would watch her step nephew, Benny, play ball and in the process, expand her bonding with her niece Kristie and step nephew James. Martha loved family and she especially loved children. Later she had a date with a young attorney who worked as an investigator for the State Attorney General's Office.

Benny's turn to play came at the end of the third inning. He was positioned at second base. Jay had played the same position from little league through junior high and still played an occasional second base as a substitute on Actions' slow pitch softball team. He shouted position instructions to young Benny while a patient and tolerant coach nodded to Benny to accept the instruction. Jay was in the game as much as Benny. He relaxed when the third out was made and Benny returned to the bench to wait his turn at bat. Jay made a quick check with the coach and learned that Benny was the number six hitter. He had time to check on Kristie and James.

The fun loving little cherubs had moved from the dirt in back of the bleachers to the gravel and dirt parking lot. Jay noticed the change and signaled Susan to get them back in the corral. Susan was on her way when Jay heard her shout at James. He turned in time to see James pitch a rock in perfect form at Kristie who adeptly stepped aside. The rock with high velocity slammed loudly into the door of an Oldsmobile leaving a prominent impression in the door and the door's owner who happened to be leaning against the opposite fender. The owner immediately moved between Susan and the car. James was hot footing it in the other direction and Kristie hid behind Susan. Jay jumped off the bleachers and headed for the scene of the crime. By the time he got to the Oldsmobile the owner was inspecting the damage to his four-year old rust marked, pitted, and now newly dented sedan.

Jay approached the victim with conciliation in mind. "I'm sorry about the damage. The kids somehow got out of our sight. I'll pay for the repair."

The gentleman stood tall and folded his strong arms across his chest. He looked at Jay as if to size his ability to pay. Perhaps he sensed an opportunity. It was certainly worth the effort to see if this sucker was good for a load. "Well, I know that kids will be kids and all that, but you see this door is dented and they got to replace it. When they do that they got to paint to match and that means the panels have to be primed and coated so we're talking considerable costs, I imagine."

Jay's boiling point was near. *Another fight—goddamn it, another fight. First Ken, then the Bitch, that idiot in the Benz, and now this jerk.* Jay knew that combat was out of the question. First of all, it wouldn't play well with Susan and the kids. Second, they were in a public park that was patrolled by the local constabulary. Third, and most important of all the considerations, was that this guy was more than big enough to eat Jay's lunch.

Susan sensed Jay's anger. She had the urge to begin proceedings by kicking the gentleman in the groin but realized that his counter attack could render Jay useless. As an alternative she took Kristie by the hand and left to pull James from under the bleachers where he had established sanctuary.

Jay recognized her departure as permission for him to work this thing out as best he could. "Look, friend, I am willing to pay to fix the door but the rest of the car is not my responsibility. I've got a friend who does bodywork who could do a quick estimate. You get an estimate on the door from whoever you want and then we can reach an understanding."

The man stared down at Jay. "First of all, I'm not your friend. You are going to pay for the damage in full. None of the compromise crap. Your kid rocked my car and you pay. It's pretty simple. I'll tell you how much. You don't tell me!"

Susan had returned to the bleachers and captured James. He began to sob and leaned against his Aunt Martha. Kristie held on to Susan and looked back at her Daddy. Both men were animated and pointing, but not shouting. Martha carefully moved James to his mother's side and then walked over to where Jay and his newfound friend were getting acquainted. She heard the last exchange and began to make her own observations as an attorney schooled in artful negotiations. She noticed that the subject automobile had a sizable crack in the windshield and that the inspection sticker on the same windshield had expired six months ago. The taillight cover was missing and the absence of the rear wheel cover revealed a missing lug nut. This gentleman was not prone to investing funds in automobile maintenance or safety requirements. Best bet is that he is a cash hound.

Jay had reverted to his classical angry stare that usually preceded a gigantic screw up. He was unaware of Martha's presence.

She caught the signal and moved in. "Sir, I'm Martha Marquart, Mr. Marquart's sister and attorney. We recognize your interest in seeing that this matter is properly concluded. I suggest that we ask the Waltham Police to come to the scene and make an official report of the damage as well as a record of the incident in case of insurance claims or litigation. Of course, I'll represent Mr. Marquart and if you have counsel you may want to suggest that he or she contact me after the police report is on file."

Martha offered her business card to the gentleman who looked at it but with a wave refused to take it. Jay was stunned at his Sister's assertion. Both men were totally disarmed.

Martha took to the offensive. "Two hundred bucks. Cash. You take it and get that piece of junk out of here. We'll forget this unfortunate incident ever happened."

She held out ten twenty-dollar bills. The gentleman looked first at the money, then at Jay, then Martha, and back to the money. Martha raised her arm as if to let the gentleman smell the cash. He paused for a brief moment and took the money. Martha nodded to the man, took Jay by the arm, and escorted him back to the bleachers.

Jay was speechless. He looked out at the field only to notice the final out of the game. He learned later that he had missed Benny's clutch single that drove in the winning run. James cuddled next to Jay in gesture of seeking forgiveness. Jay, still stunned, placed his arm around James and gave him a hug. Susan counseled Benny not to bug Jay about his outstanding play. There would be time for that later. For the time being it was best to let Daddy alone. Kristie held onto Martha because she knew that Aunt Martha did something to cause peace. Suddenly Brian appeared in their midst.

Jay, Susan and the kids piled into the Jeep and headed for the post-game team meeting at the Dairy Queen. Martha said her goodbyes at the ballpark and headed for the nearest Automated teller machine to replenish her cash supply before her date. Brian drove his beat up pickup truck behind Jay to the

Dairy Queen. He enjoyed a Buster Bar while he waited for Jay to complete his father bit. Somehow Brian remained a kid in spite of his occupation. He was Uncle Brian to the kids and a good time buddy for their parents. He enjoyed being a surrogate uncle and at work often told their natural father, Eddie the Enforcer, about his kids. Eddie seemed disinterested.

The Dairy Queen was over-run with kids from age six to sixty getting a sugar fix after a victory or defeat. It didn't seem to matter if they won or lost. Jay sat amidst the confusion and for the time being forgot about the incident at the Park. It was amazing to Jay how Dairy Queens around the world over remained indestructible to the continuous onslaught of Little League baseball teams. He pondered which came first, "Did Little League find Dairy Queen or did Dairy Queen find Little League?" What was probably more important was who was going to survive the longest. If Dairy Queen disappeared who would be next—Dairy Delight—Dairy World—Dairy whatever until the whole soft ice cream universe disappeared? On the other hand, if Little League Baseball was discontinued or went on strike like the majors, the Dairy Queens of the Universe would go without notice and eventually disappear anyway. The whole thing was much too horrible to contemplate. He looked at Brian and realized that there was one saving factor. Brian was hopelessly hooked on Buster Bars. Brian's uncontrolled consumption could be the salvation of Dairy Queen. The thought brought a smile to Jay's face. The first one since Kristie gave the finger to the nerd in the Benz. Brian noticed Jay's smile and raised his dripping Buster Bar in a toast. He also rocked his head toward the door as a signal that it was time to go fishing.

Jay caught Brian's signal and, looked for Susan. He spotted her coming out of the ladies' room with Kristie and James at hand. As he waved, she gathered the three kids and joined him. Uncle Brian also joined the group and they spent a few more minutes together. Brian complimented Benny on his game winning single. This was the first that Jay heard of Benny's heroics. Benny beamed at his step-father and accepted his great hug with pride. Jay explained to the kids that he and Uncle Brian were going fishing and he would see them in the morning. They were also going to have a party tomorrow afternoon after the lawn was cut and the house was cleaned. They were to help Susan tonight by taking a bath and going to bed when she said. He would see them in the morning. Benny wanted to know if he could go along. Jay promised him a fishing trip, kissed the three kids, added another for Susan and headed for the door with Brian.

Brian's old Dodge Ram pickup truck was filthy and cluttered. The ashtray was overflowing with cigarette butts, candy wrappers and miscellaneous pieces of paper. The floor held last winter's mud, a tire tool, and parts from the non-functional radio. Jay kicked the derbies aside and carefully cranked open the door window. It was off track forcing him to guide the window to its lowered position. Brian pumped the gas pedal and turned the key. On the third try the tired old truck came to life. He steered free of the crowded Dairy Queen parking lot and headed for the Mass. Pike. Traffic had cleared so the time to the Hingham Town Boat Dock was less than an hour.

Jay slumped in the seat. "Shit, Brian. I say shit."

Brian gave a quick glance at the sulking Jay. "Now what's buggin' you, man?"

Jay straightened up when he heard Brian's question. He pounded his fist on the dashboard and made a quick left jab motion. "Martha gave that robbin' son of a bitch two hundred bucks. How am I gonna come up with that kind of money? Shit. I say shit."

Brian casually flipped his cigarette out the window and followed it with a quick spit. Then he gave Jay another glance. "Well, I only saw the tail end of the action and it looked to me that she saved your ass. You got that man mad and he was fixin' to kick your butt, maybe. She say you had to pay her back?"

Jay lit a cigarette, fished a beer out of the cooler between them and pondered Brian's question. He took a long swallow and belched. "She's my sister. I'll pay her back. No way am I gonna stiff my sister. She can be a real pain in the ass—a real pain in the ass."

Brian seemed philosophical. "Yeah, well everybody should have a pain in the ass like that. Wish I did. How come she ain't married? Why you bitching? Everything's cool."

Jay was slightly offended at Brian's personal question about Martha. He looked at Brian and decided that he meant no harm. It was a reasonable question for Brian to ask, but it didn't deserve an answer. He finished his beer, dug in the cooler for another, popped the top, and handed it to Brian. Then he pulled another out for himself. "You know, Brian, I figure Martha will get married when she has me straight. Then she can concentrate on her own life. Right now I'm about all she can handle. Man, that son of a bitch had me hassled. I think I could have beaten him out completely if Martha hadn't bought the bastard off. He would have blinked. I was givin' him the evil eye and I could see his lip quiver. The dude had no stomach for a fight. He was a con—a goddamn con job. Yeah, I was ready to rumble. He woulda made the first move, then I roll him out. Shit."

Brian laughed at Jay's comments. He had heard Jay talk this way before. Jay talked a good fight but was slow to actually engage. "I know you ain't had nothin' to smoke, man, but you talkin' like you on the clouds. No way you gonna punch that dude. You got Susan and the kids standin' there. A lawyer by your side. That low-grade hassle could keep you in the slam all weekend. Then you got to explain at work why you got to go to court. Man, if I got into a fuss over something like that Patriot would fry me good."

Now it was Jay's turn to smile." Yeah, well, Patriot can't afford to have its employees looked at too closely by the fuzz. Action doesn't have quite the same situation. You see, that dude wasn't gonna go with the hassle I was givin' him about estimates and all that, and he wasn't about to duke it out. So, when I give him the stare down he says let's forget it happened. He was about to cave when Martha comes up and pays him off. You see how fast he grabs the cash?"

Brian didn't answer. He was occupied with trying to merge left in heavy traffic on to State Route 3. The exit to Hingham was just two miles beyond the intersection of Interstate 93 and State Route 3 which was the main route for Boston weekenders to take to Cape Cod. Traffic was bumper to bumper and barely moving. The flashing blue lights of a State trooper vehicle were visible ahead near the exit to Hingham. Brian became tense. He handed Jay his half-consumed beer and gestured for him to stash the empty cans in the cooler. Brian maneuvered the truck onto State Route 3 and carefully merged to the right lane. He was holding the wheel with his left hand and attempting to open a box of Tic Tacs with his right hand and thumb. Having succeeded he poured the contents into his mouth.

The truck swayed as Brian turned to talk to Jay. "Jay, can you see what we got up there? Is it an accident or are they doing sobriety tests? Man, I don't want them looking close at this truck. They find my stash and its iron bar city. Drink the rest of my beer. We get stopped I'll tell them you been doing the drinking and I been driving. You okay with that?"

Jay strained to look ahead. He could see two cars in the break down lane ahead of the State Trooper. Suddenly he caught the flash of a yellow light in front of the vehicles. It was either a towing vehicle or CVS Good Samaritan van.

"Christ, Brian, relax. Looks like it's a breakdown or accident. No sweat. Just act normal. I realize that may be difficult for a man of your status."

Brian was not amused. In spite of the cool sea breeze he was sweating and perspiration was evident on his brow. He feared arrest. The strain was becoming very apparent as the truck began a slow weave from the right lane onto the breakdown lane and back. Jay glanced at Brian as the truck began to move to the right. His grip on the wheel was overly tight and he appeared to be fighting the steering. Fortunately, traffic was moving about fifteen miles per hour so the irregular movement was not noticed by the busy troopers directing traffic. As the truck came close to the scene Brian moved to the left and cleared the trooper's car with little room to spare. He somehow managed to exit Route 3 without incident. Jay glanced out the rear window to be sure they were not being followed.

Brian stared straight ahead and as they came to the stoplight, he released a deep sigh. "Jay, my man, I live in fear that I' m gonna take a dive. You know I'm only carrying a little for us. Not like it's a big thing. But it seems that I freak out more than I used to when the cops are around. Wonder why."

Jay leaned out the window and looked back at the traffic jam before he answered. "I don't know what's eating you, man. You might be getting old in this business. You ever been hassled?"

"Nope, never have."

Little more was said. The Hingham Boat Dock was busy as pleasure boaters and fishermen launched and retrieved their boats. Brian's customer had tied the boat to the dock a few hours earlier and had managed to frustrate the launching process by occupying precious pier space. The Hingham Harbor Master was standing next to the boat when Brian and Jay arrived at the dock. Brian noticed him and went to the rescue. Jay began removing the fishing gear, radio tape player, and cooler from the truck.

Brian tried his best brand of soft-soap. "Sorry about the delay, Officer. We'll be loaded and out of here in a few minutes. We were delayed in traffic. There's an accident up on Three."

The Harbor Master was not convinced. He nodded at Brian and handed him a ticket for inappropriate use of Public Launching Facilities. Brian glanced at the ticket that contained a twenty-five-dollar fine. The Harbor Master walked away without saying a word. Brian shoved the ticket in his pocket and went to help Jay with the gear. In a few minutes, they were ready to go.

The boat, a twenty-foot blue Sea Sprite with a closed bow and padded seats, had seen better days. It was a pleasure boat of the run about class and definitely not built for fishing. The old Inboard/outboard power drive system displayed leaking seals, low compression, noisy water pump, and a tendency to overheat when pushed over 3000 rpm. Its most significant quality was its tendency to float. The outdated Massachusetts' registration tags were properly displayed on the bow. The Windshield held a Coast Guard Safety Inspection decal from 1988. It was typical of the boats cruising Boston Harbor on a summer Friday night. Brian nursed the engine to life while Jay tended to the lines. They were free of the dock, free of the harbor master's stare, and free of life's pressures. The tranquility of the open water with the glide of the boat through the relative calm brought both men to full relaxation.

Brian made headway for the first fishing spot just outside the Boston Lighthouse that sat on the end of a reef marking the entrance to Boston Harbor. Jay attended to his fishing tackle as Brian moved toward the outer harbor. Susan had brought the gear to the park and transferred it to Brian's truck before Jay had checked it. He kept his fishing box and rods at the ready in the basement and Susan only had to bring it along. His preparedness brought rewards as he found everything available. His next act was to pull a couple of beers from the cooler for Brian and himself. The hassle with Ken, the beef with the jerk at the ballpark, Brian's freak-out, the fine from the harbor master didn't mean a thing. Lean back and relax, man, relax. The weekend was just beginning.

The plan was to fish the structures outside the harbor around the Graves Reef, as it was called, then as the tide continued its ebb, move in to the inner reef and fish close to the edge. Mackerel, flounder, cod and possibly a sea bass were if the offing with a little luck. These areas were heavily fished by the locals so a number of boats were already in position as Brian came onto the spot. He maneuvered the boat close to the reef and signaled Jay to set the anchor. When he was confident that the anchor was holding he shut off the motor. It was dusk with the final glow of the sun behind the horizon—the time when most small fishing boats began to return to port.

Two hours later Brian and Jay had the spot all to themselves. Boats that had not returned to port had moved to the inner harbor. The fish were not cooperating. Not even a nibble had been registered since the anchor had been set. *Time to move,* thought Brian. "Jay, I guess we better move inside. They ain't hittin' out here anyway. I didn't see anybody pulling anything in. What do you say?"

Jay started to reel in. "Yeah, I'll clean the hook and pull the anchor. Crank it up and let's get outta here."

The old engine kicked in on the first try. Jay had the anchor on board. Brian carefully steered the craft past the rocks now visible and into Nantasket Roads. He followed the buoys past Boston Light and then began a gradual approach toward the reef just becoming visible above the tide.

"Brian, bring her in close to the rocks," Jay urged. "They'll be feeding on the structure. We can use drop lines if you can get next to the reef. Get right on top if you can."

The current from the ebb was particularly strong. Brian powered the boat forward until the bow hit the rocks. He kept the power forward while Jay pitched the anchor onto the reef. The night prevented Jay from seeing the anchor grasp the rocks but a pull on the line convinced him that they were secure. He signaled Brian to cut the engine. Once again, they baited their hooks and waited for results. An hour later they experienced the result of their efforts. Instead of a fish they felt an unusual rock of the boat followed by the sound of the outdrive bouncing on the rocks. Brian instinctively pushed the raise button on the outdrive control and brought it to its highest position. Now the thump was heard from the bottom of the boat. Within what seemed like a few short minutes they were firmly grounded on the reef.

Brian leaned back in the seat and relaxed. "Jay. Old buddy, guessed we're screwed here for about four hours if my estimation of the tide is near correct. We ought to be able to get off 'bout three hours into the flood if we ain't too high. We could be stuck for four maybe five hours max. This thing probably draws a foot and a half with outdrive up—three feet with it down. We just got to wait it out."

Jay had the benefit of several beers working on his attitude. "Yeah, we sure as hell ain't goin' to do much fishing in the process. Break out the stash. I could use a smoke."

Brian dug into the depths of his tackle box and produced a nickel bag. He handed it to Jay and helped himself to another beer. "Jay, you know that we sittin' here like this, there is only one boat that gonna pass us that gives us a close look. That's gonna be the Harbor Patrol. Water Cops. They come over and check us out all the way. They check for booze, pot, and everything else. They find any and we go to the slam, they impound the boat, and the whole world comes down on us. We gotta pray that they don't come around."

The thought of being hassled again irritated Jay. He felt his anger rise as he fired back at Brian, "Man, you starting that paranoid shit again? We're fishing that's all. We fucked up and ran aground. Hell, they see that all the time. Ain't no reason for them to do a body search. They don't mind us having a few beers as long as we don't hurt nobody. Stay cool. I'll finish the joint and if you want I'll throw the stash overboard. How we fixed for beer?"

Brian simply shrugged an answer to John's questions. He slowly sipped his beer. After a while he looked up at Jay. "Jay, I gotta know, would you rat on me?"

"Would I what?"

"Rat on me. You know. If a guy, say a cop, started asking you questions about me, what I do, who I work for, and all that would you tell him?"

Jay was completely distracted by the conversation. He wondered what Brian was trying to say. "No, Brian. I wouldn't rat on you. Who's going to be asking questions about you, anyway? You don't own the business. You're a truck driver that delivers packages. I don't know nothing about your business."

"But what if you got caught with some stash they want to know where you got it? You gotta think of the kids and don't wanna take a dive then you tell 'em you got the stash from me. Would you do that?"

Irritation and anger started to ebb into Jay's emotions. He tried to remain calm. "Brian, if it's a choice between you and the kids, I take the kids. Yeah, under those conditions I'll tell them where I got the stash if that is what it takes. You gotta expect that. Anybody would. You wanna take me off your list?"

"You gotta know I got insurance." Brian's expression seemed secure.

Whatever Brian had in mind was not clear to Jay. "Insurance? What the hell you talking about? Insurance. You got insurance from taking a dive? Brian, they don't sell that kind of insurance."

Brian was more confident as he fired back, "It's company insurance. The company insures me. They got insurance."

"What company insurance—hospital, life, disability, workman's compensation, unemployment, and dive. Gimme a break, Brian." Frustration mixed with anger mounted in Jay's clouded mind.

Brian assumed the role of an instructor. "No shit, man. It's self-insurance. They provide it. You see, when we get a new customer and I go to make the first delivery Eddie goes along to make sure everything is okay and the Customer is satisfied and everything. You know Eddie, Susan's ex? Well, he explains to the Customer how everything works. You know about payments and delivery and order and all that. He also explains that we got to be sure that the Customer stays satisfied and don't have no beef that they take to the fuzz cause if they do Eddie breaks both their legs. That's my insurance. The Customer knows that if he rats, Eddie gonna break both his legs or blow up his car or something. That's my insurance, man. You gotta know that."

Suddenly the small boat got very small. Jay felt the sting of an outright threat from his best friend. The surge of anger that he had felt several times earlier in the day was overpowering. This time he could be violent and succeed. He grabbed the grappling hook and took straight aim at Brian who now stood in the boat with his back turned. Jay began his swing but checked it as they became illuminated in a spotlight from a Harbor Patrol Boat closing on their position.

The patrol boat moved in cautiously. A man in the distinctive gray uniform was on the bow. "You boys okay? Anyone hurt? The boat okay? How hard did you hit the rocks?"

The patrol boat moved to within twenty feet of the Sea Sprite before it touched bottom. Close but not close enough to do a full inspection without getting very wet.

Brian waved at the officer and replied, "We're okay. We were at anchor when the tide went out. Just grounded. No damage. Guess we'll just have to wait for the flood. Thanks for checking."

The officer moved the spotlight back and forth as it to do his own check on the condition of the boat. "Yeah, we gotta check it out. We'll stop by every hour to make sure you're still okay. You got a VHF?"

Brian's response was quick. "No radio. It's on the blink so we took it in for repair. Guess we should have asked for a loaner."

The officer turned off the light and sat down. "Shouldn't be out here at night or anytime without a VHF. You got flares? Anything happens, use a flare. We'll see it and be here fast. Take care."

The Patrol Boat reversed its engine and backed away from the reef. Brian waved to the officer and sat down facing Jay. He began to sob. Jay's anger dissipated when Brian unemotionally and skillfully dealt with the harbor patrol. Now he felt deep sympathy for his friend who was experiencing what Jay thought to be a nervous breakdown. Brian's sobbing increased to an uncontrollable rate and he began to hyperventilate.

My God, Jay thought, *will I need those flares? Where in the hell are they?*

Brian began to take deep breaths. His sobbing stopped. He eventually looked up at his friend. Jay's eyes filled with tears as he looked back at Brian's exhausted expression.

Brian slowly gained control. He was no longer the instructor on matters of insurance. Now he was a lonely man and scared. "Jay, I gotta get outta this racket. I can't take it anymore. Man, it was fun when we were in high school but now it's getting to me. Man, I don't want to do no time. I'm scared shitless that somebody's gonna cop on me. Eddie gives me this insurance shit. He says don't worry cause nobody's gonna wanna mess with him. Shit. I say I wanna quit and Eddie says I ain't gonna. He says I gotta keep on muling. He says I just got to cover my ass. Says that I gotta tell you about my insurance. He won't bust Susan or his kids but that asshole might bounce Kristie if he figures you gonna rat. I try to make a move and that son of a bitch will break me in two. What we gonna do, Jay?"

Jay couldn't believe the turn in events. He now understood the bizarre conduct of his buddy. Eddie the Enforcer, AKA the Insurance Man, was leaning on Brian to make Jay's life miserable. It was unclear if Eddie was knocking Jay because of Susan and his kids. He might be trying to hurt Susan by putting the pressure on Jay. On the other hand, this might really be a business matter. Eddie and the firm might be simply pressuring Brian to tidy up his security measurers since he obviously told them he wants to quit.

The uncertainty denied Jay an answer to Brian's question. He slowly shook his head as a negative response. Brian folded his arms across his chest and cuddled into the seat. In a few minutes, he was asleep. Jay stared into the sky, had another smoke and waited for the tide.

It was almost two A.M. when Jay felt the boat begin a slow rock accompanied by the sound of water slapping the side. The tide had advanced on the reef and the boat was beginning to float.

Jay tapped Brian on the shoulder. "Brian, I think we're about free. I'll try to get the anchor loose. Damned if I know where that son of a bitch landed. It won't pull so I gotta go over the side and fish it out. We got a flashlight?"

Brian handed Jay the flashlight. Jay had a good jag on from the smoke and beer. He dropped off the side of the boat into a foot of water. The reef was ragged and the footing uncertain. He held the anchor line and followed it to the anchor securely wedged between the rocks. He pulled the anchor free but fell backwards as he lost his footing. The cold-water shock was accompanied by a nauseating pain in his lower back.

Brian saw him fall but was unable to assist since the boat had become free. Jay, realizing his predicament, struggled to his feet, cradled the anchor in his arms, and painfully returned to the boat. He was standing in water up to his thigh. Brian tried to steady the boat against the rapid current and help him back into the boat. Jay tossed the anchor into the boat and made one major effort to come over the side. Brian gave him a boost by pulling his arms. He landed in the bottom of the boat with a loud thud joined by a blast of profanity that would embarrass a sailor's parrot.

The spotlight from the Harbor Patrol boat caught them as Jay was struggling to get up. "You boys free? Everything all right? We'll stand by till you are underway."

Brian gave an affirmative wave to the Patrol boat and attempted to start the engine. After a few turns the motor kicked in. Brian hit the switch for the navigation lights that thankfully worked. He maneuvered off the reef and steered for Hingham. The Patrol Boat followed in their wake for a while then veered to starboard toward Boston. Jay was in pain but the jag made it tolerable. He noticed the turn by the Patrol Boat and nudged Brian. Brian gave Jay a big smile and the two exchanged a high-five followed by uncontrolled laughter. Their fishing trip had lasted over six hours with not one catch or even a bite. Brian had experienced a nervous breakdown. Jay had attempted murder, fell on his butt in two feet of water, injured his back, and was wet and cold. They had barely escaped arrest. This was truly a fun-filled adventure that they would talk about forever.

The Hingham Town Boat Dock was quiet as Brian made his approach to the pier. The Harbor Master was probably in town at Dunkin' Donuts. Brian purposely landed the boat in the same spot where it had been tied in the afternoon. He secured the boat as Jay removed the gear. When he was satisfied that the Sea Sprite was properly birthed he took the twenty-five-dollar ticket wrapped it around the keys and put them in the glovebox. The Customer would grease out of it.

It was four in the morning by the time Brian dropped Jay at his Waltham estate. Jay showered and managed to crawl into bed by five. In two hours Susan and the kids would start the Saturday rituals. Jay would have none of it. He slept past noon and awoke with severe pain in his back. He could barely move.

Susan responded to his pleas for help and held him upright as he dressed. There was no way that he was going to be able to mow the lawn in his condition. It didn't look too bad and could wait his recovery.

The first priority was pain control. Doctor Marquart's remedy for back pain was a generous quantify of gin in grapefruit juice taken constantly until the pain disappeared or the patient passed out. The therapy began as Susan was feeding lunch to the children. The kids accepted Susan's explanation that daddy was a bit under the weather so the usual Saturday afternoon games would be delayed. Daddy was opting for total postponement.

By three in the afternoon Daddy was literally feeling no pain. He had supplemented his therapy by taking a few sniffs of coke out of sight of the kids. Although a little stiff in the back he managed to referee the kids through a backyard run through the hose, a game of darts in which Kristie decided that James was the target, and a game of horse with Benny on the garage hoop. He was aglow and on a good high. Time to get out the old Webber. Brian and Louise were about due.

Fortunately, the fish fry was not dependent on last night's catch. The Marquart freezer was heavily stocked with the results of more productive trips. Susan had removed a generous quantity of flounder and blue fish that was in the process of defrosting. Jay pulled the Webber out of the garage, loaded it with charcoal, and placed the lighter fluid on the small folding table with his cooking utensils. He then joined Susan in the kitchen and helped prepare a special dish of vegetables in oil that they would bake on the Webber with the fish. Susan accepted Jay's offer of a tall, powerful gin and grapefruit. It was time for her to start to gain altitude. Jay was in full orbit. He stretched out a couple of lines that they inhaled.

Brian and Louise arrived at five-thirty, a little later than usual. Louise explained that Brian had to answer his page and make a few unscheduled deliveries. Jay looked at Brian who dropped his eyes. The insurance conversation of the prior evening was not forgotten by either man. A sudden anxiety caused Jay to begin to shake. He sat down. After a few minutes, he recovered and made a drink for Brian and Louise. The kids had pulled Uncle Brian into the backyard for a game of tag. Louise joined Susan in the kitchen. Jay lit the Webber. The pain returned only not in the back. It was in the abdomen, high, just below the chest and in the middle. He became dizzy. The pain grew in intensity and seemed to radiate to his arms. He was sweating. His breathing was difficult and painful. Susan came out of the kitchen with the fish as Jay fell to his knees. She ran to him and shouted for Brian to help. The pain dissipated as they placed him in a chair.

Jay had worked in the Cardiac Catheterization Laboratory at St. Anslem's for a few years after high school. He was classified as a technician but was no more than a gofer in a high-tech environment. Nevertheless, he learned about the symptoms of cardiac arrest and saw patients experience the pain associated with failure. He was certain that he was on the verge of a heart attack but he also felt that he had time to get to the hospital unassisted.

Jay took Susan's hand. "Susan, look, I think I need to get checked out. If Louise and Brian can feed the kids and look after them, you can drive me to Waltham hospital emergency. We ought to leave now. They can check me out and we can be home in a couple hours."

Louise, standing next to Jay, heard the conversation. "Susan, you take off. Me and Brian can take care of the kids. They'll be all right. Jay has gotta get to the hospital. You want Brian to take you? I can feed the kids and see they get to bed."

Susan nodded. Brian handed his truck keys to Louise. Jay gave Brian the keys to the Jeep. Susan and Brian helped Jay into the Jeep. Fifteen minutes later they arrived at the Waltham Hospital Emergency Room. Jay walked into the Emergency Room with Susan at his side. He explained to the clerk that he had experienced radiating pains in his chest and abdomen accompanied by dizziness and sweating. The clerk immediately put him in a wheelchair and pushed him into an Emergency Room. A nurse followed them in and asked Jay the same questions as the clerk while she took his blood pressure and pulse. She asked Jay to lay on the Emergency Room gurney and to take off his shirt. Jay was feeling better but remained worried about the sudden unexplainable pain. In a few minutes, a physician came into the room.

The doctor was younger than Jay and Susan. He had a boyish face and seemed a little unsure of himself.

Great, John thought. He was on his deathbed and they throw in a rookie. Obviously, a moonlighter from one of the teaching hospitals. Suddenly Jay had an anxiety attack of a different nature. *Holy Christ! Not St. Anslem's. If this guy knows the Bitch—relax, Jay—he don't know me so he won't be able to put it together even if he knows Cecile.*

The physician greeted Jay and Susan and asked the same questions over again. He then began to examine Jay closely with his stethoscope. He looked at Jay's eyes very closely, his fingernails, and tapped his body in various places. As he was completing his exam the nurse reappeared to extract some blood for the lab.

She also asked Jay to urinate in a small bottle. No small task for a guy lying flat on his back. The nurse suggested that he use the lavatory across the hall if he felt up to it. Jay's pains had gone and his anxiety level was back to normal. He felt weird but said he could make it to the lavatory unassisted. Susan helped him off the table. He had to pee in the worst way so the trip was welcomed. Hitting the bottle was the most difficult part of the whole experience. He returned to the room with the specimen and handed it to the nurse. She accepted it and placed the bottle on the counter then assisted Jay back on the table. The EGK machine had been placed next to the table. The nurse explained the process as she placed the leads on his body.

Jay knew the process very well. He had taken many EKGs in his day as a cardiac tech at St. Anslem's—no few of them in the emergency ward. At St. Anslem's any patient that presented symptoms like Jay's would be treated by a team of cardiologists, fellows, residents, medical students, nurse specialists, and technicians from the lab, cardiac care unit, and x-ray—not to mention a cardiac surgeon lurking about just in case. This cast of thousands was now being represented by a sleazy looking nurse and a kid playing doctor. She completed the EKG, made a few notes on the record and took Jay's pulse again.

The doctor came back into the room a few minutes later and casually looked at the nurse's notes before he commented, "Mr. Marquart, my name is Doctor Barker. I'm the emergency physician on duty. We've reviewed your symptoms and given you a preliminary examination. At this time I believe that you do not have cardiac failure but we need to wait for the blood and urine tests before we can come to any definite conclusions. The EKG looks normal but, again, we will have it read by a cardiologist later tonight or in the morning. We are going to admit you to the observation area for monitoring overnight. That way we can rule out cardiac distress. If everything goes as I expect you should be able to go home in the morning sometime before noon I think. Tell me, have you been taking medication of any kind or using the so-called recreational drugs? How about alcohol? My guess is that you had quite a lot to drink today. That so?"

Susan wanted to crawl under the table. *Had he used recreational drugs? Does a bear shit in the woods?* Jay had sniffed up his week's supply of coke as he knocked down a fifth of gin. She had her share too. Hopefully this guy would not test her blood. He obviously knew the answers to the questions. Jay had overdosed, plain and simple and now the jig was up. That overnight bit for observation was a polite way of saying detox. They were going to detox her Jay and then throw him into rehab or some "do-gooder" program. Maybe he would go from the hospital direct to the tank downtown. For a moment she thought that a heart attack would have been a better deal.

Jay's response to the doctor was classical. "Yeah, I started popping painkillers early this morning. I hurt my back last night fishing and the pain was killing me. They didn't seem to help so I used some dope. When that didn't help I went to booze. Sort of screwed myself up I guess. You want to look at my back—still hurts like hell." Jay turned on his side and put his hand on his lower back. A large bruise was present.

The doctor looked at the area and gave it a slight touch. "Well, we need to get a few x-rays. You would have been better off to come in this morning and have this looked at instead of punishing your body with over medication. You could have bruised ribs—maybe broken. Any sharp pains when you breathe? We'll know by morning."

The nurse listened to the conversation and made notes. She nodded when the doctor mentioned x-rays. The order forms were quickly obtained for his signature. Jay looked at Susan and winked. He had, at least for the moment, diverted further discussion about drugs.

The doctor directed his attention to Susan. "Mrs. Marquart, there's no reason for you to stay. Mr. Marquart will be closely monitored overnight. If anything happens we will call you. Do you have transportation? We can give you a ride home if you need one."

Susan explained to the doctor that a friend had brought them to the hospital. He was in the waiting room and would take her home. If necessary she could drive herself back to the hospital. Otherwise, she would bring the kids with her in the morning to collect their hero. The doctor nodded and left the room in response to an audible page. The nurse put down the chart and followed. Jay sat up on the table and asked Susan to have Brian come in. He needed a few minutes with him to assure him that nothing was wrong. Susan caught the drift that Jay wanted to speak to Brian alone. She gave Jay a kiss and left to find Brian.

A few minutes later Brian came into the room looking like the one who needed treatment. He was smiling and tried to be reassuring. "Jay, man, you scared the shit out of me. Susan says you gonna be okay. Man, what hit you? You looked like hell. Susan's calling Louise and telling her everything is Okay. Why they keeping you, man? Oh, yeah, Susan needs your insurance card for the desk. You got it? I'll take it out when I leave. You scared me, man."

Jay dug in his wallet and began to look for his Bay Area HMO membership card provided by Action. He found the card and handed it to Brian. "Yeah, well, Brian, I was scared myself. I never been hit like that before. They got me figured out I think which is what I want to tell you about. They got my blood and pee in the lab right now. What they gonna find is a lot of coke and maryjo. They gonna know that I OD'ed. That's gonna be in my medical record at this hospital. No way anybody else is gonna know so don't worry about your insurance or anything like that. You know what I mean?"

Suddenly Brian became noticeably upset. "Why you tellin' me this, man? If this thing is air tight then we got nothing to worry about, unless they got to tell the fuzz. They got to do that?"

Jay gave his friend a negative wave-off. "No way. I'm a private admit. Came in under my own steam so to speak. If I would have been in a car wreck or fell down on the street or got caught doing drugs then my record would be in the public domain. As it is I'm a private patient and these people got to preserve my confidentiality. Wanted you to know that and not worry about your insurance man. No way is he gonna know. You okay with that?"

Brian tried to look comfortable. "Yeah, man. I'm okay with that. You been in this hospital racket so you outta know. I'll take this card to Susan. She says she will get you tomorrow so I'll check in with you then. Don't get frisky with that nurse. Looks like she could eat your lunch."

Susan came to the door of the room looking for Brian and the HMO card. Brian handed her the card. She blew John a kiss and left with Brian. A few minutes later an x-ray tech moved John onto a gurney and pushed him to the x-ray room for a series of pictures. Moving around the x-ray table was painful for John but gave him assurance that the effect of his excess drugs was wearing off. After the x-rays he was pushed to the observation area and placed in a bed with heart monitoring equipment.

The night attending nurse took his temperature, pulse, and respiration rate every hour. They kept him awake most of the night. In the morning, he was served a bland breakfast of cereal, skim milk, dry toast, and hot tea. Except for a lack of sleep, he felt fine.

Around eight-thirty a man dressed in a blue suit approached his bed. "Mr. Marquart, I'm Dr. Hendricks, internist and cardiologist. How are you feeling this morning?"

Jay sat up and tried to look as if he was in fine form. "Fine, Doctor. A little tired. No problems. How do I look from your point of view?"

Hendricks rapidly turned the pages in the chart and talked at the same time. "Well, you had a good night. All signs are back to normal. I looked at the EKG and it is normal. I guess you are a lucky man. You just missed a big problem. The lab tests revealed an extremely high presence of cocaine, alcohol and other drugs. You experienced a mild overdose. Had you not had the reaction when you did and continued to consume you could be in bad shape. If you are prone to habitual use I would like to recommend a treatment program. St. Anslem's Hospital has an excellent program that is discreet and personal. The director of the program, Dr. Ron Anderson, is a friend of mine who would be glad to give you his personal attention."

That was the last thing Jay wanted to hear but he didn't want to offend the doctor. He tried to give a reasoned response. "Doctor, I know that you have my best interest in mind. Right now I don't consider my habit as being out of control. I got caught up in a lot of things this weekend and sort of lost control. I can handle it. This won't happen again, I'm sure. You think from what you saw in the blood and urine that I'm hooked. Well, so is half the world. Illicit drug use is big business and so is drug treatment. Hell, you can't have one without the other. For now I'll continue to use and eventually get the treatment. It's sort of like Little League Baseball and Dairy Queens."

The metaphor was lost on Dr. Hendricks. He looked at Jay with pity in his eyes.

Jay wondered what caused him to say something that stupid and far removed. Hendricks wondered about the comment briefly and then attempted to counter Jay's reluctance to accept counseling, "Jay, you know I hear that from a lot of patients. You're right, it seems that the whole world is addicted to something. That doesn't change biology. Eventually your resistance to the drug breaks down and you begin to experience physical breakdown. Your system collapses and you experience cardiac failure or stroke. If you are not dead you are a vegetable. That's a guaranteed outcome, my friend. You can count on it unless you get help. Drug rehabilitation and counseling works. The sooner you start the better. You are thirty-six. Well, if you continue to treat yourself as you did yesterday you won't see forty. If you have people that depend on you, that should mean something."

Jay remained determined to best the physician. "Come on, Doc. They say the same things about cigarettes. We been puffing away for hundreds of years and all of a sudden, we're killing ourselves. I admit we're all going to die from something. Cigarettes, drugs, sugar, pork or old age—when you're dead you're dead. I hear you and I'll be careful. Right now, I need some slack."

Hendricks knew he was not about to convince this patient. Unfortunately, the man would have to learn the hard way. "I'll write the discharge order, Mr. Marquart. The record will contain a note that I recommended continuing treatment and counseling. You need to know that especially if you decide later to take my advice. Your insurance will cover the treatments as they have been prescribed by a treating physician. When you check in remember to refer your treatment facility to your medical record here. I'll give you my card. Call anytime."

Doctor Hendricks extended his hand and Jay shook it. He gave a short wave and walked over to the nurses' station. Jay waited a few minutes after the doctor had left the observation area. He carefully got out of bed and walked toward the counter. The nurse looked up as he approached. She asked if he was all right and gestured for him to sit down at the chair next to the desk.

Jay stood next to the desk instead of accepting her invitation to rest. He tried to act nonchalant. "Did he write the discharge order?"

The cute but slightly portly nurse smiled and gave a positive nod. "Sure did. You can go home anytime you're ready. Is there someone who can pick you up or do you have your car here? You need to stop at Outpatient on the way out and make sure that they have all the billing info. While you're waiting for someone to pick you up you can get dressed and take care of the paper work. Let me know if I can help."

"Why outpatient? I thought admitting took care of the discharges". Jay tried to impress her with his knowledge of hospital procedure.

The nurse was not impressed. She maintained her smile as she attempted to explain. "You were admitted to the observation area that is part of the Ambulatory Services Department. You were never an inpatient. Your stay was less than twenty-four hours so it's not an admission. The face sheet on your record is outpatient/emergency service. Less cost and a better bang for the buck."

Jay, the hospital expert, was the one who became impressed. *Man, this hospital business has changed in the few years since I left St. A's,* he thought. No wonder the Emergency Room wasn't packed with white coats. This was a bare-bones cost-effective operation. Jay asked permission to use the desk phone to call Susan. She answered promptly. It would be an hour or so before she could get to the hospital since she was in the middle of feeding the kids. Jay got dressed and ambled to the outpatient desk. The clerk was efficient. His billing record was complete. Having completed the discharge process, he wandered into the cafeteria for donuts and coffee. He desperately needed the caffeine.

Susan and the kids arrived about fifteen minutes after Jay had returned to the out- patient waiting area from the cafeteria. The kids were happy to see that Daddy was healthy and happy. Kristie seemed especially pleased. Benny wanted to know about Daddy's heart attack pointing out that some of his buddies on the team had daddies with heart attacks. This caused Jay to suddenly recall his statement to Doctor Hendricks that half the world was addicted. He was tempted to ask Benny if the daddies were also junkies. Otherwise, the ride home in the overcrowded Jeep was uneventful.

Once home the excitement about Daddy subsided and the kids found other things to occupy Sunday afternoon. Susan was extremely curious about his diagnosis.

Jay attempted to explain. "Susan, the doc said I had a mild overdose reaction to cocaine. He said I was lucky that I didn't get the big one. Seems I stopped at the right time. Anyway, he figures I'm an addict that needs treatment, rehab, and all that. I told him no soap."

Susan shook her head as a sign of opposition to the doctor's advice as if it had been directed to her. "Jay, we don't do that much coke. A lot of people do more than us. Ask Brian, he knows. Louise tells me about the stuff he delivers to some people. We don't do near that much. I can't see that we're addicts. We do a lot of booze and smoke but not much coke. We don't need that goodie-two-shoes stuff, do we?"

Jay wondered about Susan's constant me of first person plural. To the best of his recollection he was the one with the reaction. Susan must have felt it as much as he. Again he had the thought that half the world was addicted. "No, Susan, we don't need that goodie-two-shoes shit. I'll be more careful about overloading. We're okay. You feeling all right? Louise get along all right with the kids?"

Susan was pleased to get off the discussion about addiction. "Louise and Brian are great. She had the kids bathed and in bed when I got home. Brian cleaned up outside then we talked past midnight. He sure seemed worried about you. What are you going to do now?"

"Sleep, Susan, sleep. I feel like a brew but I'll pass that up for now. If Brian calls tell him what I told you. I'll give him a call tomorrow night. Right now I need some sack."

Jay was in bed at two in the afternoon. He fell sound asleep in a matter of minutes. Susan entertained the kids for the rest of Sunday. The boys were pleased that they could stay up late and ride with their mother to take Kristie to her other house. At ten-thirty Sunday night Susan escorted Kristie to the front door of her mother's house in Roslindale.

Cecile answered the door surprised to see her instead of Jay. Before she could speak Kristie opened the conversation.

"Mommy, Daddy got sick and had to go the hospital. He came home but is sleeping. He was very sick. I guess he is good now."

Susan attempted to explain. "Cecile, Jay had a mild attack of something. I think it was related to the heart. They kept him overnight to check him out. He came home this afternoon and went to bed. The doctor says that he's all right. He asked me to bring Kristie to you."

Cecile's nursing instincts caused her to realize that this was not a runny nose type incident. She immediately suspected that good old John had stepped over the line and hit the wall. This might be the incident she was waiting for. She hugged Kristie and pushed her inside. Then she gave Susan a friendly and cordial goodbye. "Thank you for being so considerate, Susan. I hope Jay is feeling better. Tell him of my concern. I'll call him later this week. Thanks again."

Kristie ran into the house. Officer O'Sullivan picked her up and tousled her hair.

Susan said her goodbye, returned to the Jeep, and drove home. She was uncomfortable with the conversation with Cecile. She wondered what Cecile was going to contact John about next week.

Jay was up earlier than usual on Monday. He had slept for nearly sixteen hours. The effects of his weekend experience was not apparent. He bounced around the kitchen making coffee and slamming the refrigerator door. Susan finally appeared. She had juice and coffee with him while explaining the events of Kristie's return to Cecile. Jay actually seemed amused at the prospect of Kristie telling Cecile that Daddy was in the hospital. He really didn't give a damn about the prospect of a call from Cecile. He could handle that "Bitch." No sweat. At seven-thirty he kissed Susan and left for Action Waste Management—a half-hour ahead of schedule.

By seven-thirty Cecile had been at work for a half-hour in St. Anslem's Medical Intensive Care Unit. She had taken report from the night shift, and had made rounds with the chief resident in order to decide on the A.M. transfers to general units. The attending physicians were beginning to come to review their patients' progress and teach the residents and medical students rotating through the service. Nursing students were scheduled to arrive at nine o'clock. Patient acuity was exceptionally high. The pressure was on.

As Cecile was breezing by the desk the unit secretary signaled her that she had a telephone call. Cecile made a quick turn behind the desk, grabbed the phone, and answered with professional style, "Good morning, this is Nurse O'Sullivan. Can I help you?"

The caller was obviously not under the same pressure as Cecile. Her greeting was evident of the fact. "Cecile! Kathy Berry. Do you know what they call a nurse with two assholes? Married! How do like that one, my old Bunker Hill buddy?"

Cecile had great affection for her former classmate. They talked often and shared the events of their lives. It was a surprise that her friend would call at this busy time. Cecile suspected that behind the relaxed greeting was an important message. "Kathy, it's always a pleasure to have these deep intellectual discussions with my favorite classmate, but I'm up to your favorite part of the anatomy in alligators right now. Do you have something else on your mind?"

Kathy caught the cue. "Yes, my dear, I do. Knowing that you have a great interest in researching nursing functions in cardiac care I thought you might be interested in doing a case study on an interesting patient. I was doing a temp job at Waltham's observation unit Saturday night and encountered an interesting case that seemed to fit your research protocols. You get the drift?"

The drift was that Kathy had confidential information about a patient that she knew Cecile could use. However, it was necessary to give the message in a way that did not violate the law or nursing ethics regarding patient confidentiality. It was up to Cecile to give the good opening for Kathy to respond.

"Look, my research centers on Caucasian males, middle age, who experience cardiac symptoms from excessive use of recreational drugs. Did this patient present that way?"

The reply was right on. Kathy let it happen. "That he did, my dear. The man had a good course with discharge in twenty hours. You might want to make note that the patient came in through the Emergency Service Saturday P.M. complaining of abdominal and chest pains. Blood and urine was in orbit. Good case for your review. Anyway, you know where it's at. Know you're busy this time of the morning but wanted to get you the information. Keep in touch."

"Thanks, Kathy. See ya."

Cecile hung up and waved her fist in the air. That was it. Jay had spaced out on Saturday afternoon. Probably in front of the kids. He went to Waltham Hospital. Was discharged on Sunday. Kristie knew Daddy was sick so she probably saw what made him sick. Now the challenge was to get Jay's medical record before a judge. That would prove her point. He would lose custody. She made a mental note to call her lawyer at lunch.

Jay arrived at Action Waste Management early enough to accidentally meet his boss, Ken Ryan, in the parking lot. That had never happened before. Ken was blown away. Usually Jay arrived fifteen minutes late looking like he hadn't slept for a week.

Ken greeted his charge with Monday morning warmth. "Good morning, Jay. Looks like you're ready for another week. Have a good weekend with plenty of rest?"

Jay acted as if the world was well within his grasp. "Same-o, same-o, Ken. Got a good night's sleep last night. Bring it on."

A large notice in bold print hung on a pedestal sign at the employee entrance announcing a meeting for all non-management employees in the cafeteria at nine o'clock. A notice for a management meeting was on Ken's desk. That meeting was to start promptly at eight-thirty and conclude no later than nine. This was most unusual. Jay and Ken both realized that something big was about to happen. Both thought that the Boston project was about to begin

Ken went immediately to the management conference room. He was one of the last to arrive. The other ten supervisors were already present guessing about the purpose of the meeting. Promptly at eight-thirty, Mark Meehan entered the room accompanied by three men, two of whom looked like interior linemen for the Patriots. He invited everyone to have coffee. When everyone appeared comfortable he called the meeting to order.

"Gentlemen, let me introduce our guests. The man on my right is Robert Muldoon, President of the Boston Workers' Guild. To his right is Mr. Martin Hart, President of The Service Workers Local Number 936, and on the end is Mr. Veto Celli who has joined our staff as sales manager for the Boston area project. You will all get to know Mr. Celli better as he becomes involved in the Boston project. The primary reason for this meeting is to advise you that at the employees' meeting to begin in less than a half-hour they will be advised of their opportunity to join Local 936. We have decided not to contest an election. The Union has agreed not to obstruct proceedings in the Boston project. A contract with 936 will be worked out this week as soon as the employees have completed their enrollment. Action Waste Management will be a Union Shop. Any questions?"

The room was silent. Finally, a supervisor asked if the contract would change work hours and production schedules. Mr. Hart explained that the current working conditions were to be included in the contract without change. Of most importance would be the economic issues that would be subject of a reopened clause next year. For now, everything would remain the same. Ken asked if the contract would require management to deal with a business agent on work rules and hours. Again, Mr. Hart explained that no change in practice was intended. There would be a Shop Steward appointed who would represent Union member concerns to the local. The Business Agent would be the agent for the Shop Steward to the Local and would not generally be involved in day to day matters. When no more questions were presented Mr. Meehan thanked the Union officials for their assistance. It was nine o'clock and time for them to attend the employees' meeting.

He asked the supervisors to remain, have another cup of coffee and meet Mr. Celli. As Celli circulated among the supervisors, Meehan pulled Ken to the side for a private conversation.

"Ken, I want you to know that the Union wants Jay Marquart as the shop steward. It's okay with me. How do feel about it?"

Ryan seemed puzzled. "It's okay with me, Mark. I wonder what Jay will say. He's an independent cuss that doesn't seem to me to be inclined to join a Union. He might tell them to shove it."

Meehan was insistent. He held Ken by the shirt as he pressed the point. "Well, they won't bring it up at this meeting. You can help Jay decide. If all goes well at the employees' meeting and the cards get signed they'll ask Jay to be the Steward this afternoon. I'll let you know later this morning where it stands. Then maybe you can prep Jay to go with it. You two get along?"

"Yeah. We get along." Ryan wondered about the question as Meehan walked away.

The small company cafeteria had several tables in line with Service Workers Local 936 signs. A few clerks from the Union sat behind the tables but said nothing to the employees as they mingled about waiting for the meeting to begin. The purpose of the meeting was very evident. In spite of it the employees were careful not to express an opinion. At a time like this it was best to keep your opinions to yourself. Action's Human Resource Director was chatting with one of the clerks who seemed to be in charge. Jay noticed an absence of stress in the environment. He remembered when the Union tried to organize St. Anslem's an all-out war erupted until the Cardinal declared peace by recognizing the Union. Jay carried a Union card until he decided to go to school. He thought Unions sucked. He too kept his opinion to himself as he enjoyed the free coffee and donuts. At least the Union had provided that and he hadn't even joined.

At a few minutes after nine three men entered the room greeted by the HR Director. They proceeded to the head table while the HRD asked everyone to take a seat. He then introduced Mr. Muldoon of the Boston Workers' Guild. Mr. Muldoon, dressed in a shirt with an open collar, moved to the podium and began the pitch.

"Ladies and gentlemen, I am Bob Muldoon of the Boston Workers' Guild. I am pleased to inform you that Action Waste Management has agreed to allow The Service Workers of America Local 936 to represent you and your interest in collective bargaining. This of course will only happen with your consent. We want to inform you of the advantages of collective bargaining and to inform you about Local 936. Marty Hart, here at the table, is the president of the Local. He'll tell you all about it in a minute. With him is Dave Donovan who is the business agent for 936. He'll be working with your Shop Steward once we get organized."

Muldoon explained at great length about the history of the Union movement in the United States. He eventually narrowed his focus to the Boston Workers' Guild pointing out that The Service Workers of America Local 936 was a charter member of the Guild. The local had a long and distinguished history in rightfully representing its members. On cue, the clerks at the tables would prompt applause from the assembly. Eventually Muldoon had the assembly applauding and cheering. The time was right to introduce Marty Hart. When Hart took the floor, he was met with a standing ovation again prompted by the clerks now positioned around the room. He continued firing up the emotions. Jay stayed calm taking note that nothing of substance was being said. The meeting reminded him of the high school pep rallies that he attended to get out of study hall. No sooner had the thought crossed his mind when Hart began leading cheers. Jay couldn't believe it. He was considering walking out when Hart completed his speech by inviting everyone to sign the enrollment card. Jay got in line with everyone else. As each person signed the card they were ushered into a receiving line where they shook hands with Muldoon, Hart and Donovan in that order. As Jay was shaking hands Donovan took special notice of his name and commented that he was looking forward to working with him. Jay was surprised at the comment but made no response except an affirmative nod of the head.

It was all over by ten-thirty. Jay was in the Union. He didn't feel any different. He wondered if Ken would be upset when he found out. Certainly, the management meeting earlier was about the Union thing. Muldoon said it had already been worked out with management.

"So, everything's cool," he said out loud as he strolled past Ken's desk and gave him a wave.

Ken looked up and motioned Jay to have a seat at his desk. When Jay seemed comfortable, Ken passed him a piece of paper and explained.

"Jay, there's a note here for you from HR. They want you to meet with the Union at one o'clock. Guess I'm not going to get much work out of you today. What's up?"

Jay threw his hands in the air in mock confusion. "Hell, I don't know, Ken. This whole thing came out of the blue. You know this was up? I never had much use for the Union. It was a war at St. Anslem's. My old man said the only way to join a Union was if you could run it. Maybe they are going to ask me to run this thing. How about that?"

This was the right answer and gave Ryan the lead that he needed to carry out Meehan's order. "Well, now, Jay, you could just be right. This place will need a Shop Steward who has some brains, can respect the business, and represent the employees. You might be the right man for the job. Would you take it if they asked?"

"Yeah, if they ask. I'm not about to run for office. Anybody else is interested they can have it. I'll get along fine as I am. What makes you think they might ask?" Jay looked at Ryan with a degree of suspicion.

Ken winked at Jay and smiled. "I heard the Union guy mention it. Mr. Meehan said it was okay with him if you accepted. He thinks you're all right."

"Cut the bullshit, Ken." Jay straightened up in the chair and then stood up. "If Meehan goes along then it's because you suggested me. He don't know I exist. What's in it for you if I take the Steward job? Oh, hell, what's important is what's in it for me. Don't bother to answer I'll figure my end."

Jay walked back to his desk and began to review grant applications. Ken waited until he was sure Jay was occupied, then called Meehan's office. He reported his conversation with Jay to Meehan. Meehan thanked him for the information. Jay's interest in finding something in it for him could be accommodated with trips and time off for meetings. All this would be explained by Donovan. Things were coming together just fine.

Promptly at one o'clock Jay reported to the HR department. The receptionist ushered him into an interview room where Dave Donovan was waiting. Donovan stayed seated as Jay came into the room. He extended his hand and pulled Jay into the chair next to him at the small round table. Donovan was friendly and had a fatherly like appearance. He leaned back in his chair and tried to put Jay as ease as he spoke.

"Jay, Mr. Marquart, how are you doing? Things went well this morning. The troops selected us to represent them. Everybody signed up. No contest. How about that? So now we have to get to work. Check off of dues start the first of the month and the troops are going want to see something for it. Somebody has to be here to see that what they want is registered, put into writing and sent to the Local. Also, if anybody has a beef with management it has to be dealt with on the spot. So, we need a guy that's tough and has the guts to put it on the line. The troops think you can do the job. You up to it?"

Jay tried to look tough. He tilted himself back of the rear legs of the chair and put his thumbs in the waist of his pants. Then he glared at the Union official. "Yeah, Donovan, I'm up to it. Somehow, I don't think the troops have the slightest idea that I'm being selected for the job. You guys got your reason for picking me. That's okay with me but you got to explain to me why I should go along."

Donovan didn't need this attitude. He was not happy with the way that Muldoon and whoever had selected this person for a key and important post.

Now he had to deal with his arrogance. "Well, life's full of little surprises. Maybe a little fairy popped Muldoon on the head and told him to pick you, I really don't know. I was told that you were the Shop Steward and that's the way it is. Now, if you don't want the job I can mention it to the muscle and they will find someone else. You got a problem?"

Jay didn't pick up on Donovan's irritation. Instead he pushed further, "No problem, Donovan, except I figure there's gotta be some vigorish. This is a tough job the way you describe it. It seems I'm at personal risk. You got any insurance that keeps me from getting canned or worse yet wasted?"

The George Raft imitation amused Donovan. He saw through the phony exterior and recognized a person that could be formed to be of service to the Local. He rocked back on the legs of his chair and gave Jay a fatherly answer. "You watch too much TV. There is no vigorish. You have the protection of the U.S. government. The law requires the company to give you time to do your duties as Shop Steward. That includes time off to attend meetings. You can spend a lot of time traveling. The Union pays the expenses. What else you do want to know? Make up your mind. Are you in or out?"

Jay gave an affirmative nod. "I'm in, Donovan. Definitely in."

Chapter Six

The Honorable Robert Cowan, Mayor of the City of Boston, returned from his trip to Washington over the weekend and was in no mood for a press conference. The media broke the news on Friday that the Mayor was going to DC to chat with the Secretary of Labor and the President about the position of Under Secretary in the Labor Department. The Mayor's office at first denied the reported purpose of the trip but later confirmed that some meetings with the secretary were scheduled. There was no confirmation that the President was involved. Cowan had advised his staff before the trip about its purpose but also advised that the tentative nature of proceedings required caution if not deception in dealing with the media. When he returned, the local media had the benefit of the national press in Washington that shadowed the Mayor for the entire time. There were no secrets. There were also no definitive answers. Pressure for a news conference came from the Mayor's staff.

There were things that Mayor Cowan could not tell the press. For example, he did not want to disclose that the appointment as Under Secretary was a dead end in his quest for national prominence. Even if the President was re-elected it was doubtful that Cowan would be advanced in his administration. The President as much as said so. Furthermore, the pay as Under Secretary was slightly less than Mayor of Boston and living expenses in Washington, considering the Mayor's living allowance from the City, were higher. The economics of the opportunity did not recommend the position. Why would he bail out of his native Boston for the cutthroat Washington scene?

The answer to the question was another fact that the Mayor did not want to discuss with the media. The political scene in Massachusetts, while always cutthroat, was becoming hazardous to the Mayor's political health and personal freedom. If a scandal broke over the misuse of campaign funds he would be dead as a candidate for Governor. There was reasonable assurance that his contributors would rally in his defense should any accusations be made. He had strengthened that position by bringing Bob Muldoon and the Labor Bosses to his aid in the Party. However, the Republicans were determined to reelect Dukar and position the Governor as a potential presidential candidate. To do this they needed to reelect Dukar for another term as Governor by a wide margin. Since Cowan could carry Boston and most of eastern Massachusetts, he stood as an upset candidate and threat to the Republican plan. Cowan suspected that a deal had been cut by his friends and the opposition to mow him out of the way. Things went too well in Washington. Apparently, the skids were greased for his appointment. Who paid for the deal? Who would he really be working for? Where did Muldoon and the Labor Guild fit in? And of most importance, who was going to take the fall when the campaign fund issue finally came to the surface as it eventually would? He needed answers. So did the media. Hopefully not to the same questions.

As a first item, the Mayor requested that Alfonse Siro, President of the City Council, meet with him to discuss the change in City Government in the event that the Mayor resigned to accept the Federal appointment. Siro had routinely supported Cowan in City Council. He held the Mayor's trust but not his confidence. Cowan wisely kept his campaign and personal business restricted to a few close associates and friends. Siro didn't belong to the inner circle but was a confidant for the Mayor in dealing with the politics in the Council. Siro was also a seasoned politician who realized that it was necessary to hold certain matters close to one's vest. One of Siro's closest associates in politics and personal friend was Michael Francis Megan, Deputy Commissioner for Parks and Recreation—City of Boston. Siro had been advised by his political supporters that the Mayor would support Megan's appointment to the Commissioner of Health job should Commissioner Logan resign. Logan would resign as a result of an advantageous opportunity in the private sector. This transition would follow the initiation of the waste management voluntary privatization project.

It was necessary for Cowan and Siro to have a detailed discussion about the complex agenda of change. Once they had a meeting of the mind on dates, times, places, and people, they could begin a calculated campaign of conditioning the media that of course included the usual informal leaks for the benefit of the inquiring minds.

Siro was the first person the Mayor contacted after his return from Washington. The two met at the Mayor's office at seven o'clock Monday morning. The time and place for the meeting was well selected since Siro routinely met with the Mayor on Monday to go over agenda items for the City Council meeting held on Thursday morning. City Hall beat reporters waited outside of the Mayor's office for Siro's exit then would badger the Mayor for an advance look at the agenda. The Mayor routinely passed the reporters to his secretary who provided them a draft copy immediately after sending a fax copy of the rest of the Council members. If the agenda was not agreed upon at the time of the meeting the Mayor would truthfully inform the reporters that the agenda was not ready for distribution. This was already decided to be the case as Siro walked into Cowan's office.

Cowan had arrived at the office at six A.M. He had gone over the telephone calls, reviewed the messages on his desk and listened to voicemail. Sharon, his secretary, arrived at six-forty-five. She usually arrived at seven but the Mayor called her Sunday to ask her to be a few minutes early in case the reporters needed to be diverted with coffee and Danish. She had the usual office pot ready with a full tray of donuts. Inside the Mayor's office coffee and Danish waited Siro's arrival. Siro walked past her with a good morning nod and entered the Mayor's office without benefit of being announced. The reporter sitting on the couch in the reception area did not have time to move from under his cup of coffee and donut to ask preliminary questions. He would remain on stakeout.

Siro, as President of the City Council, considered himself an equal to the Mayor and always addressed him with informality and friendliness, "Good morning, Bob. How'd things go in DC?"

The Mayor looked up from the messages spread on his desk and extended his hand to his political colleague. "Well, it's progressing, Al. We need to talk about some things in case it all comes together soon."

Al Siro liked the comfort of the Mayor's roomy office. He thought often about being mayor and occupying the corner room. When he became Mayor he intended to keep all the furniture as is. He patted the arm of the chair as he sat down and when comfortable responded to Cowan. "I think so. You have a bird dog outside. Probably be a covey of them in a few minutes. They're going to have a million questions. What's our approach?"

Cowan plopped into his double padded desk chair and leaned back to the limits. He stared at the large ornate chandelier in the center of the ceiling. "Al, I'm not certain if this thing in Washington is the best bet for me. My people say it's the way to go. I'm inclined to take their advice but to make it work I understand that a few things need to be completed here. You have any idea what I'm talking about?"

"Yeah, Bob. I guess that the waste management thing is the key to getting things straightened out. That's probably the first priority." Siro mentally went over the facts given to him an hour earlier.

The Mayor came forward in his chair and looked at Siro with a questioning expression. "Well, I'm willing to authorize the voluntary thing for the City but it will require the support of the City Council. You guys willing to go along?"

The response from Siro was quick and direct. "Bob, you know that I can deliver the Council. I'll need a few things to keep things in line regardless if I become acting Mayor. You know that Commissioner Logan could be a problem on the political end. The kid is sincere but acts like a loose cannon. He ought to have another job. If you don't move him then I have to do it. It would be best if Logan resigns and you appoint Megan to the acting job as Commissioner of Health. Then when and if I step in I give him the permanent appointment. He's my man. I'll take responsibility. If I don't step in, you put up with him long enough for the waste project to get settled then make a decision about Megan. We can talk about Megan's permanent appointment as we go along."

Cowan turned in his chair and gazed out the window at the snarled early morning traffic moving slowly around City Hall. "Al, you know that labor will back Megan's appointment because Logan stuck his finger in their eye at Boston Hospital. They have been pressuring me to bounce the kid ever since. Do your sponsors have any opinions on Megan or Logan?"

"Labor has contacted me about Logan," Siro began as an understatement. "They want something done. I also have some word that the Boston Taxpayers Association likes the private waste management idea. They will support Megan if he's in office. I guess that means that they would back you and me if we put him there. Labor and the BTA is a tough combination to beat. That's both sides of the aisle. Don't think we could do better. Anyway, that's the way it was explained to me."

That was what Cowan was waiting to hear. Siro was in the tank. Big money had made a move on him. Good. He had it explained to him by somebody other than Labor. The contact had been made. Siro would stick to the script as long as it was the script that Big Money had written. He also now knew that the reason things went well in Washington was due to an alliance made high up in the power politics game. That gave him some assurance in accepting the Federal appointment. He had just been promoted from the rank of pawn to castle.

Siro noticed the appearance of a slight smile on Cowan's face. Obviously, the message had been received just as Patello suggested it would. Cowan was a seasoned, smart politician who heard the unspoken word clear as a bell. When Patello met with Siro he had carefully explained the approach to Cowan. Siro had rehearsed the script over and over while waiting for Cowan to return from D.C. He knew the call for a meeting was inevitable. Patello had said so.

In his mind, Siro turned the script to page two. "Bob, we need to avoid any talk about improper use of funds and things like that. Some people believe that Logan pocketed funds for you when he was in your campaign. If you drop him will he implicate you in any way? If that hits the fan the whole thing would be diverted. To me Logan seems too innocent to be guilty of stealing."

The Mayor was standing now. He calmly made his way to the coffee pot and poured a cup for himself and offered to refresh Siro's. "Not to worry, Al. Mr. Logan had nothing to do with my campaign funds. The kid never saw a nickel. In fact, he not only donated his time to the campaign he donated his own money as well. The man is a one hundred percenter. They might want to nail him but they can't. I always thought that the TPA was targeting the kid to get me to do something in his defense so that I would automatically incriminate myself. Labor picked up on the rumor as a way of forcing the kid out. I let it happen as a diversion. The more they chased Logan the further they were from the facts. It's nice to have a guy like him around. Could he take a fall? Well, you know that anything is possible in the courts but it would be a real travesty of justice."

Siro was pleased with the exchange. He had the answer to Mr. Patello's second question. Logan was an innocent man and possibly an innocent victim.

Cowan kept the kid in the dark about campaign funds but allowed the shadow of suspicion to fall over him as a diversion. Siro recognized the tactic. He knew that if things got hot for Cowan he could set Logan up for a fall by a simple adjustment to the books. Cowan's greatest crime at that point is being hoodwinked by an honest man. It happens all the time. You just can't trust honest people.

"I understand, Bob. Let's do it. Are you going to talk to Commissioner Logan about his future? It seems to me that he has to make the move in order for the rest to happen. He gets a new job. You appoint Megan to take Health as an Interim appointment. Megan announces the waste management deal. You make your decision. Then I make mine. That puts it in order. Sound good to you?"

Cowan now realized that he had to take a risk. If he appointed Megan to the Health slot it would be a signal to the boys upstairs that he could be trusted. On the other hand, if he fired Logan he would be without any insurance that the Big Boys were going to deliver the Federal job. He needed a sign from above. Logan was the sign. If Logan resigned then the game was on. If Logan had to be fired, the deal was screwed.

"Al, I think the best thing to do is wait for Logan. If he finds a job on his own in the next couple of weeks then we can proceed. If I force him to move it seems to me that he will become defensive and create a lot of media interest on his plight. You know, a young married man with a couple of kids put on the bricks by an unfeeling Mayor who puts politics in front of the family. If my Federal job comes up first then when I resign you can advise Logan that he ought to go with me or move to the private sector. You have a right to put your own people in the job. The press will understand. So will Logan. Tell you what I'll do. I'll have a staff meeting with all the Commissioners and confirm that I have looked at a Federal appointment. They know it anyway. I'll remind them that according to the Articles the President of the City Council steps is as the acting Mayor until the Council sets a date for an election. These people are politically savvy and capable of doing their own thing. Could be that I have all their resignations. You want to come to the meeting?"

Siro was shocked at the Mayor's suggestion. "Bob, the press would have a field day with that action. I don't want any part of it. Your first suggestion is right. If Logan can find a job on his own in the next week or so that would be best. I'll pass the word along and see if something comes up. That way the power base has to do its part. Let's do it that way. Speaking of the press how are you going to respond to those vultures when I leave?"

Cowan had what he needed. Siro was his messenger to the inner sanctum. In less than an hour he was certain that somebody way up would recognize that for the deal to move a sign of security was required. The sign was a job for Logan.

With a show of conciliation Cowan appeared to agree with Siro. "Al, for the time being, I think we should stick to the routine of City business. No comment about the Washington thing. I know that the President and the Secretary of Labor are only going to acknowledge that I'm being considered for the post. I'll acknowledge the same thing. No decisions have been made and none are expected soon. As for the Council agenda, we can say that we have not completed it. Frankly, I would like to move the Waste Management on Thursday but that depends on what happens relative to our discussion. Let the press hang out for a while."

Council President Alfonse Siro nodded his agreement, shook the Mayor's hand and opened the office door. A wild gang of reporters stormed the door nearly pushing Siro back into the office. He used his bulk to push forward and through the crowd.

When asked if he had a statement, he paused long enough to be courteous. His report to the media was that the Mayor had acknowledged the prospect of a Federal appointment.

No, they had not discussed succession. Several items of City business were proposed for the Council that were to have some staff analysis. The agenda was not complete. He was sure that the Mayor's secretary would furnish them a copy of the agenda when it was ready. He rendered a salute to the cameras and walked into the corridor. The Mayor had taken the opportunity to close his door and stayed sheltered from the media, at least for the time being.

Siro moved quickly to his office in City Hall and waited for the procession of reporters to dissipate. When his secretary signaled that the hall had cleared he asked her to hold all calls. Siro picked up his phone and dialed Charles Patello's direct line. Al Siro and Chuck Patello had met years ago at the Roman Cultural Society. Although they came from different neighborhoods they had maintained contact as each had progressed in their respective careers. Their occupations were different so there was no basis for a business relationship. Social occasions of the Society offered the continuing contact. As Siro moved forward in politics his friends at the Society became major supporters. They met late that night following Kevin Hardly's dinner meeting about the development of an Office for Health Affairs for the Archdiocese. Patello explained his interest in Commissioner Logan as a possible candidate for the job as well as the political advantages to Siro if Megan became the new Commissioner. He also explained that the Voluntary Waste Management Program was the underlying issue. For everyone to benefit it was essential for Mayor Cowan to accept a Federal appointment that was being arranged.

Siro was a quick study. He well understood the issues. He agreed to all facets of the transition including keeping Mr. Megan in line. His report to Patello was positive and he was pleased to give it when Charlie came on the line. "Charlie, this is Al Siro. Just met with the Mayor. He's in good form. As you thought, Logan is clean. Bob is using the kid as a decoy. Now here's the way I think he wants things to happen. First thing is that the deal in Washington has got to be right financially. He thinks the Labor Secretary will call him today with good news. Then before he makes any announcement about his leaving, the Logan kid gets another job. I guess he would see Logan getting a new job as a sign of good faith — from whom I don't know. Then he appoints Megan as interim-commissioner before he announces that he is going to D.C. Oh, yeah, he pushes the button on the waste management thing as soon as Logan resigns. I guess that's about it."

Charles Patello was not usually a religious man, but in his mind he thanked God for the apparent break before responding to Siro. "Thanks, Al. The job at the Archdiocese has to be cleared by the Cardinal. We meet with him tomorrow afternoon. If all goes well, and I think it will, we can make an offer to Logan Tuesday or Wednesday. If the Mayor waves notice Logan can start next week. The Mayor can appoint Megan as soon as Logan resigns. The Waste Management Project could pass the Council on Thursday. Is all this possible? How about Megan? Is he on board?"

Again, Siro had good news. "Megan is fine, Charlie. I've been keeping him informed. He knows the Project and is poised to contact Action Waste Management as step one. The soft spots are the Archdiocese and the U.S. Department of Labor. Sounds to me like we are violating the principle of separation of Church and State. Maybe we need a constitutional lawyer."

Patello appreciated the humor. "I hear you, Al. My guess is that the Federal thing will happen as the Mayor believes. I have no idea how the Cardinal will respond. The man is unpredictable. No way that I can get a handle on him."

"Have you tried money, Charlie? I understand he is a sucker for a buck. Let me know if I can help."

Patello hung up the phone. He thought about how much money had been invested in the Church by his various companies since he had hooked up with Hardly and his glorious Knights. It was good business to support the Church even if you couldn't own one. At least he owned Hardly and that meatball, O'Shea. The thought brought him a sudden chill. *Can those clowns put on a convincing act for His Eminence at tomorrow's briefing? My God, all this work and influence clear to the office of the President of the United States could be for naught if Laurel and Hardly did their routine at the Chancery.* Somehow, he had to direct that presentation. He called Kevin Hardly and offered to buy him lunch. Hardly accepted. Next, he placed a call to Marone to give him a status report and check on the Federal scene.

Tony Marone was in conference with Mario Capizzi when the secretary forwarded Charlie Patello's call. Patello was on the top priority list in Marone's office. That meant his calls were always put through.

Tony's greeting was energized. "Charlie, my man. How you doin'? I'm in with Mario now. We're getting ready for a meeting tomorrow on getting into the health business. It looks like Boston is the place to be. You got any action?"

Action was just the word that Patello wanted to hear. He pushed the point back to Marone. "Things are shaping up, Tony, and coming to a head rapidly. The deal with the Union went down without a hitch. Action is being organized as we speak. Muldoon is in the wrapper. Al Siro, President of the City Council and next Mayor is on board. Megan checks out. He belongs to Siro. The Waste Management Project could go by Thursday. But—we have two big ifs. The first is getting the Cardinal to go along with our scheme for an Office of Health Affairs where we stash Logan and the second is getting the Federal job for the Mayor. I have to deal with the Cardinal but you and your friends have to deliver to the Mayor. You heard anything from Washington?"

Marone turned away from the phone to ask Capizzi if he had a report from Washington. Mario gave an affirmative nod and offered to talk to Patello. Marone handed him the phone. "Yeah, Charlie, this is Mario. I had a call Sunday from the Federation. It seems that your good Mayor pissed off the Feds by asking for a deal better than the President. After a little reality check His Honor caught on that he was begging, not choosing so he narrowed his focus. What he really wanted was some dough to get his kids in private schools, a living allowance, and a little slush for moving around. The Feds got the slush in the budget for his office. The other stuff is being taken care of on the QT. He is going to get a call around noon that fills him like he wants. That should do it. He could resign anytime that makes sense. Now Tony and I been talking about what might be needed if we go into the health business. We think that you need a good wrapper on this guy Logan and that top guy at that Catholic hospital, St. Whatever. I'll let Tony explain. You need anything else from me?"

Capizzi's rapid commentary always confused Patello as he tried to follow the point. He wanted to make sure he had a good understanding of what was required. "You've answered my question, Mario. I've got what I need for now. Put Tony on. I need to understand this wrapper for Logan."

There was a pause before Marone answered, "Charlie, Tony. Listen, we been thinking that this guy Logan being clean ain't in our best interest. See, your Mayor Cowan is asking for a shelter and Labor wants to give it to him. Okay. So that gives the Mayor no collar. He can bolt from the Federal job, go back home and raise hell. That makes you look bad but also puts us at odds with the Federation who we don't want no hassle till we get our end of the health thing. What we think we ought to do is slip a collar on Logan that he doesn't know about but the Mayor does. That way if the Mayor bolts he has to drag Logan. Logan's collar serves evidence that the Mayor played with money. This keeps the Mayor in line. The Federation stays out of it."

Patello's head began to ache as he tried to follow the scheme. "I understand what you want and why you want it, Tony. You need to explain to me how we are going to get it done."

Marone seemed exasperated at Patello's comment. "Okay. Try this. We convince the Mayor to free up ten grand to reimburse Logan for campaign expenses. The ten grand will be donated by us on a special check made out to the Mayor but after the Mayor endorses it we deposit it to a special personal account that you set up for Logan in that bank you control. You tell Logan that the money is a signing bonus from the Catholic guys supporting the Church. He can draw on the account or transfer it to his own. Our accountants can cover it. We end up with a canceled check made out to the Mayor that he endorsed over to Logan's special account. That bit of evidence keeps him in line."

"How do you get Hizzoner to go along with this?" Patello's question was actually an audible thought.

Marone accepted it as if he expected the question. He hardly paused as he rapidly explained, "Logan ain't the only one getting a signing bonus. The Mayor thinks he gets an under the table twenty-thousand-dollar bonus. We show him two checks made out to him for ten grand each. He endorsees one check and gives it back to us so we can deposit it in a special account that is released to him when he properly completes his term as Under Secretary of Labor. The account will have joint signatures, his and a trustee that we appoint. When he gets to Washington the cards will be there for his signature. We take the endorsed check, altar the endorsement and deposit it in Logan's account. Then we cover the ten-grand from another source. Costs us thirty grand over all, but that's cheap for a collar. What do you say?"

"Sounds crazy enough to work. How do I figure in?"

Marone was convinced that he had given Patello a good explanation. He slowed his speech to a relaxed tempo. "We'll have a guy deliver the Mayor's endorsed check to you. You see that it gets deposited into Logan's special account. Logan won't need to sign the check for a deposit only but if the bank looks for it maybe you can have an officer initial it, that way it will go through. You got the bank guys under control?"

Patello was uncomfortable with the plan but decided to let the New York staff worry about it. For now he would do what was being asked of him, "Sure, Tony. We can get it done. The tough part is putting a wrapper on Durant at the hospital. He's innocent but not as much as Logan. Been around a little longer and is more independent. It might take a while to bring him in. I'll work on it."

"Yeah, do that. Keep us posted on the deal with the Cardinal. You doing okay?"

Patello didn't answer Marone's question. He said his goodbye and wished them well. The conversation came to a close with Charlie's promise to report on his Tuesday meeting. A glance at his Rolex signaled time to grab a cab for his lunch with Kevin Hardly in the Chairman's Suite at The Hardly Security and Trust Bank. When he arrived, Mr. Hardly's executive assistant ushered him into the private dining room. The dining room was a part of the extensive executive suite that Hardly had built for himself over the years that he directed Hardly Security and Trust Bank. The Chairman's Suite occupied the entire twenty-eighth floor of the HSTB Building. The dining room was positioned on the east side with ceiling to floor windows looking out over Logan Airport,

Boston Harbor and Massachusetts Bay. Occupants of the room became instantly mesmerized by the view. Hardly had used their loss of concentration on business matters to his and the bank's benefit on many occasions.

A waitress from the bank's catering staff was in attendance. She took Mr. Patello's order for iced tea and returned shortly with the beverage. Kevin was on the phone in his private office that adjoined the dining room. The connecting door to his office was wide open giving him a view of the occupants as they arrived. He waved to Charlie indicating that he would join him soon. Charlie acknowledged the wave and turned to enjoy the view of the Boston Harbor. As he turned away from the panoramic view Thomas O'Shea walked into the dining room. He asked the waitress for a glass of white wine, looked coolly at Charlie, and stared out the window.

Patello looked at O'Shea to give a greeting but O'Shea stared out the window seemingly ignoring Charlie. After a few cold minutes, O'Shea spoke but without making eye contact with Patello.

"Charles, Kevin had the decency and courtesy to invite me to this meeting. I cannot understand why you would attempt to exclude me from a briefing about the Archdiocese. I am an officer of the hospital. Anything you have to say to Kevin you need to say to me as well. Why wasn't I asked to this meeting?"

Charlie was about to unload on Thomas when the waitress returned with the glass of white wine. Another glass was on her tray that Kevin Hardly picked off as he followed her into the dining room. Kevin noticed that the chill in his colleagues' expression matched that of the wine. He decided to take charge.

"Gentlemen, good afternoon. A beautiful day. I truly enjoy this view. We ought to be on the water taking a cruise toward the Cape. Better yet—doing eighteen—I've got a three o'clock tee time so we'll have to make this short. Charlie, you suggested that we have this session. Let's order lunch then we can eat and meet. Tom agreed to join us at my request."

The three men sat at the dining table large enough for ten. Kevin instinctively sat at the head of the table. O'Shea moved quickly to his right. Patello waited until the others were seated then sat on Kevin's left. The waitress distributed menus and explained the very special preparations of the day. Hardly made a brief speech about the diet he had started that morning and ordered a cup of clam chowder, to be followed by a chef's salad. O'Shea and Patello both ordered a turkey club sandwich. The waitress took the orders with dispatch to the kitchen.

Kevin's expression turned troubled. "Gentlemen, I received this disturbing letter from the Alleton Club requesting that I appear before the discipline committee to explain my improper conduct on the night we had our dinner meeting. For the life of me I can't figure out what they mean by improper conduct. I thought we were well behaved. This could mean my dismissal or suspension from the club. I wonder if I should refer this to my attorney. It could be a plot by my lovely cousin to disgrace me. Did either of you get unruly?"

Patello recognized the set up. He guessed that the two experts from the bank's crack planning department got buzzed and littered up the place after the terrific trinity of Hardly, O'Shea and Patello left. No need to target the young men at this point. They might be needed tomorrow although they would be the last people he would put before the Cardinal.

O'Shea came to the same conclusion as Patello. He was less tactful in response. "Kevin, my guess is that those nitwits from planning lit up the place after we left. They were both looped to the gills. Thank God we got the report before they passed out. My suggestion is that you plead guilty and throw yourself on the mercy of the court."

Kevin looked as if he was going to cry. The humiliation of appearing before his dreaded cousin on a discipline rap was more than he could tolerate. He stared at O'Shea in disbelief.

Patello gave him a reassuring pat on the shoulder. "Well, Kevin, we have to admit that we all had quite a bit to drink. The gentlemen from planning were our guests or more properly the guest of Mr. Hardly. Whatever they did as your guest is seen by the club, I imagine, as an act of the member. I also suspect that the club manager earned a few points from your cousin for turning you in. Let me see if I can be of some help before you go to court so to speak. Can you give me a list of the members who serve on the discipline committee? A list of the Board of trustees might also be helpful. I'll have a friend of mine go over the list and see if we can find a friend in court. We can probably put this matter to rest in no time. Our major concern, I suggest, is convincing the Cardinal that the Office of Health Affairs is the way to go."

Kevin Hardly was relieved. He had the same look on his face that he had when he received his passing mark in Ethics back at good old Boston College many years ago. "Charlie, I'll have the list in your hands by the time we leave this meeting. I'll appreciate anything you can do. I didn't know who were connected with the Alleton Club.

"I'm not, Kevin." Patello did not want to pursue the matter. "But I am connected—that's usually good enough. As for the meeting tomorrow, we need to be explicit, I imagine, about the mission and fiscal benefits of the office. We have the information that we can provide but my observation is that the Cardinal appreciates a concise, to-the-point recommendation. He is decisive."

The waitress arrived with the food so time was taken to begin its consumption. O'Shea was animated while trying to eat and talk at the same time. "The key to the Cardinal is Dr. Folley. His Eminence will take his advice before any of us. He respects the Doc. Let's give him the ball and let him sell it. He knows healthcare in Boston. If any of us do the talking the Cardinal will only get confused. I say we let Richard be our spokesman."

Patello felt the sting of O'Shea's whip. O'Shea had maneuvered Folley as the spokesman in order to gain control of the operation. Folley was O'Shea's son-in-law and blood runs thick in the Irish clan. On the other hand, to oppose the suggestion could be counterproductive to the main objective. If necessary, Patello felt he could force the O'Shea clan out in the future. He wondered how much he should inform his associates about the circumstances surrounding Mr. Logan. Some preliminary information seemed appropriate. While he had mentioned the potential availability of the Commissioner of Health for the City of Boston as the first Director of the Office of Health Affairs for the Archdiocese to Hardly and O'Shea he had not finalized their support for the recommendation. This was the time to get their support.

Artfully, Patello moved the question to O'Shea as a way of gaining acceptance by letting the opposition game the idea. "Gentlemen, an essential part of our recommendation to the Cardinal is the inclusion of competent leadership of the health services within the healing mission. The corporate structure suggested by the bank's crack planning staff is essential as well as the person who is to head the organization. We must recommend both to the Cardinal. Tom, I recall that Dr. Folley was impressed with the corporate structure. He also supported the idea of a Director for the office when we had our meeting at the club. Can you check with him to see that he is comfortable in recommending that same concept tomorrow?"

O'Shea was excited to be put in control by Patello. He jumped at the opportunity. "I can and I will, Charlie. It's too damn bad that Richard wasn't included in this meeting. Why are you trying to be so secretive?"

Patello felt the burn of anger. He was certain that his face was flushed giving away his otherwise controlled emotions. He held back the profanity forcing its way through his mind. There remained more important matters to be resolved. "I apologize for the oversight, Tom. Time is so short that I felt a need to get together with Kevin and review things for tomorrow. It would be presumptive of me to call a meeting of our executive committee. Kevin is the chairman and I very much appreciate his wisdom in asking you to attend. The item that now concerns me the most is the director's job. As you remember, I agreed to make initial contact with Commissioner Logan to see if he is interested in working for the Archdiocese. 1 am pleased to report to you that he is interested in changing from public life to the private sector. I have not informed him that the opportunity is with the Church but from everything we know about him he would fit well into our organization. He is a very active Catholic. You are also aware that the Mayor is considering a post in Washington. This makes Logan very available. We should make him an offer this week if the Cardinal buys into the office idea."

Kevin Hardly listened to the exchange between his two friends. The subtle animosity between them was lost on Kevin who believed that he never had an enemy other than his cousin. Conflict was something that a gentleman of means delegated to staff. He was still somewhat preoccupied with the letter from the Alleton Club but forced some concentration on the discussion. He especially heard Patello's comment that Logan was an active Catholic. That gave cause for his reply.

"Gentlemen, we definitely need a good Catholic in the job. Mr. Logan should also be a Knight. I'll recommend him. We can have him installed at the next Knights of the Holy Cross Installation in October. It's on the Cardinal's calendar. We'll need to have him complete the application and get the recommendation of his Pastor. Do you know if he belongs to Malta or the KC's? I'll check on it. I'm sure the Cardinal will go along."

O'Shea was amazed. He sat with his mouth wide open staring at his boss. There was no room for discussion. Hardly, in his usual fog, had accepted Logan as a part of the Archdiocesan team. There was no need to look at Patello. O'Shea could feel the joyful vibration of the big wop.

"Well, bring in Logan and see if Folley can drop him out."

O'Shea maneuvered for some room. "Kevin, we agreed earlier that Dr. Folley was our spokesman. We have now apparently agreed that Mr. Logan will direct the office for the Archdiocese. All of this is contingent on the Cardinal's decision. I will call Richard immediately after this meeting and inform him of our discussion. Is there anything else he should be told?"

Patello reached into his coat pocket and produced an envelope addressed to Hardly. He opened it pulled out two copies of a resume. "Tom, I have copies of Michael Logan's resume for each of you. You might want to fax a copy to Dr. Folley. I think you will be favorably impressed with his background. He will work well with Mr. Durant, Dr. Folley, and the other Catholic hospital administrators in the Archdiocese. When and if the Cardinal accepts our recommendation, we need to make immediate contact with Logan. Salary, fringes, and perks should be decided now or no later than tomorrow."

The rush to conclude on Logan's selection was not to O'Shea's liking. He again attempted to stall. "Kevin, Charlie, I feel that we are going too far at this time. We don't know how the Cardinal is going to react. I want time to review this resume. I'm sure Richard will feel the same way. We have time after tomorrow's session to conclude the details of Mr. Logan's employment."

Kevin Hardly was leaning toward the position of his Executive Vice President because he wanted to conclude the meeting and take a pee before dealing with the more important matter of the problem at the Alleton Club. By agreeing with O'Shea, he thought the meeting would end quicker. "Charlie, I think Tom is right. Let's wait until tomorrow to deal with Mr. Logan. I'm sure Tom has to get back to work. I need to get you the list of people from the Alleton Club so you can deal with my little problem. Let's call it quits for now."

The session adjourned with little more being said. Patello was led by Hardly to the desk of his executive assistant who handed Patello a copy of the Alleton Club Year book containing a list of the Board of Directors and the various committee members. Hardly made a quick run to the men's room. All the members in good standing were listed alphabetically on following pages. Charlie counted twenty-three Hardly names and wondered if there would be one less when the book was reprinted. When he returned to his office he telephoned Philip Mondi at Patriot Transportation and Courier Service. He explained to his good friend that he wanted to cross check the Alleton elite with the special service customer list of Patriot Transport. He also explained the purpose of the analysis. Mondi was very cooperative. He sent a courier to pick up the membership lists and return it immediately to his attention.

Hardly and O'Shea's refusal to consider salary and benefits for Logan worried Patello. Time was short to demonstrate to the Mayor that the Washington appointment was secure. If the Cardinal didn't go along with the deal or if he even delayed a decision the whole basket of fruit could spoil which included the prize plum—waste management. He desperately needed a fallback position. The more he pondered the situation the more he became convinced that he was locked in. The deal with Logan was a must. If that "goddamn O'Shea" screwed around with Logan's appointment he would put in a hit order. No. That would only make things worse by drawing a big investigation perhaps closing all Uncle Frank's business ventures in New England. He needed to be patient. Maybe work for time on the other end. He thought about convincing the people in Washington through NAI that they should stall the Mayor for another week or so. That probably wouldn't fly. The NAI and the Federation were working out the health deal this week. A delay didn't figure in. He remembered Bishop Hanks advising the Terrific Trinity that the Church saw time in centuries while business measured time in minutes. The decision-making processes of the Church and of business were basically incompatible. Yet, the Church seemed to be holding all the marbles. Maybe he was in the wrong racket. His mother wanted him to go to the seminary. Instead he took Uncle Frank's advice and went to Boston College. The Jesuits taught him that time was the essence of imperfection. At the moment, their wisdom seemed to be the essence of perfection. What logic could be applied for solution?

Patello sat at his desk with his hands holding his head as if more in pain than in thought. The ring on his private line brought him out of his meditation. Phil Mondi was calling to report on the Alleton Club analysis. As Patello had thought, six Boardmembers were special service customers of Patriot. Of the six, two served on the Discipline Committee. Another committee member's spouse had used Patriot for special parties at their Cape Cod estate. The spouse was a particular client who had become well acquainted with a gentleman named Eddie in the Accounts section of Special Services. At Mondi's request Eddie had placed a call to the lady asking that the matter regarding Mr. Hardly be resolved without further consideration. The spouse in turn had a conversation with her husband. She reported back to Eddie that apparently, the whole matter was a misunderstanding. Mr. Hardly would be receiving a letter by Patriot courier this afternoon apologizing for the unfortunate mistake. Case closed. Now if the Church could be just as expedient.

Patello was about to return to his deep concentration when his secretary announced that a Mr. Muldoon was holding on line one. Great. Muldoon was hardly what was needed at the moment. Obviously, the goon wanted answers that Patello didn't have. He advised his secretary that he was on another call and would return Mr. Muldoon's call later. That didn't work. The secretary came back on the intercom and reported that Mr. Muldoon insisted on being put through. His call was urgent. He insisted that Mr. Patello take his call. If necessary he would hold until Patello completed his other call.

Patello conceded and answered the phone. "Robert, my cheery little man, what pray tell is of such urgency that you demand my attention? You know I'm a very busy executive."

Muldoon chuckled at Patello's frustration. "Ah, Charlie, you need to be busy with all you've got to do. We have it goin' now my friend but we need to get Hizzoner to Washington soon. Do you know what might be slowing things down? We have Action Waste organized as I'm sure you know. Mr. Meehan and I would like to begin selling waste management agreements to the hospitals. Time is money—perhaps you didn't know. I have it on good authority that the big boys are in New York resolving the little matters while we tend to the world's problems. What can you tell me?"

Patello really needed to hear that time is money crap. Good or Muldoon was having a ball rubbing his nose in it. He obviously figured out that the Church was the delay. He just wanted to hear Patello admit that there was a force in the world that he couldn't control.

"Bob, we have to wait for the Cardinal to open up the job for Logan. Then the Mayor moves Megan in. When that's done Mr. Cowan goes to Washington and we go to work. It should all fall in place before the weekend. You see things any differently?"

"No different, Charlie," replied an apparently relaxed Muldoon. "I'm scheduled to meet Dave Donovan with 936 this afternoon. He is going to introduce me to the Shop Steward at Action. I wanted to make sure that things were progressing according to plan so I wouldn't have to tell the new guy to pull Action's troops out on the bricks. Keep me posted."

Patello placed the phone on the hook and nursed his anger. After a few deep breaths, he transitioned to frustration. He wondered if Muldoon knew that the Marquart kid was well wrapped by the syndicate. Certainty he knew that he was wrapped by Action. That was the deal. He guessed that Muldoon suspected that Marquart was a syndicate plant and was making initial reconnaissance to determine the depth of Marquart's connection. He would learn little or nothing from his meeting with Marquart. The kid had no idea that he was a lynch pin in the operation.

Jay Marquart was elated with his new status as Shop Steward for the Action Waste Management Bargaining Unit of Local 936. Donovan had promised to teach him all he needed to know about his duties. He had even offered to buy him a few beers after work. Some bigwig from the Workers' Guild was going to join them and press the flesh. He thought about pushing his luck and asking buddy/boss Ryan for an early out so he could meet Donovan. Then again Jay didn't need a repeat of last Friday. On second thought, he would work the full shift. He would hold back on pulling rank for the time being.

Donovan had invited Jay to meet him at Stinger's Tavern in Dorchester between five and five-thirty. Jay knew he wouldn't get there until after five-thirty since he had to cross the entire City in rush hour traffic. Donovan could wait. From the looks of him he had spent a few hours in a bar before so he wouldn't feel out of place. The other stiff would probably knock down a few extras as well. Jay called Susan and reported his new status. He also advised her that his new duties required him to attend a special training session with the Union leadership this evening so don't hold dinner.

Susan recognized the ploy and reminded him of his delicate condition resulting from the weekend binge just ended. She also told him that Brian had called and desperately needed to make contact. Cecile had also called and left a message on the answering machine. She asked that Jay call her at home this evening to discuss a very important matter. Jay completed his conversation with Susan. He immediately dialed the page operator at Patriot requesting that Brian contact him at Action Waste Management.

It took a half-hour for Brian to answer Jay's page. He apologized to Jay for the delay in response. Brian was excited over his new assignment as a special assistant to Eddie. He wanted Jay to know that Eddie had chosen Brian to do special courier jobs to elite clients. This meant that he was no longer a truck driver. He was expected to wear a shirt and tie since he was going to be delivering to lawyers, bankers, doctors and all kinds of important people. He had made his first run this afternoon to some rich broad who took the delivery and gave him a letter that he took to the chairman of Hardly Security and Trust. Eddie wasn't the monster that Brian thought he was. The topper was that he was driving a four-door sedan instead of a van. He felt like celebrating and wanted Jay to join him for a few after work.

Jay tried to invade Brian's excitement with his own exuberance but to no avail. He agreed to join Brian after work if Brian would agree to meet him at Stinger's in Dorchester. Brian offered the opinion that they meet at the Waltham Tap and Keg where they had held court for years. No sense changing a good thing. As Jay hung up the phone he made a mental note to return Cecile's call between the evening's sessions. Hopefully the "Bitch" wouldn't screw up the celebrating. The clock on the wall registered four-forty-five which meant that boss buddy was out the door. Jay straightened out his cluttered desk containing grant applications pending review and headed for the door. He was now on a mission for God's own Union.

Jay found Stinger's Tavern at about five-forty-five across the street from the Boston Workers' Guild building. He parked his Jeep in the Guild parking lot figuring that it had to be the safest place in the neighborhood. His buddy Donovan was standing at the bar when Jay arrived. Donovan saw Jay as he came in. He moved away to meet Jay in the middle of the bar and escorted him to a table in the rear. He then introduced Jay to a grumpy old fart named Muldoon. Muldoon remained seated and simply nodded to Jay. Jay recalled that Muldoon had opened proceedings at the Union meeting that morning. He obviously was a member of the Union hierarchy. As a gesture of respect Jay slid into the chair next to Donovan.

Muldoon ordered a round of his favorite Sam Adams beer for the three of them and began the conversation. "I hope you like Sam Adams, son. If you don't you better learn to like it because it's Boston beer and its Union beer. Union is solidarity. We support those who support us. You know what I mean? All Union members are your brothers and sisters, not just your buddies at Action, I mean every working son of a bitch who holds a card. You been chosen to represent the members at Action in 936 but also to become a member of the team that carries the ball for every Local in this area. Donovan and I expect big things from you. You up to it?"

If it was confidence that Muldoon was looking for, Jay had plenty of it. He put a fist on the table as emphasis for his reply. "Sure, I'm up to it. I told

Mr. Donovan that when we met this afternoon. But this thing came on all of a sudden. You are going to have to explain a hell of a lot to me if I'm going to do what is expected. I don't know diddly squat about this Union stuff. How in the hell did I get this job? Was I really selected by the troops or did someone finger me? You gotta know, I been drinking Sam Adams since I was sixteen. Drinking beer is something I know a lot about."

Muldoon put his hand over Jay's clenched fist as if to imply that Jay was subordinate to the Guild. "For now, all you got to know is that you are the Shop Steward. Donovan will see that you get the right information and experience. You just check with him every time you get a question. Eventually you will be able to figure things out for yourself. We have training sessions on Saturdays and some evenings for the Shop Stewards. You'll attend those and learn more. Donovan will get you the right invitations."

Jay felt his familiar serge of anger. *Christ! Saturdays and evenings—what a lot of bullshit,* he thought. Nothing was going to screw up his weekends, not Donovan, not Muldoon or any other mother's son in or out of the Union. Weekends were sacred. He'd explain that to them later. For this meeting, the less said from him the better. Jay decided to let Muldoon have the floor.

Muldoon had already decided to take it. "Jay, what we want to do here now is begin to get to know one another. You from around here? Your Dad carry a card? Gimme a little life history. Maybe we got something in common. Let's have another beer."

Muldoon waved his empty bottle at the window to the bar. The bartender immediately responded with three brews. Jay thanked Muldoon and proceeded with his life history beginning with his first job out of high school at St. Anslem's, his marriage, college, Kristie, divorce, remarried to Susan, her family, State work and then to Action. He tactfully omitted mentioning his spare time activities with the Democratic Party and muling for party bosses.

Muldoon listened carefully and then carefully interrupted Jay. "You know, Jay, I kinda feel that you are holding something back. Were you ever active in politics say as a party worker or something like that? People who have a natural political side are usually the type that rises to the top in the Union. You seem to me to be the political type. You like politics? Ever hear of a guy named Patello?"

Jay felt the hook. He suddenly recalled Ken's comment about running junk for the mob. Now this Union chief starts with the "who do you know" games. He wondered if he should lie. Better not. This guy probably knows the answer or maybe he knows a little and wants to know a lot more. Best tact is to try to circle around the question. Lie just enough to get off the hook was his thought as he answered. “Well, there was a time right after I graduated from UMass that I thought I would try to use what they taught me in political science. I was a poli-sci major. Anyway, I did some volunteer work for the Democrats. Couldn’t eat it so I quit.”

The answer wasn’t enough for Muldoon. He pressed for more. “How’d you get with the State? Charlie Patello arrange it?”

Jay was uncertain if he was being set up. “Who? Charlie Patello. I guess I might have met him but I don’t know if he helped me get with the State. I asked the Party for a recommendation that they gave but I don’t think Mr. Patello was involved. At least I’m not aware that he was.”

Again, Muldoon pushed for information. “How’d you get the job with Action? You friendly with Meehan?”

Jay felt certain that Muldoon knew everything but Jay remained determined to force Muldoon to tell what he knew before Jay spilled his guts. “That’s the second time I heard that in the last four days. I don’t think Mr. Meehan knows who I am. I got the job at Action on my own. Applied from a notice on the State bulletin board. They liked my background and that was it. Why you want to know all this?”

It seemed as if Muldoon was beginning to back down at least for the moment. “Just trying to get acquainted, Jay. We like to know if we are working with a working stiff or a wimp from the back office. Which one are you? Take it from me, Meehan knows who you are. He might try to compromise you with goodies and special favors. You tough enough to resist?”

“Hell, Mr. Muldoon, just let him try to buy me. He’ll get the surprise of his rich life.” Jay swung his other fist as an emphasis of his tough hide.

Muldoon now seemed satisfied. He explained that he had another meeting across town, excused himself, shook Jay’s hand and left. As he passed the bar he ordered another round for Jay and Donovan. The bartender delivered the beer and explained to Donovan that Mr. Muldoon had paid the tab. Donovan exchanged small ta1k with Jay as they drank the final round. Little was said about the conversation with Muldoon except the opinion offered by Donovan that he thought Muldoon liked Jay. Donovan finished his beer in a gulp and said goodbye to Jay, offering that he had to get with the family. He promised to call Jay in the next day or so to fill him in on the contract negotiations with Action.

Jay sat by himself and relaxed. He nursed the remainder of his Sam Adams while pondering the exchange with Muldoon. The guy was about as subtle as an atomic missile. He might just as well have said that he thought Jay was a management shill. In his mind, Jay reasoned, *Well, what the hell, if that's what he thinks then there's no reason to disappoint him.*

Jay left Stinger's in plenty of time to make his appointment with friend Brian. The trip across the City was miserable. Traffic was backed up on Interstate 93 inbound and jammed on the Mass Pike outbound. Somehow Jay didn't seem to care. He wore a nice glow from the three beers. The world still appeared to be his oyster. Gradually he steered to the Waltham Tap and Keg. Brian was perched on his favorite stool holding a few beer-leads on his buddy.

As Jay pulled alongside, Brian already had one perched for him. This was Brian's night to howl. The moon was full and Brian was half the same. Jay slapped his buddy on the back and gulped down the offered beer. He quickly ordered up another for Brian and himself. The code of celebrant drinkers required a reciprocal round before conversing. This time they touched bottles in mutual salute before guzzling the brine.

Their consumption rate slowed as they began the next round. Eventually conversation about the day entered the agenda.

Jay fired the first volley. "Brian, you son of a bitch, what is this about you sticking your head up Eddie's ass? You tuning in on the big time?"

Brian had to swallow fast to respond. He almost choked. "No, man. It came out of the blue. I didn't know anything and he comes up and says they taking me off the route. I figure I'm canned. What the hell, I wanted to quit anyway. So, Eddie sits me down and says how he needs an experienced field hand to run special orders for high rollers. The swells don't like to have a truck deliver their nose candy. Guess it makes the neighbors think they got a hefty stash. They gimme a Chevy with a tape player and everything. I'm on call around the clock though. Got this damn pager hanging on me all the time. Can you believe this shit?"

Jay just smiled. "You get to keep the tips, Brian?"

"No way. I'm not supposed to accept any money." Brian seemed to assume an almost religious sincerity. "I only deliver. The collection is made by a bag man some other way. I never see the guy. That way if I get busted they can only nail me for possession not for dealing. It's an easier rap. Hell, I don't know what I'm delivering. I can only guess. None of the packages lookalike and they sure as hell don't have labels. The dudes sign for it like anything else. Special courier, that's me. Got a raise too. You ready for another?"

Another beer was produced by the hefty bartender. Jay found the barstool difficult to his seating. They moved to a remaining open booth that proved more comfortable and conducive to conversation. The Waltham Tap and Keg was beginning to get crowded. Most of the booths were filled, people standing at the bar were two deep, the pool tables in the rear were occupied and the blaring music from the corner jukebox saturated the place with Country and Western music. Conversation was difficult and required a shout to be heard. Jay played with the napkin dispenser while Brian continued to ramble in a very loud voice about his new career opportunity. No matter how hard Jay tried he could not insert his own news about his appointment as a shop steward. He was becoming bored with the celebration. It seemed time to quit. He had a nice buzz. Brian was repeating himself for the fourth or fifth time.

Maybe one more round and we split, thought Jay.

He was about to suggest this to Brian when Brian's pager let out a shrill high-pitched beep that gained the attention of the assembled faithful. Brian struggled to find the device clipped on his belt. When he finally located it, he could not find the page button. Eventually, he overcame the miracle of technology and noted the paging phone number on the small LED. With no small amount of pride Brian excused himself to answer the summons.

Hell, Jay thought, *they ought to give him a cellular phone to go with the job. That would make things easier and really boost Brian's ego.* He decided to mention it to Brian on his return.

It seemed like only a minute or two when Brian came back to the booth looking excited. "Jay, I got to make a run. You wanna go along? I could use your help."

Jay was now more than a little drunk. He thought the request from Brian was ridiculous. "You need my help? Shit, you delivering a ton of stash or something? How heavy can that stuff be? I never had any trouble lifting mine. Why you want me along?"

The sarcasm went over Brian's head. "Well, I gotta admit to being a little scared about this new deal. I mean, it happened too sudden. One day Eddie was going to fry my ass and the next thing I'm his man. He could be setting me up. I gotta be careful for a while till I get used to this action. You know, man."

"What I know is that you're still a paranoid." Jay remembered the crying jag that Brian had on the last fishing trip. "Eddie try to sell you any more insurance for the new job? Shit, Brian, you can't run scared all the time. Where we goin' and what do you want me to do?"

Brian assumed an important air and sat back in the booth to detail a reply. "Well, I got to go over to the dispatcher at Patriot and pick up the load. Then I carry it to the fruit bowl downtown. You take your car home and I'll pick you up on my way to town. It's eight-thirty now. We can be back at your place by midnight."

Jay was amused at Brian, the executive. He leaned across the table and poked Brian in the chest to give emphasis. "You bet your ass I'll be home by midnight. I got a big day tomorrow. We got a Union at Action and I'm the Shop Steward. We're into contract talks. How about that? What's the fruit bowl? Never heard of it."

Now it was Brain's turn to lean back. "Jay, I been holding a Union card since I joined Patriot. It don't hurt a thing, man. Don't worry about it. The fruit bowl is that queer bar down on Harrison. I think the name of the joint is the Troubadour or something like that. Anyway, what I want you to do is cover my ass, so to speak."

"Sick, Brian. That is really sick. Man, you need a vacation."

If Brian realized Jay's implication, he gave it little credence. "No, man. I don't mean that. What I mean is that I want you to go in first and just look around. Order a beer and case the joint. You see something that you don't think is natural give me the high sign and we split. I tell the dispatcher that I think I had a hot LZ. It's SOP. We don't always deliver on the first try. The Customer got to secure the zone or we don't come in. Eddie explains all that when the order is made."

Jay was still amused at the nature of the task. He continued to bait his friend. "Brian, when I go into that fruit bowl, I ain't gonna see anything that I think is natural. What the hell am I supposed to see that tells me we got to split? You're puttin' the wrong man on point, buddy."

Brian finally got the point but decided to ignore it. Instead he tried to flatter his friend into cooperating. "Jay, if there's one man on earth that's an expert on saloons and stash it's you. You done more pickups in this town than anybody. You been buying stash since junior high. You know what to look for. Just go in there like you was the deal and I'm the dealer. You think it's right give me the nod. Then I go to my contact. The dispatcher will tell me who to look for. They know I'm coming but they don't expect me to have a point, man. You stay clear. If the deal gets busted you stand aside and walk away. Don't get involved. If there's a bust Eddie will get me clear. Patriot only runs a delivery service and they don't deal is the way that they explain it to the law. That's somebody else that I never see or know anything about. You know I could be delivering a box of candy to some guy's sweetheart."

"Sick, Brian, really sick." Jay's response was again lost on Brian.

Jay and Brian divided the tab, waved goodnight to their friendly bartender, and processed to the dingy parking lot behind the bar. Brian insisted on giving Jay a tour of his assigned Caprice Classic with tape player and a Patriot Courier Service sign on the front doors. Jay complemented Brian on his new found status.

In his semi-inebriated condition, Jay drove home carefully. The boys were in process of preparing for bed. He supervised the baths while Susan warmed his dinner. Jay explained to her that he was going to help Brian with a job that would have him home by midnight. Susan didn't ask about the job but knew well that her hero was sticking his neck out for a friend. This was a prominent feature of Jay's personality that she both admired and feared.

Jay fixed a couple of gin and grapefruits that they consumed while waiting for Brian to arrive. A horn from the driveway announced the beginning of the mission. Jay hugged the kids, kissed Susan and left. On his way out the door Susan reminded him to call Cecile.

Jay's stomach ached from the hastily consumed meal, two gin and grapefruits, and the anxiety of having to call the "Bitch." *Damn. What was her problem?* He suspected that she wanted to hassle him about the hospital thing on Saturday. *That's none of her business,* he thought. *If she suspected an overdose, so what? The record was secure.* He wondered if she found a judge who could make him tell the cause of his hospitalization. The pain in his stomach and chest seemed to be progressing. He tried to ignore the pain and concentrate on Cecile. "Got to call Martha in the morning and ask her about this medical record thing. She is going to he really pissed when she learns about the hospital trip."

Brian took notice of Jay's pained expression. "What's the matter, man? You look like you got a fart caught sideways. See that package on the back seat. That's it. Looks like it might be a box of candy. What's inside is none of my business, man. I'm just the special courier delivering a late-night order. How you feeling?"

Jay was doubled over in the front seat but tried to answer. "Like shit. My guts are killing me. Maybe we ought to open the box and help ourselves to some of that candy. You game for that?"

Messing with a delivery package was against the code and Brian was not about to violate the code. "Yeah, sure. We just tell the Customer that it was our favorite kind so we helped ourselves to a small bite. Oh, man, Eddie would chomp us up."

It took about fifteen minutes in late-night traffic to drive from Waltham to the center of Boston. Brian took another fifteen minutes to locate the Troubadour Night Club. He pulled into a loading zone in front of the building next to the club. They could see in the front door that the place was crowded.

Brian took charge of the operation. "Jay, it looks like there's an open spot at the end of the bar. I can see it from here. You go in, sit there, and order a drink. If things look okay then turn around on the barstool and look out the door. When you turn around that's my signal to come in. You just sit there and finish your drink. Wait until I leave then follow me out after a while. They might spot you coming out but then it don't mean nothing. Main thing is that you got to act natural like you belong there. "

"Shit, Brian. Acting natural and looking like I belong there is a contradiction." Jay had his pain under control for the moment and was back at jabbing Brian. "I gotta tell ya if one of those freaks puts his hand on my knee we are going to have combat. Who you looking for?"

Brian reached into the back seat and brought the package into his hands. "Best you don't know. Otherwise, you might look right at them and blow the cover. You do a general check and give me the sign. Oh, yeah, if the place looks hot you keep looking forward, finish your drink and leave. I turn back to Patriot with a customer not found report. Eddie knows that means a hot LZ. Sometimes when that happens I make a second run."

"You make a second pass on this deal, you making it alone. I signed on for a single trip." Jay gave an emphatic point with his finger as he started to leave. He opened the car door and strolled to the club.

A bouncer stood outside smoking a cigarette. He gave Jay a quick once over as Jay opened the door and stepped in. Otherwise, Jay felt that he was generally unnoticed. He took the seat at the end of the bar as planned. From his vantage point he could see most of the customers. Surprisingly a number of women were present. Conversation was animated. People were having a good time. Whatever bizarre behavior Jay expected was not evident. The place seemed like a lively singles bar. He became comfortable. Eventually the busy bartender managed to ask him for an order. Jay asked for his usual gin and grapefruit. The bartender nodded. Jay noticed effeminate characteristics but without offense. He felt that he was in a nice place.

As the bartender was making his drink Jay, on impulse, spun around on his barstool. Just as he completed his one hundred eighty degree turn he realized with horror that he had accidentally given the all clear signal to Brian who was already out of the car and walking to the club entrance with package in hand. It was in God's hands now.

Jay turned to his left and spun his stool back to the bar just as the bartender placed a drink in front of him. He tried to sip the drink but his hand was shaking uncontrollably. He then turned to his right to place his elbows on the bar. Brian had approached two men sitting in a booth. They apparently invited Brian to sit down. As he slid into the booth he placed the package in front of the larger man.

After a few deep breaths, Jay raised his eyes to give the crowd the visual check that he had failed to do before giving Brian the all clear. He suddenly had strong eye contact with a giant of a man that looked like Rock Hudson. The man was staring at Jay with a very serious look. As Jay returned the stare the man slowly turned his head in the direction of the booth where Brian was sitting with his new customers. Rock glanced back at Jay and walked over to the booth. With a start, Jay recognized the Rock Hudson lookalike. It was Officer Michael O'Sullivan of the Boston PD presently married to one Cecile O'Sullivan, RN.

Jay was amazed at the realization. "Cecile's old man was hanging out in a queer bar. Holy shit! The guys a cop!" He made Jay with Brian. "It's a bust—a fuckin' bust."

The pain in Jay's stomach made him double over. He spilled his drink. The bartender came to Jay's aid and asked if he could be of some assistance. Jay thanked the man, paid for the drink, and tried to leave but he could barely manage to walk.

The pain brought tears to Jay's eyes. He was beginning to pray for an arrest so he could ask for medical care. He even thought about surrendering to O'Sullivan on the spot when the image of Kristie came to mind. This is what the "Bitch" needed to knock him out of custody. The combination of love for

Kristie and hate for Cecile overcame the pain for the moment. He regained his composure. A glance at the booth where Brian was seated revealed the two customers, Brian, and O'Sullivan engaged in friendly humorous conversation. There was no bust. *What the hell is going on?* surged in his mind. He didn't wait to find out.

Carefully he maneuvered out the door to the Chevy. Brian in his usual careless manner had failed to lock the doors. Jay slumped into the front seat. The pain had returned.

Brian came out to the car a few minutes after Jay. He got behind the wheel and started the engine. Brian happily chirped at his buddy. "Hey, thanks for your help, Jay. Those were a couple nice guys. That other guy must have been a user. They invited me to party with 'em. Told him I had a few other runs to make. Can you imagine that? They want me to take a few sniffs. They acted like I know what's in there. I act like I maybe know. Anyway, they gonna' ask for me special from now on. How you doin'?"

Jay didn't want to talk but he managed to answer, "Hurtin' bad, Brian. I got to get home. Man, I never want to see another drop of booze. Can you hurry up?"

In addition to the pain Jay was very anxious about being identified by Officer O'Sullivan as part of the delivery. Legally it didn't mean much. He could testily in Cecile's behalf at a custody hearing. Maybe he was undercover.

Jay had reasoned an explanation. *Yeah, that's it. He was undercover. He's going for something else. Maybe he's on to Patriot and the whole ring. Maybe he's trying to bust his queer buddies for possession. Hell, they might already be in the slammer. No good. He busts the users and they finger Brian who fingers him. Cecile wins. So how do I tip off Brian? Do I tip off Brian and he goes to Eddie for insurance? Eddie figures how I'm linked in and comes after me. I lose. Hell, there has to be a way out of this mess. Right now, I'm cornered. Maybe I'll die. Case closed. Yeah, that's it. Maybe I'll die. Brian? How does Brian work in? Those guys got his name. They going to ask for him special. Why? Oh, yeah! They are setting him up. I bet all three of those dudes were cops. Brian is their way into the Patriot racket. They get Brian on the hook and use him as a backward mule. That's not too bad if nobody gets killed in the process. Patriot goes down but Brian cops out. Man, got to get clear from the whole mess before it falls on me. Jesus, how do I get clear?*

Brian pulled into Jay's driveway just after midnight. Jay managed to get inside and sat in the living room. Susan was sound asleep. She was unaware of

Jay's misery or anxiety. She found him asleep in the chair at seven the next morning. The pain was still with him but he decided to go to work. His new status demanded the extra sacrifice of attendance.

At eight fifteen he shuffled past Ken Ryan's desk and slumped in his chair. Roughly, Jay figured he had three hours of restless sleep. The rest of the night had been constant sharp pains followed by anxiety attacks and visions of Cecile gloating over a court victory. Ken approached Jay's desk with a new work schedule for the Boston project. Jay was convulsing. He was incoherent. The company nurse responded to Ken's call. She took Jay's vital signs, asked him a few questions that he was not able to answer. She concluded that Jay was suffering from the DT's.

Ken realized that a 911 call would put Jay in the public record. He instead took the chance that Jay was not in a life-threatening condition. A few months prior Action had signed a corporate health contract with St. Anslem's that contained among many things an Employee Assistance Program for individuals suspected or known to be substance abusers. With the assistance of Action's EAP director, the health nurse, Ken, and a cast of thousands Jay was placed in the company van and driven to St. Anslem's where he was introduced to SACAP or in the complete text, St. Anslem's Chemical Addiction Program.

Jay was placed in a regular hospital room and bed. Doctors and nurses hovered around him taking vital signs, asking him questions, and taking the mandatory blood and urine samples. He signed a treatment consent form that Ken suggested was appropriate if he was to be treated for his convulsions and pain. The form specified emergency treatment for detoxification and overdose. Jay noted the words but was in no condition to object. After a time, a nurse brought Jay some liquid medication that he took without question. Within a half-hour he stopped shaking and the pain was less intense. He felt weak. The rebound that he experienced on Sunday at Waltham Hospital was not happening this time. He knew he was a sick cookie. Nailed. Tears came to his eyes as he drifted into a peaceful sleep.

Several hours later he woke soaked in sweat. The bed linen was more off the bed than on, displaying the significant restlessness of which he had been completely unaware. He felt totally fatigued and very weak. His throat was dry. An attempt to speak resulted in a burning sensation in his chest that seemed to consume what little breath he had in his lungs. As his eyes gained focus he became aware that no one else was in the room. Panic overcame fatigue as he attempted to get out of bed. His legs collapsed under him as he touched the floor. He fell on the terrazzo floor, unconscious.

An eternity later he opened his eyes. He was back in the same bed but with clean linens. The room was dark except for a small night light that seemed to be in the distance. The window offered no light causing Jay to realize that the day had passed. An intravenous pole and stand was adjacent to the bed. Jay looked up at the bottle and visually traced the line to his left arm. This time he did not panic. He recalled that somewhere within reach was a nurse call button. Find the button and a human being would appear. Unless—unless he was dead and experiencing the transfer to the life hereafter. Again, panic.

Horseshit. No angel is going to hook up an IV. Where's that damn button?

He found it clipped to the linen just below his shoulder on the left side, somewhat out of range, causing him to reach across his body with his right hand. He made a mental note to explain to the nurse about the proper position of the call button as he gave it a push.

After a few minutes, a nursing assistant came into the room. She was very pleasant and seemed quite pleased with Jay's return to a rational state. It was a few minutes after ten. She explained that Jay had been in the detox mode for nearly fourteen hours. Susan had been with him most of the time but had gone home to care for the kids. They would continue to take his vital signs throughout the night. In the morning, a physician would explain his physical condition and a counselor assigned to him would explain the course of rehabilitation. He had fought most of the afternoon but eventually came to rest. The IV was to deal with dehydration. It probably would be discontinued in the morning. The doctor wanted it to continue through the night. If he was hungry or thirsty she could get him something. The nurse was busy with a new admit but would drop in to check on him when she was free.

"Any questions?"

Jay listened to the nursing assistant with amazement. He didn't remember anything about the day. He recalled going to work and the night before at the Troubadour. He had no recollection how he got to St. Anslem's. To be sure, he asked the nursing assistant if he was in fact at St. Anslem's. She explained that he was in the SACAP Unit. He vaguely recalled that the Unit began about the time that he left St. A's. He also recalled that the doctor at Waltham had recommended the St. Anslem's program. Well, he certainly took his advice. He asked if he could call Susan. There were no telephones in SACAP rooms but phones for patient use were available at the nursing station. Jay was asked to wait until morning to place his call unless it was an emergency. He agreed to be patient and give Susan a call in the morning.

Chapter Seven

As Tuesday began with pain for John Marquart, it began with anxiety for Charles Patello. After a restless night, Charlie got out of bed at five A.M. By the time he had showered and dressed it was five forty-five. He decided against his usual juice and coffee opting instead to drive to his office arriving an hour and a half ahead of his routine schedule. He had not heard from his so-called buddy, Thomas O'Shea, since their meeting the day before so he had no idea if the good doctor Folley was on board and willing to promote Logan to the Cardinal as the director of the Archdiocesan Office for Health Affairs. The meeting with the Cardinal was scheduled to begin sometime after three-thirty that afternoon. Patello wondered if he would develop a bleeding ulcer between now and then. He wandered aimlessly around the empty office until his stomach directed him to the all-night coffee shop across the street where he devoured two cream filled doughnuts, a large orange juice, and black coffee. Slowly his anxiety transitioned to the indigestion that was more his style. The chatter in the coffee shop diverted him from the thoughts of the pending meeting with the Cardinal. He allowed himself the pleasure of pondering the favor of the young waitress as a further diversion while he consumed three more cups of black coffee. Finally, at half past eight he paid the check and walked to his office. The caffeine had him wired for action.

Things were already happening at One Park Avenue in Manhattan. Mario Capizzi, President of National Associated Investors arrived at his office at six to prepare for the Board of Directors meeting scheduled for eight A.M. His number-one assistant, Anthony Marone, arrived a half-hour later. The two executives carefully examined the Board members' information packets that had been placed on the Boardroom table the day before. Everything seemed to be in good order for the critical presentation on the prospect of NAI entering the business of healthcare. Slide projector, screen, podium, amplifier, tape recorder, television with VCR, and notepads were strategically placed to capture the details of presentation and discussion. At seven A.M. the executive assistant to Mr. Capizzi arrived and began to double check the arrangements. A few minutes later Mr. Marone's executive assistant arrived and began a test of the technical recording devices. The caterer arrived at seven-thirty to prepare the continental breakfast consisting of fruit, Danish, yogurt, nut bread, sweet rolls, bagels, jams, jellies, a variety of juices, tea, soft drinks, and caffeinated and decaffeinated coffee. The mammoth boardroom was immaculate. The plush chairs were positioned at the table. The executives, satisfied that all was in readiness, relaxed with a cup of coffee. The executive assistants moved to the outer reception area in order to greet the incoming members.

As the caterer was arranging the nourishment, Mr. Tom Callahan, Health Consultant for Debur and Tandy, retained by the Federation, arrived and began to prepare for his presentation. He and his assistant placed special notebooks that contained statistics supporting his presentation at each chair. Copies of slides to be used in the presentation were also in the packets. His assistant carefully loaded the slide projector and tested the focus. He then placed a videotape in the VCR, cueing it to the start position. Callahan placed his presentation notes next to the podium after giving them a final review. At twenty minutes before the hour Mr. Frank Patello, Chairman of the Board of NAI, walked into the Boardroom.

Patello huddled with Capizzi, Marone and Callahan to review the agenda and get a feel for the details of the presentation. The meeting plan was simple and directed to the single issue of health. After call to order and roll call the minutes of the last meeting would be brought forward for approval. They had been previously mailed to the members. No contest or amendment was expected. Since this was a special meeting of the Board, Big Frank Patello intended to ask the members to wave the routine reports and old business of the NAI in order to move promptly to the subject of Health as a new business venture. With the concurrence of the members, he would introduce Mr. Callahan who would explain the nature of the venture. The presentation would be followed by a period of questions and comments. The nature of the questions and comments from the members would give Patello a general sense of the attitude of the Board concerning the venture. After they had exhausted their inquiries, Big Frank would call for a break. During the forty-five-minute break Capizzi and Marone would lobby any apparent opposition. Callahan would be available for a one on one with any Boardmember seeking more information or clarification.

Following the break, Big Frank intended to ask Mr. Capizzi to present a sketch of the NAI Health business plan. This would give the Board better insight of the processes and methods to be employed by NAI in developing the health services programs and, of most importance, the expected profits. Again, questions and comments would be entertained after the presentation. If all went well Frank would ask for a motion to approve the venture with the capital allocation recommended in the business plan that was included in detail in their information packets. The representative of the Federation was already disposed to make the motion. If necessary, Patello would give the second but it was expected that the Federation had arranged for a second from the floor. After the vote was taken with a positive result, Big Frank would ask if there was any other business. Not expecting any other items to be brought forward he would then ask for a motion to adjourn. Following adjournment cocktails would be served in the reception area while the Boardroom was prepared by the caterer for a very delicious gourmet style lunch. The executive assistants would be available to assist any Boardmember in arranging travel, tours, or entertainment following lunch.

The four men felt that the meeting was well planned. Preparations were in order. At ten minutes to eight the first members arrived. By eight o'clock Frank Patello noticed that a solid quorum was present. Additional representatives were scheduled to arrive soon. The attitude among those present was jovial. Jim Ebber, representing the Federation, was circulating and apparently spreading the gospel. It all looked good. Big Frank decided to delay the start of the meeting in order to allow for more good will to develop and to allow late arrivals to sample the buffet. No need to press the issue since it seemed to be carrying itself.

The members of the NAI Board of Directors had all been carefully selected by Frank Patello. They came from all parts of the United States but the majority were wealthy people from the Northeast. Each person's wealth was gained by hard work, albeit somewhat less than honorable. Nevertheless, they held a great amount of personal respect in society because of their wealth which they shared generously with special charities. The twenty-one members were also heavily invested in the NAI ventures. All in all, the NAI Board of Trustees comprised a solid mutual aid and admiration society that lived the motto of one for all and all for one. At exactly eight-thirty, Big Frank asked everyone to be seated so the meeting could begin.

As planned, Big Frank moved through the preliminaries with ease and then introduced Mr. Tom Callahan. Tom expressed his gratitude for the opportunity to address the members of the Board. He introduced his able assistant then moved immediately to the subject, healthcare for fun and profit.

"In the next year, over one trillion dollars will be spent on health services," he explained. "Nearly forty percent of that amount is expected to be spent on services traditionally provided by hospitals and another twenty percent for physician services. Sixty percent to be spent on hospitals and physicians while the remaining forty percent will be distributed over a wide range of services including nursing homes, durable medical equipment, drugs, and other health-related programs."

As Mr. Callahan spoke his assistant presented slides demonstrating the statistics.

Callahan continued. "From a business perspective it is important to note that the money to be spent for hospital and physician services is ninety percent prepaid and held by insurance companies, Health Maintenance Organizations, and government agencies to be eventually distributed to the point of service. The dominate method of conducting health insurance over the past decades was by use of an indemnity form of insurance that reserved the premiums and paid to the agencies on a schedule of fees usually negotiated and discounted. The insurance companies attempted to earn a profit on investment income. This method was not successful from a proprietary perspective because there was no control on the utilization of the services. Consequently, the providers were prone to over treat the patient in order to maximize their revenue and profits. Under the indemnity program the insurance companies made little profit, physicians and hospitals made big profits, and the purchaser of the health insurance, usually employers, paid ever increasing premiums."

At this point, Mr. Callahan's assistant displayed a chart showing the growth in employer spending on health insurance compared to salaries and wages over the past thirty years. The chart displayed that over the past three decades for every dollar on increased wages another two dollars was spent for healthcare benefits.

Callahan dramatized the chart and continued. "The increasing premiums caused the rapid escalation of the health services component in gross national product. Automobile manufacturers complained bitterly to the government that the cost of health benefits in the cost of their products made them non-competitive with foreign companies. Federal initiative to reform the provision and payment methods for healthcare failed in Congress but did result in industrial attempts to modify the nature of prepaid health services. The underlying concept in reform is the modified Health Maintenance Organization as the payer networks regulator coupled with the recently introduced concept of healthcare.

"The networks are vertically organized hospitals and doctors who bid for the contracts to provide care for the Health Maintenance Organizations. Fiscal control is maintained by a capitation agreement that only allows a given amount per person in the plan to be spent in a given year. The health network agrees to provide services as needed but stands at risk on total spending. If money is leftover at the end of the year the network is given a bonus."

At this point Callahan paused. His assistant lowered the lights and immediately played a videotape of various congressional hearings on healthcare reform. Congressmen from California and Illinois spoke in-depth about the cost of healthcare. Each offered a solution that differed in form but substantially admonished physicians and hospitals as culprits. After the fifteen-minute tape was completed the assistant raised the light level as Callahan returned to the platform. He glanced at his watch and noticed that the presentation had passed the forty-five-minute mark.

Time, he thought, *to get to the point.*

"Gentlemen, for the past hour I have attempted to give you a fairly comprehensive review of the status of health services from a fiscal point of view. I'm sure you noticed that the complex state of affairs that currently exists in health provides at best a very risky opportunity. What I want to point out, however, is that the opportunity for profit is not in health per se but in the transition of health services. Keep in mind that currently a trillion dollars in cash is floating around out there looking for a place to land. That trillion dollars is earmarked for health service. My recommendation is that you take advantage of the confusion that may exist in select markets, move in, and acquire the health payer and provider base, extract the short run profits while they last, and then divest as the markets move toward stabilization. You have effectively done this in the waste management venture. The strategy used in that venture is basically the same that you may want to employ in health. I imagine the tactics will vary, however. You have what the industry needs to make its transition. What health needs is transitional dollars. I mean capital to acquire the franchise for service that includes the provider base. This acquisition gives you the cash drawer to collect the prepaid dollars. As the cash flows into the drawer you extract your return up front, then pay for the services to the at-risk providers and at the end share in the profits. Basically, you have the opportunity to make out on both ends."

Callahan had their attention. "The timeframe between confusion and stabilization is uncertain. Once you move in you will be better able to determine the time that you will want to remain in that particular market. In other words, if you have control of the market you pretty much can hold the window open for however long that you like. The dominate factor however is regulation brought by legislation. Right now, the Country in 1995 favors private enterprise and a conservative point of view toward health services. However, that could shift. For instance, a move toward any willing payer type legislation could dramatically affect your franchise and control over the provider. Once you get in, you need to keep a sharp eye on the political winds. Gentlemen, I've exhausted my material and I thank you for your kind attention. At this time, I conclude my remarks. Thank you."

Mr. Callahan stepped away from the podium and Big Frank took his place. As Callahan stepped down a hearty round of applause erupted form the Board. Frank shook Callahan's hand and pulled him next to the podium in a position to respond to questions.

Big Frank politely asked for order. "Gentlemen, as I'm sure you have observed we have one of the leading authorities in health reform with us this morning. I thank Mr. Callahan for his excellent presentation. I also want to thank our friends at the Federation for bringing the discussion on the health market to our attention through Mr. Callahan. Now Mr. Callahan has agreed to entertain your questions and comments. The floor is open."

The question-and-answer period went on for another forty-five minutes. Patello noted with pleasure that the questions were of a genuine nature. There was no sarcasm or arguments. All of the Board members were attentive to the subject and seemed attracted to the proposition. Most of the questions centered on the temporary or time limited nature of the venture. It was generally agreed that this element posed the basis for risk as it did for profit.

The meeting schedule was now running a half-hour late but otherwise in good form. Patello recessed the meeting for thirty minutes. During the break Callahan's assistant removed the charts, slides and videotape used earlier. As he completed his work, Mario Capizzi's executive assistant distributed an outline of the next presentation to the respective chairs. She also placed several charts on the easel next to the podium.

Capizzi and Marone circulated among the Boardmembers and listened to their exchange.

Again, all seemed well. Callahan was cornered by a small group who were actively exploring his mind about health transition in various parts of the country. There was no question that the NAI Board was focused on the topic.

Chairman Patello called the meeting back to order exactly thirty minutes into the break. As the members took their seats, he began the second session. "Gentlemen, we were advised in our first session this morning about the short run opportunity in the field of health services. The opportunity as I understand it requires that we select a market and move swiftly to gain control. Then as the market matures, we divest for capital gain in addition to extracting significant operating profits. We might also choose to enter several markets at the sometime depending on the opportunities. If you recall we recognized the same opportunities when we entered the waste management field. You are well aware, I'm sure, of the success of that venture. While we are not experienced in health we are well experienced in the waste management program. On that basis, I asked Mr. Mario Capizzi, our chief executive officer and Mr. Anthony Marone, President of Park Consulting, to develop a proposed strategy for our entry into the health venture. Mr. Capizzi and Mr. Marone have worked with Mr. Callahan in developing the business plan that Mr. Capizzi is about to present. The full details of the plan are before you in the blue notebook under section two. Mr. Capizzi."

Mario Capizzi stepped to the podium looking refreshed and energized. His appearance suggested confidence. The slight smile on his face and the glint in his eyes conveyed a winning attitude. He was ready to get started.

"Once again, good morning, gentlemen. You know me well enough to realize that I wasn't going to let Frank do all the talking. Now it's my turn and

I'm going to take full advantage of it. Seriously, your positive reception to Tom Callahan's presentation was most encouraging. Mario and I have been studying the prospect of a health venture in-depth and we are convinced that it is a profitable, very profitable, venture. The details of what I am about to present are in your notebook and an outline of my presentation is also at your place. You may want to follow it and make notes for questions later. I will be asking for motions to support the venture at the conclusion. This will include a request for a significant capital authorization. The name of this project is TARGET BOSTON MEDICAL. We propose to penetrate the Boston medical market with the acquisition of a Health Maintenance Organization currently serving that area. As we gain control of the HMO we will begin the process of selling coverage to employers at under market prices. As we market to employers we will through another entity, form an integrated delivery network that will appear to bid for and acquire an exclusive contract with our HMO for the provision of services to our insured. We intend to use the capitation model as the means of putting our providers in the network at risk. We will extract twenty percent of the premium dollars from the HMO up front and will also extract another twenty percent of the capitation allowance from the network up front as part of our corporate fee. We also reserve the right to a major share of any profits at the end of each operating year. In view of the fact that we are underselling the market you may wonder about the prospect of profits. Believe me, the potential for profit is great. I will ask Mr. Marone to explain."

Tony Marone took the podium looking less confident than his boss. He was unsure if he really understood the health racket. Capizzi and Callahan had it cold and had convinced Marone that it was a boomer. Now Marone had to explain it to some hard business types that knew their way around a buck. Before speaking he carefully wiped his brow.

"Gentlemen, I am an expert in converting trash to cash. I suppose I appear less than confident about my ability to convert an ill to a bill. Well, that's only because I am new to the idea and have yet to master the lingo. However, I do know a rip-off when I see it. The people of Boston have been getting the medical shaft for a long time. Regardless of our proprietary intent, what we propose is needed in Boston and will be viewed by the people as something welcome and well overdue. To demonstrate my point there are more physicians per capita in Boston than any other city in the United States. Furthermore, Boston has the highest percentage of medical specialists in the Country. The case cost per hospital admission is the highest in the country and the hospital length of stay again is number one. The number of hospital days per one thousand population is currently at eight hundred down from a thousand a year ago. This is compared to three hundred fifty days per thousand in Los Angles. With the right administration of our HMO and the network we can lower the use and cost of healthcare in Boston by forty percent in two years max, and at the same time extract our ROI off the top of the premium and get another big piece at the bottom line. Eventually the competition will catch up to our methods and true price/quality competition will create equilibrium. As that begins to occur we will begin our withdrawal."

As Tony was talking, Mario was demonstrating the points with the charts and graphs on the easel. Tony would occasionally defer to Mario who would explain in some detail how the data was created and go more into its meaning. After fifteen minutes of explanation and discourse Tony returned the podium to Mario.

Mario continued his relaxed approach. "Tony has mentioned the impact of competition as an ally in our efforts. Boston has not experienced the effect of competition in health services. The community has never questioned the extravagant over served care because the health industry appeared to be the backbone of the local economy. We will cause that to change. In fact, the change is taking place without us.

"At the present time, the major teaching hospitals are attempting to gobble up the competition at the community hospital level in order to preserve their referral base to their high-priced specialists. This has caused major disruption in the harmony of the medical community which gives us the opportunity to move in and get established virtually without notice. The existing HMO's are locally owned. The physicians and the hospitals have sucked them dry. I hasten to point out that the hospitals have the highest profit history in the country. Our first acquisition opportunity we believe is Bay Area Health Maintenance, an HMO that is in desperate need of capital. We could bail them out and gain a majority equity position. The remaining equity belongs to about a hundred physicians that we could buyout in groups or one at a time. We give them some vigorish to use in the partnership they take in the health network that we form. That same network should have an institutional partner that would eventually couple with the physicians in buying us out at the right time. Our contacts in the Boston area are well situated to deliver St.

Anslem's Hospital to the network assuming that they can overcome the Church bureaucracy. Gentlemen, that in a nutshell is Target Boston Medical."

Several questions were asked by a variety of Board Members about the estimated time to be spent in the Boston market. Most felt that the NAI venture should start in several areas in order to maximize the prospect of success in the brief window of opportunity that Callahan had described. Eventually the motion was made and passed that initial studies be prepared for Dayton, Grand Rapids, and Raleigh. The capital allocation for each project was estimated and approved by the Board. It was also recommended that Park Consulting change its focus from waste management to healthcare. The Board of Directors concluded that NAI should begin to divest from waste management enterprises. There being no further business to be brought before the Board of Directors, Mr. Frank Patello, Chairman, accepted a motion to adjourn.

Charlie Patello managed to control his emotions throughout the morning. He tried several times to contact O'Shea to learn if Dr. Folley had sufficiently prepped for the presentation to the Cardinal. O'Shea's office repeatedly reported that he was in a meeting and unavailable. A brief conversation with Hardly lacked substantive information but was reassuring enough to allow Charlie Patello to concentrate on other matters.

He left his office at noon for lunch at the coffee shop. In spite of his anxiety he sported a solid appetite. Refreshed, he returned to his desk at one fifteen in time for a call from Tony Marone. Tony was excited about the conclusion of the NAI Board meeting and wanted to give Charlie an update. Charlie listened to the report with great interest. The prospect of moving out of the waste management business in favor of the health venture seemed problematic in view of the state of affairs in Boston. The Mayor was in waiting for a Federal job. The Logan kid was being greased for the Archdiocese. A new Commissioner of Health for the City was positioned to approve the voluntary waste management program. The Union had been cut in at Action. Boston City and St. Anslem's were targeted for waste contracts. It was reasoned to suddenly back off would cause a real mess that would take years to repair.

Patello knew he had to persuade Marone to delay the retreat from waste management. Carefully he tried to counter. "Look, Tony, we can't back off this waste project and move on health. There's too much at stake. Maybe instead of Target Boston you should Target Grand Rapids."

Marone, nevertheless, got the point. He offered a compromise. "I see it different, Charlie. The waste thing is tied to hospitals. It's a natural progression. We continue to move the waste project while doing the preliminaries on health. The two overlap, but don't conflict. We'll get you the help you need. Once the Mayor is taken care of Mark Mehan becomes point on the waste project and you can steer the health thing. No sweat. We like the setup. You got control of the Catholic hospital and ought to be able to bring it in to the network when the time is right. That Bay Area HMO is ripe for a takeover. It's got a load of Docs that we can con into the deal. Our consultant is pure genius and our guiding light. In the end, maybe we give him a piece of the action. We'll have a meeting of the Boston crowd to layout a work plan next week. You see what you can do to wrap up the waste project this week. By the way, the Mayor's deal is all set. It's critical that the Logan kid goes into the wrapper. You having any problem with that?"

Feeling some relief, Patello got back on track. "I'm not aware of any problem, Tony, other than the absence of a job to put him into. It all depends on that quack, Folley, convincing the Cardinal that he needs Logan to run his health business—excuse me—ministry. We meet in a couple hours. By five or six this afternoon I'll know if we have a problem."

Everything seemed in good order from Marone's point of view. He said as much to Charlie. "Okay. You remember the signing bonus. When you have Logan let me know. I'll get the checks prepared for Cowan's endorsement. You see that an account is opened at the bank. We'll have Patriot hand carry the Logan check to the bank for deposit. To move this along Logan should resign his City job by Thursday. The Mayor will announce that Megan is the acting commissioner that same day. He also lets it leak that he is going to resign. On Monday, the Mayor meets with the President and the Secretary of Labor at a press conference in Washington to announce Cowan as the new Under Secretary. The Federation is taking care of all the details. Anything else?"

"Nothing at the moment, Tony." Patello knew it would be useless to complain about the workload. "I'll get back to you this evening or tomorrow morning. It's time for me to head for the Chancery. Say a prayer for our success."

"Yeah, right. You can count on my prayers." Marone had not said a prayer since the third grade.

Patello hung up the phone and closed the files on his desk. He moved to the outer office and announced to his executive assistant that he would be at the Chancery for the rest of the day. He expected to be in the rest of the week but asked that his schedule be cleared for a number of priority meetings that he expected to develop. It was only two-thirty. The meeting with the Cardinal was expected to begin sometime after three-thirty. Charlie knew that it would only take a half-hour to drive from his downtown office to the Chancery in Brighton. Getting there a little early would give him time to check with Hardly, O'Shea and the distinguished Dr. Folley about their state of readiness. As he entered his car, he suddenly wished that he had eaten a light lunch.

The meeting with the Cardinal was to be held in the Cardinal's Residence, a stately edifice located a few hundred yards from the Chancery office building on the same campus. While the Residence resembled a mansion, it was used in the main for administration and as a conference center. The Cardinal used only a small portion of the building for his living quarters. Patello was unaware of the location of the meeting and had to be directed to the Residence by the receptionist at the Chancery. He was the first to arrive. A receptionist at the Residence answered the door. She directed Mr. Patello to a comfortable waiting area in a large corridor, gave him a cup of coffee, and immediately disappeared. Charlie sat alone in the corridor with his thoughts, surrounded by the life size portraits of Bishops, Archbishops, and Cardinals who over the past centuries had given spiritual guidance to the faithful of Boston and Eastern Massachusetts. He noticed that each portrait seemed to stare right at him. Was that planned or was he somehow being subjected to the spirit of these spiritual ancestors who knew that evil intent was more the agenda than advancing the ministry? He put his coffee cup on the small table next to his chair and walked to the nearest window where the magnificent landscape offered less imposing thoughts.

Kevin Hardly was next to arrive. Again, the receptionist answered the door. As she escorted Mr. Hardly to the waiting area she noticed that Mr. Patello had strayed to a nearby window. This was apparently some form of misconduct. As Kevin was provided the obligatory cup of coffee the receptionist summoned Mr. Patello back to his chair. He sensed a slight reprimand as she asked if he would like another cup of coffee. The message was plain and simple. Stay in your seat. Suddenly Charlie had a flashback to his days at St. Mary's grammar school. Kevin seemed relaxed in the sullen environment.

As soon as the receptionist disappeared down the endless corridor, Kevin was on his feet inspecting the various portraits. He gave Charlie a historical review of each one noting his family's relationship with the Church during the particular reign of the Ordinary. In a way, it seemed that Hardly was right at home in the Cardinal's Residence. He, in his capacity as the First Leading Knight of the Order of Knights of the Holy Cross, had frequently visited the Residence.

Kevin and Charlie exchanged small talk as the wait extended past the three-thirty start time. It was curious to Charlie that O'Shea had yet to arrive. Kevin could offer no explanation for the absence of O'Shea or, of greater significance, the illusive Dr. Folley. Charlie's anxiety was mounting to anger and frustration. He was considering finding a telephone and searching out the missing persons when Bishop Hanks suddenly appeared from out of the darkness. Bishop Hanks apologized for the wait explaining that the Cardinal's cabinet meeting had extended well beyond its intended time allocation. The Cardinal required the extra time to resolve a number of matters before rushing for a plane to Rome. The Cardinal had asked Bishop Hanks to apologize to the distinguished gentlemen for not being able to meet with them but he was sure they would understand that the important matters waiting his attention at the Vatican required his immediate departure. Bishop Hanks asked Kevin and Charlie to follow him to the Cardinal's conference room where they could continue their discussion.

Patello was speechless. He could hardly breathe. The absolute need to settle the issue now was lost to everyone but him. He began to sweat. His stomach turned and he suppressed a belch. He was beyond anger. This was panic. No recourse. Just plain panic. As they walked to the conference room he barely was conscious of the conversation between Bishop Hanks and Hardly. Vaguely he heard something about the Cardinal's general consent to experiment with the concept but it seemed distant to the issue. He was concentrating on regaining his composure. What was the rule—never let them see you sweat. Under his coat, he was dripping wet.

As they entered the conference room, Patello got his second major shock of the day. Seated at the table was the distinguished Dr. Richard Folley with his favorite father-in-law, Mr. Thomas O'Shea. Bishop Hanks asked Hardly and Patello to be comfortable. The ever-present receptionist appeared from behind a paneled wall and offered coffee. She complemented the offer with a plate of large chocolate chip cookies that Bishop Hanks identified as the Cardinal's favorite. No one could resist taking a bite from the Cardinal's private stash. It was evident from the used coffee cups in front of Folley and O'Shea that there had been a pre-conference. Patello wondered if the Cardinal had been present. He made a quick glance around the room for evidence of another person but the efficient secretary had removed the used cups and saucers before disappearing behind the panel. He was left with the question.

As they began to sip their coffee and nibble at the Cardinal's favorite cookies, Bishop Hanks once again apologized for the Cardinal's absence. He then got immediately to the purpose of the meeting. "Gentlemen, when Dr. Folley called me to explain the purpose of the meeting this afternoon I advised the Cardinal. His Eminence requested that Dr. Folley give him a preview of the discussion and then detailed the matter to his Cabinet this morning. Dr. Folley was given permission to have Mr. O'Shea, the Cardinal's financial advisor, assist in the briefing. The bottom line is that the Cabinet agreed with the Cardinal's decision to establish an Office of Health Affairs for the Archdiocese. As an additional point, the Cardinal has asked Dr. Folley to be the secretary of Health for the Archdiocese. In that capacity, he will direct the affairs of the Health Office. He will also be a member of the Cardinal's Cabinet. There is only two other laymen on the Cabinet so this is quite an honor."

Now Patello was in a slow bum. He knew that the Cardinal would not have made up his mind in that short of time. This was a well thought out decision that could only have been reached after many discussions. Apparently, the good Dr. Folley had wisely used his clinical time with the Cardinal to foster the concept and feather his own nest at the same time. Best guess was that Folley began his campaign right after the Alleton Club briefing. That would be about the right amount of time needed to cut the deal.

Bishop Hanks finished his introductory comments and then asked Dr. Folley to detail the nature of his conversation with the Cardinal.

Folley appeared eager to explain. "Thanks, Bishop. Kevin and Charlie you know that I was completely sold on the idea of an Office for Health Affairs. I decided right after our review of the idea at the Alleton Club that it was an idea I would promote to the Cardinal. His Eminence has always confided in me his great concern that the healing ministry was losing prominence in Boston. Special emphasis on the ministry was needed. The office was perfect for that to happen. Now the Cardinal is convinced that the best way to expand the ministry is to expand our influence over the physician. That's why he wants me to place emphasis on the teaching and physician training programs at St. Anslem's. It's his idea that St. A's be identified as the teaching and tertiary care hospital for the Archdiocese. The community-based Catholic hospitals will be expected to refer tertiary patients to the Catholic tertiary base, St. A's. We have the quality to match the big centers downtown. Once the word is passed that we have a Catholic system, the physicians will fight to be a part of it. The only downside to the prospect of success is our physical plant limitations. We will need to expand our capacity to accommodate the referrals. We will also have to recruit more specialists in medicine, surgery, and obstetrics. A quick fix might be to eliminate those programs at St. A's that are not tertiary such as the SACAP. I would like to add that the research done by the bank's planning staff was very much appreciated by the Cardinal. He reviewed the material very closely. He is convinced that St. A's and the Office for Health Affairs can be very profitable for years to come. These profits will be the basis for the future expansion of the ministry. Tom gave the Cardinal a good review of the finances. Dad, would you like to comment?"

O'Shea sat back in his chair and looked directly at Patello as he responded, "Yeah. Dick. My involvement in this process was minor compared to the outstanding work that Dick did in convincing the Cardinal to accept our proposal. I hasten to add that Bishop Hanks was a champion in getting us onto the Cardinal's busy schedule. I explained to the Cardinal that St. A's was losing a ton of money because it was being mismanaged. The big money was in the more exotic procedures. To make it big you had to invest in super stars that would draw referrals from all over New England if not the Country. This kid, Durant, has no imagination or understanding of the business. He wouldn't last a week at the bank. Having Dick as his boss will overcome the administration's stupidity. I expect that Dick will want to can him in a few months anyway. We need some good marketing. Development is also a key. People will want to give to the idea of a Catholic medical center."

Bishop Hanks became visibly anxious at O'Shea's comments about Durant. He raised his hand to silence O'Shea and then began his own commentary. "Gentlemen, you need to recall that Mr. Durant was selected by the Cardinal based on the recommendation of his fellow Bishops. He is an experienced administrator with a proven track record. The Cardinal is not to be easily convinced that Mr. Durant is incompetent. You also need to recall that your first recommendation, Mr. Bauman, was a serious embarrassment to the Cardinal. I believe it important that you concentrate on establishing the effectiveness of the Office for Health Affairs first before you concentrate on compromising Mr. Durant."

O'Shea suddenly had the look of a whipped puppy. He lowered his eyes and remained silent. The pause in the conversation was pregnant.

Patello sensed the opening and proceeded to jump into the fray. "Bishop Hanks, I'm certain the Cardinal recognizes the need for competent management. Our intent is not to discredit Mr. Durant. More importantly, our intent is to ensure that the ministry remains credible to the public it serves. We indeed intend to place our emphasis on the Office for Health Affairs. Selecting Dr. Folley to be the secretary and Director of the office is genius. However, the selection could require Dr. Folley to resign his position as Chairman of St. Anslem's Department of Medicine. It will be extremely difficult for him to manage both positions without help. Ordinarily we would expect the Chief Executive Officer of the hospital to fill the gap. But as Mr. O'Shea has pointed out, the state of affairs at the hospital will require his full attention. We believe that the secretary for Health should have an administrator to work the fields in behalf of the ministry. Our intent was to propose that Mr. Michael Logan be employed to staff the office. He is an outstanding Catholic gentleman that is well recognized in the community for his dedication to the poor. His presence and identification with the Catholic ministry will only help our efforts. I have it on good authority that Mr. Logan will resign from the City when the Mayor accepts a Federal appointment. Apparently, Mr. Siro intends to appoint a new Commissioner of Health. I know Mr. Logan and am confident that he would accept a position with the Archdiocese."

Bishop Hanks nodded in agreement.

Folley recognized that Patello had scored. He decided to parlay his own gains. "Bishop, I agree with Mr. Patello. I will definitely need some help. As you know I am very active in State and City programs that include our ministry. My presence is necessary in many places with frequent conflicts in schedule. Mr. Logan could well represent me on such occasions. I hope we can move on Charlie's recommendation with dispatch."

It was now Kevin Hardly's turn to get into the action. He had sat quietly while Bishop Hanks, Charlie and Dick were discussing Logan's appointment. When Bishop nodded his head in apparent agreement Hardly saw that as his cue.

"Bishop, I have listened with great interest to the discussion regarding Mr. Durant and Mr. Logan. There is no doubt that these are two fine Catholic gentlemen valuable to our ministry. It is my intent to see that these men are made Knights of the Holy Cross at the next installation. We will need their pastor's recommendation and a complete file on them as soon as possible. With your permission, I'll contact them immediately for the necessary information."

Bishop Hanks looked at Kevin in a questionable manner but supported his comments. "You have my permission, Kevin. I wonder if we should be a little more discreet and wait until we know that Mr. Logan wants to join us. We also have a Board meeting at St. Anslem's next Tuesday. I assume the details of the office will be discussed there. Mr. Durant has a lot of things to think about in that regard. He or rather St. Anslem's will have to foot the bill for the office which will include Dr. Folley and Mr. Logan. That might not make Durant very happy. What do you think, Tom?"

O'Shea waved his hand as if to dispel Durant's anticipated opposition. "Bishop, it makes no difference if the administrators are Knights or not. They still have to produce a positive operating result. I believe Durant is incapable of coming up with a positive margin. Okay, let's make him a Knight and see if that helps. As far as supporting the office, St. Anslem's has no other choice. We have decided that's the way it is. Durant has to get off his butt and produce. One other thing I'm certain about is that Durant is not a leader. If we bring him into the Order of the Knights of the Holy Cross then he should be held as a member without opportunity for advancement. We don't want him to become an officer and destroy our work. We have to keep him silent."

Patello struggled to suppress his laughter. The words of the famous Christmas carol jumped to his head: *Silent Knight—Holy Knight all is calm. All is bright.* The irony was diverting him from the intensity of the discussion. That stupid fool O'Shea completely missed the humor of his comment. Bishop Hanks either missed it or chose to ignore it. Probably the latter. Hardly was in his usual fog and Folley was busy, as usual, counting his trump.

Bishop Hanks lowered his head then raised it slowly as a signal to reorder the meeting. "Gentlemen, we seem to have come to an agreement. As the Cardinal expects, we will establish an Office for the Healthcare Ministry. Dr. Folley will serve the Cardinal as his Secretary for Health Affairs. Mr. Logan will be employed as the director of Health Affairs reporting to Dr. Folley. St. Anslem's Hospital will provide the fiscal support for the office assisted, as appropriate, by the other Catholic hospitals in the Archdiocese. Dr. Folley, I trust you will take care of the details of locating the office. Mr. Patello, I take it you will assist Dr. Folley in obtaining the services of Mr. Logan. We will announce all of this at the St. Anslem's Board meeting next Tuesday. Is that about it?"

"Excuse me, Bishop. You forgot to mention the Knights." Hardly fired his last salvo.

"Oh, yes, thank you, Kevin." The look on the Bishop's face was not one of gratitude. With the meeting concluded, Bishop Hanks escorted the participants to the door.

Patello and Folley lingered in the parking lot to discuss the employment of Logan. Folley agreed to offer Logan a salary of one hundred twenty-five thousand dollars plus an automobile and the usual benefits enjoyed by executives at St. Anslem's. Patello agreed to contact Logan and make the offer. If Logan was agreeable, Patello would arrange for a meeting between Folley and Logan to close the deal. Patello was satisfied with the outcome of the meeting but was uncomfortable with the amount of control held by Folley and O'Shea.

This deal could still go south, he thought.

Early Wednesday morning Patello placed a call to Commissioner Logan's office. He asked for an immediate appointment on a very urgent matter. The secretary put the call directly into Michael Logan's office. Logan agreed to meet Patello at the Coffee Shoppe in South Station at ten o'clock.

Logan had no sooner completed the call from Patello when he received a call on his private line from the Mayor.

Cowan was excited and breathless as he spoke. "Michael, I have it from a confidential source that you are considering a job with the Archdiocese. Look, I want you to know that this is an excellent opportunity. I'll be resigning within the next week so it would be to your advantage to take the offer. I can arrange for you to resign immediately in good standing. It will look natural since I intend to leak my resignation today or tomorrow. How does it sound to you?"

The call was very perplexing to Logan. "Your Honor, I'm grateful for the call and your support. Honestly, this is the first that I knew that the position was with the Archdiocese. I haven't any idea what the job is all about. Of course, an association with the Cardinal would be viewed as an honorable position so on that basis I'm prone to give it positive consideration. I expect to hear more about it in a few hours. Things seem to be moving at a fast pace."

Cowan began to push. "Michael, this is an excellent opportunity. I've been very involved in its development. The Cardinal is a close friend. I mentioned you to him on a number of occasions and he has been waiting for an opportunity to bring you on his staff. You go along with this. It will be a big advancement to your career. The Catholics collectively are the largest provider of healthcare in the State. That might be changing because of the new mergers and such but they will always be on top. I'm sure the money and benefits will be better than the City. Let me know how you decide. If possible I would like to announce your change at the Council meeting tomorrow. What do you think?"

Logan caught the drift. Essentially the Mayor was telling him in a nice way to resign or be fired. The sequence was simple. Scenario one, Logan finds a new job this morning and resigns this afternoon or, scenario two, the Mayor resigns to go to Washington and Logan gets fired by Siro. Better to resign with a bird in hand than get fired.

As Mayor Cowan hung up the phone he winked at Council President Siro. The deal was certain in the Mayor's opinion. He and Siro then began to work out the various tactics ordinarily employed in the transition of political power. At the City Council meeting on Thursday the Mayor would announce the resignation of Commissioner Logan coupled with the announcement that Commissioner Megan would be transferred from his post in Parks and Recreation to be acting Commissioner of Health. With that business completed the Mayor would announce the plan to immediately implement the voluntary privatization of waste management for the City. The Acting Commissioner of Health would detail the plan to the Council. Mr. Siro, as President of the City Council, would move support for the plan. Other routine business of the Council would follow. However, by this afternoon the agenda for the Council meeting would be in the hands of the media as well as the members of the City Council. Obviously, the agenda would raise speculation that the Mayor's resignation was in the immediate offing. This speculation would be prompted by a leak from Washington. The Mayor would have no comment but Siro would confirm to the media that he expected the Mayor to resign within the week. The Mayor would announce his resignation the following Monday to be effective after the Council meeting the following Thursday. Siro would take office as acting Mayor at the close of the Council meeting.

Siro called Patello from the Mayor's office to let him know that Logan had been prepped for the ten o'clock meeting. The Mayor called Muldoon to let him know that the transition plan was being implemented. Patello called Marone to let him know that the waste management project was taking off. Marone called Meehan at Action to advise him to be ready for the implementation of the Boston project. Meehan called his management team including Ken Ryan in Quality Control and Veto Celli, Boston Project Sales Manager, to prepare them for the all-out effort. Muldoon called Celli as well to discuss personal business following which he called Donovan to press Action on the bargaining agreement. Donovan tried to call Marquart but he was not at work.

The meeting between Logan and Patello took place at South Station as planned. Patello arrived first and managed a small table away from the general milieu of patrons. As Logan entered the Coffee Shop, Patello waved him over to the table.

Logan was uptight and a bit irritated. "Mr. Patello, in our first meeting you gave me no indication that the opportunity you had in mind was with the Archdiocese. It was a shock to learn that the Mayor had actually arranged this with the Cardinal. What I don't understand is why you are involved."

Patello, on the other hand, was amused to learn that the Mayor had told Logan that he had arranged the deal with the Cardinal. Quickly, Charlie easily concluded that Hizzoner was feathering his nest as usual. Nevertheless, the Kid's attitude was disarming. Setting aside the Mayor, Patello decided that a direct and almost truthful approach was best.

"Michael, the Cardinal, like all good executives in big organizations uses staff and delegates to carry out the details of direction. In the case of the health ministry the Cardinal has recently established an Office for Health Affairs under the direction of Dr. Richard Folley, Chairman of Medicine at St. Anslem's. Dr. Folley has the title of Secretary for Health Affairs for the Archdiocese. Several of us who also serve on the Board of Trustees for St. Anslem's also serve to advise Dr. Folley. My assignment is to lead a recruiting effort to select and employ a Director for the Office of Health Affairs. We have counseled with the Mayor, the Cardinal, and several additional influential people in Boston. They have been unanimous in recommending you for the directorship. As a public figure, we found it easy to gain perspective on your attitudes, manner, and so forth. Interviews were not necessary from our point of view. We are prepared to offer you the position. Hopefully, you are in a position to want to take it."

Reflecting on his recent conversation with Mayor Cowan, Logan seemed positive. "Mr. Patello, as a leading citizen in Boston I suspect you are well aware that events to take place in the next twenty-four hours will put me in a position where I cannot refuse your kind offer. However, I have no idea what your kind offer consists of. Furthermore, I have never met Dr. Folley much less the Cardinal. You are asking me to go into this deal blind. I'm willing to take a chance but I need some protection. I'll require a salary of one hundred twenty-five thousand plus two times salary in life insurance, full health insurance for myself and my family, guaranteed pension, and an automobile. I will also require the option to leave the position at any time in the first year of employment with one year salary and benefits extended from the date of my resignation. After the first year of employment the extension is only applicable if the Archdiocese requires or requests my resignation."

True to his negotiating instincts, Patello tried to shave the request. "Michael, your salary request is higher than we expected to pay. However, I can understand your request. The other items are also understandable. I would like to suggest another item that may help. The general employment agreements with the Archdiocese requires a thirty-day probation period. Usually no benefits or perks are provided during this period. I feel that I can get a wavier to the thirty-day elimination period with the exception of the salary extension. To offset this, since I am going out on a limb on the salary, I will see that you are paid a signing bonus of ten thousand dollars. This amount is yours today with absolutely no recourse. We also will provide you with private banking services at Hardly Security and Trust without charge. We can have the account opened and the money deposited this afternoon. You can go home tonight ten thousand dollars richer. Tomorrow you meet with Dr. Folley. If you decide after the meeting that you don't want the job you can still keep the ten grand. How's it sound?"

This was an unexpected twist. Logan had never heard of a signing bonus paid without signing. He decided to look the horse in the mouth. "It sounds like something out of *The Godfather*. If I wasn't dealing with the Church I would swear that you were working for the mob."

"That hurts, Michael." Patello appeared to be greatly offended. "I am trying to meet your requests. If you want to turn me down just say so. We have other candidates but none with your civic background."

Logan feared that the offer would be withdrawn leaving him unprotected. He made a quick grab. "Okay, Patello. It's a deal. You have the employment agreement to me this afternoon. Keep it confidential. Deliver it to me for my eyes only. I'll review it and sign it after I have the ten thousand dollars in the bank. Let me know where and when I meet Dr. Folley."

"Done, Michael. We'll be in contact this afternoon. Are you going to be in the office?"

Logan nodded in the affirmative and shook Patello's extended hand as he departed.

A waitress appeared as he was walking away. She noticed that Patello was also standing to leave so she turned away. It was a free rent day at the Coffee Shop.

Patello returned immediately to his office and placed a call to Capizzi regarding the ten thousand dollar signing bonus. Capizzi informed Patello that the Mayor had endorsed the check for the ten thousand dollars that morning. The check had been taken by courier to Patriot dispatch where it was being held for further delivery instructions. Capizzi reasoned that Patello should direct the check into the bank account for Logan.

To that end Patello called Kevin Hardly and told him that he had offered private banking services at no charge to Mr. Logan. He asked Hardly to make the necessary arrangements. If Hardly could have the necessary account cards prepared, Patello would have a courier pick them up and take them to Mr. Logan for signature. The courier would bring the signed account cards and an initial deposit of ten thousand dollars back to the bank before close of business today.

Patello knew that Hardly would want to be as helpful as he could be. He also reasoned that an account opened through the office of the Chairman of the Board would not be subject to scrutiny. This way the initial deposit with the Mayor's endorsement would have little if any notice. Also, the lack of endorsement by Logan would not be an issue since the total amount was for deposit. He thought about having Hardly initial the check for good measure but dismissed the idea after realizing that it would set a trail back to the Terrific Trinity.

Hardly, as Patello expected, was very pleased to hear that Logan had accepted the Archdiocese's offer. Of course, he would see that Mr. Logan was given the benefit of private banking. He would see to the account personally.

After he finished talking to Patello, Kevin Hardly immediately set about arranging the private banking service for Mr. Logan. Hardly had no way of knowing how to arrange such service. He immediately sought council of his efficient executive assistant. She advised Mr. Hardly that opening an account in the private banking service was not at all complicated. She would take care of the arrangements. Hardly was relieved to have her in charge of the assignment. He then left for an afternoon of friendly poker at the Alleton Club.

The executive assistant checked the bank's procedure manual for private banking and discovered that all private bank accounts required the approval of the Treasurer. No problem. She would direct the courier to Mr. O'Shea's office. She than called the executive assistant in Mr. O'Shea's office and advised her that a VIP private banking account would be coming from Mr. Hardly's office this afternoon that required special attention and prompt dispatch. Mr. O'Shea's executive assistant assured her that he would be available to handle the matter.

Patello also called the bank's Human Resource Department. The HR Director had been of great help in the initial phase of the Logan recruitment. Patello outlined the terms of employment except the signing bonus and asked the HR guy to prepare a legal type employment agreement. He then called Folley to advise that the deal was cut. The employment agreement would be in his hands this afternoon and, hopefully with Dr. Folley's signature, in Logan's hands an hour later, Folley listened to the employment terms short of the signing bonus but including private banking services. He agreed to the terms and said he would sign the agreement. A courier would transport the document.

Next Patello called Phil Mondi at Patriot Transportion and Courier Service. He explained to his buddy, Phil, that he had a rather complex courier assignment that required a man used to details, who could follow orders, and get the job done no matter what. Mondi asked for time to review his staff and give him a call back. Patello explained that this was business for Marone and that the item was already at his dispatch center. Mondi knew immediately what the item was and promised to call Patello back in less than ten minutes. During that time, Phil met with Eddie who advised that the best man to handle this special assignment was Brian. Mondi returned the call to Patello and advised him that they had a man standing by. Patello said he would fax the courier instructions to Patriot dispatch in fifteen minutes.

Brian was in process of spending some quality time with Louise when his beeper let out its annoying screech. He first had to find his pants then the damned beeper. He dutifully returned the call to Dispatch and was told that Eddie wanted him on the spot now. He was to "drop whoever he was doing and double time it back." Eddie seemed to have a sixth sense about Brian's whereabouts. Without delay Brian quit his conversation with Louise and powered the Chevy Caprice with tape deck back to station. As he arrived Eddie, waved him into the office and presented him with a list of assignments:

- Item 1: Pick up item envelope at Patriot dispatch center.
- Item 2: Pick up item envelope at Chairman's office Hardly Security and Trust. See executive assistant.
- Item 3: Pick up items envelopes at Human Resource Office (Director) Boston Security and Trust
- Item 4: Take item 2 to Commissioner Public Health—City Hall—Wait for his response in envelope (Commissioner's eyes only).
- Item 5: Take item 3 to Commissioner Public Health—City Hall—Wait for his response in envelope (Commissioner's eyes only).
- Item 6: Take item 1 and item 4 back to Chairman's Office Boston Security and Trust—Wait for response in envelope.
- Item 7: Take item 3 to Dr. Richard Folley—St. Anslem's Hospital—Wait for response in envelope.
- Item 8: Take item 6 and item 7 back to Commissioner Public Health—City Hall (Commissioner's eyes only).
- Out time EST 1400. Assign comp: EST 1630

Brian was used to the complex type assignment. He also recognized the tight timeframe for completion. Two and a half hours to move around heavy City traffic was tough enough but waiting for response was always dependent on the secretaries' breaks and other delays as the subjects quizzed each other about the documents. This was obviously some hot stuff that some bigwigs wanted done in quick order. Well, he would do his end. The rest was up to the subject items. As he departed, Eddie requested that he phone in at every stop.

Brian checked out of Patriot dispatch with the envelope containing the ten-thousand dollar check in his courier pouch. He aimed the blue Chevy toward the financial district and Hardly Security and Trust. The trip took about twenty minutes in midafternoon. He parked the car in the loading zone and headed for the twenty-eighth floor's executive suite. The executive assistant in Mr. Hardly's office presented Brian with a very large promotional type folder that was to be delivered to Commissioner Logan's office. In addition, he was given a smaller envelope containing the private banking account signature cards. He was instructed to wait for Mr. Logan to sign the cards and then bring them back to Mr. Hardly's office. This was generally in accord with Eddie's orders. On his return trip, he would also deliver the envelope listed as Item one. Brian couldn't figure out why he couldn't deliver Item One now but his was not to reason why and orders were orders. He left the Executive Suite and dropped down to the tenth floor per instructions to pick up Item three from the Human Resource Office. The envelope was waiting for him at the reception desk. First phase completed he telephoned Eddie that he was on his way to City Hall.

When Brian arrived at Commissioner Loan's office he was escorted into the Commissioner's office. Mr. Loan asked Brian to sit in a comfortable chair while he examined the documents. It took about twenty minutes for the Commissioner to review the material. Mr. Logan made a phone call to someone who seemed to answer his question about a bank account. Item two was signed and placed back in the envelope. Item three took another twenty minutes of scrutiny before it was signed. Both items were given to Brian after Mr. Logan made copies. Brian called Eddie to report that the stop at the Commissioner's office had consumed an hour of the precious schedule. He departed City Hall and made his way back to Boston Security. He was actually doubling back over his original track. Brian would cover the same route three times. Again, he realized that his job was to follow Eddie's orders. He made a mental note to critique the process with Eddie at his first opportunity. To Brian the process seemed like "pure bullshit."

Again, Brian managed to avoid the usual downtown traffic snarls. Fortunately, the unloading zone in front of the bank was vacant. He ran for the elevator destined for the twenty-fifth floor just managing to squeeze past the closing door. As he entered the executive suite the assistant waved to him to move ahead of others waiting her attention. At last he sensed some expediency toward restoration of the vital schedule. Then things began to unravel. She explained that the material for Mr. Hardly had to be taken to Mr. O'Shea's office on the twenty-second floor. Mr. O'Shea was waiting for the material. He would complete the transaction and authorize the transfer of information back to Mr. Logan. Brian dutifully retreated from the executive suite and caught the elevator for twenty-two. The executive assistant in Mr. O'Shea's office took the envelope containing the check and the envelope containing the signature cards into Mr. O'Shea's office.

The door to O'Shea's office was left open. Brian saw that O'Shea seemed irritated with the material. He made a few telephone calls. Yelled at the ceiling and sent the executive assistant packing the material to an unknown location. Before she departed she made copies of the material and asked Brian for his log sheet that she also copied. She then disappeared and returned in less than fifteen minutes with a few slips of paper in her hand that she gave to O'Shea. O'Shea gave out with a blast of profanity that shocked Brian. Then he came out of his sanctuary with a sealed envelope in his hand. He pushed the envelope into Brian's hand and ordered him to tell Mr. Logan that the money "wherever it came from" was now in his new account. Brian sensed that the messenger had just been shot. He didn't respond to O'Shea. Verbal messages by courier went out of vogue when Bell invented the telephone. Instead, he quietly retreated to the elevator, got into his car, and headed for his next destination, St. Anslem's Hospital.

Brian's attitude deteriorated completely when he attempted to park at St. Anslem's.

The traffic at the hospital was usually complex but today it was compounded by an unusual number of ambulances delivering nursing home patients for therapies. When he attempted to park in the fire zone next to the main entrance a burley security guard chased him out. He offered little consolation to Brian's plea for temporary parking. Eventually he found an unoccupied handicap slot. Once inside, he found the information clerk busy assisting visitors. She finally found time to direct Brian to Dr. Folley's office located a floor below the main entrance.

Brian was feeling his way toward Dr. Folley's office when he met Cecile. She glared at Brian in her usual manner. Brian had actually never seen Cecile that he could remember, without her hateful stare. He gave her a weak wave and attempted to pass.

Cecile blocked his way. She pushed him against the wall and put a clench fist in his face. "Brian, you worm, where is Jay? I've been trying to contact him for two days. He better return my call. You see to it, dimwit."

The fist was less alarming than her attitude. Brian untypically became somewhat sarcastic. "Cecile, I'm so happy that we had this pleasant chat. As soon as I leave here I'll let Jay out of my trunk so he can give you a call. Now if you'll go back to your cage, I'll get back to work."

The comment accelerated Cecile's anger. "You don't know the meaning of work, you crawling epidemic. Get out of here before you contaminate the place."

Having fired the last volley, Cecile popped back into the Medical Intensive Care Unit. Brian stood in the corridor totally disarmed. His mind was blown. He leaned against the wall pondering the exchange with Cecile. Gradually he remembered the task at hand and proceeded to locate the office of Dr. Richard Folley. The receptionist took the package from Brian and invited him to be seated. Dr. Folley was in conference but had left instructions to be interrupted when the courier arrived. The receptionist reappeared and told Brian that Dr. Folley would be with him in a few minutes. Then she went on break. Thirty minutes later Brian took the initiative and knocked on Dr. Folley's door. Dr. Folley responded with an invitation to come in. When Brian inquired about the package Dr. Folley nodded to the out box on his desk. He stated that it had been ready for the last twenty minutes and waiting for someone to pick it up.

Brian thanked the good doctor and headed for his handicapped parking place. He headed for City Hall, the final destination. Eddie said he would call the Commissioner's office to let him know that the package was on its way.

It was nearly four-thirty-and traffic was becoming impossible. Brian arrived at the Commissioner's office at five-fifteen. The Commissioner was alone in the office. He was packing files and personal affects in boxes that were stacked in the outer office. Brian handed him the envelope from the bank and the envelope from the hospital. He waited patiently as the commissioner looked them over. Finally, the Commissioner looked up as if to ask Brian if "there was anything else."

Brian caught the signal. "Ah, Sir, the gentleman at the bank asked that I tell you that the money, wherever it came from, was in your new account."

Logan nodded as if relieved. "Thank you. Do you remember who at the bank gave you that message?"

"Yes, Sir. It was the gentleman on the twenty-second floor, a Mr. O'Shea. He signed for the material I just delivered. Anything else, Sir?"

Michael Logan said nothing in response. He simply gave Brian a wave as a sign of dismissal and continued to pack.

Brian left the Commissioner's office after he had used the secretary's desk phone to notify Eddie that the run was complete. Eddie immediately informed Mr. Meehan who called Patello. Patello was already aware of the matter having, first, been informed by Logan who wanted to know why Mr. O'Shea was so caustic. Patello covered the matter by informing Logan that the signing bonus was provided by anonymous benefactors of the Archdiocese who did not want to reveal their identity. He offered that Mr. O'Shea was irritated that he did not know the source of the donations. He offered to calm Mr. O'Shea by giving him some insight to the signing bonus.

Logan accepted the offer. He also advised Patello that he had signed his letter of resignation and sent it by special courier a half-hour ago. He had called the Mayor earlier. The Mayor was going to inform the media tonight and present the resignation as a matter of business at the City Council meeting in the morning.

Patello was furious. Everything had gone fine except that idiot Hardly had to involve O'Shea. O'Shea obviously took careful note of the deposit check. He most certainly realized that the Mayor's endorsement on the check signaled foul play. Nevertheless, he let the deposit go through. Why? Regardless, O'Shea was in the know. This made him a big problem in the conduct of the Waste project and possibly a bigger problem in the future health initiative. The guy had to be reported to the boys in New York. Since it was now a matter concerning the Waste project, Patello thought it best to advise Meehan as well as Mondi. He first called Meehan and told him about the conversation with Logan. Meehan was not aware of the way that Capizzi had arranged the wrapper so could offer little comment. He, nevertheless, did recognize the potential for a massive screw up. His recommendation was that Patello check with Phil Mondi at Patriot to see if the courier experienced anything unusual. Patello took the advice and called Mondi. Mondi promised to interview the courier and get back to him.

As Brian was about to take up where he had left off with Louise earlier in the day, his pager once again let out its annoying tone. This time Brian was being summoned by Mr. Mondi who wanted to meet him in the office immediately. Brian bid a quick farewell to his main squeeze and pointed his trusted Chevy back to the coral. Big Boss Mondi was very kind and grateful to Brian for returning to the office at the late hour. He asked Brian several questions about his afternoon run. Brian gave detailed answers about every stop. He left out the exchange with Cecile but was very explicit about the hassle in Mr. O'Shea's office including the verbal message that he relayed to Mr. Logan. He noticed that Mr. Mondi took careful notes on the part involving O'Shea. Mondi also was interested in the fact that O'Shea's secretary made a copy of Brian's log. He asked Brian for his log and then made a copy for himself. Brian became increasingly nervous during the interview. He wasn't sure if he had screwed up or not. If Eddie suddenly came through the door, Brian would know that he had messed up and Eddie was going to rearrange his anatomy. That never happened. To the opposite, Mr. Mondi shook Brian's hand, gave him five twenty dollars bills, and told him to take his best girl out to dinner. This was definitely a day and night to remember.

Mondi called Patello at his home around nine-thirty that evening. He gave him the courier's report. Patello was now very certain that O'Shea was holding some very incriminating evidence. As he pondered the matter the local television stations were reporting the resignation of Commissioner Logan combined with information from a Washington source that Mayor Cowan was to be named as the Under Secretary of Labor. The Mayor acknowledged that Commissioner Logan had resigned to accept a post with the Archdiocese of Boston. However, at this time the Mayor would neither confirm nor deny the Washington report.

In an on-camera interview, Commissioner Logan stated he was very pleased to be joining the Archdiocese as the director of the Office of Health Affairs. Cardinal McMahon was in Rome and unavailable for comment but a spokesman for the Archdiocese confirmed that Mr. Logan had been employed. No additional information was available at this time from the Archdiocese.

Sister Elizabeth was glued to her television set. The creation of an Office for Health Affairs was a recommendation that she and Sister Celest had made to Cardinal McMahon when he was first installed as the Archbishop of Boston. He rejected the proposal out of hand stating that it represented too much bureaucracy. At the time Sr. Elizabeth had recommended that Sr. Celest could run the office as a part of St. Anslem's Hospital thus avoiding additional expense and bureaucracy. Again, the Cardinal rejected the idea because of more pressing matters. She now recognized that politics of some nature created the moment for the office. However, the fact that she and the other members of the Board of St. Anslem's were not consulted gave her a stomachache. Her pain and discomfort was compounded with the realization that the director of the office was selected without any input from the Board. Indeed, she would again have recommended Sr. Celest for the job. She suspected that the Terrific Trinity had a hand in this and vowed to raise no small amount of hell at the Board meeting on Tuesday.

Chapter Eight

Jay woke early Wednesday. The light of the new day was beginning to filter through the dusty venetian blinds on his shabby hospital window. The previous two days were still a blur. He did recall several conversations with the hospital staff on Tuesday. Nothing of great substance. A few residents checked the progress of his treatment that consisted in the main of medication and bed rest. The lab jockey stuck him a few times and there was the persistent demand that he pee in a bottle. He recalled that Susan was with him for a few hours last night. Boss and buddy, Ken Ryan, also dropped in, said little and left. Susan mentioned that Brian inquired about his health and wished him well. The kids, Benny and James, wanted Dad home for the weekend. Kristie hadn't been told about Dad yet. He and Susan reasoned that Cecile would push Kristie for answers that she didn't have. Besides Jay wasn't sure what his diagnosis was. Nobody had given him the word. Today was supposed to be the day that Jay learned all. The real doctor was supposed to show up early in the morning to explain to him why he had been in captivity for the past two days. Jay had made up his mind that this was his last day in internment. He was going to bust out at noon, doctor or no doctor. He felt fine.

He was just beginning to dig into his breakfast tray when a distinguished gentleman with stethoscope in hand came into his room. He was the first physician that appeared to be over thirty that Jay had encountered since he was admitted. The doctor introduced himself as Doctor Kenneth, an internist in private practice and part time attending with the St. Anslem's Chemical Addiction Program. He explained to Jay that he had been assigned to his case on the rotation schedule. If Jay preferred another Physician, Dr. Kenneth would make all the necessary arrangements. Otherwise, he would continue to direct Jay's care as he had been doing since Jay had been admitted to the Unit. Jay did not have a primary care physician although the HMO required him to name one. He knew that Susan and the kids had docs but Jay couldn't remember their names.

Jay reasoned that accommodating the doctor would be the best tact so he offered a proper reply. "Look, Doctor, I'm sure that you'll do fine. In fact, I think you have done wonders. I feel fine and think I can go home and back to work. I thank you for all that you have done. The staff has been wonderful. About all I need is a discharge order and I'll cease being your problem.

Doctor Kenneth shook his head from side to side as Jay talked. Then he answered, "Jay, you are not well. I'm here to advise you about your illness and work out a treatment plan. You have a long way to go for recovery. We might be able to discharge you from this bed but we cannot in good conscience discharge you from treatment. You have an illness that needs treatment. On the other hand, we cannot force you to follow our direction. This has to be a voluntary decision on your part."

The doctor's comments frustrated Jay. He wanted out of the hospital. He did not want to hear about an illness that he did not believe he had. This time he answered with sarcasm, "What, pray tell, is this terrible disease? Am I going to die? I don't feel like I'm what sick. If you are referring to my boozing, I've heard that song before. Some guy at Waltham Hospital handed me that line on Sunday. Said his name was Hendricks. Know him?"

Kenneth sat on the edge of the bed and looked out the window. "Mr. Marquart, you told the resident about your admission to Waltham's ER on Saturday. You also signed a consent release for us to access your records. We brought your records forward and have consulted with Dr. Hendricks. If you would like him to continue your treatment that can be arranged. Dr. Hendricks and I trained here at St. Anslem's. We share a private office practice. In summary, you have a chemical dependency based on a deficiency in your blood. This deficiency causes you to use drugs to offset the imbalance in your system. The problem is that the chemicals that you are using while giving you emotional satisfaction are causing an increasing deficit in the quality of your metabolism. We intend to treat your deficiency with the right chemicals and restore your chemical balance. You also need to know that we suspect that you are developing ulcers. That is very consistent with addicted people. Without treatment, you will continue to experience physical as well as mental breakdowns."

Jay got out of the bed and began to pace around the room. His irritation was now very obvious. "Let me get this straight. You want me to start taking drugs in order to stop taking drugs. That's interesting. You guys have a neat thing going for you. Hendricks scoops 'em up in Waltham's ER and you take a chunk out of 'em at St. A's. Between the two of you every junkie in town gets fixed. Not."

Dr. Kenneth stood up and followed Jay. Eventually he got in front of him and looked Jay in the eye. "Mr. Marquart, I don't intend to argue with you about this. I also don't intend to take any of your crap. Your disease is the most difficult to cure. The main reason is because you and many like you do not believe that they are as sick as they are. A person who experiences cardiac arrest doesn't have to be convinced. They get religion real fast. An addict, in spite of the pain, wants to keep right on punishing himself because he thinks it feels so good. The cost isn't money. The real cost is the loss of dignity, family, and the love and respect of those close to you. You think you can handle it. Well, friend, look around you at your wife and kids and ask if they can handle it. They have to carry the burden."

"Doctor, I'm sorry if I offended you." Jay realized that he had angered the physician and probably lost his chance to be discharged. "You've got a tough and thankless job. Yeah, I know that I have a problem. I like to party. Who doesn't? But I pull up short of saying I'm a junkie. I also realize that over doing it can screw me up big time. So, I'll slow down. No reason to quit. Just a little self-control and I can go on living. You take care of the poor bastard that's zonked out in the gutter. I'll take care of good ol' Jay and stay out of here. Tell me again how you got my record out of Waltham."

Dr. Kenneth backed away and seemed to regain his composure. "Mr. Marquart, I want to treat you now so you avoid being zonked out in the gutter. Your denial of the problem is very typical. I won't bother you anymore today but I will ask our counselor, Bob Markley, to have a chat with you. Will you see him?"

Jay sensed that things were about to go his way. "Sure, if it will make you feel better. Send him around. How about that discharge order? I don't want to walk out of here today against medical advice or AMA as you guys put it. That could screw up the insurance. We can both appreciate that."

Dr. Kenneth closed Jay's chart folder, put his pen in his pocket, and with a sigh followed by a slight wave to Jay walked out of the room. Jay watched the doctor walk out. In a way he felt sorry for the guy. He had tried his very best to sell Jay a continuing treatment program. The effort and passion that the doctor displayed suggested to Jay that there had to be big money involved. Why else would the doctor try so hard to convince him that he needed the cure? Jay also recognized that the doctor's compassion was genuine. Several of Jay's verbal blasts almost brought the man to tears.

Why couldn't the guy just back off? he wondered. *No need to make such a big deal out of the problem.*

Suddenly, he remembered that he had to make some telephone calls. The first one to Susan would be to arrange for her to pick him up this afternoon. He also had to call Ryan and, "oh, yeah, the Bitch. Must not forget the Bitch."

Jay dressed and packed what few items he had in a hospital container that he found in the closet. Satisfied that he was ready to go, he ambled to the front desk to get permission to use the patient telephone. The desk was unattended except for a gentleman in whites that, because of his somewhat unkept appearance and relaxed posture, gave Jay the impression that he was a male nursing assistant. The man also looked a little shop worn and long of tooth. His ID badge was clipped on backwards so the name was not visible. His hair was overdue for a trim, the mustache drooping slightly to starboard, and his belly pulled the shirt buttons to maximum tension. The uniform was clean and the white shoes were spotless yet old. When Jay asked for permission to use a phone, the man flashed Jay an infectious grin and passed him the desk phone. Jay punched nine for an outside line and received a weird screech.

The man gently reached over and depressed the button causing disconnect. "Sorry, buddy, no need to punch nine. We now have the most marvelous advanced state of the art telephone system in the world. Administration bought this miracle of modem technology with the money usually paid to us slaves. Now we can call anywhere in the world without punching nine. Try again. Just dial your number. All the comforts of home right here in St. A's. Would you ever have guessed? Just look at the excellent device before you. We still have to train it to say only what we want to hear. I guess that will be part of next year's expensive upgrade. We can hardly wait."

Jay returned the man's smile. He loved the guy's sarcasm. This was the kind of person Jay was attracted to, a real cynic. This time he dialed correctly. Susan answered on the second ring. Jay explained to her that he was "busting out of this funny farm by four-thirty at the latest." The man heard the comment, smiled, and leaned back in his chair as if he was a party to the conversation. Jay noticed his interest and gave him a wink in acknowledgment that also served as an invitation to monitor Jay's particular style and humor. Jay appreciated an audience. He performed well using the best street terms in describing to Susan the quality of care at St. Anslem's. He talked about how he humbled Dr. Kenneth and now was waiting for his next victim, "some dweeb named Markley." After he polished off this guy, he was leaving.

Susan was very pleased that Jay was being discharged. Trying to handle Benny and James, make visits to the hospital to see Jay, and run the household was no small challenge. She was looking forward to Jay's homecoming and the coming weekend party. She desperately needed a few belts and a couple of good laughs with Brian and Louise.

Her excitement was evident. "Jay, I'll be there to pick you up at four-thirty. I'll bring the kids. They have been concerned about you. Cecile called several times but I told her you were on the road for Action. I think she smells something. Brian met her at the hospital today when he was delivering something. Anyway, she chewed him out about you not returning her call. He called about a half-hour ago. He doesn't know where you are either. He thinks you are out of town. Maybe you ought to call him tonight after you get home."

Jay acknowledged the need to call Cecile. He also said he would call Brian that evening. His intent was to call Ryan after he finished his conversation with Susan but the fact that Cecile was making such a fuss motivated him to retaliate. He cut short his conversation with Susan. As he hung up the receiver he asked his newfound buddy if he could place an in-house call. The man nodded in the affirmative and instructed Jay how to locate the number in the house directory. It was a simple matter of dialing the four-digit number.

The unit secretary in the Medical Intensive Care Unit Answered the phone immediately and in response to Jay's inquiry, informed him that Mrs. O'Sullivan was on duty. He was asked if he wanted to hold for a minute until she was available or she could return the call. Jay opted to hold. He reasoned that a return call to the SACAP unit could complicate the conversation.

In less than a minute Cecile answered the phone with her usual professional greeting. "This is Nurse O'Sullivan. How may I help you?"

"Nurse O'Sullivan, this is Mr. Jay Marquart. The question is, how can I help you, as if I really cared?"

Cecile was not in the mood for Jay's smart mouth. She fired back with a blast of her own. "Well, Mr. Marquart, your antics of the past week are of sufficient note that my lawyer is preparing the necessary papers to return you to court. You have placed Kristie in harm's way with your habitual and excessive alcohol and drug use. I am advised that I have an obligation to bring your conduct and Mrs. Marquart's conduct as well to the attention of the court that way protecting Kirstie from harm and undue negative influence. You will lose your custody. My call was to advise you that papers would be served to you in the next few days. I will add the information that for the past few days you have obviously been in treatment at St. A's drug unit. We will subpoena your medical record. You know, Jay, I don't care if you and Susan dope yourselves to hell. But there is no way that my daughter is going to be subjected to the influence of her drunken, spaced out father and his junkie wife. You can try to ignore me but that won't matter once we get to court. This time you have really screwed up."

Jay was speechless. He feared that Cecile was on his trail after Kristie spilled the beans about his trip to Waltham Hospital on Saturday. How did the Bitch know that he was at St. Anslem's? Everything was supposed to be so confidential. He thought he was in a protected unit. Suddenly he realized that he had accidentally violated his own confidentiality. As he stared at the marvelous marvel of modem technologic telephone he noticed the small screen LED on the top of the instrument flashing the number of the station he had called and the name of the unit secretary that had answered. Apparently, Cecile was now looking at the LED on her telephone that was flashing the number and name of the Unit from which the call had been placed. He was nailed. He was at the moment too shocked to get angry. Tears filled his eyes and he sobbed. His tough cocky attitude dissipated. Gone was the humor that he had exchanged earlier with the man at the desk.

The man at the desk took note of the change. He got out of his chair, walked around the desk and stood at Jay's side. Gently he placed his hand on Jay's shoulder. The touch of compassion was welcomed by Jay. God, how he was in need of a friend.

Jay struggled to regain his composure and best Cecile. "Cecile, you and your lawyer can cram it. You have no right to my medical records and you have no knowledge that would give cause of improper influence on Kristie. I'll have you out of her life for good if you try to disrupt my relationship with Kristie. Kiss off."

Jay slammed the telephone on the desk. Now he was enraged. Inadvertently he swung his fist at the man whom he had befriended a few minutes before.

The man with the skill of a prizefighter gracefully dodged the blow. Jay threw a chair across the room that crashed against the wall then bounced into a lamp that it destroyed. His anger accelerated. Three more pieces of furniture were pitched across the room. The office, reception desk, and adjacent area were systematically reduced into piles of debris. Jay raged, shouted, cursed and beat his fist into the wall.

A Code 777 SACAP was called by the unit head nurse to the hospital communication center and relayed through the entire institution via the audible paging system. Three massive security guards responded, well trained in handling violent patients. As they appeared Jay's new friend waved then out of sight. He allowed Jay to wear out his anger. Eventually, Jay tired. He sat down in the middle of the room, exhausted, and began to cry. His friend sat down next to him among the broken furniture, glass, torn paper, and various personal items from staff lockers. Gently, he placed his arm around Jay. Jay reached up and took the man's hand as a gesture of relief. He was asleep within a few minutes.

Jay's new friend sat in the chair next to the bed and waited. It was well past time for his lunch break but he had missed that many times before. He waited, as he had also done many times before.

After a few hours, Jay opened his eyes. He was still very tired and emotionally drained. He was also bathed in sweat. His clothes were damp and he felt a chill. The very dry condition of his throat was stark contrast. He was in desperate need of water. The shame of his outrage clouded his mind. Above the discomfort and shame was the overriding issue of the pending court fight with Cecile. Martha was his only counsel. He desperately needed to talk to her. Carefully he raised himself up and sat on the edge of the bed. It was then that he noticed the man in the chair next to the bed. It was the same guy that was with him when he lost it at the nurses' station.

The good dude with the quick smile and wicked sense of humor that Jay had tried to cold crock with his famous right hook sat peacefully watching Jay struggle to the edge of the bed.

"How you doing, partner? Thirsty I bet. I'm usually thirsty when I come off a tear like that. Man, you messed up the place. Administration's going to flip. Well, they have to have something to do to earn the big bucks. What set you off, anyway? Here, I got you a glass of water."

Jay accepted the glass of water with noticeable gratitude. He raised the glass in salute before he gulped it down. He handed the glass back to the man who poured him another from the pitcher at his side. Again, Jay drained the glass without taking a breath.

On the third glass Jay sipped the contents slowly. He was beginning to regain composure. "You know, buddy, you seem to have been my constant companion for the past several hours and we haven't even been introduced. I'm Jay Marquart, patient extraordinaire and self-appointed interior decorator of St. A's drunk tank. Who might you be?"

The man's quaint smile returned. "My name's Bob Markley. I used to have your job and, I might add, did a much better job on a regular basis. Now I'm confined to the payroll as a counselor. I think before the action started that you referred to me as a dweeb. Doctor Kenneth wanted me to chat with you this afternoon. I have to admit, it was an interesting interview."

The comment surprised Jay. He leaned forward and supported himself by spreading his arms to his side and placing his hands on the side of the bed as he sat. "Yeah. You aren't what I expected either. I don't know what to do now. This fucking hospital has messed me up big time. I came in here thinking that I was protected by the usual code of confidentiality. Now that goofy telephone has told the world including my ex-wife that I'm a junkie. Man, I'm gonna sue their ass. She's taking me to court knowing that I'm in here. The goddamn records are open for public scrutiny, she thinks. Where does she come off as a nurse in this hospital exposing the records of a patient? My sister's a lawyer. Man, she is going to sue your ass."

Markley was shaken by Jay's comment about litigation but he remained calm. "Jay, I can't comment on the status of the hospital in your dispute with your ex-wife. I can say that under Federal law if a patient seeks or receives treatment at a general hospital that operates a certified substance abuse program recognized by the Federal Government then the patient's treatment and the patient's records in the program remain confidential. No one, including the courts, can access that information. Any member of the hospital staff in any capacity that uses that information outside of the treatment program is subject to criminal action. St. A's program is fully accredited and certified by the Federal government. You are protected as a recipient of our care. The only way that your records would transfer out of here is if you were never admitted to the program. While you have been in the Unit for the past two days you have been classified as a general hospital patient. What Dr. Kenneth tried so ineffectively to explain to you this morning is that we want to admit you to the program. You rejected the idea but you might want to reconsider in view of recent events."

Jay wasn't sure he had heard what Markley said. "Okay, let's see if I got this straight. I join your little dance party and my records get locked up. Nobody gets to them. But if I don't join, then my records are treated like general hospital records. Hell, what's the difference? General medical records are supposed to be confidential."

Markley got out of his chair and placed his hand on Jay's shoulder to emphasize the point. "General medical records are easily subpoenaed by the courts. Lawyers force disclosure through discovery all the time. It's not as easy in substance abuse programs. You can have your lawyer check it out. Anyway, it gives you better protection than you have now. My suggestion is that you voluntarily admit yourself to the program as of your date of admission on Tuesday. You can do that since you have not been discharged. We simply transfer you and your records out of general hospital into the program. Everything is locked up including your trip to Waltham hospital because Dr. Hendricks made a referral in your record to St. A's program. It's a nice neat package."

"What's the catch?" Jay was suspicious.

Markley sensed that he had Jay's attention. "Well, you have to be serious about your treatment. If you admit to the program and then withdraw or refuse to accept treatment, which is the same as withdrawal, then you lose the Federal protection. Your records flow back to general hospital for whatever consequence."

The thought of protection was appealing but the thought of continuing treatment was discouraging. "Man, what am I getting into? I thought Dr. Kenneth wrote the discharge order. How we going to get around that?"

Markley waved his hand in the air as if to brush away a fly. "No sweat. I asked him not to make any entry on your chart until we had our little chat. I really didn't have any idea things would shape up this way. I thought maybe I would just beat the hell out of you and leave it at that. So, what do you say? Try it. You'll like it."

Jay was caught by Markley's comfortable manner. "Okay, sign me up. Did you ever sell used cars or do recruiting for the Marines?"

Bob Markley invited Jay back to the nursing station. Housekeeping had cleaned the place up. Some of the broken furniture had been replaced and there was an odor of fresh paint. Jay attempted a weak apology that Markley discounted. Apparently, the nurses' station and lobby were frequently rearranged by irate clients.

The two men entered a very small office in back of the nurse station. Markley produced an admitting form to the Program that Jay signed after giving the small print a quick glance. He also signed another series of consent and release forms. Markley back dated the forms to last Tuesday. He handed Jay several pamphlets about the program that he instructed Jay to keep and use if he ran into questions from family and friends about his disease and treatment. Otherwise, there was no need to advertise his condition.

One pamphlet was strictly for the employer. Markley noticed that Jay seemed to be staring at this one. "Jay, you worried about your job?"

"Yeah. My boss and the company nurse brought me in here. They know about me. How they gonna keep this out of my employee file?" Jay's eyes were closed as if experiencing some pain as he mouthed the question.

Markley made a quick check of Jay's medical record. "It says on the record that Action Waste Management referred you to us through their Employee Assistance Program. The only thing that should ever appear in your work record is the time that you are off the job for illness, vacation, and things like that. If you had a medical problem at work that the company nurse assisted with then that would be a part of her daily log. There should be no indication in your work file regarding your dependency problem. If it concerns you, I'll have our staff check your file or you can do it yourself when you get back to work."

The response brought Jay out of his temporary depression. "When can I go back to work? I got things stacked up. I was counting on being there tomorrow."

"Monday at the earliest. That wild spree that you went on a few hours ago is apt to hit you again. We need to get better acquainted over the next few days. You can go home this afternoon but I want you to spend your days here for a while. When you get over the hit that detox gives you then we can let you take a little more mental pressure. It's hard to tell at the beginning what might light your fuse. Apparently, your ex-wife lights you up real easy." Markley knew he had made an understatement.

Anger flared in Jay's eyes. He stood and pounded his fist on the counter. "Yeah, well, she's gonna drag my ass into court over custody of my daughter. This goddamn place gave her the information she needed to fry my ass. You gotta know that I'm going after her big time. This hospital is in deep shit, I'll own this goddamn place before it's over. That fucking telephone system is gonna cost you big bucks. I thought hospital employees were supposed to keep patient information confidential. Seems to me that I could have her nursing license revoked."

Markley tried to appease his patient. "Jay, you are getting agitated and in a few minutes your anger will erupt into violence. I'll see that it doesn't happen. You and I can talk about something else, or if you want, we can talk more about your concern. The key here is that we talk out your anxiety and anger. That's why I want you to spend a lot of time with me over the next few days. You'll meet some other people who understand your problem and the disease that causes it. In time, you will realize how beneficial it is to have someone to turn to when the pressure moves you to a breaking point. You will get to know a lot of people in the many support groups that are available."

The thought of a full-blown counseling program was not what Jay had in mind. "Look, Bob, you know that I'm not really big into this stuff. I'm hiding my record so my Ex can't take my daughter away from me. You gave me the idea. All the rest of this stuff is a little far out. Sounds like you figure me for a head case."

"In a way, you are," Markley came back at him. "What makes you different from a psycho is that the cause of your anger is very evident. You are going through a form of withdrawal. The change taking place in your body chemistry causes a psychic reaction that manifests in violent behavior. Dr. Kenneth will monitor your chemistry and give you supplements that moderate your emotions while your body adjusts to what we expect to be a permanent change in your lifestyle. However, the type of disease that you have cannot be cured medically. It can only be controlled by a combination of medicine and a strong dose of individual will power. Dr. Kenneth will evaluate your physical needs and prescribe the appropriate therapy. I'll be your buddy during this process and together we can work on the will power bit. Take it from me, it's not going to be easy."

It was apparent to Jay that the price of protection from Cecile was cooperation with Markley. With some degree of courtesy, he tried to explain his position, "So you think that between now and Monday I'll get religion. Man, that's far out. I can't wait to get out of here. The only thing that will bring me back is Kristie, that's my daughter. No way am I going to swallow Kenneth's medicine. I told him this morning that taking drugs to stop taking drugs was bullshit. I'll listen to you but I'm not going to start taking those weird pills. You know I used to work in the cath. lab here. I saw those docs pump up the charges on those patients with a lot of stuff that didn't mean shit. What did the patient know? Nothing, man. They just wanted to live. Well, I just want to keep my daughter."

"Okay, Jay, we'll take it one step at a time." Markley was satisfied that he had a taker.

One of the first procedures in the first step involved a telephone call to Ken Ryan at Action Waste Management. Jay's call was warmly received by Ken who emoted about the prospect of the Boston project. It was expected to start as early as tomorrow. Ken was in hope that Jay would be back on board. Jay reported that he had to continue treatment through the weekend and would possibly be back to work on Monday. His new buddy, Bob Markley, got on the phone at Jay's request and explained in careful terms that Jay's condition required careful monitoring for the next few days. The call concluded with Ken reporting to Jay that a Mr. Donovan desperately needed to talk to him. He gave Donovan's phone number to Jay.

Jay called Donovan and explained that he had been sick and in the hospital for the past couple of days. He had to stay home for another few days and would be back to work on Monday. Donovan asked Jay to call him tomorrow since it was noised about that the Boston project at Action was going to kick off. The Union contract had to be worked out so that the workers got a piece of the rewards. A good health plan was definitely a part of the discussion. Jay agreed to give Donovan another call in the morning.

At four-thirty Susan came into the Unit. Benny and James were left in the main lobby with coloring books being carefully watched by the volunteers on duty. Susan was anxious to get back to her charges and became noticeably irritated when Jay asked her to take a few minutes to meet Bob Markley. She became increasingly agitated as Bob explained that Jay was not being discharged but allowed to go home in the evenings. His days were to be spent in the Unit through the weekend. Susan realized that somehow Markley had got his clutches on Jay. She feared the goody two shoes lifestyle that often accompanied the reformed. This could mean a damper on the weekend party that she desperately needed.

On the way home, she noticeably pouted about the days ahead. Jay didn't appreciate her attitude. He was concentrating on the legalities ahead of him while trying to form the details in mind so he could give Martha the material to hang Cecile and St. Anslem's in the bargain.

The happy Marquart family arrived home and proceeded to enjoy a welcome home dinner that Susan prepared for their hero. Jay was in very good spirits. In similar circumstances, he would have had two or three gin and grapefruits. Now he was sober and intent on staying that way. Susan missed the usual jag that accompanied the family's good times. Somehow things just didn't seem the same. After dinner Jay moved in front of the TV to take in the sports report on the evening news. His timing was perfect to see and hear the headline story about the pending resignation of the Mayor and the resignation of the Commissioner of Health who was to become a part of the Archdiocesan staff. Jay caught the comment that the former Commissioner was to be the director of Health so he made a mental note to sue the Church as well as St. Anslem's although he wasn't too sure what he would do with a Church if he won. The kids hung around Jay until they were certain that he was home for the night. Then they disappeared to other haunts.

As the sports reports began, the Marquart telephone broke Jay's attention on the latest Red Sox win. When he answered the phone his concentration remained focused on the interview with the relief pitcher who managed to get the final out on three straight strikes. His attention shifted immediately, however, to Martha's greeting following his bland hello.

Martha was insistent on penetrating the events of the past few days. "Well, my dear brother, what have you been up to the past five days? My guess is that you have teased your former wife to a state of frenzy."

"Martha, thanks for calling." Jay was excited and began to ramble. "We got to talk. Man, that bitch really messed up this time. I want you to sue her ass and St. Anslem's Hospital. We goin' to nail them big time."

The strength of Jay's reply caused Martha to try a countermeasure. "She apparently thinks you are the one who messed up. I don't know what to think. Your lawyer that handled the divorce was advised by her lawyer that you are going to be served with papers tomorrow claiming that you are an unfit parent, an alcoholic, drug abuser, and a few other things all of which is intended to return you to court for a custody hearing. He called me and asked me to tip you off. I wanted you to know that you will be served and advise you not to beat the shit out of the process server. Remember that he is a court official. Please be a good boy and accept the papers without contest or comment. Bring them to your divorce lawyer and we can take it from there. What have you been up to, anyway?"

Jay detailed the events of the weekend beginning with his trip to Waltham Hospital. He proudly added his new status as Shop Steward with Local 936 and the Action Union as prelude to the event Tuesday morning that caused his trip to St. Anslem's. He omitted telling Martha anything about his experience at the Troubadour with Cecile's husband but he did explain that his illness of Tuesday was prompted by a drinking and smoking spree with Brian the night before. The big event, from Jay's point of view, was the telephone call with Cecile and the telephone system at St. Anslem's. Jay was confident that he had complete immunity from Cecile's charges because of his enrollment in the St. Anslem's Chemical Addiction Program. Martha remarked that she was not familiar with the Federal law regarding substance abuse program immunity. She would check it out in the morning. She also advised Jay to stay cloistered in the SACAP during the day but to expect that the process server would find him at home or at work when he returned.

After some more thought, Martha conceded that Cecile may have compromised herself. Guardedly, she explained, "Jay, off the top of my head, I think that you may have a point about Cecile. She could be in big trouble. The hospital is another story. I'll talk to some plaintiff attorneys about the malpractice issue. If you have a case they'll grab it on contingency. We need to talk about it some more. Let's plan on getting together as soon as you can without messing up your participation in the program at the hospital. You need to maintain your status in that effort. Let me know when you are going to get sprung."

Martha was relieved that Jay was participating in the SACAP program. She and the rest of the Marquart clan knew that Jay needed help for years. Any mention of this to Jay was always ignored or met with angry response. In her own way, Martha prayed that Jay would stick with it this time. She was certain that without the benefit of the program he was without a defense to

Cecile's custody challenge. Jay, on the other hand, concluded the call with Martha, encouraged over the prospect of gaining full custody of Kristie, receiving a generous settlement from the hospital, and forcing Cecile on to welfare as a consequence of losing her nursing license. Things were definitely looking up. He felt good enough to give buddy Brian a call.

Brian answered the phone on the first ring and Jay fired a greeting.

"Brian, my main man, I hear tell that the Bitch worked you over yesterday at St. A's. Man, you don't have to take nothing from her. I got her good this time. I been spending some time at St. A's myself, following up on Sunday. How you doing?"

"Hey, Jay. I'm fine, man. How about you? Why they hang on to you so long? You can't pay or something? I got a few bucks and maybe Louise can chip in. Say we get the crowd down at the Waltham to have a charity drink me down for your benefit. What do you say, man?"

The idea of a charity drink fest to help a drunk struck Jay as very funny. He decided to humor his friend in reply. "Well, Brian, the hospital says that I got to cut down on the partying. They got me coming back during the day for a while until I get straighten out. I'll be fine in a week or so. I just been hitting it too much."

"It's nothing. Hey, we goin' fishing Friday night? I got the boat out at Hingham. I hear from the Customer that the Blues are running. It's time we get out there, man. We got skunked last time. Time to get even."

"Not this time, Brian. Benny's got a game again and I got to rest after. The hospital wants me to come in on Saturday. They do a test and I got to be clean. I'm gonna be very dry for a while. Let's get together on Saturday evening as usual. Susan and the kids are looking forward to it."

Brian still didn't quite get the message. "Yeah, man. Louise and I enjoy it to. You want me to come packing? There's some quality joy in town."

"Oh, Brian, my man, you are the party mule. I just told you I got to stay clean. You bring what you think you and the girls will want. I'm not having any, thank you."

Thursday morning was warm, bright and clear. The Mayor enjoyed his stroll to City Hall greeting well-wishers along the way. He was in very good spirits.

The night before he had received final notice that he was the Nominee for the position as Under Secretary of Labor for the United States Department of Labor. Washington would release the information from the President's office before noon. The matter had been leaked to the wire services late last night and, therefore, would be the topic of interest by the media at the City Council meeting. His official resignation would take place next week at the Council meeting but would be a matter of routine for him. Siro would gain the spotlight next week. Between now and then it would be Mayor Cowan's time to celebrate and be celebrated by the Boston media. It was a real story about a local boy making it big on the national scene. Just what the Mayor needed to pave the way for his eventual return as the Democratic candidate for Governor. His plan was working well.

As Mayor Cowan entered City Hall a *Boston Globe* beat reporter came by his side and began asking questions about the transition. The questions were more for the reporter's information than as a matter of report. The Mayor invited the reporter to walk with him to the office where they chatted about several items in the process of resignation. The Mayor appeared successful in cultivating the young reporter. Sharon, the faithful secretary, filled their coffee cups and maintained the process of cleaning the files, packing personal items, and answering the phone that was now constantly ringing. At eight-thirty she invited the reporter to step outside while reminding the Mayor that he had to prepare for the Council meeting scheduled for ten o'clock. As the reporter was leaving the office, Council President Alphonse Siro and Commissioner Michael Francis Megan, currently of Parks and Recreation and soon to be of Health and Hospitals, walked in. The reporter decided to wait around in the outer office.

Al Siro had in hand several press releases regarding the appointment of Megan to the Commissioner of health position. Of even greater importance, was the resolution supporting the initiation of a voluntary waste management program for the City of Boston. The resolution made the program effective immediately upon acceptance. The Mayor was quick to approve the resolution and press release. He was also delighted to begin to pass the routine of the Mayor's office to Council President Siro. The two men had conspired to have Siro actually run his office and the Mayor's for the past week and now going forward until after the special election that the City Council had to arrange. The tact was obviously to establish Siro in the minds of the voters so that he would be the choice for Mayor elect.

The three men conferred for about an hour. At nine-thirty they left the Mayor's office for the City Council Chambers. *The Globe* reporter strolled with them as if one of the party, much to the chagrin of the reporters from the electronic media crammed in the Council Chambers. The other members of the Council were already present. They surrounded Cowan and Siro as they entered the room. The Mayor accepted the individual acknowledgments with excellent poise. Everyone was very well behaved. Even the media seemed to respect the collegial order that prevailed this important meeting. At exactly ten A.M., President Siro called the meeting to order. Several matters of routine business were handled with dispatch. Next on the agenda was the resignation of Commissioner Michael Logan.

Council President Siro asked Mayor Cowan to report the resignation of the Commissioner and to announce his interim successor. Mayor Cowan reported that Commissioner Logan had long sought an opportunity to enter the private sector and become involved in the direct provision of health services.

"It is to his credit and to the credit of the Boston Catholic Archdiocese that their mutual interest can be served by integrating the Church's healing mission with the dedication of a health professional committed to the public's interest" was the opening theme of the Mayor's report. He concluded by praising the work of the Church in carrying for the Boston community saying in conclusion that. "Michael Logan is truly an honorable public servant that deserves credit for his attention to the health needs of the community."

When the Mayor concluded his report, President Siro introduced a resolution of gratitude to Michael Logan. The resolution was passed unanimously.

The Mayor requested the floor again and announced Megan as his choice to replace Logan as Commissioner of Health. Megan needed no introduction to the Council, the media, or to the residents of Boston. His very active manner and enthusiasm for his job had endeared him to the public. He was a budding politician who was cutting his teeth in public service. Someday he intended to be mayor. As for now he was content to share in the bright lights of the office transition. He was at this time becoming a prominent matter of record. At the Mayor's beckoning, Megan stepped to his side. The Mayor embraced the new appointee as the media cameras recorded the event.

President Siro called the meeting back to order at which time he accepted a resolution to endorse and support Mayor Cowan's appointment of

Commissioner Megan as the interim Commissioner of Public Health. Again, the motion was passed unanimously.

The Mayor thanked President Siro and the Council for their supporting resolutions. He then baited the media by stating that the replacement for Commissioner of Parks and Recreation would be announced in the future. Perhaps next week. He, however, had no one in mind at his time. The media became drawn to the reality that the Mayor's own resignation would be the topic of the next City Council meeting. The media seemed to surge at the inference. Siro noted the interest and immediately called a twenty-minute recess. The media swarmed to the Mayor and began asking questions about his Federal appointment, his resignation, and plans for transition.

Things were going exactly as planned by Siro and Cowan. They had decided at their morning conference to create a media diversion before the introduction of the voluntary waste management program to the Council. They reasoned that by creating interest in the Mayor before the recess, the media would have filled their notebooks and cameras with sufficient material. As expected, the majority of the electronic media were folding their equipment at the end of the recess time. When President Siro called the meeting back to order only the assigned beat reporters from the local newspapers remained.

Council President Siro introduced the subject of waste management as a matter of concern for the City Council. He explained the history of the project going back at least ten years when the City found it necessary to begin an expensive process of harbor clean up and water reclamation. He pointed out that the project although funded in the main by the Federal government had nevertheless required the City and surrounding Communities to experience the highest water rates in the nation. Now it was time, if not past time, to continue the cleanup of the area through a process of waste control and management of waste disposal. This included a recycling program for the City but more important it had to include a recycling and waste management program for private industry and private residences.

Siro concluded his remarks by pointing out that improper control of waste material and toxic agents was the fifth ranking cause of death in the United States last year. "These agents," according to Mr. Siro, "could be traced to environmental pollutants, food and water contaminants, ingredients in commercial products and many more related health problems." He proposed that the City had a large responsibility dealing with asbestos, childhood exposure to lead, as well as the new large-scale changes that the City needed to contemplate. "Therefore," he concluded after twenty minutes of information that he read from an Action brochure, "the City requires the assistance immediately of a qualified private company to assist in the protection and maintenance of a high standard of health for the citizens of Boston."

Following the presentation by the President of the Council, the Mayor explained that the City was particularly blessed to have the Nation's leading private waste management company located in Boston. This company, at the invitation of the Mayor, had submitted a bid to cover the Boston Hospital's waste management process at a saving of thirty percent under present costs. The City Budget Office had confirmed these savings. With the concurrence of the City Council the Mayor would sign the contract with Action Waste Management to implement a waste management program at City Hospital immediately. President Siro then called for a motion to approve the Action Waste Management/Boston Hospital agreement. Again, the motion passed without opposition.

After the vote on the City Hospital contract, and on cue, a member of the Council called for a vote supporting the voluntary privatization of waste management for the City. "This vote," he explained, "would open the door for private waste management companies such as Action to promote a healthy environment without imposing higher taxes on a community already overtaxed."

This time there was some dissension as several Council members argued that the citizens were not overtaxed but perhaps under-served. The debate made for good theater and also served to tire the remaining reporters who were faced with deadlines. Siro allowed the debate to continue until it was obvious that the reporters had enough. He then called for the vote which passed by a sound majority exactly as planned. As the Council meeting came to a close, Siro noted with pleasure that the meeting had extended well beyond the two-hour schedule. It was nearly one-thirty. The Council had worked through the lunch hour. No one could say that the people were not getting their money's worth from the City Council.

Mark Meehan sat in the back of the City Council Chambers for the entire meeting. He had supplied Council President Siro with pages of material on environmental control. Most of the information had been published by Park in a sales handbook for their respective agencies. With Meehan was the company attorney who noted the time and date of the Council's votes regarding waste management. After the meeting the attorney went immediately to the office of the City Clerk to obtain copies of the resolutions. Meehan went straight to his office filled with the excitement of the Boston Project. It was now official. The project was underway. At his direction, his secretary called another management meeting on the Boston Project. These meetings were turning into daily affairs.

Bob Muldoon was also at the Council meeting. He sat with Meehan and commented from time to time about the actors on the stage. He seemed pleased with their performance. After the final curtain call Muldoon moved to the front of the Council. He sought out his friend, Megan, and congratulated him on his new assignment. Siro noticed Muldoon from across the room and made special effort to come to his side. Siro was very obvious about securing Labor's support in the mayoral special election. Muldoon did not hesitate to offer that support. Their relationship extended over Siro's entire political career. Marty Hart, President of Local 936, the only local in Boston having a contract or near contract with a waste management firm, was also at the meeting. With him was Dave Donovan, Business Manager of 936. They sat apart from Muldoon but moved to his side as he began to talk to Siro. Otherwise, the two 936 officials chatted about the situation at Action Waste Management concerning their new shop steward. Donovan was concerned that Marquart was sick at a very critical time. Hart advised him to give it another week. Muldoon introduced his associates to Al Siro who seemed genuinely pleased to have their acquaintance.

Charles Patello was also in the back of the Council Chambers. He and Meehan intended to meet there but Patello steered away when Muldoon moved into the chair next to Meehan. Muldoon was Meehan's problem now. Patello had other matters at hand now that the Waste Management project was underway. There remained the mystery of O'Shea's interest in the check deposited in Logan's account. He left the Council Chambers as the meeting concluded and walked back to his office where he immediately placed a call to Mario Capizzi. Mr. Capizzi was very pleased that all the details for implementing the Action project were now complete save the minor issue of the Mayor's resignation. That was simply a matter of timing since the Mayor had publicly announced that he had accepted the Federal appointment. Capizzi gave Patello a well done and concluded with the question of what was next on Patello's agenda.

Patello saw the question as an opportunity to discuss the O'Shea matter. "Mario, we have one glitch that could be trouble. Boston Security's Executive Vice President, a guy named O'Shea, looked over the bonus check. He apparently noticed the Mayor's endorsement. He sent a verbal message to Logan via the courier that the money wherever it came from is in Logan's account. He essentially told Logan that he thinks the money is dirty. Logan called me to ask what's going on. I told Logan that O'Shea's nose is out of joint because he isn't in the know about the donors. Logan seemed to buy this. Then I told Mondi who checked the courier who tells him that O'Shea made copies of the check, the courier's log and I don't know what all. You know that O'Shea is a member of the St. Anslem's Board. Hardly, O'Shea and I control the place along with a Dr. Folley, who happens to be O'Shea's son-in-law. Anyway, O'Shea and Folley pull a fast one on me and convince the Cardinal to make Folley the head of the Office of Health Affairs."

Capizzi was very confused at Patello's rambling explanation. "Charlie, you need to take a little time off. I can't follow you. About all I understand is that some bigwig at the bank is aware that the money in Logan's account came from the Mayor. Now the son of a bitch may have some ulterior motive in pimping Logan about the account. That motive is not clear. He knew that you were involved in cutting the employment deal with Logan but he didn't bother calling you about the check. In fact, he didn't bother calling Logan about the check. He chose, instead, to send a cynical message to Logan that essentially said that he was in the know. You think he might want a piece of Logan? He probably figures that Logan and the Mayor are in a deal. He knows that you arranged for the private bank account but he doesn't know, at least not yet, that you or we paid him a signing bonus. It seems to me that the best thing to do at this stage is nothing. You play it straight like you know nothing about a signing bonus. I doubt that Logan will bring it up to anybody but you. If he does, then we'll come up with a cover story. Right now, the trail is to the Mayor just like we wanted it. This O'Shea guy, I bet, is on that trail for his own good."

"That's probably true, Mario." Patello began to relax and realized that he had pushed the panic button. "I've been a buddy of O'Shea's since our days at Boston College. I'll tell you this, the guy is just smart enough to make him dangerous. Right now, he has the information about Logan's account that is just like a loaded gun. The fool could pull the trigger without thinking and screw everything up. Remember you put the wrapper on Logan as a trigger to nail the mayor. Now O'Shea has the same gun but doesn't know who or how to fire it."

Capizzi was pleased that Patello had regained control of his emotions. "That's right. If he was straight he would have made an issue about the check and never have processed it into Logan's account. My thought is that he might be smarter than you think and have a target in mind or he might realize that the information has great potential for future return. That's what you would expect from a banker. The bastards are all crooked at heart. Let's wait him out. Keep a close eye on him. Say nothing to anybody about this. Anything else?"

Patello answered, "We have a Board meeting at St. Anslem's on Tuesday. That's when we put Logan into the lineup. We'll see then if O'Shea has anything immediate in mind or is playing for the long run. I'll keep you posted."

In Capizzi's mind he thought it time to end the conversation, "Okay. I'll brief Marone and Big Frank. Big Frank doesn't like surprises. You best tell Meehan and Mondi its business as usual. We play out the string as planned. Anything comes of this O'Shea issue we'll deal with it from New York. You keep me posted. You also got to play it cool with O'Shea. He may be looking at you just like you are looking at him. Don't tip your hand."

Patello felt relieved after his telephone conversation with Capizzi. He cleaned up his office, dictated a few letters, and placed a call to Siro for a round of golf later in the afternoon. The courting had begun.

Joseph Durant sat at his desk studying the Boston newspapers. Both *The Globe* and *The Herald* devoted the entire front page to the pending resignation of Mayor Cowan. Cowan was glorified by both papers as a visionary Mayor that brought the City to new heights with his programs in environmental control, health and safety, and public recreation. Both papers featured pictures of the Mayor during his campaign talking to the man on the street or riding a fire truck. *The Globe* also carried a side bar story about Commissioner Michael Logan's resignation and his new appointment as Director of the Office for Health Affairs for the Archdiocese. This was the main point of interest for Durant. He was both angry and offended that the Archdiocese hadn't informed him of the new Office. He also wondered if the office would absorb any of the functions of the hospital President. The newspaper accounts centered on the accomplishments of the Commissioner with little information about his new assignment.

The Herald carried the same stories about the Mayor but differed in its inside report about Commissioner Logan. It implied that the Commissioner was over his head in dealing with the complex problems of the City. It pointed out that his extreme dedication to the inner-city health problems was admirable but he left healthcare in general get out of hand. The provision of health services was the City's third largest industry next to State government and Private education. That industry, according to the *Herald* report, was shameful due to the outrageous profiteering and gouging of the public trust by private hospitals. The report called for the new Commissioner and the Interim Mayor to appoint a special Blue-Ribbon Task Force to investigate the deteriorating status of health services in the Boston Metropolitan area.

The Boston Business Journal was published twice a week. It had been focusing stories about healthcare in Boston for over a year. For the most part, they watched the action of the major downtown teaching hospitals as the barometer of the industry. Hospital profits and executive salaries were a common focus. Their editorials were sharply critical of the major hospital Boards and Presidents. Reporters followed executives on weekends taking special note of their extravagant homes, yachts, and golf club memberships. In recent editions, the *Journal* had begun a series of reports about the excess utilization of Boston Hospitals. It predicted that Boston's over capacity of hospital beds would be eliminated by the new reimbursement methods currently being implemented by the Health Maintenance organizations. One writer described it as a gigantic meltdown of the healthcare industry that would eliminate over a third of the hospitals in the area and displace over six thousand employees. While not stated, the implication was that the smaller hospitals in the City would succumb to the change. It appeared that the rule of the jungle was being applied to healthcare reform in Boston.

Durant knew that the *Journal* articles, while colored in rhetoric, were based on fact. The future of St. Anslem's was a matter of great concern to him. He felt a desperate urge to express his anxiety and emphasize the need for survival planning at the Board meeting next Tuesday. Unfortunately, the great Thomas O'Shea had pre-emoted the agenda with his microscopic attention to the details of finance.

Durant nursed his frustration. He told himself over and over again that he could regain control by cooperating with the ridiculous demands of O'Shea.

He also resolved in his mind to welcome Logan and the Office of Health Affairs. His intent was to capture the focus of the office on the survival issue and in that way hopefully redirect the Board to the big picture. He decided not to make an issue about not being informed or included in the formation of the office. It was best to make sure that his trusted vice president for finance was well prepared with every detail in response to Mr. O'Shea's criticisms of the hospital's fiscal status and operational deficiencies. After about three hours of contemplation he regained his composure and asked his Executive Assistant to arrange a time for him to have a pre-board briefing with Rod Weaver, Senior VP for finance. He also asked the executive assistant to invite Mitch Daly, the hospital's Senior Vice President for strategic planning to attend the briefing.

It was Durant's intent to have Daly well informed on the Board's focus on the fiscal item while Daly prepared the appropriate analysis on strategic issues. Durant intended to redirect the Board's attention to strategy for survival over the next three months as the new fiscal year approached. Strategic planning was an excellent complement to budgeting. The fiscal year for St. Anslem's began on October first. Between now and then Durant intended to combine the talents of Weaver and Daly into the most reliable authority on health services in the area. That team combined with his leadership would be the means by which Durant would lead the Board of Trustees and St. Anslem's into its future as the premier Catholic Hospital in New England.

While Durant pondered the future of St. Anslem's Hospital, Bob Markley pondered the life and times of Jay Marquart. It was nearly nine o'clock and Mr. Marquart had not appeared in the Unit. Markley was questioning his judgment in letting Jay go home last night. He was still very brittle. If his ex-wife hassled him or if his current wife began to mope, Jay could easily revert. He had not yet taken the first step toward recovery. That precious first step required the addict to admit that he or she was hooked. Markley knew that it would take Jay a while to come to that important conclusion. Durant also recognized in Jay an inner strength to meet the challenge of recovery. He was a fighter and a man with passion. He easily displayed compassion and love for others. On the other hand he required love from others. These were the qualities that

Markley recognized as prospects toward recovery. He sat at the desk staring at Jay's chart and said his daily prayer for his friends, the recovering patients.

The telephone in front of Markley reminded him of a more immediate concern. From his point of view, "that damn thing" had indeed violated the rule of confidentiality when it signaled to Jay's ex-wife that he was in the unit. Certainly, the lawyers if they got involved would come up with a thousand mitigating circumstances that obliterated the hospital's liability. In the argument the patient would be lost from recovery. Markley was certain of that. However, Jay's determination to litigate the matter forced Markley to prepare an official hospital incident report that had to be submitted to the Risk Management Director who would notify the hospital's malpractice-practice carrier who would notify a defense attorney who would assign a claim manager who would do whatever it took to blame Jay for the whole thing.

Markley knew he had no choice but to prepare and submit the incident report. But he decided to send the matter through the director of the SACAP Unit, Dr. Ron Anderson, for review before it was channeled to Risk Management. Dr. Anderson was Bob Markley's hero. He, in Markley's eyes, was a miracle worker with addicted persons. A kind and compassionate man who was adept at moving around rules that obstructed patient care, Anderson would recognize the problem and find a solution to the administrative dilemma. Markley inserted the required form in the typewriter and began to peck out the answers to the numbered questions. He was pondering the wording and description of the incident when a shadow moved across the desk.

He looked up into the smiling face of Jay Marquart. He extended a hand to him and commented, "Jay, you're late. Good to see you. Have a good night?"

Jay appeared in good spirits. "Yes, I did, Bob. Nice of you to ask. I don't recall that you mentioned a starting time. We on a timeclock?"

"Not exactly. You do remember that hospitals operate on a certain routine. It's rather convenient to have the patient around when the lab tech shows up to draw blood. Little things like that are seen by some as important. I'll call the lab and tell them that you have arrived. They'll be so pleased. Dr. Kenneth will be in shortly. Glad you arrived before him. Otherwise, he would have to make a house call."

Jay was not impressed. "Yeah, right. Look, I talked to my sister last night about this flap with my ex. Seems that I'm going to be served some papers. Can they do that to me in here?"

Markley was not about to let Jay worry about the presence of a court order. "Jay, no one knows you're here but us chickens. The front desk has you as discharged from general hospital. They don't know where you are. If, by chance, the process server gets by the front desk he won't get into this unit. We have a security force that loves to throw people into the street. You will probably be served at home or at work next week. And, by the way, could you manage to check in here by eight o'clock? We would appreciate it. Here, go pee in this bottle."

Jay complied with the request and returned the specimen to the desk. A Lab tech in a white coat two sizes too small met Jay at the desk and took the urine specimen. He then escorted Jay to a small room where he extracted a small vile of Jay's blood. Jay's attempt to make small talk fell on deaf ears. The tech was not a friendly sort. Jay was prone to suggest that the tech needed a stiff belt but thought differently as he saw Dr. Kenneth enter the Unit. The doctor began reviewing several charts that Markley had selected for his review. The two men were conferring when Jay walked back to the desk. Markley nodded to Jay and then asked a nursing assistant to take Mr. Marquart to the patient library to view the video presentation. Jay obediently followed the attractive young lady to a former patient room now equipped with a couch and a few recliners facing a television and a VCR. All of the furniture had seen better days. On each side of the room were battered bookshelves containing a few books and a lot of pamphlets.

The nursing assistant invited Jay to have a seat and be comfortable. She offered him a cup of juice or water that he declined. She then pulled down the tattered window blinds, turned on the television and started the VCR. As the video began she left the room. Jay realized that they only way he could escape the approaching propaganda was to leave the room or turn off the set. Either option would be seen as discourteous, rude, and obstinate, he thought. There was no need to be that offensive to kind people who seemed eager to be of service. Jay decided to go along with the game. He settled back in his recliner to enjoy the video. The flick began with an assortment of down-and-out bums aimlessly through littered streets and then panned to a well-dressed, up and coming, Harvard type sitting in a BMW smoking a joint. The scene shifted to a group of business types having lunch with several drinks. As the group departed one member walked to the bar instead of out the door. He ordered a drink and began a casual narrative about his decision to enjoy life by his standards. The key to the good life, according to the drinking narrator was maintaining control of your own destiny. He hastily drank his drink and ordered another. Following the consumption of the second drink and more narrative about his staunch independence he dropped the money on the bar and left, apparently in full control of his destiny. Following scenes depicted his failure to make appointments, loss of customers, arguments with his spouse, divorce, unemployment, fiscal disaster and eventual transition to the street aimlessly walking and looking for his lost destiny. He appeared in poor health. As he collapsed a friend picked him up and escorted him into a shelter where he was given nourishment, clothes, and assistance in his recovery.

The concluding scene showed the recovering alcoholic regaining his dignity and control of his destiny. He explained that controlling his destiny required control of his addiction. That type of control required the understanding of his disease and the benefit of support from others who understood the many difficulties faced by an addicted and dependent person. The final scenes pictured various support groups in the conduct of their meetings and providing individual support. The now recovering narrator praised the work of the groups and offered to be of assistance to the viewer as the telephone numbers of the groups rolled over the screen.

Jay, for lack of anything else to do, watched the video with mild interest He recalled the same type presentations in high school. Then he thought the corny acting was funny. He and his buddies would mock the flicks as they partied after school. Now he began of wonder if the film had some message for him. His life carried some of the tragedy depicted in the story but he had reasonable comfort and happiness. The struggle he had with Cecile over Kristie was rooted, he admitted, in his determination to party above all else. He also realized that his family and his life with Susan were centered on the good times associated with the high that he and Susan so often sought. They were always financially distressed. They were compatible. Were they addicted? He was holding the question in his mind when Dr. Kenneth greeted him from the hall.

Dr. Kenneth's inquiry about Jay's current state of body and mind brought a courteous response from Jay. The good doctor noticed Jay's change of attitude from their first meeting. This was a definite sign of progress. He invited Jay to walk down the hall to his office. Once there he gave him a standard physical exam. A nurse appeared and stuck a thermometer in Jay's mouth. As Jay's temperature was being recorded, Dr. Kenneth flipped through the chart making various notes.

Kenneth eventually closed the chart, removed the thermometer, looked at it, and put it aside as he addressed his patient. "Jay, your body is responding well to treatment. Your lab and urine tests show that the presence of alcohol and cocaine use are substantially gone. This is normal. But you are in a fragile state. If you consume any substance of that sort over the weekend you could have another incident like the one that brought you in here. Your blood still carries very evident traces of marijuana. That shows little or no decline over the time that you have been with us. This does not necessarily mean that you have used marijuana in the last few days. The chemical trace of that substance in a habitual user will remain for a long time even if the person completely refrains. We should begin to see a decline after a week. It could be a month or maybe two before you test completely clean. That should be your goal. Test clean and then stay that way. In the interim we will provide you with the support that your body needs to adjust to the new you. I would like you to take some medication that will help you overcome your craving for these substances. We also have something that will help you control your anger. Mr. Markley told me about your incident yesterday."

Dr. Kenneth offered Jay three pills and a paper cup filled with water. Jay looked at the pills and reluctantly put them in his mouth, drank the water, swallowed, and attempted to talk.

"Doctor, I'll give this medication thing a try. I don't know why but as long as I'm here I might as well play your game. If these things mess me up then you got to know that I won't take another one. I've heard about guys being hooked on methadone. They are as spaced out as dope heads on opium. I'll go cold turkey before I get hooked on that treatment."

Dr. Kenneth explained, "Jay, you are going through withdrawal from three substances, cocaine, alcohol and marijuana. You have used these substances in increasing quantities over the past several years. Your dependency obviously was increasing so now we are reversing that biological trend. We are uncertain how you will react to this transition mentally and emotionally. Our attempt with the medication is to fortify you against a convulsive reaction like you experienced Monday and an emotional breakdown like you experienced yesterday. We know from experience that every patient experiencing withdrawal has physical and mental side-effects. We can't predict the severity of those side-effects. Your situation is better than most because we are treating you before you totally overdosed and experienced a severe major physical and mental breakdown. That's the up side. The down side is that we are faced with greater uncertainty about withdrawal side-effects than we would be in treating what you describe as dope heads on opium. We do know that you are experiencing side-effects. Markley watched you do it. We are confident that you will have more."

Jay tried to act sincere. "So how long am I gonna be a head case?"

Dr. Kenneth continued. "Well, cocaine withdrawal which is the substance having the greatest impact is generally not predictable. We have recognized that cocaine abstinence syndrome has three stages. Phase One could last only a few hours. In some cases, we have seen it last up to nine days. Phase One is the most serious. This is when a patient becomes violent and does physical harm to himself or someone else. In Phase Two the patient becomes less violent but may experience severe depression. The depression eliminates harm to others but may cause the patient to harm himself. Phase One and two may overlap. There is no clear cut line between them. The second phase may take from one to ten weeks. Phase three is that time when the patient recognizes the problem and struggles to be free of the addiction. A failure in the attempt triggers the effects of one and two. Phase three has an indefinite time phase. It just goes on and on. What is important to the patient's recovery, just as it is to people addicted to alcohol, is the recognition of their addiction and the ability to seek the support from others in helping them avoid the crash. What I'm telling you is that there is no known cure from addiction. The disease can be controlled."

Jay seemed to modify his doubts. "Man, this is weird. I been hanging around this place for the past four days and all of a sudden I got an incurable disease."

"Correction. You've been hanging around this place for four days and now know that you have an incurable disease. You were sick when you came in here, remember. You just didn't believe it." Dr. Kenneth tried to regain Jay's attention to the point

Jay remained skeptical. "Yeah, I'm still not completely convinced that I'm sick as you put it. Another way of looking at it could be that I was on a weekend drunk and took a bad trip. You know—like a bad hangover. Otherwise, I feel fine."

"I recognize your disbelief." Kenneth attempted to be tactful but direct. "You weren't hit hard enough to be a believer. The guys that get hit the hardest are the first to admit the problem but are usually too far gone to do anything about it. You, at the moment, don't fully admit the problem but have the strength to do something about it. Hopefully you won't wait to get the big hit. This is the time to start your recovery."

"I'm here, aren't I? What's the drill?" Jay's anger started to flare. "I give you my blood, pee in a bottle, and watch a class B video—that's it? Where's the beef, man?"

"Good questions, Jay. The drill is rather loose except for the medication and observation. We will see that you get plenty of rest over the weekend. Mr. Markley will explain the support methods in place to assist with your recovery and I'll keep tabs on you medically. If you seem to be in control by Monday we will recommend that you go back to work. We'll know for sure by Sunday evening. Depends how you behave over the weekend. That medication that you took will make you drowsy. The nurse will show you a room where you can sleep if you like. Otherwise, feel free to go back to the lounge, have a cup of coffee or whatever. Read or watch television for a while. Bob Markley will catch up with you in an hour or so. He'll start you on the reinforcement. By the way lunch will be served in the lounge. You'll meet some other people there. I'll check in with you tomorrow."

Jay left the doctor's office in a quandary. He still didn't accept the idea that he had a disease. He was beginning to accept the thought that he raised a little too much hell. He began to feel sleepy. A little sack time seemed like a good idea. The nurse at the desk was very responsive to his request to lie down and rest his eyes. She escorted him back to the same room he was in the day before. Jay popped off his shoes, laid down, and fell asleep

The next thing he experienced was someone gently shaking him awake. He opened his eyes to the friendly smile of Bob Markley who extended a friendly greeting.

"Wake up, Sunshine. You have been pounding your ear for nearly two hours. Another half-hour and you would have missed lunch. Let's go. Got some people I want you to meet."

Jay gave Markley a light jab on the shoulder as he rolled out of bed. It took him awhile to find his shoes since he couldn't remember taking them off. Then he went to the powder room where he discovered that he forgot his comb. After straightening his hair with his fingers, he joined Markley for the walk to the dining room lounge. As they entered the room Jay noticed that the buffet lunch had been well consumed. Markley's estimate that Jay would have missed lunch in a half-hour was off by a half-hour. Jay picked up some bread, a slice of cheese, and the crumbs of a few potato chips that the swarm had mysteriously overlooked. Some sliced vegetables were all that remained in abundance. Jay filled his paper plate with the residue and took the remaining empty seat. Markley walked around the room greeting each person. Then he walked to the podium placed at the back opposite the food table.

"Good afternoon, folks," Markley began. "My name is Bob and I'm a recovering alcoholic. How's everybody today?"

Everybody applauded Bob's greeting and seemed to be in good spirits. Bob raised his hands asking for silence. Gradually the group came to order.

Markley then continued his greeting. "Ladies and gentlemen, it's always nice to have you here for our weekly meeting. It's especially nice to see so many of you attending on a regular basis. Now there are a few things, however, that the administration has asked that I point out. First is that you are using too many napkins. If this keeps up the vice president in charge of napkins is going to cut us off and we'll have to go back to using the drapes—that is if they ever get around to replacing the drapes that they took away from us last winter. Also, they have reminded me that we have used up our allotment of used and broken furniture for the remainder of the fiscal year. We will have to wait until next year before we will be given any more broken furniture. Until then we will have to make out with the good stuff. That means we will have to be on our worse behavior. Can you handle it?"

Again, the remarks were answered with laughter, applause, and cheers. The remarks about the furniture caused Jay to blush. He felt as though everyone in the room was looking at him but when he raised his head he saw that he was not being noticed.

As Bob paused in his remarks he looked directly at Jay. "My friends, we have a guest today. I hope my comments made in jest have not given him the wrong impression. You are a wonderful group dedicated to your own recovery and the recovery of those around you. You have done a marvelous if not miraculous service for one another. Some of you will want to talk about that today but before we do I want you to introduce yourself."

Following his comments each person in turn rose and faced Jay. They introduced themselves giving their first name only followed by the comment that he or she was a recovering addict. At the end of the introductions Bob asked Jay to introduce himself.

Jay carefully stood before the group uncertain what he was going to say. "Ladies and gentlemen, ah, I'm Jay. Bob, ah, I mean when Bob said he was going to buy me lunch I didn't know that, ah, he had this in mind. You see, I'm, ah, I mean I been getting some treatment here and he said he wanted me to meet some wonderful people. Well, ah, I know what he meant. You are great folks. Thanks for having me."

The people responded with a loud round of applause. A few waved a sign of acceptance to Jay. Another person reached out and shook his hand. Jay was somewhat embarrassed at the friendliness of their reaction. When the group came back to order Bob asked if anyone had anything that they wanted to report or discuss. One by one individuals stood to report on the success or failure of their efforts to stay sober. One man reported in detail about his fall from the wagon and how a friend rescued him. He was back on the road to recovery. Others commented on the days, weeks, or months that they had been clean. They all thanked each other for the support to continue.

After the reports were completed Bob congratulated the group for their continuing success in recovery. He mentioned that the meeting would be held again next week at same time and place. He encouraged them to return and bring a friend in need. As the meeting concluded several of the attendees approached Jay and shook his hand. They stated that they hoped to see him again.

Jay accepted their expressions of friendship with courtesy. He noticed that the group consisted of people several years his senior. They were clean, poorly dressed, but well groomed. Their age was more in line with his parents. He realized that these were not his kind of people. Bob was beginning to pick up the paper plates and cups from the tables so Jay broke off his thoughts and began to help.

Markley, at first, seemed to take Jay's help for granted. Then he casually asked, "So Jay, what did you think of our little gathering?"

Jay was waiting for the question. "Nice people, but I felt really out of place. I mean these people were old enough to be my parents. That really threw me off. I was surprised to hear you admit to being a drunk. You gave me enough hints over the past few days that I should have realized it. Anyway, it was an eye-opener. I couldn't believe how many of these people fell off the wagon. Man, I guess when you been sopping it up as long as they have there ain't no way that you're going to quit. Right?"

"Wrong!" Markley fired back. "Many of those people have been dry longer than you have been alive. They come here to give help and be an inspiration to the rest of us. We need all the help we can get. The key to recovery is to admit that you are sick and be willing to get help when you need it. Age makes no difference. An addicted person experiences the same difficulties. Help is the answer. That's what I wanted you to see and hear. I want you to have confidence in the ability of others to help you when you are under pressure."

"Man, you guys have been pushing this sick shit at me since I came in." Jay reverted to his defensive style. "I'm not ready to buy it. Sure, I overloaded and had a bust. You guys can dry me out and everything is Jake. I go back out on the street and take care of myself No way I want to go through this again. I got that religion, man. Don't need this gang-bang routine, no way."

The response caused Markley to put down the paper plates and directly confront Jay. "Jay we know what we know about you. You can't take the street. Eventually you'll find that out. Here's a card with the Unit's call number. Keep this in your wallet.

"Right now, I'm your friend as well as your counselor. When the pressure builds call this number. If I'm not in, somebody else just as qualified, if not more qualified than me, will come to your aid. We can even pick you up and bring you in if necessary. Things might get rough for you in your free time this weekend. Remember, Dr. Kenneth explained that you were in Phase One of your recovery. You could experience a serious reaction to your detox. You need to be on guard. You mentioned that you had religion, well, say a few prayers that you get by without taking a big hit. I'll say a few for you myself."

"Screw that religion stuff, partner. I'm supposed to be Catholic. Went to a Catholic grade school and had that God stuff crammed down my throat. Never bought it either. This is a Catholic hospital, right? How come they screw me over with their goddamn telephone letting my ex know that I'm in 'Dope-Ville'? It's nothing but a freaking racket, man. All they want is money. Bring in my insurance. Too bad you ain't on the cash side of this deal, partner. They got you suckered. Looks like the Pope trained a drunk to dance to his tune and bring in the trade. Shit, I ain't buying."

Jay's anger accelerated. He suddenly grabbed a chair and threw it across the room into the food table. He kicked violently at another chair, missed and slammed his foot into the wall-mounted air conditioner. The resulting pain brought his emotions to overload. He screamed and sat down in chair. As he rubbed his aching foot he shouted continuing profanities at the top of his lungs. The head nurse and a nursing assistant heard the commotion and rushed to the aid of Bob Markley. As they entered the room Markley was calmly leaning against the wall waiting for Jay's temper to cool. They opted to stand across the room at the door out or Jay's sight. Eventually Jay began to run out of steam. He placed his face in his hands and his elbows on his knees. He sat that way in silence taking deep breaths.

As his breathing began to slow Markley sat in the chair next to Jay and gently put his hand on Jay's shoulder. "Jay, you've had a long day. It's time for a rest. Let's go back to your room. It's time for another pill. Then you can sleep for a few hours before you go home. I'll be with you and check on you before you go leave. We can pick up on all this conversation in the morning. What do you say?"

"Yeah, okay. I'm sorry about messing the place up. Okay?"

"Sure, it's okay, man. It's nothing. Let's go."

Jay got out of the chair unassisted. Markley waved the nurse and her assistant out of the room before Jay noticed their presence. As Bob reached to assist, Jay indicated to him that he could, actually preferred, to walk unassisted. Markley wondered if Jay was signaling that he still denied that he need for help in his recovery. However, Jay did not seem to object to Bob walking beside him to his room. As they neared Jay's room Markley noticed that Jay's energy and good nature had returned.

Jay picked up the pace and gave Bob a smile as they entered the room. "That was a short trip. Hope I didn't break anything expensive."

"Not likely, Jay. The administration gives us the hand me downs that are usually shot to hell by the time we get them. If that stuff wasn't in SACAP in would be in the junk. Feeling better?"

"Yeah, sure. I don't think I need that pill."

"Take it anyway. That way the Pope won't get upset when the cash is low. I'll check you out about four. If you feel all right then you can go home for the night. Okay?"

"Sure."

After Jay took the medication Markley busied around the room until he was confident that Jay was relaxed and under control. Then he returned to the nursing station and completed his work on the incident report concerning Patient John Marquart and the St. Anslem's telephone system. He read his description of the incident over several times, uncertain on the emphasis given to the apparent misconduct-conduct of a certain staff nurse. Finally, he put the report in his confidential file for safekeeping. He intended to think it over some more before sending it to Dr. Anderson.

Joseph Durant, President of St. Anslem's Hospital, habitually arrived at his office every day at seven A.M. This Friday was no exception. His diligent executive assistant somehow always managed to arrive at least fifteen minutes before the boss and routinely had the lights on, voicemail recorded, and coffee perking when he came in. Durant's routine was to go through the messages, read correspondence, dictate replies, review the appointments for the day and then begin shouting usually about "that son of a bitch, Folley," followed by whoever else came to mind. He could never quite handle the fact that while he arrived at seven most of the other executives began filing in after eight. The executive assistant could only shrug when he demanded a stat meeting of his executive staff at seven-thirty. The only one available was Dr. Folley who was the last person Durant wanted to see.

Durant's frustration centered on the lack of information for the Board of Trustees meeting agenda next Tuesday. O'Shea, Folley and "the rest of those bastards that had screwed things up royally with that crap about the expense reports and now the prospect of this Logan character getting into the act" made for more uncertainty. He had tried to call Hardly, Chairman of the Board, on Thursday but he was out playing golf. Hardly eventually returned the call through his secretary who advised Durant to consult with Mr. O'Shea about the Board agenda. Durant had that experience last week. No further contact was necessary.

He sat at his desk with his head in his hands wondering who on the Board might have some interest in an agenda and be available for a telephone conversation before eight A.M. Suddenly he remembered Sister Mary Elizabeth. Nuns always got up early, went to Mass, and then to work. She would know about Logan and the Office of Health Affairs. After all she was part of the Official Church. He hastily dialed her number. Sr. Mary Elizabeth answered with a cheery good morning. After that it was all downhill.

Sister Mary Elizabeth became emotional when Durant asked her if she could give him any information about the change at the Archdiocese. She pulled up an inch short of using gutter terms in describing the basic intellect of the male-dominated Board and the Chancery. She had tried to discuss the matter with Bishop Hanks who said that he would report in full at the St. Anslem's Board meeting. Until that time, he in effect told her to cool her jets. He did explain that Dr. Folley had been anointed by the Cardinal as the guru of Health and would be the king of kings as far as the health ministry was concerned. End of report.

As a closing comment Sister mentioned that she had talked recently to Sister Celest who would be calling Mr. Durant in the next week. She concluded by telling Joe that he was constantly in her prayers.

Durant's next move was a call to Bishop Hanks at the Archdiocese. He felt certain that he would get a better reception than Sister Mary Elizabeth. In fact, he got no reception at all. The switchboard operator at the Chancery reported that the Bishop was not available. She took the name and number for an eventual return call. She had no idea when the Bishop would be available.

Charles Patello was a mystery to Durant. He was, on the surface, a very friendly type who always had a useful opinion when asked. At Board meetings, he seemed content to let Hardly get pushed around by O'Shea and Folley. Durant felt that Patello was not a part of the inner circle that ran things for the Archdiocese and the Universe. He observed that Mr. Patello preferred to be removed from the politics of business and government. He was a successful self-made man, content in his own right. It, therefore, seemed inappropriate to call him for an opinion on the agenda and the Office for Health Affairs. On the other hand, Mr. Patello was a member of the executive committee. Durant had already called O'Shea, Hardly, Sr. Elizabeth, and Bishop Hanks. To omit calling Patello would appear improper and look like a selective omission if the matter became a topic of discussion. He realized then that he needed to call Mr. Patello and the remaining Boardmembers as well. He would first call Mr. Patello. After that he intended to call Mr. Mondi and Mr. Meehan. With luck, he would have made contact or at least attempted to make contact with the entire Board before noon with the exception of that jerk, Folley.

The medical staff was scheduled to have its monthly meeting in the auditorium at noon. Durant usually gave a brief report at the meeting. Folley always showed up for that part. Durant decided to collar him after the medical staff meeting and after he had talked to the other members of the Board.

Durant had seldom called Patello in the past since Patello always seemed as though he preferred to remain distant from the administrative chores of the hospital. However, on this occasion Patello seemed pleased that Durant had called. He answered the phone with a cheery greeting followed by an immediate offer of assistance. Durant first apologized for having to call then explained that the purpose of the call was to determine Mr. Patello's preference in dealing with the formal and informal items that were becoming apparent for the St. Anslem's Board meeting. Charlie Patello replied in a gentlemanly manner with complete courtesy. He stated that he felt the most immediate concern of the hospital and of the Board was the deteriorating fiscal position. He was aware that Mr. O'Shea was very intent on that point. He also mentioned that he had met Logan and felt that he could be of great help to St. Anslem's especially in getting the hospital into a better competitive position with the leading Teaching Hospitals of the world.

As Patello talked his mind was searching for an opportunity to link Durant's apparent anxiety to Capizzi's suggestion that Durant "be put in a wrapper." It seemed to Patello that Durant needed a friend in court. There was the opportunity to compromise him. Durant had suddenly walked into his arms. The question was how best to embrace him.

Patello needed time to consult with New York. For the moment he would compromise Durant. "Joe, my friends Mr. Hardly and Mr. O'Shea have been very active with the Archdiocese in bringing about these changes. They have given me some insight to the duties of Mr. Logan but I really don't know enough about it to comment. Dr. Folley has also been involved I believe and as you know he has the ear of the Cardinal. I suspect your best source of information is Dr. Folley. If you haven't talked to him about it I suggest that you do before the Board meeting. Personally, I'm confused how your position and Logan's interact. I consider the CEO of the hospital as the key person in the health structure. We need to make sure that is the way things are structured."

Durant was relieved to gain a friend on the Board. "Thanks, Charlie. Obviously, you realize that I'm concerned about this new structure. Of course, the Cardinal has every right to make whatever changes he wants in the conduct and direction of his health ministry. I'll go along no matter what but in this very competitive environment we cannot afford expensive duplication of executive talent and complicated levels in decision making. The Mass General and Brigham merger has eliminated a big hunk of bureaucracy. They are streamlined. Our decision making must be very accurate and timely."

"Joe, I know far less than you do about health reform and what's going on in Boston," confessed Patello. "The newspapers carry a story every day about the changes taking place. St. Anslem's is never mentioned in the new networks that the downtown hospitals are forming. It seems to me that we need to move rapidly before we are left out completely. With all the pressures, you have in just trying to make ends meet it must be nearly impossible to keep up the pace. Mr. Logan will be able to help I'm sure. However, we need to develop a plan that fits the future. We need a true strategic plan. I have used national consultants in my business and have been amazed and pleased at the amount of insight that a large national firm can give you. I would like to recommend to the Board that we form a strategic planning committee and hire a national consulting firm to help us. I'll fix it so you direct the effort. What do you say?"

"Yeah, that's great." Durant was elated. "Mitch Daly, our Planning VP, as you know has been bugging me to hire a consultant to help us do a strategic plan. The problem is money. We are struggling to meet payroll. O'Shea is constantly raising hell about the deficit. I understand that a major consulting job could go over a hundred grand. In all good conscience, I couldn't spend that kind of money when I'm laying people off. How are we going to justify it?"

Patello saw the opening but decided to play it slow and easy. "At the moment I don't have an answer. Let me explore some options. I have some contacts with national organizations that have provided grants and planning assistance to charitable agencies in various parts of the Country. I'll make a few phone calls and see if I can come up with something. I'll get back to you on Monday. In the meantime, just enjoy the weekend. You're a boater, aren't you? I understand that it's supposed to be a great weekend for sailing."

"Actually, I'm a power boater. We don't always appreciate high winds like the rag flappers but I expect to get out for a few hours on Sunday. How do you intend to bring this planning effort up to the Board?" Joe asked.

"Tactically, I think it best that the agenda remain as loose as possible," commented Patello. "That way I can slip it in when the opportunity presents itself. My guess is that Kevin will let things just happen as he usually does. Tom will want to beat you on the head about money. Bishop Hanks will want to tell us about Folley and Folley will tell us about Logan. The combination of all of this will create enough confusion for me to suggest that we bring about order through a strategic plan. The other Board members will welcome the comic relief."

Durant was relieved. "Okay. I'll stop worrying about an organized meeting and agenda and let things just happen. I was going to call Mr. Mondi and Mr. Meehan for their input. Should I still do that? What does the Bishop have to tell about Dr. Folley?"

The question about the Bishop brought Patello up short. Suddenly he realized that by pressing his interest to compromise Durant he had inadvertently tipped his hand that he was in the know more than he wanted Durant to realize. At this point Folley's appointment as Secretary of Health for the Archdiocese was only known to a few insiders. Patello did not want Druant to see him as a member of the Cardinal's gang. On the other hand, to deny having any knowledge about the appointment and have Durant learn later that he was one of the first informed would destroy the trust with Durant that he was now trying to firmly establish. Patello opted to give an honest reply.

"I'm sorry, Joe. I thought that Dr. Folley might have informed you. The word I got from Bishop Hanks is that the Cardinal has named Dr. Folley to be his Secretary of Health. Logan will be reporting to Folley as I understand it. I expect that the Bishop will report that to the Board on Tuesday."

The news was a real downer for Durant. "Christ! That really sucks, Charlie. How in the hell can I run this hospital to the satisfaction of the Cardinal, the Board, that jerk Folley, and Logan, who I've never met? That really sucks!"

Patello recovered. "Well, it only serves to justify the need for an organized plan of action. Let's get the planning committee organized. Maybe Mondi and Meehan could serve on the committee with you and me. That would create some balance while Logan, Folley, O'Shea and Bishop Hanks handle the fiscal crisis. Hardly can be the mediator. Why don't you let me talk to the others? That way you won't be seen by O'Shea and his associates as an insurgent."

Suddenly Durant remembered, "How about Sister Mary Elizabeth? Where does she fit in? Her nose seemed well out of joint when I talked to her about an hour ago. Think she would fit into the planning committee?"

"Good question, Joe. I'm not really sure. Let's give it some more thought and talk on Monday."

As the conversation ended Patello felt certain that he had gained the trust of Durant. Even more important he felt that Durant had allowed himself to become dependent on Patello for leverage against the apparent power play that Folley had engineered by his appointment as Secretary of Health. A side bar advantage is that the counter move the planning committee could cause O'Shea to expose his motive for holding the evidence about Logan's bank account. This was a long shot worth taking. Now Patello needed the assistance of Park consulting. Tony Marone wasn't in to answer his call but got back to him within the hour. Charlie detailed the conversation with Durant to Marone who immediately opted to consult with Capizzi and get back to Patello. Three hours later a meeting had been arranged for Monday morning in Patello's office. Capizzi and Marone would be there. Tom Callahan, world-class health consultant of Debur and Tandy, would also be with them.

Durant was fuming mad. Twice he picked up the telephone to call Folley. Each time he thought better of it and returned the phone to the receiver. He pounded the desk in anger, shouted at the ceiling, and yelled for his executive assistant. She walked into his office and calmly sat in the chair in front of his desk. Her matronly deportment and professional style caused the near mad executive to reign in his own emotions. They sat looking at each other for a few minutes before he spoke.

"Damn it, that jerk Folley has got me by the shorts. I need to have a stat conference with Weaver and Daly. Get 'em here in the next fifteen minutes. Tell 'em whatever they are doing can wait. Have you mailed out anything for the Board meeting?"

The executive assistant was very curious about the Folley remark. Some rumors about the good doctor becoming Durant's boss had been circulating among the secretaries. Obviously, this was not the time to engage the boss in small talk about a trivial thing like his job. She thought it best just to answer his question. "The only thing that has been sent to the Trustees is the meeting notice, Mr. Durant. I expected to fax an agenda to everyone today. Do you have it ready?"

"Negative. We'll surprise them with some of Hardly's mystic commentary. Folley can do the dance of the Seven Veils and I'll do some slight-of-hand tricks with the cash balance. For my big finish, I'll make Weaver disappear. That ought to make 'em go bananas."

This was the opening the Executive Assistant had been waiting for. Now was the time to pop the question. "You are obviously upset about the meeting. What has Dr. Folley done this time?"

Durant's anger brought him out of his chair. He paced back and forth as he began to explain to the faithful executive assistant, "God's gift to the medical profession, one Dr. Folley, has apparently used his clinical relationship with the Cardinal as a means to achieve prominence and glory in the Chancery. He got himself appointed Secretary of Health for the Archdiocese. I think the son of a bitch is running for Pope. The Cardinal had to be drunk when he made that decision, Jesus!"

Having extracted the information of interest, the executive assistant redirected Durant back to the business at hand. "Mr. Weaver called earlier for an appointment. I gave him one o'clock. Usually Mr. Daly prefers to meet with you on Monday morning. Should I cancel his Monday meeting and bring him in at one with Mr. Daly?"

The relationship between Weaver and Daly had always been strained. Weaver by nature and profession was cautious. Every detail needed to be accounted for in an exact fashion. Accounting was an art that Weaver mastered and bookkeeping was an exact science that he commanded. Daly was an artist of a different sort. Since his days as a student activist during the Viet Nam War, Daly had used estimates and trends as a gauge of measurement. Details were always contained but hidden in the packaged conclusion. Durant had discovered that Weaver's exact nature in budgeting and Daly's wide lens approach to planning often led to the same conclusions. When that happened the hospital could set a course with accuracy. When the two perspectives differed, Durant took the time to analyze the differences in-depth before proceeding. During the analysis of the difference Durant would attempt to get the two executives to collaborate and come to a uniform compromised conclusion. Collaboration was difficult and often forced. The two men were not only professionally different but were on the opposite extremes politically. Weaver epitomized the arch conservative while Daly was an outspoken liberal who still wore a Castro style beard. Bringing the two together in a small conference or in a general executive staff meeting was always potentially explosive. Apart each man was extremely competent and possibly the best in their respective positions in all of the Boston area hospitals, a fact not fully known therefore not appreciated by the Board.

Durant intended to inform Weaver and Daly about the conversation with Patello at the same time. He wanted to measure their individual reactions and see if they could come to an immediate common perspective on the conduct of a strategic planning process.

It was important that the executive staff have a united effort in order to keep planning under management control. He would emphasize that point by telling the executives about Folley's latest claim to glory. The political strategy within the Board would be obvious. No need to explain all of this to the executive assistant.

Instead Durant gave a simple answer to her question. "No. Let Daly's Monday meeting stand. Tell him to be here at one for a discussion with Rod on strategic planning. We can detail today's meeting on Monday. Schedule Rod to come back on Monday. That way they'll both be upset."

Actually, one P.M. was the best time for Durant to meet with Weaver and Daly. The General Medical Staff meeting was less than an hour away by the time he had finished his morning routine, called the Boardmembers, ranted and raved, then had a discussion with his executive assistant. For the next thirty minutes Durant would busy himself making notes for the President's report to the Medical Staff. The meeting would begin at noon and usually conclude by one. He could then move immediately to the meeting with his two senior vice presidents.

At eleven-forty-five Durant entered the hospital's main auditorium. Several physicians had arrived and were enjoying the buffet lunch. Physicians are customarily attracted to a free lunch. It is an integral part of their residency training that lasts through out their entire career. Hospital Presidents are taught to always cater to the physicians. Gradually the room became crowded as the teaching faculty, hospital-based specialists, and community-based physicians assembled for their obligatory meeting. Some signed the attendance forms, ate lunch and left. Most stayed obediently through the reports and presentations. The agenda for the general staff meetings is purposely short since the physicians attend a number of departmental quality review sessions on a routine basis. In addition, the medical staff has a major scientific session each month called grand rounds that is always very well attended. Actually, the general staff meeting was more of a social gathering where the elected leadership of the medical staff would report on medical administrative matters and the members of the medical staff could register a complaint about parking, medical record transcription, or anything else that came to mind. The president of the medical staff moved quickly through the agenda to the concluding item, The Hospital President's Report.

Durant's style in dealing with the general medical Staff was to be concise, factual, and always upbeat. His years of experience had taught him that placing a burden on the physicians with a lot of crape hanging always generated a negative reaction. This was especially true in the current environment where the specialists were losing income because of the increasing denial rate by Health Maintenance Organizations. The primary care physicians were becoming busier but they were also being held far more responsible and accountable under the capitation payment method.

Durant cautiously steered around conflict between members of the staff. He began his report by thanking the physicians for their continuing support during these difficult times. He noted that the occupancy of the hospital was nearing a record low but the diagnostic and therapeutic procedures were running ahead of last year. From a fiscal perspective, the hospital's cash flow was excellent. Days in the accounts receivable were slightly under this same period last year. The employee to patient ratio was on the decline. Spending was being modified to become consistent with revenue. He concluded his remarks, as he began, by thanking the physicians for their loyalty and support.

As Durant was giving his report, most of the physicians were finding another cup of coffee, talking to a colleague, or lining up a consultation. No one seemed to realize that the President's report was packed with bad news. The hospital was losing money. Admissions were at a record low. Intensity was declining. Expenses were being cut. Employees were being laid off. Revenue was declining. As always Durant asked if anyone had any questions or comments. Hearing none he returned the podium to the President of the Medical Staff who adjourned the meeting.

Durant lingered in the auditorium as the physicians filed out. Some of the doctors remained in little groups chatting about matters of practice and referrals. Others socialized and talked about the Red Sox, golf, or vacations. Often individual physicians would take the time to whisper the latest gossip in Durant's ear. He wondered if anyone would bring Folley's latest escapade to his attention. None did. He also noticed that Dr. Folley, Chairman of the Department of Medicine at St. Anslem's Hospital, Member of the Board of Trustees, Professor of Medicine Tuft's University School of Medicine, Distinguished servant of the Commonwealth and City, gentleman, scholar, man of letters, and soon to be announced Secretary of Health for the Boston Catholic Archdiocese was not present.

Good, thought Durant, *this is not the time or place for a confrontation.*

While Durant was hanging around the auditorium, Weaver and Daly had arrived at his office. Daly was the first. He properly announced himself to the executive assistant and took a chair in the office reception area. Weaver arrived within minutes of Daly. He walked past Daly without comment, waved to the executive assistant, entered the President's office and sat down. Both executives remained in their own solitude until Durant arrived. As the boss entered his office Daly walked in and took a chair opposite Weaver at the small conference table. Durant joined them and sat at the end of the table so that he was flanked on both sides by his capable assistants. The boss tried to warm the meeting by commenting about the weather, the weekend relaxation, and some trivial gossip about who was doing what to whom. As the execs took to the discussion with their own commentary Durant carefully measured the compatibility scale.

When he determined the time was right, he brought their attention to the purpose of the meeting. "Boys, we have another interesting challenge given to us by the great Dr. Richard Folley. This time he has managed to get himself appointed Secretary for Health on the Cardinal's Cabinet. He has also been appointed boss of the new Office for Health for the Archdiocese. I'm sure that you have heard that former City Commissioner Logan is going to direct that office. What we don't know at this time is how all of this impacts on our work in administering St. Anslem's. I expect to be enlightened at the Board meeting on Tuesday. There are some Board members who feel that the CEO of St. Anslem's should be the principal agent for the Board of St. Anslem's. They are going to recommend that St. A's establish its destiny through a strategic planning effort led by the administration of the hospital. We need to be prepared to take charge of the planning effort. I wanted to have an initial discussion about this with the two of you today so you could begin to prepare your thoughts over the weekend. We will meet again on Monday morning to begin to flesh out our approach."

Daly sat up straight and began to be energized by Durant's comments. His black eyes flashed from Durant to Weaver and back. As Durant finished his comments Daly jumped in.

"This could be the opportunity that we have been looking for to focus the Board on the changing pattern of health delivery going on in Boston and away from the micro perspective of money. The only reports they ever see are financial. Has anyone thought about a planning committee?"

Weaver slumped in his chair and began rubbing his temples. He seemed irritated by Daly's eagerness. With a quick flick of the wrist he popped open his ever-present Briefcase, laid copies the draft financial operating statement for the recent month on the table, and began his commentary.

"What we need to plan is how we are going to get out of the toilet. We went down a million two hundred and change the past month. If this keeps up the only viable plan is bankruptcy. Folley and that goddamn Department of Medicine is way under budget in revenue and way over on expenses. That jerk needs to start cutting losses. Why don't we start with him and bounce his ass full-time to the Archdiocese? Another cut could be in administration by chopping back on wild hair planners who only know how to plan to spend. We need more tertiary admits to cover the overhead load. O'Shea will jump all over this planning shit."

Durant took quick notice of Weaver's slam at Daly. Daly hadn't missed it either. He was leaning forward in his chair as if he was about to lunge at Weaver. Durant came forward in his chair in an attempt to separate the two. "Look, guys, what I need is your collective wisdom not your antagonism. We know that this place has got warts. We also know that O'Shea is screaming about the losses. If our only answer is to gut this place with layoffs and cutbacks then we are in a death glide. I'm not ready to admit that, although it might be the fact. We owe it to the Board to do a very careful review of our situation and look for viable alternatives. Maybe the Office for Health can help generate more referrals to St. A's. We ought to at least get the Catholic market."

With a wave of his hand Weaver dismissed Durant's comment. "Boss, you are kidding yourself if you think the Catholics are going to let the Archdiocese tell them where they are going to get healthcare. Have you been to Church lately? The place is nearly empty on Sunday. People listen to the HMO's. Our docs have to sell their excellence to the HMO's. That's where the action is. The only thing you are going to get from that stupid Health Office at the Archdiocese is a bill to pay for Folley and Logan. That's the only kind of plan they care about."

Daly remained focused on Weaver but directed his remarks to Durant. "I believe the only way out of the fiscal crisis is to reposition the hospital into new markets. Our emphasis on cardiac disease has brought us into the most competitive market. We might have the best product but who knows it. If we are going to stay with that emphasis then we have to put big bucks into the marketing end. We could be a small player with high quality in cardiac and create another high-profile service that draws the referrals. A planning effort would help determine where the new markets are. Again, my learned fiscal wizard, you better be prepared to open the purse strings because a real planning effort costs money."

As Daly concluded his comment, Weaver leaned forward and put his fist in the middle of the table. He glared at Daly. "If I'm a wizard you're a mystic. What in the hell do we need to spend money on? We need to stop spending, not start, for Christ's sake. Your goddamn planners and consultants are not going to tell us anything that we don't know. What we need to do is kick some ass. Let's start with Folley."

Daly sat back in his chair and seemed to relax. He looked at Weaver with a slight smile before commenting, "Rodger, my dear friend, you are a real asshole."

Before Durant could call for order, Weaver jumped from his chair and made a move for Daly. Daly, the smaller of the two but far quicker, was on his feet in time to duck Weaver's blind punch. Weaver's second punch landed harmlessly on Daly's upraised arms. The two combatants then went into a clinch and proceeded to waltz around Durant's office knocking pictures off the wall and rearranging the top of the boss's desk.

Durant was at first speechless and then began to repeatedly shout, "Knock it off!" to little avail except to draw the executive assistant into the office. She watched the dance for a few seconds before announcing, "You two jerks couldn't get noticed at a walrus convention." That comment ended the fray.

Weaver and Daly picked up their material and left together. Durant wondered if they were headed for the parking lot to finish the battle. As the door closed he joined his faithful executive assistant in putting the office back in order.

Another executive conference brought to a productive conclusion, he thought.

It was now three-thirty on Friday afternoon. Time to start the weekend. Durant turned out the lights in the office and went home.

As he drove home, Durant worked over in his mind the exchange between his two capable Vice Presidents. He dismissed the physical combat as something of no consequence. Instead he searched for a common point to base a planning review. Points of agreement were the fiscal crisis and low occupancy. There seemed to be mixed attitudes about the hospital's emphasis on cardio vascular disease. Yet, putting the insults aside, the two executives seemed to acknowledge that as the hospital's strong suit. Neither seemed to suggest that the hospital had any other area of prominence. Daly would not acknowledge that cost reduction methods were required. Weaver, on the other hand, felt that immediate cutbacks were necessary. On the last point, Durant completely agreed with Weaver. Monthly losses of over a million dollars could not be sustained. The hospital was required to drastically scale back its spending. The challenge was to reduce spending without impacting the revenue base. On the other hand, revenue enhancement would be served if the doctors would become salesmen to the HMO's, as Weaver had suggested, and if the hospital would find new profitable markets as Dally had suggested.

In summary, Durant focused on three combined efforts. The first would be a detailed fiscal analysis of all hospital functions. Those that were not essential would be eliminated. The second analysis would be a review of all hospital services from a revenue to cost perspective. Those services that were not profitable would be eliminated unless they materially contributed to enhancing revenue for another service such as the cardiac catheterization laboratory in medicine contributing to the volume of cardiac surgery. The third analysis would be the strategic planning effort. The intent of that effort would be determining new markets that offered opportunity for growth and prominence.

This last analysis is where Durant intended to focus the planning committee. He prayed that Patello would find a funding source for the planning program. Such a find would eliminate the objection that Weaver raised about the cost of consultants. In his heart, Durant felt that Weaver was being the Devil's advocate as a conditioner for O'Shea.

Yes, all things considered it was a productive meeting, was his last thought on the subject as he turned into his driveway.

Part Two

Chapter Nine

Jay Marquart was in a funk. Friday, his second-favorite day, was spent at St. Anslem's chemical dependency unit talking with Dr. Kenneth about his "disease" as the doctor described it, listening to a variety of lectures about physical and mental deterioration caused by substance abuse, and chatting with seasoned veterans in the struggle to recovery. It was hard to deny the logic of the presentations. He was convinced that he was going to die a painful death and bring no end of hardship and ruin to those who loved him if he gave no effort to reform.

Okay, you got me, he thought as he looked at the fourth video in a series of six.

But recognizing the problem and doing something about it seemed impossible. It was Friday and for as long as Jay could remember, Friday afternoon he went on a jag that carried him to Monday morning. His lifestyle was built on the practice of substance abuse. He smoked and drank when he went fishing on Friday night. Or was it more correct to state that he fished when he went smoking and drinking. Jay was puzzled over what came first.

It's that damn medication, he thought, *it's messing up my head.* If he was going to be a recovering addict, as everybody seemed intent on making him, then he would design his own method of recovery.

He began a careful reflection of his lifestyle and decided that he could maintain the practices that he enjoyed absent of the excessive consumption of substances. A troublesome point in the analysis was that his spouse was a happy participant in his excess. There was no way that Jay was going to disrupt the loving relationship that he had with Susan. They shared good times centered on booze, pot, and coke. That's what brought them together and nothing, especially abstinence, was going to separate them. Jay concluded that for the sake of his family he would need to continue to consume some form of intoxicating substance. He would explain that requirement to Bob Markley at their next session.

Staying off the stuff on a Friday night wasn't enough of a downer but he had to check out of his fishing trip with Brian in order to meet with Martha about his intent to sue the hospital and "nail dear old Cecile to the wall." Martha had researched the Federal law on record confidentiality and wanted to go over it with him. She wanted to make sure that while he was hanging around the hospital over the weekend he did not do anything that would void his protection. Their meeting was scheduled to follow Benny's baseball game.

Cecile's process server had yet to catch up with Jay and give him the summons to return to court for the custody battle over Kristie. That was another downer. There was a big legal fight brewing that Jay did not have the money to sustain. Lawyers, other than Martha, expected to be paid. She and Jay were also going to discuss that monstrous problem at their Friday night session.

If he survived Friday night, he had to look forward to coming back to St. A's and hanging around in the morbid surroundings while his yard was left unattended. Saturday morning was the time that Jay had dedicated to mowing the lawn and trimming the place to perfection. He was proud of his yard. He also enjoyed the three or four beers that it took for him to complete the job. Afterwards it was playtime with the kids until Brian and Louise arrived. Then it was party time all night long. Brian was scheduled to show up with the usual goodies. Sunday morning, instead of sleeping off the jag, he was scheduled to check in again at St. A's.

"Bummer. This is a goddamn bummer. Ain't no way that I'm gonna make it through the weekend. No way!" was the thought in his mind as Jay lay down for his afternoon nap.

Bob Markley had purposely avoided Jay on Friday. He had a legitimate reason. It was time for Jay to reconcile his dependency in his own mind by coming to grips with the activities in his lifestyle that catered to his problem. Jay also needed to build support relationships on a broader base than Markley. However, if Jay entered into a crisis, the staff had been informed to call Bob to the scene. Markley and Dr. Kenneth felt that Jay was not out of the woods emotionally but could still experience a violent reaction to the detoxification.

Another reason for the distance that Markley sought from Jay was to establish some objectivity in thinking about the incident report sitting in his desk drawer. Markley feared that the report once submitted to the risk manager would bring Jay's former wife under investigation by a nursing review board. This would give her reason to create a defense, he thought, that would subject Jay to intense pressure. He feared that Jay would crack under the pressure and revert to substance abuse. On the other hand, if Markley did not submit the report and Jay sued the hospital the same pressure would be caused as the hospital applied its defense. Markley's interest in Jay as a patient was overshadowing his obligation as an agent representing the institution's best interest. The pressure of being in the middle was very familiar to Markley. He had cracked under that same type of pressure in the past and well understood the familiar sensation to find an escape.

About the time that Joseph Durant was pulling into his driveway in Hingham after an exciting day at St. Anslem's, Jay Marquart was entering his driveway in Waltham after a non-eventful day at the same place. As Jay left the Jeep, he was mobbed by Benny and James. Kristie was not scheduled to visit until Sunday night. Susan had prepared a snack for him that he gobbled before he changed into shorts and a Tee shirt. Once properly dressed, the whole family piled into the Jeep and headed for the Waltham Little League Ball Park. This was the final game of the schedule. Rumors around the dugout indicated that if Benny had a good game he would be selected as the first alternate on the League All-Star Team. The prospect of such an honor registered little with Benny as he toyed with his brother in the back seat. Jay, however, was visibly excited about the prospect. He kept explaining the fine points of the game to Benny as they negotiated around the usual five o'clock traffic. Susan listened to Jay and observed that Benny was not at all on the same wavelength. When they arrived at the ballpark, Benny jumped from the Jeep and ran to his team mates already taking in-field practice. Jay gave him a parting pat on the back and shouted encouragement to the back of the running boy.

As Jay was walking toward the bleachers he noticed a familiar person sitting prominently in the third row where Jay usually perched. It was none other than his newfound friend of last Friday, the owner of the Oldsmobile that James had marked on the door and forever in Jay's mind.

"What's that son of a bitch doing in my place, Susan?" was his first verbal reaction. "I'll kick his ass," was the second.

Susan tried to direct Jay around to the other end of the bleachers while trying to calm him down. “Jay, the man can sit wherever he wants. We don’t own the ballpark. Let him be.”

Her appeal had the right effect as Jay followed her lead but continued to mumble. They found a vantage point behind home plate but with an obstructed view of second base where Benny was positioned.

As the game began with Benny in the starting lineup, Jay began pacing in front of the bleachers shouting encouragement to Benny while standing for brief periods in front of his former advisory. Eventually the Oldsmobile owner moved to the top of the bleachers above Jay’s intended obstruction.

As the inning came to a close and Benny returned to the dugout, Jay returned to his seat beside Susan. “Fixed his ass good, Susan. Did ya see him move? Man, he knows I ain’t gonna take nothing from him,” Jay proudly announced loud enough to cause people near them to turn around. With his emotions in high, Jay stood on the bleachers and directed more remarks toward the top row. “Hey, man, you want to talk about this? We can do some battle or we can wimp out? Shit, man, I know what you want to do.”

The man to whom Jay had directed the remarks looked toward the field in apparent disregard of Jay. Susan’s embarrassment was at its peak. Gently she pulled at Jay’s trousers in an attempt to get him to direct his attention elsewhere. Fortunately, before the matter reached a climax little Benny was at bat. Susan brought this to Jay’s immediate attention. Jay became focused on the ball game once again and seemed to forget the Oldsmobile owner. It took seven pitches for Benny to earn a walk. Jay yelled base stealing instructions, told him when to tag, suggested he keep his eye on the pitcher, and generally announced strategy to all within ear shot. Benny made it to third on a throwing error to second by the catcher and two pitches later ran home on a pass ball. Jay was elated. At the end of the first inning Benny’s team held a comfortable six run lead. Jay was now relaxed and focused on the rest of the game without incident.

Benny’s team coasted to victory in four innings thanks to the merciful eleven-run rule. As the team assembled at the Dairy Queen, Benny’s manager informed Susan and Jay that Benny had been selected as an alternate to the All-Star squad and would be assigned as a regular since another player was forced to drop out due to a conflict with the family vacation. Benny was an All-Star. Susan and Jay were proud parents. Normally this would be cause for a few drinks and a family celebration into the wee hours of Saturday morning followed by the ritual of Saturday night. Jay couldn't wait to tell Brian but it would keep until tomorrow when he and Louise came over.

As he sat in the Dairy Queen pondering the glorified status of Susan's son, Jay lost all thought of St. Anslem's, Cecile's lawyers, and a disease that he didn't think he had. None of that for now. It was a time to rejoice.

The Marquart family Jeep pulled into their Waltham estate about seven-thirty. Susan was primed for a grapefruit and gin in Benny's honor. Jay was still in a good mood but stuffed with a quart of frozen yogurt and hot fudge. Normally he would have forgone the ice cream for a few stiff drinks but suddenly he remembered the blood and urine test in the morning. He realized that one drink would lead to another and then to countless others ending in a super jag. This was the picture vividly explained to him over the past three days in his rehabilitation. Some of it was beginning to sink in. As an alternative, he ordered the largest serving of frozen yogurt that was available and loaded it with hot fudge. He tried to get Susan to join him in the quasi-celebration but to no avail. She appeared to Jay to be somewhat depressed.

The prospect of a continuing celebration at home diminished more as Susan noticed Martha's car parked on the street in front of their home. Jay made the same observation but with positive interest since Martha had promised him information about the Federal law on patient records and the prospect of a malpractice-practice action against the hospital.

As the family piled from the Jeep, Martha walked into the driveway from the backyard where she had been sitting on a swing enjoying the summer sunset. James was the first to greet Aunt Martha with great news that Benny was going to be in the sky with the moon because he was going to be a star. Martha accepted the information with parallel happiness to James' but was confused as to what was actually being said. Susan greeted her sister-in-law and detailed the good news. She also offered to fix Martha a refreshing drink as an adjunct to her relaxing moments. Martha was quick to accept. Jay interjected a request for an iced tea that Susan promised to supply as well. Jay and Martha returned to the backyard swing to watch the final hour of a beautiful sunset. Within moments Susan joined then with a tall iced tea for Jay and a couple of equally large gin and grapefruits for Martha and herself.

Jay felt the surge of anger toward Susan and Martha. It seemed to him to be totally inconsiderate of the struggle he faced. *Don't they realize that I am in a world of hurt?* he thought. *How can they drink in front of me when I need their help and support?* was the question that raced through his mind as his anger surged toward an uncontrollable rage. *This is a test,* he reasoned, *yeah, a goddamn test. Markley said I would be tested over the weekend. If I break now and get pissed then I fail the test and will probably have to start that rehab crap all over again. I'll have something to tell Markley in the morning. No way am I gonna let these two broads mess me up.*

He felt an inner strength and frustration at the same time that caused him to stand. He at first turned away from the women then turned to face them. "Martha, I need to be briefed on the deal about the Federal law. You thought you would know something about the Suit I want to bring against the hospital. Maybe we ought to go inside where it's cooler and better light."

With a nod Martha and Susan carried their drinks inside to the kitchen table where they sat with Jay. Susan placed a bowl of pretzels on the table as Martha began her report.

"Jay, the hospital gave you the straight dope on the Federal law. Essentially, the law enacted in 1975 established that any patient in a Federal qualified substance abuse program was guaranteed confidentiality. However, the Department of Health and Human Resources was charged with enforcement of the law and with establishing the appropriate regulations for implementing and enforcing the law. A revised set of regulations was published by the Department in 1987. These new guidelines apply to any hospital or treatment program operated under Federal License or certification. The guidelines do allow a general hospital to determine that only the distinct substance abuse program falls under the regulations."

Jay was eagerly following Martha's commentary. He held up his hand as if to ask a question but began with an explanation. "Okay, so Markley was right in telling me that I had to sign in the program. Otherwise, they could have released my general medical record. Sounds like we got 'em by the short and curly. They blew my cover with their damn telephone."

Martha gave a slight shrug and continued her report. "Jay, as we know the law is seldom black or white. According to the regulations, the focus of enforcement depends on how the hospital organizes its substance abuse program. If a patient receives treatment in a general hospital that does not operate a program or have specialized personnel whose primary function is treatment, diagnosis or referral of substance abuse patients then the record is not protected under the law. On the other hand, if the hospital does have an organized program with the requisite personnel and certification, then the law does apply, St. Anslem's has all the necessary qualifications to bring it under the Law. Now we have to be aware that the regulations allow for exceptions."

Jay's face reddened as Martha mentioned exceptions. He stood and began to pace around the kitchen. "Martha, what exceptions? They flat out broke the law, right?"

"Jay, there are always necessary reasons to except rules and regulations." Martha straightened her glasses and looked at Jay as if she were talking to a client. "The law recognizes this. In this case the Federal regulations allow for patient information to be given if the patient authorizes it. Most patient authorizations are to qualified service organizations such as research firms, data processing organizations, insurance payers, and laboratories, legal or medical professional services, even collecting agencies. However, once the information is given to the agency, they must agree to retain its confidentiality. You can see that as the information gets spread around to so many different places the ability to enforce the law becomes mute."

"Hell, Martha, I ain't gonna authorize any release of information to anybody." Jay pounded the table to give emphasis. "They can't make me, can they?" Jay's expressed concern brought him back to his chair.

Martha looked at Susan and pointed to her glass for a refill. Susan was quick to oblige. Jay's iced tea was half full but Susan topped it off. This time Jay didn't notice. He was concentrating on Martha's every word.

She continued to explain. "There are other exceptions for minors, incompetent patients, and such that don't apply to you. And there are a lot of wrinkles in the patient authorized disclosure that we need to be careful about. You may have authorized certain agencies to receive information when you signed the admitting form to the program. For example, your insurance company may be an authorized agency. We'll have to check it. The point is that your release of information on the admitting form may give the hospital its defense."

Jay hit the table again with his fist and scared both Susan and Martha. "That's bullshit, pure bullshit. That's no defense against their damn telephone; I didn't authorize that telephone on my admitting form. No way!"

Martha raised her hands as if to calm him. "Jay, I'm only trying to demonstrate the complex side of the issue. We will have to explore the hospital policies of patient confidentiality on and off the substance abuse unit. There's a lot we don't know and will need to know to determine if we have a case that will stand up in court. I'll need to talk to a few more med-mal lawyers. This is a legal specialty in which I have limited experience and then only on the side of the defense. Now before you go off on another tear let me advise you that there is another category of exception known as disclosures without patient consent that allows for access to your record in case of a medical emergency. That's an obvious one except you need to know that if you are severely injured from whatever cause the treating person or institutional is entitled to your medical history. The last category is one that merits our careful concern. Your records could be disclosed on a court order if you refuse to voluntarily disclose your medical history to the court. This allows an attorney, even in a civil suit, to apply to the court for a court order to release the information. What I fear is that Cecile's attorney could make that application in your custody hearing. You see how complex this can be? You also need to know that if you are involved in any sort of criminal action the judge can order the immediate release of your medical records. Do not, I repeat, do not get involved in any violation of the law—even a speeding ticket or worse yet using or trafficking drugs—until we have a chance to sort all this out."

Jay was visibly shaken by Martha's last remarks. He felt a familiar pain in his stomach as he remembered the episode on Monday night at the Troubadour Lounge. Was he at that time involved in a criminal act? Should he tell Martha about the incident? Did Officer O'Sullivan have enough information to link him to Brian and the delivery? Did that cop tell Cecile about her ex running dope to a queer bar?"

Jay decided on the spot not to tell Martha about his escapade but to ponder the questions for future response as Martha advanced his cause. "Martha, I'm off the stuff I hope for life. I don't want any more to do with it. I'm sober and intend to stay that way. I admit that I'm habitual and will need a lot of help and support to stay clean but I'm gonna do it. It's like a disease that can't be cured but only controlled. I'm gonna control it. It's not going to control me anymore."

The three sat in silence. Martha's eyes filled with tears as she reached across the table and put her hands over Jay's clenched fists. Jay sat slumped with his head down and eyes closed. Susan sat wide eyed with her mouth open as if she had just had the shock of her life. In fact, she had just received the shock of her life. She was firmly convinced that Jay's daily trek to St. A's was simply a front to dodge the obnoxious pressure from the docs who wanted him on the wagon. She thought that as soon as he could ditch their action it would be back to party time. Now he had bought into their routine and was swearing off. This was serious if true. On the other hand, he might be playing out the magnificent hoax. Jay was a great actor. Could be that he was acting serious to build up Martha's confidence in representing him. Susan remained confident that Jay would repent his newfound ways as soon as the coast was clear. He would let her know when.

Martha saw the expression on Susan's face and decided that the evening conference was over. After a few minutes of silence, she stood up.

"Susan, thanks for the hospitality. It's really nice to visit a family and relax. Benny and James are the cutest. Tell Benny that I'll try to make the All-Star game."

Jay and Susan both stood as Martha was speaking and walked with her out to her car. Martha kept the conversation alive with small talk about the yard, neighbors, and the heat and humidity.

As she opened her car door Jay shook her hand. "Martha, thanks for everything. I'll call you when and if I ever get those papers from Cecile's lawyer."

Susan nodded her agreement with Jay.

Martha closed her car door, opened the door and started the car while making a parting comment. "Well, I'm certain that the two of you will be served by Monday night at the latest. They usually don't deliver legal documents on Saturday or Sunday. Don't be shocked at what they say. Remember, the other side has to make the case. We defend. I'm not worried. Don't you be worried."

After Martha left Jay and Susan walked into the backyard and sat together on the swing. Jay put his arms around Susan and held her close. She returned the embrace with a kiss. Their evening ended in love. The weekend had begun.

Jay got up early on Saturday and drove to St. Anslem's. It was raining and cool so he really didn't mind the imposition on his time in the yard. If it wasn't for this hospital thing he would be sitting around the house bored stiff waiting for the rain to stop. He parked his car in one of the free outpatient parking spots next to the doctor's office building and casually walked in the hospital's main entrance. The hospital was routinely quiet on Saturday. Ambulatory service was about half the volume of a weekday and inpatient occupancy was about forty percent of capacity. General staff on weekends was reduced to the minimum. Everything was slow and easy.

Jay remembered the hospital weekend drill well from his days in the cath. lab: Check in early. Tidy up the lab and the lab office. Make sure everything is set for the occasional emergency. Do the odd jobs scribbled on the notepad by the supervisor. Check the battery in the beeper. Let switchboard know that the lab was on stand-by. Head for the cafeteria for donuts, coffee, and to place a bet.

Placing a bet in the cafeteria was one of St. Anslem's unusual qualities that set it apart from just about any other hospital in Boston. It was not, however, a featured service of the institution since only the rank and file employees were aware of its availability. Administration seemed to be in the dark about the little man who sat in the cafeteria every morning except Sunday, seven to nine reading the sports page from the *Herald*. He nibbled on a donut, slowly drank his coffee, and had an occasional conversation with the hospital employee who would make a brief stop at the table and chat about the prospective outcome of the Bruins, Patriots, Celtics or Red Sox. He wore a Boston College cap that served as his advertisement. Indeed, the BC Eagles were the focus of his enterprise. He, as a special service to his established customers, would scalp tickets to the big games such as Notre Dame or Michigan.

Jay, while employed at St. Anslem's, had used Tommy the Tout on several occasions and at one time found himself seriously in Tommy's debt. When he became delinquent on payment a rather large muscular patient transporter took a few minutes of his time to explain to Jay that Tommy expected prompt payment and that Jay should perhaps borrow the necessary funds to cover the debt; otherwise, he might have a sudden accident. Jay got the message and mooched the money from his Dad. Tommy was impressed with Jay's immediate response and from that day forward held Jay in high esteem.

The thought about his old friend Tommy caused Jay to amble into the cafeteria for a cup of coffee and donut before checking into SACAP. He was still early and Saturday was casual time. Not surprisingly, Tommy was on his perch with the *Herald* spread on the table before him. Jay paid the cashier for the donut and coffee and took the table directly across the aisle from Tommy.

Without looking up Tommy greeted his old friend. "Jay, how you doing? Looks like the Sox are on a run. They win 'em both this weekend and they are in third place. Looks to me like they got a good shot at it. What do you say?"

Jay was practically knocked off his chair by Tommy's comments. He hadn't seen Tommy for nearly eight years since he had graduated from UMass. The fact that he remembered Jay's name was remarkable. Before responding Jay picked up his donut and coffee and moved to Tommy's table for a chat. Just like he had done many years ago.

"Tommy, how in the hell did you remember my name? Man, that's remarkable."

Tommy liked the praise but decided to be humble. "Not so remarkable, Jay. You remembered my name. Why? Because we had dealings that left a lasting impression. Some people you never forget."

Tommy never looked up from his newspaper as he spoke.

Jay stared at the unseen face and pondered the remark about Cecile's cop before he answered. "Tommy, Cecile and I couldn't make it work. Happens to a lot of couples. That cop is better for her. Seems to be more her type."

"Yeah, well maybe so," commented Tommy. "You know I do some business with the boys over at the Precinct and the talk I hear is that he's a switch hitter. Maybe he should play for the Sox. You want any action?"

Jay noticed that Tommy looked up when he mentioned action. "Not today, Tommy. I'm just passing through. Got an appointment in a few minutes. I'll be back and we can chat some more. Maybe you'll give good odds on BC making it to the Sugar Bowl"

"Don't laugh. They been there before. See ya around, Jay. Stop back when you got time."

Jay walked toward the SACAP Unit thinking about his conversation with Tommy. He realized that the hospital cafeteria was the universal communication center for all things personal and private. Talking to Tommy was a mistake, he thought. *If he mentions the conversation to an employee who mentions it to another eventually the whole world will figure out that ol' Jay is in SACAP working off a drunk. Nothing is confidential among hospital types just like nothing is confidential among cops. Put the two together and nothing is sacred. Pretty soon Cecile will hear from her hubby that I was at the Troubadour and she'll tell him that I'm on junk then the two of them will throw me in the slam and take away my kid.*

Jay's depression was beginning to mount when he checked into the Unit. It climbed another notch when he was told by the nurse that Bob Markley had the weekend off. Another counselor would work with him today. She gave him his morning medication that he took reluctantly. A lab tech obtained the usual specimens and disappeared down the hall toward a room with a screaming patient going through initial detox. Jay wondered if he had made such horrible sounds. The nurse informed him that Dr. Kenneth would be making rounds in about a half-hour. She suggested that Jay rest in a room assigned for his use today. Instead he opted to walk up and down the corridor while he continued to ponder his awkward predicament involving Officer O'Sullivan.

There was something wrong with the picture that he couldn't figure out. Gradually he began to realize that Tommy, with reason or not, was sending Jay a message of some kind. Jay's mind was spinning as he tried to reason the situation. *What was it he said about Cecile's cop? He's a switch hitter! The guy is half gay maybe even full-time. Yeah. Okay. What about it? Was he in the Troubadour for business or pleasure or both? What if the guy is a gay user cop? Man, that's heavy. So could be that he's as scared of me as I am of him. That so, then he ain't gonna say nothing to Cecile. I'm safe.*

The thought of being off the hook with Officer O'Sullivan gave Jay a boost out of his depression so he thought. Actually, the medication he had taken a few minutes before was more of an assist. He began to put a little bounce in his step as he paced in front of the nursing station. The nurse made a clinical note about his obvious change in attitude. Jay started another lap around the Unit as Dr. Kenneth came through the door. He greeted Jay but made no attempt to interrupt the wandering soul. Jay was actually humming a song as he returned Dr. Kenneth's greeting with a wave. Kenneth was pleased with Jay's demeanor. It Action with the positive progress notes in his medical record. It seemed possible to Dr. Kenneth that Jay would escape from Phase One of his detoxification in another day and return to work on Monday in reasonably good shape. He reviewed the nurse's notes on the record and followed her comments with his own entry about Jay's progress. Just as he completed the daily entry Jay rounded the comer in front of the station. Dr. Kenneth flagged him down and invited him to go to his office for a chat.

Dr. Kenneth sat at his desk. Jay was hyped and chose to stand. He continually rocked back and forth as the good doctor talked to him.

"Mr. Marquart, you have made steady progress over the past few days. We note that your depression and anger have become more controlled. The medication that we have been using is having the right effect. You're a little manic right now so we will have to make some adjustments in the dosage. If we can keep your chemistry in balance you will have a much better chance of building your will power to stay clean. Congratulations. You seem to be on the way to recovery. We'll watch you for a few more hours today then you can go home early and enjoy the rest of the day with your family. You haven't seen much of them this week. Tomorrow will be a short day as well. We want to give you some more medication. If the dosage seems right then you can go home. Monday it's back to work. Bob Markley will set you up with the right amount of support for your continuing recovery. You'll check in with us once a week for a while then you can fly on your own and just call when you need help."

Jay listened to Dr. Kenneth and was recalling his conversation with Martha the night before at the same time. The prospect of being out of the daily clutches of the Unit was excellent. Being on his own was trouble. Martha had warned him that screwing up in public would void his Federal protection. He knew that he was still very attracted to the "stuff." Markley understood the problem. Jay wanted Markley at his side. He wanted his freedom but he wanted help. He suddenly realized that he was beginning to act like a recovering addict. He was not the same belligerent that broke up the place a few days ago. He had developed respect for the very people who he had ridiculed. Had he inadvertently taken that first step that Markley had talked about? If so he didn't remember taking an oath or pledge that put him officially on the wagon. Dr. Kenneth was great but he was no junkie. That was for sure.

Jay wanted to talk about this with Markley before he stepped back into the cold cruel world and Action Waste Management. He tried to explain this to the doctor. "Dr. Kenneth, I appreciate all that you and the nurses have done. I feel pretty good right now. Staying off the stuff ain't going to be easy. I know that. I told you when we first met that I didn't want to take drugs to help with my recovery. I still feel that way. That medication messes me up. I need to be able to work things out in my own mind. I'll come in tomorrow for my last dose. Let's see what happens without any drugs after that."

Kenneth sensed that Jay was trying to escape. "Jay, going bare is a mistake. Your chemistry is still subject to wide fluctuations that could cause you severe depression and violent behavior. We want you to avoid that."

"But you said that I made good progress. Hell, I haven't busted up a thing or anybody for a couple of days now. You think I'm bye Phase One. So let's go with the flow."

"There could be a relapse," commented Kenneth, "you know, an overlap between the Phase One and Phase Two cycles. These things aren't exact. If you insist on going bare then we will probably have to double or even triple the usual support base. You up to that?"

Jay gave an emphatic nod. "Whatever it takes. But no drugs. Where's Markley? He's never around when we need him. He ought to be in here holding my hand. Seriously, I want to talk to him about this before I go back to work on Monday. Is he available?"

Dr. Kenneth thought for a while before he answered. As he pondered Jay's question he slowly shook his head from side to side in a negative fashion. "Bob Markley, for, ah, personal reasons, has been given every weekend off. He takes call but doesn't come in except for extreme emergencies. I know how to reach him so I'll call him tonight and try to arrange for him to meet you tomorrow. When you check in tomorrow we'll let you know the arrangements. You coming in after Mass?"

The question caught Jay off guard. He hadn't been to Mass since he graduated from the eighth grade. He gave Dr. Kenneth a look that caused the learned man of science to blush. "Yeah, right, after Mass. I'll see you about ten. Okay?"

Jay escaped the confines of St. Anslem's at noon. He arrived home in time to join Susan and the kids for lunch. On impulse, he called Cecile's in an attempt to talk to Kristie and to arrange for her visit on Sunday evening. Cecile was not in but Michael O'Sullivan obligingly gave Kristie the phone to talk to her Daddy. The conversation centered on her many activities of the week that included swimming, dance lessons, and a visit to a preschool that Kristie had attended. Daddy reminded her that she was coming to Daddy's house for dinner Sunday evening. Kristie seemed excited about the event. At Jay's request, Michael got back on the line to talk about the arrangements. Michael explained to Jay that Kristie would be at Cecile's parents on Sunday for a visit and Jay could pick her up there at five P.M. The arrangement was fine with Jay as long as he didn't have to spend time chatting with Cecile's parents. That was always a painful experience. Jay completed his conversation with the man of the house and hung up. He had been tempted to make some small comment about the Troubadour but could not find the right approach. Afterwards he was relieved that he had not opened the subject. More research on the mysterious Michael O'Sullivan was definitely in order.

Susan seemed to be in a rare sullen mood. She appeared cool toward Jay but attentive. Her facial expressions signaled Jay that something was amiss. He took special care to show extra affection to her as he sought out the cause of her suspected malady. Susan recognized Jay's very obvious attempt to communicate with affection. This was a pleasant change in his usual disregard. She decided to nurse him along and get the most mileage out of his affectionate maneuvers. After a while of being exceptionally nice Jay seemed to tire of the effort. The sun was breaking through the clouds and the temperature had risen to near normal. The grass was still too wet to mow but the driveway was dry enough for some hoops. Jay dismissed his attention to Susan and joined Benny and the basketball, Susan nevertheless enjoyed the past hour stringing him along. She also knew that she had him hooked for the rest of the day. He was set to be her obedient servant.

By late afternoon the skies had completely cleared. It was going to be a beautiful evening but a little on the cool side, a definite reminder that September was less than a month away. The usual backyard cookout with Brian and Louise was right on schedule. The party couple had arrived exactly at five. Brian and Jay had enlisted Benny and James for a two on two basketball game while the charcoal in the old Webber began its progress to white hot. Brian would break out of the game now and then for a quick sip of beer. He hadn't given any notice that Jay was sipping an iced tea carefully placed near the grill.

Inside Louise and Susan sat at the kitchen table chatting about Jay's recent illness. The standard tall gin and grapefruit was placed in reach as they conversed while preparing salad and side dishes. Louise opened her hand bag to show Susan the small bag of cocaine that Brian had supplied for a late-night sniff. Susan was pleased to see that the usual party was in the offing. Her concern was that Jay in his new temperate mentality would deny the recreation to the rest of them.

She felt a need for reinforcement that caused her to talk to Louise about Jay. "Louise, I'm worried about Jay. You know that he went back into the hospital for two days and has been going in for treatment every day this week?"

Louise was taken back by Susan's concerned expression. After a deep breath she responded to Susan. "Brian mentioned that Jay had to go back in on Monday. Jay told him about it the other night. Is he really sick? How serious is this, Susan?"

Susan laughed at the question and tried to imagine the seriousness of sobriety. "Oh, Louise, he isn't going to die or anything like that. He's decided to go sober. I mean he thinks that he can quit booze, pot, coke, and whatever just like that. I can't believe it! I mean how am I going to live with him in that condition? I don't know how to handle this."

Louise closed her handbag before she responded, "Well, knowing Jay you won't have to live with it for long. He'll have his nose into the candy tonight I bet. We both know that Jay and Brian have been using since they were thirteen maybe before. They won't quit. Jay especially. He's got to have a mighty big reason to keep him sober. I mean a mighty big reason."

Suddenly Susan's sense of humor disappeared. She appeared to have tears in her eyes. "Kristie is the big reason, Louise. He's doing it for Kristie. Cecile is taking him back to court on custody. Jay thinks that she is going to convince the judge that he's a drunk and an unfit parent. Jay is determined to stay sober to keep Kristie. I don't understand it all but Martha tells Jay that he's got to stay out of trouble or the kid is lost. I want to help him, Louise, but I'm not a drunk. Why should I have to give it up?"

Louise took Susan's hand in sympathy. "Did Martha say you had to give it up? How about Jay? Did he ask you to go sober? I don't think you have to enter into this, do you?"

"Oh, Louise, I just don't know." Susan's depression increased. "I don't want something like this to come between us. It shouldn't matter if I have a few drinks. Jay can stay off it. I'll even help him if I can. I love him. But you got to remember that I've been using since I was thirteen too. We were in the same class."

The conversation was interrupted by the sudden ring of the telephone. Susan answered it immediately. Bob Markley was calling for Jay. Markley was a familiar name to Susan. Jay had mentioned his new friend to her several times during the past week. Hearing his voice made her feel like he had been listening in on the conversation she had been having with Louise. She almost made a comment about him not taking her seriously but managed to simply extend her greetings with the comment that she had heard Jay mention his name. Bob responded with the hope that would have the opportunity to meet in the near future. Susan gave a polite response and asked Bob to please hold until she could call Jay to the phone.

Jay came quickly to the phone as Susan announced that Mr. Markley was holding.

The two ladies noticed Jay's relieved expression as he greeted the caller. Jay, noticing their intense interest in his conversation, moved out of the kitchen to the living room stretching the phone cord to its maximum length. After thanking Bob for calling he unlaced a barrage of criticism about his goofing off on weekends.

Then in a conciliatory manner Jay got to the point. "Bob, I appreciate you getting back to me. You see, Kenneth says that I can go back to work on Monday. That's great except he wants me to stay on the meds. I think that stuff messes me up and I don't want to be screwed up at work. So he says that I can stay off the meds if we can triple the support. Hell, I don't know how we can do that. I figure I got to talk to you about it. You got time tomorrow?"

Markley seemed to hesitate before he answered, "Sure, Jay, we can get together and talk about it. The support that you will require is not all that time consuming. It just requires that you get help at the first sign of pressure rather than trying to tough it out. You partying now?"

"Yeah, we got some people in. No big deal. Why?"

"Well, I imagine that some of you are having a few drinks and such. As the night goes on you will feel like having a belt or two yourself just to join the fun. That leads to trouble. I don't know how long your friends have been with you but if they have started drinking you are already experiencing pressure. If not right now then in a little while. So what Kenneth was saying is rather than wait for the urge to down a few, you use your will power when you expect pressure and call for support. I thought that maybe you were calling for help now."

Jay was impressed with Markley's ability to understand what was going on. "Yeah, in a way I am. This action will go on for a while. Iced tea won't make it past dinner, then I'll look to kick back. But you got me peeing in a bottle in the morning so I'll stay off the stuff. It's not much pressure—just a little."

Markley moved to conclude. "Well, if you think you are in trouble later on give the Unit a call. There's someone on duty that can help you. If you need me they can reach me. Otherwise, I'll see you at St. A's about ten. Okay?"

"Yeah, that's okay. Ten is fine." Jay tried to lighten up the conversation. "Gives me time to go to Mass like the doctor ordered. You going to Mass?" quipped Jay.

Markley was quick in reply. "Sure thing, my man. See ya at ten sharp. Don't be late."

Jay pushed the disconnect button and walked back into the kitchen to replace the phone in the wall-mounted cradle. It was obvious by the look on Louise's face that she had heard his part of the conversation. Susan was standing by the kitchen counter preparing some vegetables. Jay stared at Louise for a brief moment to register his dislike for her eavesdropping, then gave Susan a sharp slap on her behind as he moved out the door to rejoin the basketball game. He felt rejuvenated. The party would be the same and he would have a good time without the need of a buzz.

Let the good times begin, he thought.

The party followed its usual format. The steaks were done to everyone's preference by a sober chef. Brian swilled his usual eight beers waiting for the food. After each one he offered to bring one to Jay as he opened the cooler for another. Jay's constant refusal did not make an impact until he began asking Brian to run into the kitchen for a refill of his iced tea. After a second trip Brian asked if Jay was on the wagon. When Jay answered yes, Brian took it as a matter of the moment and hardly let it register.

However, both Susan and Louise were carefully monitoring Jay's actions. Neither one mentioned it during the dinner. They were preoccupied with getting the kids fed and after a while directed to a shower and bed. By the time the ladies returned to the picnic table Brian was well past sobriety and Jay was still nibbling on a piece of Susan's chocolate cake. The two women had been on a constant intake of gin and grapefruit for the past three hours and were sharing a nice glow. As was customary at this hour on a Saturday night Louise opened her purse and put the little bag of white powder on the table. She opened it carefully and stretched the lines to accommodate the consumers. Brian immediately inhaled the first line. Susan followed and then Louise. Jay sat at the table and watched the action. He leaned toward the remaining line then stood and walked to the opposite end of the table. Susan followed him and gave him a loving hug and kiss. She felt him tremble and saw that he was sweating. In spite of her now heavy jag she recognized his need for compassion and understanding.

Louise recognized the situation and placed the cocaine into her purse. Brian saw that Jay was abstaining so he began to inhale the remaining line. Louise gave him a quick jab in the ribs that caused Brian to suddenly realize that the party had experienced a mood change.

"What's going on?" was his flustered reaction to Louise. Then he saw Susan holding Jay as she helped him sit down. "Jay getting sick again?" was Brian's second question that went unanswered.

Susan sat next to Jay. Louise steered Brian onto the bench across from them.

Jay regained his composure and spoke to Brian. "Brian, I'm feeling better now. I was hurting a few minutes ago because I'm on the wagon and I desperately wanted to take a sniff with you all. But I ain't going to 'cause I got to test clean in the morning. I'm hooked on dope. Hell, I guess we all are. But I got to get clean and stay that way or I stand a chance of losing Kristie. Can you dig that?"

Brian blinked and put his hands on his head. "Wow, yeah, I can dig that. How is Cecile gong to bust you, man? You got rights. Shit, she can't just walk in and take the kid. She's got to go to court, man. How they going to know that you been flying? Shit. She mess with you and I'll have Eddie bust her ass. Shit!"

Brian's expression of support was refreshing to Jay. All evening he felt that he was being criticized for attempting to stay sober. He extended a high-five to Brian who responded with a double grip. Jay was pleased that he had his friend's moral support if not his understanding.

Jay gave Brian a nod and commented. "Brian, my main man, I'll need you to carry me through this. I don't know if all this is really necessary. Last Saturday you and Louise carried me to the hospital when I was in a world of hurt. Tuesday the same thing. Now I feel fine but the doctor tells me that if I keep hittin' it I'm gonna bust. I think I got to stay clean for a while till my insides get better than I can go back on if I stay low. You know, kinda nice and easy. Cecile is serving papers that say, I guess, that my boozing and partying is a danger to Kristie. That way she can take her away from me. I ain't gonna let that happen. I got to stay completely clean till the legal stuff is resolved. You dig? Hey, man, you been back to the Troubadour and see those dudes you met last Monday?"

Jay's sudden interest in the Troubadour crowd escaped Brian. He was more intent on his friend's struggle to retain the partial custody of Kristie. "Jay, man, you got whatever help I can give. That Bitch, Cecile, worked me over good at St. A's. Hell, I was only there trying to do my job. She yelled at me like I was some scuzz or something. Man, that broad has a big problem. Somebody got to take her out. Maybe Eddie's got an idea. You want I should ask him?"

Susan listened to the conversation in silence until Eddie was mentioned. She stood, walked in front of Brian and proceeded to get in his face. "Let's keep things in proper perspective, Brian, my good fellow. Eddie has two sons that have a pretty good life right now without him around. We don't need his help and we certainly don't need to be in his debt. You have to work for the bastard and you have my sympathy. I'm free of him and I want to keep it that way. I have custody of my kids. There's no way I want him to even think of getting next to them again. Keep him out of our family affairs!'

Jay put his arm around Susan's waist and pulled her back from Brian while giving her an affectionate hug. He felt her relax. She was on a heavy jag that caused wide emotional swings.

Jay realized that it was time for the party to come to hopefully a peaceful end. "Yeah, Brian. Susan's right! We don't need Eddie to get involved. I think I got Cecile anyway. She screwed up big time last week. I can't talk about it now 'cause the lawyers got to work it through. We're in good shape. Hey, I really appreciate the way you all are backing me on this. Things will be back to normal in a few weeks. What do you say we call it a night? I got to meet a guy in the morning."

Louise was pleased with Jay's suggestion that the party end. She had been uncomfortable with the affair since she first learned of John's intent to remain sober. In her own mind, she harbored a fear that he would in some way influence Brian to change his ways. In a protective way, she put her arms around Brian and expressed her concern that Brian needed his rest after a long day making special trips for Patriot. She properly avoided mentioning that Brian was making the trips at Eddie's direction.

In custom with their usual routine the two couples busied themselves cleaning up the backyard, putting things back in order, and taking the remaining food back into the kitchen. Usually the cocaine had been consumed on previous Saturdays. This time Louise opened her purse and placed the half-used bag on the kitchen counter. She then asked Susan if she wanted the remainder since Jay had always split the cost with Brian. The leftover was rightfully Jay's since he was the only one who didn't take a sniff Susan was grateful to Louise for making the offer. She took the small bag and placed it high and deep in a kitchen cabinet.

When the cleanup details were completed Brian and Louise bid their farewells and left. Jay and Susan sat in their living room completely exhausted. It was eleven-thirty and time for bed, nearly four hours ahead of the usual Saturday night schedule.

Sunday morning at Mass Joe Durant followed his wife back to their pew after receiving Holy Communion. His mind repeated the standard prayers of thanksgiving and praise. He knelt in the pew with his head bowed in the same fashion that he had been taught by the good Sisters when he first received this Sacrament over fifty years ago. The peaceful meditation quickly bounced his mind back to the St. Anslem's fiscal crisis and political reorganization that he had been concentrating on all morning. As the Priest descended the altar to give the final blessing, Joseph Durant was damning the stupidity of the terrific trinity of Hardly, O'Shea and Patello and the inflated ego of one Dr. Richard Folley. He thought of the open warfare between his two vice presidents on Friday afternoon with the resolve to kick them in the butt if it happened again. His anger was at a flash point as the Priest, servers, cantor and lecturer processed from the altar to the back of the Church in the concluding act of the service. Indeed, Joseph Durant had fulfilled the obligation of the faithful to attend Mass on Sunday but his attention was at best divided between matters spiritual and temporal or perhaps moral and immoral if subject to penitential reflection. He felt the subtle nudge from his wife signaling time to leave the pew and depart the Church.

The warm sun felt good after the overly cooled air-conditioned Church. It was a typical failing of New Englanders to run the air conditioning at full blast when the temperature outside hovered at the seventy-five-degree mark.

They don't know heat, Durant thought. *Cold, they know; heat, they don't. They put in air conditioning and think it's going to make it snow in August. They should spend a summer in Cincinnati.*

As he walked by the elderly Priest greeting the parishioners on the way out of the Church, Durant was tempted to complain that the Church was too cold. However, the good nature of the Priest gave him pause to reconsider. He decided against the complaint and moved to his car parked across the street. His wife had preceded him to the car and was waiting for him to unlock the doors. He saw her waiting and pushed the unlock button on his security case. The double beep of the alarm system caused his wife to jump and then to give him an angry look as she opened the door. That look was his first humorous event of the day and caused him to focus on the freedom and relaxation of a beautiful Sunday. After he slipped behind the wheel he lowered the windows on his BMW to enjoy the refreshingly warm breeze. His wife promptly raised the window on her side.

Ten o'clock Mass was too late for Joe. By the time Mass was over and they returned home it was almost Noon. Mrs. Durant would fix some brunch and proceed to read the Sunday *Globe*. Joe's preference was to go to the earliest

Mass possible, run home, change clothes, and buzz down to the marina. Joe loved to spend time on his twenty-eight-foot Carver cruiser. An early start gave him time to set up the electronics, tinker with whatever needed tinkering and shoot the breeze with adjacent boat owners. Unfortunately, his routine on this Sunday was restricted due to his wife's insistence that they attend ten o'-clock Mass. By the time they got through brunch, read the paper, and drove the three miles to the marina it was nearly two P.M. Another hour of tinkering put him out of the marina on a cruise of Boston Harbor as other boats were returning. To be running against the trend was frustrating to Durant and caused his emotions to begin to peak. Besides the late hour of the afternoon signaled his physic to begin to prepare forthe usual intellectual combat that a hospital administrator experiences as the week begins.

As they returned from their afternoon cruise Joe's mind was dealing with the problems of St. Anslem's. He was making an approach to the marina's gas dock to refuel and miscalculated his speed. The marina's dock hand made every attempt to signal Joe to back down and then to slow the boat with his own weight on the line that Joe's wife had passed. Joe came too just as his cruiser began to climb the stern of an ancient blue Sea Sprite tied up at the forward pumps. He immediately reversed both engines but not in time to avoid giving the old boat a bump sending its owner over the windshield onto the bow. Dockhands successfully secured both boats without further incident.

The owner of the Sea Sprite crawled off the bow of his boat and onto the gas dock. He began shouting at the dockhands who seemed willing to take his wrath. Suddenly he turned to Joe and began calling him everything but human. Joe at first attempted to apologize but saw that the man was not about to be placated. Joe also noticed, as did everyone else, that the man was totally stoned. His threats and vulgarity caused the gas attendant to call the harbor master who arrived immediately. The Harbor Master somehow managed to calm the man and then suggested, since there was no apparent injury or damage to either vessel, that the two boat owners exchange names, addresses, telephone numbers, and insurance carriers as required by law.

Joe's wife had anticipated the information and had it prepared on one of Joe's business cards. The owner of the Sea Sprite grabbed a piece of scrap paper from the glovebox on his dash and scribbled out the information that he handed to the Harbor Master who handed it to Joe. He looked at the information and found it barely legible but adequate. Then to his surprise he noticed that the man had written the information on the back of a delivery receipt for a package from Patriot Transportion and Courier Service that had a special thank you note on the bottom from Philip Mondi, President of Patriot and parenthetically a trustee of St. Anslem's Hospital. The package had been delivered on Friday by a special courier named Brian who had also signed the receipt. Joe thought he might get an insight on the man from Mr. Mondi at the Tuesday board meeting. Carefully he placed the information in his wallet.

Jay slept in Sunday morning. It was almost nine-thirty when he jumped out of bed remembering with a start that he had an appointment with Bob Markley at St. A's at ten. After a quick shower, he dressed and jumped in his Jeep. Susan and the kids were at the breakfast table as Jay made his Dagwood exit. They waved to their disappearing Dad and accepted Susan's assurance that he wouldn't be gone long. Jay pointed the Jeep toward Brighton and hit the gas pedal.

He pulled into the outpatient free parking at ten fifteen, bailed out of the vehicle and ran to the Unit. The nurse at the station was unaware that Jay had an appointment with Markley. It wasn't on the schedule. She was also not aware that Markley was coming in. She was aware that he had not yet appeared in the Unit. Nevertheless, she invited Jay to be comfortable in the "lounge." She also offered to notify another counselor if Markley didn't show.

With his confidence in Markley beginning to slip Jay nursed his anxiety as he waited in the lounge. He had managed to beg a cup of coffee from the nurse at the station and was beginning to relax when he heard Markley greeting the nurse down the hall. A few minutes later he stuck his head into the "lounge" and invited Jay to meet with him in Dr. Kenneth's office. When they were both seated Markley offered an apology for being late but did not attempt any explanation.

Jay did not require an explanation but felt slightly offended that none was offered. He, nevertheless accepted the apology and began the conversation. "Bob, like I explained last night, Kenneth has released me to go back to work tomorrow and that's great. But he wants me to stay on the meds. I don't want any more of that shit, I got to go bare and he says that I'll need triple support".

"Right, Jay," Markley was reassuring. "I talked to Dr. Kenneth last night. He feels that you are not completely through your detox. Something could trigger a violent response that you might not be able to control. You have a temper that gets out of control very easily. That's because you are an emotional guy. You love and hate to extremes. When you go on a hate you could hurt someone or someone could hurt you. The worst result is that you would seriously hurt someone that you love. Some guys have never come back from that kind of a trip."

Jay was not convinced. "Well, I haven't lost it in a while. You know that I've taken all kinds of crap without bustin' anybody. You know I'm under control."

Markley was reassuring. "You're under control because you have been taking medication for the past six days. You have a buildup in your system that will carry you for an indeterminable amount of time. As that stuff wears off you will either go back on drugs and/or go crazy and hurt someone. Believe me. I've been there. We can't make you take the medication. You can do as you please. What Kenneth wants me to do is keep a real close check on you, like every couple of hours, to see if we can anticipate when you are going to crash. Then we send over a truck and haul you back in here for a dope job."

Jay was not amused. "So how is this supposed to work? You call me every couple of hours at work to see if I'm still among the sane and living. Suppose I ain't at my desk? Then what? You send over the dope mobile? People will think the place has turned into a trauma center. You got to come up with a better system."

Markley gave Jay a direct answer. "The best system is for you to take the medication. That way we can trust your emotions. Otherwise, we have to keep you in a net. We don't have the high-tech stuff like cardiology. There are no Holitor monitors in our arsenal. Just plain old infantry is all we have. Here's what we can try. Your medication has been given once a day at around ten A.M. You're just overdue. Suppose you take a dose now and another tomorrow morning before you go to work. Then I check on you tomorrow afternoon around three or so. If things are cool, then we try to get by Tuesday but I check on you throughout the day just to be safe. You take another dose on Wednesday and we try to stretch it out to Saturday. Gradually you come off the stuff in about two weeks."

"Ween me off is what you mean." Jay was adamant. "No way. I'll take a dose now like you want. Then we talk about it some more on Wednesday. If I'm still in good shape then we go another couple of days. You can call all you want in the meantime."

Markley was now on the defensive and looking for an out. "Jay, I just thought of something. Suppose we do it like you just said except that you come to our support groups on Tuesday and Thursday nights. You take a little extra time to pee in the bottle like you do now. That way we can keep tabs on each other and maintain the emotional support therapy as well. Is it a deal? Think about it. You have the weekends free."

Jay heard the sound about the weekend. He was growing weary of the haggling over the medication. The meeting with Markley had not been as sympathetic as he had hoped. He was being pressured to continue a process that he wasn't convinced he needed. Yet he knew that the legal fight over Kristie would require him to have some demonstration of sobriety. Grudgingly he accepted. "Okay, Robert, you got a deal."

Markley was pleased that Jay was willing to attend two support groups during the week. That was actually his goal in the first place but he had to get Jay to buy the idea. There was one other point that needed to be accomplished. "Good, Jay. It's not the ideal method but it will do, I suppose. You drive a hard bargain. Remember, this is in your best interest. I don't get a damn thing out of helping you. You're just like any other drunk to me. You see it any different?"

Jay's anger peaked. "Don't get anything out of helping me! Markley, you hypocritical son of a bitch. You get off helping drunks and dopers. You need me and everyone like me. Man, you are so full of shit."

"Yeah, right," Markley fired back. "I really need you. You and this load of junkies. You think that you qualify as an addict? Man, you got to feel that hook before you know you're on."

Jay countered. "I'm on, baby. I know that. I'll admit it. But I'll control it. Yeah, you watch."

That's it, thought Markley. *The kid just said the magic words, "I'll admit it." Now if I can just get him to admit that he needs help to control it then he is on his way in the never-ending struggle toward recovery. Yeah.*

The conversation between Jay and Markley lasted about a half-hour. As they were completing their discussion Dr. Kenneth came in to make his Sunday morning rounds. Bob and Jay both reported the outcome of their conversation after which Dr. Kenneth gave Jay his last dose of medication. Then he wrote the appropriate note in the record authorizing Jay's return to work. The nurse on duty filled out the form for Jay to turn in to the EAP supervisor at

Action Waste Management. The form stated that Jay had received treatment at St. Anslem's for a medical disorder and was now able to resume duties.

Markley gave Jay a schedule of the support groups that meet on Tuesday and Thursday evenings at seven P.M. in the hospital cafeteria. He explained to him that he could report into the Unit at six-thirty and give his urine specimen before the meeting began. With sincere appreciation Jay shook Bob Markley's and Dr. Kenneth's hands and left the Unit to drive home. He turned into his driveway at about the same time that Durant arrived home from Mass.

Kristie was waiting on the front porch of her maternal grandparents at precisely five P.M. as scheduled. Jay drove the Jeep into the driveway and waved for Kristie to get in the Jeep. She ran immediately to the car but Jay had second thoughts. As she entered on the right side Jay exited on the left. He went to the front door and knocked. Cecile's father answered after a brief wait. Jay explained that Kristie was in his care. He thanked the old man for having her ready. Cecile's father appreciated Jay taking the time to come to the door. He offered a cold beer to Jay and seemed to want to talk. Jay again thanked the man for his kindness but used the excuse that dinner was waiting for back home. He concluded the conversation with a promise to take Cecile's father fishing in the near future. With that finished he reentered the Jeep and headed for Waltham.

When they arrived home, Susan had a well-prepared dinner waiting. The Marquart family enjoyed the meal. Afterwards they played in the yard until dark. Susan supervised the baths and Jay read stories. When the right hour came, Susan put Benny and James to bed while Jay drove Kristie to Roslindale. She was in her mother's arms by ten P.M.

Chapter Ten

Summer haze destroyed the view of Boston Harbor as Charles Patello drove North on Interstate 93. The sun was barely visible as it appeared to rise out of the distant ocean in the east. In a couple of hours, the heat from the rising sun would dissipate the fog and give way to a clear warm day. For the time being motorists would occasionally use their windshield wipers to clear the damp fog. Headlights were on and speeds were moderate except for a few reckless souls seemingly in a hurry to begin the day's labor. It was only six-fifteen in the morning but traffic was bumper to bumper caused by late weekenders returning to Boston for an early Monday morning start. Patello was on schedule, however, as he pulled off the Interstate at exit 19 and into the financial district. His office was only three blocks from the main traffic artery giving him easy in and out to the City.

The first order of the day was preparation for an important meeting with Frank Capizzi, Tony Marone, and Tom Callahan. The New York trio was due in on the shuttle from LaGuardia at nine o'clock. The time from Logan Airport to Patello's office was less than an hour in traffic which meant the meeting could begin before ten. Between now and then Patello intended to pull his extensive file of St. Anslem's for review by Callahan, He would also make copies of special items like the work done by Hardly Security and Trust's planning wizards that justified the Office of Health Affairs for the Archdiocese.

Another item on Patello's agenda for the week was to further conversations he had over the weekend with several prominent, wealthy individuals who held stock in Cambridge Banks. Patello spent most of Sunday in the locker room and bar of the exclusive Oceanview Country Club courting the ear of the investors. Everyone he talked to in friendly and informal conversation was attracted to the idea of merging the two banks held by the Hardly boys. Patello had offered to expand the idea with some initial fiscal analysis that he promised to provide in a very confidential way. Uncle Frank's idea had taken root.

Joseph Durant left his home in Hingham at six-thirty and arrived at St. Anslem's at seven-fifteen. He did his usual routine and then checked with his faithful executive assistant to be sure that Abbott and Costello, otherwise known as Daly and Weaver, would be in his office at exactly eight AM. She confirmed that both executives had been notified on Friday that the meeting was so scheduled. Durant became tense. He ordered his assistant to begin immediately to find the executives and make sure that they were on time. He was determined to make them disciplined.

Ken Ryan was in the shower at six-thirty. He intended to be at his desk at Action Waste Management an hour ahead of his usual start time in order to prepare the day's work schedule. The Boston Project was in process. Boston Hospital had signed on Friday thanks to the enlightened Commissioner of Health, Michael Megan. Now the wandering intellect of Action's crack sales manager, His "Worthlessness," Mr. Veto Celi, was to be displayed at the President's office at St. Anslem's Hospital to explain the advantages of a waste management contract with Action. Considering that Mr. Celi was an expert in propositions that one could not refuse, it was a forgone conclusion by Mr. Ryan that he would have his staff actively engaged in the St. Anslem's contract by noon. Ryan intended to use Jay Marquart as the lead technician on the St. A's agreement.

By seven-thirty Dr. Ron Anderson, Medical Director of SACAP, had reviewed the Medical Record of Jay Marquart. He had also studied the incident report clipped to the back of the chart. If anything, he felt that Bob Markley had understated the importance of the incident. Dr. Anderson asked his secretary to call Mr. Markley to come to his office for an urgent conference on the Marquart affair. He also asked her to invite Dr. Kenneth to the meeting. For the present time, however, he felt the matter should be restricted to the three of them.

Bob Markley came into the Unit just as Dr. Anderson's Office called for the meeting. The unit secretary handed him the phone. After he hung up, he informed the nurse that he was headed for the Big Office. On the way, he popped into the cafeteria for a cup of coffee and a donut. *Anderson wouldn't mind a twenty-minute delay en route*, he thought. *He takes that long to come up with his next word.*

As Bob sat munching his donut he noticed the hospital chaplain having a conversation with Tommy the Tout. "Geez, there goes the Mass card money," was his first reaction. Then he saw Tommy give the Priest some money. "My God, Father won!" was his second take. On his third glance, he noticed that Tommy held a Mass card in his hand. Obviously, Tommy the Tout had invested in the spiritual welfare of the dearly departed, most certainly one of his customers who hadn't welched. In Tommy's mind, he was covering the spread.

With renewed faith in God and man, Bob Markley finished his donut and coffee, took his cup and saucer to the dish conveyer, and walked to Dr. Anderson's office. When he arrived, the secretary ushered him into the office of his leader. Ron Anderson was a diamond in the rough. He hated administration but was a very capable administrator in his own right. That is to say he did things by his own rules instead of the rules of the institution. The Jay Marquart incident frustrated him because he couldn't figure out a resolution to the problem without using the standard administrative procedure for potential malpractice claims. His reason for inviting Markley and Dr. Kenneth to a meeting was to see if the three of them could conjure up a better way of disposing of the incident.

As Markley entered his office, Anderson gave him a typical Anderson greeting. "Well, pickled brain, you got this one really messed up. What's your answer to this mess? What took you so long to get here, anyway?"

Markley was accustomed to the gruff talk of Anderson. Indeed, it was his frank nature and direct approach that had contributed so well to Markley's road to recovery. After which Markley found that his own personality was a good match for Anderson. As a team, they had formed the SACAP program that was just beginning to be recognized by the medical staff as successful. Anderson had carefully selected community-based primary care practitioners to be the medical staff in the Unit while Markley had carefully worked with nursing to develop the support staff. Dr. Kenneth was one of the first physicians to join the team. He had completed a medical residency at St. Anslem's several years before. During those years he was seen as one of the most promising physicians in his class and was elevated to the position as Chief Resident. In that capacity, he and Dr. Anderson quickly established a strong sense of mutual admiration that carried forward into his private practice.

As Markley was attempting to respond to Anderson's opening inquiry, Dr. Kenneth arrived. Kenneth greeted both men and immediately inquired about the nature of the meeting. Without saying a word Anderson handed Kenneth the Incident Report and Markley's notes. The three men sat in silence as Kenneth reviewed the information.

Kenneth completed reading the report and placed the information on Anderson's desk. As he did so Anderson began to offer his analysis. "This is the first I was aware that Jay was thinking of suing the hospital. He is somewhat difficult but manageable I thought. He never said anything to me about the conversation with his ex-wife. The fact that she works here is in the notes. Bob charted the incident when Jay broke up the lounge the first time. The record does note that he reacted following a telephone conversation. I didn't know that crazy telephone system was really the cause. It seems to me that the nature of this incident could cause the hospital a lot of trouble. There does not seem to be any basis for professional malpractice which would make this a general liability case. I guess the lawyers will decide that."

Markley nodded his agreement before commenting. "Jay signed into the program in an attempt to maintain confidentiality of his medical record. The hospital through its telephone system violated the patient's right to confidentiality. We screwed up plain and simple. I think the man has a good case that could cost the hospital big bucks but worse than that we could lose our Accreditation and Federal Certification. We lose that and there goes the revenue. Durant would close us down in a New York minute. Count on it."

"A couple of things come to mind," commented Anderson. "First I think there is a professional malpractice act by the patient's ex-wife. If she uses this information for her personal intent then she has violated her professional ethics and the ethics of the hospital as well. Secondly, I agree with Bob's observation that Administration would close us down. Even with our accreditation in good order, I'm being badgered to cut the program back to nothing in order to break even. A big law suit would take us off the Board for good. Anybody have an idea how we can get around this?"

Anderson's two colleagues looked at one another in silence. This was the first time that either of them had ever heard their leader ask them for a way around an administrative problem. He was the one who always had a way of dealing with the issue at hand. He had never lost in an administrative contest of rules. Now it appeared that he was helpless in circumventing the incident.

After a brief period of silence, Kenneth made a suggestion." This may seem reckless, Ron, but why don't we play it by the book. You know, send in the report through channels and let administration find a way out. Hell, we didn't buy the phone system. Durant and his band of merry men put the thing in. Nobody asked us if it violated patient confidentiality. My guess is that the hospital lawyers will do everything they can to avoid looking stupid as rocks. This thing will never get to court. How can Durant justify the stupidity of administration? If he tries to close us down as a cover up he really sticks his foot in it. I bet the lawyers will tell him to keep us going no matter what. This thing could really be our salvation."

Markley realized that it was his turn to speak. "Dr. Kenneth, if we do as you suggest then we are hanging a nurse out to dry. This thing will fall on her like a ton of bricks. It seems to me that a lawyer would reason that the telephone system, as faulty as it is, is inhuman and therefore incapable of violating confidence. Only a person can do that and the person who did it is a nurse in the employ of St. Anslem's. She has a reason for using patient information for her own intent. The hospital will have to defend her but only to the point that she violated the hospital rules. After that she is on her own. She could lose her license over this."

Kenneth felt uncomfortable defending his point considering Markley's comment. He gave a slight wave of his hands as a signal that the nurse was not his concern.

Anderson caught the signal and decided to speak to the idea. "Bob, the nurse is responsible for her own actions and therefore her own defense. She is not a nurse on our Unit so we have no control of her actions. She is the one who committed the malpractice, allegedly. If we try to cover this matter then we become an accomplice to the act. I think Kenneth is right. Maybe we should do it by the book. That, at least, would throw administration. They hardly expect me to follow procedure. I might go one better than expected and bring this matter personally to the attention of Folley and Durant. I'll ask them both to meet with me on an urgent matter. That way I'll have them off guard. Just as soon as I get the meeting, I'll see that risk management gets the incident report at the same time so they can't blame me for hiding anything. On the other hand, once Risk Management has the report they have to process it so Durant can't cover it up by sticking it in my ear. I'll try to move this thing this morning. It'll make Folley's day."

Markley saw the lights go on. The Old Man was back in charge. He would blow administration away with the realization that their decision to install a stupid telephone system was the cause of a major problem that not only threatened the hospital's reputation but brought into question the professionalism and ethics of its nursing staff.

Kenneth could be right, he thought. *This might be a blessing in disguise.*

Mitch Daly walked into the President's office at seven fifty-five. He was always early. Rod Weaver by contrast was always late. Daly intended to make Weaver's delinquency evident by his early arrival. In his usual aggressive manner, he announced himself to the executive assistant and walked immediately into Durant's office acting as though he expected the meeting to be in session. Durant was still fusing to himself about Folley and at first tried to ignore Daly's presence.

Daly, detecting the cold shoulder, asserted himself into the Boss's presence by making conversation. "As usual Rod is late, Joe. If you like we can begin to discuss the planning process. I don't think Rod will be able to contribute much to the conversation anyway. That was pretty disgusting conduct on Friday. You handled it well. I made some calls on Friday and have some good advice on strategic planning. I have copies of my notes that we can go over anytime that you want."

Durant realized that he could not easily escape this conversation without throwing Daly out of his office. This would not only frustrate him but would cause more delay in developing a planning format for presentation at the Board meeting tomorrow morning. Since he did not want to start the meeting without Weaver, he decided to humor Daly until Rod made the scene.

Durant stood up and walked over to his office door. "You want some coffee, Mitch? I'm going to have some. That was a very unsatisfactory scene Friday. I hope you two have gotten it out of your system so we can have a productive session this morning."

Daly was relieved that the subject had been brought up. He was not the type who apologized but who always sought out the opportunity to rationalize his every action. He walked with Joe to the coffee pot in the reception area but did not accept the offer of the senior executive to pour him a cup of coffee. Instead he commented, "Joe, you noticed I'm sure that the confrontation was initiated by Rod's refusal to accept the need for a strategic plan developed by market analysis. He will not accept any data that he hasn't had the opportunity to massage into his own format. I believe he refers to it as 'cooking' the facts. He does it every month with the financial statements. You know that. Well, if we are going to have an objective planning effort I'll have to be put in charge of the data gathering and Rod will have to keep his hands off."

Durant was intent on keeping the team approach intact. He was not interested in excluding Weaver from the data. "Mitch, we can discuss the details of information at our gathering when Rod arrives. I'm sure each of you has sources that are unique to your position. I know, for instance that Rod has some very reliable data concerning the cost of operations in the various Boston teaching hospitals. I imagine that information will be very helpful. You have shown me market data and utilization reports for the entire State that we can incorporate in our analysis. I believe that both of you are vital to this project."

"But somebody has to be in charge," insisted Daly. "That corn-fed accountant will procrastinate forever. I said Friday that we had to regain control. We have to move fast to compile a set of facts that are objective so we can formulate an objective plan. Creative accounting won't work in these changing times. You know that I'm right."

The two executives walked back into Durant's office and sat at the small conference table. Durant was thinking about how to respond to Daly's comments when the executive assistant came into the office and announced that Rod Weaver had called in to report that he was caught in traffic the Mass Pike. He estimated his time of arrival at ten A.M. She also informed Mr. Durant that a Mr. Veto Celi of Action Waste Management was waiting to see him. She placed Mr. Celi's card on the table and left.

Durant had completely lost his concentration on Daly's suggestion. He was barely able to control his anger toward Weaver who should have left home earlier to avoid the usual traffic snarls on the Pike. This only tended to authenticate Daly's point about Weaver. It also meant that without Weaver the present meeting was a Daly benefit. It seemed to Durant that to continue the discussion with Daly was useless unless he was willing to put Daly in charge.

"On second thought" he concluded, "maybe if I give the lead to Daly, Weaver will be more responsive to protecting his turf and therefore more of a contributor to the process." With that in mind he responded to Daly. "Mitch, we are obviously not going to get much accomplished in the time we have this morning but I want to be prepared to give the Board a review of our planning process tomorrow. You put one together for me to review later this afternoon. If it looks okay then you can present it to the Board. I'll explain this to Weaver when he shows up."

Daly was elated with the charge. He immediately pulled an outline out of his briefcase and put it on the conference table.

Durant waved his hand across his chest to cancel the move. "Mitch, I'm pressed for time right now. We can go over this later today. There's a gentleman waiting to see me and I guess a few others that are pressing the schedule. We'll talk about this later. Please excuse me."

The expression on Daly's face was reminiscent of a scolded child. He slowly retrieved the outline and placed it back in the briefcase. As he walked out of the office he reminded Durant that he had put him in charge of the process. He also reminded Durant that it was vital to the conduct of the strategic plan for Weaver to be subordinated. Durant had his orders.

As Daly left the office Durant collapsed in his desk chair. His emotions were about spent in one meeting trying to corral the slippery intellects of Daly and Weaver. Unfortunately, he had no choice but to continue the effort since the pressure caused by O'Shea, Folley and now Logan had to be offset by a dramatic counter move. He scribbled a note to call Patello before noon. As he moved the notepad next to his telephone his eye caught sight of a short burly gentleman with no neck and a flat bent nose standing at this desk.

When Joe looked up the man sat down and introduced himself. "Joe Durant, I'm Veto Celi with Action Waste Management. You probably forgot that I was here so I came on in. We got to talk about your waste. You got a problem."

Joe Durant felt the intimidation as it was offered. He also realized that this was no ordinary salesman. "Mr. Celi, I apologize about the delay. I had an appointment with a gentleman who just left and I was making a few notes. What is this problem about waste? St. Anslem's has a very satisfactory arrangement with the City for waste handling that we intend to keep in effect."

Veto leaned forward and placed a small plastic bag on Durant's desk. "Yeah, well, you had an arrangement with the City. You got canceled this morning. No more waste handling. Here's why."

Celi popped opened the plastic bag and dumped the contents on Durant's desk. Several syringes, IV tubing, bloody bandages, and various pieces of paper with the St. Anslem's logo were spread before the hospital chief executive.

"You see, all this was found in your last load that was supposed to be clean waste. You ain't separating your trash right so the City ain't gonna haul it no more. We're gonna do it for you and we are gonna see that you do a good separation job. We'll take care of everything. No hassle. You sign now and we can have our guys on the job tomorrow. You got no worries. The press ain't aware of any of this cause the new Commissioner is looking out for the hospitals."

More intimidation, thought Durant. *This thug has got a pair. He also has me by the trash if he is right about the City canceling the waste contract.*

In response Durant attempted a counter bluff. "Mr. Celi, we have no information about this from the City. If they do intend to cancel our arrangement then they have to give us proper notice. I believe the contract calls for a sixty-day notice of cancellation. If we are to use a private service we would select the company on a bid basis. Your offer of immediate support is appreciated but I don't think it's necessary."

Veto Celi leaned back in the chair and rested his large folded hands on his portly expanse. "Durant, you got no contract with the City. They been doing the trash because of the Ordinance that got changed last week. Private companies are in the business now. The City can cancel who it wants anytime it wants. Now, you want to do business with someone else. Okay. Find another company that's ready to go. There ain't any. So, you haul your own trash, or let it pile up and face a big fine, or do business with us. You probably got called from the City on Friday. You take the day off?"

Durant was uncertain about Celi's comments. It was true that he had not seen a contract with the City for trash hauling. The subject had never come up before. The arrangement was taken for granted. If the City had called to cancel on Friday, a message would have been noted by the executive assistant or if the call came after hours it would have been registered on the voicemail system.

Durant tried to reason again. "Sir, I can assure you that I have not received any call from the City canceling our waste hauling agreement. As far as I know we still have the service."

Celi remained unmoved. "Okay. Look, maybe they talked to someone else. Who you got in charge of trash? They got a call I bet. You better check with them."

Without hesitation Durant hit the speed dial button for the hospital's chief operating officer. The COO was making administrative rounds when Durant called. However, the secretary in the office acknowledged that the hospital's Director of Environmental Services had been notified by the City just an hour ago that they had discontinued the waste hauling service. She also reported that the COO and the DES were going to meet in an hour to determine how to solve this crisis. Durant explained to her that he had the solution near at hand and asked that the two managers meet with him in his office at the scheduled time.

As Durant hung up the phone, Celi again propped himself on the desk. "You got the word like I said, right? Now we can do business. Here is the standard contract that you sign. We send in some people to do a special review then we write up the extras. You always got to have extras. Like I said, we can start today or tomorrow on a handshake. You can trust me and I know that I can trust you. We gonna get along fine."

Durant took the contract from Celi's extended hand. He gave it a fast review and noted the unilateral advantage to the seller. The price was pre-printed in the contract as a base on which the extras would be added. The initial fee was thirty thousand dollars plus a monthly service fee of twenty-five thousand dollars. Before any extras were figured in the annual expense in the first year of the agreement was a minimum of three hundred and thirty thousand dollars. This was pure expense add on. No replacement of existing costs or revenue offset. The total amount fell right to the bottom line as another increase to the rapidly growing deficit.

Weaver would love this deal, he thought. *Just one more item to make the fiscal wizard an unhappy camper.*

The irritation had to be evident on Durant's face. Nevertheless, Celi gave no solace. He, instead, pushed the point. "You want to talk it over with your people? Okay. Call me this afternoon so I can arrange for a pickup in the morning. Like I said we can do business now on a handshake. That number on my card will go directly to Mr. Meehan's office. He's the big shot at Action. He tells me he knows you and the hospital. Anyway, he'll let me know when you decide. It's a pleasure doing business with you. I got to run along. "

As Celi stood to leave he extended his hand to Durant. Joe was sensitive to Celi's prompting him to do business on a handshake. He doubted that this clod recognized the fine points of contract, but a handshake at this point was establishing a contract. Joe did not take Celi's hand but put his own hand on Celi's back and politely escorted him out of the office with the understanding that Mr. Durant would call Mr. Meehan's office with a response in the next few hours.

Rod Weaver had finally arrived and was chatting with the executive assistant when Celi walked out of the office escorted by Durant. As they passed, Weaver hastily moved into Durant's office and settled down. He had the up to date financial report spread out on the conference table when Durant returned.

"Boss, we went down another million five last month but I covered some of it with prior period adjustments," Weaver explained without looking up from the report. "We still lost over a million at the operating line and about three hundred thou bottom line. That's what I was working on this morning early. I figured you would want me to finish this instead of bullshitting with Daly."

Durant couldn't make up his mind on where to begin. His first instinct was to chew Weaver out for disregarding the directive to attend the meeting with Daly. He also had to find the appropriate way to tell Weaver that he had put Daly in charge of the planning effort. More pressing was the matter with waste hauling that was going to add over three hundred thousand dollars to the operating loss now projected at fifteen million dollars.

Durant chose to initiate the discussion about the waste. "Rod, we have been blessed with another challenge. It seems that the big change in City Hall last week not only gave us Mr. Logan but it also gave us three hundred thousand dollar increased expenses in the environmental services budget. We have, or are about to have, an exclusive agreement with Action Waste Management to haul our waste and manage our waste control. You have the assignment to find the money to pay for it."

Weaver remained calm. "The only way is to start cutting out programs that aren't self-sufficient. That means we have to take on the docs especially Folley. He pisses it away faster than anybody. Hey, isn't Action owned by one of our trustees? We can't do business with them. It's a breach of the conflict of interest regulation. You going to bring that up tomorrow?"

Durant looked at Weaver with shock. "Come on, Rod. The whole damn board is one big conflict of interest. We do our banking with Hardly Security run by Hardly and O'Shea. Sr. Elizabeth and Bishop Hanks have spiritual equity and Dr. Folley earns his daily bread here, more or less. Now that Meehan is dipping in, that only leaves Patello and Mondi without a piece. I bet if we look hard enough we would find that they have something going for them too. Best we don't look and I sure as hell am not going to raise the conflict of interest issue. I'll report the waste contract matter and see what happens."

Carefully, Weaver folded the financial report and placed it back in his briefcase. "Boss, three hundred thousand is going to look like a good deal compared to what I figure the Cardinal's Office for Health Affairs will cost. I estimate it at over a million dollars for salaries, wages, supplies and rent. We don't have that in the budget either. Two months of that will add another couple hundred thousand to this year to date deficit with only two months left in the fiscal year. Next fiscal year, starting in October, we predict another twenty percent drop in revenue. Something has got to give. We better let the Board in on this disaster."

Durant was quick to reply. "Rod, I suspect that Mr. O'Shea will expand on that topic quite adequately. How Folley and Logan will react is beyond me. I do know that Patello is going to work with us in an attempt to regain control through the planning effort. That's what I needed you for this morning. Since you were engaged in other happier things like the deficit I told Mitch to take charge and develop the process. I'll see his outline this afternoon and he'll present it to the Board with Patello tomorrow."

Weaver began to react but was cut short by Durant who moved to answer the phone. The executive assistant reported that Dr. Anderson was holding on a matter of urgency. He insisted that she interrupt the meeting with Weaver adding parenthetically that Weaver never had anything of substance to talk about anyway.

Durant excused Weaver, subject to recall later in the day, and took the call from Anderson. "Dr. Anderson, and good morning. What pray tell is of such great urgency that you would interrupt my discussion about the deficit to which you contribute so generously?"

Anderson accepted Durant's jab in good humor since he was often prone to taking a few good-natured shots at the President. "Joe, we have a situation in SACAP that could mean big trouble. I've filed an incident report but think that you, Folley and I should review this matter and decide how we keep it under control. It's either a big malpractice mess or gigantic general liability problem. Apparently Folley is available now if you are."

Durant's many years as a hospital administrator had sensitized him to malpractice and the delicate process of discovery so rigidly applied by plaintiffs' attorneys. He had often painfully collected all records pertaining to an incident in response to interrogatories and had sat for hours giving depositions or serving as witness at trial. If the incident that Anderson was reporting was as serious as it seemed then the meeting that he was asking for would eventually be discovered and subject to examination by the plaintiff. The only way to avoid having the meeting subject to discovery was to meet under the hospital's professional review and quality assurance process that was privileged from discovery under Massachusetts law. Until that could be arranged Durant knew that it was best for him not to be informed or involved.

The Risk Manager at St. Anslem's reported to the Director of Professional Review and Quality Assurance who reported to the Professional Review Committee of the Board of Trustees. The President of the hospital served as a member of the committee but like all other members could not influence the agenda of the meeting. That method of organization assured that all incident reports regardless of nature or severity were reported and reviewed by the committee. The only way an incident could avoid review was if it were not reported to risk management or if risk management omitted the incident from the committee report. In either case the individual responsible for the omission became personally liable. As a consequence, the risk management process at St. Anslem's was excellent. Conversely the quality of care at St. Anslem's was also excellent. The entire staff took great pride in the very low frequency of incidents and the very rare malpractice law suits.

Durant was very curious about Anderson's incident report but did not want to violate the privilege process by having an impromptu meeting. Instead he offered an alternative approach. "Let's have your meeting, Ron, but do it under the auspices of the Professional Review Director. That way the meeting will be a part of his investigation that he will report to the Board Committee. If this thing is as hot as you say then we don't want to get caught outside of privileged communication. We have to keep it under wraps. Okay? Now as far as a big rush is concerned, the Professional Review report for the Board is complete for tomorrow. The next full meeting of the Board is two months from tomorrow so if any Board action regarding the incident is necessary it will have to wait that long. In the interim, we'll have the insurance company involved and the lawyers and whoever else is necessary to keep it in control."

Anderson remained insistent but amiable toward the process. He, nevertheless, had to suppress his anger as he responded to Durant. "Joe, I realize the need to keep this thing privileged so if you want to have the Quality Director at the meeting that's okay with me. My only concern or I should say my greatest concern is that the people involved will be in a civil action that will bring us to the front in less than the two months it will take to get this to the Board. I don't think it matters if you report it to the Board tomorrow or not. What really matters to the hospital is our reputation that could be smeared all over page one. We have employees violating patient confidence. We have a goofy telephone system that does the same thing. We have a possible violation of Federal Law and our Joint Commission Accreditation at stake. Now, do you want to talk about this or not?"

Durant was not persuaded. "Ron, for the second time this morning I have been given a proposition that I cannot refuse. I'll try to arrange something today or first thing tomorrow after the Board meeting. As usual, it's been a pleasure talking to you."

Durant hung up the phone and glanced at his watch. It was almost eleven-thirty. In the past few hours he had been conned by one vice-president, snubbed by another vice-president, shaken down by a hitman turned salesman, told that the place was going bankrupt, and informed by a physician that the hospital had screwed up royally. All things considered it was a fairly typical Monday morning.

A brief walk in the summer air before lunch seemed like a smart idea. Durant waved to his executive assistant as he passed her door. Once outside his office he sensed the freedom to think. The walk around the hospital campus at noon always gave him time to reflect on the morning's events. The most important thing in his mind was the need to formulate a planning proposal for the Board. Daly had to be the front man. He knew that Weaver would be supportive in the meeting. Weaver in spite of his unusual character was loyal and a team player especially when the chips were down. He made up his mind not to attempt to change the spots on his two vice presidents at this critical time. The hospital's fiscal problem was certainly obvious to everyone on the Board. O'Shea could scream and holler all he wanted but it would not make a difference. It was curious how O'Shea could support the idea of an Office for Health Affairs if Weaver's projections were right that a million dollars were to be added to the hospital's expenses. Durant from Action Waste Management bothered Durant. One of the hospital's trustees had apparently sent this goon over to break St. Anslem's leg. Since there was obviously no alternative for the hospital, it seemed that the approach could have been more subtle. He made a mental note to ask Meehan about it in the morning.

All things considered the Anderson matter seemed to be the least significant. He intended to ask the Director of Professional Review and Quality Assurance to pull the incident report and call a special meeting as part of his routine investigation. *No sense making it a Federal case just yet,* he thought. *These malpractice matters take a long time to resolve anyway.*

As he returned to his office, the executive assistant handed him a note to call Dr. Folley immediately on a very urgent matter. Durant's first inclination was to throw the note in the waste basket which he did. Talking to Folley was the last thing he wanted to do in view of the morning's events. As he began to read the day's correspondence the private line to his office lit up as the phone rang.

The private line by passed the executive assistant and was seldom used except in extremely important and highly confidential matters. Its main function was for outgoing calls. Since incoming calls was not the purpose of the extension, the number was not listed in the hospital's directory. To Durant's knowledge the number was known only by his executive assistant and his wife. Most of the time incoming calls were wrong numbers. He casually lifted the handset and said hello.

There was a pause before the caller reacted to the bland greeting. "Hello! Is that how you answer your phone? You're supposed to be the chief executive officer of Boston's most prestigious Catholic hospital and you answer with a stupid hello. It's no wonder people have no respect for us. Did you get my message that I wanted to talk to you?"

Durant took a deep breath as a way of warding off the temptation to slam the receiver down. "Yes, Dr. Folley, I did get your message and I intended to call you at the first opportunity. How's Mrs. Folley and the kids? Well, I hope. And does all go the same with you?"

"Durant, don't hand me any of your smooze. Save it for the Nuns. They buy it. Where do you come off telling my Director of SACAP that you're not going to meet with me about the screw up in the Unit. Now let me tell you how it is. I'm not going to meet with you. No Sir! You are going to meet with me. For the record, the SACAP incident is a matter of concern to the Cardinal and his Director of Health Affairs. As Secretary to the Cardinal, I will conduct a personal investigation of this incident. You see to it that all the appropriate records are on my desk this afternoon. This is now Archdiocesan business. Your job is to serve the cause. Do you understand?"

Durant was totally disarmed by Folley's outburst. Carefully he tried to recover from the apparent emotion of the caller to a point of reason. "Look, Richard, I don't know what happened in SACAP except that Ron thinks it's serious enough to prompt malpractice litigation. My response to Ron was in the interest of putting the discussions into a privileged forum. You might want to consult with the Archdiocesan attorney before you get too involved. Right now, the Cardinal is not likely to get sued but you could change that very easily. I'll have all the records dumped on your desk by this afternoon."

"No, I don't need the records as long as I have your report," responded Folley. "You look into this thing and give me a report. I am a trustee of this hospital entitled to this kind of information when and if I want it. Just do it and report to me," Folley demanded.

"As you wish, Herr Doctor. But if you want fast information why don't you act like a Department Chairman and talk to your Director of SACAP? Seems to me that you would be getting firsthand information rather than something I might edit. I'm sure Dr. Anderson would want to fill you in. You really don't need me in the conversation. I'll get involved when you need a solution to whatever the problem is."

Suddenly Folley was silent. The reality that he could be involved as the Chairman of the Department of Medicine had never occurred to him. It was beginning to be evident that his many hats as Secretary of Health, Hospital Trustee and Department Chairman was confusing his already complex and gigantic ego. He was now caught up in the confusion and desperately needed to retreat.

The circumstance caused Folley to have a sudden mood change. "You make a good point, Joe. I'll talk this over with Ron. We'll keep our conversations off the record. You don't need to be involved at this stage. I'll call you if I need you. Thanks for returning my call."

With all the confusion surrounding the SACAP incident Durant forgot about the meeting he had requested with the Chief operating officer and the Director of Environmental Services. After he had finished his conversation with Dr. Folley the executive assistant advised him that she had delayed the COO meeting until he had a break. They were now available and waiting in the reception area. Durant asked them into the office and again the small conference table became the locus for decision making. In response to Durant's questions the DES advised that the City had canceled the waste hauling agreement effective at eight A.M. this morning. There were no other private waste management companies in Boston other than Action that was capable of handling hospital waste. And finally, the price was high but under the amount estimated for the hospital to handle its own waste disposal.

The Chief Operating Officer offered the concluding comment: "We have no choice, Joe. Let's take the deal and look for a way out down the line. As soon as Action gets some competition the price will become more reasonable. In the meantime, we pay through the nose."

Durant nodded in agreement. After the two executives left the office Durant called Action and confirmed the acceptance of the contract.

Mark Meehan wasn't in his office when Durant called to accept the Action offer. Joe was disappointed in not being able to attempt to negotiate some improvement to the arrangement. The need to get the agreement in place immediately caused him to give Meehan's secretary the message that St. Anslem's Hospital was now a customer of Action and that Mr. Durant would like to speak to Mr. Meehan about the contract terms. The secretary took the message and, as previously instructed by Mr. Meehan, relayed the message to Mr. Celi. Celi just grunted and notified the back office that St. Anslem's was now an Action Waste Management Customer.

The back office at Action had been notified last week that the Boston project would start with hospital contracts at Boston Hospital and St. Anslem's. The Boston Hospital agreement came in on Friday and a project team had been immediately assigned. On Monday morning they had moved on site to begin to scope the project. St. Anslem's was expected to be in place on Monday so the back office was standing by waiting for the signal to begin.

Celi's call to Action's production manager triggered the first phase of the St. Anslem's project design. Kevin Ryan, as director of quality control for Action, had the assignment of doing an assessment of each project in the pre-design phase. The assessment was conducted by a team of waste management technicians who would go to the project site and completely review the existing waste handling methods and waste requirements. After the review, the technicians would present a list of recommendations for the project that Ryan would in turn present to the production manager who would send the project design to cost accounting who would determine the cost of the add-ons to the base price that also included the standard thirty percent markup. This final document would go to Mr. Meehan for signature.

Celi would not see the final contract. That was a confidential matter between Meehan and Muldoon. Meehan would add Muldoon's cut to the contract as part of the markup before letting Muldoon see the final price. When the Customer signed the contract, Action gave Muldoon his ten percent and Muldoon would think about giving Celi a piece.

Jay Marquart returned to work Monday morning on time. He felt good but was uneasy about his reception in the office. His exit last Tuesday was a bit spectacular as he experienced the trauma of detox. To his surprise and comfort, he soon realized that only Ken Ryan and the EAP director knew the true nature of his illness. The others could only speculate and few seemed to be interested in the nature of the illness but many inquired about his health while welcoming him back. It was refreshing. Jay dug in to the unfinished work on his desk and was well on the way of catching up by lunchtime.

When he returned form lunch Mr. Donovan, business agent for Local 936, was waiting at his desk. For the first time Jay felt the pressure that Markley had warned him about. Donovan had a cheery smile on his face when he greeted Jay.

"Hey, how are you feeling? Good to see you back on the job. You know I'm sorry to have to come here on your first day back but we are a little behind on getting this contract thing worked out. You know?"

"Yeah, I'm okay. Good to see you too, Donovan." Jay was immediately suspicious. "What's the agenda? I'm still new at this you know. Only been in the Union a week and sick most of the time. Any connection?"

Donovan dismissed the humor. "No connection, Jay. The purpose of the Union is to make the workers well and whole at the same time. Best we get to it."

Donovan opened his briefcase and placed a copy of the standard Union agreement form on Jay's desk. He explained each article to Jay and how each point was intended to benefit the workers. The distinctions between the non-economic and economic issues were explained in a manner that began to detail the preliminary bargaining strategy.

Jay became fascinated with the information and the relevant process. Several times he interrupted Donovan to ask questions. Donovan tolerated the interruptions as a coach would accept strategy questions from a quarterback.

The relationship between the two men was growing stronger. Jay though his fascination was rapidly becoming an advocate for the collective bargaining agreement. Donovan was a true labor pro who took note of Jay's attitude with growing pride.

Jay and Donovan had been in session for about an hour when Ken Ryan came by the desk and asked Jay to meet with him. Donovan courteously greeted Ken and acknowledged that he and Jay had about finished their conversation. Jay told Ken that he would be with him in a few minutes. As Ken left the desk Donovan continued the conversation by pointing out that a meeting of the Action Union members would be held in a few days. At that meeting Donovan would explain the contract form to the workers. Jay's assignment would be to take special note of the questions asked and by whom. Then in the next few days after the meeting he was to circulate among the employees and get their opinions and answer their questions. Then, in a week or so there would be another meeting where Donovan would present a list of Union demands that would be presented to management at the first negotiation session. Jay would be present at the negotiations and communicate progress to the employees. Donovan concluded the meeting by saying that he would keep in close touch with him over the next few days.

Jay walked Donovan to the door and then returned to Ken's desk.

Ken seemed frustrated with the workload of the Boston project. Boston Hospital's administration was apparently not cooperating with the Action project team. Staff in the Environmental Services department had refused to take the project team on tour they were forced to undertake an unguided exploration of the mammoth institution to find the various trash collection points. Nursing personnel were equally uncooperative in giving time to the surveyors for review of the waste management processes in patient care areas. All things considered the first day of the Boston project was turning into a disaster. Action's production manager had called an emergency supervisors meeting to regroup the effort when it became apparent that the Boston Hospital staff was intent on sabotaging the program. As the meeting was in process the manager received word that St. Anslem's had accepted the Action proposal and trash pickup and disposal was to begin tomorrow.

Ken Ryan was instructed to have a survey team ready to go to St. Anslem's for initial analysis in the morning. Ken explained all of this to Jay before informing him that he was to be the lead technician on the St. Anslem's part of the Boston Project. Jay couldn't believe what Ken was saying. The lead technician would be required to spend two or three weeks at St. Anslem's in the design phase and another month on a part time basis helping with the implementation. He would practically be a member of the St. Anslem's staff again but with complete freedom to roam the house looking into every nook and cranny. Ken's main concern was that St. Anslem's waste management program be designed and implemented without conflict. He had selected Jay because he was knowledgeable about hospital routine and was acquainted with the staff at St. Anslem's. Jay seemed like the perfect choice to head the project. Ken was unaware that Jay intended to sue the hospital. Jay, on the other hand, felt that piece of information was not germane to the discussion so he didn't mention it to Ken as they discussed the St. A's program.

Neither Jay nor Ken was aware that Veto Celi had conned Durant into accepting Action's contract. No one except Durant and Weaver was aware that St. Anslem's could not afford to pay for all the good service that Action intended to provide. Ken and Jay decided to outline the study phase of the program for St. A's this afternoon and go over to the hospital in the morning to meet with the appropriate members of the hospital staff to discuss the project. Ken had asked Mr. Celi to arrange the meeting. So it was that Action's finest trash men, Ken Ryan and Jay Marquart, leaped into the fray confident of success.

After Jay had accepted the assignment Ken moved to another subject. He carefully inquired about Mr. Donovan's visit. Jay felt that the matter would soon be general knowledge when Donovan distributed the contract form to the employees so he filled Ken in on the process of negotiation that Donovan had described. He also mentioned that he was a member of the negotiation team. Ken commented that with Jay's assignment at St. A's and his Union position he was a man of dual status.

Not bad for a drunk, Jay thought.

As Jay returned to his desk he received a call from the receptionist informing him that a gentleman was in the lobby who wanted to discuss a legal matter. Jay's first thought was that the person was a cop waiting to arrest him for drug trafficking at the Troubadour. When he asked the receptionist to tell the man that he wasn't in she said that he was aware that Mr. Marquart was at his desk and had asked permission to meet him there. Jay knew the day was going too well. Something like this was bound to happen. Suddenly he felt the rush of pain and concurrent anger that caused him to destroy the SACAP lobby last week. Jay told the receptionists to "send the son of a bitch in" and slammed the phone. He stood at the side of his desk and clenched a paperweight in his right hand.

No way I'm gonna take a dive from that queer bastard O'Sullivan, he pledged in his mind. *I'll knock that weirdo silly. Then they can send in the SWAT team to get me out of here.*

A small man with glasses dressed in an open collar shirt, no jacket, with faded blue jeans walked up to Jay from the opposite direction that he was facing. "Good afternoon, Mr. Marquart. Thank you for seeing me."

Jay turned abruptly and dropped the paperweight when he saw the small man. He broke into a wry smile as he greeted the alien. "Well, how do you do, little fella? What pray tell brings you to my den? Need your ashes hauled, perhaps?"

The grunt looked at the paperweight on the floor and then into Jay's eyes. "Mr. Marquart, I am an official of the Court here to present you process and notice ordering you to appear before a Judge on the date and time specified in the documents as noted. My I see your driver's license as identification?" The man sat at Jay's desk and pulled several sets of legal looking documents from his heavy bag.

Jay was stunned at the sudden direct manner. He pulled out his wallet and without any comment produced his driver's license for the man's inspection. The runt looked at the license with a nod returned it to its owner. Then he handed the papers to Jay who took them without comment. The little man then asked Jay to sign a paper certifying that process had been served. A copy of the signed paper was given to Jay and the little man disappeared.

The papers, as Jay had realized when they were presented, were the anticipated summons from Cecile's attorney. He recalled Martha's warning that they would get to him on Monday. He also remembered her warning him not to kill the messenger. She said that they would be cutthroat documents that would be very irritating. Carefully he began reading the first document and wondering if his emotions could take it. He was not up to it. Halfway through the first document he let out a scream that brought Ken running to his desk. Jay was shaking with anger as Ken put his arms around him and walked him out of the building.

After two laps around the employee parking lot Jay seemed to regain composure. Ken stayed by his side but said nothing.

Gradually Jay began to open up. "Christ, Ken, I'm sorry about that outburst. That dirty bitch, Cecile, has served me with papers to take Kristie away. Goddamn it, the things in those papers are bullshit, Ken. Pure bullshit! Man, she has started a war that she is gonna lose. I'll fry her ass. Goddamn it, Ken, she can't do that. She's gonna pay."

Ken was sympathetic. His divorce had been pure hell. The hatred between him and his first wife was intense for the first two years but gradually disappeared. Now they were friendly and occasionally met on social occasions. The fact that no children were involved in Ken's divorce made it easier to adjust the anger. That was very different from Jay's situation. Ken's second marriage produced a child that brought him to focus on the happiness of marriage and family. The pain of the first difficult experience was over. Jay's anguish brought back the memories of that experience.

Ken knew how Jay felt and he was intent to ease his pain. "Jay, I got a pretty good idea what you are going through. I'll give you whatever help I can. How you fixed for a lawyer? You need a mean legal jock that will ride her ass. My man might be the guy you want. He hits hard and takes no prisoners."

Jay was grateful for Ken's assistance. It was very necessary support that caused him to remember that he was due to attend a support session at St. A's that evening. "There's no escaping the place," came out as a sudden burst from Jay that caused Ken to give him a bewildered look. Jay continued. "Ken, I've got a ton of problems with this damn divorce thing. I need to call my sister and arrange to have her go over these damn papers. She'll help with the legal stuff and probably hook me up with the guy I used the first time. If not, then I'll mention your attorney. She knows who's who. If you can spare me for the rest of the day I'll come in early tomorrow and prep for the St. A's meeting. I won't let you down on the project, I promise. Right now, I got to start with the legal stuff. By the way I'll be over to St. A's tonight. Sort of a therapy session."

Ken looked at his watch. The day was about shot. He patted Jay on the back and told him to get lost. After Jay drove out of the parking lot Ken returned to his desk and began planning the approach to St. Anslem's management. A quick check with Celi revealed that the earliest Action's crack sales manager was able to arrange a meeting with the hospital administration was Wednesday morning at nine o'clock.

Good, thought Ken. *That gives me an extra day to prepare and extra time to get Jay back on track.*

Tom Callahan, Mario Capizzi, and Tony Marone walked into Charlie Patello's office a few minutes after ten. They looked refreshed and ready to work. After an exchange of greetings, the four men went into the conference room and spread out around the large round table. Patello had purposely removed chairs from the room in order to give each participant lots of elbow room. Fresh coffee, juice and Danish were on a side table. In front of each chair at the table was a set of documents pertaining to St. Anslem's Hospital. Audit reports, minutes from board meetings, the famous Boston Security Trust planning review, organizational charts, and a file on the top executives including Joe Durant, Rod Weaver, and Mitch Daly were at the ready. Patello had also prepared a summary report of each of the Boardmembers. Dr. Richard Folley's report was extensive and was his father-in-law's report by Thomas O'Shea. The rest were one page documents extracted from the Boston Register.

Patello suggested that the first hour of the meeting be spent in silence while each person did their own review of the documents. After the review, he would answer questions about the information or as requested get additional data to supplement the information at hand. He then suggested that following the data review: The meeting would be divided into three segments. The first segment would be a tactical discussion about Park's entry into the Boston healthcare market. The second segment would be an analysis of St. Anslem's potential as an assist to Park's objectives. The third and concluding segment would be a detailed plan for the invasion of the Boston Healthcare market using St. Anslem's as a resource when and if appropriate.

Torn Callahan was impressed with Patello's organization of the meeting. He complemented Charlie and suggested that some additional information that he had brought along regarding the Health Maintenance organizations be distributed and included in the first hour information review session. Charlie was quick to agree. He also asked Tom to lead the discussions in the following three segments. Tom, true to his consultant status, was pleased to accept the assignment.

Mario took off his coat, filled his coffee cup, and directed a comment to Tony. "Christ, I guess we are back in school. You and I will sit here with our hands folded and do our homework. Sounds like we are in for a serious session."

The real Boston Project was about to begin. The document review session took less than an hour. It was apparent to Callahan that the three men were ready for discussion after about forty-five minutes. Patello had left the room to make a phone call, Capizzi was staring out the window at Boston Harbor, and Marone was in the men's room. As soon as they returned, Callahan brought the document discussion to order. Callahan offered the first observation that St. Anslem's seemed to have a complete lack of corporate direction. He also observed that the Health Maintenance organizations were moving into exclusive arrangements with providers that could offer organized delivery or health service networks. St. Anslem's had no affiliation with the existing area networks. He reasoned that St. Anslem's absent of a network affiliation would experience rapid market decline to the point of dissolution. Since this was so obvious, he asked Patello if the hospital had developed a plan for becoming part of a network or developing a network of its own. Patello reported that he and the hospital's CEO had discussed the need for a planning effort. The conduct of that effort would be the center of the discussion in the third session.

Mario Capizzi was openly disgusted at the lack of fiscal stability exhibited by St. Anslem's. In his opinion, the Archdiocese would be better off closing the place and going into some other "racket." He expressed the concern that if Park used St. Anslem's as the entry to the Boston health market it would be a venture destined to fail.

Tony Marone was silent. He seemed depressed after reading the information. Patello noticed his body language and asked him to comment. Tony kept his eyes down as if in deep thought as he responded, "I was told by my mother that if I couldn't say anything nice I should keep my mouth shut. May Mother forgive me, this is a big freaking mess. Charlie, you been hanging out with this Catholic gang for a long time. What's with it? These board meeting minutes are all about politics. Who's watching the store? O'Shea sounds like a real hitter but that's the guy we got some trouble with. Right? What about Hardly? Who owns him?"

Patello was about to respond to Capizzi and Marone when Callahan interrupted.

"Gentlemen, your questions are well directed. They express the obvious point that St. Anslem's is not moving progressively with the changing Boston market. Without redirection, the hospital will dissolve. I believe we all agree on this. Now our purpose is to find opportunity in the market, not to invest in St. Anslem's as our own. Let's hold our opinions and concerns for now and deal with them after we consider Park's interest in Boston healthcare. Allow me to reflect on the decision of the NAI Board. This is in tune with Charlie's agenda for our second topic. NAI recognized that the disruption in the healthcare market place was caused in the main by payers modifying the insurance coverage in order to tap into the profits of the providers, especially hospitals. Because of the success of that effort hospitals are now losing money and the HMO's are making it.

"Things have gone nearly one hundred eighty degrees in just a few years. Now the hospitals are countering with networks in order to force the HMO's into sharing the wealth. Meanwhile, the purchaser, area employers, are demanding a piece of the action by a reduction in the premium. Things are very confused. NAI is looking for the opportunity to profit by the confusion. NAI's intent is to tap into the revenue stream of the HMO's and the networks, extract maximum return, and divest at the first sign of order or regulation that is bound to happen."

This was the first time that Patello had heard the details about the NAI decision. He immediately recognized the wisdom of a fast hit into the market and running with the money when the slow down became obvious. The history of healthcare suggested that government regulation would follow as soon as the big investors had accumulated the maximum return. Some politician would see the advantage in demanding that the poor be given equal access to healthcare financed by a method of indirect or direct taxation.

That would socialize the industry and cause private enterprise to divest. Then the healthcare business would return to the not for profit status that it originally had with rigid government regulations. Insurance would be replaced by a government controlled single payer mechanism that would shut off cash flow to the private HMO's and insurance companies. At the present time healthcare was enjoying a period of deregulation that offered the window of opportunity. He and Callahan entered into a lengthy dialog about the timing of a Federal sponsored health reform and then evolved into discussion about the prospect of a State reform effort that would close the window of opportunity in the near future.

Patello reported that Governor Dukar was solidly controlled by private enterprise, especially the insurance industry. His reelection assured that private investment in healthcare would be protected through his next term. On an even brighter note he pointed out that it was the intention of the party to move Dukar into the National picture as a Presidential candidate by the year 2000. Key to his reelection as Governor, however, was moving Mayor Cowan out of the picture as an opponent. NAI's assistance in placing Cowan in a Federal post was very much appreciated by the local establishment who would be, therefore, supportive of NAI's adventure in the Boston health market as long as it did not conflict with the progress of the other major players.

Callahan jumped on Patello's comments. "There's the opportunity to get in and out of our window, Charlie. We get involved in the segment of service that the other networks can't crack or don't want to crack. We do it with the understanding that eventually the market that we control will be dissolved to the benefit of the major participants. They let us alone until we finish milking the cow then it's all theirs. I'm talking the Catholic market. No one wants to compete with God. So, we become God's agents and eventually integrate with the unholy. There are three pieces to this puzzle. The first is the payer. That's where the cash flow originates. The second is the physician who inadvertently directs the distribution of dollars by directing care. The third piece is the institution that still demands the lion's share of the money. We want to tap in at all three points."

Capizzi was beginning to track on Callahan's evolving strategy. "If I'm following you right, Tom, you are beginning to make the point that the weaker elements in the three categories offer us the opportunity to get involved. Seems to me that speed is important. We probably have to buy in at all three levels. That's going to mean heavy cash. The ROI will be stressed."

Callahan was quick to respond. "Not necessarily, Mario. We can use leverage on the buy in and, in St. Anslem's case, we might not have to spend a dime. I think we can acquire that hospital in time by relieving the Archdiocese of the debt Then we sell the assets at a profit to another provider, like the doctors. You see, the doctors, especially the primary care guys, are the main support of the hospital and the specialists. We get control of the hospital by buying the practices of the primary care docs then organize a network of physicians that includes the key specialists at St. A's. Once we get control of the docs, we have control of St. A's. After that we set up a system where the cash flows through the network that we own before it flows to the hospital. We got the hospital by the shorts and it doesn't cost us any more than we had to invest in the docs."

The conversation was moving too fast for Tony Marone. He waved his pencil back and forth as the three other men injected their comments. Finally, he held up both hands as an appeal to be heard. "Look, I'm only the trash man in this outfit so you gotta excuse me if I get lost in this medical stuff. I'm interested in how we get control of the cash flow in the first place. Seems that we got to start an insurance company and sell policies to employers. You got to understand that I haven't done any policy work since I was helping my old man run numbers. How we going to get into this end of the business, Tom?"

"We take over an existing HMO that's on the edge," was Callahan's quick reply.

Callahan was prepared for the question. He asked the participants to open the HMO information that he had distributed at the beginning of the meeting. Inside the folder were summary financial statements of the major competing HMO's in the Boston market. All of the reporting payers displayed significant improvement in operating results except Bay Area Health Maintenance. Their five percent operating deficit the prior year had slipped to seven percent in the current year in spite of increased enrollment.

Callahan brought this distinction to the attention of the assembled. "Gentlemen, Bay Area has grown in number of lives enrolled every year. Yet it continues to lose money. Their figures show the highest case cost per hospitalization, the longest length stay, the most hospital days per thousand enrollees, and the highest charge per physician visit. In view of their lack of provider discipline they are obviously pricing their product below cost and below market. Why? Because the shareholders realize that a high market penetration will attract a takeover if they get a buyer before they face bankruptcy. At the moment, they lack the market penetration to make them a favorable hit. They are also facing a significant cash squeeze. If their financial institution forces them to lose their line of credit then we ride to the rescue."

Patello smelled the smoke.

"What bank is on the hook, Tom, as if I didn't have a pretty good idea?"

"My up-front opinion is that the bank's Board of Directors to which I belong will be anxious to support the takeover," responded Patello. "If Hardly can be easily convinced. O'Shea will have little to say about the deal but he might smell what is happening if he realizes that I'm directly involved. We have to be very careful of Mr. O'Shea right now."

Callahan was not aware of the intrigue involving O'Shea and Mr. Logan's special account. He nevertheless knew by the look of agreement on the faces of Capizzi and Marone that whatever the issue it best not be discussed. Instead he continued to explain the plan.

Callahan continued. "The doctors must believe that they are in charge of the process. To give it the right look we set up a holding company that owns a subsidiary HMO. We manage the subsidiary and charge a management fee. That fee comes off the top. We also share in the profits that will eventually result when we get the utilization under control."

"That's the same process that we use in the waste management business," quipped Marone,. "Park rakes it in on the consulting fee and comes back in for a piece of the profit. Same game, right?"

"Right," answered Callahan. "The Catholic hospitals sponsored by religious Orders have essentially used the process ever since Medicare began. That's how they were able to support the Sisters' retirement and maintenance. They are now dissolving their operations because the new organizations or networks won't carry the extra cash load that the system office used to put on the hospitals. The hospitals aren't the revenue centers anymore. They are simply another element of cost. The Catholic hospitals and others like them are going through a lot of change. The Sisters are getting out of the business. There's more opportunity for us."

"Things are a little different in Boston," Patello asserted. "St. Anslem's is the major Catholic hospital. It doesn't belong to a system. All of its profits and cash have been held for its own use. Now the Archdiocese, at our urging, has set up a central office that Logan is going to run. That could be expensive for the hospital. How do we cut ourselves in?"

"That Archdiocesan office has all the importance of an udder on a bull," quipped Callahan. "Logan will have to find something to do. We need to make him our friend very fast so he appreciates the advantage to the Catholic market in associating with the Park Medical Service Network that we form and has control of the primary care physicians at St. Anslem's and the other area Catholic hospitals. By the way Park Medical Service Network is a subsidiary of none other than Park Medical that also holds Bay Area."

Patello held up his hand as if asking permission to speak. Callahan noticed the gesture and give him the opportunity. "Actually, Tom, Logan is a tool of ours as it is. He is also under the control of an egomaniac. I'm speaking of my very good friend, Dr. Richard Folley. Folley won't let Logan take a pee without permission. If we concentrate on Logan we will be wasting valuable time. I suggest that we go all out to compromise Folley. Logan will fall right in line."

Capizzi, taking his cue from Patello, jumped into the conversation. "This stuff Charlie gave us about Dr. Folley tells me he is a sucker for a pat on the back. No brains but a hell of a lot of pride. What's his thing, Charlie, broads, booze or bucks?"

Patello laughed at the thought of the great Dr. Folley being compromised by a cheap whore in a waterfront tavern. "I don't think the standard methods are applicable, Mario. The man is a pseudo intellectual that feeds his ego from a position of prominence. He needs to be in charge but never accountable. That way he gets all the glory of success and is the first to condemn others for failure. He hates Durant, the hospital CEO, because Durant has a higher position from a social perspective. So he managed to gain a higher perch by convincing the Cardinal that he should be the secretary of health overseeing the so-called health ministry. The secretary, you see, has no accountability for the conduct of the hospital. That's Durant's job. If the hospital fails, Folley tells the Cardinal that Durant is incompetent. The Cardinal admires Folley's perceptive wisdom and cans Durant. Now Folley has another kind of problem. If he is put in charge of the hospital directly he becomes accountable and subject to criticism. Criticism is something he cannot stand. He desperately needs to appoint another shill as the hospital CEO to insulate him from the heat. All we need to do to push Folley over is in some way make him accountable. On the other hand, if we want to keep him in place as our shill then all we have to do is be his protection from accountability."

Callahan was actively making notes as Patello described Dr. Folley. He suddenly looked up and interrupted the conversation. "I think this all fits together rather well. We give the good Dr. Folley a prominent position at the corporate board level of Bay Area and another corporate board position with Park Medical Services Network. We convince him that a man of his prominence is important for our success. He then becomes our advocate for the development of the network and our ally in the implementation of utilization control. If he steps out of line we expose his gigantic conflict of interest. He could go to jail because of his ego but he probably will just melt from humiliation."

Patello felt a need to review the plan as it had developed so far. "Okay, Tom, let's review where we are. The first priority is to acquire the Bay Area

HMO by underwriting its loans with Boston Security. We have to discuss how we are going to sell this to the bank. The second priority is to establish a holding company known as Park Medical Services. This will become the holding company for Bay Area and eventually for Park Health Services Network. Third, but concurrent with the second priority, is to establish the Park Health Services Network. Fourth is activating PHSN to acquire the primary physician practices affiliated with St. Anslem's and other Catholic hospitals? Is that it?"

"Generally, that's it," replied Callahan. "The details of each priority need to be worked out. Let's make some assignments. The bank deal with Bay Area should best directed by Charlie, I think. Corporate formation belongs to Mario and Tony. Anybody have a suggestion how we proceed with the primary docs?"

"Let me provide some input," offered Patello. "I think I should be the invisible man getting things pointed in the right direction. The bank deal and Bay Area is tricky. My suggestion is that we get a brother Knight to call on Hardly. Hardly controls the Board of Security. If his brother in arms wants the deal for the good of the Church. Hardly will go to hell and back to deliver. Mario, we can discuss who in New York should contact Hardly. I can arrange for the details of incorporation of the holding company and the subs but Mario and Tony will square the set with Park and NAI. Now as far as getting to the docs, I think we could do that with the cooperation of the hospital's Board of Trustees. You see, St. Anslem's CEO wants me to help form a long-range plan. I suggested that we required a consultant to steer the process. I also said that I could possibly arrange for a planning grant. My thought is that the affiliated companies of NAI employ Debur and Tandy to do a strategic plan for St. Anslem's. Callahan comes in and does a complete review of the hospital. The outcome of the review points the hospital the way we need it to go. However, in the process of the review Callahan gets to know where the docs are. He feeds the information to us and we go after the docs. Folley could even be our front man. How's it sound?"

"Sounds like a go to me," offered Marone. "How long before we get it squared away?"

Callahan eagerly responded to the question. "We can get the business set up in less than a month. Cash should start coming our way in six months. That means late winter early spring. I'll have to clear with corporate to do the St. Anslem assignment. They might want to use our Boston office. Maybe NAI should consider it part of the National contract. Charlie, can you get this approved by the St. Anslem's Board very soon?"

Patello gave a quick reply. "Hope to get the strategic planning proposal approved at tomorrow's board meeting, Tom. Okay if I use your name?"

"Sure, Charlie. Let me know when they want me to start. Give me as much lead time as possible," answered Callahan.

Mario Capizzi noticed that the discussion had evolved to a point of conclusion. At his suggestion Callahan was delegated to formalize the morning's discussion into a corporate plan for the directors of Park. That plan would be the document authorizing the development of the corporate structures. He suggested that the meeting was concluded. Then the New York contingent called a cab and rushed to Logan Airport in an attempt to catch the one o'clock plane to LaGuardia.

Jay drove directly to Martha's office after he left work. He bolted into the waiting room like a man on a mission. The apprehension on his face more than his demand for immediate service caused the receptionist to inform Martha that she had a client with an emergency. Jay appreciated the extra attention. His anxiety level had been on a steady increase since leaving work. The legal language in the documents served to him seemed oppressive. In spite of the cooperation given to him up front, he still was asked to wait until Martha finished her conversation with a client who was in the middle of an appointment. The wait lasted twenty minutes during which time Jay paced back and forth in the small reception area. Only the receptionist was more relieved than Jay when Martha finally appeared.

Martha allowed Jay time to emote about Cecile, her crooked lawyer, and his vengeance to the "Bitch." When he began to settle down due to physical exhaustion she asked to see the documents that he was clutching in his hands. Jay timidly gave her the papers then renewed his wrath.

"Martha, that bitch has really done it this time. You got to nail her. That crap in there is not true. I mean it's bullshit. What's gonna happen now?"

The documents were about as Martha had expected. She noted that Cecile's attorney was regarded as one of Boston's leading divorce lawyers. Not the same one that had represented her in the divorce. That was significant. It signaled that Cecile was going for it all by retaining a respected and very expensive attorney. The pleadings were designed to force Jay into economic ruin in defense. This was a very expensive case that Jay could ill afford. The stage was definitely set for a compromise rather than a bare-knuckle brawl in court. Without some unknown leverage Jay would lose more than he would gain if a deal had to be struck. Martha realized that this was not the time to inform her brother that he was in deep trouble. The original divorce decree had contained a Judgment of Dissolution governing the relationship of the parties to the divorce in matters of child support, custody, and visitation. Cecile through her attorney was asking for modification of the original judgment to revoke joint custody and increase support payments based on the allegation that Jay's income had increased substantially over the amount he was making at the time of the divorce. Cecile was asking at minimum the twenty percent allowed by law of Jay's current income. The second modification request was revocation of custody based on the allegation that Jay and Susan were not fit to care for Kristie because of their substantiated use of chemical substances. Martha noted with particular concern that the petition to the court made special mention that Susan was a habitual user of intoxicating substances.

The surprise package that concerned Martha the most at this time was an Emergency Petition to the Court to immediately revoke custody because of immediate endangerment to Kristie based on the substantiated information that Jay's use of chemical substances has resulted in an overdose. This would require that Jay's medical record be presented as evidence to the court. To that end, a Discovery Document was included that required Jay to present all of his medical records from all doctors and medical institutions from whom and in which he had received care in the past five years. The discovery specifically mentioned Waltham Hospital.

Another clever part of the pleadings was a Petition to the Court for ruling to show cause that Jay had missed several support payments. This was a diversion to create the perception that Jay was, in addition to being a junkie, a deadbeat dad. The discovery document requested that he present all of his financial records for the past five years to include paychecks, bank statements, loans and mortgage documents, and all other personal financial documents.

Finally, the package included two notices of Hearing. The first hearing was of an immediate nature to deal with the Child Endangerment Emergency. The second Hearing was attentive to all other matters of petition pertaining to the modification of the Judgment of Dissolution. Martha realized that the emergency hearing could be scheduled within two weeks from time of service.

The Petition for Modification would be heard by the Court sometime in November was her first guess. She was consumed with anger over the issue affecting Kristie but also realized that Cecile was being represented by a professional who knew that emotion served his cause. Job number one at this time was to keep Jay under control and get him properly represented on the custody matters,

Carefully, she began her explanation of the issues. "Well, my brother, we have our work cut out for us. I'll get with a good divorce lawyer in the morning. Mark Addison, the man that represented you at the time of your divorce, is with another firm so I'll have to see if he is interested in continuing, I recommend that you stay with him. He has an excellent reputation in these matters. He'll have to charge full fees so we will have to talk about that after he gives me some idea about what to expect. I'm going to suggest to him that we team up on the defense in the Emergency Petition. I'm probably better prepared on the medical record confidentiality issue. We'll see."

Jay's anger seemed to abate but he remained emotional. "Martha, I don't have any money. I'm supporting three kids and a wife on my income. Cecile makes nearly twice what I make. How can she expect me to pay more support? Between her and her weird cop husband they must be knocking down a hundred grand. I'm barely meeting expenses. How am I going to pay Addison? I think he ripped me off last time."

Martha was extremely sensitive to Jay's remarks about Mark. He had given Jay every possible consideration in fees to the extent that the Firm had been critical of him continuing the case. Only Martha's association with the firm had prevented him from withdrawing. Carefully, she commented, "Jay, you have to realize that lawyers need to get paid for their work. I'll try to work something out for you but it's still going to cost. You need to be prepared for that."

"Well, he needs to be prepared to deal with a guy that runs a little short. Maybe he'll take my credit card if it isn't over the limit," was Jay's reply.

For the first time since last Thursday Jay felt the surge of uncontrollable anger that caused him to react violently. Suddenly he experienced the familiar pain in his chest and a sudden shortness of breath that caused him to double over.

"Jay, are you all right? Should I get you some help? What's going on?" were three rapid questions asked by Martha that Jay could not answer because of the increasing pain now moving from his chest to his stomach. He could only look at her with a very painful expression.

Gradually Jay relaxed and the pain decreased. “Deni, I think I’ll be all right. I’m might go over to St. A’s. I have to do a urine test and then hang around for a support group session. If I get in trouble someone there will help. Otherwise, I’ll just drive home. Could you do me a favor and call Susan? Tell her what’s going on just in case I decide to go in. I don’t think I will but I can’t tell. Man, my gut hurts.”

“Sure, I’ll call her. You want me to drive you to the hospital?” Martha offered.

Jay had managed to stand and was feeling less pain. He felt certain that the physical crisis had passed. His emotions were also stable at the moment. “Thanks, Den. I just had some sort of a jolt. I’ll be all right, I think. I can drive. Tell Susan that I should be home soon. Are you going to call me tomorrow after you talk to Addison?”

Martha moved to his side. “I’ll call you early afternoon. You had better be prepared to give this matter a lot of time. We’ll talk tomorrow.”

She took Jay by the hand and gave it an affectionate sisterly squeeze. Then she escorted him through the now vacant reception area. Jay gave her a hug and went out the door. By the time he arrived home the pain was gone.

Joe Durant was pleased to see Monday end. It seemed that nothing good had happened. Tomorrow’s board meeting appeared to him as the mother of all disasters. Monday’s little problems were nothing compared to the battle that awaited the mom. He was holding his head in his hands while sitting at his desk in apparent deep contemplation when Rod Weaver and Mitch Daly walked in. They seemed to be in a collegial mood as they jointly greeted their depressed mentor. Joe had forgotten that he had demanded that the two appear before him to discuss tactics for the A.M. onslaught. With a pained expression, he returned their greeting and moved with them to the well-used small conference table.

Eagerly, Mitch Daly distributed his plan for planning that he had tried to force on Durant earlier in the day. With a nod from Durant he began his explanation. “Boss, since you put me in charge of this project I thought we ought to have a common understanding of the approach I will take at the Board meeting. I want to be sure that you and fiscal are in sync in case any questions are directed at you during or after the meeting. Okay? Now I will distribute this outline that has three major phases. The first phase is organization. As I understand it, Joe, Mr. Patello has agreed to chair a planning committee. We'll let him pick the Boardmembers who will serve but I think we should name the administrators. Obviously, the three of us would be the ones to serve. Medical staff should be represented on the committee. The president of the medical staff should be invited or his representative. I imagine Folley will want to play God and name the physician. Anyway, the committee should be in place within a week after the meeting. Second phase is plan function. I will select a consultant with the approval of the committee. Several firms have been contacted that are sending me information and ballpark prices. We definitely need a consultant to move this along. The last phase is timing. You notice that I intend to complete the planning project in eight months. That includes the conferences and special interest reviews that will need to take place. How's it sound?"

"Expensive," was Weaver's quick answer. "How in the hell do you intend to pay for an army of consultants hanging around her for eight months? God created the universe in seven days. That ought to be good enough for you."

"Actually, it was six days, Rod. Remember, he took Sunday off," commented Durant. "Your plan for planning outline has some merit. Mitch, but I anticipate that Mr. Patello has a consultant in tow that we will use. If I'm right, he also has a means to pay for the process. That being the case then we'll take our directions from the consultant, I imagine. Patello called me about an hour ago and said that he had what we wanted. His only concern was convincing the rest of the Board. I guess he is taking care of the politics. We can only wait and see."

"Well, the price recommends it," said a smiling Weaver. "If Patello wants to pay the fiddler it's only right that we let him call the tune."

Daly was showing signs of depression. "So if I'm supposed to be in charge of the process and Patello and his consultant are actually running it what do I do?"

"Whatever they ask," responded Durant.

With that comment, the meeting came to a close. Weaver left first. Daly followed in a few minutes after starring in silence at his boss. Durant was unmoved by Daly's silent emotion. His day had been a sequence of disasters. A disgruntled vice president was the least of his concerns.

CHAPTER ELEVEN

Kevin Hardly was up by five A.M. He did his usual exercises, showered and had breakfast before six. He drank his coffee, had some juice, and read the paper as he sat on the patio of his mansion on his well-landscaped estate. This was to be Kevin Hardly's day. He was to conduct the meeting of the St. Anslem's Board of Trustees, an assignment bestowed on him by the Deity. Otherwise, his position as Chairman of one of Boston's most prestigious Banks was somewhat mundane compared to the responsibility of doing God's work at the leading Catholic Hospital in the area, if not the world. The Cardinal had impressed him with the awesome responsibility when he asked Hardly to serve the Church in that capacity. He had accepted the assignment just as eagerly as he had accepted the leadership of the Knights of the Holy Cross. This was God's work that had to be done and he was the man to do it. The Cardinal, himself, had said so.

At exactly six-fifteen he backed his Mercedes out of the garage and aimed it toward St. Anslem's Hospital. The half-hour drive would put him there fifteen minutes before the seven o'clock starting time. *Plenty of time to get organized,* he thought.

Joe Durant had a different perspective on the Board meeting. He had arrived at the hospital at six A.M. and began to assist the housekeeping and food service personnel arrange the hospital's spacious boardroom for the meeting. Durant felt that the Boardroom was obscene but his opinion was of no consequence. Its think panel walls, expensive drapes, false sky lights, religious art, plush chairs, and a custom-built table that would hold thirty-five people was way beyond good taste. The adjacent kitchen and serving area with wet bar that opened into the main room also seemed pretentious.

The entire board suite was commissioned and paid for by Kevin Hardly as a gift to the hospital following his appointment as Chairman of the Board. Three adjacent storerooms had been absorbed by the designer and decorator for the project. Walls had been removed. New ceiling, carpet, thick panel walls and a full kitchen with food serving area added. Hidden microphones recorded every word spoken and amplified every sound. Picture screens descended from the ceiling at a touch on a control panel at the Chairman's place. Television, VCR's, and projectors all were at the ready in a rear projection booth also commanded by the Chair.

Hardly had assigned the interior decorator of Boston Security to the task of designing, building and equipping the suit without regard to cost. Consequently, the room was named the Hardly Board Room. A portrait of the great and generous man hung in an ornate frame on the wall at the end of the mammoth table. On the wall, opposite and above the chairman's position, hung a picture of His Eminence, Francis Cardinal McMahon.

The food service personnel were assigned the task of preparing the extensive breakfast buffet that was the trademark of the Board meetings. Grommet dishes were always plentiful. Delicious Danish, bagels, and sweet rolls from the City's best bakeries adorned the table as did a variety of juices. A chef was available to prepare custom omelets for those with expanded appetites. Waitresses were assigned the task of replenishing beverages and removing the dishes.

Customarily the people attending ate and discussed the business of the hospital at the same time in a rather informal manner. The conduct and ambiance of the meeting was Kevin's idea because he thought that God would have conducted the meeting in a friendly relaxed way. Occasionally the discussions were replaced by a formal presentation but that was rare. A staff of six people from the Environmental Services department had arrived at five-thirty to thoroughly clean the entire suite.

Durant could not remember anytime that the Board meeting ever included material of such consequence that environmental and food service personnel could not be present. Hardly ran an open and informal meeting. Rarely did the minutes reflect the actual conduct of the meeting since Durant wrote the minutes to accommodate the regulatory requirements. Confidential matters were always slipped into the minutes after the fact and authenticated by approval of the minutes at the following meeting. Everyone seemed content with the loose conduct. This time Durant expected a rather large explosion of emotions as the hospital finances were discussed, the waste management contract was reported, the planning committee was proposed, and the Bishop announced the impact of Dr. Folley's and Mr. Logan's positions with the Archdiocese, as well as the ongoing discussion regarding the serious fiscal plight of the hospital.

This was a very important meeting that Durant felt required the Chairman to conduct in formal fashion. So convinced was Durant that he had placed a copy of Robert's Rules of Order at the Chairman's place. He had also directed the food service and environmental staff to leave as soon as the Chairman began the meeting.

Hardly was the first member of the Board to arrive. He strolled into the Boardroom and extended a cordial greeting to the employees. Then he walked over to Durant, shook his hand and presented him with a thick envelope that held the crest and return address of the Knights of the Holy Cross.

Joe looked at the envelope with question as Hardly began to explain. "Joseph, it's time that you became a Knight. That envelope contains the application form and information about the Order. It's true Catholic action that you will want to be a part of. We'll give it fast process. I'm sure the Cardinal will approve it. We can have you ready for the October installation. Your wife will become a Lady in the Order and join with you. It's all explained in the material. Don't forget to give us your sizes so the good Sisters can have your capes ready for the installation. The capes are made to order by a cloistered order of Nuns in Canada. They need a month lead time at least. It will be good to have you join us. I expect that Mr. and Mrs. Logan will be installed in the same class with you."

Durant was taken off guard by Hardly's invitation. He could only express his gratitude to Hardly for considering him for the honor. Hardly seemed pleased with Durant's attitude and followed with a lengthily explanation about the New England Platoon of which he was the Leading Knight. The discussion became extended and offered no time for Durant to prepare Hardly for the coming onslaught.

Just as Durant sensed an opening in the conversation, Dr. Folley arrived with a gentleman unknown to Durant but who was recognized from his picture in the media as Mr. Michael Logan. Folley ignored Durant as he introduced

Logan to Hardly. Hardly graciously greeted Mr. Logan and invited him to be a regular guest at all St. Anslem's board meetings and functions. He then produced another Holy Cross envelope that he presented to Logan with the same lengthily explanation.

Bishop Hanks was next to arrive. He noticed Folley and Logan talking to Hardly and immediately joined them. Hardly informed the Bishop of Logan's intent to become a Knight which sparked another round of conversation about the Order. By now Durant realized that any preparation time was lost. The remaining Board members were now present and seated at the table where breakfast was being served. Patello was among them but distant from Durant denying them the opportunity to communicate.

Sister Mary Elizabeth was the last to arrive. When she greeted the Bishop, it diverted Hardly from his recruiting speech. Hardly noticed that the Board had assembled in their usual informal fashion so he took his place at the head of the table and ordered his favorite omelet from the waiting chef.

Although the meeting lacked formality there was a customary seating arrangement that was always adhered to: Kevin Hardly sat at the head of the table with the portrait of the Cardinal looking over him. Thomas O'Shea sat on Hardly's right and Charles Patello sat on his left. Durant sat next to Patello and Folley sat next to O'Shea. The remaining Boardmembers sat anywhere they pleased but never in the designated chairs. Durant was moving to his customary place when he noticed that Dr. Folley had placed Logan in the chair that Joe usually occupied. Hardly seemed pleased with the arrangement that left Durant to find a place most distant from the Chairman. This caused him to take a place at the end but next to the friendly Sister Mary Elizabeth. Sister Elizabeth greeted Joe warmly. She had noticed the social slam by Folley and expressed her resentment of the action as she gave Joe an affectionate pat on his hand.

Joe had desperately wanted to inform Chairman Hardly about the special features of the meeting not the least of which was that he had invited Rod Weaver and Mitch Daly to attend as guests. Weaver and Daly walked into the Boardroom unnoticed by Hardly. Durant motioned them to join him at the table. He then hastily explained to the two executives that they were there at his invitation only since he had not had the opportunity to clear their attendance with Hardly. Weaver was his usual casual self and ordered a lavish breakfast. Daly became very nervous. His hand seemed to shake as he attempted to drink the glass of juice put before him.

Another custom of the Board was the prayer used to start all of their gatherings. Kevin had the prayer composed by a Trappist Monk for which he had made a sizable contribution to the monastery. He tapped his water glass to get everyone's attention and then asked Bishop Hanks to lead the Board in the recitation of the special prayer. The good Bishop always accommodated Kevin's request to recite the Monk's prayer and routinely added a few prayers and petitions of his own that served to allow everyone's eggs to get cold. Following the prayer Kevin invited the members to continue enjoying their breakfast. He then invited Dr. Folley to introduce a very special guest.

Dr. Folley remained seated and continued to hold his fork that he pointed at Logan as he began the introduction. "Kevin and members of the Board, it is with pleasure that I introduce you to Mr. Michael Logan who I'm sure you already know because of his outstanding work with the City. Michael has accepted the challenge of working with me as we start the much-needed Office for Health Affairs for the Archdiocese. Bishop Hanks will explain the Cardinal's intent for this important office. Allow me to say that Mr. Logan will be instrumental in organizing and directing the various health institutions and services provided by the Archdiocese. Putting it all together makes us the largest provider of healthcare in the State bar none. Mr. Logan's background and experience will be of great help as we expand our Catholic network."

The Board gave a muffled applause as Dr. Folley concluded his remarks. He turned to Logan and asked if he had anything to say. Michael felt inclined to stand and make his comments but he succumbed to the informality and remained seated. "Thank you for the warm greeting. I am excited about this association with the Church and its health ministry. Dr. Folley has told me about your dedication and I am most anxious to join you in carrying out the mission of St. Anslem's and the Church. I look forward to getting to know each of you personally."

As Logan concluded his comments, Dr. Folley again took the lead in the discussion. "Kevin, I think that this is the right time for us to hear from Bishop Hanks about the Cardinal's decision to establish an Office for Health Affairs."

Kevin simply nodded at the request. Bishop Hanks wiped his mouth with his napkin and prepared to speak.

Dr. Folley then signaled that he had a few more words to say causing the Bishop to yield. "Before you get to that, Bishop, I suppose that I ought to express my gratitude to you and the Cardinal for listening to my recommendations about the function of the secretary for Health. Cardinal McMahon asked me to meet with him on several occasions last month to work out the details of the assignment. I can say to you that he is very excited about this post and I am very excited about being the first person, religious or lay, to be selected for the task. Bishop Hanks was most kind in recommending me for the job and I thank him for that. Bishop, please continue."

Bishop Hanks seemed skeptical that he was actually being allowed to speak. He recalled that he had actually recommended that the Cardinal appoint a priest to the secretariat post instead of Dr. Folley. He hadn't said as much to the Cardinal but he thought Folley was a "pompous ass." The Cardinal had already promised the job to Folley when he asked the Bishop's opinion.

Carefully he thought out his comments so that the Cardinal would be protected from any bad consequence of the decision. "My friends, His Eminence has a very high regard for the laity. We have more laypeople in key posts within the Archdiocese than any other diocese in the United States. We also have the largest percentage of Catholic population of any major metropolitan area in the Country. The services provided by the Church to the people of Boston are numerous. That is why the Cardinal felt that a professional such as Dr. Folley should be the one to guide those health services in the true interest of the Church and the community the Church serves. We are fortunate that Dr. Folley can find the time from his very pressing duties here to attend to the challenge offered by the whole Archdiocese."

Sister Mary Elizabeth was unconvinced. With no hesitation, she fired a shot across the Bishop's bow. "Bishop, it seems to me that the Cardinal sought little counsel on the need for the office. Many of us would have advised him against it. Healthcare is going through a massive restructuring that may move the ministry in an entirely different direction. I believe the matter should have been discussed openly in the Priests' senate if nowhere else. Where is the office to be located and how are we going to pay for it? It seems to me that these are questions that should have answers before men are appointed to new positions."

Bishop Hanks had feared Sister's reaction. He took special note of her use of the word "men" in the spicy retort. The flush in his cheeks betrayed his embarrassment as he fumbled for an answer.

It was at this point that Thomas O'Shea saw the opportunity to relieve the Bishop and redirect the focus of blame. "Kevin, before we get into much more detail I want to know why certain uninvited people are in this room.

Aren't the Board meetings supposed to be confidential? We have two vice presidents sitting at the table who usually don't come into these meetings until they are called and then excused. Why are they here?"

Kevin hadn't noticed that the hospital wait staff, per instructions of Durant, had disappeared when the discussion started. He also hadn't noticed that Weaver and Daly were seated at the end of the table. He had no idea how to respond to his friend and associate, O'Shea.

Durant relieved him of the pressure by firing back at O'Shea. "These gentlemen are here at my direction to serve as resource to this Board on two very important subjects, finance and strategic planning. Perhaps we should get into these items and then they could be excused."

Hardly responded, "Yes, all right, we can do that. Joe would you like to lead us through the latest financial report. Is that all right with you, Tom?"

Thomas O'Shea was determined to control the discussion of the finances. He had studied Weaver's report to the last item. "Kevin, as Treasurer of the hospital's corporation I think it would be more in tune with my responsibility if I gave the report and then we can ask management to reply. There are significant problems apparent in the operating statement that Mr. Durant will need to address. If you will so allow me, I'll pass out a copy of the latest statement and a copy of my own notes. I want you to know that I had to make a demand for this information to Mr. Weaver who finally sent me the statements late yesterday afternoon. One of our major problems, as you can see, is the lack of current information."

Hardly nodded his consent as O'Shea began distributing the documents. Weaver leaned over to his boss and in a stage whisper stated another problem was "the Treasurer didn't know his ass from third base about a hospital financial operating statement." The people seated near Durant chuckled when the comment was made. Sister Mary Elizabeth simply nodded. Durant actually blushed.

O'Shea paused when the humor became apparent but he had not heard the comment. He could only stare at Durant with contempt. Weaver was gratified that the Treasurer had been disarmed by the interruption He sat back in his chair and flashed a big smile at Mr. O'Shea that brought him back to the task of distributing the material. Thomas O'Shea, regardless of Weaver's opinion, was an expert in financial analysis. His many years directing the fiscal affairs of Boston Security had made him expert in all forms of fiscal reporting. The hospital method of accounting had been foreign to him when he first became involved with St. Anslem's but he soon mastered the information. He knew that St. Anslem's was in a "death glide" as he described it to the Board. The escalating monthly deficits were pointing to a year end disaster that would reduce the hospital's equity by nearly twenty million dollars. This equity reduction would break the bond covenants and require extensive debt reduction that the hospital was ill-prepared to do.

The immediate requirement proposed by Treasurer O'Shea was "an all-out reduction in spending by a minimum of thirty percent within the next thirty to sixty days. While that reduction could not offset the expected loss for the current year, it would be sufficient to convince the Rating Agencies that the hospital could regain stability with a projected break even or better result in the next year. What we need from management is their plan for expense reductions and a positive margin." When his remarks were completed the mood around the table was somber.

Hardly was unsure what to do or say next. No one seemed ready to ask questions or even move.

Durant realized that, ready or not, he had to seize the moment before the Board turned their attention to O'Shea's demands and took management to task. He pulled his emotions under control and formally addressed the Chair. "Mr. Hardly, I thank Mr. O'Shea for his excellent analysis of the many challenges facing St. Anslem's. Our fiscal position has deteriorated rapidly this year. We have been adjusting our spending to match the declining revenue but, unfortunately, the change in the case mix intensity has reduced the average case revenue faster than we can adjust costs. To accommodate the thirty percent reduction that Mr. O'Shea proposes requires elimination of programs that are not carrying their own weight and/or are not feeding patients to the more profitable services. What I'm proposing is that St. Anslem's only provide those services that are profitable. However, those services that we provide must be suitable to our mission of teaching and research. The determination of our service base must be carefully reviewed."

Patello had been silent up to this point. Suddenly he caught the cue from Durant about the determination of service being an overture to the planning program. Without pause or permission he injected himself into Durant's comments. "We have the prospect of a major disaster if we cut expenses without reason other than to offset the deficit. If making money was our mission then we would sell this place and put the money into a saving account at O'Shea's bank. Mr. Durant is right about the need to analyze our services in respect to our mission. I also think that we need an expert to assist us with the process. This is a major consulting job."

Kevin Hardly suddenly came to life at the suggestion of a consulting job. "We have a great amount of expertise at the bank that could be used by the hospital at no charge. Our planning and marketing staff has two very well qualified people who did the work for the Archdiocese on the Office for Health Affairs. They could be made available to assist the hospital and this Board."

The look on Patello's face at the mention of "Laurel and Hardy," crack planners from Boston Security, made O'Shea laugh out loud. Normally O'Shea was a man completely divorced from humor but when Hardly trumped Patello's ace, he couldn't control the expression.

Patello was rendered speechless by Hardly's remarks so O'Shea took up the void. "Kevin, the bank's staff is involved in a major project at this time that would prevent them from giving the hospital the attention it deserves. My thought is that Mr. Logan could direct the planning effort. He could use our marketing and planning staff for special reviews."

Durant sensed the loss of control as Logan was mentioned. He interrupted as O'Shea was about to speak. "Excuse me, Mr. O'Shea, but we have a qualified planner on our executive staff who is prepared to direct the planning effort. Mr. Daly is not only a qualified and experienced planner of health facilities and functions he is also knowledgeable about St. Anslem's, I would like to propose that Mr. Daly be empowered to formalize the planning effort and that a consultant as offered by Mr. Patello be used as back up to the program."

"The point I'm trying to make is that we have no confidence in management to lead us in anything," O'Shea stood and pounded the table to give emphasis to his verbal reaction. "Joe Durant has led this hospital to the point of fiscal failure and now he wants us to trust him to lead us out of it. We need new leadership to give us a better focus on the impact of health reform. Joe is old school. Let Logan, a fresh face, take over and preserve the ministry. That's what he is supposed to do under Richard's guidance. Right, Richard?"

Sr. Elizabeth suddenly jumped into the debate. The little nun had a hot disposition that tended to explode when she became frustrated. The discourteous assault on Joe Durant by O'Shea brought back to her mind the same mean tactics that the Cardinal's "men" had employed to discredit Sr. Celest. *No more of this,* she thought and rose from her chair. "Mr. Hardly, I am ashamed to be party to this juvenile bickering. Why are we being so critical when we have never expressed any dissatisfaction with our managers in the past? Yes, we have good reason to be concerned but Mr. Durant has stated that concern and has requested an opportunity to undertake corrective steps. We, or at least Mr. O'Shea, seem determined to replace Mr. Durant with Mr. Logan. I'm certain that Mr. Logan is a fine gentleman but so is Mr. Durant. Mr. Durant is also known to us as a capable administrator is spite of Mr. O'Shea's opinion. I, for one, will not go along with Mr. O'Shea's suggestion. I implore you, Mr. Hardly, to bring this discussion under control. It's your job as Chairman to properly direct this meeting and I suggest that you do it."

Hardly had the look of a second grader being scolded by the Sister. He sat with his hands folded in good parochial school fashion. He lowered his head when Sr. Elizabeth leveled her criticism at him. His embarrassment was obvious as the room became deathly quiet. Hardly was emotionally wounded and rendered speechless. The great lay member of the Church's nobility was now a silent Knight divorced of sword or speech. He had no quick response to this professed Lady of the Church who had humbled him and now stood before his table in his court demanding that he be responsible to his charge.

The silence continued. No one seemed to move. Sr. Elizabeth remained standing and took time to look into the eyes of each member of the Board. Some made eye contact. Others like Hardly and O'Shea kept their eyes lowered. Sr. Elizabeth was for the moment in charge of the meeting. Hardly, unable to respond, had effectively abdicated to Sister.

It was an opportunity to correct a wrong. Sister took full advantage of her position and began her commentary. "As a Board of Directors we have been lax in our responsibility. This hospital has been governed by a process of absentee decision making that we have accepted without question. Why was the Office for Health Affairs established without our input? Why was Dr. Folley appointed to the Secretariat without consideration being given to other interested people, religious or laity? Why was Mr. Logan employed without the benefit of executive search? Why, then, should we be held accountable for the status of this hospital if we are not to be involved in the major decisions affecting our responsibility? How can we plan the future of this hospital as a service to the ministry when we are excluded from ministerial direction? I believe we need to have direct communication with the Cardinal in order for us to fulfill our responsibility."

Sister Elizabeth looked directly at Bishop Hanks as she paused. The Bishop was now staring back at Sister and opened his mouth to speak. Sister was not ready to yield. Still standing she continued her filibuster. "I want to know what the Office for Health Affairs is going to cost and who is going to pay for it. Do we have a say in that? We are expected to maintain fiscal stability. In view of our current instability I presume that the Cardinal has found other resources to support the office that has so much importance. Where is this office to be located? Several months ago, we agreed to hire more surgeons and cardiologists. They have occupied every available space in the hospital. Are we now expected to reduce our patient capacity to accommodate the secretary and director as well as a supporting cast of thousands? Do we have any say in this? Indeed, we need to plan. But we cannot plan in a vacuum. The Cardinal must be part of the planning process and be transparently honest in dealing with us. We cannot be expected to guess at his interests. The preservation and conduct of the healing ministry requires total cooperation and honesty. I am determined to see that this Board has every opportunity to fulfill its responsibility. Therefore, I request, no I demand, to be given the Chair of a Planning Committee for this Hospital that will deal with the full scope of the healing ministry as it may apply to St. Anslem's."

Hardly had regained some composure but was still emotionally off balance. Sister's demand to be named Chairperson of the yet to be formed Planning Committee was ringing in his ears. He desperately needed help.

Bishop Hanks seemed to be riding to the rescue when he began to counter Sister's comments. "Sister, I apologize for not communicating with you and the rest of the Board when the office was formed. The Cardinal asked that I attend to all the details. Obviously, I was lax in several matters. The Cardinal has no funds to support the office. The expenses are to be paid by St. Anslem's at first and as the other Catholic hospitals in the Archdiocese join the system they will help defer the costs. Mr. Logan is very qualified to create the system of Catholic Health Services. That's why he was employed. It was not intended that he would be directly involved in the management of St. Anslem's. Your point is well taken. I, for one, welcome your leadership in the development of the health ministry. You are the right person to orient Mr. Logan on the scope of the ministry and the content of the health system. As we form our recommendations, I'm confident that His Eminence would join us for discussion. I'll tell him that you and your committee will be working with Mr. Logan and Dr. Folley on the plan for the System. I know that he will be pleased."

Sister felt the all too familiar kick upstairs. By moving her to the System formation the Good Bishop had effectively moved her away from the details of the hospital plan. However, she was unsure if that was his intent or if he was just being the usual tactful clergyman. She decided to test his sincerity. "Thank you for the vote of confidence, Bishop. I assume that you will join us on the committee. Have you any suggestions for other members?"

The Bishop had played the game of Church politics many times. He was a seasoned veteran of the clerical wars and recognized the clever move of this cagey nun. If he yielded to her intent to block involvement by the terrific trinity he would gain counsel in dealing with the problems of the women religious' defiance toward the official Church. On the other hand, if he suggested one of the terrific trinity it was a message to her that the committee was a chosen battle ground for the conflict of the religious sexes in the Boston Archdiocese. That was a war for a different time and place.

In reply he opted for the middle ground. "Sister, I have no specific recommendations. Please choose whoever you think will best serve the purpose. Of course. I'll be on the committee as you ask."

Sister received the Bishop's communique and acknowledged it with a smile. The Bishop signed off the net with a nod of respect leaving her to play the next card. That card was selection of another member to the committee that would be an acceptable party to the Bishop and still supportive to her cause. That meant someone with influence but apparently neutral to the terrific trinity.

Sister replied, "Thank you for the support, Bishop. I suggest that Mr. Mondi would be an excellent addition to our committee. You, Mr. Mondi and I will team with Dr. Folley and Mr. Logan to plan the purpose and function of the Office for Health Affairs. We can coordinate with the planning function at St. Anslem's that Mr. Durant will conduct."

Not only had the good Sister taken over control of the Arch Diocese Office for Health Affairs, she was now moving in as chairman of St. Anslem's. Hardly realized what was happening but was a victim of his informal style. He was at a loss to recover the mantle from this black clad whirlwind. O'Shea also recognized that the Bishop and Nun had worked a combination that effectively moved the terrific trinity to the sidelines. This could be bad for business if left alone. Mondi was unknown to O'Shea except that he was a loyal knight that Hardly had recommended to the Cardinal. For the moment O'Shea counted him on the side of the trinity. O'Shea concluded that the new Committee was controllable. He opted not to create any obstruction to its function. Of greater importance was to maintain control of St. Anslem's governance.

To that end O'Shea decided to form an alliance with Patello. "Sister, your idea of relating the plan for the Health Office with the plan for the hospital is excellent. But it seems to me that the office and the hospital are somewhat at opposite extremes. The hospital is in desperate need of a business plan to offset the growing deficit. Related to this, as we heard from Mr. Durant, is the need to determine the appropriate products for the hospital to deliver. Therefore, I suggest that the hospital plan be held separate from the office until it is concluded and then be coordinated. Otherwise, we could be out of money before we have these things properly thought out. Earlier Mr. Patello suggested that we use a consultant to assist the hospital. I now believe that we should accept that suggestion in order to expedite the planning process."

O'Shea's comments keyed Hardly's return to authority. Before Sister Elizabeth could respond, the Great Knight regained the Chair.

"Thank you, Tom. You have brought us back to the original concern of the hospital's finances. Let's give that matter some thought before we decide to use a consultant. Tom, I believe you said that we needed to reduce our expenses by sixty percent in the next thirty days. Correct?"

"Actually, it was thirty percent in sixty days, Kevin," was O'Shea's glib response.

"Well, whatever, we need to be at it," continued Hardly. "Now Mr. Weaver is here. Perhaps he can give us some insight as to how we might accomplish this."

Rod Weaver had been enjoying the heated exchange and political maneuvering of the Boardmembers. It was better than Monday Night Football of which he was an avid observer. The sudden call to participate came unexpectedly. He was caught off guard.

A quick look to Durant signaled his panic and caused Joe to respond in his behalf. "Mr. Hardly, I can speak for Rod on this matter. He has studied our fiscal situation in-depth but is not prepared at the moment to make any definite recommendations. I asked him here today to explain what Mr. O'Shea has eloquently stated and to ask the Board to allow us to prepare a cost-reduction program as Mr. O'Shea has proposed. With your permission, we can be prepared to present that plan to the Board by next week. We have already advised management in all areas of the hospital to prepare for significant reductions in the work force. Unfortunately, as we prepare for the reductions our situation becomes worse by changes in the local environment. The recent modification in the City ordinance regarding waste management will add another three hundred thousand dollars to our expenses in the next year. Sister has also raised the question about the expense of the Office for Health Affairs. Mr. Weaver has estimated that will cost us another one million dollars. These additions compound the thirty percent reduction already required."

Hardly's response did not garner the sympathy that Durant was seeking. "Joe, every business in town is affected by City Hall. We have to accept it as the cost of doing business. So should you. If these additions require more belt tightening then we just have to do it. If the members agree, we can have a special meeting of the Board next week to review the cost-reduction plan. Tom, I expect that you and the Finance Committee will review the plan ahead of our meeting."

Tom O'Shea was quick with a reply. "You can count on it, Kevin. Remember that the Finance Committee consists of Dr. Folley and me. I suggest that Mark Meehan join us. That gives the committee good balance. Okay with you, Mark?"

Mark Meehan had been quiet and comfortable during the meeting. He was confident that ultimately the great Charlie Patello would surface and destroy all this political intrigue. Durant's comment about the waste management costs caused him some anxiety. Now O'Shea, either purposely or accidentally, had put his feet to the fire by asking him to serve on the Finance Committee. Perhaps O'Shea had done this to give Meehan some protection since the committee would control the cost analysis. The impact of the waste management contract could be covered by other reductions. He reminded himself of Hardly's comments that sought to admonish administration's criticism of the change in Civic policy. Without speaking, Mark Meehan nodded his agreement to serve as a new member of the finance committee. If necessary he could always resign.

Kevin Hardly felt that he had regained control. His intent was to adjourn the meeting before he lost it again. The time served that purpose well. Kevin had always promised that the seven AM start time for the Board meetings allowed those attending to be at their offices by eight-thirty providing the meeting ended by eight. He had never failed to close the meeting by that time. Today was not to be an exception. A glance at his watch registered the time to quit. He then began his closing commentary. "Bishop Hanks, Sister Elizabeth, I want to thank you for your leadership today. You have advanced the ministry with your commitment to assist the new Office for Health Affairs. I also want to thank the Board members who have agreed to accept new committee appointments. Indeed, all of you are to be commended for your commitment to our ministry. This has been a very important meeting. It's now eight o'clock and time to adjourn. Mr. Durant's office will inform you soon about the date, time and place of our special meeting next week. Thank you for coming."

The Board members reacted without hesitation at Hardly's call to adjourn. They stood almost in unison and began to exit. However, each one took the time to shake Michael Logan's hand as they departed. Michael was unsteady in his response to the welcome comments. His mind had been blown by the conduct of the Board meeting. Certainly, as a public servant and a member of the Mayor's cabinet he had been subjected to vicious political in-fighting. He had expected it and was prepared for it. However, he was not prepared and certainly did not expect to experience the scope of bickering that seemed to pervade this Catholic hospital. He kept reflecting in his mind that on his second day on the job, at his first meeting of the St. Anslem's Board, he became the target of a Sister's wrath. Her anger caused the creation of a committee that had the prospect of replacing him or at least reducing him to an errand boy. He felt that he had been had. He wanted out.

Joe Durant was also frustrated as the meeting came to a close. He had hoped to initiate a planning process that would give administration the opportunity to continue managing the hospital. Instead he had to be content with Sister Elizabeth's system planning i.e. watchdog committee and a cold-blooded cost reduction finance committee that expected miracles in a week. Remarkably, Rod Weaver seemed pleased with the challenge. He positioned himself at the door of the Boardroom and exchanged pleasantries with the members as they left. Mitch Daly was in a quandary. He simply hung back waiting for the chance to reconcile with his boss.

Charlie Patello was the big loser. His intent to establish a planning committee under his control with the consultants was deterred by a crafty Nun who had another agenda. Now the inside track to the healthcare business sought by Park was on hold until another avenue could be found. Charlie noticed that Joe was hanging back waiting for the room to clear. Hardly and O'Shea had already left. Logan was still chatting with Sr. Elizabeth and Dr. Folley.

As Charlie approached the door he caught Durant's eye and motioned for him to step into the hall. Durant made an immediate move for the door with Daly following. Outside and out of sight from Folley, Charlie offered the services of the Consultants to Durant at no cost. Patello proposed that the consulting expertise could be a valuable assist to the hospital's administration in developing the cost-reduction plan. Durant was elated with the offer and accepted on the spot.

Daly listened intently to the conversation between his boss and the Board member. Afterward, he reminded Durant that he had been placed in charge of the planning process which meant that the consultants were to be in his charge. Durant again explained to Daly that the immediate problem was cost reduction in concert with planning. That meant that he and Weaver would be working in tandem with the consultants. Durant decided that he would personally direct the process.

Rod Weaver was finished working the crowd. He was noticed by Durant as he escorted Sr. Elizabeth toward the door. Since Daly was already standing by lobbying for control, Durant thought it a good time to get his two senior executives primed for the task ahead. He asked Daly to follow Rod to the door and then escort him back to the President's office for a brief post mortem. Daly obediently went after Weaver as Durant returned to his office.

A few minutes later Daly and Weaver came into the President's office already engaged in heated debate over the process of cost reduction versus strategic planning. Weaver was adamant that the process as requested by the Board should be led by the Fiscal officer. Daly insisted that the cost-reduction program was a feature of a bigger effort in strategic planning and therefore should be lead and coordinated by the professional planner. Durant patiently listened to the debate until he suspected that his two valued assistants were about to resume physical combat.

At this vital point he explained the process by handing out specific assignments accordingly: "Gentlemen, the Board in its usual fashion was not clear what it expected to see in the next week. It did mandate a plan for a thirty percent cost reduction over the next year. That means immediate cutbacks. Rod, pull together the other members of the executive staff for an emergency session. Operations will have to carry the ball with the initial layoffs. After the first hit of a general cut we'll go after the programs that are free standing and in deficit. SACAP is one that comes to mind. The next level of cost reduction is modification of those programs that are high cost and primary to our mission statement. Things like teaching, research, and tertiary care are examples of the third level. At the third level we will want to consider spreading the cost of programs by arranging affiliations with other teaching and research institutions in the City. This means a loss of autonomy. It might also lead into a merger. Mitch, this is where you come in. I want you to become very valuable to Sr. Elizabeth and her committee. Give them all the staff support they can handle. Become valuable to Logan. He has no staff for planning so you become his staff. Just remember, you still work for me. When the consultants get involved they will function out of my office but will work with each of you as we progress through the three phases. Now, gentlemen, you have the outline for the cost-reduction plan that will be explained to the Board next week. I'll have the consultants put this forward as their recommendation so we can bypass Folley's usual objection to whatever we suggest. Any questions?"

Daly was energized by the assignment. Durant's organized approach to the effort was exciting. It seemed to create a clear path that everyone would follow. This was Daly's style. He loved having everyone marching to a common drummer even though he preferred to march to his own beat. He seemed confident in his assignment but sought some clarification. "Joe, if I'm reading you right you want me to contact Sr. Elizabeth and offer her help with her committee. That will bring us into some discussion about phase three details in the cost-reduction program including affiliations and possibly merger. You think the Bishop will even allow us to talk about that?"

Durant took some time to think before he answered. "I don't know, Mitch. You recall that Sister mentioned that we couldn't plan in a vacuum. She wanted the Cardinal's input and direction. Talk of a merger will force him to speak although it may be in Tongues. I read in the last issue of Health Progress from the Catholic Health Association that some religious Orders of Women are restructuring their health ministry and repositioning away from the institutional acute care business to non-institutional services for the poor such as halfway houses, nutritional support, and daycare centers. If His Eminence wants to make that switch in Boston, the next year seems to be the open window."

Weaver sat wide eyed listening to the conversation. When Durant mentioned repositioning to non-institutional service Rod broke in.

"Not in a million years! He can't afford to get out of acute care. We've got too much debt. He'll never file Chapter Eleven. That's the only way he could dump the bond holders. St. A's balance sheet after this year's deficit won't be able to satisfy our capital debt out of equity. We would have to dissolve. The Cardinal wouldn't have a nickel to support those charity programs. That could take down the whole Archdiocese. He's broke as it is. It seems to me that we are in one hell of a bind."

"We'll never know unless we force the conversation to the surface, Rod." Durant remained pensive as he responded. "The ethical issues are also beginning to mount. Assisted suicide is going to be as big as abortion. If State or Federal action supports that as a right I question if the Church will be able to remain in the acute care business regardless of the fiscal issues. That's something else that Sister's committee will need to discuss, I guess."

Suddenly Daly appeared uncomfortable. "Joe, I don't think I can lead any discussion on the ethical things. I don't know anything about the Church except what I hear around here." Daly's agnosticism was well known throughout the hospital. He was firm in his social stance that belief in a Supreme Being was a very personal matter not requiring an open ecclesiastical forum. Therefore, Church in any form was not a part of his thinking.

Durant was tolerant of Daly's point of view and sheltered him from the ritual of the Catholic hospital in order to avoid any mutual embarrassment. "Don't worry about leading that discussion, Mitch. It will happen without your urging. If nothing else the Cardinal and Bishop Hanks will work it out in a closed session and then bring the answers if there are any to the committee. All you have to do is make sure that the ethical issues are recorded when they come up."

"Let's get back to the cuts," urged Weaver. "You want me to get operations to chop across the Board on the first run then we go back and knock off the losers. Why don't we do 'em both at the same time?"

"That's fine. Do them both at the same time if you can." Durant was agitated at Weaver's apparent criticism. "Do you know or are you sure who the winners and losers are? It seems to me that some review is in order before we just chop off a department or program."

"Not all of' 'em," quipped Weaver, "but we have some that are no-brainers. You mentioned SACAP. That's a big loser. We could save a ton if we closed it today. Not only do the dopers not pay but they routinely bust up the place. I think we should convince Folley to fold it up. First cut I think we should ask for a twenty percent cut back in staffing then settle for fifteen. How's that sound?"

Durant was skeptical. "Rod, it sounds like a wild guess. You probably have reason for suggesting that number but I beg you to support it with fact. We'll have a hell of a time convincing the management staff to do the cuts not to mention the skepticism of O'Shea. Work it up and be prepared to present it at a general management meeting in a few days. Meanwhile, I'll see that Human Resources gets with you to work out the proper notices and placement services. You have any trouble with that?"

As Durant finished his reply he signaled the end of the meeting. Daly and Weaver left abruptly without further comment. The cost-reduction program had begun.

Dr. Folley quit the Board meeting in good spirits. He always maintained an appearance of self-esteem and control no matter what pressures he might be facing. This was in stark contrast to Michael Logan who Folley had in tow. Logan was visibly distressed after the meeting. His depression was apparent in his manner and his conversation with the trustees who took the time to speak to him. Folley noticed his state of mind and decided to change the young man's attitude with a little counseling in the great man's office.

The office of the Chairman of the Department of Medicine at St. Anslem's Hospital well represented the status of the Chairman and well as the incumbent's ego. Originally the single office was adequate to hold a desk, credenza, small conference table, and several comfortable chairs. Soon, after being named to the post Dr. Folley removed the adjacent walls of the office tripling its size. He added paneled walls, thick carpet, expensive bookshelves, a miniature library, communication and entertainment center, two comfortable sofas, and innumerable pictures of the great Physician with heads of State, Cardinals, Popes, Corporate Presidents, Athletes, Royalty, and Television Personalities not to mention one picture of his wife and daughter.

Logan was welcomed into the plush accommodation and given an in-depth commentary about each person with whom the great man was pictured. Then they sat on the comfortable couch and had a father to son type conversation.

Folley intended to convince Logan that they were in control of the hospital and its administration. Sister Elizabeth had distorted that concept in the Board meeting and somehow had manage to wrestle the control of the Office of Health Affairs hack into the arms of the clergy. He began the conversation with a direct approach. "Michael, regardless of what this morning's meeting might lead you to think, I am in charge of the health affairs of the Archdiocese. That position takes precedence over any board or committee. As far as you are concerned, you only report to me, not to Sr. Elizabeth or anyone else. I'm the boss. St. Anslem's is run by Tom O'Shea and me. Hardly is our support. No one else counts. What we say goes."

This type of reaffirmation was very much needed by Logan. His confidence was lost by the conduct of the meeting. Folley seemed to reinstate some of the foundation but he retained an uneasy feeling about the ability of Folley to exercise the authority he claimed to have. His inclination was to directly question the great man on the stability of the secretary appointment and his own position as director of the office. Instead he opted to be polite and talk around his concerns.

Logan began to comment. "The meeting was an eye-opener, Richard. The quality of the people on the Board is very impressive. Everyone seemed eager to participate. You must enjoy the collegial activity."

The attempt to catch Folley in a soft contradiction by referring to collegiality was missed by the great doctor. He responded with a flurry of compliments about the members of the Board and concluded with praise for his counterparts. "You know, Michael, we have some of the best minds in healthcare gathered at St. Anslem's. The people on the Board respect that and add to our excellence. They are the true leaders of the Boston community. It's an honor to be part of this organization. They have attended to the needs of the institution and have guided us to greater heights. We are truly blessed to have a Board with such dedication and influence. You will come to appreciate them in a very short time."

Logan could see that his meeting was more "bullshit" than "applesauce" as they used to say at City Hall. He began to plot his escape from the den of greatness. "We need to get our office set up, Doctor. I have an appointment with a rental agent who wants to show us some new space in Wellesley. I understand that would be close to your home. Would you like to see it with us?"

The good doctor hated these details. He preferred to be accommodated in accord with his status. Shopping was not part of that accommodation. "Michael, I know that you will do an excellent job in choosing the right spot. Wellesley would be very nice. If it looks good to you sign the deal. I'll arrange for the bills to be paid by the hospital."

Michael Logan said his goodbye to Dr. Folley and walked to the hospital's lobby.

Mitch Daly spotted him near the door and ran to catch up. He reintroduced himself to Logan in a friendly way. Logan was impressed with Daly's professional demeanor and his friendship. The prospect of friendship was more the attraction since Logan felt a strong need for a friend in what he believed to be a hostile environment. Daly sensing the acceptance walked with Logan to the parking garage. The two men chatted generally about the Board meeting. As they were about to go their different ways, Daly nonchalantly offered to help Logan with the work of the planning committee, Logan accepted without hesitation.

Within minutes after Logan departed for his appointment with the real estate agent, Daly informed Durant that he had infiltrated the Office of Health Affairs. Durant was pleased.

Durant, while pleased with Daly's initiative, could not give him much time to relay all the details of his successful encounter with Logan. Waiting outside the President's office were two representatives from Action Waste Management who had arrived for their appointment to discuss the design and implementation of the waste control program for the hospital. Durant had summoned his Operations Officer and Director of Environmental Services to join them. Neither had arrived as yet and Durant was reluctant to meet with the Action "hoods" alone. *They can wait*, he thought as he began to scribble the first paragraphs of what would eventually be the minutes of the recently concluded Board meeting.

Outside of Durant's office Ken Ryan and Jay Marquart waited patiently for the meeting to begin. Ken was nervous about the presentation that he had outlined the day before and explained to Jay that morning. He and Jay had rehearsed for about two hours before driving to the hospital. Jay was excited about the prospect of meeting the hospital "big shot." He had mentioned to Ken that after they made their pitch he intended to tell the "cheese" some things about his hospital that needed "some work." Ken at first pleaded and then emphatically instructed Jay to set his own problems aside and attend only to the task of the company. Jay, with a hurt expression, promised to behave himself and stick to the script as Ken had it written. He still nursed the fantasy of convincing the boss that a certain nurse in the Medical Intensive Care Unit was "a big-ass problem that had to go."

The hospital's Chief Operating Officer and the Director of Environmental Services arrived about five minutes after the time of the appointment. As they entered the President's waiting area, the Executive Assistant introduced them to Ken and Jay. They were involved in conversation when Joe Durant opened his office door and invited them to come in. The five men sat around the well-used small conference table. Ken introduced Jay to the hospital President as his assistant and technical advisor for the St. Anslem's contract. Jay, in very proper businesslike fashion, shook Durant's hand and commented about the excellent reputation of the hospital. He concluded his statement with an expression of pleasure in being associated with this premier institution.

Durant was pleasantly surprised at the quality of Action's representatives. He had expected another "knee capper" like Veto Celi. Ken Ryan was, first of all, a gentleman and secondly a true expert in the process of waste management. *The technical guy is a bit of a bullshitter but seems like he could adapt to the hospital scene*, was the mental note that Durant made as Jay was introduced. He also realized that he was captive to the contract so to make the most of it he decided to listen rather than argue with the presentation. If any contest was in order he knew that he could rely on his COO and DES to carry the ball.

Durant countered Ryan's remarks with an explanation of the hospital's organization and conduct. He emphasized the priority of patient care while pointing out that the hospital functioned around the clock. Therefore, all patient support services, especially sanitation was a perpetual need. Waste services had to be continuous.

Ryan was attentive to the admonitions of the chief executive. He addressed the need to be always supportive of the patient and the caregiver. To accomplish the intent of the contract which was in another sense a patient care activity, Action intended to do a complete review of the hospital's waste handling systems to insure the sanitary quality of the institution was maintained and enhanced.

Ken Ryan explained, "The company's leading technician. Mr. Jay Marquart, will supervise a team of four people who will spend two weeks around the clock reviewing all procedures of waste disposal. After the review has been completed we will make specific recommendations on improved methods that we will discuss with the hospital. We will also train your personnel on the new methods of dealing with hazardous and infectious waste products. After the training is complete we will do continuous spot reviews and upgrades on methods and equipment. We have a twenty-four-hour on-call service that will respond in case there is a special problem like a radiation spill or contamination. With your permission, Mr. Durant, I would like Jay Marquart to explain more about the survey process."

During the rehearsal Jay had been short and bland as he explained to Ken how he thought the survey should be conducted. His descriptions were not very impressive compared to Ken's style but adequate to convince the hospital management that Action had some idea what it was about. Durant's nod to Ken's suggestion for Jay to proceed created a transformation of Jay's rehearsed stoic personality to the great orator. With persuasive animation he walked and talked about the details of the hospital's systems. He knew the trash collection regimens of the environmental services personnel, the location of the trash chutes, and the special handling of waste from the infectious cases, surgery, and post anesthesia recovery. He talked about double bagging, red bagging, incineration, liquid waste, and equipment sanitation. He even talked with knowledge about the Joint Commission on Accreditation of Healthcare Organizations' safety and sanitation standards and the State regulations pertaining to AIDS. He was in his element and he knew it. After about fifteen minutes he had blown their minds.

The hospital's Director of Environmental Services was amazed at Jay's detailed knowledge of the housekeeping policies and procedures. His instinct was to offer Jay a job on the spot. The Chief Operating Officer was equally impressed and, in his mind was thinking that Jay would be an excellent replacement for the DES. Durant was wondering if Jay's knowledge would lead to significant cuts in the Environmental Services staff that would offset the cost of the waste management contract. For the first time Durant was optimistic about the invasion of the hospital by Action Waste Management. "These guys are pros," he said to himself. "Where in the hell did they get that thug, Celi? That part still doesn't fit."

The presentation plan that Ken had prepared called for him to follow Jay with more rhetoric about the depth of Action's quality control. As Jay concluded his comments, Ken realized that Jay was a tough act to follow. He recognized that the hospital's executives were literally "in the bag" as far as Acton was concerned. To belabor the pitch would be overkill that could possibly dull the edge that Jay had so skillfully honed. Instead he opted to conclude the promotion and move into details.

Ken concluded, "Mr. Durant, we can have our team here tomorrow to meet whatever staff you would like to have involved with us in the survey. Mr.

Marquart has been cleared from his other assignments to give St. Anslem's first priority. We are ready."

Durant was sold as was the COO and DES. He actually thanked the Action representatives and then asked the COO to take charge of the project. The COO immediately bucked it to the DES who responded to Ryan.

"Gentlemen, I suggest that you have your team available to meet with supervisory staff from environmental services, nursing, engineering, and ancillary support services tomorrow afternoon at one-thirty. I'll arrange the meeting. Here's my card. If your secretary could contact my office after ten tomorrow we can tell you where the meeting will be. I expect we will have present about fifteen or twenty persons. That will be the first team. Others will come on board as you move through the house. You'll find St. A's people a delight to work with."

Ryan recognized a good ending. He rose from his chair and shook the hand of each of the hospital executives. "We will be here tomorrow at one-thirty. This has been a very enjoyable and productive session. Action is honored to be a part of the St. Anslem's tradition. Thank you very much."

As Ken spoke he passed out his business card. Suddenly he realized that the star of the show, one Jay Marquart, had not been blessed with business cards since he was not a part of management or sales. Awkwardly he asked Jay to write his name on the back of his card so that the hospital executives would be able to contact him. Jay obediently retrieved the cards and printed his name and desk extension on the back of Ken's card.

Durant was amused at Ken's embarrassment. "You'll have to get the kid a promotion so he can have his own cards," he quipped.

As Durant was concluding his meeting with the Action reps, Dr. Ron Anderson was entering the sanctuary of Dr. Folley. He carried the medical record of Jay Marquart and a copy of the incident report filed by Bob Markley. The Board meeting and the postmortem session with Logan had caused Folley to forget the little problem in SACAP. When Anderson entered his office Folley was curious why he was there. Anderson impatiently explained that the meeting was Folley's idea. Apparently the great one felt a need for an off the record report about the Marquart incident. Gradually Dr. Folley's mind adjusted to the particulars of the incident. He asked Ron to sit down and give him a full verbal report.

Anderson was irritated that the matter had not been officially reviewed by the administration. He let Folley know in no certain terms that the hospital was running a major risk if it did not take proper steps to offset what could be a major lawsuit. "If it is necessary to protect the investigation from discovery by classifying it as professional review then let's get it done!" shouted Anderson. "Risk management should have been on top of this the minute they got my report."

Folley listened patiently to his super star for a few minutes and then held up his hands to call for a pause. "Ron, so far you've told me how upset you are, how administration is dragging its feet, and what a hell of a mess we're in. Somehow you have managed to avoid telling me what happened to cause this sad state of affairs. Could you possibly get to the details?"

Anderson reacted. "Yeah, sure. In a nutshell this fellow, Marquart, a patient in the program, uses the unit phone to call his ex-wife, a nurse in MICU. She sees on the caller screen that he's in SACAP and runs to her lawyer who files to revoke his joint custody of their kid. Now I think he's got us on violation of the confidentiality provisions, both State and Federal, and I imagine he's got her on several violations of the nurse Practice Act. She could lose her license. We could lose ours. He could get a big settlement. That's it in a nutshell."

Folley sat up in his chair. His eyes opened wide at first and seemed to begin to squint as he thought about Anderson's comments. "If what you say is true then we need to reach a settlement with this patient. On the other hand, if the telephone made the mistake, then the hospital is not at fault but the nurse is in deep trouble. My thinking is that he used the phone for his own benefit, not for ours. In a way, it was an unauthorized use of hospital equipment. I could argue that he doesn't have a case."

Anderson stood and began to pace as he responded to Folley's observations. "I thought of that too. Then Markley busted by bubble when he told me that he gave Marquart permission to use the phone. I think that brings us back into the problem."

The complexity of the issue caused Folley to have a headache. He wanted to delegate this mess but his immediate subordinate to whom he would refer the matter stood before him seeking guidance. The pressure of accountability caused him to abdicate. "Okay. Let's give this to risk management and professional review like Durant wants. I'll tell him that it's being forwarded by Department so he has to keep me involved as the Chairman and referring party. You and Markley are parties to the fact. We point at the nurse. I imagine that the hospital will eventually have a disciplinary hearing and will be forced to report the misconduct of the nurse to the State. That could screw her out of her career."

Without further comment, he dialed the number of the Risk Management office and directed the manager to refer the incident report to the director of Quality Assurance for immediate review. Dr. Folley also advised that he would sign the report as Dr. Anderson's supervisor.

Susan Marquart hated the summer. During the winter Benny was in school and was the teacher's problem. Now he was hers. James wasn't old enough to realize that Mom needed a few drinks in the afternoon to move her from one hour to the next. Benny was old enough to understand and even ask questions. He was out of the house at the moment, playing ball with the neighborhood kids in a vacant lot. James was taking a nap. Carefully she recovered the bag of white powder that Louise had so generously left after the party Saturday night. She inhaled the cocaine and felt the pleasure with relief from the problems of the day. She, for the moment, couldn't even remember the problems.

Carefully she stretched another line. Life was comfortable again. The ringing seemed distant so she attempted to ignore it. Then it started again and seemed to be closer and closer. Awkwardly she grabbed the phone and gave a mumbled greeting. The person calling her tried repeatedly to communicate with her. She also tried to cooperate but her mind was not functioning on what was being said.

"What? Who is this? This is Susan. Who are you calling? What? Who. Is. This?"

"Susan, this is Eddie. You know. Eddie, the father of your boys. Hey, you on something? Hey, com'on now. You sober up. I wanna talk. Man, you ain't changed at all. You gotta be missin' old Eddie now that your hero is goin' clean."

The fog covering Susan's mind was beginning to clear. Eddie's name registered strong with her. He caused her to tremble and chill. "Eddie, why are you calling? I don't need you."

Eddie laughed. "You'll always need me, honey, or someone like me 'cause I got what you need to face your miserable life. But that's not the only reason I'm calling. I hear from our mutual friend, Brian, that my kid is on the All-Star team. So, when does he play? I gotta see the game."

Susan's emotions bounced from anger to calm. Eddie had not exhibited any interest in the boys from the time of their birth. He had beaten her when he learned that she was pregnant claiming that she purposely conceived to trap and enslave him to a responsibility that he didn't want. Now he seemed to want to be part of the boys' life. Benny had asked her about his real father on several occasions. He was interested in his father even though his father did not seem interested in him. Jay had attempted to be a true surrogate with reasonable success. Benny liked Jay and well appreciated the special attention that Jay gave him, especially in baseball. If Eddie attended the game Jay may become offended and retreat from the close affection that had developed between the two. She also realized that she could not stop Eddie from attending the game. He could easily find out from the Waltham Recreation Department when the game was going to be played. He had called her for another reason. Benny, the All Star, was his excuse.

"The first round is Wednesday at six," she reported. "If they win they play again on Saturday. Are you really going to be there? Why don't you bring your support payments with you? That way I won't have to bother the judge."

The comment caused Eddie to chuckle. "Well, darling, you know that I don't need a hassle with a judge. Maybe you and I could work out some sort of trade. You know, maybe I could supply you with a needed commodity. Brian tells me that your old man isn't buying anymore. That means you are on the wagon unless you have resources that we don't know about. I can start hanging out with Benny and James now and then like a good daddy. They could deliver the mail between us. It sort of gives the kids a sense of responsibility. Can't get 'em started too early. What do you say?"

Susan was furious. "Eddie, you no-good son of a bitch! You want my kids to be a mule for their goddamn worthless father. You son of a bitch! Maybe I will explain this to the judge when I drag you into court." Her audible sobs caused her to choke as she tried to scream her response.

Eddie seemed unmoved by her emotional outburst. "Whoa. Hold on there, Sweetheart. I'm trying to make things simple and easy for us. Now if you bring the judge into the deal he's gonna expect that you have mended your sorrowful ways. I might go to the slam but you, my dear, go on the wagon with your hubby. From what I hear that's the last thing you want to do. Right? So, what I suggest is that you and me come to terms. Like, I give you a reasonable discount on your personal needs and you lay off on the support thing. You don't want the kids as the go between, that's okay. Then we got to work something else out. I think it's best we do it my way. I still am going to Benny's game. You want to talk some more there? I'm willing to listen. See you Wednesday?"

"Yeah. Okay. We can talk Wednesday!"

As Susan hung up the phone she broke into a sweat. Her hands trembled. She knew that she had to accept Benny's offer. The problem was explaining to Jay that Benny's real father was taking an interest in his son and then explaining why the support payments stopped. The inconsistency of the two actions would cause Jay to eventually discover that Eddie was her supplier. She would also have to pay the balance to Eddie from the meager house allowance that Jay was able to afford her. This was a very dangerous and delicate operation that required a cool approach. She also reasoned that Benny as the go between might inadvertently say something to Jay that would cause the upset. An alternate was necessary.

Perhaps Louise could help, she thought. *She seems to understand the problem.*

Susan was uncertain about Louise as a friend. She was very supportive of Susan in dealing with the pressure that Jay's reformation was causing her. But could she be trusted to be a mule for her in bringing the goods from Eddie? Brian, as a professional mule worked for the syndicate under Eddie's supervision. Would Eddie tell Brian about the link? Then Brian would tell Jay because of their long standing friendship. The set up was full of faults but there seemed to be no alternative. She decided to call Louise and discuss the proposition when the telephone rang.

When she answered Jay greeted her with bubbling excitement. "Suse, I really scored big! Ken Ryan asked me to be the lead tech at St. A's so we made the proposal this afternoon and I wowed 'em. They want me bad. Anyway, I met the head guy who thinks I'm great. I'm gonna be spending a lot of time surveying the joint. Hell, maybe I can convince the boss to can Cecile. Then I'll sue his ass with less prejudice. Anyway, I called to let you know that I'm doing some overtime then I'll go direct to St. A's for my support therapy. Oh, yeah, Martha called. Seems my emergency hearing is set for Friday morning. I'll meet with my lawyer tomorrow. Then Martha and I are gonna have a special session on Thursday before I go to my support thing. That means I won't be able to make the start of Benny's game but I'll get there before it's over. How's things with you?"

Susan sensed an opportunity to set the stage for her own arrangement. Jay's good mood allowed her to inject the presence of Eddie at the game without causing Jay depression or anger. Eddie would serve as Jay's substitute. It was worth the gamble. "Jay, I've had a bit of a shock that I'm still trying to recover from. That bastard, Eddie, called and told me that he was going to Benny's game. He said that he wanted to watch his son play in the All-Star game. I told him that I thought he had a lot of nerve."

Jay reacted in a strong but calm manner. "Boy, that takes a pair. He doesn't even give the kid a birthday present but he wants to take pride in the fact that his son is on the All Stars. He's really messed up. You better tell Benny that his father is gonna be at the game. It's probably a good thing that I'm gonna be late. I don't want to have to talk to the guy. You can do that."

Susan was surprised and more than a little hurt at Jay's reaction. While it was what she had hoped for it nevertheless left her with the definite and distinct impression that she was secondary in Jay's life. He cared not that Eddie was reentering her life and the lives of Benny and James. He definitely was totally focused on Kristie and his legal bout with Cecile. She felt the pangs of jealously. After a few minutes of contemplation, she called Louise.

Jay and Ken Ryan sat at a table in the cafeteria at Action Waste Management. Food service had been discontinued for the day except for the coffee pot that was always available for employees on break. Jay talked incessantly about the St. A's project. He explained the survey approach, waste collection points, employee training programs, and recycling. Ken took extensive notes as Jay rambled and occasionally inserted his own observations. The two men were as excited as college students planning a road trip. They were having fun being a success. Ken needed this session with Jay in order to compile the program plan for the St. Anslem's project. That plan, formally prepared and submitted under Ken's signature, would go to Mr. Meehan for final approval and pricing. Then the final document would become a part of the contract including all the extras that Celi would deliver to Mr. Durant by the end of the week. Ken expected to have the draft of the plan completed this afternoon and had asked Jay to hang around to review the draft. Jay, contrary to his usual reaction, was eager to participate. His only concern was that he not be late for his evening therapy support session at St. Anslem's.

Ken Ryan was a quick study when it came to creating a written proposal. He picked up Jay's ideas and polished them to perfection. Within an hour after he had returned to his desk the first draft was being reviewed by Jay who made several suggestions. Jay was equally excited about the creative function. He sat with Ken as the proposal went in and through the word processor. Another draft was produced that required little revisions. By six P.M. the team of Ryan and Marquart delivered the final proposal for the St. Anslem's project to the in-basket on the secretary's desk in Mr. Meehan's office. There was no doubt that the two men had prepared a masterpiece for the company. Under usual circumstances they would have washed down their euphoria with several beers before arriving home late and too tired to explain to the waiting spouse what caused this celebrate binge.

That was the way a working man, or woman perhaps, was expected to give emphasis to the import of their labors. It is a long-respected custom. But no longer is it the custom for Mr. Jay Marquart. Mr. Marquart's excitement for the day is followed by a rush trip to St. Anslem's Hospital where he will pee in a bottle and cavort with his fellow junkies and drunks. Jay Marquart is establishing a new ritual in an attempt to rid himself of the habitual effect of an old custom.

The adrenaline was flowing as Jay made his way back to St. Anslem's. He arrived a few minutes late for his lab test but sufficiently ahead of the time for the start of the support group session. Bob Markley met him in the Unit and offered Jay the specimen bottle. That was all Jay required in the way of instruction. He proceeded to the restroom, filled the much too little bottle with urine, applied the safety cap, and returned the specimen to the waiting Bob Markley.

Bob noticed the spirited attitude of Marquart and had to comment. "Jay, you look like a high school kid that just landed his first date. You really that turned on about going to a support group?"

"Oh, no, man. I scored big at work today," bubbled Jay. "As a matter-of-fact I set this place up with a hell of a deal. You are going into a waste management program that will make this place the talk of the town. Man, you are going to have the best recycling system in the whole Country. Count on it, baby. And old Junkie Jay set it up. You may applaud."

Markley shook his head in disbelief at the pride his patient exhibited. Then he glanced down at the memorandum on his desk from Mr. Weaver's office that summoned him to a crisis meeting to discuss and implement a minimum twenty percent cut in expenses. Now he learned from a popular drunk that the hospital was adopting a waste management program on top of a twenty percent cutback. "Durant has really lost it this time," he mumbled as Jay marched around the room acting like a proud Caesar.

Markley took a deep breath that caused his emotions to gain control. With some remorse, he looked at Jay now perched on his elbows across the desk. "Okay, Napoleon, let's go join the party of our peers."

Somehow Markley had persuaded the hospital administration to let the SACAP Support Group use the hospital cafeteria for its Tuesday and Thursday night sessions. This meant that the cafeteria had to be closed to the public by seven o'clock on those particular evenings. It also meant a loss of revenue from the regular use of the cafeteria coupled with the fact that the support group did not pay for the use of the room or the coffee they consumed. This was another coup for Markley over administration. Weaver had wanted to charge the revenue loss to the SACAP budget but Dr. Anderson raised so much hell that Durant caved in. Markley was concerned that the mess that the group caused plus the occasional fight that broke up the furniture would give emphasis to Weaver's point and cause Durant to change his mind regardless of Anderson's wild temper. Fortunately, Durant was far too occupied with the escapades of Dr. Folley to worry about a few broken tables and chairs. At the moment, the party seemed secure.

Bob Markley and Jay entered the cafeteria a few minutes after seven. The meeting was well attended. At least thirty qualified members were present who politely applauded when Bob arrived. Instead of moving to the podium as Jay expected, Bob took a seat in the third row next to several elderly participants. Jay hastened to sit next to him. The room came to near order as an elderly gentleman, facilitator for the evening, came to the front. He asked everyone to rise and join him in the opening prayer. Jay was not ready for a religious experience. The idea of a prayer seemed to turn him off from a party that he was not overly excited about to begin with. With reluctance he stood and prepared himself for the usual Our Father, Hail Mary, fair for which Catholics were famous. Instead the assembled stood and began to recite The Twelve Steps of Alcoholics Anonymous from small pamphlets that were on each chair. Markley was most vocal in his recitation, from Jay's observation.

The elderly gentleman asked for order following the opening prayer since several members decided to have another cup of coffee and continue to socialize. Gradually the members returned to their chairs. Once order was returned, the facilitator asked each person to introduce themselves. As usual each person began with the admission that they were a drunk or an addict, gave their first name, and then reported how long they had been sober. The times ranged from over twenty years to less than a day. To Jay's surprise, Markley reported only a ten-month period of sobriety. Some members omitted the statistic that caused Jay to recognize that the information was not obligatory.

When it was his turn, Jay made the admission and reported one week of success on the road to recovery. As he was speaking he noticed for the first time that several of the attendees were close to his age. That gave him some encouragement and comfort in realizing that he was not confined to an old man's club. Following the introductions, the facilitator asked the audience to take time to meet and become acquainted with the person near them or if already acquainted then find a new friend. The purpose, as everyone seemed to know, was to create a network of acquaintances who could help in a crisis.

Again, the meeting became animated and seemingly unruly. Jay wanted to converse with Bob who had turned to the person on the other side leaving Jay to find another friend. He sat in silence for a brief time until he felt a tap on his shoulder.

The man introduced himself as Herb. He was dressed in an open collared sport shirt and a pair of Dockers. His Rockport dock siders covered sockless feet. Jay estimated his age at around forty. He was well spoken and conveyed a professional attitude. Jay shook the outstretched hand and accepted the suggestion that they move to a less crowded part of the room. Herb told Jay that he had worked the investment desk at a large investment firm and was well on his way to making big money when he was caught by his boss coming in an hour late after a liquid lunch. Fortunately the boss recognized the symptoms of a problem drinker and sent him to the company employee assistance program. Herb objected to the inference that he had a problem and resigned. After several weeks of unemployment and constant drinking he found his way back to the program. He was reemployed on a probationary basis and now was on the way to recovery.

Herb had also found Jesus as he traveled the way on his journey. Jesus was his inspiration and his guide to a new life and the life hereafter for there was no life without Jesus. He wanted Jay to understand that Jesus could be his friend as well and help him through the pain and suffering that was part of the recovery process but more important Jesus would be his strength as he faced the temptation to again use the destructive substances.

Jay became increasingly uncomfortable as Herb continued to ramble about his born-again status. He looked for an opportunity to break off the conversation. Several times Jay glanced over toward Bob Markley who was engaged in conversation with several people. No chance for rescue.

Jay sensed that the only way to divert the conversation was to become confrontational, a method that well fit his personality. "Herb, I guess that Jesus is the right way for you but I believe in myself as the only source of power to overcome my problem. You see, I'm responsible for what I do. No other person or God directs my will. What I do I do myself. If I need help then I get that help from my friends."

To Jay's surprise, Herb seemed pleased with the comment. His eyes brightened and he again took Jay by the hand. "You see, my friend, how you admit that an inner strength is necessary for recovery. I felt the same way but eventually I realized that the inner strength was the true Spirit of Jesus Christ born within us. That's the answer to the problem we face. By increasing our faith we build inner strength of mind and soul that carries us through our trials. You will come to realize that the dependency that you have on yourself is really a dependency on Christ Our Savior. Study His life and you will see yourself. Then you will have strength because you will have knowledge and inspiration."

Jay realized that Herb was very serious about his religious perspective. He was not evangelizing. He stated his opinions about Jesus in a calm but definite manner. Herb was a true believer. The man deserved respect. He was sincere in presenting Jay with a perspective that he believed would help his recovery. It was difficult to simply confront the man.

On the other hand to accept his point of view could result in an acquaintance that Jay did not really want. *What the hell?* Jay thought. *I guess I'll just have to give it to him straight.* "Herb, as I understand this session we are supposed to be getting acquainted so we can help each other when we are about to fall off the wagon. Now it seems to me that you and I have different attitudes about who gives us our strength when we need it. I say it's strictly up to me and you say it's Jesus. Now with that difference I don't see that we could be of help to each other. Hell, man, if you start preaching to me about Jesus you can be damned sure that I'm gonna take a stiff drink and keep on rollin'. In fact, I feel like one right now."

Herb was not about to be deterred. "The truth is, Jay, we always feel like taking a drink and keep on rolling. Falling off the wagon is what we do best, I guess. It takes strength to hold on. You know that Jesus fell three times on His way to His death and resurrection. His crucifixion is a reflection of our own.

We can be renewed through Him. Think about it. Maybe we shouldn't be together at the time of our crisis but we are together now and you have been an inspiration to me to keep my faith. Perhaps I have been of some help to you. I pray that this conversation creates an awareness that Christ is your strength and that someday you will realize that. Anyway, we have met as fellow travelers. We'll see each other again. Remember, live and let live."

Herb stood, gave Jay a pat on the shoulder, and walked across the room where he easily entered another conversation. Jay was left alone and somewhat bewildered. Now that the conversation had ended he was a bit remorseful. It didn't seem that he had offended Herb. Jay actually hoped that he would have the opportunity to meet him again. The fact that he had been influenced by a "Jesus freak" was fascinating.

Anxiously he sought the opportunity to review the experience with Bob Markley who was roaming about talking to everyone he could. Jay walked toward him and was about to corner him when the facilitator again called for order. When all were seated he introduced a lady by her first name who came forward to lead a review in "The 24-Hour Plan" The "plan" was a simple process of concentrating on keeping sober for the current twenty-four-hour period. Essentially the plan was to merely put off taking a drink until tomorrow. Jay found the concept amusing but controlled his expressions. Others in the room nodded their agreement with the concept but humorously chided the presenter who also took humor in her presentation.

For a bunch of drunks, Jay thought, *these guys are a ton of laughs.*

The meeting concluded exactly at eight. Markley and a few others policed the cafeteria and rearranged the tables and chairs. Jay assisted Markley with the cleanup detail. He wanted to talk to him about the meeting anyway. It only took about a half-hour to complete the detail. Jay noticed that the Environmental night staff was poised outside the cafeteria waiting to finish the process so the cafeteria would be ready to reopen for the night shift. Markley did a final check and then signaled the cleaning staff to come in. He put his arm around Jay's shoulder and thanked him for his help. Jay acknowledged and asked if Bob had a few minutes to chat. Markley looked at his watch as if to signal limited time and suggested that they go over to the Unit.

They sat at the desk since the staff was busy making patient rounds. Markley asked Jay what was on his mind.

Jay wasn't sure how to address the subject but made a straightforward attempt. "Bob, this session tonight was a little weird from my point of view. I mean I can't see how this buddy-buddy shit does any good. I've been sober for only a week so why make a big thing out of it. Those guys seem like they want to celebrate every minute off the stuff. I'm not sure that I belong. Then I meet this guy Herb who gets off telling me about how he found Jesus. Man, I know that I don't belong. You got to help me in a different way, man. This is definitely not my style."

Markley gave Jay an understanding glance. "Jay, you do belong but we don't want to force you to realize your dependency on others. We want you to discover it by becoming acquainted with people who you can depend on to help you in a crisis. Sooner or later you will want someone to help you through a situation. You will reach out for them. I expect that, at this time in your recovery, you would call me since you know me the best. Eventually you might find reason to call Herb or somebody else that you will meet in future sessions. As you become better acquainted you will have a circle of associates and will only come to the meetings occasionally. A lot of people come now only to offer to be of help to others. They have their problem under good control but none of us are ever cured. You have to remember that. That's why we emphasize mutual support. You may not believe this but you are still in a withdrawal stage. Hopefully you have moved to phase three where the impact of the change in you physically is minor. However, you could be at the Phase Two level where your emotional reaction to the physical withdrawal could be severe. In other words you could be a living time bomb emotionally. Something could set you off and you could become violent. You have demonstrated your temper to us on a few occasions. What I am attempting to do by having you attend these sessions is to build a network of people who you can call when you feel a violent reaction coming on. Most if not all of the people at the meeting tonight have experienced this kind of reaction. They know what to do."

Jay waved his disbelief at his friend. "Yeah, right. I've got some poor sum bitch by the neck ready to pound on him and buddy Herb shows up and gives me a Jesus lesson. That's really gonna help, man. Why can't I just rely on my on mental strength to get through? How come I got to have all this help?" Jay's climbing irritation served as a good case in point as he banged the desk for emphasis.

Bob recognized that Jay was losing his control. He thought of bringing that to his attention as an example of the emotional imbalance that could erupt into violence but opted to pursue the content of Jay's remarks. "Eventually you will build more inner strength, Jay, but until you have that strength you will need help from others. At this stage of your recovery you are emotionally weak. You need to condition yourself emotionally. It's like training for the Olympics. Right now you have the desire to win but you haven't a prayer of pulling it off. You need to train for the event. Many people use religion as a platform to build their inner strength. It's a very good base. Herb discovered that. Another good base to stabilize the emotions is prescribed medication. A combination of the two is a very good choice. Remember you have already decided against that medical advice. Now you seem to want to reject social support. Well, I assure you my friend, you will need all the help you can get. Don't cut yourself off completely."

Jay decided to take one more jab. "So if I'm gonna train for the Olympics in Doping Off I need a good coach. Don't tell me Herb is my main man. I need you. You gonna be my coach?"

Markley was reassuring. "Sure. Jay. I'm your coach at least for a while. You still need a network in case I'm not available. Come to the sessions for a while. Eventually you'll get with the program."

Jay noticed that Bob glanced at his watch as he made his last comment. This was definitely a signal that their session was coming to a close. With a polite "thank you" Jay stood and began to leave. Bob remained seated but smiled at Jay as a sign of friendship and encouragement. It was enough to restore Jay's confidence in the program at least for the moment.

Jay said goodbye to Bob and walked toward the main lobby. As he passed the President's office Joe Durant and Rod Weaver were standing in the corridor. Jay greeted the President who seemed pleasantly surprised to see him. He introduced Jay to the Senior Vice President for Finance as the chief consultant for Action Waste Management. He also assumed that Jay was in the hospital as part of his consulting assignment. The three men chatted for a while until Durant commented that it had been an exceptionally long day. Weaver and Marquart were both quick to agree as they separated to find their cars in the nearly vacant parking garage.

When Jay arrived home Susan had his dinner waiting. She asked about his day and he was anxious to tell her every detail. He emoted over and over about his presentation to the hospital's executive staff and his participation in the contract proposal for Mr. Meehan. It seemed to be a near perfect day from Jay's point of view. He even made favorable comments about his support group session commenting briefly about his Jesus freak friend.

Susan sat listening to Jay ramble. She sipped slowly on a tall gin and grapefruit. Jay, in his excitement, had not even noticed. As he stopped to take a bite of food Susan reminded Jay that Benny's father had called to inquire about the All-Star game. Jay seemed as though he was going to choke but then swallowed hard before he reacted. This time he was less controlled than when Susan had mentioned Eddie to him on the phone. Jay became agitated. His eyes narrowed and he pounded the table. Without a word he left the table and walked into the living room where he stared out the window.

The anger consumed him to a point of violence. Had Susan followed him into the living room he most certainly would have struck her. He was out of control but had not yet acted. Eddie was a hot button and Susan had punched it. His mind suddenly focused on the gin and grapefruit that Susan was drinking. He hated her for having that drink. He wanted to punch her senseless. His mind made a quick shift again and the nerd Herb came flashing before his eyes. He hated Herb and he hated Jesus. The thought of Jesus made him sick and he felt a need to get to the bathroom. Then, as he closed the door behind him the anger began to dissipate. He broke into a cold sweat, lay down on the hard tile floor, and fell asleep. It had been an exceptionally long day.

Chapter Twelve

At first the Senior Partner for Corporate Accounts at Debur and Tandy said no to Tom Callahan's request for him to be exclusively assigned to the Park account. Callahan was a big producer. His monthly billings had set company records and had been on the increase every month. Furthermore, his reputation as an expert in healthcare was becoming wide spread. His excellence became the spearhead for the acquisition of new accounts in the health industry. With the consulting assignment came the audit account where more big profits were found. In the old days it was the audit account that created the consulting account. Today, consulting was the front runner. Tom Callahan was too valuable to be assigned to a single account.

Callahan answered Patello's call and, in response to the request that he meet with the CEO at St. Anslem's, informed Patello that Callahan had not been given the go ahead to shepherd the account. Patello immediately called Marone who talked to Capizzi.

Capizzi managed to have a word with Big Frank who placed a call to the President of Debur and Tandy. An hour later Callahan telephoned Patello to inform him that the company had a change of heart. In fact, Tom Callahan had already booked his flight to Boston. He would arrive that evening and would be available to meet with Joe Durant on Thursday. Patello was very pleased with the change. He proposed to meet Callahan at his hotel Thursday morning and accompany him to the hospital. Patello would make the arrangements with Durant.

Durant was not available to take Patello's call. He was in the auditorium listening to Rod Weaver explain to the entire management staff of the hospital that expenses would have to be cut by twenty percent from present spending levels over the next two months with another ten percent off the reduced amount in the following two months. Weaver emphasized that salaries and wages amounted to eighty percent of the hospital's expenses therefore it was reasonable that eighty percent of the required cuts would be applied to reduced staffing. Each manager was given a form to list the names and positions that they would eliminate. The form was to be completed and submitted to the Chief Operations Officer in forty-eight hours. The lists would be analyzed to see if the required quota was met and to measure the impact on the hospital's operational quality. When all reviews were completed, notices of layoffs would be given to each employee on the cut list. Weaver completed his matter-of-fact presentation and was followed by the hospital's Human Resources Director who gave an in-depth explanation of the process of termination with some insight into the laws that protect individuals with unemployment compensation. The hospital would also attempt to provide assistance with out-placement services.

St. Anslem's auditorium with its bland off whitewalls, worn gray carpet, and uncomfortable folding chairs was always very warm when filled to capacity. Today the auditorium was hot and very uncomfortable. The pictures of past Presidents of the Medical Staff hanging unevenly on the side walls seemed to reflect dour expressions equal to the mood of the live attendees. The hospital's management staff remained silent as the presentations were made. Some hung their heads as if trying to duck the impact of the information. Others glanced at the person next to them and exchanged a look of disbelief and anger.

Bob Markley attended the meeting as a representative of the SACAP program. As the lead Counselor, he was not considered a member of management in the strict terms. Dr. Anderson routinely asked him to cover the management meetings in his place. In addition to Markley, the Nursing Supervisor for the Unit also attended the meetings. Markley sat next to her and noticed her hands trembling as the quota was announced. It was apparent to all the managers that the cuts would affect them as well as the non-managerial ranks.

One out of every five people in the room could expect to be laid off. Bob realized that the SACAP Nursing Supervisor was expecting to be on the hit list. She had only been at St. Anslem's for a year and had not been held in very high regard by her boss, an assistant director of nursing, who felt that all members of the nursing management staff should have a bachelor's degree. The

Supervisor had been selected because of her experience in treating substance abuse patients. Now she felt that she was about to be selected out because she lacked a collegiate experience. The fear that she exhibited was contagious. Markley began to wonder about his own security but brushed the thought aside. His reputation with the clients and the physicians gave him enough status to survive.

Durant sensed the mounting anxiety. He was scheduled to be the last speaker with the assignment of forming an esprit de corps to meet this difficult challenge. He realized that it was an impossible task. The audience was helplessly lost to their own emotions. No one could bring them to a collaborative pitch. They wanted to escape. Durant wanted to escape. There was no way out. Hospital employees by the thousands had already been laid off in the City and Metropolitan area. St. Anslem's had avoided a general layoff by choosing attrition as the preferred method. Now the ax was falling hard. Durant held the ax. He had to chop. As he was announced to the staff he slowly walked to the podium. The room was silent Eyes were mostly downward. No one wanted to look at him.

Durant first looked directly at them and noticing no eye contact in response, he glanced at the ceiling as he began his remarks. "Every day you and your associates face the very difficult task of caring for people who are in need. Often that care requires us to inform the patient that they must stop doing the things that they enjoy doing the most. The patient, for their own benefit, must change their way of life. Sometimes the patient's life depends on their ability to make the change in their lifestyle in order to keep on living. Eventually the patient recovers but with a significantly modified lifestyle. The hospital is a reflection of the process of caring. It too has a life that has to be maintained. When change is required it must change in order to survive. That change requires a discipline that is most difficult for the human quality of the institution to accept because the human quality is where the institution contains the compassion and sensitivity required in patient care. The information that you have received this morning coupled with the assignment to reduce staff is indeed a bitter pill to swallow. In fact, it is not as simple as taking medication. It is more in the order of a surgical amputation. It, nevertheless, must be done or St. Anslem's will not survive. Even if we do survive, and I am confident that we will, we will be a different hospital than we are today. The change may not be to our personal liking but that is something that we have to accept."

He paused briefly and continued. "Change is apparent in all aspects of health services. Patients are treated with technological excellence that produces a cure in less than a third of the time required just a few years ago. Unfortunately, the cost of that cure has escalated beyond the level of public acceptance. We are now expected to match one miracle with another. That is our challenge."

As he concluded his remarks Durant stepped away from the podium without offering to accept questions. The room remained silent. A few people glared at him as if they felt he was the cause of their problem. Such is the role of a chief executive officer.

Durant knew their feelings. He wanted to hide for the rest of the day but other appointments waited him. He walked out of the auditorium and went directly back to his office where his executive assistant handed him a list of telephone calls. Charles Patello wanted to talk to him about a meeting with a consultant from Debur and Tandy. Wellesley Real Estate wanted him to sign a lease for the office suite of "The Catholic Health Services Network." Dr. Folley had called to inform him that he would receive a call from Wellesley Real Estate. The Director of Quality Assurance had called an emergency meeting of the Quality Assurance Committee to discuss the SACAP incident. Mark Meehan had called to report that the contract with Action was ready for his review. Ken Ryan would deliver the contract when he came to the hospital for the afternoon meeting. Thomas O'Shea had called demanding to know the date, time, and place for the Finance Committee to review the cost-reduction plan. He also wanted to know the date time and place for the special Board meeting. Sister Elizabeth called asking for a place to hold a Planning Committee meeting. Mrs. Durant had called to report that the drain for the washing machine was clogged. Kevin Hardly called to inquire if the application for the Knights of the Holy Cross could be completed and in his hands in the next two days. Curiously, Durant had also received a call from Sr. Celest.

Durant sorted the messages in priority of response. He made a note on his appointment book to call Meehan after he had reviewed the Action contract. He instructed his executive assistant to call Wellesley Real Estate and have the agent bring the lease to his office so it could be reviewed by administration, finance, and legal counsel. He also asked her to have Rod Weaver come to his office ASAP to discuss the cost-reduction plan and set the time for the Finance Committee and the special Board meeting. It was his intent to return O'Shea's call by late afternoon. He noted that the Quality Assurance Meeting was scheduled for three P.M. in the Boardroom. Hopefully he could make the O'Shea call after that session. He had the executive assistant forward Sr. Elizabeth's request to Mitch Daly with the direction that he was to use the Board Room for the meeting and assist Sister to the fullest extent. That left calls to his wife, Charlie Patello, and Sr. Celest that he began to return in that order.

The first call to his wife was to provide moral support since she had already employed the plumber's helper to relieve the clogged drain and to ask her to complete the application forms for their admission to the Knights. The floor had been drained, washed, and dried by the time he had returned the call. The application forms were ready and waiting his signature plus a check to cover the initiation.

His next call to Patello was equally expedient. They agreed to meet Thursday morning at nine A.M. in the President's office. Durant would have Weaver and Daly attend as well.

The last call to Sr. Celest was a local call that surprised Durant since the good Sister had been banished to the Retreat House and House of Prayer at Cape Cod nearly eighty miles from Boston. The good Sister answered after the second ring with a simple greeting. "This is Sister Celest."

"Sister Celest, this is Joe Durant. How are you? More important, where are you?'

Celest was quick to reply. "Joe! God love you. Thanks for returning my call. I'm here in Boston. Can you believe it! I'm loose and loving it. We have to talk."

Durant was shocked at the good Sister's use of street talk. She was always very proper but feisty. He smiled as he responded. "Celest, you know you can talk to me anytime. Even if you are loose as you put it. Just who are you running from? Certainly not our good friend, Sr. Elizabeth.

Sister Celest explained, "No, Joe, not Sr. Elizabeth. Pardon my rhetoric. I'm sort of hiding out with Sr. Elizabeth's permission. She knows where I am and what I'm doing. In fact, it's partly her idea. I can explain the whole thing. See, she and I decided a long time ago that this idea of ministry in healthcare was misguided. Instead of running a big hospital mostly for the rich we felt that the healing mission of Christ should be concentrated on the poor. His Eminence was more inclined to accept Folley and the three stooges in their teaching hospital thing. So when I went to the House of Prayer it was with the intent that I would secretly organize a voluntary non-denominational soup kitchen in Roxbury. Now it's about ready. I've got a license. The space is under lease thanks to the Sisters' treasury. I could be open by sometime next week except for a few minor details. That's where you come in. I need a few things that I think St. Anslem's could easily provide."

The big bite was coming and Joe knew it. It couldn't have been at a worse time. Having just announced the staff cuts and cost-reduction program there was little ability for the hospital to get involved with a renegade nun running a soup kitchen.

Sr. Celest was disarmed by Durant's apparent reluctance. She had expected more enthusiasm from her colleague. Carefully she began her appeal. "Joe, I know that St. Anslem's throws out enough food every day to feed hundreds of people. All I want is the food that you prepare every day and don't use. With your leftovers I can nurture a lot of starving, needy people. Instead of throwing it out, you have it sent to me. My people will make delicious and nutritional meals. How does it sound?"

"It doesn't sound right at all, Celest." Joe mounted a defense. "If you recall you initiated a portion control system as one of your last acts in administration. We have very little surplus. Certainly not enough to feed the hungry in a soup kitchen. You will have to find several additional sources for your needs even if we do ship you our leftovers."

Durant was about to continue his point when Sr. Celest quickly interrupted him. "Yes, I did put in a portion control program. I know how much food was saved as a result. I also know that from a cost perspective it didn't amount to a tinker's damn. You could increase the amount of food preparation to meet our needs without adding a cent of preparation cost. The only thing I'm asking for is the cost of the food itself. You wouldn't notice it on your operating statement. You know I'm right. Stop being such a tightwad. You're beginning to sound like Tom O'Shea."

Suddenly Durant got the message. The good Nun wasn't asking for the leftovers. She was asking him to increase the amount of food preparation to include the needs of her soup kitchen. The mention of O'Shea caused Joe to enter a note of caution. "Does Sr. Elizabeth know that you want me to provide food to your kitchen? Somebody's got to cover me. If O'Shea got wind of this he would fry me on the spot. I don't think we can pull this off, Celest."

Sr. Celest was not to be denied. "That a boy, Joe. You keep thinking positive. Sure, Sr. Elizabeth knows that I'm putting the squeeze on you. We are all taking a risk in this venture. Nobody has any armor plate. Elizabeth promised the Cardinal that she would keep me in stir. If he found out that she let me loose she would be in sack cloth. I promised that I would stay in retirement and pray up a storm on the Cape. Officially I am being disobedient which violates my vows, kinda. I could get kicked out of the order with no place to go if His Eminence ordered it. You are asked to kick in a little food and you want a cover? Get with it, Joe. This is the new Church and you are on the ground floor. Take the risk! Find out what it really means to be a missionary."

Celest's scolding was what was needed to bring Joe over. He felt the spirit of adventure in contrast to the demoralization of the previous day. It was an opportunity to participate in a new adventure that seemed to be proper and; while a variation of proper procedure, positive in nature. On impulse, he told her what she wanted to hear. "Okay, Celest. You got me. How do we get started?"

"Great, Joe. It's a simple scheme. We work together on two meals, lunch and dinner. Breakfast is another story. I'm working on a deal with Dunkin' Donuts. Here's how St. A's fits in. Get me a copy of your menu cycle. I'll plan our meals to follow yours. For example, your lunch menu becomes our dinner. Dinner at St. A's becomes lunch the following day at the kitchen. See how it works? You ship us the food as leftovers after lunch and the dinner leftovers on the following morning. Pretty simple. We have the equipment to warm the food and distribute it."

Joe was now with the program. He was turned on to the idea of working the scheme as a form of new mission divorced of the burdensome bureaucracy. Then he thought of a problem. "Celest, we've got a glitch here, I think. Transport is expensive and involves too many people from our side that could spill the beans. No pun intended. Could you arrange to have the food picked up?"

The good Sister was frustrated. "We don't have any transportation, Joe. Eventually I'll have to have a van but for openers I have to rely on others. Say, why don't we put the bite on Phil Mondi? He could use one of Patriot's vans to move the food twice a day. It wouldn't cost him much and he could write it off at twice the amount. You could swear to it."

Sr. Celest's comments reminded Joe that he had not as yet asked Mr. Mondi about his friend at the Hingham Marina. Now he had cause to contact Phil on official business and, in the process bring up the obnoxious boat owner. He came up with a plan. "I think what I'll do is talk to Mondi about transporting the food at a reduced charge. I can cover the cost out of petty cash for a while. At least we won't have to assign St. A's personnel to the task. I'm confident that Phil will give me a deal. Tell me again when this is supposed to start."

"I'm not real sure of the exact day, Joe," said Celest. "For planning purposes why don't you figure on next Wednesday. That's probably the earliest. I'll call if there's going to be any delay. Meanwhile, you have my phone number. Call me anytime at that number I'm living at one of our Small Group Houses but working at the kitchen."

As Joe hung up the phone he was wearing a broad smile. This was going to be fun. Without hesitation he called the hospital's director of Food and Nutrition and instructed her to be prepared to increase the food preparation amounts in order to support a voluntary agency. The increased costs were to be charged to the President's office. He followed the telephone conversation with an official memorandum to the director with a copy to the Senior Vice President for Finance. Then he placed a call to Phil Mondi and arranged for the transportation of the food.

Phil was pleased to have the opportunity to be of additional service to the hospital. The transportation of food from St. Anslem's to a Roxbury address on a twice-a-day schedule was no problem except on the weekends when on call drivers would have to be used. He agreed to charge the hospital half of the usual rate on week days but would have to charge the full weekend rate. Durant accepted the proposal and arranged for the bills to be sent directly to his attention.

With the arrangements for the Soup Kitchen complete Joe mentioned to Phil Mondi that he had a personal matter to discuss. He then described the event of the prior weekend when his boat bumped into a smaller boat at the Hingham Marina and that the owner of the other boat became near violent. He added that the other boat owner had made threats to him and his wife. He concluded by explaining that when they exchanged insurance information the man had written the information on a personal note and receipt from Phil Mondi.

Mondi expressed no emotion after Durant's description of the information. He simply said that he knew of the man and assured Durant that no further action would be taken by the individual. Mondi made the statement as a guarantee. Durant thought that Mondi had unusual control over his customers.

The conversation with Sr. Celest and Phil Mondi brought Durant back from his funk caused by the management meeting. He was actually starting to feel good about his plight when Rod Weaver walked in causing the anxiety pains to return. A quick glance at his watch suggested that he was experiencing hunger rather than anxiety so he offered to buy Weaver lunch in the cafeteria. Weaver was not one to turn down a free lunch. However, he advanced the caution that the mood around the hospital was quite somber and that they might want to have a food tester with them. Durant explained that was precisely why he had invited Weaver to dine with him.

With slightly elevated spirits the two executives walked to the cafeteria. The place was crowded as usual but the noise level was unusually low. The hospital employees were speaking in whispers as they speculated about the forthcoming layoffs. All eyes turned toward Durant and Weaver as they paid the cashier for their food and took a seat at a nearby table. People surrounding them fell silent and seemed only intent to consume their lunch and depart. Durant felt the emotional chill. Weaver looked around the cafeteria and received cold stares in return. Now the whispered conversation seemed to stop all together. It was as if the assembled expected the executives to perform their dastardly acts on the spot. Durant began to nibble at his sandwich trying to act unruffled by the lynch mob. Weaver glistened with sweat and nervously sipped an iced tea.

The sound of a voice behind him caused Durant to noticeably jump in his chair. Defensively, he spun around expecting to fend off an attack. Ken Ryan was standing behind Durant with a tray of food. Durant made a quick turn in his chair as he heard Ryan's greeting. The reaction by the executive caused Ryan to step back and bump into Jay Marquart who spilled his coke on his lunch.

Ryan quickly regained composure. "Good afternoon, Mr. Durant. Hope we didn't startle you. Can we join you or are you engaged in a discussion?"

Durant was surprised to see the two Action representatives in the cafeteria. Then he remembered that they were to meet with several managers in the early afternoon to discuss the waste management project. He saw them now as comic relief from the tension of the moment. He came close to breaking out in hysterical laughter but instead stood and invited the two to join them.

Weaver recognized Marquart from the chance meeting of the prior evening but he had not met Ryan. Instinctively he took the initiative and introduced himself. Durant, pleased that Weaver had made the self-introduction, motioned for Ken and Jay to sit at the table.

Jay was busy trying to avoid dripping his spilled Coke off the food tray onto the men. He clumsily held the tray with one hand while attempting to soak up the sticky liquid with a supply of napkins. His balancing act reminded Durant of a scene from an old Charlie Chaplin movie that added another comical segment. Eventually, Jay managed to avoid further embarrassment and sat down.

Ken ignored Jay's balancing act and concentrated on making conversation with the executives. "Mr. Durant, I have the contract with me. If you have time this afternoon I'll go over it with you and answer any questions that you might have. We think you will be pleased with it. It contains a number of special features that we discussed but the price is less than we had anticipated. I know that will come as good news. Mr. Meehan asked that I offer you full support in this project. He has instructed me to see that you are satisfied."

Durant was in no mood to deal with the Action shakedown. If the employees seated around them realized the cost of this deal they would lynch all four of them on the spot. It was best that the matter be delegated, he thought as he responded, "Thanks, Ken. I am certain that Mr. Meehan has the best interest of St. Anslem's in mind and heart. I regret that I won't have time to meet with you this afternoon. It might be more expedient if you gave the contract to Mr. Weaver for his review. He could discuss the matter with me and then we could get back to you in a day or so."

Weaver was quick to pick up on his boss's lead. He said he would review the document later this afternoon and have his comments to Durant by the next morning. Ryan was satisfied with the response and handed Weaver a large envelope containing the contract ready for signature.

Weaver, contrary to his usual practice, did not open the envelope but placed it on his tray for future review. Durant hoped that the conversation would now shift to another subject. It did.

Jay had been nibbling on his soaked taco when he spotted Cecile and Officer O'Sullivan sitting with another couple at the far end of the cafeteria. Without warning, Jay took his best shot. "You know, Mr. Durant, there are a lot of wonderful people working here. I know many of them. I also know that there are a few leeches in this place that you would be better off without. You want a list of the deadbeats in here, just let me know."

Ken Ryan was blown away by Jay's unexpected outburst. He stared at him with his mouth wide open but unable to speak. Weaver smiled and remained silent. Durant at first was insulted by the remark but recalled that the young man had unusual insights about the hospital. He decided to explore Jay's comment. "Jay, you continue to amaze me with your knowledge about what goes on at St. A's. Pray tell, what instinct causes you to conclude that we have leeches on board?"

Jay wanted the opportunity to expand on his remark but he was taken back by Durant's question. He was not ready with a reply. There was a long pause before he spoke. "Well, I might have been out of line with what I said. I'm sorry about that. I know some people who work here and a few of them are weird. They don't have the best interest of the patient at heart. I guess I got upset when one of them came in a few minutes ago. I would like to take back what I said. I'm sorry I popped off."

Durant thought for a minute. He was uncertain if he wanted to let the young man off the hook. There was something about what he said and the way he said it that signaled to old pro executive that Jay had a problem with the hospital. The Action technician was scheduled to review the entire hospital and in doing so come in contact with a highly demoralized staff. If he made any adverse comments to them it could cause a major employee relations crisis.

Carefully, Durant directed his response to Action's senior representative. "Ken, you and Jay need to know that we informed management this morning that there was going to be a major layoff over the next month. People are very demoralized. They are not going to be very receptive to the waste management program when they realize that it is absorbing dollars that could be used to retain employees. You will be seen as a villain. Please be very careful how you handle the troops and be extra careful what you say."

Ken was uncertain how to respond. He knew that Jay was embarrassed over the whole episode. There was little he could do to repair the damage. His immediate goal was to regain the confidence of the hospital executive and avoid further erosion of the relationship. For a brief second he thought of offering to pull Jay off the project but dismissed the idea with a quick reflection that Jay was the one who had won the hospital's confidence in the first place.

Ken tried the sell. "Mr. Durant, I know that Jay regrets his comment. He has apologized and I add my apologies as well. We now better understand the situation and will be very careful not to cause any employee problems. Jay will deal strictly with the technical details of the project and will not be in routine communication with anyone other than the director of Environmental Services. He and I will have a daily meeting on this project. Any major issues will be immediately brought to your attention."

Jay sat with a remorseful look on his face as Ken maneuvered to regain confidence lost. Durant was extracting as much as he could out of the situation. He had been at a disadvantage since the day that the thug, Celi, walked into his office. It was very apparent that neither Ryan nor Marquart had any inclination of the strong-arm methods used by the sales agent in obtaining the contract. Durant had his fun. Now it was time to let these little fish off the hook.

"Okay, Ken. It'll be all right. Please be careful. Don't call anybody a leech even if they are. That's my job. You guys do the project and leave the rest up to us. Now if you will excuse us, Mr. Weaver and I have some important business to discuss in my office."

Having finished their lunch and gained the last word, Durant and Weaver left the table, bussed their trays, and returned to the President's office. Ken and Jay continued to sit at the cafeteria table in silence. Jay knew that he had screwed up. He also knew that Ken was plenty upset with his outburst. Ken ate his lunch and ignored his associate. Giving Jay the silent treatment was the most effective discipline that Ken could impose. O'Sullivan gave Jay the same cold stare that he had given him in the Troubadour Night Club just a few weeks ago.

Jay recognized the stare and felt the same chill that he had experienced then. *O'Sullivan was up to something—something about Brian something about the delivery business. So why would he bug me? I'm clean,* was Jay's thoughts interrupted by Ryan who pointed to the clock. It was time to meet with the Environmental Services folks.

Weaver and Durant sat at the small conference table in the Chief Executive's office and pondered the cost-reduction plan. The morning meeting with management had started the process. Everyone was now working on the cut list. Word had circulated around the hospital within minutes after the management meeting concluded. Weaver was optimistic that the requested cuts would be provided by the management group. Durant, on the other hand, felt certain that the management team would make a token list and force the executive level to arbitrarily complete the cuts. That would reduce the effort to "a scientific wild-ass guess," as Durant called it, in making the decision about who goes and who stays.

Weaver countered Durant's concerns by suggesting that the executive level should restrict its decisions to program cuts and not be involved with individual layoffs. This again prompted Weaver to insist that the SACAP program be eliminated as an example of those hospital activities that do not carry their own weight. Durant was becoming more sympathetic to the idea but wanted more time to review the total impact of program cuts on the over-all mission of the hospital. Weaver agreed to have a list of programs for Durant to review with the consultant at the meeting scheduled for tomorrow. With the consultant's help the two executives projected that they could review the first draft of the cost-reduction plan with the finance committee next Monday and set the special Board meeting for the following Wednesday. Weaver said that he would be ready.

Durant quickly placed a call to O'Shea's office and left the message that the Finance Committee meeting was scheduled for Monday at nine A.M. in the President's office. He then directed his executive assistant to send out notices that the special Board meeting to discuss the cost-reduction plan would be held at seven A.M. on Wednesday in the Hardly Board Room. The executive assistant suggested that Mr. Hardly approve the time and date before the notices were sent. Durant accepted the suggestion and asked the executive assistant to clear the date with Mr. Hardly.

Ken Ryan and Jay Marquart left the cafeteria and found their way to a small conference room located next to the auditorium. The director of Environmental Services greeted the Action representatives and introduced them to each of the ten people selected to attend the meeting.

The DES brought the meeting to order. He then explained that St. A's was the first hospital in the City to initiate a waste management program in response to the new City ordinance requiring a recycling program in all public service institutions. He noted that Action Waste Management was the Nation's largest and most successful waste management company as a part of the Park System. Ken was pleased that the DES was following the script that they had provided with the company literature. He waited patiently for the DES to complete the commercial and introduce him as the project director for the St. Anslem's project. After fifteen minutes the DES got around to giving Ken a full introduction. The floor was his.

Ken began by explaining the many aspects of the program. He went into the benefits of waste control and management. He explained how society would be improved by the process. Jay was carefully observing the audience. None of them seem remotely interested. They were preoccupied with the assignment given to them at the morning management meeting. Jay noticed that each person had a list on which they scribbled and erased names only to scribble them again. Ken's comments were hardly heard if at all. After about twenty minutes he introduced Jay as the lead technician who would design the St. A's program with their help.

Jay took ten minutes to explain the process of survey and returned the floor to Ken. Ken thanked the group for their attention and asked if they had any questions. There was no response. No one even moved. Finally the DES, somewhat embarrassed, thanked Ken and Jay for the information and adjourned the meeting. The room emptied within a minute. The DES also beat a hasty retreat leaving Ken and Jay alone to pack their notes and ponder the next move. It was apparent that the Waste Management Project at St. Anslem's Hospital had functionally hit a brick wall.

Jay was also preoccupied. His outburst at lunch about the "leeches" on St. Anslem's staff was directly related to his mental state in preparation for the emergency court hearing now only forty-eight hours away. The pressure was definitely on. He had a meeting with his attorney this afternoon and a court rehearsal with Martha to follow. Even without the preparation by legal counsel he mentally played the events of the hearing in his mind. He had a few points to make and he was damn determined to make them. Carefully he played out the strategy based on "if she says that then I say this." He anticipated that the judge would let Cecile and him have a debate with the Judge eventually ruling that Jay was the victor, sending Cecile into a confined state. The more he thought about it the more convinced he became that he would demolish his ex.

However, the good officer O'Sullivan kept coming to mind as Jay played out his fantasy. He saw O'Sullivan as a hidden force that without warning would charge into the court and make serious accusations causing the Judge to reverse his favorable decision casting Jay to a life where Kristie became only a memory. The thought made him shake with fear. How could he neutralize O'Sullivan? What was O'Sullivan up to? He had nothing to pin on Jay. Why even worry about the guy? Was he closing in on Brian and had Brian implicated John? Hardly. Brian was a very small potato. *Busting Brian is like handing out a parking ticket. Who cares?* he thought. Nevertheless, he couldn't eliminate O'Sullivan from his mind.

Mark Addison, Attorney at Law, had agreed to again represent Jay Marquart in his marital difficulties because of his professional friendship with Martha. He had found Jay very difficult to represent when he obtained his divorce from Cecile. When Martha called, he at first declined then reconsidered when she offered to assist him at no charge. In fact, she advanced fifteen hundred dollars of her own money to Addison unbeknownst to Jay. With money in hand the divorce attorney again accepted Marquart as his client. He and Martha had discussed the situation in-depth without Jay. He was aware that Cecile had based her complaint on Jay's alleged use of drugs and that she apparently was prepared to introduce Jay's medical records as evidence. It was apparent to Addison that Cecile's attorney was determined to drive a very hard bargain, if any, under these circumstances.

Jay arrived at Addison's office precisely at three P.M. Right on schedule. Martha came in a few minutes later much to Jay's surprise. They both sat in the waiting room waiting for Mark Addison to complete a telephone call. Martha took the time to give Jay an update on the prospect of malpractice litigation against St. Anslem's. She had previously reviewed the matter with Addison and, at his suggestion, had contacted a number of attorneys in the Boston area that specialized in medical malpractice. Each one had given the same advice. Essentially, the prospect for a damage settlement was very small. In fact, it was so small that none of the attorneys would consider taking the case on contingency. They also felt that the client would have to front a lot of money on a fee for service basis and in the end not recover the cost. A court settlement in favor of the plaintiff was very iffy. However, all the attorneys wanted to be considered in case the Plaintiff decided to pursue the matter. Martha's advice to Jay was to do nothing at this time. She felt that time remained their ally.

As Martha was explaining the prospect of litigation to Jay, the Professional Review Committee of St. Anslem's Hospital was beginning its special meeting to officially review the "SACAP Incident," Dr. Ray Sutton, St. A's Quality Review Officer and the hospital's Risk Manager had both investigated the incident before the meeting. They had invited Dr. Anderson and Bob Markley to appear before the committee as witnesses.

Dr. Sutton had also requested that Ms. Cecile O'Sullivan, RN, appear before the committee. However, Ms. O' Sullivan through her attorney had declined to appear. Her attorney had explained to Dr. Sutton that since Ms. O'Sullivan was taking legal action against Mr. Marquart on a domestic matter it would be inappropriate for her to participate in a hearing of this type. He offered the cooperation of Ms. O'Sullivan when the issue now before the court reached a settlement.

In view of Ms. O'Sullivan's position, Dr. Sutton had contacted the hospital's law firm that concluded the hospital was subject to litigation and that Ms. O'Sullivan had violated the hospital's patient confidentiality policy. It was the recommendation of the hospital's lawyers that the hospital's offshore captive insurance company establish a reserve account of $100,000 against a potential claim and that disciplinary proceedings be initiated against Ms. O'Sullivan in order to preserve the integrity of the hospital's policies.

Joe Durant listened intently to the description of the incident and the results of Dr. Sutton's investigation. He was impressed with the account given by Mr. Markley and the sincere concern expressed by both Dr. Anderson and Dr. Folley. Throughout the presentation and discussion of the incident the patient's name was not used. This was the usual custom anytime a case was presented in a hospital forum. However, a copy of the incident report was always available for review upon request by any member of the Professional Review Committee. As the hospital's risk manager was attempting to explain the fault of the telephone system in the incident he inadvertently used and mispronounced the patient's name. Durant casually corrected the mispronunciation and suddenly realized that the patient was the same person with whom he had lunch. The shock registered noticeably on his face causing the others to become silent.

Dr. Anderson looked at Durant's wide eyes and easily concluded that the President had some connection with the patient. "Joe, you look like this thing has fallen right on your big toe. What's the matter?"

The opportunity to hit the administration was too much for Dr. Folley to avoid. He swung around in his chair to look at Dr. Anderson and at the same time put his back to Joe Durant. "The connection is obvious, Ron. It was Durant and his band of merry men that bought that damn telephone system. Now their great administrative wisdom has got us into a hell of a jam. It's a wonder that something like this hasn't happened before. What we need is a capital review committee made up of doctors that reviews all of these things before administration screws up. I'll see to it that the Board hears about this."

Folley's obnoxious comment transferred Durant's shock about Marquart to anger toward Folley. He was not easily prone to violence but he wanted to punch the good doctor "right in the puss." He actually turned red with anger before he took a deep breath that signaled to all in the very silent room that Durant was regaining emotional control.

After an extended pause Durant began a response to Dr. Anderson's question. "Before Dr. Folley interjected his usual useless comments I was going to comment that the patient in this incident is now a contractor working at the Action Waste Management Company, a company owned by Mr. Mark Meehan, one of our trustees. The part about Meehan is probably irrelevant but I thought I would add it so Dr. Folley would have something to think about. Otherwise, I will be having occasional meetings with Mr. Marquart and his associates as they install a waste management program in the hospital. He will be surveying the entire hospital and analyzing our waste processing systems. It causes me to wonder if he could use any of this information against us if we end up in some litigation."

Dr. Folley still had his back to Durant but he suddenly spun around and glared at the administrator. "What waste management! What crazy thing have you done now? You're starting a waste management program without consulting the medical staff! That's the problem! The administration has gone nuts. They start and stop things without any consideration for the doctors. Where in the hell do they think the patients come from? The doctors support this hospital so the doctors should run the hospital. We should get rid of all these expensive administrators."

Dr. Sutton was embarrassed at Folley's outburst. He sat looking downward and wondered how he could steer the discussion back to the purpose of professional quality review. Certainly, the conduct of the meeting was anything but professional at the moment. He noticed that Durant now looked very angry and seemed ready to fire back at Folley.

Quickly Sutton began to speak in an effort to diffuse the impending confrontation. "Gentlemen, is seems to me that the patient's presence in the hospital as a contractor after the incident is a simple coincidence that has little impact if any on the incident and any resulting litigation. Many people provide services to the hospital every day. Many of them become patients and afterward continue to provide service here. An incident report on a patient should not be cause for us to avoid or discontinue using the services of that person or person's company. I think our attorney would suggest that to discontinue the working relationship may prejudice our position.

Dr. Anderson spoke in support of Dr. Sutton's tactic. "We need to continue to do things in a normal way. That means we make changes but we don't penalize the patient in the process. If we decided to not let Marquart work in our building then we would be punishing him for our mistake. A plaintiff attorney would love that. We also need to remember that Marquart is still a patient in the SACAP program. He has tests done twice a week and continues to get some therapy. We don't want to do anything to make him think that we screwed up more than we did."

Joe was very grateful for Dr. Sutton's attempt to restore the purpose of the meeting. He was also appreciative of Dr. Anderson's use of the word "we" in admission of the hospital's mistake. Folley was a battle that had to be fought eventually but at a time and place more appropriate to the hospital's governance. For now, it was best to decide what steps should be taken to correct the hospital's conduct relative to patient confidentiality. Durant opted to sidestep confrontation with Dr. Folley and properly respond to Sutton and Anderson.

"I agree that we should adopt a business as usual approach, with Marquart," Joe began, "but I am going to minimize my involvement in the waste management program. It also occurs to me that waste management is a quality item that should involve medical staff involvement as Dr. Folley suggests. Dr. Sutton, would you consider it a part of your responsibilities to monitor the program as the physician representative to the department of Environmental Services?"

Dr. Sutton was quick to respond in the positive. "I would be glad to become involved with the program, Joe. I'll contact Environmental Services as soon as we adjourn. Also, with the committee's consent, I'll notify the Senior Vice President for Nursing that Mrs. O'Sullivan has violated hospital rules and ethics. This will activate a meeting of the Nursing Review Board. The outcome of that hearing and our review could require us to report O'Sullivan to the State Board. They might suspend her license which, as you all know, could result in litigation by Mrs. O'Sullivan against the hospital for defamation of character and obstruction of professional practice. You may be sure that I will keep in close contact with our attorney and insurance carrier as we move forward. Also, the minutes of this meeting will be carefully prepared and preserved as a privileged matter. I suggest that we adjourn before our discussion gets us into complications beyond our control."

"Not so fast, Sutton!" shouted a rejuvenated Dr. Folley. "We still haven't dealt with the stupidity of administration in buying that damn telephone system. That's what got us into this mess—not some stupid nurse. I move that this committee condemns the goddamn telephone system and recommends firing the idiot who bought it."

Durant jumped to his feet and moved quickly to where Folley was sitting. He placed his hands on Folley's arms pinning him to his chair. "Listen, you worm. I'm not going to take any more of your shit. This mess was caused by the incompetence of people in your department—not the goddamn telephone system as you refer to it. If anybody gets canned it should be you and the guy who gave Marquart permission to use the telephone. Maybe we should have a Board hearing on that. What do you say?"

Folley's political skills suddenly came to the front. He realized that to continue an emotional confrontation would only reduce him to the level of the now brawling Durant. A retreat to the status of a gentleman would better serve his cause. With emotions under control he addressed the Chair. "Dr. Sutton, I apologize for distracting you. Certainly, you are the one who should investigate and report on all aspects of this most unfortunate incident. We can rely on your professional ability and gentlemanly conduct. Since the lay member of this committee has become so emotional I support your suggestion that we adjourn. We should schedule another meeting when you have completed your review of this entire matter."

No more was said. Dr. Sutton simply nodded as Dr. Folley completed his remarks. The others in the room, speechless by the actions of the past few minutes, quickly filed out. Dr. Anderson was the first to leave. He was embarrassed by Folley's conduct but angry at Durant's suggestion that Markley be made the scapegoat of the whole affair. He wanted to be alone.

Durant held Folley in his chair. He wanted Anderson to escape before he allowed Folley up. Sutton was concerned that Durant was restraining Folley and offered to walk the good doctor back to his office. When Sutton made the offer, Durant released Folley's arms. The two physicians walked out together leaving Durant to ponder the event. He sat alone in the conference room until his emotions settled. Then he returned to his desk to ponder more pleasant things. The thoughts of Sister Celest and her renegade mission spirited his good humor. Life did have its amusing moments even if he was condemned to being a hospital administrator.

Mark Addison greeted Jay and Martha and escorted them back to his small office with a single window overlooking the brick wall next door. His desk was cluttered and files lay scattered around the room. He invited them to sit in the small plastic chairs abutting his desk as he crawled over the mess on the floor and sat in his well-worn desk chair. Martha carefully removed the files on one chair placing them carefully on the floor before sitting down. Jay followed her example. His shock at the disorganized, untidy office was obvious in his behavior. Suddenly all the lack of confidence that Jay held in mind toward Addison came to the front forcing him to experience a sudden depression. Addison seemed unaware of Jay's mood and proceeded to explain the strategies and tactics to be employed before the Judge in the morning.

Addison explained that Cecile's attorney would not consider any compromise before the hearing. Even money would not alter his position. He was going for the kill. Jay was becoming less confident as Addison continued his approach. The one saving point that seemed to weigh heavily in Jay's favor was the apparent breach of confidentiality committed by Cecile in bringing this to the attention of the court. Otherwise, Jay's behavior could be judged inappropriate and possibly a threat to the safety of his child. This could result in the dissolution of the joint custody. On the other hand, Addison explained, no harm had come to the child. Furthermore, Jay had voluntarily admitted himself to a treatment program. Therefore, the possibility of harm to the child was removed and the child was in a safe and loving environment. That point could be made if the medical records noting any violent behavior or prospect of violent behavior were not submitted as evidence to the contrary. Therefore, it seemed very likely that Cecile's attorney would push to have the medical record entered as evidence.

Failing that, the next best thing for Cecile would be a review of the record by the Judge off the record as material to assist in the decision. Therefore, Addison concluded, that it was imperative that Jay's medical record be held in confidence. It should not be used in any fashion to decide the case.

To accomplish this he felt that Jay should propose a number of things that would give confidence to the court that the child was safe and secure in his custody. These things included first of all continuing evidence of his sobriety and abstinence from chemical substances and increased child support payments. The other matters such as continued employment and home ownership were important but less significant in forcing the necessary compromise.

Jay listened carefully to Addison's explanation. When it was completed he took a deep breath and then erupted into a near violent state. He pounded Addison's desk and kicked the files littering the floor. Then he pushed himself into his attorney's face. "Goddamn it, Mark! How in the hell do you figure I need to pay that bitch more money? She and that fag husband make twice what I'm paid. Christ, if I have to give her all that I make there's no way that I can keep my house. She's got me, man. You're supposed to get me out of this mess—not in over my head."

Addison's first instinct was to throw Jay out of the office. He needed this case like a hole in the head. Jay was a loser if he ever saw one. Even if he managed to pull this one out he probably would not get paid and certainly there was no glory in the win. He glanced at Martha and saw from her look that she was pleading with him to stay cool. With guarded tone, he attempted to respond to Jay. "The reason we are offering some increase in the child support payment is to set a platform for compromise. We need to disarm her attorney. If we can convince the Judge that the medical record issue is inappropriate then he has to see that other matters involving custody are intact. The support payment is always the first consideration after matters of child safety."

"Shit, Addison. We're just buying our way out, right?" Jay was back in his chair and beginning to settle down.

Addison sensed that the meeting was now under control. He wanted to move on so he agreed with Jay's observation. "Yeah, Jay, you might say that. We need to redirect their thinking away from the medical record to the common denominator, cold cash. That usually works but it will only work if we can keep the record out of the Judge's hands. That's where I need you, Martha. I have little experience in this medical confidentiality issue. You have researched it and I imagine could be very convincing on the subject. Would you be willing to come in as co-counsel?"

Martha had anticipated Addison's request. In fact, she was going to bring the matter to his attention if he had not raised it first. She had prepared an entry of appearance form to submit to the Judge for the record that would officially give her recognition as co-counsel. Without a word of reply she handed the prepared form to Addison. He was surprised but elated. The two attorneys shook hands. Jay's confidence began to return. From that point on the conversation was between the two lawyers. Jay sat in meek silence. Finally, the session concluded around six P.M.

As Jay left Addison's office he seemed on an emotional high. He was pumped and ready for combat. Martha decided to use this momentum to better prepare her brother client for the morning. She bought him a sandwich and afterwards took him back to her office. There they jointly researched the firm's library searching documented cases of the medical confidentiality issue. Jay was most adept in the research. His speed reading capability, perception and understanding of legal precedence was remarkable. By midnight lawyer and client were jointly prepared to defend the issue. Jay was convinced that they were unbeatable. He would carry Addison through this thing.

After nine hours of preparation for the court hearing Jay arrived home. It was close to one A.M. The house lights were on as he pulled into the driveway. Good. He wanted to tell Susan about the day and explain the legalities that he had mastered. He found her sleeping on the couch still in her usual outfit that she wore to Benny's baseball games. Suddenly Jay remembered the game and wondered about the outcome. He attempted to wake her but could not get her to a state of consciousness.

Stoned, he thought. *Stoned out of her freaking mind.* He turned out the lights and went to bed.

Jay was up early on Thursday. However, this was not the usual working day when he thought anxiously about Friday, his second-favorite day. This was the day that he was scheduled to appear in court and begin the tedious process of protecting joint custody of his beloved Kristie. Nothing else registered in his mind. He was ready. The eight A.M. meeting with the judge was less than two hours away. He dressed in his best slacks, shirt and tie. His hair was trimmed and mustache neat.

The eyes! Damn the eyes, he thought. They were red and strained. Would the Judge recognize this as a sign of a junkie? Not much he could do about it now. Just look neat and act like a civilized person. He was aware that this first session was a hearing about the child endangerment issue. The medical record was key at this time. His lawyers would convince the Judge that he was an ordinary hardworking slob that was no threat to anybody especially his own daughter. Sure, he had a little problem with booze and coke. Who didn't? That was being taken care of He would agree to give evidence going forward that he was on the wagon. The judge would buy that. His lawyers said so. That would end the first round. Then he would proceed to kick Cecile's ass. He had her cold. She violated the patient Confidentiality Act and that was the end of her career. "Yeah, satisfaction guaranteed. Bring it on!"

The thoughts of success rolled over and over in his mind as he finished dressing and walked to the kitchen for his starter cup of coffee. A glance into the living room found Susan still dressed and sound asleep on the couch where she was when he came home. Jay, until now, had not been aware of her absence from their bed. He recalled her stupor and thought it best to try to raise her if for no other reason to determine if she was alive. A kiss on the cheek caused her to moan and roll away from Jay's affection. Satisfied that she was alive but not yet conscious, he moved on to the kitchen and prepared a large pot of coffee. Susan would need it soon. Jay knew from his own experience that the first hours of reentry were painful and difficult. Coffee helped.

Susan would need a lot of coffee. She had been on a long trip.

Jay arrived at the Court House at seven-fifteen. Addison wanted to meet him and go over the strategy one more time. Martha was there when Mark and Jay arrived. She was prepared to the hilt with the patient confidentiality research.

As they were talking, Mr. and Mrs. O'Sullivan came into the waiting room with their attorney. Immediately, Cecile's attorney challenged Addison about Martha's presence. Addison informed him that Martha was submitting an entry of appearance as co-counsel. Cecile, listening to the conversation, became very angry and pulled her attorney aside. Shortly he returned to Addison and asked that they meet with the judge in chambers prior to the initiation of a formal court hearing. Addison readily agreed. This was the first step in reaching a compromise off the official court record and avoided having Jay's medical history put on the public record. Addison felt that they had won the first round before the bell had rung. Together the three attorneys asked to meet with the judge. They were admitted to his chambers.

Jay and Cecile were omitted from the meeting with the Judge. They sat in the dingy waiting room trying desperately to avoid eye contact with each other. Cecile sat next to Officer O'Sullivan in silence. Jay paced back and forth on the opposite side of the room. He was very careful to avoid looking at Cecile. Occasionally he would seek a quick peak at her husband and be met with the same cold stare that he had experienced on the two other occasions. Jay then realized that Officer O'Sullivan was staring at him, constantly. He could not escape the gaze. O'Sullivan was on to something and Jay was very curious in finding out what. He came close to speaking to the good officer but realized that any conversation with O'Sullivan at this time could only be used by Cecile in the Kristie matter. It was best to leave it alone.

Perhaps another conversation with Tommy the Tout was in order for more inside dope on Cecile's cop, registered in his mind as the next move.

Judge Roper had only been on the bench a few months. He was still learning "the tricks of the trade," as he put it. Prior to his appointment as Judge he had been a very successful and well respected criminal lawyer. His experience in civil matters was therefore limited but the prospect of a child in danger caused him great concern. Consequently, he was less that sympathetic to an alleged addicted father who put a child at risk.

Cecile's attorney made Jay's escapades sound as if Kristie had been held by the neck as Jay devoured drugs to a point of being violent. He assured the Judge that if Jay had not fell unconscious he most certainly would have done physical harm to the child. The only safe course for the child was to remove her from the joint custody and place her in the safe arms of her loving and protective mother.

Martha patiently explained to the Judge that Jay readily admitted to having a substance abuse problem and in the interest of the child and his own health had voluntarily admitted himself to a treatment program. There was no evidence that the child had ever been in any danger and was in fact in a very safe and loving environment.

Judge Roper became very interested in Martha's explanation of the applicable laws that protected Jay's confidentiality as a substance abuse patient. He accepted the argument that Jay's medical record could not be used as evidence to support Cecile's contention that Jay's conduct put Kristie in harm's way. However, he advanced the idea that, as the Judge, he may find it necessary to review Jay's medical record off the record to determine if he was in fact a violent person and potentially harmful to Kristie.

Martha then suggested to the Judge that Jay's medical record was a record of treatment for a recognized illness, nothing more. What was more pertinent to the issue was Jay's status as a loving father and respected citizen, who was employed and working in a vital service. She proposed that of more benefit was evidence of Jay's continuing sobriety and offered to provide the Court with continued reports supporting his cure. She emphasized that Jay had no record indicating that he was a violent person in any regard. He was in fact a peaceful citizen and loving father who had a medical problem for which he was under treatment.

Cecile's attorney tried repeatedly to inject comments about the violent nature of addicts who robbed and killed to support their uncontrollable habits. The signal that Martha had well made her point came when the Judge explained to Cecile's attorney that Jay was not a criminal or accused of a crime. The issue at the moment was to determine if a formal court hearing was necessary to officially determine if Kristie was in danger. The Judge then concluded that there was no need for a formal hearing since he was convinced that Kristie was not in immediate or pending danger.

However, the Court would require that the circumstances be continually monitored. He then required that laboratory reports from Jay's treatment facility supporting his abstinence from chemical abuse be submitted to the court twice a month for a period of one year or until the issue of joint custody changed. In that regard, the hearing of joint custody was placed on continuance pending a review of all other allegations made by Cecile and her legal counsel.

Cecile's attorney, realizing that the child endangerment issue was lost, explained that an extended delay in dealing with other important matters such as increased support payments was not in the Child's best interest. He proposed that the matter be dealt with expediently realizing that Jay would be on the defensive and in a position only to accept a compromise in favor of Cecile.

Mark Addison quickly proposed to the Judge that the issues raised by Cecile could be addressed by the two parties and solutions reached. Attorneys for both sides then accepted the Judge's suggestion that the remaining issues be negotiated and an agreement be submitted to the Court for official determination. The matter was placed on continuance for six months pending submission of the compromise document. After being excused by the Judge, the three attorneys stood in the corridor away from their clients and agreed to propose to their respective clients that the support payments be increased twenty-five dollars per month. They also agreed that the compromise document requested by the Court would be drafted by Cecile's attorney. This gave him the opportunity to include many stipulations that would place Jay at a disadvantage. However, it was a necessary concession to resolve the matter of child support.

The attorneys parted to confer with their respective clients. Martha and Mark were pleased with the outcome so far. They had managed to dodge the endangerment issue, had protected Jay's medical record and were in neutral on the continuing issue of joint custody.

When all of this was explained to Jay he became very agitated. The increase in support payment overshadowed all of the positive results. His first reaction was totally negative. "Not another goddamn cent!" he yelled loud enough for Cecile to hear across the room.

Mark escorted Jay into the corridor where he explained that the increase payments was, as they had discussed the day before, a buyout of the problem. The issue was nevertheless still at hand since it was scheduled for a court hearing in six months. Between now and then, Addison further explained, it was necessary for Jay "to be a good boy, stay out of trouble, remain sober, and, make the goddamn payments on time." He pointed out to Jay that it was only out of respect for Martha that he refrained from "punching him out" and if he didn't like the deal than he could get himself another lawyer if he could find one that "would put up with his shit."

Jay got the message. The two men returned to the conference room where Addison announced to Cecile's attorney that they would proceed as agreed. Jay noticed that Cecile was looking very depressed at the outcome. He took immediate consolation from her appearance.

Maybe I can get her fired, too. That would really piss her off, he thought as a smile crossed his face for the first time that day. After all, Friday was almost here.

Joe Durant, St. Anslem's CEO, was not smiling. Wednesday night had been sleepless as he tossed in bed replaying his fight the prior afternoon with Folley. His mind continually played out scenarios about getting even or better yet embarrassing the "Great One" in a way that would crush his gigantic ego and tumble him from his "lofty perch." The anger continued as he drove to the hospital in the morning. He was so engrossed in thought that he almost didn't make the stop at the toll gate at the turnpike exit. Fortunately, the flashing red light caught his attention before he rammed the lowered gate arm in the automatic lane. Quickly he deposited the fifty cents and moved through the exit onto Cambridge Street where he proceeded to run the next three stoplights. Screeching brakes and violent oaths of cross traffic drivers caused him to temporarily focus on his driving until he arrived unharmed at the hospital parking garage.

As he walked from the garage to the hospital entrance and then to his office he felt the cold stares of the other arriving employees who by now were fully aware of the pending reduction in staff. *To hell with them*, he thought. *The freeloaders have had it made since Medicare began. Now it's time to pay the piper. Christ, how I wish that I could get out of this messed-up business. It's nothing but bad news.*

Durant's ever-present and always efficient executive assistant was waiting as he entered the office. She handed him the messages from the night voicemail then reminded him of his early meeting with Mr. Patello and Mr. Callahan. Mitch Daly had already arrived and was waiting in Durant's office. He was an hour early for the meeting but wanted to talk to Joe about his on-going conversations with Mike Logan and other discussions with Sister Mary Elizabeth. Joe was in no mood to hear about Logan. It just rekindled his irritation with Folley and the whole can of worms created by "that damned Archdiocesan Office for Health Affairs."

The mention of Sister Elizabeth caused him a moment reflection of Sister Celest's breakout and guerrilla war against hunger in which he was now engaged. Maybe there was some small reason to smile. He sent his assistant on the usual early morning task of liberating a fresh pot of coffee and then entered the office where he greeted Mitch Daly with a surprising cheery good morning. Daly was in good spirits. The past few days had been exciting as he romanced the young Michael Logan. Logan seemed eager to get established and was most wining to use Daly's services in the formation of the Archdiocesan Health Services Network. Daly excitedly reported to Durant that Logan had agreed with Daly that St. Anslem's should be the centerpiece of the network. Consequently, the conduct of the network should be to support the advancement of St. Anslem's. He had the same conversation with Sr. Elizabeth who agreed with the idea that St. Anslem's should be the focus of the network.

"Actually," reported Daly, "Sister thinks that the office should be a part of the hospital's organization instead of the other way around. I get the idea that she is going to explain this to Mr. Hardly and Bishop Hanks. I took the liberty of telling both Logan and Sr. Elizabeth about our meeting this morning with the Consultants. Logan might show up. Hope you don't mind."

At first Durant reacted negatively to Logan's presence at the meeting with the consultant. He said so to Daly who offered to call Logan and tell him the meeting was canceled. After a moment of reflection Durant changed his mind. He felt that it might be well for Logan to meet with the Consultant, Patello, himself and his two vice presidents in an atmosphere that represented the authority of the President of the hospital. This had the prospect of bringing the young Mr. Logan under control. The missing ingredient was Sr. Elizabeth and Phil Mondi from the recently formed Strategic Planning Committee but they could be involved at the next meeting that Durant intended to schedule in short order.

The Executive Assistant arrived with a fresh pot of coffee as well as some Danish intended for the meeting with Patello. It was Durant's standing order that any meeting involving a trustee should have proper refreshments. Folley was an exception to that rule. After she had placed the coffee and Danish on the small conference table she handed Durant a file folder that she had been carefully holding under her arm. She explained that Dr. Folley had sent the folder to the office a few minutes ago with the instruction that it was to be brought to Mr. Durant's attention immediately and was very urgent. It required his immediate action.

Without a word Durant open the folder to find a check request for the security deposit and first month rent for an office suite in Wellesley to house the Archdiocesan Office for Health Affairs. Another check request was for furniture and equipment for two executive offices, a secretary's office, a reception area and a conference room that included table and chairs for twenty people. A memo from Michael Logan to Dr. Folley was also included requesting a working capital fund for twenty thousand dollars. Folley had approved the request and had written a note to Durant ordering the hospital to establish the account. The office payroll would be paid by the Archdiocese since officially the employees were employed by the Archdiocese but the Archdiocese would submit a bill to the hospital every month for the payroll and benefits plus an additional administration fee. On top of the file was a note from Bishop Hanks stating that the Cardinal had approved the business arrangements?

Very quickly Durant calculated that the total annual cost would run in the neighborhood of one million dollars. He recalled that Rod Weaver had predicted that amount when news of the office was first mentioned to him. Weaver's fiscal instincts deserved respect.

Durant marveled at Folley's timing. There was no way that he, as CEO of St. Anslem's, could deny the request for funds now before him. The entire matter had been pre-approved by the Cardinal. Durant's only task was to apply the rubber stamp and sign the checks. Folley, on the other hand, was in the envious position of criticizing Durant's every move. Folley was the master of the healthcare universe but had managed to avoid any accountability for the outcome of the healing effort. Another million dollars of expense was about to be loaded on patient revenue and the backs of the hospital employees who were now being denied employment. "Is this truly the healing mission of Christ?" he mumbled aloud as he signed the check request.

Daly wasn't aware of the contents of the file folder that had captured his boss' complete attention. Neither did he understand Durant's comment as he signed the documents. Not sure if the remarks had been directed to him, Daly asked him to repeat what he had said. The question brought Durant back to Daly and the pending meeting. He began an explanation of the folder's contents when Rod Weaver announced himself and took a seat next to Daly.

Durant handed Weaver the folder. "Well, Rod, you came just in time to be given another million dollars of expense for the bottom line. That seems to be in line with what you said the Archdiocesan Office would cost. My congratulations on your perceptive judgment."

Weaver accepted the comment as casually as he accepted the folder. "Not to worry, my leader. I think I got it covered for now. I pumped up the accruals last month in order to create a reserve against unexpected year-end adjustments. I'll fudge Folley's Folley against the cushion and things won't look much worse than they are. But we got to be sure the troops don't get wind of this. Man, they are pissed! The big problem is working this hit into the new budget. Somehow, we got to lay this cost off on the other hospitals in the Archdiocese or cover it with another round of layoffs. Maybe we should get rid of the senior vice president for planning. That would just about cover it."

Daly was not amused at his colleague's sick attempt at humor. He turned red and began to fire back at Weaver when Durant, wanting to avoid the brawl of the previous Friday, declared peace on the entire assembly. Daly obediently tucked away his anger and chose to avoid Weaver's silly smile. Weaver, too, decided to discontinue jabbing at Daly's excitable nature for the time being.

The declaration of a truce coincided with the announcement that Mr. Michael Logan had arrived for his nine o'clock meeting with Mr. Durant. No sooner had Mr. Logan been escorted into Durant's office, then the Executive Assistant returned with Mr. Patello and Mr. Callahan of Debur and Tandy. The meeting was now in session.

Durant made the necessary introductions and after that seemed to lose control. Daly tried to assert his plan for planning while Weaver locked in on the cost-reduction program. Logan, at first, was impassive but noting the lack of order pushed for more direction by the Archdiocese and physicians in developing a health services network.

Callahan and Patello listened carefully to the disjointed conversation for about fifteen minutes. Suddenly Callahan interrupted all the participants with the announcement that he could offer a solution to all of the problems being discussed. Even if the comment had little substance it served the purpose of bringing the participants to a point of silence. Callahan had been well briefed by Patello about the disaster at the St. Anslem's Board meeting. He was very much aware of the politics between Folley and Durant, Sister Elizabeth, Bishop Hanks, Hardly and O'Shea. The overall purpose of Target Boston Medical as it had been named by the combine of National Associated Investors and the Federation could be well advanced by using the disjointed enthusiasm of St. Anslem's and the Archdiocese.

Skillfully, Callahan moved to compromise each person by agreeing with each one's basic premise. "Yes, the doctors were the key to the formation of a primary care network," he said to Logan. Then without taking a breath he turned to Weaver. "It is essential for a hospital to be lean and mean in the new era. Low cost and high quality are the essentials for survival. Now is the time to trim back. Once the network is formed the high cost hospital win be left wanting." Then he turned quickly to Daly. "What is the product line of tomorrow's acute care hospital? We know that the services provided today in St. Anslem's are declining in volume and to some degree may be unnecessary in a few short years. How are we going to redesign the hospital's function to meet future demands? The foundation for change must be set now. We could already be obsolete."

"Let's begin with the doctors," Callahan continued. "Our first task should be to bring the physicians of St. Anslem's into a self-styled organization that supports their interest in practice, teaching and research and, at the same time, gives them an advantage in the competition for prepaid healthcare dollars. This means becoming a preferred provider of physician services to major payers such as the HMOs and what remains of the indemnity health insurance business. It seems that the Archdiocese would want to concentrate on the physicians and the physicians' organization. St. A's administration would, of course, be involved in the physician bit but would concentrate in cost reduction and quality management. This suggests that the hospital would incorporate many of the re-engineering concepts now being introduced across the country. We could provide assistance in that. Mr. Daly, your expertise could be very helpful in the interface between the formation of the physicians' network and the hospital re-engineering. Perhaps you could be staff liaison between the two projects. Debur and Tandy will be the consultants and supply the research with recommendations for progress. Mr. Durant, do you have any comments?"

Joe Durant had sat in silence listening to Callahan make himself indispensable. He also felt that the trend of Callahan's process led the CEO of St. Anslem's out on a limb to be sawed off by the Office of Health Affairs as the physician's network took root. In his mind he foresaw a competition for survival between himself and the good Dr. Folley as the transition to network took place. The option to try to obstruct Callahan's recommendation would place him squarely in the camp of the unthinking which would only hasten his professional demise. The right tact at this time would be to go with the flow and take Folley's folly on head to head when the opportunity presented itself. Chances were good that Folley would give him a shot at bringing the office down.

Carefully, Joe picked his words in response to Callahan's question. "Tom, your summation of the situation is right on. My only question is, how do we get this whole thing started? This is a big job. We need your help but we cannot take the time to regroup at this stage. Our staff reduction and cost control programs are well underway. They can't be stopped. It's like trying to change tires while the car is running."

Joe's dodge seemed to work. Callahan did not suspect that Durant was reserved in his response. Instantly Tom began to detail a plan of action. "I know you are well underway, Joe. The cost-reduction program must be continued and I suspect accelerated. I'll get together with Mr. Logan right after this meeting, if he has time, and set up a process for getting the doctors informed and involved. I'll have my research staff begin to look at the area HMO's to see if we can find a friendly one that will help us in our transition. If you don't mind,

I would like to assign a staff person to work with Mr. Daly in the accumulation of data, conducting interviews, and doing market reviews. Is that okay?"

Durant nodded in agreement before Daly had a chance to react. Mitch Daly, not unlike his boss, recognized that he was being subordinated. He fumed at the prospect and wanted to react. He saw Durant's nod of agreement and realized that the simple gesture had eliminated any chance for him to recover leadership status. Obediently, Daly expressed his acceptance of the supporting role. As a last attempt for prominence he began to explain to Callahan how the strategic process should be conducted in an iterative manner that involved a cast of thousands. Callahan listened politely to Daly but was clearly not impressed.

As Daly finished his commentary, Callahan brushed aside his input and began his own description of the planning process. "Things will happen fast now that the cost reduction is underway. It's important for that to succeed. I suggest that the first round of layoffs be announced in the next twenty-four hours. That will get everybody's attention including the doctors. Logan and I will meet with Dr. Folley and do a quick evaluation of the hospital's primary care base. I suspect that we will have to expand the primary side and contract the specialists. That will set us in motion to form a separate practice corporation to acquire private primary practices. Start up and working capital will be required and I suspect that the hospital will provide that unless the hospital wants to form a joint venture with an investor or other proprietary healthcare provider. Callahan stated he could make those kinds of arrangements. We are talking about an entirely new type of organization that places the hospital in a network where it functions as a cost center instead of its conventional role as a revenue center."

Weaver was energized by Daly's comment to accelerate the cost-reduction program. Looking at Patello, he injected his concern about the trustees, especially Mr. O'Shea's interest in closely monitoring the cost-reduction process. "Mr. Patello, if I'm correct I don't believe we can proceed with cost reduction until the Finance Committee has reviewed our reduction plan. If you recall their recommendation had to go the full board. That's going to take a week at best before we can announce any layoffs."

Before Patello could respond, Durant superseded Weaver's comments. "Rod, we'll be meeting with the Finance Committee on Monday. Between now and then Mr. Callahan will be having some in-depth discussions with Mr.

Logan and Dr. Folley. They will understand the need to expedite the cost-reduction process. It seems to me that we can make an announcement on Friday and then bring the Finance Committee up to speed on Monday. I assume that you will be with us at the finance committee, Tom. We also have a special meeting of the Board scheduled for next Wednesday. Between now and then it will be important, I think, for Mr. Callahan to meet with Sr. Elizabeth and bring her up to speed on the relationship between cost reduction and strategic planning."

Patello sensed that Durant was passing the ball to him in order to deal with the combination of O'Shea and Folley. His reaction was exactly what Durant was looking for. Patello was quick to assure the CEO that the trustees especially the Father and Son in Law duo of O'Shea and Folley could be contained.

Patello was reassuring. "I'll be meeting with Kevin Hardly on another matter this afternoon and will tell him about our meeting this morning. Hopefully, he will have time to meet Tom at that time. Somehow, we will get the message to O'Shea that the cost-reduction program is being expedited. He should be pleased with that."

Rod Weaver seemed pleased with the prospect of the consulting process but it was evident to Joe Durant that his fiscal officer was nursing some concerns. Recognizing the need to make sure everything was put on the table he asked Weaver to comment.

Weaver always took the opportunity to raise the penetrating questions that were the trademark of CFO's throughout the world. "I just have a few minor concerns that I believe were bypassed. The first is the need for an engagement letter or contract with Debur and Tandy for Callahan's services. We want to be sure that he is recognized properly as a vendor to the hospital under the Medicare provisions. Also, Tom, you mentioned earlier about the prospect of some kind of joint venture with a proprietary organization for the startup and working capital requirements. I am certain that with the kind of deficits that are coming, we will not be in a position to finance the network. We will definitely need a partner. That means we will require permission of the Cardinal. He has very specific guidelines about partnerships with non-Catholic organizations. My thought is that we start early to work this matter through the Chancery. Otherwise, it might never get off the ground."

Rod's comments gave Callahan the perfect lead. "Mr. Weaver, I'll have an engagement letter ready for you this afternoon. Please understand that I am retained primarily as a health planning consultant for Park, Inc. of New York.

They are considering health services as a new venture. Mr. Patello's interest in that firm brought me to Boston to review the local market. I will be assisting St. Anslem's as a part of that agreement and with their consent will only be required to charge the hospital for any staff other than me who are specifically assigned plus specific expenses related to the St. Anslem's study. As the study progresses it may prove appropriate for Park to joint venture with St. Anslem's in the network. That, of course, remains to be seen. Park, as you may know, is an internationally known leader in environmental services and waste management. They are looking to expand and diversify. Health services on the surface looks like a natural for them."

Now it was time for Michael Logan to assert the authority of his office. He almost stood as he began to speak but contained his emphasis and remained seated as he began, "I think we must realize that the Office of Health Affairs for the Archdiocese will represent the Cardinal in all proceedings with the network idea. While we cannot speak for the Cardinal, I believe it appropriate to state that His Eminence has complete faith in Dr. Folley. Whatever the doctor recommends will be supported by the Cardinal as long as it avoids scandal. In other words, we need not be timid about this thing. As soon as Dr. Folley is informed you can be sure that we will have the green light to proceed."

Joe Durant felt the strong undercurrent of Logan's remarks pull the hospital resources away from his control into the waiting ego of Dr. Folley. It was more than evident that the Cardinal had put complete faith in his physician to develop and expand the healing ministry in a contemporary fashion as the healthcare market in Boston wallowed in the heavy seas of transition. A quick glance at Weaver revealed the same question pounding in his own mind. *Who in the hell was Park and how did they fit into the scheme?* He decided to explore the matter with Patello using very careful tact.

"Charlie, we have had an excellent meeting thanks to you. This was a much-needed step to put the hospital into a position of remaining competitive. I have to confess that I don't know anything about Park, Inc. that Mr. Callahan mentioned as being interested in providing health services in Boston. Can you fill me in?"

Patello was, as always, gracious in response. He explained that Park was both a service and consulting company that specialized in public service and municipal projects. It realized that the provision of health services was consistent with its overall mission and sought the services of Debur and Tandy to do an in-depth analysis of the market potential. Boston was a selected market not only because of its quality healthcare but because several of Park's principal investors were in New England. He concluded by pointing out that in his capacity as an investment banker he was assisting Park in its analysis of the Boston area. It was opportune that St. Anslem's was also looking at repositioning itself by possibly forming a medical network.

Patello decided not to mention that Park was the parent of Action Waste Management. That would not be conducive to maintaining an open mind. He also excluded mentioning that several of St. Anslem's trustees were vested in the success of Park. Durant was certain to object to that point and may even cloud the prospects with questions about conflict of interest. He had enough information about Park for the present. As he neared the end of his response to Durant about Park he thought it best to beat a retreat from the meeting before the questions became more penetrating.

Patello continued. "Joe, I guess that gives you some understanding of Park and its interest. I'm serving as their investment banker and advisor. Because of my relationship with them we have the opportunity to use the consulting services at practically no cost to the hospital. We can work together for our mutual benefit. Tom will provide you with a sub letter to our contract that will give you some assurance of service. That will serve as the engagement letter that Rod asked for. We ought to hold for now until Dr. Folley is brought up to speed and we get through the finance and planning committees of the hospital. The whole matter can then be explained at the special Board meeting."

He then stood to leave. Callahan followed Patello's lead as did Logan.

Durant continued to sit as he pondered the impact of' Patello's comments. Weaver also sat in silence. Daly appeared excited about the whole matter and rose immediately to shake Callahan's hand while expressing his interest in working with him. Slowly, Durant got out of his chair and then thanked Charlie for the excellent support he was giving to the hospital. He then escorted everyone to the door of the administration suite. As they were leaving he caught hold of Weaver's arm and gently pulled him back. After the door closed Joe requested extra time with Weaver to review the status of the cost reduction and staff cutbacks.

Rod was most pleased that his boss was taking an immediate interest in the cost project. The number of layoffs required to stabilize the hospital's finances were considerable and far more than had been determined by management after the meeting earlier in the week. Drastic action was required. The two executives returned to the President's office where Rod began without prompt to explain the status of the cost-reduction plan.

"Boss, right now we only have a beginning of the required reductions. The management gave us about one tenth of the amount requested. We're just going to have to chop across the Board. Let's begin with management. We cut out the obstacles and go with force. What do you say?"

"Have you discussed this with the COO, Rod? We need him in these decisions," Durant asked.

"He's the first one you should lay off, Joe. That would get their attention. I don't think he believes we're serious. I tried to get him to kick ass on the cuts and he buzzed me off!"

St. Anslem's Chief Operating Officer, Nick Samuel, was known for his methodical yet easygoing style. He eventually got things done but at a pace that suited him. On several occasions Durant had warned him about his attitude. His last evaluation contained special comments about his approach to special projects with a warning to improve. On the side Durant had suggested that Samuel begin a job search. Samuel had responded in his usual manner. Now faced with another example of slow response to duty from his COO, Durant nodded his in agreement with Rod's suggestion.

"Okay, Rod, he goes with the morning tide. I'll give him notice this afternoon. Any other examples of how we might give this thing emphasis?"

Rod knew when he had Durant in an action mode. This was it. Without hesitation, he lined up the next target for cuts. "I've got a million of 'em. The one that makes the most sense is reduction scope if not complete elimination of the SACAP. Those drunks are pissing away the revenue in greater amounts than surgery. We don't need the program. It doesn't do a damn thing for the hospital. Tell Folley that it's a goner."

Joe sat silently as he pondered Weaver's suggestion. He, too, felt no special attraction to the SACAP. Its elimination would have the least impact on the total medical staff who were bound to react when some of their favorite nurses got the ax. But the SACAP staff had only a few physicians involved who had their own private practice and volunteered coverage in the unit because of the persuasive ability of Dr. Anderson. Dr. Anderson, of course, would be very offended and the good Dr. Folley would go bananas.

"Unless he made the decision," Durant suddenly blurted out. "Yeah, that's it. We somehow get that jerk to make the decision. How are we going to do that, Rod?"

Weaver was taken by surprise. He had no idea what his boss had been thinking. He had taken the silence as a rejection of the SACAP cut. "How we gonna do what, Joe?"

Durant stood and began pacing around his office. He seemed obsessed with something but Rod was not sure what. "How are we going to trick Folley into cutting SACAP, Rod? That's what I want to know. If he makes the decision than he takes the heat. The only way he would do it is if it fed his goddamn ego. That's what we have to figure. How does the SACAP cut make that crazy fool look good if that's possible. You got any ideas?"

After Patello, Logan, Callahan, and Daly left Durant's office Logan and Callahan proceeded immediately to Dr. Folley's office. Daly returned to his own office while Patello rushed to Kevin Hardly's office at Hardly Security and Trust to attend a very important meeting that had been in process for the past two hours. Patello had arranged for Mario Capizzi to meet with Hardly and the CEO of Bay Area HMO to discuss the possible acquisition of the HMO by Park, Inc. Michael Logan completed the introduction of Tom Callahan to Dr. Folley. The three men sat in the doctor's plush office at his expensive desk. Callahan scanned the many pictures and plaques on the wall and praised the grand man on his many accomplishments and important associations. Folley listened and accepted the praise with a broadening smile. He immediately regarded Callahan as a very perceptive and intelligent person.

As the atmosphere thickened, Logan began to recount the meeting just concluded in Joe Durant's office. He made sure that Folley was paying very close attention when the idea of a primary care physician network was mentioned. "Of course," he explained, "only a physician could be the head of such an organization. Mr. Callahan thought you might be instrumental in forming the network. Perhaps I should let him explain."

Callahan caught the ball and began running. "Dr. Folley, the key to the future of health services is to restore the physician to their proper position of leadership. You are an example of that. Obviously, His Eminence recognized your ability when he chose you to direct his healing ministry. Now it is necessary for you to lead your fellow physicians and form an organization that guarantees their future and the future of the healing ministry. That organization needs to be one that can deal with the many managed care companies in a way that creates a foundation for quality care, efficiency and economy. Only the physician can direct care that will result in quality, efficiency and economy. The primary care physician is the initial source of all of those elements. An internist, such as yourself, who has proven management ability, communication skills, and strong political instincts is important to the formation of the entity. Our proposition is this. We suggest that the Office for Health Affairs for the Archdiocese concentrate on forming the Arch Diocesan Health Services Network. It will be essentially a medical services organization that brings together primary care practices and specialists that serves the managed care corporations with capitation type agreements. In effect, the physician network handles all of the revenue from the payers and buys services from hospitals and other institutions as appropriate. You see, in this form the hospital is simply a cost center instead of its traditional role as a revenue center."

Folley could barely contain his excitement. He recognized potential in the network far beyond Callahan's description. But being the consummate politician, he appeared reserved, almost skeptical, as Callahan finished his commentary. Then in Churchill fashion he carefully reacted.

"Mr. Callahan, you propose to organize St. Anslem's Medical Staff when in fact St. Anslem's physicians are already organized under our own bylaws and in specialty departments. We have established referral patterns that are long standing. We have some of the most outstanding specialists in the area. Any attempt to modify the relationships between our primary care practitioners and the specialists will create professional disharmony. This change will have to be gradual and will have to be cautious in its approach. As the Chairman of the Department of Medicine it will undoubtedly fall on my shoulders to steer this program through the cross currents of opposition. I consider this a great challenge. I'll need to make basic changes in my own organization in order to accommodate the formation of the network. In addition to Mr. Logan I expect that I will need to recruit some key physicians to the cause—especially a primary care physician who can preach the gospel to the private practitioners—Dr. Anderson is very highly regarded in the private community and could well serve as the new Director of the primary care section of the Medical Services organization. I'll speak to him about it."

Callahan knew the great man was hooked. In fact, Folley was reeling himself in and crawling into the boat. Nothing more was necessary except to set the stage for the next act. Callahan commented, "Dr. Folley, I suggest that we use the hospital's Planning Committee as the way of coordinating the transition of the hospital to the network. I'll be involved with them and will be in a position to steer their analysis. Mr. Logan and Mr. Durant will work together, I'm sure, to see that things move along. It's important that we keep things in motion and not get bogged down in extensive committee meetings as is usual Board behavior. Finance Committees have a tendency to delay transition pending audits and so forth. We can supply finance information as we progress so we won't be delayed by committee."

Dr. Folley was having trouble tracking Callahan's disjointed comments. Finally, he waved his hand to silence Callahan. "Mr. Callahan, I am a trustee of St. Anslem's as well as the secretary for Health Affairs for the Archdiocese. Both the Chairman and Treasurer of St. Anslem's Board rely on me for advice and counsel. You can be sure that I will move the decision process. I control the hospital's corporation. Please understand that."

That was all Callahan needed. He now had a power base to further the advance on Target Boston Medical. Gaining control of the provider base was well in motion.

Getting a foothold into the payer base was being conducted by National Associated Investors. Kevin Hardly, at Charlie Patello's request, had arranged an introductory meeting in his office between Dr. William Hall, President of Bay Area Health Maintenance Organization and Mr. Mario Cappi, President of National Associated Investors headquarters in New York City. Dr. Hall and three other physicians had originated Bay Area primarily as a Health Maintenance Organization for communities outside of Boston. It prospered for about five years and then fell on hard times as the competition from the Boston based HMO's began to move into its territory. Bay Area countered by marketing in Boston with exceptionally low rates that resulted in a number of large accounts but increasing deficits.

Hardly Security and Trust backed Bay Area with extensive loans and was now faced with non-performance loans. Dr. Hall and his associates had advised the bank of their intent to sell the business and pay the loans. Patello, as a director of the bank, brought NAI forward as a potential buyer. The meeting lasted four hours including lunch. At the conclusion NAI agreed to buy Bay Area for an amount equal to sixty percent of its current accounts payable to all lenders and healthcare providers. The bank agreed to write down the Bay Area debt by twenty percent. NAI intended to dissolve the balance and finance capital reserves by applying write downs of thirty percent to the providers' accounts.

Dr. Hall and his associates were given a scandalous severance and told to disappear. Hardly assigned the bank's crack legal staff to complete the details of the sale and to see that NAI's subsidiary, Park, Inc. was established to do business in Massachusetts as Park/Bay Area HealthCare.

Dr. Hall resigned, effectively immediately, from his post as President of the HMO. An interim CEO was required to primarily act as the company spokesman. Kevin Hardly suggested that a top-flight executive who was between opportunities could well fill the bill. Capizzi looked to Patello who nodded in agreement. Hardly placed a quick call to the Emerald Tap where Joseph Bauman was holding his daily ritual. After he hung up the phone, Joseph Bauman, former Executive Vice President of St. Anslem's Hospital and new interim President of Park/Bay Area HealthCare, bought a round of drinks for the house. Surely the CEO of a major Health Maintenance Organization would have an expense account for such purposes and it was very unlikely that he would not encounter another Chapel door in this new position. It was time to celebrate. Slowly he sipped the whiskey and followed it with a beer. The few well-wishers available gave him a pat on the back in gratitude for the free drink although they had not the least idea what had brought this good fortune their way. Bauman knew, however, that his fortune was tied to his dedication to Mother Church and the Knights led by Kevin Hardly. It was to Kevin and his brother Knights that Sir Joseph Bauman raised his glass repeatedly that afternoon.

Weaver pondered Durant's question. It was not easy to con the great Dr. Folley. His natural attitude was to oppose anything that was suggested to him. The only thing that he favored was his own idea. Therefore, eliminating

SACAP as a cost cutting move would not fly. After a few minutes of silence Rod made a suggestion. "Let's spin it off. I mean, we suggest to Logan that The Office of Health Affairs should have its own service base. We give the program lock, stock and barrel to the office and take it off our books. They will try to pass the losses back to us but it will be so embarrassing that Logan will convince Folley to scrap the idea. If Logan doesn't do it, then the Cardinal will when he gets wind of the loss. Folley will buck everybody except the Cardinal. How's it sound?"

Durant's reaction was spirited. "Sounds possible. That would mean that we close the inpatient unit and layoff the nursing and counseling staff. Logan could set up an outpatient type service and pay us rent for the space. You know, Rod, under those conditions the program might be able to break even or even make a few bucks. I'll take a run at Logan and Folley with this afternoon. Right now, I've got to give Samuel his pink slip and work out a severance deal for him. That's going to be rough. You go back to your office and rework the numbers. Let's figure on reducing management by fifty percent." Weaver gave his boss a high-five and left.

Durant called Nick Samuel and asked him to come to his office. When Samuel arrived, he seemed already solemn as if he anticipated the worse, When Durant gave him official notice of termination the middle-aged executive lost his composure and began to sob uncontrollably. All Durant could do was close the door and wait for him to regain his emotion. That took about forty-five minutes when the sobbing was replace with anger. He damned Durant, the hospital, the Church, and concluded with a threat to "unionize the whole fucking place." His parting shot was an announcement that "the Cardinal was going to hear how people were being treated at this place."

As Samuel opened the door to leave, he suddenly turned around and walked back to Durant. Samuel extended his hand and commented that he understood that Joe was "just doing what was necessary." He asked for one year of salary and benefits plus out placement services and positive recommendation to any prospective employer. Joe offered him six month's salary and benefits plus out placement services. He advised him that "his record of service at St. Anslem's deserved only the highest of recommendation." Samuel accepted Durant's offer, shook his hand for the second time and left to clean out his desk.

Durant was upset by his encounter with Samuels. His own emotions were at an edge. He wanted to retreat to his boat and soak up the sun and have a few stiff drinks. That would have to wait for the weekend. For now he desperately needed to advance Weaver's idea of spinning off the SACAP program to Folley's folly. The idea was so intriguing that he suddenly abandoned all reservations and decided to approach the great doctor with the proposition. *To hell with caution*, he thought. *This has to happen now!*

After Callahan left, Dr. Folley and Michael Logan discussed the formation of the physician health services network. It seemed like the perfect program to give the Office of Health Affairs immediate purpose and importance. Any delay in implementation could only jeopardize the prospect of success. Folley became more convinced that Dr. Anderson was the man to lead the primary care division of the network. To move him to that post would require that he give up his post as Director of SACAP unless he could take the program with him. He immediately arranged to meet with Dr. Anderson the first thing on Friday morning to advise him of his new assignment. SCAP would become part of the new service base for the Office of Health Affairs effective tomorrow. "The only hang up could be Durant and his bungling band of administrators," he said aloud. "I'll have to take care of them now so Anderson won't be screwed by their messing around with this. You give anything to those suits and it gets really messed up. Especially if Weaver has to analyze it sixteen different ways."

Logan sat in silence as his boss ranted about the incompetence of the hospital's administration. He offered no opinion or comment. In his mind he felt the urge to tell Folley to cool down and let the matter be handled by someone experienced in politics such as himself. All things considered this was more of a political move than managerial. Folley could benefit by using Logan's skills to assist him in fulfilling his political ambitions which Logan estimated as being the first non-ordained American Pope. Logan recognized in Folley the same critical ambition that was apparent in Mayor Cowan. They are both people of extreme ambition who have no self-control or compassion when their ego is involved. Such people usually succeed in their social quest for prominence and often end in disgrace because they try to devour the public by containing the God-given gift of free thought. Folley was destined for a big fall but not until he had gained greater prominence than what was available at St. Anslem's. Logan realized that he could share the ride to the top by hanging on to Folley. The trick was to get off before the fall.

Folley instructed Logan, "You go back to the office. I'll be there in the morning after I talk to Anderson. We can set things up then." Folley was speaking to Logan who heard only the last part as he began to come out of his fog. He had to ask the great doctor to repeat which caused Folley to get irritated. "Goddamn it, I said for you to go back to the office I'll be there sometime tomorrow morning. Right now, I intend to tell Durant about the change for SACAP. Do you understand or do I have to have it explained to you?"

Logan didn't respond. Instead he picked up his briefcase and walked out the door.

Folley paid no attention to Logan's irritation. He put on his tailored full-length lab coat and moved post haste toward Stairway five. Stairway five was one of those things that happen in building programs that defy explanation. Somehow a stairway was built as a change order to the plans that connected only two floors of the hospital. That stairway was located a few feet from Dr. Folley's office and terminated on the floor above adjacent to the door to the doctors' lounge. The doctors' lounge was less than fifty feet from the door to the President's Suite. Few people used or even knew about stairway five. Those in the know, aside from Dr. Folley and Mr. Durant, included the members of the Department of Medicine, resident physicians, and the environmental services staff.

Samuel had a thing about stairway five. He used it every day as his own escape. He would linger on the landing between the floors sometimes for a half-hour before someone would come along. In winter, he used the landing for a place to sneak a smoke in violation of the hospital's strict no smoking policy. Today he sought the isolation of the landing in stairway five to regain his emotions before informing his staff that he was the first member of the top management staff to get the ax. He leaned against the wall on the landing and held a lit cigarette in his cupped hand. A large "No Smoking" sign appeared just above his head. As he thought about his official announcement to his staff he began to sob again uncontrollably as he did in Durant's office. He was sobbing loudly when he heard the door below the landing open and within a few seconds later heard the door above open. Loud pounding footsteps came from both directions.

Suddenly Durant and Folley met face to face on the landing in front of him. Neither man seemed to notice him. Their eyes were fixed on each other. Both were trying to speak without listening and soon they began shouting. Samuel's sobs continued even at greater intensity but were not audible to the men in front of him who were now nose to nose and screaming.

Durant was saying, "SACAP was done. It was being transferred out of the hospital. The Office of Health Affairs could have it if it wanted but it could not continue as a part of the hospital. The inpatient Unit would be closed this weekend."

Folley didn't hear a word. He shouted back at Durant, "SACAP was really a service better provided by affiliated practitioners in a setting away from the acute hospital. The inpatient Unit should be closed now and the physicians put into primary care."

Both men were poking each other in the chest with their index fingers. The conversation was repetitions of their opening statements still unheard by either party except that various references to the marital status of their respective parents was providing emphasis and punctuation.

Samuel found the scene distracting to his own deliberations. He stopped sobbing and began to concentrate on the senseless debate before him. The sudden cessation of who cleaned the area every time that Samuel found it cluttered with surgical booties and masks. Otherwise, it remained a safe haven for those who wanted a few minutes isolation. His background sobbing caused Durant and Folley to stop shouting. The silence was deafening.

Durant and Folley looked at Samuel for the first time realizing that he had witnessed their confrontation. They then looked at each other in silence while out of the recesses of their minds they now heard the message that each man had been trying to deliver. They were saying the same thing. They were in agreement. They experienced intellectual shock.

After a few minutes of silence, Durant was the first to speak. "I'll take care of the hospital side first thing in the morning."

Folley nodded. "I have to tell Dr. Anderson. He's out this afternoon so I won't get to him until tomorrow. Better we not say anything about this until I talk to him. I'll call you after that and then you can do what you have to do to close the inpatient unit."

Durant agreed. "Okay, we'll hold off until we hear from you. Health Affairs wants the outpatient service?"

Again, Folley nodded. "Yeah."

The two men parted and retraced their steps out of stairway five.

"There go a couple of aces," Samuel said aloud as the doors above and below him closed. He leaned back, lit another cigarette, thought about his comments to the staff and began to sob.

Jay felt exuberant after his morning in court. He took his time but eventually found his way to his desk at Action Waste Management. Boss and buddy Ken Ryan spotted Jay's entry as a bit of a surprise since he figured win or lose Jay would take the day off.

Curiosity brought Ken to Jay's desk with the inevitable question. "How did it go?"

Jay was eager to recall all the details for Ken with the editorial commentary about how he "kicked butt." According to Jay's point of view good 'ol Cecile was left in the wake of overpowering legal excellence delivered by his crack team of lawyers that he had schooled to perfection. Now all Jay had to do was "pee in a bottle every couple of weeks and stay clean." Cecile, on the other hand, was going to lose her job and probably her nursing license for "stepping on the cape of a legal superman that took no shit from his ex. No way was she gonna walk away from this without paying a price." After listening to Jay explain his great victory, Ken was surprised to hear him say that the matter of joint custody was on continuance with a hearing date pending in six months. Ken didn't have the heart to explain to Jay that the battle had just begun.

Among the many things cluttering Jay's desk was a memo from Ken reminding him that he was to do routine inspections and attend supervisory meetings at St. Anslem's at least twice a week. In his absence Ken had arranged for Jay to attend the first contract review meeting at St. Anslem's on Friday. Jay liked that. It would give him a chance to sit with Tommy the Tout for a brief discussion about Cecile's "queer cop husband."

Another item on his desk was a draft collective bargaining agreement between The Service Workers of America Local 936 and Action Waste Management. A note attached to the draft document, From the Desk of David Donovan, Business Agent Local 936, advised Jay that the document was being circulated to all members of the Union for their review in lieu of the standard agreement form given to him on Monday. Jay was to circulate around the shop and remind the members of the importance of the agreement and ask them to bring their questions and concerns to him. They would have a meeting soon to discuss the progress of negotiations. There was also another note on the draft agreement from Ken Ryan asking for a copy of the agreement. Jay noticed that the draft document contained a list of concessions apparently "granted" by management in the past few days. Donovan's promise of a meeting with the employees prior to the start of negotiations seemed to have been forgotten. It was apparent to Jay that some kind of negotiation was already taking place without any input from the member employees at Action Waste Management.

Notes on the document carried the initials of Marty Hart, President of the Union and none other than the exalted Mr. Bob Muldoon, of the Boston Workers Guild. *This thing has been up and down the line and the troops have yet to see it*, thought Jay. *Man, this is democracy in action.* Without hesitation, he copied the document and left it on Ken's desk. Then he phoned Donovan and left a message on his voicemail that he had reviewed the document and would do as he had asked.

The afternoon seemed to fly by. Jay was looking out the window when he saw Ken's car exit the parking lot. At first, he thought that Ken was leaving early but a quick glance at the clock indicated that Jay was staying late, much later than usual. In fact, if he delayed much longer he would be late for his appointment with Bob Markley and the Thursday night version of his support group. Jay offered his apologies to the couple he was talking to about the contract negotiations and beat a hasty retreat to his Jeep. He was anxious to meet with Markley and recount his success in court.

The drive to St. Anslem's frustrated Jay because of numerous traffic delays. He shouted his usual obscenities to slow drivers especially those intent on obeying the law. Some received the benefit of a prominent thrust of his finger in their direction as he wheeled around and through stalled traffic. Miraculously, Jay arrived at St. Anslem's at the appointed time without doing harm to himself or anybody else.

As Jay entered the SACAP Unit Bob Markley greeted him from behind the desk and handed him the obligatory specimen bottle. Jay waved a greeting to Bob, took the bottle without a word and proceeded to the hall lavatory. He returned a few minutes later and handed the bottle well filled to Markley who labeled it immediately and placed it in the lab call container. With that task done the two men now had a chance to chat before the start of the support session in the cafeteria.

Ken, sensing Jay's exuberance, opened the conversation with a pointed and leading question. "Well, Mr. Marquart, did things in court resolve to your satisfaction or am I to be tormented by a solid state of depression that only you can produce?"

It was the perfect lead for Jay to emote, as he had done with Ken Ryan. He covered his day in court in detail and added his own color commentary. He concluded that he was generally off the hook except for the small matter of routine testing.

Ken sat patiently listening to Jay's commentary. He realized that Jay's quest for sobriety was motivated by the prospect of losing joint custody of Kristie. Yet, Jay did not mention Kristie. Often he mentioned Cecile and his hate for her. Yet the love that he apparently held for his daughter was shadowed by the hate for her mother. This same type of confusion led him to substance abuse as an alternative to proper conduct of a healthy lifestyle. Markley also knew from his own experience that unless a change in attitude took place Jay would soon revert to his old practices.

As Jay began to wind down, Bob began a careful approach to the subject.

"Jay, have you talked to Kristie today?"

"No, didn't have the chance. I've got her this weekend. We'll have a great time. Man, I bet that bitch will hate to let her come over. Yeah, man, she's gonna hate it."

Markley continued. "I'm sure Kristie will enjoy being with you now that you are relaxed and in apparent good health. You going to stay healthy, Jay?"

Jay felt the sting of the question. He had no intention of violating his sobriety. He really hadn't given the matter any thought until Markley's penetrating question. His face became grim as he pondered a reply. Gradually Jay responded, "Markley, there's only one reason that I joined your daisy chain. That was to keep my relationship with Kristie. I've got that made. I'll stay as sober as I have to. But I don't think I'll need all the hand holding and back slapping that you build into this party. I'll hang out tonight but after that you won't see me around except to pee in the bottle."

Markley was quick to answer. "That really wasn't my point, Jay, although I would like to discuss that with you later. What I was attempting to do was remind you that, in addition to your addiction, you have some related physical problems that could become severe if you fall off the wagon so to speak. I know you love Kristie. As she grows older she will become very dependent on you. Your health will be very important to maintaining your relationship with her. Your habitual use of coke, pot, and booze could cause a stroke or cardiac arrest.

You still are nursing a chemical imbalance in your system that could cause you to become emotionally unstable. What I'm trying to suggest is that you stick with the program here until you regain complete health."

Jay felt like Markley was trying to sell him a used car. He told him so. He also told him that he was "in good health now and I feel fine, man. If I get sick I'll give good Doc Kenneth a call. He can send you over to my house so you can hold my hand and make me well. Hell, Bob, I'm gonna be all right. You worry too much."

Markley saw an opening in Jay's tight defense and he moved to penetrate it. "Jay, our approach is to keep you well by offering you moral support that will keep you from reverting and becoming ill. You know I would prefer to hold your hand before you get sick rather than after. That's the idea of a support group. There's a lot of people who care about you. Get to know them. You also have a lot to give. You could be a great help to someone else. Caring is what it's all about."

Jay moved close to Bob. He looked him in the eye. "Go on, Markley. Go on and ask me."

Markley became puzzled. He lost his point as a result of Jay's bewildering question. He fell into the trap that Jay had set. "Ask you what, man?"

"Ask me if I care, man. Yeah, you ask me if I care." Jay's eyes filled with tears as he fired his last volley. Abruptly he walked out of Markley's life, out of SACAP, and out of St. Anslem's. He was in control now. He had returned from the hell of the legal wars. It was time to repair his normal life.

Markley watched Jay walk out the door and made no attempt to stop him. The experienced Counselor knew that Jay cared about others. For some reason Jay had built a barrier between his compassion and the people around him. That barrier was fortified by chemical dependency. Markley knew the feeling. As a young man he decided to dedicate his life to caring for others spiritually, mentally and physically. Educated and professed he began his career only to experience occasional rejection by those he tried to help the most. To relieve his frustration, he started drinking. Eventually he became a helpless drunk very much in need of his own medicine.

Jay had rejected his assistance. Markley felt very much in need of a drink now. It was that old feeling that brought him to relieve his frustration with a good extended binge. Had he been alone now he would have to fight the strong temptation to go to the nearest tavern for a drink that would start a binge. But he wasn't alone. It was seven o'clock and the St. Anslem's Support Group was waiting for him to begin their meeting.

"Thank God, Thank God, Thank God," he repeated aloud over and over as he entered the cafeteria.

Jay was not there but Markley knew he would be back for his twice monthly urine analysis. Hopefully, Jay could be convinced that total sobriety was the best if not the only answer. Markley had overcome temptation. He was renewed. He felt good.

Ask me if I care, he thought. *Yeah, ask me if I care. You're damn right I do and so do you, Jay Marquart, so do you. Someday I'll prove that you care but for now I'm going to have to be satisfied with caring for and about you.*

Chapter Thirteen

Dr. Anderson was furious. Normally his anger was evident by his very red complexion that signaled to all that he was about to emote in a near violent fashion. This was different. He was very mad. Steaming mad. He could hardly speak because of his anger. In fact, he felt sick to his stomach. There was no reason for two patients enrolled in the SACAP program brought to the Emergency Room in the early morning hours to be admitted to the Psychiatric Unit. The SACAP inpatient unit was empty but staffed to accept patients. Yet, the emergency physician on duty admitted the patients to the Psych. unit.

This had happened on rare occasion in the past usually by a new ER physician who confused the treatment methods of chemically addicted patients between medicine and psychiatry. Anderson would correct the physician the next day by a simple tirade sufficient to cause the young doctor never to make the mistake again. This time when he began to make his point with the experienced emergency physician on duty he was presented with a directive signed by Dr. Folley announcing that effective at six PM the previous evening the In-Patient Service of the SACAP Program was closed. All patients requiring substance abuse treatment on an inpatient basis were to be admitted to the Psychiatric unit.

Anderson had not been informed of the memo. Folley had not even given him the courtesy of a phone call until after the fact when his secretary informed him that Dr. Folley wanted to see him in the Chairman's office.

Choked with emotion Anderson placed a call to the SACAP Unit and spoke to the Nursing Supervisor who again verified that the Unit was empty and she had not been notified that the service was closed. Markley also reported that he had checked with the Unit as late as nine P.M. on Thursday evening and no notice had been given.

The Nursing Supervisor called Anderson a few minutes after their conversation to report that she had been summoned to the Office of the Vice President for Nursing at nine A.M. She confided to Anderson that she expected to be laid off at that time. She also expected most of her staff to go as well.

It was at this point that the heat of Anderson's anger moved from red to white. He charged out of his office into stairway five, actually jumped down the stairs, and landed loudly in the Great One's office. As Anderson stormed by the secretary he inadvertently grabbed a paperweight and held it tightly in his fist. The secretary, alarmed at his violent appearance, summoned hospital security as Anderson slammed the door to Folley's office.

The Great Dr. Folley sat at his desk in the far corner of the gigantic office and watched Anderson charge at him. In order not to provoke any violence he purposely remained seated. Anderson stopped a few feet in front of the desk and glared in heated silence at his mentor. Finally after what seemed to be a prolonged period of silence, Anderson was able to choke back his emotions and began to speak in surprisingly civil tones.

"Dr. Folley, I have been informed by the Emergency Room staff that you ordered all SACAP patients admitted to the Psych. Unit effective nine P.M. last night. I suppose you had a reason for such nonsense but I would at least have expected that you would have informed me, as the director of SACAP, of the need to close my service or is that expecting too much from someone of your elevated status."

Folley sensed that it was safe to stand before he gave a reply—a reply he had been carefully crafting all night. He also noticed that Anderson held a paperweight tightly in his right hand so he decided to stay behind his desk safely out of harm's way. "Ah, good morning, Dr. Anderson. I was going to come to your office in a few minutes to explain this whole situation. Actually, I had to make a sudden decision in order to save the service. It certainly isn't my intent to close the program. No way. Closing the program is strictly the decision of Durant and his band of merry misfits. Last night in a chance meeting with Durant he let it slip that he was laying off your whole staff this morning. He was going to close the inpatient service as an administrative decision last night. If we had transferred your patients to another hospital we would have effectively surrendered our license as an approved substance abuse program. I upstaged our CEO by diverting your patients to the Psych unit. That at least keeps the Feds from pulling the program approval. What we have to do now is transfer the program out of St. A's control. My thought is that we keep it under the same sponsorship but spin it off to the Archdiocese Health Services Network."

Anderson seemed shocked at the explanation. He stared at Folley in apparent disbelief and then moved forward to sit in the plush chair in front of the desk. Slowly he relaxed as he pondered his next move. The paperweight in his hand became heavy so he placed it on the desk and sat back in the chair. He felt the perspiration on his body and took out a small pack of tissues from his lab coat pocket. He wiped his forehead and then cleaned his glasses. He stared into the corner avoiding eye contact with Folley.

"Dick, we have known each other since residency. I have worked in the department longer than you have been Chairman. I was home last night. Didn't go to bed until after the news. You could have given me a call at any time. Why the shock treatment? I don't deserve to be treated this way."

Folley sensed that it was safe to come closer to his colleague. He cautiously moved from behind his desk and sat in the chair next to Anderson. He was now in perfect clinical position to continue the treatment. Anderson was emoting over the disregard for his position rather than the patient transfer. Folley took note of the attitude and sought to press Anderson's anger into an advantage.

"You are absolutely right, Ron. Nobody deserves to be treated the way the doctors are being treated by the administration. We need to do something about it. That's what I was about most of the night. I had to take things into my own hands in order to avoid a disaster. It took hours of negotiating before I got around Durant. When I felt that I was in control I made some unilateral decisions. In the heat of battle I didn't think to keep you informed. I had hoped that no patients would need admission so I could bring you up to speed first thing this morning. It's unfortunate that those two patients were admitted but as you can see they desperately needed care. Can I tell you about how I think we can salvage this whole thing and gain control at the same time?"

Anderson was now relaxed and prepared to listen. Folley pressed the intercom button and asked the secretary to bring in some coffee and Danish. The meeting was now in civil form. When the door opened, the secretary entered with the coffee and two burley security guards who stood at attention while she placed the refreshments on the table near the physicians. As she left the security guards backed out of the room giving surveillance and security to all present. Anderson stared at the guards in a bewildered gaze.

Folley appeared to give them no consideration as he casually poured the coffee. When they had gone he continued his explanation about the new organization that he had devised. "Here's how I plan to set this up. We form a physicians' service organization as a part of the Archdiocesan Office for Health Affairs. The organization will be separate from the hospital's control. The doctors will own and run it. We will control the admissions to the hospital and in that way control the hospital. Furthermore, we eventually take over all the diagnostic and therapeutic services. The hospital only provides the nursing and hotel functions. Medical and Surgical services are then completely in the control of physicians. No more lay fiscal wizards. We are also in control in negotiations with the HMO's. We decide how much the hospital gets paid after the physician fees are determined. This is the way healthcare is going and we are on the ground floor. What do you think?"

Only Napoleon could have conquered the hospital with such speed, thought Anderson. Folley's physical resemblance to Bonaparte caused Anderson to begin to smile but he suppressed the urge opting instead to attempt to focus Folley's explanation to his particular program. He recovered and replied. "Dick, your plan is very ambitious but how and where does substance abuse fit in. We seem to be hanging out in space right now. I understand that administration is laying off the nursing staff as we speak. Who's next? Where will the program be tomorrow or tonight for that matter? Patients in the program will need to be directed. How does all this fit together?

"Yes, correct," replied Folley. "The deal I cut with Durant is that he can close the inpatient unit today. Psych will take your inpatients. This afternoon you and your medical staff will go to work for the Archdiocesan Office of Health Affairs. You will be named the Director of Physician Services which includes the formation of a Physician Primary Care Network. I thought the first physicians in the network would be your physicians that are in private practice and part of your substance abuse network. It's a natural. The substance abuse program will grow as the primary care network expands. Eventually, we can reestablish the inpatient service as we acquire leased space from the hospital corporation. This has to happen now. I've got the lawyers working on the contracts. The chaos surrounding the hospital cutbacks present our opportunity. If we just stand by, we physicians will just have to accept the watered-down operation that administration has to offer."

Anderson's head was spinning. He came in to complain about inadvertent decisions affecting his program and now he was being offered a new job for a new organization that he was expected to create. Perhaps "offered" wasn't the right term. It sounded more like he was being forced into the new position. He tried to sort out options in his mind as Folley continued to expound about his newfound source of capital and the prospect of being aligned with a national health conglomerate. Anderson was a primary care physician who had developed an interest and specialty in substance abuse. That's what he wanted to do. Now the program was being disassembled by economic forces that excluded his involvement except through his association with Dr. Folley. To refuse to go along with Folley would obviously mean his resignation that would force him back into primary practice where he would only see an occasional substance abuse patient. Under Folley's plan he would at least have the opportunity to keep the program alive on an outpatient basis and would also keep his substance abuse physicians together. Going along with Folley seemed to be the best decision at the moment. He could opt out in the future if necessary.

Reluctantly, he bought in. "Okay, Dick, I'll go along. You've got to promise me that I can do this primary care network with a principal focus on substance abuse. Is that a deal?"

"Of course, Dr. Anderson. That's the whole point. We are actually expanding the healing ministry in the Archdiocese by giving emphasis on the substance abuse problem in society and bringing the physicians into an organization that has the flexibility to focus on this and other problems. The hospital becomes a servant to the system rather than constrict the mission as it now seems to be doing. The hospital as the focus of the health delivery network is a thing of the past. Isn't this exciting?"

Anderson remained reserved as he commented, "Well, I have to confess that I'm more apprehensive than excited about this grand change. We have a monstrous logistical problem just notifying people registered in the program about the change. Support sessions, counselor visits, crisis calls, therapy, testing, the whole nine yards will have to be redirected today. If the nursing staff is given notice of termination then it will fall strictly on Markley and my office staff to administer this change over. I better get with Bob stat and start the process. You're sure that you want this to happen?"

Dr. Folley gave him a slap on the back. "Ron, there's no other way. Let's get it done!"

Anderson left Folley's office in a totally different mood than when he entered. His anger had been replaced by confusion and mild depression. Nevertheless, he was sedate and in deep thought as he slowly climbed the stairway five steps.

Folley, on the other hand was on a high. He placed a quick call to Durant to inform him that he and Dr. Anderson had agreed to move the SACAP program to the Archdiocese. He also advised Durant to transfer Anderson to the Archdiocese payroll immediately. He then called Logan to inform him of the change and to see that Dr. Anderson had office space at the Office of Health Affairs. His last euphoric call was to inform Tom Callahan that the primary care program was initiated and to request that Callahan give it special mention at the forth coming meetings of the Board Finance and Planning committees. All three calls were made before Dr. Anderson had returned to his office.

Tom Callahan was amazed at the progress as he reviewed reports in his temporary office provided by Charlie Patello. In less than a week Target Boston Medical had acquired an HMO, penetrated the planning and fiscal functions of an acute care teaching hospital, and established a base for a physician primary care network. In a stable market this type of penetration could take a year. Fortunately, the instability of the Boston market caused by the wild competition of the managed care systems allowed for a quick takeover. But the rapidity of the change at St. Anslem's was unusual. Consequently, it was a fragile state that would require careful cultivation.

St. Anslem's and the Archdiocese were mere pawns in the process of gaining access and front-end control of the prepaid revenue streams of the major manage care companies in the Boston area. Bay Area, St. Anslem's and Folley et al would be used as currency to buy or merge with the larger providers and payers. Central direction, medical service organizations, and other corporate services would open the door to unlimited opportunities to skim huge sums from the gross revenues of the HMO's and the providers, especially the physicians who were always gullible. Callahan had outlined this for the people in New York, his clients, who would be most pleased with the progress to date. Carefully he prepared a detailed report and faxed it to Tony Marone. President of Park, Inc., New York City.

The report from Callahan was most timely for Tony Marone. He was due for a meeting with Mario Capizzi and Big Frank to discuss the Boston project. Action Waste Management was the primary topic of concern but the medical thing that Tony didn't completely understand was also on the agenda. He intended to use Callahan's report as evidence that he was on top of a project that was advancing well ahead of expectations. With copies of Callahan's report tucked in his meeting folder he rode the private elevator to Big Frank's penthouse office. Capizzi had arrived just moments ahead of him and together they entered Big Frank's spacious, plush environs.

Frank was genuinely pleased to see his associates. He enjoyed early morning meetings with his trusted executives. Both men had proven their loyalty to Frank on several occasions and Frank had rewarded them with prestige, power, and wealth. His acknowledgment of their good work created further incentive for then to press even harder for the benefit of the organization but more for their boss and friend. Mario and Tony were known to be the key players in the organization but everyone, including the dynamic duo, knew that the successor to Big Frank would be his favorite nephew, Charlie Patello. Charlie's picture, as usual, faced Mario and Tony from atop Frank's desk as he greeted his two executives and invited then to join him for breakfast. This was to be one of Frank's famous working breakfasts which meant that you listened to Frank, answered his questions, gave commentary, and reached conclusions while sipping juice, maneuvered Eggs Benedict from plate to mouth, and drank coffee. Tony had become accustomed to changing his shirt when returning to his office after a breakfast meeting weather he had spilled eggs on it or not. The resulting perspiration from the pressure of the meeting recommended a change.

"Things are moving pretty well in Boston," was Frank's opening comment. "We've been approved by the Attorney General's Office to do business as Park/Bay Area so that gives us a legitimate base for operations. Action Waste Management is moving with the hospital contracts and we seem to be gaining business from other industries. Target Boston Medical is in process but it's probably too early to expect noticeable results."

Frank's last comment seemed to be Tony's cue. Awkwardly, he dropped his fork and stretched to reach his folder slightly out or reach behind his chair. Frank waited patiently for Tony to recover.

When he did he distributed copies of Callahan's report and began commentary. "Frank, we seem to be well ahead of expectations on Medical. Apparently, we have an unusually cooperative associate in one Dr. Folley. Tom seems to think that the doctor's motive is simply ego but we need to be alert to how far we can compromise this dude. Anyway, he seems to have a leg up on the doctor thing. He also is determined to bring the hospital down which I guess will help us when we sweep up the pieces."

When Tony finished his report, Frank nodded his approval. Tony sat back in his chair and felt the perspiration seep through his no longer fresh shirt. Mario gave Tony an approving glance and began to comment.

"Frank, we've got this plug, Joe Bauman, set in as the President of Bay Area. He can take a fall anytime we want him to. As far as I can tell the guy is clueless as well as harmless. We'll feed him a few things to say, dress him in a new suit, get him in Rotary, and then push him over. It's a good set up. He's already got his hand in the cookie jar."

"That's all very good," commented Frank, "but we got some other things to consider here. The first is that Boston seems to be our base of operations now. We aren't doing squat in New York. Anyway, not enough to keeps us here. I've talked to the executive committee and they want us to study the prospect of moving our base to Boston. I like it because that gives Charlie the opportunity to take over. I'm getting up there you know. Anyway, here's how I think we could do it. Boston is a lot smaller than New York and the banking is being gobbled up by the Nationals. We have the capital to move in and gain a prominent place in the finance business in the Boston area. You see, Charlie tells me that this guy Hardly is on the edge of retirement and he owns the big piece of Hardly Security and Trust. His cousin, and they hate each other's guts, owns the big piece of Cambridge Banks. So, we declare peace on the two cousins, buy them out and merge the two. Bingo! We got the cover. We also got a handle on most of the big bucks in town."

It was usual for Big Frank to shoot out these grand schemes as fuel for his Execs. They knew he was searching for criticism.

Mario was the first to react. "Frank, you say the Nationals are already scooping up the Boston market. Seems to me that if Hardley Security and Cambridge were hot targets they would be gone by now. It also seems to me that if we are going to move our base to Boston and penetrate the entire commercial base then we need to get out of some of our smaller scams so we don't compete with ourselves.

Frank was ready with an answer. "Good point, Mario, I raised that when Charlie suggested this move. It seems that both banks have been on the takeover list for some time but the cousins are tough guys who are stuck in the past. They won't move because of the family thing and the hate they have for each other. Goes way back. Anyway, Charlie is close to Hardly and has an angle on his cousin. Charlie even has a good piece of Hardly Security. So what it is, is that Charlie thinks we can work a back door deal with Hardly and his cousin separately to buy them out. Then we gradually buy a few pieces until we have control. A simple takeover. Just takes a little time. Charlie thinks this guy Hardly is going screwy or something so we ought to get his piece before his family puts him in a home or something like that."

Mario nodded his understanding of the strategy but pursued his point. "Frank, we have Action Waste Management, Park/Bay Area Medical, and Patriot Transport all functioning as legit businesses in Boston. Patriot also fronts for a drug distribution business tied to our operation in Queens. Now we also have a soft spot with our tie to the Workers Guild and this guy Cowan in Washington. That set up ties back to some big wig at Hardly Security, O'Shea, who holds some information that could implicate us if we have to ice Cowan. My concern is that we need to tie off some loose ends before we get to far out front in Boston. We could get nailed if some nosy reporter looks very deep into our moves on the banks. The Boston Business Journal would have a field day with wild speculation. We just got to be careful."

Big Frank was quick to agree. "Yeah, we got too many loose ends. I'll tell Charlie that we are going to tie a few things down. We'll take care of it from here. Mario you figure out how we settle this Cowan and O'Shea bit. Charlie will get into Hardly's knickers for a buy. You think we should move Action and Patriot?"

"I'm not sure, Frank." Mario pondered, "Let me give it some thought. We might have to bring Meehan and Mondi into the loop to figure this out. You think that's okay?"

Big Frank nodded. "Sure, but not now. You do some analysis on how we are going to move around. Then we can have a meet with the Boston execs and get their input. No need to get everybody worked up until we have a better idea on the process. I'll keep Charlie in the know. You're right. We got to take our time. No big rush. What so you say, Tony?"

Tony Marone had been content to let the top dogs do all the speculation. He had little to offer in addition to what Mario had said. While he listened to the exchange he busied himself with finishing the Eggs Benedict and was in process of devouring an extra portion of rolls and coffee when Frank penetrated his solitude. He had to swallow fast and the forced suppression of a loud belch brought tears to his eyes. Unable to speak, he waved for time as he rapidly pushed his linen napkin over his red face. In a matter of seconds that seemed like an eternity to Tony, he was able to utter a fragile response.

"Uh, Frank, I think Mario has said most of what I could offer. We got to be careful. I heard from one of our mules in Queens that Boston PD has a snooper cop working undercover on the distribution. Queens is watching him while he is watching Patriot. Nothing new. Just another hassle. They got this cop chasing shadows right now but he could find out about this O'Shea trip if he gets to the records of the local mules. It's really a remote possibility though. We just got to be careful."

Big Frank's eyes opened wide in shocked surprise. "Christ, Tony, that's the first I heard of any hassle by the Boston PD. Is Mondi aware of this? Who's handling the cover? They got this cop channeled off the hunt?"

"Queens is on top of it, Frank." Tony was relaxed. "They picked it up from an inside tip from Boston's Narcotic Unit. Apparently, the cop on the sniff is a fag that isn't fully appreciated by the boys in blue. They know we are supplying Boston out of Queens so one of their guys blows it to one of the NYPD narcs who lets it leak to the Queens. They put a tag on the dude. So far he's not close to anything. They got him watching some user who is clueless. If the cop strays off the false lead then they get Mondi covered with a fall guy or two. Right now, Mondi isn't in the know because they don't want Patriot to make any move that would create a bigger rift in the Boston PD. Mondi has a muscle man that might overreact."

The prospect of a cop from Boston PD sniffing around the Patriot operation made Frank nervous. He feared that a penetration of the drug distribution system could eventually lead to his favorite nephew, Patello. The meeting was held in silence as Frank thought about the situation reported by Marone. Holding his head in his hands he began to give his staff some direction.
"Okay, look, this probably isn't a big deal but we want to be sure that Charlie and Phil are covered. Maybe we should isolate the distribution and set a trail. If the cop gets close we give him the unit, sacrifice the cover, and reorganize. We done this before."

"Frank, if you're very concerned we could set up a competing distributor now," offered Mario, "then if the Patriot route has to go we already have a replacement in business. From a business point of view the Patriot route is the cash cow."

Big Frank wasn't sure of the value in the suggestion. Cautiously, he reacted. "Action is a good laundry, Mario, and Medical is looking like a big producer. Maybe we don't need the drug distribution in Boston. We got other distribution points in New England and most of the East Coast. I got to think this over. Maybe we could bring it in through Maine. Portland might be a good center. Mario, you and Tony look this over."

This was Frank's last word on the subject for now. He took a final sip of his coffee and stood. Mario and Tony knew that the breakfast meeting was concluded.

NOAA Weather predicted a perfect boating weekend—sunny and clear with winds around ten knots from the southwest, temperature in the low eighties. Clouds were expected to form by Sunday evening followed by light rain late Sunday night. Durant had listened to the report on his car radio's weather band on the way to the hospital. The thought of a peaceful weekend on his boat caused him to forget, at least for a moment, the tragic circumstances at St. Anslem's. He drifted into his office and continued to dream about the peaceful cruising until he received the call from Folley.

Unexpectedly the Great One was not in his usual insulting mood. He actually complemented the administration on the progress being made in the cost-reduction program. Then he followed with a report of his meeting with Dr. Anderson. Durant listened in shock and scribbled notes as Folley announced the process underway to close the SACAP unit and transfer the program to the Archdiocese. Abruptly, Folley hung up leaving Durant immobilized.

As if on cue Rod Weaver appeared at Durant's desk with a list of layoffs reported to him by middle management. Prominent on the list was a number of management personnel who had been notified by Nick Samuel that their positions were eliminated. It was obvious that Samuel had played the role of the grim reaper after he regained his balance following his own dismissal.

Weaver was elated with the results. "Boss, this thing is really taking off. I mean heads are rolling all over the place. Our first run of the cuts had us about eighty percent of what we need. My suggestion is that we hold at this point and take stock of the impact. We probably got to reorganize now that nearly a third of the management staff is on notice. We should be able to start the second round in a couple of weeks. I hear tell that nursing is closing the inpatient SACAP unit and laying off the staff. I've already figured that in but frankly I never thought Folley and Anderson would let it happen. Man, this is unbelievable."

"I have more news for you Rod," interrupted Durant. "Not only is Folley closing the Unit, he is moving the doctors including Anderson to the Archdiocese. We'll probably be paying as much if not more for their services but as least it reduces some more personnel with big numbers from the payroll. You better give Folley a call and find out how and when all this stuff is to happen. On second thought, you better call Anderson. He will be far more rational."

Weaver was shocked. Folley was actually cooperating with the administration. Something was wrong with the picture. He thought for a minute and then offered his comments. "Joe, he's up to something. It sounds like he's on board but I'll bet he's working on a deal for himself Think about it We take out all the cost of the program and give him the revenue such as it is. He gets Anderson to organize the docs in a way that he gets a piece of their action. I bet he's going to organize a practice plan and set himself up as the CEO. If he succeeds, he could take over the hospital by controlling the docs. We got to stop that."

Durant nodded and then commented, "Yeah, but who really cares about that? Nobody except maybe you and me because we have our little war with Folley. Who cares, Rod? Hell, I'm beginning to wonder if I should give a damn about this mess. We're gutting the place and the Board seems deliriously happy about it. We need to remember that come Monday morning we will have the opportunity to explain to the Finance Committee that we have things under control. Then on Wednesday the full Board gets to hear about the new tomorrow from Callahan, the boy wonder from Debur and Tandy. I tell you, Rod, it's hard to take all this good news. You remember that Callahan proposed the acceleration of the cost-reduction program with special emphasis on the physicians to get their attention. You also remember that he, not Folley, mentioned the formation of a physician organization with special emphasis on primary care. So, my friend, I don't think we are in a position to fault Folley on the events of the last twenty-four hours. We bought in to Callahan's idea. He will lead us through this even though it isn't clear how we will come out of it. You tracking on this?"

Weaver's head was spinning as he attempted to track on Durant's commentary. He wanted to react but could not collect his thoughts fast enough to inject them. In response, he could only shake his head from side to side as if to protest what he was hearing. It was very uncharacteristic for his boss to excuse Folley for minor aggressive behavior but to be oblivious to a major takeover of power was shocking. He took a deep breath as Durant directed the question to him.

After a few moments, he attempted a reply. "There's no way that Sister Elizabeth will let this happen. She hates Folley more than anybody on the Board. When she hears about this switch she'll take the issue right to the Cardinal. There's no way that she'll let Folley take over this hospital. You know that's right, Joe!"

Weaver's mention of Sister Elizabeth triggered a quick reflection in Durant's mind. He suddenly remembered that not only was Wednesday the day for the special Board meeting, it was also the day that his special arrangement for sending food to Sister Celest's soup kitchen was to begin. He also recalled that Celest had mentioned Sister Elizabeth's full support for the new ministry. Perhaps Elizabeth wasn't as committed to the tertiary acute care male-dominated teaching and research ministry as she was to storefront healing missions.

Cautiously, he reacted to Weaver. "I'll guess we'll have to wait and see how she reacts, Rod. My guess is that the Sisters are committed to caring in whatever way is the most effective. They see things differently than you and me. We shouldn't try to guess. Let's wait and see."

Officer Michael O'Sullivan was very frustrated. As an obedient public servant, he had accepted his orders to work undercover and explore the distribution network of the largest suspected drug supplier in the Boston community. The dealers were strictly consignment agents using various suppliers to purposely create cross trails for the weary police. The primary supplier was unknown by name. The process that a well healed user followed to obtain a fix was known: A call was placed to a dealer who called a supplier. The supplier used a parcel delivery service to bring the fix to the user. When the dealer received a verification of delivery notice he then contacted the user for payment. On no occasion did drugs and money change hands at the same time. Equally important was the fact that the dealer did not possess the drugs. He simply served as a middle man or order taker and collector.

There was a well-conceived legal gap between user, dealer and supplier that prevented the police from breaking up the ring by its usual methods of surveillance and raids. The only way apparent to Officer O'Sullivan's superiors was to interrupt the influx of cocaine to the supplier and/or identify the supplier and nail them with an inventory large enough to warrant a major conviction. An additional difficulty was that the distribution system was specially designed to accommodate the rich and famous who had their own ways and means of safeguarding their habit.

O'Sullivan had been given a no easy task. However, it was supposed to have been made easier when the Brass passed on an anonymous tip that the coordinator for the entire Boston operation was none other than O'Sullivan's wife's ex-husband, Jay Marquart.

Officer O'Sullivan was flabbergasted by the information. He, nevertheless, obeyed orders to maintained a constant vigil on the suspect. This was not hard to do since the suspect showed up at O'Sullivan's house several times a week, was in court with his wife over the custody of their child, was a patient at the hospital where his wife worked and was working under contract at St. Anslem's where O'Sullivan would often see the suspect at lunch. O'Sullivan was very tired of watching the apparent brains of the Boston underworld stumble in and out of his life. Furthermore, it seemed unlikely that the coordinator of the drug distribution system would be in a drug rehabilitation program.

There was some consolation in believing that perhaps Marquart was using the other members of the SACAP as dealers. If he could prove this theory then he could also nail the hospital before the hospital could bring his wife before the State Nursing Licenser Board for violating patient confidence. O'Sullivan's plan was to get the goods on Marquart and implicate the hospital so the hospital would cop a plea in exchange for forgetting about the incident involving Cecile blowing out Jay's medical record. This was very unlikely but it gave the good Officer something to dream about as he made vain efforts to offset his boredom.

The alternate lifestyle experienced by O'Sullivan in contrast to married life was punctuated by frequent visits to the Troubadour Lounge. It was at the Troubadour that he had enlisted the assistance of some acquaintances in exploring the drug distribution system in Boston. In the beginning, O'Sullivan was probably the only person to frequent the Troubadour who wasn't a known user. Nevertheless, he had little trouble finding volunteers to set out on the dangerous mission of acquiring illicit drugs especially when the acquisition was paid for and protected by an Officer of the Law.

O'Sullivan was not surprised when suspect Marquart walked into the Troubadour the front man on the first of the exploratory purchases. The delivery man who entered after Marquart arrived was obviously some dupe who was unaware of the nature of the delivery. O'Sullivan and his friends chatted with the delivery man for a while and succeeded in formulating a friendship that would carry them through several additional buys. Brian, the delivery man, was very friendly and intent on serving his customers. He was very generous in passing on whatever information he had when asked about his relationship with the suspect, Marquart. Unfortunately, he gave O'Sullivan nothing that would assist the law in pinning Marquart as the head of the Boston dope business. In fact, the information that Brian provided would cause an investigator to completely discount the idea that Marquart was involved at all.

In a very guarded fashion, O'Sullivan would discuss the information that Brian provided with his friends at the Troubadour. They cautioned him that many dealers would lead the police up blind alleys in order to cover the main trail. Frequently the carrier would be given packets of sugar instead of cocaine to deliver to a known set-up. On this basis O'Sullivan agreed to allow his friends to open the pouch delivered by Brian and sample the product. They reported to him that the product was of excellent quality.

They also convinced Officer O'Sullivan to sample the product as well so in the future he could identify the real thing. O'Sullivan, after many additional buys, became an expert in identifying high quality cocaine. His expanding circle of loyal friends would eagerly assist him in sampling the evidence that rapidly disappeared. Brian, as a consequence, made frequent trips to the Troubadour.

Jay had no idea that he was the focus suspect of the Boston Police Department's investigation of the drug distribution system. He was only aware of O'Sullivan's constant stare and penetrating look every time they were in the same vicinity. Jay also felt that O'Sullivan was a bit goofy for marrying Cecile. Jay had made that mistake but rectified it with a divorce. Why O'Sullivan fell into the trap of the black spider was a mystery.

Jay only considered the matter as a secondary concern to O'Sullivan's interest in him. Was the crazy cop intent on nailing him as a user? Jay reasoned that O'Sullivan could shake him down anytime for possession. If so he would find nothing since Jay had eliminated all traces of drugs from his body, clothes and Jeep. There was only one answer that made sense to Jay: O'Sullivan was looking for an excuse to bust him on any charge that would cause the court to determine that he was an unfit parent. Anything and everything could be used against him—driving under the influence, running a stoplight, flipping off a meter maid—anything. The law held all the cards. The only protection Jay could think of was to get an angle on O'Sullivan that he could use to get that crazy cop to back off.

O'Sullivan was in the back of Jay's mind as he drove toward St. Anslem's on a beautiful Friday morning. Foremost in his mind was the prospect of resuming his weekend ritual with a fishing trip on Friday night. He was intent on giving his main man, Brian, a call as soon as he completed his eight A.M. conference. Many other thoughts also occurred to him. Last night, his first night at home with Susan and the kids in over a week without the pressure of a pending court fight, had been most relaxing. It was far better than hanging around with the wacked out members of his support group. However, the incident with Bob Markley was an irritation to Jay that entered his every thought. Consequently, Jay held a mental note to square things with his SACAP friend before the day was out.

He was also upset to learn that Benny and his All-Star team had been trounced by eight runs in their initial playoff game. Jay had missed the event because of his preparation for the court hearing. The baseball season was officially over for the Marquart clan which put a little different perspective on the weekend festivities. Benny seemed well adjusted to the outcome as he detailed his play to Jay. Susan added some color commentary including the fact that Eddie gave Benny several helpful tips on fielding.

Eddie the Enforcer seemed to cross Jay's mind with Markley, O'Sullivan, and a cast of thousands that crowded his thinking. Eagerly he pushed them aside and concentrated on Brian. It was Friday. Let the games begin.

It was only seven A.M. when Jay entered the hospital cafeteria. As expected, Tommy the Tout was at his usual table, chatting now and then with the "trade" as they dropped by. He nodded a greeting to Jay as he slid into the chair at the Tout's "office." Jay purposely arrived an hour early to have a few minutes with Tommy. This was the first move of many that Jay had conceived to learn the inside about O'Sullivan. Tommy was the man. If there was any dirt on O'Sullivan, the Tout would be in the know.

Jay threw Tommy an opening. "Hay, Tommy, what's the best line?"

"Take the Sox on tonight's game by two. Pitching is right. How much you want? How's it been goin', Jay? I hear you done good in court. The nurses been talkin'."

"I'll take five on the Sox. What do the nurses say, man? I'm okay. They think Cecile got screwed?"

"I got you down for five. They don't say much. You got to piece it together. Most of them are scared about the layoffs so what they say is how they gonna keep their jobs. Word is that your ex is gonna get it for some rap that you hung on her. Guess the Union is getting involved."

Jay was impressed that the hospital grapevine had Cecile as a topic. "Yeah, well, maybe she's got it comin'. I'm thinkin' that her old man could get her out of the jam. Hell, he's a top cop, right?"

Tommy made a note of the bet but didn't look at Jay. Instead he continued his comments. "Don't think it's a police matter, Jay. Besides, that man of hers ain't got any pull. He's downtown and the boys at the precinct think he's a fink. Some say he's queer and now the word is that he's on the stuff. Nobody knows for sure. He's a narc so he might be doin' a con. You know. Trying to lead a fly to honey. You know what I'm sayin'?"

"Yeah, well, the guy bugs me. I see him around here a lot," was Jay's response.

The Tout cut in. "He's got no buddies. Comes out here to have lunch with the Mrs. She picks up the tab. He don't come by here. Not a sporting man I guess. The other bulls come by—they say he's trying to make a big bust that gets him a desk job. He's a college grad that took criminal justice. Really ain't cut out for the street. Guy like that would arrest his own mother if it would get him promoted. The boys think he's the kind that would trump up a charge against some fool to make the grade. Don't get too close to that clown, Jay. He's a little too hungry. If he comes by here the boys say that I shouldn't take his action. He would put a collar on me for sure. Man's a pure asshole."

Tommy paused, took a sip of his coffee, and waved to a resident in green. Jay knew this meant that it was time for the next customer. With that he gave Tommy a nod and moved away from the table. Then he went back to the serving counter where he picked up a jelly donut and a cup of black coffee. He tried to joke with the cashier but was rebuked by her solemn mood. Sitting at a small table, he glanced around at the cafeteria customers. Nearly all of them were employees. They were divorced of their usual humor. Few spoke. They sat in groups of two or three as if they were attending a wake.

It was not the same happy St. Anslem's that Jay was used to. The atmosphere made him shiver.

No one from the SACAP Unit was in the cafeteria which seemed strange to Jay. He had hoped that Markley would stop by for his usual morning caffeine fix. Jay's plan was to give him a casual good morning and then slowly move to an apology for the brushoff he gave him yesterday. Jay waited as long as he could for Markley to appear. At seven-forty-five he disposed of his empty coffee cup and left the cafeteria.

Jay walked slowly through the corridor attempting eye contact with passing hospital employees. Everyone had their heads down and avoided greetings or conversation. They were very scared. As he passed the entrance to the SACAP Unit he had the urge to walk in and give his buddy, Markley, a big hello as if nothing had happened. However, a glance in the Unit revealed an empty desk where Markley would normally be at this hour. Not only was Markley missing but there was no staff in view. The Unit was very quiet. The lights were out in the inpatient section. This caused him to wonder if by some miracle all the drunks and junkies in the world had been cured.

Not likely, was his second thought. *I don't feel cured—as a matter-of-fact I feel like a belt right now.*

The thought of a cold beer triggered the thought of Friday and fishing with his buddy, Brian. With that in mind he entered the small conference room in the Environmental Services Office where Ken Ryan had told him the meeting of the Environmental Service's Supervisors would be held. Jay was to attend as an observer and to respond to any technical questions that might come up. He saw it as an opportunity to plan the rest of the day since the progress of the St. Anslem's Waste Management Program was not expected to be a hot topic among the housekeeping staff.

Typically, Jay expected the staff to arrive five or ten minute's late, soak up some coffee, listen to a rah-rah talk by the director, and then split. Little if anything would be asked. This was going to be a no-brainer. Surprisingly, the conference room was dark Jay turned on the lights to find a cluttered room with paper cups half filled with stale coffee apparently from the previous day. The chairs were in disarray and the floor was littered with paper and other debris. He brushed aside the mess and waited for the arrival of the supervisors. Fifteen minutes past the hour no one had arrived.

Jay decided that the meeting was over before it began and started to leave when a small man in a white lab coat walked in. The man had a very pleasant and warm smile. He greeted Jay with a handshake and introduced himself as Dr. Ray Sutton, Director of Quality Assurance. His warmth and friendly attitude was stark contrast to what Jay had observed in the cafeteria and corridors. He reminded Jay of the St. Anslem's of old with friendly, confident people who loved their work and loved the patient. Jay eagerly shook Dr. Sutton's hand and introduced himself.

Sutton's eyes sparkled when he heard Jay's name. He commented that he had heard Jay mentioned in several conversations lately and would like to know all about the Waste Management Program being implemented at St. Anslem's. Jay loved to talk about waste management and Sutton appeared to have a willing ear. From that point on the conversation was one sided as Jay waxed eloquent about the environment, the fine qualities of Action, and the grand program that he had in mind for St. Anslem's.

Sutton maintained an obvious interest in Jay's commentary. When the part about St. Anslem's came up the doctor's interest heightened. He would interrupt Jay now and then for more explanation and in-depth description of some features. Eventually, it was Sutton who had the floor explaining to Jay about the Quality Assurance program at St. Anslem's and how the waste management program was very important part of the hospital's quality effort. Sutton detailed to Jay how the medical staff directed the hospital on quality matters and the administration implemented the quality assurance program as prescribed by the medical staff and as approved by the Board of Directors.

Jay was fascinated with Sutton's commentary. As the doctor talked, Jay's mind departed from waste management and centered on the matter of patient confidentiality. He wondered if he dare ask this man about the stupid nurse who had no regard for the patient, the hospital, or the law. Maybe he could get Sutton to bring down the whole organization on Cecile's head. The guy seemed like a person that Jay could trust. As he was about to raise the issue, the Environmental Services office clerk stuck her head into the conference room. She seemed surprised to find the room occupied. In response to her question Jay explained that he was the Action representative to the supervisors' meeting.

The clerk nodded a greeting to Dr. Sutton and then explained to the two gentlemen that the meeting had been canceled. No one knew that Jay and Dr. Sutton were to attend and she apologized for not notifying them of the cancellation. The clerk's interruption diverted Jay from his about to be asked question. Sutton was also diverted. He stood and shook Jay's hand, commenting about how glad he was to have had this conversation. He hoped he would have the opportunity to learn more and be a participant in the waste management program for the hospital. Then he gave Jay a parting smile and left.

Jay sat for a while and pondered the conversation with Dr. Sutton. The little man seemed very sincere and interested not only in waste management for the hospital but for the entire wellbeing of the hospital as well. He was the first person in the administration of the hospital who seemed genuinely concerned about the matter of quality patient care. Dr. Sutton had refreshed Jay's enthusiasm. It was a great start for a Friday. Things were definitely on a high. It was time to return to Action Waste Management and go to work.

In another part of the hospital Bob Markley sat and listened to Dr. Anderson in total disbelief. The task being given to him was simply stated but impossible to perform in the time allotted. Essentially, Anderson had directed him to transform the SACAP program from its hospital base to a non-institutional program in less than twenty-four hours. Dealing with the personnel had been simplified by administration who was at that very moment laying off the entire inpatient contingent. The tough part was notifying the patients and rescheduling their appointments. Major logistical problems presented themselves not the least of which was continuity of care and billing for services under a new name—a name yet to be determined. Then there was the crisis patient—the poor soul who crashed with DT's, or went on a bender, and/or was brought or found their way to St. A's expecting the usual compassionate reception but instead was going to be locked in the Psych. Department's rubber room.

Markley tried vainly to dissuade Anderson. "Ron, this is insane. This can't be done. Hell, it shouldn't be done. You know this is a great disservice to the patients. A transition of this kind, if it is going to be done at all, requires a month at least. You have to explain this to Dr. Folley. If you want I can get a petition from the patients. They won't like this at all."

Dr. Anderson listened patiently to the passionate pleas of his main man. Markley always thought first of the patient. The pressure of administration was not his to bear so it was natural for him to give the patient the very best of care without regard to efficiency, cost, or the bottom line. Anderson, on the other hand, was equally compassionate but sufficiently imbedded in management to realize the necessary balance between compassion and resources. Markley's attitude was registering with Anderson until he suggested the patient petition. This was a form of anarchy that Dr. Anderson despised. It basically informed the patient that things were so out of control that a riot was necessary to regain order.

Anderson turned red with the thought. "Markley, if you so much as breath a word of our problems to the patients I'll can you in a New York minute. We care for the patients in spite of our problems and without passing on our burdens to them. Do you understand? Now you get your butt back to the Unit or what's left of it and start the transition process. I have to deal with the SACAP medical staff. You deal with the rest. That can't be too difficult. There's hardly anybody left except you, the docs, and me. Give that jerk that heads the Archdiocesan Office for Folley a call and make sure he understands what's happening. Maybe he can give you some logistical support. Logan is his name. You can get the number from Folley's office."

Markley shook his head in disbelief. "Yeah, right. I bet this guy is a real winner. What's a bureaucrat going to know about running a program for abusers? Say, what about the support groups? Are they still going to meet in the cafeteria or has the administration pulled the authorization?"

Anderson was mad and very impatient. He shouted at Markley, "All the more reason for you to call Logan. He's our administrator now so you can ask him to arrange for the support group sessions. You are supposed to be on his payroll by this afternoon."

The sudden thought of leaving the employ of St. Anslem's registered with a bang. Markley felt fear then anger. He and thousands of patients and employees were being pushed around without knowing about it or having any say about the changes. This seemed to be a massive affront to his personal dignity and worse yet, a violation of all those principles that St. Anslem's and the Church he loved seemed to promote. Again, he protested. "Ron, for Christ's sake, don't I have any say about this change? What if I don't want to work for Logan's office? I usually have a right to pick my employer. It was my choice to work at St. Anslem's. It doesn't seem right that I can be pushed over to another employer without some options being available."

Anderson became calm and tried to reason with the distraught Markley. "Look, Bob, You say you chose the hospital as a place to work. That's true.

But you need to remember that the hospital and I chose you. We both had options. You can go to work anyplace else at any time. No one is holding you here. You won't leave the program because the patients are in the program. It doesn't make a bit of difference who runs it as long as the patients are being cared for. That's why we are here and that's why we are going to make the best of this change. The patients have confidence in us and they have confidence in the professionals and the counselors. We need to preserve that confidence and uphold the spiritual dimension that supports that confidence. Fortunately, the continuation of the Church sponsorship and identity is not lost in this transition. You, better than anyone, should understand that."

Markley felt the sting of the scolding that Anderson, his boss and personal physician, was giving him. He remembered the many times in the past when Dr. Anderson had challenged him to gather his inner strength to overcome his struggle with alcohol. It was the Church that Markley loved as a young man with all its subsequent changes that confused Markley and caused him to use booze as a crutch. It was also the authority within the Church that recognized his problem and brought him to Dr. Anderson for help. Markley was grateful to Anderson and to the Church for reinstating him to society. He knew that his mission to care for those afflicted with substance abuse was God-given. He had an obligation to serve his Church and to serve those most in need of help. Anderson had just reminded him of that obligation.

"Okay, Ron, you're right," Markley acknowledged. "I don't have a choice, although I may have options. I'll get busy and start the change. Lord knows, I hate change. If Logan and that wizard you work for screw up the program I'll use whatever influence I can muster to bring them down and get the program on the right track."

Anderson knew that Markley had friends in high places. Those friends were the ones who brought him to St. Anslem's. Properly they stayed distant as Markley reconstructed his life. Markley, in turn, did not pursue the rise to power but remained content to work with the poor and afflicted.

Anderson, nevertheless, was surprised at Markley's threat to use his holstered firepower. "You sound like Wyatt Earp, Robert. What the hell has gotten into you? If this thing fails at this point it's because you and I sat on our collective asses and let it happen."

Markley seemed pensive. "Right again, Ron. I'm not blaming you. I'm just a little upset."

Markley left Dr. Anderson's office and returned to the Unit. Nurses who had been notified of the "right sizing" on the Unit were silently walking about cleaning out lockers, removing notices form bulletin boards, and returning supplies to pharmacy and general stores. Markley convinced the Supervisor to keep the outpatient and counseling rooms stocked and ready for the walk-in patients over the weekend. He hoped to be able to talk Logan into obtaining use of the rooms from the hospital until the new service could be relocated.

He also made a list of probable patients who he suspected might need emergent help in the next seventy-two hours. This list was strictly a guess. He simply went down the list of current patients undergoing treatment in the Phase One condition. Then he went over a list of patients who were judged to be between Phase One and Two and added them to the list. As a last check he looked at the list of Patients who were in Phase Two. Jay Marquart had only been added to the Phase Two list yesterday before he bugged out of the support session. Now Markley toyed with the idea of returning his name to the intermediate list but at the last moment decided to keep Marquart on the advanced recovery list.

The Phase One and intermediate list was sent to the Emergency Room with the instructions that if any of the patients on the list called or presented themselves for care, the SACAP Counselor on call should be notified. Markley thought that a patient undergoing advanced treatment would seek assistance from someone on the support team rather than present themselves at the Emergency Room. The support person would then initiate the care process as they had all been counseled to do.

Michael Logan was ill-prepared for the call from Bob Markley. The Office of Health Affairs was greatly disorganized to say the least when he was notified by the great Dr. Folley that they were to become instant healthcare providers. Logan knew enough about the regulatory process and realized that you just didn't start giving care without some kind of a license from the State. Application and approval of a license would take weeks. Now he was being badgered by someone named Markley who claimed that the office was in the drunk and dope business effective now.

Carefully he sorted out Markley's comments to the point that he recognized the direction that was given the caller. It traced easily to Folley and his insistence for immediate acquisition of the primary care medical practices. He thanked Mr. Markley in a very courteous and cooperative manner for bringing the questions and concerns to his attention. Both men agreed that it was very important for Logan to have an immediate conference with Joe Durant and work out the logistics of continuing care. At the conclusion of their conversation Logan promised Markley that he would be back to him that same afternoon.

Logan's call to Durant prompted a quick face to face meeting that included Mitch Daly and Rod Weaver. Daly was expert on the State Licenser regulations and Weaver, of course, was there to serve as the cost cop for the hospital. Daly took the position as the mediator between Durant and Logan since he had the confidence of both executives. It was obvious that the Archdiocesan Office for Health Affairs was not legally prepared to provide any form of care. Additionally, the office lacked clinical facilities. Daly proposed that a letter of understanding be prepared that agreed to transfer the operation to the Archdiocese as soon as the Archdiocese could obtain a license. In the interim the Archdiocese would become the operator of the SACAP as an agent of St. Anslem's operating under St. Anslem's license. The Archdiocese would lease the SACAP facilities from St. A's and employ the staff as appropriate.

Weaver loved Daly's idea. It not only relieved the hospital of the operational cost of the program but through the lease returned a portion of the lost revenue. Weaver also knew that by some clever manipulation of indirect costs he could actually derive a profit from the rent income. It was hard for him to maintain a poker face as Logan agreed to Daly's suggestion. His wink to Durant was the signal to go along with the deal.

Durant promised Logan that the letter of understanding and the draft lease documents would be ready sometime on Monday. As the meeting ended, Logan asked Daly to show him the SACAP Unit and introduce him to Bob Markley.

Daly loved the idea that he was coordinating the transition of the SACAP from the hospital to the Archdiocese Health Affairs Office. The function gave him visibility that he felt would surely give him status with whoever won the inevitable power struggle between Durant and Logan. As he left Durant's office with Logan in tow he flashed a quick okay signal to the hospital executive and placed his arm on the Logan's shoulder. Daly was certain that he would survive and possibly gain a promotion in the process.

Markley was very busy with the dismantling of the SACAP Unit when Daly and Logan appeared at the Unit reception area. Markley knew Daly but never had any opportunity to get acquainted. The other gentleman was a complete stranger who appeared very much ill at ease in the clinical setting.

Daly greeted Markley as if they were longtime friends. "Hi, Bob. Meet Michael Logan. He runs the Archdiocese Health Affairs Office that is taking over SACAP. I guess today. Is that right?"

Markley ignored Daly's question and offered to shake Logan's hand. "Good to meet you, Mr. Logan. Things are in a mess right now and I expect will remain that way until we get things organized. I need to know if you or the hospital will authorize the on-call schedule for the weekend. Truth is we don't have anybody left on staff to cover."

Daly was quick to reply before Logan could speak. "It's got to be the hospital, Bob. Michael doesn't have a license so any patient treated will have to be a hospital patient in order to be legal. You don't have a problem with that, do you?"

"I don't have a problem, Sir." Markley's agitation began to surface as he answered. "But I think the hospital does. You see, they relieved all the staff from duty effective three-thirty this afternoon. The hospital may have a license and they may have the program designation but the hospital doesn't have any help. So maybe you and Mr. Logan can staff the Unit yourselves."

Logan realized that Markley's temper was heating up as a result of Daly's casual attitude. Carefully he stepped in front of Daly to signal his assertion into the discussion. "Mr. Markley, it seems to me that we are both at a disadvantage in trying to make this change on such short notice. That makes it difficult but loss of temper will not help. I desperately need your cooperation and your assistance. Is anybody left on the hospital payroll who could assume the on-call responsibility?"

Logan's refreshing tone began to calm Markley. He then attempted to cooperate. "As of now I'm the only one who hasn't received notice of termination. Even Dr. Andersen has been told that he is being transferred to the Archdiocese this afternoon. He and the other physicians remain a part of the hospital anyway because of their medical staff appointment. They can continue to treat patients as private practitioners. Their own license will cover them. The hospital can admit the patients to the Psychiatric unit or a general medical unit and still cover the acute phase of the illness. Basically, the patient is protected but does not have the benefit, as of three-thirty this afternoon, of a coordinated response to the many needs of a chemically dependent person. The patient needs social care, psychological counseling, spiritual intervention, support therapy, transportation, and maybe even a hamburger. Somebody has to be there to assist the patient. It takes more than one person to cover twenty-four hours seven days a week. Right now, we have nobody!"

Markley's temper began to flare again as he completed his answer to Logan's question. He was losing it. He threw his pencil across the room just missing Daly who began to take the matter personally. Markley's face was red and his eyes glistened with tears that caused Logan to wonder if they were from sentiment, anger or tension. Bob Markley, Alcoholic, was on the verge of a temper tantrum characteristic of a recovering addict. It was that uncontrollable surge of temper often resulting in a violent act that he had counseled his patients about. Suddenly he remembered the smiling face of Jay Marquart as he stood at the same place last night. Jay had gladly reported his win in court but refused to accept Bob's counsel about his anger. Jay left Markley in defiance flatly refusing to participate in supporting others who needed help. "Ask me if I care" was Jay's parting shot. Now Markley was being asked that question but in a very different way.

Under control Markley made an offer. "All right, Mr. Logan, let me suggest this. I'll cover the program this weekend as best I can. Nobody gets drunk on weekends so it should be a snap. I've prepared a list of the people in the program by category for the ER. So, if anybody checks in who is on the Category One list the ER staff gives me a call. I'll evaluate the situation from a non- medical perspective and see that the patient is covered. But for this to work I've got to stay on the hospital's payroll at least through the weekend. Can you handle that?"

Logan was relieved that Markley's anger began to subside. "Sure. If you haven't received notice of layoff yet I can guarantee that you won't until we are ready for you to transfer to the office. It seems to me that you should stay with the hospital until we are ready with license and all the appropriate approvals. Mr. Daly is working on that part for me. You mentioned that you would cover category one. How many categories are there and who if anybody will cover their needs?"

The question was music to Markley's ears. Logan actually expressed interest in the welfare of the patient. The question of money, expense, charges and all that other administrative stuff had not yet surfaced. Maybe Logan was a blessing.

"There are two additional categories, Mr. Logan," offered Markley. "The patients in those categories are less acute. We have a volunteer staff who support them. The hospital only gets involved if one of the volunteers thinks it necessary to bring the patient to the hospital. When that happens patient is upgraded to the category one list and I'll be notified. I think we've got it covered."

Chapter Fourteen

Jay Marquart had a great day. Things at Action went smoothly from the time that he returned and reported to Ken Ryan that St. Anslem's was screwed up to the moment he met with Donovan and learned that the Union was about to sign a contract with Action. It seemed that everything that was supposed to be under his control was now out of control. Somehow, he couldn't care less. His thought was on the afternoon and buddy Brian and a cold beer and fishing and Saturday night and all the good times. Let it roll! Nothing seemed to bother him. He was relaxed for the first time since before he "got sick" He felt good. He felt like a high. Brian was ready. The boat was available. It was a warm calm evening.

Brian picked Jay up at his home just after five-thirty. They pointed Brian's truck down the Mass Pike toward I-93 and then onto Route 3 arriving at the Hingham Boat Dock an hour and a half later. Jay had consumed three beers in the process. Brian matched him. Jay proceeded to the Deli across the street from the dock to replenish the beer supply while Brian carried the fishing gear to the boat illegally tied to the launching ramp pier. When Jay returned he found Brian standing by the boat shouting profanities at departing fisherman.

Jay regarded Brian's temper as a bit of an annoyance and he let his buddy know it. "Brian, my man, please refrain from such vulgar talk. You offend and unnerve me. What could the citizen have done to arouse your anger, pray tell?"

Brian raised his fist. "Jay, the son of a bitch called me an idiot for parking the boat where it is. Hell, I didn't put it there. He's got no right to get upset like he did and call me names. I just gave it back to him. Screw him, that's what

I say. Who the hell is he anyway? Anyway, we got screwed. That goddamn customer of mine not only parked the boat where it ain't supposed to be, he also didn't put any gas in the thing. Now we got to fill the tank before we go out. You got any money or did you use it all to buy the beer?"

Brian always had enough money for beer and gas. His question to Jay was Brian's way of letting Jay know that he was watching the amount of beer Jay was consuming. Brian hadn't said anything about Jay's trip on the wagon. He also hadn't said anything when Jay grabbed his first beer and guzzled it down. It was then that Brian realized that his old buddy was back on the sauce but there was no indication how far Jay was going to go. Brian was just curious.

Jay was taken aback by Brian's question. He had also taken it for granted that Brian would stand the expense of the evening as he had always done. Jay's gesture in buying the beer was gratuitous, he thought. Brian's sarcastic question embarrassed Jay. Slowly and in dramatic fashion Jay opened his wallet and extracted a five-dollar bill, the one he had reserved to cover his bet with Tommy the Tout, and handed it to Brian. To Jay's dismay Brian took the money without any hesitation.

Five dollars was less than a quarter of the cost of the gasoline that they would use that evening but to Jay it was much more than he had expected to spend considering that he had already spent over twice that amount to replenish the Sam Adams supply. He noted in his mind that since he couldn't drink the gasoline he most certainly would see that no beer was left for the benefit of the unworthy boat owner who left them with an empty tank. Defiantly Jay opened another beer as Brian prepared to cast off for the nearby marina gas dock.

The Hingham Marina was very busy. It seemed as though every boat moored in Hingham was trying to buy gas at the same time. Troubled attendants hurried to assist with the boat lines, pass the gas hose to owners, pray that no one would spill gas in the bilge or light a cigarette, and make out credit card receipts. Several boats waited in the stream for an opening at the gas dock. Tempers were high as some discourteous skippers attempted to move in ahead of their turn. The attendants were just too busy to referee so on occasion angry words were exchanged between the boat operators.

Joe Durant and his wife were waiting to approach the dock for fuel. Joe was being very patient as he held his thirty-foot Carver in position to approach. He knew he was next. A twenty-eight-foot Bay Liner was taking aboard lines and backing off Cautiously Joe started forward. His wife was passing the stem line to an attendant when the current caused the bow of the Carver to swing away from the dock. Before he could adjust the throttles to bring the bow back to the dock a beat up blue Sea Sprite squeezed into the spot leaving the Carver with stern tied fast and bow swinging in the current. This time the attendants moved quickly to push the Sea Sprite away from the dock so the Carver could be promptly secured. The operator of the Sea Sprite seemed to want to cooperate with the attendants in order to avoid the inevitable crunch but the passenger flashed a heavy bird at Joe Durant.

Durant caught the gesture out of the comer of his eye but was too occupied with bringing his boat to the dock to react to the insult. However, with the aid of the attendants he was soon tied fast. Then he moved to the boat's swim platform and began filling the craft's twin seventy-five-gallon tanks. The blue Sea Sprite had moved behind and was now resting its bow against the swim platform edge of Durant's Carver. Durant could not avoid knowing of the close proximity of the blue boat. He tried to ignore it as best he could. He was also determined not to lose his temper over such nonsense. His week at St. Anslem's had been difficult and the day had been climatic as reactions over the layoffs reached peak emotional state. This was his time to relax and he was determined that a discourteous inexperienced operator of a navigational hazard was not going to upset him. Very carefully he looked over his shoulder and saw Jay Marquart sitting on the engine box of the Sea Sprite, drinking a beer.

In the same instance that Durant recognized Jay. He also recognized the blue Sea Sprite as the one that he had confronted on a previous stop at the fuel dock. He took a quick look around to see if its belligerent owner was on board the boat or anywhere in sight. The man standing on the dock next to the boat was the operator but not the same one that Durant had nearly come to blows with last week. Satisfied that the present crew of the Sea Sprite was non-confrontational. Durant made eye contact with Jay and gave him a friendly nod choosing to ignore Jay's earlier "finger" salute.

The fact that Jay was drinking a beer and appeared a little tipsy registered with Durant since Jay was now a celebrated graduate of the SACAP and was a major topic of discussion in the Quality Assurance meeting.

Jay at first attempted to ignore the man fueling the boat in front of him. He had flipped him the bird as a reflex but now he was embarrassed and didn't want to look at the gentleman. He caught Durant's friendly nod out of the corner of his eye and again out of reflex he saluted the man but this time by elevating his beer can. It was then that Jay recognized Durant. His mouth fell open in surprise and he blushed. Then in typical Marquart fashion he regained his composure and moved to the bow of the Sea Sprite to engage in friendly conversation.

"Hey, Mr. Durant. How you doin'? Man, it's a great night for a little fishin', you goin' fishin'?"

Joe gave a friendly response. "I'm fine, Mr. Marquart. We're just going to take a little cruise around the harbor. It's a chance to cool off and unwind. Looks like you're going fishing."

"Yeah, well, my buddy knows this guy who lets us use his boat. It's a business relationship you might say. Usually he's got gas but not tonight. We got to fill the thing before we head out. Man, you got a nifty boat. You sleep over night on it?"

Joe noticed Jay's friendly attitude. "We can but seldom do. Where are going to fish?"

Jay seemed positive. "Out around Graves Light. Maybe out to B-Buoy but that's kinda far and I don't think we got enough beer for the voyage." He suddenly realized that he was talking to the administrator of St. Anslem's and the SACAP. The comment about not having enough beer registered with him as being inappropriate but he wasn't sure if Durant fully realized that he had been enrolled in the SACAP. Instinctively he placed his beer behind him and out of sight.

Durant had made careful note of Jay's inebriation. He followed each word of Jay's slurred speech with full intent to enter a special memo into the Quality Assurance Committee through the good office of Dr. Sutton. He felt confident that Jay's break from therapy would alter the significance of the breach of confidentiality charge that Jay held against the hospital since Jay was now engaged in public inebriation. If by chance he would get arrested for DWI or a similar charge then the hospital would be in a good defensive position. Durant toyed with the idea of notifying the Boston Harbor Patrol of a suspected drunken operator.

Jay was now alert to the possibility that he was compromised although he had no definite information that Durant was aware of his patient relationship with SACAP. He straightened himself up and did everything possible to offset the appearance of drinking. He even attempted to assume a professional posture with the hospital executive as he expanded the conversation to business matter. "Mr. Durant, I was going to call you today regarding the hospital's waste management program. We have a problem with getting it underway. The initial supervisory meeting this morning was canceled. So we are now about a week and a half behind the original schedule. I realize that the hospital is undergoing some cutbacks but I would like to know if I can work around this and get the project completed on time. Is that possible?"

Durant admired Jay's recovery. It was a very clever tactic well executed. Furthermore, the comment about the hospital's cutbacks registered with Durant as he recalled the problems of the day dealing with a demoralized staff. This caused him to think about his trustees and especially Mark Meehan who was on the Budget Review Committee. It would be well to keep Meehan satisfied. He also recalled that in his first encounter with the blue Sea Sprite and its doped-up owner he had appealed to Phil Mondi to moderate the issue. Mondi had promised that there would be no trouble from the boat owner. It wouldn't pay, thought Durant, to turn this boat in and alienate Phil Mondi.

Both Meehan and Mondi were expected allies in the upcoming finance meeting. He also recalled Folley's insistence that the doctors be involved in the Waste Management program and that Dr. Sutton had been drafted to represent the medical staff in the effort. Durant decided to play it straight.

"John, I think we can get the project back on track but we may have to change its focus. I'll ask Dr. Sutton, our quality review officer, to get in touch with you about setting up a new time line. You'll like Sutton. He'll keep it moving. If you think of it give him a call on Monday afternoon."

"Thanks, Mr. Durant. I met Dr. Sutton today. He's a good man. I'll give him a call and mention that we had this conversation. Thanks again."

Jay was pleased with the progress of the conversation. It was really the most he had accomplished all day. Ryan would be a happy camper when Jay reported in Monday morning. Instinctively, Jay picked up his beer and took a long slow drink draining the can.

Durant was quick to cut off the conversation. His last tank was filled with gas and spouted into the stream. The attendant took the hose and passed it to Brian who began filling the Sea Sprite. Durant eagerly accepted the charge ticket, signed, and moved to the bridge to start the blowers. His discussion with Jay was over, the blue Sea Sprite was literally behind him, and it was now time to relax and enjoy a peaceful evening cruise.

Jay opened another beer as he watched Brian sweat and struggle with the gas hose. Compassionately, he handed the beer to Brian who nodded for Jay to put it on the small aft deck next to the gas port. Jay did just that and then opened another beer for himself as he heard the gas hose click shut indicating that the Sea Sprite had accepted its maximum fuel capacity. He gulped the beer and hit the blower switch. Brian was now on the pier handing cash to the attendant Jay noticed that the pump registered twenty-five gallons of fuel for a total of thirty-seven dollars. His five-dollar contribution seemed insignificant to the total cost of the evening. Buddy Brian was fronting the activity, causing Jay to realize that Brian was indeed a true friend. Brian smiled at Jay as he handed the attendant the money. Then he jumped into the boat and started the motor. The attendants passed the lines to Jay as Brian skillfully moved the boat off the dock. The fishing trip was underway, at last.

Brian brought the small boat into the channel and proceeded across Hingham Bay. Jay sat aft and prepared the tackle. He noticed for the first time that the Sea Sprite had unusual rigging stored on both sides of the engine box. The equipment was heavy and consisted of several winches and cables. The inner hull on the boat had been reinforced to accept clamps that apparently were used to hold the winch in place as it raised or lowered objects into the water. A boom made out of pipe and pulleys laid on the deck next to the rigging. Jay's analysis of the equipment was interrupted by Brian who requested another beer be brought to the helm. Jay complied with the request and slipped into the seat next to his friend. Brian nodded his gratitude to Jay but was too busy to speak. The traffic was heavy with large boats throwing high cross wakes compounded with sailboats tacking back and forth. The small Sea Sprite bounced across the wakes and slid into the swells caused by the thirty- and forty-foot cruisers. Brian smiled at Jay as a wave broke across the bow and covered them with a refreshing spray. Soon they would be out of harm's way and into the peaceful solitude of the rocks surrounding Graves Light. Then they would drop their lines for the expected catch.

The sun was at half-mast and sinking fast as Brian brought the Sea Sprite into its fishing position. Jay set the anchor and sat back to enjoy the sunset. The many beers that he had consumed had produced a comfortable glow. He felt good and decided that he would maintain a binge through the weekend. Brian was also high. He produced a small bag of grass from the recesses of his tackle box and lit a joint that he passed to Jay. Jay was tempted to accept the pass but remembered that the trace would be evident in his urine test scheduled for Tuesday. He waved the joint back to Brian who seemed to understand. Then Brian dug deeper into the tackle box and brought out a small bag of cocaine. He fixed two lines on the engine box and inhaled one while inviting Jay to enjoy the other. Jay recalled that cocaine passed through the system in less than twenty-four hours. He could enjoy the coke without it being discovered in urine analysis. At first, he paused then inhaled the line.

The sky was red with the passing sun. A warm breeze blew from the west. The Sea Sprite rocked easily like a baby's cradle. Jay and Brian had escaped the madness of the working world. They were at peace, comfortable, and secure in the solitude of the evening. Jay felt the rush of the cocaine mixed with the alcohol. It felt good.

Brian saw Jay's peaceful smile. It was the first time he had seen his good friend so relaxed since before he had been notified of the court battle over Kristie. That battle was over at least for the time being. His buddy had won and was now back to being his buddy. Brian didn't like to worry about Jay. He liked to see him at peace. When Jay was cool, everything was cool. Skillfully he cast his line over the side. Then he took Jay's rod and cast the line for him. Jay accepted the rod from Brian and immediately fell asleep.

Within a few minutes Brian saw Jay's line grow taut. He shook Jay awake and pointed to the strike. Jay reacted with skill and brought the catch aboard. This was the first of many strikes over the next several hours. Cod and flounder seemed to alternate and by midnight the boat was loaded with catch. Brian suggested to Jay that they call it a night since the time required to clean the fish would make it a very long night. Jay agreed. Without incident, they cleared the rocks for the trip back to Hingham Boat Dock.

As Brian maneuvered out and away from Graves Light a Boston Harbor Patrol Boat came along side and put a spotlight on the Sea Sprite. It came in close and seemed to study Brian and Jay in the light. Brian waved to the Patrol Boat but did not receive any acknowledgment. Brian and Jay were still very high and if stopped would definitely be subject to arrest. Brian, in spite of his mental state, maintained a steady hand on the helm, carefully obeying all the rules of the road. Jay sat motionless next to Brian. Out of the corner of his eye Jay saw that one of the crew in the Patrol Boat was pointing a video camera at the Sea Sprite. He shouted to Brian that they were on Candid Camera. Both tried to hide their faces as the spotlight suddenly went out and the Patrol Boat moved ahead and away.

Neither man said anything about the unusual action of the Patrol Boat although both had the matter well in mind. No law had been broken. Aside from being smashed out of their mind, the crew had performed in good fashion. The Harbor Patrol had not hailed them or made any attempt to board them. They just put them in the spotlight and took a video of the boat and its occupants.

Brian brought them back to the Hingham Dock and tied the boat in its usual illegal spot. They unloaded the tackle and catch and prepared for the trip back to Jay's house where they would spend the next few hours cleaning the fish. Saturday night would be the backyard fish fry of the season. Aside from the usual conversation necessary to secure the boat and move toward home, Brian finally raised the question about the Patrol.

"Jay, what do you suppose that Patrol Boat thing was all about? You didn't give 'em the finger like you usually do, did you? Man, that was weird."

Jay had pulled the top off the last beer and had taken a sip. He acknowledged Brian's question by offering him a sip of the beer.

Brian shook his head in the negative. "Jay, I could use something to eat. Man, that pot gives me the urge for the munchies. You got anything to eat at your house?"

"Yeah, Brian, we always got munchies. It's the only way we keep the kids happy. We can pig out while we clean the fish. I can't figure that thing with the Patrol. Why they want to take our pictures? I mean weird, man. Maybe that cop is queer for you. You been making more friends at the Troubadour?"

"That's not funny, man. As far as I know there ain't no sea cops hanging out at the Troubadour. And I ain't been hanging out there either. Just make a delivery now and then. They treat me right. You know, man, queers ain't all bad. That's got nothin' to do with tonight. Those sea cops got no right to take our pictures. I'll talk to Eddie about it on Monday. He might have an answer."

Jay let out a shout. "Eddie! Shit, Brian. What's Eddie got do with anything. That goon hasn't got a clue. He don't know about sea cops."

Brian tried to explain. "Eddie knows the Customer, man. Maybe the sea cops like the Customer. So I'll tell Eddie and he can figure it out Maybe he needs to talk to the Customer. That ain't my boat they takin pictures of. That boat belongs to the Customer. Eddie's the one that set me up with the guy to use his boat. Eddie and the Customer get along."

Jay was pensive. "You know, Brian, I think I got it figured. That guy that owns the boat keeps parking the thing where it don't belong. So the cops get pissed and want to get the goods on whoever is parking the boat in the wrong place. Hingham gets the Boston Patrol to follow the boat and picture the operator so they can hang a high price ticket on 'em. They got you and me on video driving the boat so they figure we tied it to the dock. We probably got a big fine coming. Think the Customer can get us outta that."

Brian was not convinced. Instead of arguing Jay's theory he dropped the subject but remained intent to bring the matter to the attention of Eddie the Enforcer as he had been trained to do.

It was nearly two A.M. as the fisherman arrived at Jay's house. Brian prepared the catch for cleaning in Jay's backyard while Jay brought cookies, pretzels, cheese, cupcakes, and candy from the kitchen. By four the fish had been wrapped and put in the freezer.

Susan was half awake, and heard Jay moving about the kitchen. His entry to the bedroom following a noisy shower brought her to full consciousness. She recognized his inebriated state as he fumbled and belched. Jay was home and had returned to his former self—a drunk on a weekend tear. He was like her—an addict—and they were compatible. His trek into sobriety was bothersome since it threatened their marital harmony. He was home now. It was good to have him back. She listened to his loud snores, occasional belch, and returned to her slumber. It was good to have him back.

Saturday morning was warm, calm, and peaceful. The cool breeze allowed Susan to open the windows and let the fresh air fill the house. The air conditioner was given a rest. Benny and James were eagerly eating breakfast. They were anticipating the usual Saturday antics with Jay although this was not the weekend for Kristie to be with them. Jay was not as playful when Kristie was not around but the boys knew that he would be ready to romp anyway. Susan changed the kids' anticipation by announcing that their real father was going to take them for the afternoon. It was an arrangement that she had worked with Eddie at Benny's game.

Eddie was, for some unexplained reason, now interested in becoming acquainted with his two sons that he had purposely ignored since their birth. Benny appeared skeptical that the afternoon would be as much fun as romping around the yard with Jay. James was impassive and seemed confused at the prospect of being with his father. Following breakfast, Susan turned the boys outside to consider the day. She then waited with some anxiety for Jay to waken and learn that they were to be childless for several hours. This was not typical and Jay was not one to adjust to a lifestyle change albeit for only a brief time.

Jay slept the entire morning and woke just as Eddie drove into the driveway to pick up the boys. Jay was hung over with a miserable headache. He desperately needed coffee and a cigarette. Then he would repair to the garage where the ice chest with the remaining beer from last night awaited his attention. Carefully he moved from his bed and staggered to the kitchen where Susan always had a coffee pot in waiting. The house seemed unusually quiet for a Saturday. Jay, clad only in his jockey shorts, tried to maintain the peace by tip toeing into the kitchen. He entered just as Eddie came into the kitchen from the side door and surprised Jay. Jay could not ever remember Eddie being in his kitchen for any reason. Now the Enforcer, his wife's ex, was standing in front of him and, worse yet, blocking Jay's path to his much-needed cup of coffee. Jay was too shocked to be belligerent but not in any condition to be cordial.

Susan had met Eddie in the driveway and had followed him into the house. She was behind Eddie as Jay entered the kitchen and not visible to Jay or in a position to offer an explanation. Eddie was dressed in tight jeans, black boots, and a T-shirt that exhibited his bulging biceps. His black curly hair was well groomed. Several heavy gold chains hung loosely around his large neck that was hardly visible between the bulk of his shoulders and the large square face. Pilot style sunglasses completed the picture. He flashed a sarcastic smile as Jay staggered in shock.

Jay's first thought was that Brian had somehow got to Eddie about the Sea Cops filming the boat. Eddie apparently felt it necessary to pay Jay a visit and get his version of the incident so Jay decided to explain. "Eddie, man, this is unnecessary. You can get what you need from Brian, man. You don't need me. Shit, it wasn't nothing to get excited about. I told Brian that. What you want from me, man?"

Eddie looked back at Susan as if she had allowed the inmate to escape. She made no attempt to intervene. Eddie then turned to Jay and smiled at the little man standing before him in his underwear. "My friend, I don't want nothing from you except maybe a cup of that coffee. You look like you could use a cup or two yourself. Now what I'm about is to take my boys for an afternoon. You got a problem with that?"

Jay was blown away by Eddie's comment. Benny and James with their real father was beyond consideration. How could it happen? Jay knew he was in no position to argue the point. That was Susan's responsibility and she seemed content. He decided to go with the flow. "No, man, I got no problem with that. You gonna bring 'em back later or we gonna pick 'em up?"

Susan recognized her cue and carefully squeezed around Eddie in order to be between the two men. She poured each a cup of coffee as she spoke. "John, I'll pick the kids up around five this afternoon at the zoo. Eddie's going to take them there later. So, the boys will be with us tonight for dinner. Okay?"

Jay seemed more attentive to the cup of hot coffee than Susan's explanation. He slumped into a kitchen chair and said nothing. Eddie saw that the conversation with Jay had concluded so he suggested to Susan that they collect the boys so he could leave. The two left Jay alone with his misery. He watched the boys climb into Eddie's sleek, shiny black, four-wheel drive pickup complete with roll bar and spotlights. Eddie made sure the tires squealed as he powered down the street.

The rest of the day was a downer for Jay. He nursed one beer after another as the day wore on. He paid no attention to the yard due for a mow and trim. He felt depressed and occasionally would shout profanity as he thought of Eddie and the boys. Susan was also depressed. She drank her usual gin and grapefruit throughout the afternoon and said little to Jay. She frequently looked at the clock anxiously waiting the time to go to the zoo and pick up the boys. Eddie had promised her a supply of coke when she met them at the zoo. She was becoming desperate for the fix.

At three in the afternoon, almost by reflex and habit, the two began to work together to prepare for the evening. Jay drove to the store and bought more beer and ingredients for his special sauce that he prepared over the grill with the fish. Susan prepared a large salad and made sure that the picnic table and chairs were clean and ready. The preparation brought both of them out of the doldrums. They sensed the fun of the night and again entered a high.

It took Susan about a half an hour to drive to the zoo and find Eddie at the appointed time and place. The boys gave their Dad an affectionate hug before jumping into the Jeep. Eddie seemed uncomfortable with the sign of affection and did not reciprocate. Instead he turned to Susan and handed her what she so desperately needed.

"Flyaway, my little bitch," Eddie sang as Susan left. "Remember, this covers the support payment. You're making out like a bandit. You know that. Now in case you let this slip your mind, I've made sure that Brian comes empty-handed to your little party. You only got one source, baby. It's me. Wonderful Eddie, the true love of your miserable life. I'll let you know when I want the boys again. Otherwise, we can work something else out. Oh, yeah, don't call me—I'll call you."

Susan said nothing. She tucked the packet into her bra and turned toward the Jeep. Benny had watched his parents closely to see what his real mom and dad were like together. He was disappointed at the absence of affection. He had hoped that the afternoon with his real father was the start of a normal life like his friends on the team seemed to have with their parents. What Benny did see was the packet that his mother slipped inside her blouse. He instinctively knew that was not a sign of normal parenting. His curiosity was peaked but his disappointment caused him to refrain from questions. Instead he remained silent. James took the whole day in stride and fell asleep.

Susan was home by five-thirty. Jay had everything ready for the feast. The faithful Webber was hot and ready. A square pan with vegetables, cooking oil, and spices was simmering on the grill. Many fish filets were in the refrigerator waiting to be breaded and placed on the waiting fire. The cooler was stacked with enough beer to last well into Sunday and soft drinks were ready for the kids. Susan's special potato salad rested in the refrigerator. Cheese and salty snacks were on the kitchen counter ready to be taken to the picnic table. Jay had also moved his boom box with a generous supply of tapes onto the patio.

The only thing seemingly missing at the moment was good friends, Brian and Louise. They were due soon and with their arrival Jay anticipated the arrival of the white powder that always put a special cap on the night.

Jay knew that something else was also absent from the event—his attitude. Usually he was on a high in anticipation of good times. Tonight, for some reason he remained solemn and depressed. No matter how hard he tried to elevate himself to the event he found that he would suddenly slide into brief fits of anger and a feeling of guilt. He rationalized the sensation was caused by his encounter with Eddie that morning. He also would have mental flashes of Markley that caused Jay to think that he was perhaps feeling contrite about falling off the wagon. All these thoughts created anger that he could not completely overcome. In his mind he would damn Eddie, Markley, and St. Anslem's. He would come to peak anger when he thought of Cecile. Then he would sob as his darling Kristie came to his mind. He would shake his head from side to side in a rapid fashion trying to remove the thoughts and focus on the good time in the offing. It didn't seem to work. Frequently he would lock himself in the bathroom so Susan would not see his depression, hear him sob, or notice his tears.

Brian and Louise arrived at a time when Jay was on an upswing. It was an additional lift that powered him out of his depression. He gave Brian a high-five and hugged Louise so hard that she actually had to gasp for breath. Susan was also happy to see her friends since Jay had been unusually silent all day and seemed to be nursing the stomach flu. As usual the two women retreated to the kitchen for final preparations of the feast. Jay and Brian moved to the grill and the adjacent cooler of beer. The boom box was started. The good times were back. The fish fillets were brought forth, battered and placed on the grill. Drinks were served. Benny and James snacked on the goodies and held their soft drink cans in reflection of the adult style. Brian would raise his beer in mock salute of the kids and then proceed to chase them around the yard. Jay tended to the cooking and soon produced a feast fit for royalty. They ate well and drank a lot. The hour drew late.

Benny and James were tired but went unnoticed. Finally, James went inside and lay down on the sofa where he fell asleep. Benny recognized that this was one party where he could stick around to the final inning. Carefully he retreated to the background where his mother would not recall her duty to throw him in the sack.

The adults were very drunk. They laughed uncontrollably and seemed to be having a good time. Benny was impressed with their freedom and wanted to be like them. It seemed wonderful to be able to laugh and not have things like school to worry about. He couldn't wait to grow up.

Jay maintained his high all night long. Thoughts about Eddie, Markley or anybody else that came to mind were easily pushed aside as he consumed more booze. Obviously, the answer was to stay smashed. He saw Brian next to the grill trying to warm a piece of garlic bread on the simmering coals that seemed to produce some tragic relief to a comical evening. The fire was about out.

Jay moved to his side and pushed for the next level. "Brian, my main man, it seems that we reed to fire our booster rocket. What say you spread the lines, man. I know you got to be packin'."

Brian at first seemed not to hear Jay's call. Then, after what seemed like an eternity to Jay, Brian ate his piece of garlic bread and walked back to the picnic table where Jay, Susan and Louise were seated. He sat next to Jay and placed his arm around the shoulder of his buddy.

"I ain't packin', Jay. Eddie, he shut me off. Says that I got to buy my stash from now on. I can't carry it, man. Even with the raise I got. Eddie, he says that freebies ain't policy no more. I told Eddie that I always carry stash here and he says that you got all that we need. Hey, man, you got it?"

Jay was very confused at Brian's comment. His drunken expression became very sober and he struggled to understand what his friend was saying. Brian had never failed to supply cocaine for the Saturday night trip. Why did Brian think that the supply would be provided by Jay?

Susan noticed Jay's shock. Her drunken temperament caused her to interject a response. "Sure, we got some stash, Brian. My man is one hell of a good provider. We got stash. I'll get it. Louise, you got to help. It's leftover from our last bash. You don't mind leftovers, do you?"

Susan stood and staggered toward the kitchen with Louise in tow. Brian sat with a silly smile admiring the moving posteriors. Jay felt like he had been kicked by a mule. His stomach was suddenly in a painful knot and his head began to throb with pain. He concluded that cocaine would cure the painful rush but until it arrived from the kitchen he struggled to swallow another beer. Something didn't add up in his mind. He could not understand how Susan could have stash when she had been on a high several times since their last bash. Drunk as he was, the logic seemed to suggest that Susan had her own supplier. But Susan didn't have the where with all to buy coke. What then did she use to get the stash? The prospect of what Susan bartered tor drugs threw Jay over the edge.

Susan and Louise had each inhaled a line in the kitchen. Susan explained her arrangement with Eddie to Louise and swore her to secrecy. Then they took the packet to the backyard and spread several lines on the picnic table. Brian, Louise, and Susan inhaled the coke. Jay sat motionless. His eyes were glazed and filled with tears. The pain was intense. Frustration mounted. He began a low barely audible groan that grew slowly louder. Brian noticed it first then Louise and finally Susan.

Jay looked possessed. His face became contorted as the groan advanced to a wild scream. Suddenly he grabbed the kitchen knife that had been used to slice the garlic bread. He swung the knife from side to side as he moved toward Susan.

"You bitch! You filthy bitch! You're gonna die! You're gonna die. Goddamn it. You gotta die! I'm gonna cut your miserable fucking guts out. You dirty, filthy bitch!"

Jay was screaming his threats at the top of his voice. The summer air carried the sounds and lights went on all over the neighborhood. Benny was in shock at the sudden change in the party. His mother was being attacked. She was about to be killed. He had to help her. Carefully he moved to be out of Jay's view then he attempted to attack Jay from the rear. Jay was swinging his arms and fists from side to side as he approached Susan. Benny was caught hard on the jaw by Jay's wild swing and knocked to the driveway pavement. He seemed to be unconscious. Susan made a sudden move toward Benny. Jay raised his knife and lunged at Susan.

Martha had a date on Saturday night that had been a bust. The other party had only one thing in mind and revealed his intentions early in the evening by explaining that his wife didn't understand him. That bit of information resulted in her immediate departure from dinner at The Venicia. She didn't need a complication of that kind to compound a difficult career with a law firm that kept its glass ceiling well-polished and reinforced. She took a cab home and spent the evening watching television with her faithful golden lab, Molly. After the late movie, she went to bed only to be awakened by Molly's restless behavior, whining and occasional bark. A glance at the bedside clock revealed the hour as three-thirty. Molly never required an outside visit at that hour. Molly was also pawing around the front door. Normally she went to the back to be let out for nature's call.

With no small amount of trepidation Martha moved from her bedroom to the front door and peered through the security window. She saw a man's form slumped on the steps. Her first thought was that it was the weirdo from the dinner date. She prayed that he would go away and that she would not have to call the police. To be safe she grabbed her portable phone and returned to the window. The man attempted to stand but fell backward off the porch onto the lawn. He struggled to stand but fell to all fours. When he looked up at the door, Martha recognized Jay's distorted pain ridden face.

Martha carefully opened the door allowing Molly to run out first. The dog went to Jay and cuddled next to his fallen body. He felt the warmth of the animal and struggled to stand. Again he failed. Martha moved to his side and tried to help. He pushed her back and attempted to strike her. She tried to reason with her brother. "Jay, for Christ's sake, I'm trying to help. Let me get you inside. Please, Jay, let me help you."

Jay seemed to hear but could not comprehend. He was destroyed with anger, depression and fear. He had found his way to Martha's house by instinct since it had often been his haven in troubled times and Martha had always sheltered, protected, and defended him. He needed her now more than ever before and he was incapable of telling her why. He again tried to stand but fell for the third time. This time he passed out.

Martha dragged and carried him into her house and laid him on the living room floor. A few minutes later he regained consciousness and tried to speak.

"Oh, God—oh, God—Martha, I killed them. I killed them. She had it coming. I killed her, Martha. Oh, God, I'm sorry. I want to die. Kill me, Martha. Please kill me. I don't want to live anymore. I want to die. I want to die."

It was obvious that Jay was very drunk. But never before had Martha seen him in a totally depressed mental state. She was frightened. His claim to have killed somebody accelerated her fears. She was uncertain if he was still violent or harmless. A call to the police first entered her mind as she struggled to remain calm. Then she reconsidered. If he had already committed the crime and there was no prospect of immediate harm to herself or anybody else it would be best for his defense if he was in a better mental state when he turned himself in. On the other hand, if he should suddenly bolt from her house and/or attempt to kill her or himself she should have help. At the moment, he had passed out again. This gave her time to think the matter through.

Carefully, she searched through his pockets for the keys to the Jeep that he had parked on her lawn. Not finding them she hastened to the car and found them in the ignition. Without starting the motor, she placed the vehicle in neutral and let the Jeep roll pack into the street in a near perfect parking position. Then she rushed back into the house to find Jay still passed out. She hid the keys to the Jeep in her kitchen.

Martha knew she was in desperate need of help. Once Jay regained consciousness he would make a move that would most certainly be violent. Some intercession was required other than the Police. Jay had mentioned his respect for the St. Anslem's program. A call to them seemed like the ideal way to get assistance. A quick look in the yellow pages gave her the number of the hospital. Her first attempt produced a wrong number. Carefully, she dialed the number again and waited for someone to answer. The telephone rang over and over before a click indicated to Martha that the incoming call was being routed. Then a recorded voice announced that she had indeed called St. Anslem's and "if she did not know her party's extension she should stay on the line for operator assistance. Otherwise, if it was an emergency she should press three."

Martha was near panic. Hurriedly, she hit three and waited. After the third ring the phone was answered.

"This is St. Anslem's Emergency Service, how may I direct your call?"

In her panic Martha had not thought how she would describe her problem. Now that she had made contact with the hospital she seemed tongue-tied. "Well, I need help. I mean I need help for someone else. This person is very drunk and I think very sick. Can someone help me?"

"Has the person been treated by St. Anslem's before, Ma'am?"

"Yes. He was in the Alcohol Treatment Program. Can you send someone to help me? I mean someone to help me help him. Oh, Christ, I don't know what to say!"

"Ma'am, are you the one providing support to the patient?"

"Of course I am. Damn it, that's why I'm calling for help!"

"Ma'am, we require under these circumstances that the patient be brought to the Emergency Room. If you don't have your own transportation we suggest you use a cab."

"Will you get real? This man is unconscious! There's no way I can get him in a cab. Don't you have a counselor that I can talk to for some help?"

"I'm sorry, Ma'am. Our service has been closed. You can bring the patient to the Emergency Room or have EMS bring him. Just dial nine-one-one. Our Psychiatry resident in the Emergency Room will perform an evaluation. We do not have anyone that we can send to your home or wherever you are."

Martha sensed from the last comment that the hospital Emergency Room was becoming belligerent. There was nothing that could be gained from continuing the conversation. Without further response, she hung up. Her fear had turned to anger. She was intent on bringing the hospital to court and forcing it to expose its incompetence. Jay was right about the damned telephone system and the people who use it.

Jay was half awake, and mumbling. He shouted Brian's name and swung his fist in the air as if to battle his friend. Martha watched his antics and began to cry. She was without solution to this dilemma. Suddenly she realized that Jay had given her the answer. Brian! Brian, his best friend, could help. If she could find him then the two of them could guard Jay until it was timely to turn him over to the police. She also thought that getting him admitted to St. Anslem's Psychiatric Unit might serve to his defense unless they determined that he was mentally competent at the time he committed the crime.

One thing at a time. She found Brian's number in the book and dialed it perfectly. She was regaining her professional composure. To her relief, Brian answered on the second ring.

"Brian, this is Martha. Jay's sister…have you…."

"Oh, man, Martha. You got Jay?" Brian was near panic. "He just took off and I don't know where. We were drinking and having a good time when he just went nuts. Man, he is really screwed up. You got him?"

Brian's comments brought a surge of fear to Martha. Brain was apparently a witness to Jay's actions. Could she ask him for help under these circumstances? What role he had in the crime played in her mind as she tried to evaluate the situation.

"Brian, Jay is incoherent and hasn't been able to tell me much except he gives me the impression that maybe somebody got hurt or killed tonight. Do you know if anything like that happened?" she asked with fear.

"No way, Martha. Some bad things went down. Susan and the kids are gone from Jay. But nobody got hurt. Jay tried to croak Susan with a bread knife but he was too drunk and fell on his face. Lucky, he didn't stab himself. Susan ran in the house and grabbed the kids. That was after Jay punched Benny. Louise loaded them up and took them someplace safe. She won't tell me where. I guess that's best. Well, when Susan ran in the house, I took the knife out of Jay's hand while he was lying there but he woke up and busted me one. Before I could get up he was in his Jeep and roaring down the street. That's the last I saw of him. Then the neighbors started showing up.

Martha's fears increased. "The neighbors! How about the police? Did anyone call the police?"

"Yeah, somebody did," Brian recalled. "What happened is after Jay went tearing down the street Louise and Susan and all went roaming the other way. They both made a hell of a lot of noise. I was left there so I just started cleaning up like nothing happened. Got rid of the nose candy and stuff. Well, Jay's next-door neighbor, a nice guy, came over about the time I had things half put away. He said he heard the shouting and all and wondered if everyone was okay. I told him that there was a family misunderstanding that was taken care of so he sort of nodded and went home. The cops showed up about a little later. I was waiting for Louise. They said they had a complaint about a domestic disturbance and loud music. I let them look around. They couldn't find any problem so they left. They asked me who I was so I gave them my name and said I was a guest. Hey, you need any help with Jay? Man, he is one messed-up dude."

Somewhat relived, Martha gave a response. "I don't know, Brian. Jay is sleeping now. I have to figure what to do with him when he wakes up. I don't think he is going to sleep very long. He is very restless. Are you going to be home?"

"Martha, it's just after four A.M. I think I'm in for the evening. You thinking of giving me a call if you need help or do you want me to come over now?" he offered.

Martha was uncertain. "I've got to think this out, Brian. I'm not sure what the best thing is at the moment. I'll call you if I need you. Okay?"

Brian agreed to stand by if needed. Martha sat on the couch and studied her brother in his drunken slumber. This time he had apparently messed up good. Child abuse, battered spouse, assault with a deadly weapon, intent to kill, possession of a controlled substance, and probably several other offenses were all the result of his latest trip. On the other hand, as yet no one had filed a complaint. There was no arrest and no basis in evidence for a criminal charge. The police were called to investigate a domestic disturbance that included loud music. They found nothing and left. End of report. Jay, true to his drunken luck, was still in the clear. No one had been hurt.

Then Martha remembered that Brian had said something about Jay punching Benny. Was Benny hurt? How about Susan? Where was Susan? If she had been taken to a shelter for battered women they would listen to her story and certainly encourage her to file assault charges or at least seek a restraining order against Jay. Then the whole incident would become a matter of public record. That would lead Cecile back to court to protect Kristie. Jay's whole world would explode. The tension built in her mind and she was soon overcome with mental fatigue. Her eyes closed and she slept.

Jay's eyes were open. He laid quietly studying his sister and trying to remember how he got into her living room. He vividly remembered attacking

Susan but wasn't certain what happened after he grabbed the knife. The thought that he might have killed or even harmed her compounded the intense physical pain in the chest and abdomen. He had to move. Carefully he came to a sitting position. He gagged and gave a loud moan that caused Martha to jump. Yet she seemed to remain asleep. He rolled over and came to all fours. He was now determined to escape. Martha would most certainly want him to turn himself in for whatever he had done. In his mind, it would be better to run. To run with Kristie to a far place where they would never be found—where they could live an uncomplicated life away from Cecile and the courts. Yes, he would kidnap Kristie and they would run. Carefully, he crawled to the door and rolled onto the small porch. Then he used the handrail on the steps to raise himself to a standing position.

He was hardly able to walk yet he managed to get to the Jeep. He slid behind the wheel and reached for the ignition only to discover that the keys were not in place. Painfully he searched his pockets. The keys were gone. He realized that Martha had taken them. Anger surged as did the pain. He would have to return to her living room beat her until she returned his keys. He knew that she would not give them to him at his request. He would most certainly have to beat them out of her. He had no choice. He had to harm his Sister in order to capture Kristie and escape.

Martha was awake. She was aware of Jay's struggle to get out of her house, but was uncertain what to do to stop him. He was probably still in a violent state and she was alone. She thought about calling 911 but realized that would bring down everything that had been avoided so far—an arrest and a public record of the whole affair. As Jay staggered across the lawn toward the Jeep she walked to the door and stood on the porch. She saw him try to find his keys and saw him get out of the Jeep to return to her house.

It was then that Jay saw Martha on the porch looking at him. John felt like he was going to pass out again. Martha was staring at him but said nothing. He wanted to grab her and beat her but he was physically unable to move. He tried to yell but could only choke and vomit on her lawn. Martha was frozen with fear. She could not move to help him out of fear for her own safety.

The standoff ended suddenly when Jay remembered the spare ignition key that he had placed in a plastic container in the fender well of the Jeep. He had put the key there a long time ago as a precaution against losing his keys. He had checked it several times to make sure that the magnetic clip had not failed but he had never before had to use the emergency key. Now with reflex thought and action he turned back to the Jeep and reached under the fender. The key container fell easily into his hand but he had difficulty opening it because his hands were shaking uncontrollably.

Martha thought that his return to the Jeep meant that he wanted to rest his body against the car in order to avoid a fall. Instinctively she moved to help him. Jay sensed her approach. "Don't come near me, goddamnit!" he yelled. "I'm getting outta here. Don't try to stop me. You can't help me now. I'm too messed up. You can keep those goddamn keys. I got a spare."

Martha attempted to calm him and tried to explain that he was not in a hopeless situation. Jay did not hear a word she said. He had crawled back behind the steering wheel and had managed to start the motor. Martha moved to the side of the Jeep and tried to remain calm.

"Jay, you don't have to leave," she pleaded. "Things aren't as bad as you think. You haven't hurt anybody. Please come back into the house and we can try to reason this out."

For the first time since he had tried to leave Martha's house Jay seemed to hear what she was saying. He sat behind the wheel with the motor running and thought about her comment that he had not hurt anyone. He felt somewhat relieved but was uncertain of the truth. "Martha, I got to get outta here. I never should have come to you anyway. It's too late. I gotta go."

"Where are you going, Jay? Where do you want to go?" asked Martha.

Jay was determined. "Home. I got to go home. Pick up a few things. Then I don't know. But I got to go."

Jay slipped the Jeep into gear and drove away. Martha watched for a few minutes and then returned to the house. She went to the kitchen and recovered Jay's keys from the cupboard. It was a full keyring containing his car keys, various cabinet keys, and his house keys. Unless he had another spare container, Jay might be locked out of his house.

The drive from Martha's house back to Waltham normally took less than a half-hour. This time Jay seemed to get lost at every turn. He wandered through the streets still absent of traffic. Occasionally the Jeep would hit the curb. Traffic lights and stop signs were of no concern. His speed was very slow and deliberate. Eventually, he found himself on the west bound side of the Mass Pike approaching the first toll gate. Jay aimed at the automatic lane and glided through. The toll offender bell rang immediately as he exited but the attendant seemed disinterested. God indeed was protecting this drunk. As he approached the Waltham exit Jay unconsciously found a dollar bill in his pocket. He entered the attended lane and thrust the dollar at the lady taking tolls. As she turned to make change Jay abruptly drove away leaving the attendant wondering what to do with the fifty-cent tip. An hour and a half after leaving his Sister's house Jay pulled into his driveway.

Jay was still in a stupor as he entered the house that Brian had left unlocked. After he was inside it occurred to him that Martha had his house keys. Hardly a matter to dwell on. At the moment, he felt the need to rekindle the glow that was rapidly dissipating and being replaced with intense abdominal pain. His search for booze was not difficult since Brian had lined the bottles from the night before neatly on the kitchen counter.

Two bottles of gin, one with less than a quarter left and the other nearly full, stood easily within sight. Jay drank the remaining contents of one and took the other under his arm as he walked into the living room and sat in his favorite chair. The deafening silence of the house caused him to realize that Susan and the kids were gone. Kristie, his beloved Kristie, was not with him. He was alone, drunk, and entering deep depression.

The booze seemed to lessen the pain and he felt the return of a glow. His mind wandered back to the evening festivities and he began to recall the events that led to his violent actions. Susan was stoned on coke. It seemed that Louise and Susan were taunting him. Then he thought that Eddie was here.

No, Eddie was not here, he recalled. *He was a part of something that pissed me off. What was it? Eddie was at the house sometime. When? When was Eddie here? Yesterday. Yesterday to pick up the kids. Take them somewhere with Susan. No. Susan didn't go. What was it with Susan, the kids? Eddie. That's it. Eddie took the kids. Susan went after them. They came home. Susan got stoned. She got stoned because Eddie gave her some stash. Yeah! Susan got her high from Eddie. Eddie got the kids but what else did he get from Susan. Yeah, that's it. That's what got to me. It's getting to me again. Susan, that damn slut made it with Eddie. I got to kill him. Eddie, Susan, and the kids, they're probably together now. Susan is telling Eddie that I attacked her and beat the kids. Eddie, that gorilla, is plenty pissed. Figures to bust me up good. Maybe even waste me. He'll come here looking to bust me up. That's when I get him. I'll wait for the bastard and I'll be ready. He'll get a full load from the shotgun. I'll be ready and Eddie will get his big time. I'll be ready.*

Jay's mind was spinning with rage. He drank the gin in rapid fashion. His eyes widened as he thought of blowing Eddie away with his shotgun. In his mind, he rehearsed his moves as Eddie came into the driveway. At first, he thought he would wait until Eddie came through the side door into the kitchen. Then Jay would raise the gun from behind the counter and blast him. The thought of Eddie's brains and blood splattered all over the kitchen bothered Jay. His second thought was to wait until Eddie got out of his pretty truck and walked toward the house. Then Jay would rush out the front door and blast him on the driveway, carry Eddie back to his truck, and let him bleed all over his clean cab. That would be a fitting end.

The thought of blowing Eddie away and messing up his pretty hot wheels truck in the process seemed to give Jay some satisfaction. He relaxed in the chair and now slowly inhaled the gin. His thoughts and comfort were disturbed by two inconveniences—he had to urinate and the gin was almost gone. He decided to react to the matters in order of priority. First, he retreated to the kitchen to replenish the gin only to discover that the gin supply was extinguished. An exhaustive search of the kitchen produced a half bottle of sour mash whiskey, some peppermint schnapps, and a half gallon of Thunderbird wine. Jay carried his collection into the living room and placed the bottles next to his chair in easy reach. As he was about to sit down he again felt nature's call causing him to quickly rush to the bathroom only to be a step or two late. He finished the job and went to the bedroom to change his pants.

He left the bedroom and stumbled down the basement steps to his gun cabinet. Automatically, he reached into his pocket for the keyring that held the cabinet keys. For the second time that morning he discovered the keyring missing. He remembered that Martha had the ring causing him to explode in rage. Screaming at the top of his voice he ran up the steps and out to the garage where he found his ax. Then he returned to the basement and chopped the front of his precious gun cabinet.

With the ax, shotgun, and a box of ammunition in his arms he returned to his chair, exhausted. He gulped the whiskey that made him gag but he kept on drinking. Within minutes he began to relax. Carefully, as if on a hunt, he picked up the shotgun and gave it a full load, made sure the safety was on, and laid it across his lap on the armrests of the chair. It was like being in a deer stand. He was ready.

Martha sat in her kitchen drinking coffee and holding Jay's keyring in her hand. She wondered if her brother had made it safely home and what harm was in store for him. The thought that he might try to take Kristie out of Cecile's house was foremost in her mind. He would botch it up for sure and might even get killed in the process since Cecile's husband was an officer of the law and authorized to have and use a weapon. She thought about calling Cecile and warning her about Jay's state but realized that if Jay made no attempt then Cecile would have cause to bring the matter to the attention of the court without evident action. This was a disservice to her brother and her client. Some action was definitely necessary, however, since Jay was not in a rational state.

Martha knew she was alone in the attempt to find and convince Jay to retreat to sobriety. Brian was in reserve and she made up her mind to call him only as a last resort. Jay said that he was going home so Martha decided she would start looking for him there. She showered, dressed, put his keyring in her purse. It was almost noon as Martha left her house and began to drive to Waltham. In spite of her anxiety she drove slowly as if she were afraid of what she might encounter at her brother's house. When she arrived, she parked in the driveway close to the street and slammed her car door as she got out. Her intent was to make some noise in an attempt to give notice of her arrival. What she experienced was beyond her intentions.

Jay had sat near motionless in his chair for nearly four hours. His only movement was to reach for the nearest bottle and take an occasional gulp. He was maintaining his intoxicated state at full capacity. From time to time he would sob uncontrollably and then his anger would cause him to scream. Then he would lapse into a shallow sleep until some slight noise would cause him to awake. He would grab the shotgun and snap off the safety expecting to see Eddie walking up the driveway. Then he would relax, take another drink, and regain his slumber. The sudden sound of a car door brought him to full alert. He brought the shotgun across his chest and snapped off the safety. This time he saw movement in the driveway. The hour had arrived. Eddie, the bastard, was in view and was about to be wasted.

Jay sprang from his chair, held the shotgun at high port, and charged out the door screaming profanities as he moved to Martha. He stopped a few yards from her and brought the shotgun to his shoulder.

Martha was terrified as Jay ran toward her. She could not speak. Instinctively, she backed against her car and closed her eyes. Her head shook from side to side as if she expected to dodge the blast of the shotgun. She had no time to think of contrition, hate, or even remorse. This was to be her end. All her faculties triggered her to defend but she had no means of protection. The slaughter was now.

Jay sensed satisfaction as he raised the shotgun. His finger moved to the trigger and he glanced over the bead at the end of the barrel. He took a brief second to view his victim before the execution and noticed a figure foreign to his preconception of a cowering Eddie. He held back another second as the difference registered in his troubled mind. Then he took a step back from his intended target to evaluate. It seemed as if a doe had strayed in the path of the buck. Instinct told him he could not shoot. Be patient. The target would return.

In that same instant Martha gained strength enough to shout, "Jay! Oh, Christ, don't shoot. Don't shoot me. Please, Jay, don't! "

Jay lowered the shotgun and looked at Martha with disgust. "What the fuck you doin' here, Martha. Go away! You got my goddamn keys?" Jay snapped the safety back on. He seemed to have regained a rational state at least temporarily.

Martha was soaking with sweat. For the moment, she could not answer Jay. When she tried to speak she could not breathe. She doubled over from fear and began to hyperventilate. Jay moved to her side and took her by the arm.

Jay seemed to gain some control. "Come on, Sister. We got to go inside before the neighbors see you like this. Besides, I could use a drink. You look like you could use one yourself."

Martha glanced around. None of the neighbors seemed to have noticed. They were in their backyards or inside watching television. A wild man shouting profanities and pointing a shotgun at a defenseless woman was part of the landscape. After all it was Sunday afternoon in a Waltham neighborhood. Without further conversation, she followed Jay into the living room. He regained his position in his favorite chair with the shotgun resting across the arms of the chair. Martha took the chair in the far comer of the room, in his view, but opposite to the business end of the Thunderbird and said nothing.

Martha waited until she had regained some composure before she tried to speak. She also took time to evaluate the situation. Jay was still very drunk and expanding that status. The gun was a mystery. Who was it for? Himself or Susan or who? She wondered if he had talked to Brian or Louise about Susan. She had no idea where Susan was and wondered if Jay did. She felt it best not to discuss Susan until she had some idea about Jay's state of mind. The first priority, she thought, was to persuade Jay to put away the gun.

"Jay, I brought back your keys. I'm sorry about taking them but I was worried that you might hurt someone or yourself if you tried to drive. How are you doing now?"

Jay did not answer at first. He continued to stare out the window into the driveway. After a long while he looked at Martha as tears began to roll down his cheeks. "I guess I'm really fucked up. I really don't care. I work my butt off all my life and haven't got a thing to show for it. Shit. Kristie is gone. I guess Susan took off probably with Eddie. It's all over for me. But I'm gonna get me one before I go. Just one. That's all I want."

Martha decided to try to ease Jay out of his mental state. "We aren't in so bad shape, Jay. Nothing happened that can't be fixed. Kristie isn't even involved. She's okay. You're okay. We got to sober you up. Then we can fix everything else."

"What's with the 'we' shit, Martha? I'm all by myself and that's the way I want it. You can go back home. I'll take care of 'Jay and one or two others."

Martha was adamant. "I'm going to stay with you for a while, Jay. We need to talk. I'll help you anyway I can."

"You can help by going away. You want to see me blow my head off then just stick around. Otherwise, buzz off!"

Now Martha heard him say that the gun was for himself. Was it a feint to make her go away or was he serious. The ability to deal with Jay's possible suicide was beyond her. She needed help. Carefully, without further conversation, she moved out of the chair and into the kitchen where she found the telephone book and looked up the number of the Suicide Prevention Hot Line. Acting as if she were making a professional call she dialed the number. A calm female voice responded and asked how she could be of service. Martha took a chance and in low tones described the situation that she was experiencing. The SPH counselor reacted as if she had experienced this with regularity. She asked Martha a number of questions about the situation and then about Jay. When she had the information that she needed for background she asked Martha if she could speak to Jay. Martha agreed to try to get Jay to pick up the phone on the table next to his chair.

"Jay, can you pick up the phone? Someone wants to talk to you."

"No. Who wants to talk to me?"

"It's a friend of mine who thinks she can help you. That way you won't feel like you are all alone. Okay?"

Jay refused." I am alone, damn it, and that's the way I want it. Tell your friend to buzz off." Then, unexpectedly, he picked up the phone and in a remarkably calm voice said, "Hello, this is Jay Marquart. How can I help you?"

Suddenly his sense of humor came forward as if he intended to placate his sister by talking to her "friend." Martha was surprised at the smile on his face as he began the telephone conversation. Jay listened to the caller with apparent interest. He kidded around, even joked as if nothing were wrong. Martha could not make much sense out of the side of the conversation she was hearing. There seemed to be no reference to suicide or harm to another. She wondered if Jay might be trying to line up a date with the counselor. Then she realized that this might be a planned technique to get Jay to return to a positive mental status. Martha could only speculate and pray that something good would result. The conversation lasted only about ten minutes, far less than Martha had expected or hoped for. At the end, she heard Jay say he would call her again sometime but he did not write down a telephone number. He thanked her for her call and hung up.

After Jay put down the telephone he spoke to Martha in a conciliatory manner. "Sister, you got this all wrong. I intend to blast some son of a bitch away. I don't intend to use this shotgun on myself. Relax. Go home and get some sleep. You look terrible. I'll be okay. Just let me be. I'm screwed up good and you can't change it. Let me alone. I'll gonna be okay. You didn't have to call for help. She was a nice person and I let her know that I was okay. She said she might call me again. So, everything is okay."

Jay took another sip of the wine bottle now nearly depleted. He put his head back in the chair and closed his eyes. In a while he was breathing deeply indicating to Martha that he had fallen asleep. She watched him for several minutes and then fell asleep herself. She awoke with a start after what she thought was only a few minutes. To her surprise the room was dark. Only the light from the streetlight was giving a shady visibility sufficient for Martha to notice that Jay was not in the room. She fumbled around the room until she found a lamp that she managed to turn on. Then she noticed the shotgun was propped against the wall next to the chair. Suddenly the side door of the house slammed and she heard Jay give out a blast of profanity. A few seconds later he walked into the living room with his arms full of beer cans that he placed next to chair. The other bottles of booze that he had consumed were out of sight and the room had been tidied up.

When all was readied he again sat in his chair and opened a beer that he consumed without pause. He left the shotgun against the wall and seemed to give it no mind. He looked at Martha and offered a friendly gesture. "That damn Brian tried to clean this place up but he sure made a mess. He had all the beer stashed in the garage and didn't take any out of the cooler. Now I have to drink it all before it gets warm. What a bitch. I think I'm up to it. Feel like a drink?"

Jay was calm. Still drunk but in a pleasant mood. His sense of humor appeared to have been restored. He sat in the chair and sipped his beer in good spirits. The crisis apparently had passed.

Martha was relieved. Carefully she tried to measure if it was safe to leave him alone. "Jay, I have to go home and get ready for the week. Things are hectic right now and I need to get my rest. You going to be all right? I want you to call me in the morning. Let's try to have lunch and talk things over. We have to consider this situation in view of the court. You have to remember that St. Anslem's will submit urine test results. If you fail the test or don't show up as required the Judge will call us in. That could mean trouble. You understand what I'm saying? You're scheduled for a urinalysis this week."

"Yeah, I understand. I don't know if I give a shit anymore. I'll think it over. Maybe I can give you a call. You go on home and get some rest."

Jay's response wasn't what Martha wanted to hear. He again seemed to be in despair and depressed. She only had a half promise from him that he would call her. He ignored her lead about work, suggesting to her that he wasn't intending to go to his job on Monday. Above all else the one person that held him together, Kristie, had apparently slipped in importance. On the other hand, he was apparently in better control of his emotions and somewhat rational. He was still drunk. The shotgun was out of mind albeit not out of sight. Things had improved.

Martha decided to take a chance and leave. She walked over to her brother and gave him a kiss on the cheek. As Martha stepped out the door Jay got out of his chair and followed her to her car. He actually held the door for her as she moved behind the wheel. She closed the door and lowered the window. Jay reached in, gave her a pat on the shoulder and thanked her for all her concern and help. She noticed the tears in his eyes and for a moment thought of getting out of the car and going back into the house with him.

Jay seemed to read her thoughts. "Go home, Martha. I'll call you tomorrow. Get some sleep. Thanks for everything. Don't worry. I can take care of myself."

He watched her back out of the driveway and pull into the street. Then he walked around the yard as if inspecting the grass and shrubs. It was a dark night but pleasant. The sky was slightly overcast and he watched the clouds move under a full moon. After a while he returned to his chair in the living room and opened a fresh beer. Then he picked up the shotgun and placed it across his lap. He turned off the lamp and sat in the dark. Tears flowed freely. He began to sob. He drank. He sobbed. His thoughts moved from his loved Kristie, to Susan. Then he thought of Eddie. Anger coupled with sadness caused him to shout and moan. He rocked from side to side in the chair. The shotgun banged against the arms of the chair and hurt his knuckles.

Suddenly he grabbed the gun at the small of the stock with one hand and around the barrel with the other. He pointed the gun at his head and put the barrel in his mouth. He tasted the gun oil and it made him choke. He removed the barrel from his mouth and took a long sip of beer. Beer was definitely a better choice than gun oil. He thought that he could soak the gun in beer so that he could tolerate the taste long enough for him to pull the trigger. First, he would drink some more beer. He opened a fresh can, put the shotgun back against the wall and seemed to relax.

After a few minutes, he began to experience a loud ringing sensation in his ears. The noise would not stop. It was constant and irritating. It was the telephone. With difficulty, he found the receiver and brought it to his ears. The ringing stopped but a voice now was penetrating his privacy. It was a female voice, friendly, familiar, but without a name. She was calling to see how he was. She had talked to him earlier. How was he doing? What was he doing? She somehow managed to hold him in conversation when he didn't want to talk. They chatted for a longtime. He sipped beer and answered her questions. Eventually he told her about his thoughts and possible intentions. She suggested he call a friend to be with him. She even offered to call someone. He declined her offer but listened to what she said. They reached an agreement. He hung up the telephone and picked up the shotgun. He studied it a longtime and then carefully removed the shells from the magazine and chamber. Jay walked to the basement and placed the gun back in the chopped-up gun case. He .went back to the living room and picked up the beer cans. He tidied up the house. Then he got into his Jeep and drove to St. Anslem's Hospital.

The drive to the hospital was difficult. Jay was very drunk. The Jeep was almost out of gas and he didn't have any money. He had to avoid the toll way and go across town. Running stop signs almost caused him permanent damage. Suddenly the tall patient towers of St. Anslem's appeared before him and he steered toward the Emergency entrance. Once there he parked in the space reserved for ambulances.

At first, he could not get out of the Jeep. Then he managed to push his legs out of the door. He staggered into the Emergency entrance and approached the clerk at the reception desk. When she raised her head, Jay leaned on the desk and made an announcement.

"I'm Jay Marquart and I am a drunk."

The receptionist called a nurse assistant who called a nurse who called a resident who consulted the Emergency Room physician who called the first-year Psychiatry resident who consulted the Chief Resident in Psychiatry who called an attending psychiatrist on call who consulted with Director of Psychiatric Services who admitted Jay to the Psychiatry Service where he was to stay for at least two weeks.

Chapter Fifteen

Things were either coming together or coming apart. Mitch Daly wasn't sure. In either case he thought he could create an opportunity for himself. The Archdiocesan Office for Health Affairs had arrived and was flexing its authority all over his boss, Joe Durant. Mike Logan's youthful, almost naive personality was appealing to many including Sister Elizabeth who took well to the new genius. Dr. Folley was lord and master of the Cardinal's Court in matters of health. All this became very evident at the joint Finance and Planning Committee meeting.

Daly and Rod Weaver had spent all day Monday with their boss preparing materials for the Finance Committee. Durant had called Mr. O'Shea several times that day to discuss the agenda. Materials for the meeting were first faxed to O'Shea for his approval and then faxed to the committee. O'Shea had seemed cooperative to Durant and had approved the material without comment or criticism. On this basis, the administrators felt that the issues were answered and matters in control when the committee assembled early on Tuesday morning.

The planned agenda called for an opening prayer by Sister Elizabeth, then an update on the cost cutting measures enacted by the hospital over the past week. Joe Durant was scheduled to make this presentation with Rod Weaver backing Joe's commentary with slides and graphs. This would lead to organization changes, specifically in SACAP, that would allow Dr. Folley to have the floor. He would explain how the change was prelude to the expansion of the Archdiocesan Office for Health Affairs to services that would lead to a network of integrated medical care under physician direction. Dr. Folley would then introduce Mr. Callahan of Debur and Tandy who would make an expanded presentation of the network plan.

The goal was to gain acceptance of the plan by the finance committee who would recommend it to the Planning Committee who would recommend it to the Board of Trustees. Since the Planning Committee could not approve it before Wednesday's special Board meeting it was suggested by Callahan that the Finance Committee could recommended it in principle to the Board pending final recommendation by the Planning Committee. Sister Elizabeth had agreed to that idea on Michael Logan's suggestion. However, to be safe and politically correct, Logan suggested that the Planning Committee members be invited to the Finance Committee and that the meeting be billed as a joint committee. Sister Elizabeth thought that was a wonderful idea. What Sister Elizabeth did not know was that only she had been invited. The stage was set and all was ready.

The well-laid plans soon went astray. Mr. Thomas O'Shea, Treasurer of St. Anslem's Hospital, Knight of the Holy Cross, and self-styled protector of the Faith, sat as chairman of the hospital's Finance Committee determined to advance the cause of the Archdiocese and his son-in-law, Dr. Folley. From O'Shea's position Folley was the Archdiocese where healthcare was concerned. Folley had briefed his father-in-law on the many mistakes made in recent time by the administrator. A correction was in order.

The committee was crowded into Durant's office instead of the spacious Hardly Boardroom. Kevin seemed displeased at this and said so. Durant had purposely scheduled the meeting for his office to force some control to his position. It wasn't working. O'Shea's disruptive attitude spread to Hardly. Sister Elizabeth was also uncomfortable.

Durant managed to make his presentation without incident. Weaver's backup material generated some questions and more criticism as O'Shea challenged the accuracy of the numbers. Finally, O'Shea openly called Weaver a liar. Durant tried to defend his vice president only to the effect of generating accelerated anger from O'Shea who began shouting and pounding the table. His ranting made no sense but the members of the committee sat quietly as if terrified. O'Shea emphasized that the blundering administration had spent outrageous amounts of money on a telephone system that didn't work and a waste management contract that was nothing more than a rip-off. He claimed that the administration was self-centered without any concern for the doctors' interest.

Mark Meehan, President of Action Waste Management and newly appointed member of St. Anslem's Finance Committee, sat in silence as O'Shea condemned the waste management contract. O'Shea was either guilty of very bad manners or had forgotten that Meehan was the other half of the waste management agreement. Meehan suspected the latter even though O'Shea wasn't known as the master of tact. Meehan simply made a mental note to discuss the matter with Patello and have the issue relayed to New York.

Eventually, O'Shea settled down and then introduced Tom Callahan as a special consultant to the Archdiocesan Office of Health Affairs. Callahan explained the formation and purpose of the integrated medical network pointing to Dr. Folley as the lead person in the effort to develop the organization.

After Callahan had finished his presentation and responded to a number of rhetorical questions posed by Folley, Mr. O'Shea closed the meeting with the announcement that the committee report to the full Board at its meeting Wednesday morning would include as a major issue the recommendation that an integrated medical delivery network be formed under the direction of the Archdiocesan Office of Health Affairs. Kevin Hardly announced that he would support the formation. Sister Elizabeth looked confused but said nothing. Callahan smiled.

All the members of the Finance Committee walked out of Durant's office without speaking. No one said goodbye or good day to their Chief Executive who sat motionless at his desk not even rising as the Board Members departed. Weaver was crushed at being called a liar. Never in his long career as a finance manager had his integrity been so openly assaulted. After the committee members had left the office he also walked out without saying a word.

Mitch Daly sat like a mouse in the corner during the course of the meeting. He saw his boss crucified by the O'Shea, Folley combination. It appeared to him that Durant was soon to be gone. It also occurred to him that Durant's staff would experience the same fate perhaps even sooner. Weaver was dead meat. That hung Durant out in the open for Folley to cut to ribbons. Logan was the executive back up. Folley could stick him in at any time to fill a void in leadership when Durant got the ax. How about Mitch Daly? Should Daly make a formal move on Logan and bailout of the Durant camp before he got caught in the crossfire?

Maybe I should wait another day, Daly thought as if talking to himself, *and see if Joe can come back at the Board meeting. If he regains his position then I'm still in and if he loses then I can always make my move to the Logan camp. Right now, I'm in the middle and it feels like the place to be.*

Mark Meehan was furious. Not prone to showing anger to others, he waited until he was in his car driving back to Action. Then he exploded. He called his office and told his secretary that he wanted Ken Rayn who was supervising the St. Anslem's project and his lead tech, Jay Marquart, in his office when he arrived with a complete report on the status of the project. The secretary recognized the apparent anger in his voice and immediately relayed the message to Ken Ryan noting the sense of urgency.

Ken Ryan was in a sweat. He had practically nothing to report to Meehan on the progress of the St. Anslem's project. He knew that Jay had met with someone about the project and had run into a lack of response because of the hospital's morale problem. That was last week. Yesterday Jay Marquart had been reported missing in action by Action's human resource office that apparently got a call from St. Anslem's informing them that Jay Marquart was ill and unavailable for work.

Ryan's call to the hospital only produced the fact that Jay was a patient but no additional information concerning diagnosis, condition, or even his location was available. When Ryan called Jay's house the telephone was unanswered. Ryan informed the Human Resources Office to place Jay on sick leave until further notice.

Meehan arrived at his office to find Ryan waiting for him. Meehan liked Ryan. He felt that the young man had good judgment and was very loyal and reliable. Because of his attitude he was able to curb his anger. Ryan stood as the boss entered. Meehan sensed his anxiety and attempted to put him at ease.

"Sit down, Ken. Relax. I hope you had a good weekend. It looks like we are going to be very busy. You by yourself? Where's Marquart?"

Ryan knew he would be asked that question. Yet he wasn't sure how to answer. "He's ill, Sir. Apparently a patient at St. Anslem's. I called but the hospital wouldn't give me any information. I also placed a call to his home but no one answered. If I don't hear anything from Jay by this afternoon then I'll call his sister. She should know."

"Okay, Ken." Meehan wanted to get on with it. "What I wanted to talk to you two about was the status of the St. Anslem's project. I caught a lot of flak this morning from a fellow Board member who thinks we are ripping off the hospital. We have to be careful about how we are perceived. Just where are we with the project?"

Ryan opened his St. Anslem's file that contained his notes from the original meetings with Durant and Weaver. There were also a few comments about the first supervisors meeting. Nothing had been added to the file since. All Ryan had to report was from memory of his last conversation with Jay who apparently had met some doctor who was going to help the project. Ryan couldn't remember his name.

"Mr. Meehan, the project is very difficult because of the severe layoffs that the hospital is experiencing. We aren't able to find anyone who seems to be in charge. Meetings have been canceled. Jay apparently made contact with a doctor in administration who said that he would help move things along. I'll have to see if I can contact Jay. Then I'll have a better idea. Actually, I'm not sure that the hospital signed the contract. The last I saw of it a Mr. Weaver was going to review it and get back to us. I wonder if they made any payments."

Meehan smiled at Ryan. "Who's ripping who off?" he thought out loud. "If we have been working on the project without a contract then that son of a bitch, O'Shea, has no basis to claim he has been ripped off. Even if we have a contract and they haven't paid us then we are the ones getting the shaft. Right?"

Ryan nodded. "Sir, I believe the hospital did give us the initial payment but I'm not sure. Mr. Celi made the initial arrangements then Jay worked out the action plan under the contract. He and I presented the whole package to Mr. Durant who gave it to Mr. Weaver for review and action. Durant seemed to approve it first and I thought that Weaver was going to log it and start the payments. Isn't Mr. Celi in charge of collections? We never bothered to see if the hospital made any payment. We just thought that accounting or Mr. Celi would give us the word either way. We haven't heard anything."

The thought of Celi paying a call on O'Shea and breaking his leg amused Meehan. He put the idea aside and thanked Ryan for his report. "Thanks, Ken. That project has got to move. We'll get paid, I'm sure. You get your staff together and push forward. Don't wait for Marquart. We don't have time to wait for anybody. Just go in there and implement the process as if it were all approved. If you get any opposition let me know. In the meantime, I'll have Celi check on the money thing. "

After Ryan left his office Meehan reflected on the Finance Committee meeting. Then almost on impulse he called Joe Durant. The two exchanged greetings and then Meehan moved to the purpose of the call. "Joe, I wanted to let you know that I was shocked at the way O'Shea pushed you around this morning. You took it like a real gentleman and professional. I expect that he will try something like that again tomorrow. I want you to know that I am available to back you up if you think you need help."

Meehan's comments refreshed Joe who before the call was busy reviewing his resume and considering his resignation speech. "Thanks, Mark. I'm going to need all the help I can get. Mr. O'Shea has some false impressions that he probably got from talking to Dr. Folley. It's hard to counter that stuff in front of the whole Board when they have no idea what is being said."

"Right, Joe," Meehan countered. "I was particularly upset with O'Shea's comments about the waste handling contract being a rip-off."

Durant felt the irony. For him to gain a friend and supporter he would have to defend the waste management contract as a valuable program. He knew from the beginning that the contract had been a shakedown and a rip-off. Now the head con man was becoming his ally in his fight with Folley and O'Shea over control of the hospital. It seemed like a compromise worth the effort.

Durant replied, "Mark, you may recall that I informed the Board at its last meeting about the waste management contract and its cost. Mr. Hardly pushed it aside saying that it was the cost of doing business. If they make a point of it tomorrow I'll remind the Chairman of his previous position."

"Great! You do that, Joe," Meehan quickly reacted. "I'll see what I can do to take some of the other pressure off your back. Oh, and Joe, I think that the hospital may be a little behind on its payments to us. Can you look into it? I'll certainly appreciate it."

After completing his call to Durant, Mark immediately dialed Patello's private number. The phone rang several times before he heard the familiar click of a transfer. Mr. Patello's private secretary answered immediately. She informed Meehan that her boss was very busy with several meetings around Boston. He was due to call in about twenty minutes and she would be sure to tell him that Mr. Meehan would like a return call.

Then Meehan called his accounting office and asked for a payment report on the St. Anslem's project. He was informed that the hospital was making regular payments for trash collection. The contract had not been returned and the thirty-thousand-dollar initial payment was delinquent. In spite of the delinquency, Mr. Celi had been paid his full commission.

Patello was indeed a busy man. He had been directed by Uncle Frank Patello to shepherd the merger of The Hardly Security and Trust Bank with the Cambridge Banks controlled by the Protestant side of the Hardly clan. The effort required intense political maneuvering and undercover work in order to avoid premature publicity by the Boston business media. To accomplish the merger it was, first of all, necessary to keep the matter focused on stockholder gains and away from family disputes. This was accomplished by having companies owned or controlled by NAI buy stock in both banks. The stockholder representatives would cultivate Board members who would move management to propose merger considerations. Gradually the prospect of personal fiscal gain for the individual stockholders would make the idea of merging with their competitor palatable.

Patello had been very successful in infiltrating the respective Boards of the target banks. Secret merger talks between the two finance giants had now moved to specific proposals penned by legal counsel and analyzed by independent auditors. The focus in true business fashion was squarely on the resulting payout to stockholders and the new value per share. Nothing as yet had been mentioned about customer service. That was always an after the fact matter devised by the public relations staff as fodder for the news releases. A point also left not mentioned was the staff reduction that would affect both institutions.

Another factor assisting the merger prospect was that the heirs of the Hardly fortune on both sides of the religious issues were not particularly intent on their churches. Typical of the rich and famous they paid homage to God by enjoying the warmth of the Caribbean and the beauty of the Rocky Mountains leaving the details of fortune to hired expertise.

Kevin Hardly and his opposite cousin sat alone in their respective offices advancing in age and declining in health. They still had no love for each other but saw no reason to pass the family custom of hate that they had enjoyed on to their heirs. Instead they would leave them miserably rich without a cause to inspire them to greater wealth. While they never discussed this point it was known to God alone that it was the only time they had like ideas in their lives. Consequently, without family opposition, Patello simply had to make the deal seem like good business without National Associated Investors being identified in the offering.

Big Frank Patello and the Board of NAI knew that their identity of ownership in the new corporation formed after the bank merger would be a matter of public record. That was not a problem after the fact. However, NAI's combined power coupled with a major piece of the Boston finance market would cause concern in political circles that would motivate an ambitious attorney general to push hard on anti-trust issues. To come up front as the instigator of the merger would be potentially self-defeating. Additionally, Big Frank knew that his Board was not fully convinced that they should move their headquarters from New York to Boston as he had proposed. The bank deal was effectively the overture to establishing New England as the NAI base. Frank believed that the bank merger would cause the Board to see that New England was more accommodating to NAI and presented a very favorable environment for its operations.

On this basis he had directed his nephew to move the merger to a final point with the realization that from NAI's position it was not completely a done deal.

Charles Patello was fascinated with the idea of merging the banks. He carefully planned his approach and then gradually played it out. His schedule was at first filled with arranging accidental meetings with key people at social events and clubs. Then he advanced to lunches and dinner meetings. From there he began to arrange talks between interested parties who eventually moved their discussion into Board committee meetings as an after-agenda item. Committees then made study recommendations that were followed by motions. Now formal studies were underway. Corporate lawyers were collecting outrageous fees. Auditors were raising skeptical issues. Bank executives were becoming anxious. The whole project had generated tremendous momentum and was at a point where it had to go. Patello knew that he had to get Uncle Frank to bring it to a formal vote at NAI. The media was certain to get wind of the merger in the next few weeks.

While Frank had his nephew working almost full-time on the bank project he had only mentioned it briefly to his top executives in New York, Mario Capizzi and Tony Marone. They seemed lukewarm to the idea of moving to Boston but seemed willing to support the move. In the discussion Frank learned for the first time that the drug distribution business was under surveillance by the Boston Police Department. If the drug business was busted and traced in any way to NAI or any of its affiliates then the Boston bank deal would never happen and some top lieutenants in the organization could take a fall.

Frank was personally convinced that he should fold the drug operation in Boston and move to another area in New England under less pressure. Mario and Tony were developing a plan that would change the operation to Portland, Maine. That Plan would have to be approved and implemented before the Boston bank deal went down.

Patello had called Uncle Frank every day with an update on the bank project. Today, he intended to report that formal action was immediately necessary by NAI and that Boston media would be on the story in the very near future. He came back to his office from a series of morning conferences that gave him even greater concern that the project was about to become public knowledge. As he moved toward his office his secretary informed him that Mr. Meehan had called with an apparently urgent matter. She suggested that Mr. Patello return his call before he got tied up with his routine call to New York. Patello took the note from the secretary and moved into his office where he placed the call to Meehan on his private line.

Meehan answered the phone on its second ring and was very pleased to hear the friendly voice of Charles Patello return his greeting. "Charlie, damn. Thanks for returning my call. I know you are very busy but I think we might have some problems brewing at the hospital."

Patello looked at his watch and wondered if this call would cause him to miss Uncle Frank before he went to lunch. Nevertheless, he was cordial in reply to his friend. "The hospital is one big problem, Mark. What, pray tell, could make it any worse?"

"It's not a what. It's who and who is your buddy and BC classmate, Mr. Thomas O'Shea," shouted Meehan. "He and that stooge nephew of his are beating up Joe Durant. That's not the issue. The issue is that they are using the waste management contract as a club. If O'Shea keeps yelling that the hospital's deal with Action is a rip-off, the citizens might get interested. We don't need any public scrutiny at this stage of our implementation of the City's waste handling ordinance. The deal with Boston Hospital is very fragile. O'Shea's big mouth needs a muzzle. He went 'a little nuts' on the subject at the hospital's Finance Committee this morning and I suspect he will do a repeat performance at the Board meeting tomorrow."

The timing of this incident was very bad for Patello. O'Shea, as the Senior Vice President and Chief Fiscal Officer of Hardly Security and Trust would be the person who the bank's Board would look to for final recommendation of the merger offer. Patello had been plotting his compromise by various means for some time. Consequently, he did not want to confront the man over the damn waste management thing at this time. However, Patello recognized that Action Waste Management was a valuable asset that carried the Park label and the NAI identity. Meehan was right. A scandal over the waste handling thing could bring down Action and inadvertently the bank merger. Furthermore, that idiot, O'Shea, held in file evidence of the deal made with Logan and the Mayor over the waste ordinance and the big shots in Washington.

Time had to be invested in working this out. His call to Uncle Frank would be late today. He needed to talk this out with Meehan.

Portello asked, "You got any ideas, Mark? I don't think we can just hit the bastard. Tom is the chairman-elect. It would screw up the Alumni Association. We have to be concerned about good old BC."

Meehan was not sympathetic. "Yeah, well, I would like to schedule a hit but that is a little over kill. No pun intended. What I think we got to do for now is get him diverted to something else. Now your consultant, Callahan, has got Logan by the ears. What say you get to Callahan and have him tell Folley that the waste thing is a stupid windmill so he should lay off. Folley gets his num-nuts father-in-law to dummy up on the subject. If they want to chew up Durant—okay. They can get him on a lot of things. The telephone thing and moving the drunk tank are big things that they can nail him on any time they want. So, for the Board meeting tomorrow you, me, and Phil support Callahan's proposal and the Finance Committee's report to start the medical network thing. Only we applaud Durant and his boys for all the good work they did in getting things started. We take the ball away from O'Shea but give him what he wants. You can tell O'Shea what a great guy he is for setting up the Archdiocese thing and he agrees to back off the waste contract. Does that sound doable?"

Patello recognized that Meehan's suggestion made Durant expendable. He vaguely recalled that at one time Mario Capizzi had insisted that they put a collar on Durant. Now effectively Meehan was putting a noose around his professional neck. *Such is life*, he thought before responding positively to Mark. Then he hastily concluded the conversation and placed a call to Tom Callahan.

Callahan had not heard of the Waste Management agreement but was quick to agree that it was not an issue with the formation of a health services network and should not be used by Folley as a club to beat Durant—at least not at the present time. He agreed to call Folley in preparation for tomorrow's meeting and tactfully get him to back off the waste management issue. With that done Patello returned to the more pressing matter of merging the two banking giants.

Thomas O'Shea was very busy and very frustrated. His massive mahogany desk was overflowing with reports from the legal consultants and auditors about the prospects of merging with Cambridge Banks. All the reports were positive and conclusive. The merger was a win-win for both organizations.

O'Shea also realized that he would be a corporate casualty. He was working on his own deal. The inevitable golden handshake had to be lucrative enough to pad his already plush retirement plan and move his income beyond his current earnings of over six hundred thousand dollars per year. That could be a hard sell to a new organization that would-be intent on immediate efficiency. Politically he realized that he would be better off supporting the merger as the Chief Fiscal Officer and that way gain the favor of the Security and Trust Board whose members stood to gain a great deal. O'Shea's shares in the new organization would have great value but he didn't want that to be considered part of his severance. He felt that he had earned that increase. Now he wanted a plush deal that would accommodate the lifestyle that he had long dreamed of—a life away from the long cold Boston winter.

His thoughts about retirement were interrupted by his secretary who announced that Dr. Folley was on the phone. O'Shea always accepted the good doctor's call. Perhaps a diversion was necessary. He relaxed as he answered. "Hello, Richard. What can I do for you?"

Dr. Folley sounded casual but intent as he reported to his father-in-law that in conversation with his consultant, Tom Callahan, they had decided that making an issue of the Waste Management Contract at the St. Anslem's Board Meeting tomorrow was potentially contrary to establishing the plan for the health services network. The Waste Contract could be derisive and detract from a final conclusion on the network. Therefore, he was calling to suggest to Tom that they back off the issue for now. They could always pick up on the matter after the network idea took root. Dr. Folley also added that he thought Durant would be an easier target once the network under the direction of the Archdiocese was in place.

O'Shea listened intently to the doctor. However, in the back of his mind he was trying to piece together the puzzle of Waste Management, Tom Callahan, and Charles Patello. It didn't all fit but something told O'Shea that Patello, the bank merger, and the hospital thing had some kind of a tie. Patello had pushed for a consultant to the Board but settled for a consultant of his choosing to help Durant. The Consultant had easily compromised his son-in-law with grand ideas about leading a network of physicians.

Then there was the arrangement that Patello engineered to have the defunct Bay Area Health Maintenance organization acquired by National Associated Investors that relieved the bank of a non-performing loan. He also remembered the information about the mysterious transfer of funds directed by Patello to Michael Logan formally with City Hall and now working as the operations chief for the Arch Diocese Office of Health Affairs.

O'Shea had watched from a safe distance as Patello cleverly maneuvered the Security and Trust Board toward the merger with Cambridge. Patello was weaving a large and profitable web for someone other than himself. Who was directing Patello and what exactly was their intent? That question centered in O'Shea's mind as Dr. Folley continued to ramble. Suddenly there was silence. O'Shea heard Dr. Folley ask if he was still listening. O'Shea quickly responded that he had understood Dr. Folley's request and that he would make sure that the waste management thing did not become an issue at the hospital Board meeting.

About the only difficult part of the St. Anslem's Board Meeting on Wednesday was keeping Chairman Kevin Hardly to the agenda. He was disoriented and couldn't seem to remember what was happening. Some wondered if he knew where he was. He rambled about the Knights, the bank, his family, and his friends. He invited everyone to the installation Mass and ceremony for the newly selected Knights of the Order of the Holy Cross that was scheduled in October. Then he sat down and remained silent.

After an extended pause, Tom O'Shea offered a report of the Finance Committee.

O'Shea's report was short, factual, and concluded with a recommendation that the Board consider the formation of the health services network. He also mentioned that administration had initiated a series of cost reduction measures that had noticeably moved the hospital toward fiscal stability.

Hardly accepted the report and asked if there was any other business. Dr. Folley suggested that the Board should receive a report from Mr. Callahan about the formation of the network.

Without acknowledgment from the Chair, Tom Callahan moved to the front and gave a very scientific report about the future of healthcare, He concluded that St. Anslem's would be well served with the formation of a health services network under the direction of Dr. Folley, Mr. Logan and the Archdiocesan Office of Health Affairs. They accepted the report. Sister Elizabeth then moved that the Board endorse the recommendation of the Health Services Network as recommended by the Finance Committee and supported by the Planning Committee. The motion was seconded by Mark Meehan who winked at Durant. Without further discussion, the motion was accepted unanimously.

The Board meeting adjourned one hour after it started. Only Kevin Hardly remained to have breakfast. He sat alone in the spacious Hardly Board Room except for the single food service assistant who fixed his eggs and poured his coffee.

Mitch Daly was impressed with the outcome of the Board meeting. Somehow Durant had survived without a scratch. He had not been questioned or challenged by O'Shea or Folley. Durant seemed to be a survivor except he had not been praised or even mentioned as the reports and recommendations were presented. Durant was virtually nonexistent from the Board's perspective. Daly's political instincts told him that Durant was being left out to dry and eventually would be cut off by the Folley machine. However, Durant still had the sting of authority that commanded loyalty from his subjects. Daly was determined, therefore, to continue to serve the CEO of St. Anslem's but at the same time become invaluable to Michael Logan. He was certain that he could serve two masters.

Weaver was very frustrated and angry after the Board meeting. He would have preferred to battle it out with O'Shea. The facts were there. He had cut expenses even beyond what he had predicted and had not received any personal credit. Weaver came to the Board meeting with a wealth of reports showing the reductions in dollars and cents. The reports were without question. Weaver wanted a fight with O'Shea. It didn't happen.

Durant showed little emotion during and after the meeting. He chose to remain quiet especially when it became obvious that Meehan had arranged for peaceful conduct and presentation of the Finance Committee's report. Hardly's incompetence tended to contribute to anarchy but today even that was controlled by some mysterious staging that Meehan and probably Patello had arranged. It was obvious to Durant that his time at St. Anslem's was limited. He had lost control and now the inmates were running the asylum. He was approaching his sixtieth birthday which made the prospect of another position very unlikely. Best if he remained at St. A's until the right moment and then negotiate a package that would carry him to normal retirement. Timing would be very important. He needed to be very cooperative with the formation of the Network and give support to Folley's ambition. Durant theorized that if he could capture Folley's ego he could better negotiate a lucrative severance arrangement.

What seemed more interesting if not more important to Durant at the moment was making sure that the first shipment of food to Sister Celest's Food Kitchen got off on time. The truck from Patriot Transport was scheduled to pick up the food at the service entrance in less than an hour. Joe wanted to watch the loading and then follow the truck to the Food Kitchen and see Sister Celest's operation first hand.

To hell with the rest of the day, he thought. *I'll spend some time with the poor since I'm likely to join them.*

It was something different for Brian and he liked the idea. Eddie had asked him to park the Chevy and drive a van on a special assignment. He was to report to the service door at St. Anslem's Hospital and pick up a load of hot food that was to be delivered to a soup kitchen in Roxbury. This seemed like a fun assignment devoid of the pressure that he always felt when delivering the special packages for Eddie. At eleven A.M. sharp the shiny white van with bold black letters spelling out Patriot Transport backed into the hospital's service entrance.

The hospital's receiving clerk asked Brian to move the van to the side until the food was brought to the dock by the kitchen crew. Brian obliged and then sat on the clerk's small desk while another shipment was being processed into the hospital's inventory. The food arrived at the loading dock in wheeled insulated carts pushed by sweating kitchen employees in white uniforms stained with the remnants of processed food. They were noticeably silent as an acknowledgment of the executive in a tailored business suit that followed them.

The Suit returned the greeting of the receiving clerk and then turned to Brian. "Are you the Patriot driver?" the Suit asked.

Brian stood up straight and almost came to military attention as he responded with a prompt, "Yes, Sir!"

"Good." instructed the Suit. "Back your truck to the dock and we'll get it loaded. Wait for me to come here in my car. It's a black BMW 325. I want to follow you to the soup kitchen. Okay? You look familiar. Have we met?"

Joe Durant's face was familiar to Brian as well. At first, he thought that Joe was one of Patriot's special customers that always wore expensive suits. They seldom wanted to admit that they had ever met him before. His memory was blocked by the man's appearance that suggested that they had met in an informal place.

Brian leaned his head to the left as if he were searching his mind. "I think we have met, Sir, but I can't seem to place it. Maybe at the store or something. I go fishing a lot. Maybe at the dock?"

Durant slapped his thigh as he remembered Brian on the back of the Sea Sprite pumping gas as he conversed with John Marquart last Friday evening at the Hingham Boat Dock. "Right, that's it. You and Mr. Marquart were going fishing and I was at the dock getting gas. Mr. Marquart and I had a conversation but I didn't really have the opportunity to meet you. I'm Joe Durant. Haven't seen Jay since then. How's he doing?"

Brian was embarrassed when Joe mentioned the night at the gas dock. Jay had been rude but then seemed to recover. It was uncertain in Brian's mind if Mr. Durant was considered friendly or not. Jay had never clarified that point in his many tirades about St. Anslem's. Brain had also been told by Martha that Jay was a patient at St. Anslem's but the hospital had refused to give out information or even give him his room number. Obviously, Mr. Durant was unaware that Jay was a patient.

"I am pleased to meet you, Mr. Durant." Brian straightened up and extended his hand. "Jay, well, he's been ill I guess. I think he was or maybe still is a patient here. They won't tell me anything when I call. I guess he's okay. You can follow me to the Soup Kitchen on Melina Cass in Roxbury. It's easy to get there from here. No problem. I'll wait until you get your car."

Durant nodded and walked toward the parking garage without further comment. He realized that the hospital's refusal to give Brian any information about Jay indicated that he was admitted to a confidential service which could be SACAP or the Psychiatric unit. The SACAP inpatient unit was closed over the weekend so obviously Mr. Marquart was now residing in Psych. The names of the psychiatric patients were not included on the daily census list for confidentiality reasons so Joe would not have seen Marquart's name as he scanned the list each day. The only person who had access to a complete census list was Dr. Sutton who held it in complete secrecy. Durant made a mental note to discuss the Marquart case with him.

Sister Celest's Soup Kitchen was in a run-down non-descript brick and frame structure on Melina Cass Boulevard within a block of the truck yards and warehouses adjacent to Interstate 93 that penetrated the center of Boston's business district. The area was also the center gathering point for the homeless who took shelter beneath the viaduct that held the highway above the City streets. They gathered there and made shelters out of packing cases or simply lay on the ground in the comfort of the summer nights. During the day, they would stand at the intersections of the frontage roads feeding the Interstate and panhandle from drivers waiting to creep onto the expressway jammed with rush hour traffic. Occasionally they would perform services for the drivers such as washing their windshields with muddy water or offering newspapers saved from the gutters. Most of the time they were waved away by the savvy citizens but once in a great while a kind soul would give them some change or a dollar that went in their personal treasury marked for a bottle of wine. As night fell they would disperse and use whatever they had acquired from the day's efforts to find food, drink and, in inclement weather, a shelter that was warm with a clean bed and an opportunity for a shower.

There were plenty of places to go. Few places, however, were attentive to the free spirit that was dominant in the character of the street person. Sobriety was the main requirement of most shelters. In addition, many required religious practice. Others sought to educate them. Some expected labor in return for food and shelter. Typically, the person seeking shelter was fiercely independent. They also had sufficient intelligence to accept assistance and render gratitude. But the strength of their independence required only a voluntary response in gratitude for the kindness they received. This was the basis for their dignity and pride that they guarded with passion.

The lifestyle of the homeless was conducive to poor health, chronic disease, and injury. Unfortunately, the discipline of hygiene, diet, and self-control required to sustain health were viewed as oppressive to the independent residents of the Viaduct. As a consequence, they, in no small numbers, were often found unconscious on street comers, sometimes deceased, by police patrols who traveled the area with routine frequency. The City Ambulances would take them to the municipal Boston Hospital where they would be treated and released after health was fully or sometimes only partially restored with instructions to return for more treatment.

Most chose not to return for the continuing care. Some came back for the medicine that they took for the high or sold to others. Basically, they feared the hospital because it gave them a label in Medicaid or welfare files that intruded their privacy. The same was true for the City sponsored health centers operated by the large teaching hospitals that sent young physicians in training to experiment in the cure of the socially disadvantaged. Illness to the street person was as much if not more of a curse as it was to the affluent. But to both ends of the economic spectrum trying to escape from sickness was not nearly as difficult as trying to escape from the processes associated with treatment. Demanding bureaucrats held each person's identity as a file determined to keep the record and the person therein confined for life.

Countless individuals, foundations, churches, and voluntary organizations had opened shelters, food kitchens, clothing stores, halfway houses, and free clinics in the area. Each had its own gimmick to enhance the street person to partake of the available services. There was open competition for the body and soul of the person who had no means of compensating or gratifying the provider. Consequently, there was no temporal reward for those who gave of themselves to serve others in need except for the satisfaction of caring for and about the people of God. In spite of all the good intentions, there was still plenty of room at the inn. Compassion was a hard sell.

This attracted Sister Celest as an alternative to being the administrator of a hospital once considered a place of mercy but now a business. This was her salvation and her passion. Her little mission was crammed into a former greasy spoon and bar adjacent to and connected to a flop house. The large front windows were cracked at the comers but were clean, offering a passing soul a good view of the opportunity to find food and compassion. Inside, the bare wooden tables and creaky chairs sat unevenly on a plank floor long since divorced of any protective covering. The old bar was used for the serving line. The ancient kitchen with its sometimes-functioning equipment gave the only sign of past quality in the worn environs. The placed was immaculate. Sister Celest regarded it as a castle and a true temple of the Holy Spirit.

Joe Durant followed Brian and the white Van down Massachusetts Ave past Boston University, then around the Longwood Medical complex, past Northeastern to Melina Cass Boulevard. As the Interstate came into view, he noticed that the buildings on both sides of the Boulevard were well used by health services such as blood purchase programs, pregnancy counseling, clinics, and miscellaneous healthcare providers who spoke several languages.

A block later he saw a flop house hotel and next to it an old battered storefront that had been a restaurant. The hand painted lettering on the window had been applied over the old letters that were still visible. Now it simply stated, "A Little Portion." They had arrived at Sister Celest's food kitchen. Brian parked the Van next to a fire plug and entered the building to find Sister Celest. Joe made a left turn and parked directly across the street.

"A Little Portion" was crowded with panhandlers on lunch break and stragglers from the flop house. They seemed annoyed at the apparent delay in service. Brian sensed the anxiety and moved quickly to find Celest so he could make his delivery and move on. He found her in the back of the kitchen spreading jam from a large jar on pieces of bread. She was elated when he told her that the food had arrived. Without delay she moved to the front door and assisted him in bringing the hot meals to the bar serving counter.

Joe arrived just as Brian was beginning to take the food into the front door so he grabbed the extra hand cart and assisted the delivery. Sister Celest was very impressed at Joe's presence and much more with his participation. They hardly exchanged a greeting. Soon, Sister had him in an apron behind a serving tray passing out boiled potatoes. Brian brought in the last container and was gone in a flash. Two hours later the last of the food had been distributed and the cleanup was in process. Again, Joe assisted. Sister Celest and two elderly Sisters from the Mother house comprised the entire staff of the kitchen. Joe was well used.

Conversation had been light during serving and cleanup. Sister gave directions and Joe followed her commands. It was a very simple arrangement. Now it was time to relax for a few minutes before preparation for the evening meal that because of limitations was only a sandwich. Celest was hoping and praying for the where with all to provide three nutritional meals a day but that would have to come in time. For the present, thanks to St. Anslem's, she was able to give one good meal at noon and some sustenance in the morning and evening. No questions asked.

Joe sat at one of the worn tables and sipped a cup of very black coffee. Sister Celest sat across the table. Her coffee was untouched as she seemed to be admiring the soup kitchen.

Joe read her thoughts. "Celest, this place is wonderful from the point of service but it's a real dump. If the City Health Department comes by they'll close you for sure. I have to hand it to you though. You are fearless."

Celest dismissed Joe's comments with a wave of her hand. "Don't worry about the City, Joe. I've got it covered. No politician will ever close down a soup kitchen run by a poor old nun. They may be crooked but they aren't crazy. Besides, I have the possibility to expand. The man that owns the hotel next door wants me to take over his operation except for the prostitutes. How about that?"

Joe was flabbergasted. "Why! Why for Christ's sake would you take over a flop house that's a fire trap that will probably fall down if it doesn't burn down first?"

"You said it, Joe—for Christ's sake."

It was difficult for Joe to understand the Sister's ambitions. "Get serious, Celest."

"I am serious," argued Celest. "We just opened and the word is all over the street that we give and don't take. We let these people alone. Just feed 'em. That's all—for now. Next, we provide shelter. They are human beings, Joe. Out of kindness they will be served and then they will, on their own, seek God's mercy and salvation. Oh, I know only a few will choose to change but everyone counts. Think of it, Joe—a true mission of caring—filled with the risk and challenge that life is meant to be. It can't get any better than this."

Durant thought briefly about Sister's comments. Her sincerity was not easy to deny. "Well, I have to admit it sounds more exciting than running a hospital."

Sister Celest began to lighten up. "That's the spirit, my friend. I am very grateful that you came in to get a firsthand look at things. How about becoming my first volunteer from the other world? It will do you good. Eventually, I plan to form a Foundation and you can be its first chairman. We'll keep the money changers like Hardly, O'Shea, and Patello on the outside. Their kind screwed up the temple anyway. Right now, I do need some money and I was going to call and see if you could manage to push a little of St. A's cash my way till I get on my feet so to speak."

"You got to be kidding." Joe was shocked. "I could go to the slammer for that. O'Shea wants my ass in a sling now. He would have me shot for pushing money into this venture. I'll give you twenty bucks from Mrs. Durant's egg money."

"Okay, I'll take it." Sister chuckled. "But I still want some from St. A's. They owe it to me and to the Sisters. We worked there for decades for little or no wages. Now those fat boys on the Board want to steal the place for God only knows what. What the hospital has in the bank is really the sweat equity of the Sisters. We want to cash in. Look at it this way. The healing ministry is repositioning and we need capital."

Joe sat back down and put his hand over Sister Celest's arm. "Celest, you know that what you are asking is beyond me. Just this morning the Board voted to reposition into a medical network. Sr. Elizabeth made the motion. You have to talk to her about this. I can't help you. If she can pull a resolution out of the Board to give you some startup capital then I can do the rest. Without support of the Board I'm tied down. "

Sister nodded. "I understand, Joe. But I know that you have authority to make donations and gifts to charitable organizations within limitations. What I'm asking is that you simply exercise your given authority to make an occasional contribution to A Little Portion. It isn't like you were supporting Planned Parenthood. Even the Cardinal would have to back you on this."

"How much do you want?" Joe knew that Celest was not to be denied.

"Just five grand, Joe. That's five grand for openers. I used to spend that much on the Cardinal's Christmas present. Nobody ever complained about that. What do you say?" The good Sister was very serious.

Durant was blown away. He came to the soup kitchen out of personal curiosity and now he was being drawn into an act of ecclesiastical malfeasance that could send him to jail but gain him a higher place in the hereafter. On the other hand, the Board had committed to supporting the Health Service Office which was a ruse of the same. A contribution to A Little Portion was equally justified.

"Okay, Celest. You got to me. I'll send you a contribution from St. A's but you can forget the twenty bucks from Mrs. Durant. I've got enough trouble."

That was enough for one day. Joe had, for all practical purposes, been handcuffed in his efforts to run St. Anslem's Hospital and later had been asked to exercise his supposed authority to provide hospital funds to another charitable function. The Church and its application of the Corporal Works of Mercy were becoming a mystery to him. He remembered that Sister Celest, when she was the hospital President, had used hospital funds without Board approval to establish programs for the poor. That was one of the excuses used to move her out of the job. Now she was doing it again only he was the conduit. This time he was accountable. Sister was in the clear.

When Joe Durant arrived home, he found an official letter from the Chancery Office of the Boston Catholic Archdiocese addressed to Mr. and Mrs. Joseph Durant that appointed them Knight and Lady of the Order of the Knights of the Holy Cross. It was jointly signed by Cardinal McMahon and Kevin Hardly. The installation was scheduled for the second Saturday in October and was to be an all-day affair beginning with registration and lunch at the Sheraton.

The installation would follow in the afternoon at the Cathedral. Afterwards they would return to the Sheraton for a reception and cocktails. Dinner would be at seven followed by entertainment. Kevin Hardly would conclude the event with his annual report to the Knights followed by the Cardinal's response.

Richard Folley, M.D., had not waited for the decision of the St. Anslem's Board of Trustees. He began to organize the Archdiocesan Health Services Network well in advance of its official authorization. Dr. Anderson had been directed to schedule a series of meetings with individual primary care private practitioners on St. A's medical staff to explain the new organization. The hospital was buzzing as physicians openly speculated about the concept. Anderson took the blunt of response from joy to anger as doctors confronted him in his office, the doctors' lounge, parking lot, or cafeteria. Private practice groups secretly negotiated to sell their practice to the hospital. Specialists became sensitive to the prospect of managed care type contracts giving control of their revenue to the primary practitioners. By the time of the Board meeting the hospital's medical staff was about as disorganized and confused as the hospital employees were demoralized. St. Anslem's was not a happy ship.

Dr. Anderson was becoming a loyal disciple of the network concept. He maintained constant communication with Tom Callahan in the week following the Board meeting. Callahan became a familiar figure in the halls of the hospital as he moved from meeting to meeting with physicians in support of Anderson's appeals. Michael Logan worked equally as hard in developing the network operations. He made contact with the payers and purchasers of physician and hospital services to inform them of the Archdiocesan Health Service Network. He also made contact with other Catholic hospitals in the Archdiocese and advised them of the potential of becoming part of the Network.

Logan's reception at the other institutions was cool and indifferent. Each hospital enjoyed its independence or had been in process of establishing an affiliation with a major teaching hospital in the Boston area that would bring them greater prestige and market potential. Logan knew in his mind that only St. Anslem's would support the project but his reports to Folley and Anderson were always politically correct and therefore optimistic.

Dr. Folley enjoyed watching the activity. He frequently attended the Anderson meetings and openly announced his authorization of the project by stating his leadership of the network. At the same time, he would explain that this was a physicians' organization, owned by physicians and led by physicians. "The physicians are to be in control of their own destiny," he would exclaim. "While change is necessary in the delivery of healthcare, that change is best designee and directed by physicians. It is time to be liberated from the oppressive corporate control of lay organizations." His remarks always brought applause.

For an encore Folley would raise a clenched fist and shout, "The hospital will be only a cost center in the delivery of care that the physician will direct. We will not only prescribe the care. We will control all the revenue. The hospital will have to negotiate with us for money to operate. We will have the final say on what they buy and for what reason. We will contract with the managed care companies for the entire package."

Callahan was delighted with Folley's flamboyant and naive commentary. He was leading the sheep to the slaughter but more time was necessary to fix the plan for Boston Target Medical. In his reports to New York, Callahan estimated at least six months to the point that the Network would be fully active and another six months after that for it to be fully controlled by Park Medical.

Within a few weeks from now, however, it would be advantageous to bring the Bay Area Health Maintenance Organization and its illustrative President, Joseph Bauman, into the act as a very interested partner to the Network.

Bauman, under Callahan's tutelage, would convince Folley over an appropriate period of time that the Network would be best served by having a qualified fiscal intermediary handle the funds provided through the lucrative capitation contracts from large employers, State Agencies, Medicaid and Medicare that would be forth coming. Additionally, the Intermediary would provide the Network members with the obligatory automated information systems, especially the billing systems that are necessary to maintain adequate cash flow. All of this service would be provided for a small percentage of the gross revenue to be skimmed off the top.

The progress of Target Boston Medical was good news to Big Frank Patello. He enjoyed discussing the plan with Tony Marone and Mario Capizzi at their morning strategy sessions. The fact that the drug distribution business was under surveillance by the Boston Police still caused him great concern. If the drug business was busted all the other cards would fall bringing an abrupt end to the Patello empire. Therefore, it was essential that actions be taken to avoid the penetration of the business by the Boston Police. Capazzi and Marone were resigned to the Boston move and the major reorganization of NAI. Although Big Frank had not actually said it, they were certain that Charlie Patello would be the next boss. That too was okay with them. Charlie was Frank's family and the family had always been good to them.

The more pressing matter was the prospect of moving National Associated Investors from New York to Boston. Preliminary discussion with the Board of Directors suggested that the plan would be approved. The Board also vigorously supported the merger of Hardly Security and Trust with Cambridge Banks. However, the foundation for the move was shaky because of events taking place in Action Waste Management and the cocaine distribution business that served as the primary revenue producer for the various NAI ventures. Big Frank's idea was to equate or even exceed the cocaine revenue base with other quasi legitimate ventures such as banking, medical care and environmental services in that way provide NAI with profitable cover to continue. New York, with overdeveloped finance systems and underdeveloped medical systems, offered little opportunity for the diversification. Boston on the other hand gave great opportunity to move in and take over.

Big Frank maintained daily communication with his nephew. Patello was the key man in bringing about the transition. The NAI Board was well aware that Frank intended to step down once the organization completed the Boston move and they were also supportive of naming Patello as his successor.

To insure success Big Frank had pushed Capizzi to develop an alternative to their method of supplying New England cocaine dealers through the Patriot Transport network in Boston. Mario in response had used his extensive connections in the Boston and New York Police Narcotic Units to determine how close they were to making an arrest or infiltrating the supply and distribution system in New England. His latest report to Frank was not encouraging. The two met alone in the Big Office as it was called. Frank listened intently as Mario detailed the situation.

"Frank, what we got is the Boston PD needing a big narcotic bust to get the press off their backs about the gangs running wild all over town. The neighborhoods say that the gangs are dealing and so drugs is the reason for all the shooting and killing. The cops are looking at the trade in the neighborhoods and really aren't after the high-end dealers and suppliers."

Mario continued. "The bad news is that the cops are close to stumbling into our operation by mistake thinking that our systems is supplying the gangs. Hell, we don't work the neighborhoods. We haven't been in the low dollar stuff for years. Johnny Law, he don't know the difference when he gets the scent. He simply goes for the bust. Where it is, is that the Narcs have been watching our supply intake for at least two months. They could take it down but they don't have it channeled to the neighborhoods so they are trying to make it link. Sooner or later they are gonna find the passage to Patriot and from there to the trade. It will be disappointing for them when they can't tie it to the gangs but they will then realize that they got a bigger catch because a lot of high rollers in Boston will be in the net. One of them cuts a deal with the DA and our ass goes on the line. I think we got to cut and run before that happens."

Mario concluded, "We can arrange for the cops to get a link up to the neighborhoods through our supply system. That gets them what they want and off the hunt. We sacrifice our supply system in the process. That's the cost of doing business. Afterwards we reorganize through Portland as you suggested."

Big Frank nodded in agreement. "Mario, if we sacrifice the supply system who is going to go down? We need to protect our people,"

"Right, Frank," Mario replied. "The way we work it is to have the intake guy make a direct delivery to a guy from the neighborhood. They do it at the dock. The fuzz use an undercover guy on station who makes the bust. That's it. The Sailor and contact go down. The Sailor only knows how he gets the stuff He don't know anybody else except how he buys his own stash that he gets from us. That's the only risk. That dopey Sailor might talk about his own habit but he'll keep mum if we back him with legal help. The contact isn't our man. He is just making a buy for the gang. He'll go down but he don't know anything about us. The cops can brag that they shut down the drug racket in Boston by cutting off the supply."

The idea seemed to have some appeal to Big Frank. "How long do we lay low, Mario? We don't want to lose the Boston market. You think we should hit the Sailor and keep him quiet?"

Mario gave a wave. "That's the beauty of it, Frank. We don't miss a beat. What we do is set up the Portland operation in advance of the Boston fall. We simply reroute our navy except for the drone we send in to meet the Sailor. Right now, we supply Portland customers by Patriot. We simply reverse the process and supply Boston customers. What we do is buy a courier service in Portland that buys Patriot in Boston. The Patriot operation is completely legit. Portland simply routes its Boston deliveries through Patriot. No fuss. You might be right about the Sailor. He might have to go."

"I think it best that the Sailor don't talk about anything. He's the only link to Patriot. How long will it take to get this organized?" Frank asked.

"We got the big piece in place, Frank. Our company in Maine bought *The Portland Courier* last week, just in case we needed to move fast. Now we got to have Portland buy Patriot. Oh, yeah, we need to get Mondi brought up to speed. I suggest that he move to Portland and take over as President of both companies. Boston only needs a general manager from this point on. How's it sound?"

Big Frank nodded his approval. "You take care of it, Mario. Let Charlie in on it when you tell Phil. We want the top in the know but not involved if you know what I mean. Okay?"

Mario stood. "It's done, Frank. Like you say. It might take a few weeks to get everything in place. You'll know when."

Mario Capizzi was told to take care of it. That was all he needed to start things rolling fast. First order was to arrange a meeting in Boston with Phil Mondi and Charlie Patello. Then he scheduled a meeting with some of the operatives in the "Navy."

"The Navy" was an international smuggling operation under contract with various major organized crime families in the United States and several other countries. Equipped with jet planes and cargo ships, the Navy brought cocaine, marijuana, and other substances from the Orient, South and Central America, and the Caribbean to the United States and delivered them by central distribution cargo ships cruising outside the territorial waters. The ships would be met at predetermined points by locally owned trawlers or large speed boats that would down load the supply to small boats that would take the stash to local dealers operating legitimate businesses at Fishing Docks, marinas, and harbor towns along the Easters sea coast. From there the drugs would make their way into the retail trade by whatever way was locally established.

The Patello Family was the established importer for Central and Northern New Jersey, New York City including Westchester County, Eastern Connecticut, Rhode Island, Massachusetts, and Maine. It was considered the best "franchise" in the United States by those in the trade. It was also the envy of several competitors who would be most available to take over when and if Big Frank would experience any misfortune. To avoid any such event, Big Frank was very attentive to pressure from the authorities.

The supply routes to Jersey, New York City, and Connecticut came through New York Harbor. Rhode Island, Massachusetts, and Maine were supplied through Boston Harbor. At both intake points, Frank and his operatives had designed a system that was sufficiently complex with intent to confuse any civil authority that might become suspicious. As the first step in the import process, a fishing boat registered to a large commercial fishing company out of Cape May, New Jersey would conduct a month-long cruise to fish off Newfoundland. En route it would rendezvous with a Cargo ship and take aboard a large cache of illegal substances. The fisherman would then cruise inside territorial waters corning within five miles of the coast near Sandy Hook, New Jersey, and Boston. At predetermined times and coordinates that were never the same the fisherman was met by lobster boats seemingly running their traps. Another handoff was made to the lobster men. They in turn would load special traps with the material to be imported and mark the traps with specially marked buoys. These traps would rest in a lobster field for a short time until a local "Sailor" made a run in a small craft, emptied the traps and carried the drugs to shore, landing at an area away from high traffic and police observation.

The United States Coast Guard working with special reconnaissance aircraft flown by the U.S. Navy had been attempting to monitor the Oceanic Supply System for some time. They were aware that the drugs were coming in through Boston Harbor but had not spotted the hand-off to the lobster boat or the "Sailor." Furthermore, they were not certain how the drugs were relayed from cargo ships to the locals since the use of a commercial fisherman fell into usual traffic on the high seas. On at least one occasion, the U. S. Navy had spotted the rendezvous of the fisherman with the cargo ship but did not observe any transfer of cargo. The Navy informed the Coast Guard who informed the Drug Enforcement Authority who informed the Boston Police Department who directed the Boston Harbor Police to monitor small craft traffic during late night and early morning before dawn. The Boston Police Department also alerted their Narcotic Division to be on the alert for any information that might give them a lead on how the drugs were actually coming into the City.

The Narcotic Division filed the request. They were banking on the success of their crack agent, Officer O'Sullivan, who, it was said, was hot on the trail of a prime suspect in the drug distribution racket.

In fact, O'Sullivan had no idea where his prime suspect was. Jay Marquart had disappeared. O'Sullivan's wife knew. She knew Jay was in the St. A's Psych Unit an hour after he was admitted. This time she was keeping the information to herself. She was still due for a disciplinary hearing that could cost her a career and her nursing license. There was no way that she was going to further incriminate herself. Furthermore, Cecile was unaware that Jay was her husband's prime suspect. She was not even aware of her husband's antics at the Troubadour Lounge and his acquaintance with Brian, who she despised. Her main interest was always Kristie's welfare. Jay was proving to be emotionally unfit even if he was attempting to be sober. For now the judge was only interested in his sobriety. If Cecile raised the issue of his emotionally instability to pry Kristie away from joint custody then Martha would certainly raise the issue of patient confidentiality that was even greater for psychiatric patients than substance abuse. This time Cecile was determined to keep her mouth shut and wait it out. She was confident that Jay was certain to "screw up big time."

It had taken Martha much longer than Cecile to discover Jay's whereabouts. After she had left his house on Sunday evening she went home and tried to rest. At about ten P.M. she called Jay's house and was responded to by an answering machine with Susan's voice saying that they would get back to the caller shortly. Martha recognized the message as one that had been on the Marquart answering machine for nearly a year. Fearing the worst, she drove back to Jay's house only to find it dark and his Jeep missing. That meant that her brother was on the prowl. Where, was a mystery. She decided to return home and wait for a call.

Meanwhile, Susan and the kids were hanging out in a rundown shack owned by a relative of Louise. The place was a billed as a furnished rental. Louise had convinced her aunt to allow Susan and the kids use it for a week until the domestic thing could be worked out. Louise's aunt agreed to the deal providing Susan came across with a week's rent in advance. Susan had half the money and borrowed the rest from Louise. It was now early Monday morning and Susan had no money for food much less another week's rent. With her next to last dime she placed a call to Eddie.

Eddie took the call with great reluctance. He blasted his ex-wife without letting her explain. "Susan, I told you never to call me at work. In fact, I don't want you calling me anywhere. Make it fast. This is a company phone."

Susan did her best to explain how Jay had attacked her and Benny and how she was hiding out and desperately needed help and money.

Eddie was not the least impressed. "Look, coke head, you got stoned and pissed off your husband who tried to sober you up with a pig sticker. I don't know why he punched Benny. Probably because you pushed him in front of you. Anyway, I don't intend to get involved. And don't you get me involved. You best get back home and try to fix this mess. If you go to court then Jay tells how you got stoned and the law comes to see me and my friends. You get re-habbed and I go to the slam. The kids go to foster homes 'cause you and your hubby are unfit. That might be true but I guess it's something you don't want to admit. Is it?"

Susan knew Eddie had it figured. She could only react. "Eddie, you are an ass. I just remembered why I hate your guts."

"Yeah, well, the Virgin Mary, you ain't," quipped Eddie. "Take my advice and suck this one up. You be a good little girl. Go home and make everything square. I'll see that you get some more stuff. But you got to be good or it's no more for Susan. You dig?"

Susan took Eddie's advice. She also convinced Louise's aunt to refund part of the week's rent that Susan used for the cab back to Waltham. Once home it was evident to her that Jay had left for some unknown destination. Suspecting that he might have gone to St. Anslem's she placed a call to the hospital and asked for Bob Markley in the SACAP Unit. Markley was unaware that Jay had been admitted to Psych since Jay's name had not appeared on the list of Chemical Dependent Patients treated by the Emergency Department. They only included those patients that Markley had indicated were currently under treatment and might need help. Jay was not on that list either. Markley expressed his sincere concern to Susan and offered to check area hospitals and chemical treatment facilities to see if Jay had been admitted. Susan thanked Bob for his assistance. Then in desperation she called Martha.

Martha was very pleased to hear that Susan had returned home. She was equally pleased to hear Susan explain how she wanted to make things right. Now the problem was Jay who was somewhere with the impression that his wife and family were gone. Martha promised Susan that she would attempt to locate Jay. After she hung up Martha dialed St. Anslem's and asked if Jay Marquart was a patient. She was told that he was but no other information could be given. She was about to call Action Waste Management to see if Jay had checked in with his employer when, to her surprise, she received a call from Ken Ryan asking if she had any information about Jay's condition. Ken had already called the hospital and knew that Jay was a patient but, as Martha had learned, no information on his condition was available.

Furious about the lack of information, Martha again called St. Anslem's and asked to speak with the President. President Joseph Durant's executive assistant had been well schooled and experienced in handling complaints. The first rule was to get accurate information from the caller about the incident and the caller's involvement. The second rule was to direct the call to an appropriate person who is expert in handling complaints. Third rule is not to admit any harm. And the fourth rule is never to allow the person calling to speak to the ultimate authority, the hospital President.

Martha triggered all defenses when she identified herself as an attorney. She then explained that she represented a patient in the hospital and was being prohibited from gaining access to her client. The Executive Assistant informed her that Mr. Durant was out of the hospital but she would be most willing to forward her call to Dr. Sutton, Director of Quality Assurance. Out of frustration and realizing that she had no choice, Martha agreed to talk to Dr. Sutton. The Executive Assistant asked her to hold while she made the transfer.

In truth the hospital's state of the art telephone system allowed for the transfer of the call without placing the caller on hold but the Executive Assistant used the guise in order to call Dr. Sutton and give him a quick and brief message about the nature of the call being forwarded. Dr. Sutton was in, fortunately, and when he heard the Marquart name eagerly accepted the call. The Executive secretary then returned to Martha and informed her that she was forwarding the call to Dr. Sutton's office.

Dr. Sutton answered on the first ring. Sutton was the only person in the hospital who had a complete list of admissions from the previous day regardless of the confidential nature of the illness. As Martha was explaining her interest and concern about Jay, Dr. Sutton was scanning the Psychiatric patient list and found Jay Marquart voluntarily admitted at ten-thirty-three the previous night.

"Ms. Marquart, your client, Jay Marquart, voluntarily admitted himself through the Emergency Room last night. We protect the confidentiality of the patient because of the nature of his illness. I'm sorry that we can't give you any more information at this time. I'll inform his physician of your call and ask him to contact you when appropriate."

Dr. Sutton sounded very sincere to Martha. He was not trying any medical con that was a trademark of the medical profession. She realized that he was tied by the law so she accepted his promise with gratitude. "Dr. Sutton, I very much appreciate your help. As I'm sure you recognize, Jay is my brother who keeps me involved not only in his legal problems but to a large degree in his medical problems as well. While we now have several major grievances with the hospital that will require resolution at the moment my main intention is to see that Jay receives proper care from this point on. I believe that I have some information that is vital to his care and would like to give him that information or give it to his physician. Please understand that I consider contact with Jay or his care givers as urgent. If I don't make contact within the hour I'll resort to every legal process to force this issue."

Sutton was gaining respect for Martha as well. He recognized the sincerity of her request and accepted her urgent plea. He promised to personally contact Jay's physician and ask him to call her. If she didn't hear from the doctor within the hour, Dr. Sutton politely asked Martha to call him back. Martha thanked him for his attention and agreed to wait for a call from someone caring for Jay.

Dr. Sutton then placed a call to Bob Markley to find out if he had any information about Jay's voluntary admission to the Psychiatric service and, more importantly, to inform him that the Jay Marquart incident file had just got bigger. This was the second call that Markley had received about Jay in less than two hours. However, it was the first information that he received acknowledging that Jay was a patient. Obviously, the well-conceived plans to coordinate the psychiatric and substance abuse services of the hospital had a few cracks that Jay had managed to fall through. This was the second major incident involving the same patient and it gave both men cause for concern. They agreed to have a stat meeting.

Bob Markley met Dr. Sutton at the elevator. Both men moved quickly to the Psychiatric Unit where they had a quick meeting with the staff attending to Jay. Within fifteen minutes an attending psychiatrist was on the phone speaking to Martha. Indeed, the information about Jay's family was important to his care. The psychiatrist promised to advise Jay of the information and allow, with Jay's permission, for eventual visits from Susan and Martha.

Martha called Susan with the news about Jay. She suggested to Susan that she be kept informed of any information that the hospital might give to Susan regarding Jay's condition. Martha was intent on pressing the hospital legally.

Officer O'Sullivan was very upset. His boss in the Narcotic Division had chewed him out big time. Nothing had developed from his constant surveillance of Suspect Marquart over the past several weeks. Now the Suspect had disappeared. To make matters worse the Harbor Police and the Downtown Precinct were following leads that may make the case and embarrass the Narcotic Division. In fact, Narcotics had been told to support the Harbor boys in what was expected to be a major bust. O'Sullivan's boss was enraged. Narcotics backing the Water Cops was like being put on uniform foot patrol at a Gay Rights Parade in South Boston. There was no way you could look good.

O'Sullivan left the top office and went to lunch at the Troubadour Club. His buddies were assembled at their customary rear booth taking turns in the restroom where they sampled the evidence acquired by O'Sullivan's last buy. Without hesitation, the good officer of the law took his turn and inhaled a line. Afterwards he felt relaxed among his friends who sympathized over his plight. Two hours later O'Sullivan left the Troubadour and drove to St. Anslem's where he decided to set up a one man stakeout of the hospital's cafeteria. There was very little to see in the cafeteria. The lunch hour traffic was long past. Over the next four hours O'Sullivan watched mainly hospital employees on afternoon coffee break. The conversations that he overheard were of no significance. The cafeteria staff stared at him from time to time but left him alone since it wasn't unusual for someone waiting on word about a relative or friend to spend hours drinking coffee.

At five in the afternoon, Officer O'Sullivan left the hospital cafeteria and returned to the department where he filed another "no contact" report. Then he left the building and walked into the mall where he found a bank of pay phones. Carefully he deposited a dime and called a frequented number. Eddie's special clerk answered and took the order to be delivered at the Troubadour that evening at nine.

The news of Susan's return to the Waltham pad got around fast. Louise's aunt called Louise to complain about Susan's abrupt departure and being stiffed on the balance of the week's rent. Louise called Susan to verify the return. Susan gave Louise the details of her conversation with Eddie which was more than she ever intended to tell Jay. Louise called Brian and gave him the whole story adding that she thought Brian's boss was a masterful son of a bitch and that Jay was in the loony bin at St. Anslem's.

Brian was relieved to hear that the Marquart family was back to normal. Otherwise, he made no comment other than to inform Louise that he had several deliveries to make that evening and the last was a scheduled drop at nine o'clock downtown. He expected to be home after ten.

The Jay Marquart incidents had Dr. Sutton fully energized. He and Markley left the psychiatrist attending to Jay and marched into Dr. Anderson's office. Anderson, typically, flew off the handle when he heard the account. The three then barged unannounced into Dr. Folley's office. Folley, as expected, claimed the whole thing was the fault of the administration's cockeyed telephone system. Then the four moved expeditiously to Joe Durant's office. Durant had been informed by his executive assistant of the call she had referred to Dr. Sutton. He was contemplating his next move when the four charged into his office.

Folley took change of the impromptu meeting. He began by degrading the hospital's administration in general and then concluded with a sizzling blast at Joe. He emphasized the importance of transferring the leadership of the hospital immediately to the Archdiocesan Office for Health Affairs and Michael Logan.

When Folley paused long enough to take a breath, Dr. Sutton cut into the Great One's monologue. "Richard, you might want to rethink the idea of bringing the Archdiocese into this too soon. The patient's lawyer and Sister is pretty sharp and would realize that the Archdiocese has deep pockets. You know that we are separately incorporated from the Archdiocese in order to create a corporate veil so the Archdiocese and the Church don't get sued. Now if we let it be known or act like the Archdiocese was in anyway responsible for the screw up this weekend then the plaintiff will no doubt have cause to name the Cardinal and the Archdiocese in any litigation that might result. Bob Markley told me that all the procedure changes were ordered by your central office. I think we want to make that known."

Folley stared at Markley who was staring at the floor with a simple slight smile on his face. Failing to get eye contact with Markley, Folley glanced at Anderson who stared back.

Now Folley had his mark. "Ron, this is your program. I'll expect you to clean up this mess."

Dr. Anderson was not amused. "Dr. Folley, at your direction we transferred the SACAP to your command two days before this latest incident. You took me along for several reasons that convinced me that we were doing the right thing. Now we have a problem and you think you can dodge the accountability by dumping the matter back on the hospital. I doubt that the facts once revealed in court will support your position. It seems to me that the hospital is primary but I don't think the Archdiocese can escape the issue. We had better get the Cardinal's office informed as well as the hospital's Board of Directors. This could make big headlines. Cardinal bashing is in season."

Up to this point everyone had been standing around Durant's desk. When Dr. Sutton indicated he had an approach to the issue, Dr. Folley invited everyone to sit down at Joe's conference table. Then he ordered Durant to provide notepads. When the meeting seemed to be in order, Dr. Folley asked Dr. Sutton to proceed with his suggestion.

Dr. Sutton rocked back onto the rear legs of his chair and placed his thumbs in his belt. He purposely took the appearance of being in charge from this point forward. "Let's begin with the issues that need resolution," began a confident Sutton. "The first is the apparent breech of patient confidentiality caused by improper telephone conduct or improper conduct by a nurse. Some person is responsible for the issue and that person seems to be the nurse who gained access to confidential information by whatever means and used it improperly. If the hospital addresses that issue and resolves it, we tend to resolve the patient's issue at the same time. So far we have advised the nurse about disciplinary review but we have not moved on the matter. I suggest we have a disciplinary hearing as soon as possible. Joe, if you agree I can have the nursing office start the process today. What do you say?"

Sutton's clever tactic of throwing the question to the hospital's Chief Executive did not go unnoticed. Now the direction was back in the hospital and away from the grand Director of the Archdiocesan Office for Health. It again became a hospital matter. Folley realized that he needed to be content with the direction.

Durant sensed his reinstatement as the decision maker. "I urge that the disciplinary hearing be expedited, Dr. Sutton, but how will you deal with the problem of the patient now being in Psych. Doesn't the patient have to be involved in the hearing?"

"Not really, Joe." Sutton maintained his authority as he explained. "We have all the information necessary to proceed including the patient's statements made to Bob. Remember the Quality Assurance Committee referred the matter to me and directed that we have the disciplinary herring. That can be incorporated into our review. The patient doesn't have to be involved unless we dismiss the complaint. Then we have to inform the patient who can seek legal recourse."

Durant sat in silence and watched Dr. Folley break into a cold sweat. The Great One was in a thick gooey jam. Now the room was silent as Folley pondered the issue. After a long pause he took a very humble posture. "Tell me, Dr. Sutton, has the patient or the patient's attorney made any comment that suggests litigation is imminent?"

Up to this point everyone had been standing around Durant's desk. When Dr. Sutton indicated he had an approach to the issue, Dr. Folley invited everyone to sit down at Joe's conference table. Then he ordered Durant to provide notepads. When the meeting seemed to be in order, Dr. Folley asked Dr. Sutton to proceed with his suggestion. Dr. Sutton rocked back onto the rear legs of his chair and placed his thumbs in his belt. He purposely took the appearance of being in charge from this point forward.

Anderson shook his head as if to give a negative reaction. Sutton saw the body language and paused to let him speak.

Anderson was prone to challenge Sutton. "Dr. Sutton, the way you propose this seems to suggest that the hearing is a kangaroo court. We seem to be intent on deciding that the nurse did violate patient confidentiality. If we decide that we also have to report her to the State Board who could pull her license. That's pretty severe."

Dr. Sutton did not blink at Anderson's challenge. "You're right, Dr. Anderson. I'm convinced that the nurse is guilty. If we come to any other conclusion, I believe that we will be subject to a law suit that we will lose. The nurse is the problem and the hospital cannot afford to take the blame. We have to sacrifice the nurse."

Anderson accepted Sutton's point but expressed another reservation. "I accept the fact that the nurse violated hospital policy and for that matter the terms of her license. This matter becomes public information once it is reported to the State. We cannot escape that. That's why I believe we need to inform the Board or at least the Executive Committee. Richard, I guess you have to decide what to tell the Chancery. That brings me back to the latest incident. How do we resolve that?"

Sutton again seemed to be in command. "The attorney didn't specify the grievances. In order to adequately set our defense we need to respond to those matters that we recognize as real. We know that Mr. Marquart's admission process was bungled but that in itself doesn't cause malpractice. It only gives basis for a complaint. So far, I believe that the patient is being properly cared for and has no legal grievance. We need to be sure that nothing happens to cause any malpractice allegation. Eventually we can apologize for the actions that caused a complaint. The patient will have no recourse beyond that if the care provided was appropriate. I suggest that Bob be assigned to work with Psychiatry as a member of the care giving team for Mr. Marquart. He knows the patient from the psychological standpoint and can assist Psychiatry is avoiding anything that might cause litigation."

Bob Markley had been a silent participant in the meeting. He rather enjoyed the exchange between the giants of the medical profession. His contentment and near slumber was interrupted when he heard his name mentioned. He awoke to see everyone looking at him for a reaction to Dr. Sutton's suggestion. Actually, he had only heard his name and was not sure in what context. Blandly, he replied, "I agree. I'll do it."

Jay Marquart's first few days back in hospital captivity were generally uneventful. At least that's what his medical record indicated. Jay had little understanding of what was being done for or to him. His severe depression and intoxicated state combined caused his medical handlers to keep him sedated as he worked himself back to sobriety and then to consciousness. It was almost two days after admission that he began to have some sense of his surroundings. Then he gradually began to feel the severe sense of loss associated with the incident involving Susan and Benny. His recall of that situation was carefully analyzed and recorded. The Psychiatric staff monitored his emotions and they encouraged him to talk about the night and events leading up to his crash. Medication was used to prevent him from becoming depressed. His physical state was also being carefully evaluated by consultants from the Department of Medicine. He willingly accepted the care provided without challenge.

On the fourth day his sense of humor returned and with it his usual personality trait of criticizing authority. Some anger was also evident as he complained about the food, other patients, and absence of television in his room. Jay seemed to be returning to his former state of near rationality. He asked for permission to call his sister and his boss. He mentioned his friend Brian. Then he wondered out loud about Susan and immediately began to cry.

The sudden depression caused his physician to talk to Jay about her and to inform him for the first time about Martha's call and Susan's return home. The physician encouraged Jay to call home first and talk to Susan. It was the boost Jay needed to counter depression without the need for medication. It worked. After his telephone conversation with his wife Jay was a new man or at least the man that he used to be. Susan and the kids, including Kristie, came to visit him that same day.

Jay was out of the woods but his cure was uncertain. His physicians were concerned about his habitual use of drugs. They were determined to discover which characteristic was primary and to design his therapy specific to the principal problem. The organic treatment of his disease seemed to be the most complex. Special drugs had to be carefully selected to avoid a physical reaction that would trigger his substance dependency. Meanwhile, the non-organic form of therapy involving Jay's functioning by psychological means, such as psychotherapy and by altering the social environment was being pieced together by careful review of the patient's habits and social activity.

Essentially, the Psychiatric Unit was continuing the process of the SACAP Unit but with a greater depth analysis of the potential psychiatric disorder apparent within the dependency on substances. The Psychiatric service welcomed Bob Markley to the team working on Jay's non-organic therapy. They were in desperate need of someone who knew and understood Jay's personality traits. Markley volunteered that he could understand exactly where Jay was coming from and where he was apt to go.

It was Friday, Jay's second-favorite day and six days after his admission that Bob Markley paid his first visit to Jay in the Psychiatric Unit. Jay seemed upset with his therapists, friend and fellow drunk. They sparred in jest and anger as they renewed an acquaintance short and lost.

Markley stayed focused on reconciliation. "Jay, old Buddy, I'm pleased to report that I'm back on your case both figuratively and literally. You got to love that."

Jay tried to act disinterested. "Well, the first thing you can do for me is drop that old buddy shit. Where were you when I needed you? Hell, I had to drag myself in here—drunker than a lord—and get my ass hauled into this nut farm. Big help you are. You want to help? Get me outta here. Why can't we go back to the drunk floor where we belong? These people up here are all messed up. They can't decide if I'm a crazy that got drunk or a drunk that got crazy. You got any ideas about that?"

Markley recognized Jay's attitude as a return to his normal aggressive state. "No. But I do know that you are a drunk. That's for sure. It takes one to know one. We work together, now—Psychiatry and Medicine—in combination to cure disease. That's modem consolidation in the corporate form. Two for the price of one. You are getting a good deal. We can't go back to the old Unit because the old Unit is gone. I mean out. The program is operated by the Archdiocese as one of their central office things. I'm still with the hospital probably until we complete the transition. After that I don't know where I'm gonna go."

"I know where you'll go. You'll go a little nuts like me and end up in one of these rubber rooms. This place sucks. You know what the bastards did? They towed my Jeep. Yeah, they towed the damn thing to the tow truck garage and then wanted to charge my wife a hundred and fifty bucks when she went to claim it. We haven't got a hundred and fifty so she left the thing there until I can come up with the money. Every day they add another twenty. Man, this place really sucks. I been off work for over a week. My sick leave is shot and my vacation is gone. I missed last month's mortgage payment. Shit."

Jay's anger was building. Markley was concerned that his presence was contributing to Jay's potential depression. "Jay, why did they tow your car? Where was it? Give me some facts and maybe I can square this. Okay?"

"Man, I don't know where it was. I must have driven it to the hospital because there was no other way I could have gotten here. I just don't know where I put the thing. Hell, I might have parked it in Mr. Durant's office. If you can help get it back at no charge I sure would appreciate it."

This was the opening that Markley was looking for. If he could liberate Jay's car he would regain Jay's confidence. "Jay, let me check this out and get back to you. I'll drop by later with the word. Get some rest."

The first visit was brief and not very clinical but it had its effect. Markley had gained an opportunity to reinstate himself in Jay's confidence. That same confidence he had when Jay agreed to attend support group sessions after his first admission into the SACAP. Marquart had forgotten about his assignment to compromise Jay's litigious attitude. That would be a side benefit to rebuilding the patient's determination to stay healthy.

Markley returned to his old desk in the SACAP and placed a quick call to the hospital's Security Office. They acknowledged that last week they had a Jeep towed from the Ambulance parking area. They had not checked to see if the vehicle belonged to an inpatient. The hospital regulations stated very clearly that any vehicle improperly parked for over four hours and in a manner that disrupted patient care would be towed at the owner's expense. Exceptions could only be approved by the hospital President. End of conversation. The only recourse was to persuade the president to have the car brought back to the hospital parking lot without charge. It seemed a simple task in view of the circumstances.

Simplicity is not a part of bureaucratic vocabulary. President Durant was not available to deal with Markley's request. The Executive Assistant suggested that the matter be referred to the Vice President for Finance who had the policy established in order to set internal control on parking revenue. Rod Weaver was not sympathetic so Markley called Dr. Sutton for assistance. Sutton bucked the request to the hospital's Risk Manager who felt that any deviation from hospital policy was detrimental to the hospital's position of maintaining standard procedure in dealing with Mr. Marquart. He strongly advised against freeing Jay's Jeep. The fact that returning the Jeep had clinical merit for the patient was not accepted by either Dr. Anderson or Dr. Folley. Both men suggested that Markley forget his promise to Jay and concentrate on getting the patient out and away from St. Anslem's.

Markley believed that Jay needed to believe in his caregivers and returning the car would establish that belief. Therefore, Bob Markley, Chief Counselor and Drunk, resorted to his own initiative. The towing company that the hospital used was located on Cambridge Street less than a mile away. First, Markley called the office at the towing company and identified himself as a member of St. Anslem's administration. He explained that the Jeep in question had been towed by mistake and should be returned. The garage owner was understanding but explained that he could not return the car since money was due to him. In fact, he was considering putting a lien on the vehicle. After a lengthily discussion Markley agreed to pay the seventy-five-dollar towing charge and the garage agreed to forget the daily parking fee if the money was paid and the car was picked up today.

Bob made a quick stop at the lobby ATM and liberated seventy-five dollars from his nearly depleted checking account. Then he popped up to Psychiatry and got the keys for the Jeep from Jay. Afterwards, he did a quick step down Cambridge Street to the Garage and paid the towing charge, got a receipt marked paid in full and drove Jay's car to Waltham. Susan was delighted to have the family car back and was pleased to meet Bob Markley. Then she loaded the kids into the small back seat and drove Markley back to the hospital.

As a last administrative act of the day, Chief Counselor Markley filled out an expense reimbursement request for seventy-five dollars of out of pocket expense for patient care items. He forwarded it to The Archdiocesan Office for Health Affairs where the man in charge, Michael Logan, stamped it approved. On his way home that night Markley thought about writing up his adventure and putting it into the TQM Suggestion Box that Mitch Daly had placed in the cafeteria.

The next morning a voicemail message was waiting for Bob Markley. It was Jay Marquart calling at about ten the previous evening. "Hey, Markley, my main man. Want you to know that Susan came to see me tonight. She drove here in the Jeep. Did my heart good to see her and to know that someone in this place really cares—you know, man, really cares."

Chapter Sixteen

Cecile O'Sullivan, RN, reported to the Office of the Vice President for Nursing Services precisely at nine A.M. as directed. She had been on duty for two hours taking care of critically ill medical patients. One person had died, the one with the highest probability of rapid recovery. Unexplained blood clots caused a sudden crash that was fatal. The code team tried their miracles but to no avail. Afterwards, there was the cleanup, the emotional restoration of staff, and more patients. The Medical Intensive Care Unit was a high-pressure area. O'Sullivan had seen it all and was a seasoned veteran. She could take pressure. However, the sudden call to leave her duty station and report to the top Nurse was enough to make her sweat.

The Vice President for Nursing was very direct. She sat erect in her starched whites and explained to the medical intensive care nurse, Mrs. O'-Sullivan, that she had been accused of violating patient confidentiality. The matter had been reviewed by the Nursing Ethics Committee who supported the allegations brought forward by the hospital's Quality Assurance Committee. The next step was a formal hearing that would finally decide the matter. The Hearing Committee would be comprised of the Vice President for Nursing, two Nursing Supervisors, Dr. Sutton, and a general duty staff nurse. Cecile was given a summary report of the allegations. The hearing was scheduled two days from now. She would be excused from duty with pay to prepare for the hearing if she would like. She could be represented by an attorney if she wanted. Otherwise, or in addition, representation from the St. Anslem's Bargaining Unit of the Massachusetts State Nurses Association, Local 350, was customary. The matter was reportable to the Massachusetts' State Licensing Board who, after reviewing the outcome of the hearing, would determine independently if Cecile's nursing license would be temporarily or permanently suspended. The Nursing Vice President finished the explanation and seemed to be waiting for Cecile's reaction.

Cecile, as tough as she was, broke under the pressure of criticism. She sat on the hard wood chair in front of the small scared desk in a hot, dingy executive office the size of two closets, barely able to breathe. The tears were uncontrollable. She could not speak—only sob—as the nurse executive with little compassion handed her a box of tissues.

After a few minutes, the strength of the professional returned and Cecile straightened herself in the chair. She had taken this first hit. More would follow at the hearing committee. She became determined to deal with the matter in a dignified manner and prove her ability as a nurse deserved consideration over the inconspicuous error. She was willing to admit making the mistake because of her motherly concern for the safety of her child.

Her attempt to give a preliminary explanation to the Vice President was rejected with a wave of the hand and she was excused. On her way out of the office the secretary informed her that her supervisor had been informed Cecile was excused from duty until further notice. She returned to her Unit and went directly to the nurses' locker room where she removed the MICU Blues and slipped into her street clothes. Then she did a makeup job to cover up the traces of her emotions. MICU nurses did this as a matter of routine. Carefully, she avoided eye contact with the other nurses who came and went. By now most of the staff had heard about the hearing committee via the hospital's super-efficient grapevine communication system. They were just as interested in avoiding Cecile. Few if any of them could say that they had not violated patient confidentiality in one way or another. They hadn't been caught and they didn't want to be near anyone who had. Prayerfully, Cecile wouldn't use any of them as examples in her defense.

The cafeteria was Cecile's next stop. She desperately needed a cup of coffee. The MICU nurses' lounge would have provided it free but the close association with staff and her duty station would have been over powering. Besides there was a good chance that her husband would be in the cafeteria on his official business. His counsel could be invaluable. The matter of using a lawyer and the Union in her defense needed Officer O'Sullivan's expertise.

As she entered the cafeteria she saw her faithful hubby intently studying the ceiling from his perch at a comer table. Cecile made a rapid pass through the coffee line and slid in the chair next to him.

Michael O'Sullivan was a trained observer. His wife's red eyes, sad face, and civilian dress immediately caused him to conclude that she was not on a scheduled coffee break and that something was possibly wrong. As she sat down, he took her hand and then gently gave her a loving kiss on the cheek. His compassion brought back the tears that she had tried so hard to control. Now O'Sullivan was certain that Cecile had a problem. His love for her had grown as their marriage matured. Even though he ventured into an alternate lifestyle from time to time he held his wife in high regard and freely admitted his love for her. To see her in distress caused him to become her protector. In his mind she could do no wrong. He continued to hold her hand as she explained about the hearing committee and the charges that if proven could end her professional career. He became angry at the apparent injustice of the event. He decided that he would use his influence to deflect the imposition of shame on his loving wife, dedicated mother, and nurse.

After Cecile had completed her description of the morning's events and circumstances, they sat in silence. Officer O'Sullivan began working out a plan in his mind that he concluded would resolve the matter in his wife's favor although it had the possibility of ending his career as a policeman. In truth O'Sullivan had been contemplating his resignation from the Police Department since he had been chewed out by his boss for not cracking the narcotic supply system. Cecile's circumstances justified radical action on his part to save her reputation. Without explaining his ideas to her, he suggested that she go home and try to rest. He also persuaded her to not call her attorney at this time. Perhaps the lawyer could be useful latter. For now it would be best if she allowed her husband to try to use another route to bring this matter to a mutual satisfactory conclusion. Cecile finished her coffee, said goodbye, and left.

O'Sullivan was energized. The anger that he first felt when Cecile told him about her situation was now replaced with a strong emotion to charge into the fray. He wanted to get involved. He wanted to do something other than sit in the hospital cafeteria looking for a suspect that had disappeared. Now that suspect held the key to solving his wife's problem and saving her career. There was nothing more important. The damn drug bust was insignificant. O'Sullivan was ready to compromise his own career to preserve his wife's reputation. Moved by his love for her he slid out of his chair and walked toward Tommy the Tout.

Tommy the Tout was nearing the end of his morning stand. He usually arrived at the hospital around six-thirty every morning except Sunday and stayed at his usual table in the cafeteria until nine-thirty. The three hours seemed to adequately cover the night shift going off duty and the day shift coming on. Then he returned for dinner in the evening around five-thirty and stayed until six-thirty so the afternoon people could also place a wager. Tommy was a very accommodating bookie. However, on this particular day he had stayed an extra half-hour to wait for the residents to finish grand rounds. Residents were rabid players who made notoriously bad choices. Tommy loved to accommodate them. Now he was wondering if he had overplayed his stay as he saw Officer Michael O'Sullivan walking toward him. Without hesitation or the time of day O'Sullivan sat down in the Customer's chair next to Tommy.

O'Sullivan didn't hesitate to get to the point. "Tommy, I guess I can call you that. Everybody seems to know you as Tommy. I need to find Jay Marquart. You seem to know what goes on around here. Where is he and how soon can I see him?"

The approach was not what Tommy had expected. He had expected the hard-nosed cop to flash a badge and arrest him for bookmaking. The days that O'Sullivan had been sitting in the cafeteria were in Tommy's mind a stakeout of his operation by the cop. Now he thought the time had come for the pinch. Instead he was being asked for information about a customer. It was the code of his profession never to reveal personal information about a customer especially if that information could lead to a customer's arrest.

Tommy was torn between protecting Jay and or protecting himself. He decided to explore the situation without giving any direct answers. "Sir, I really don't know who you are and I don't know who Jay Marquart is. If you want information about the hospital or anybody in it I suggest that you inquire at the desk in the lobby. They are very nice and will tell you what they can."

O'Sullivan became irritated. "Cut the bullshit, bookie. You know I'm a cop and you know that I can bust your ass anytime I want to." O'Sullivan grabbed Tommy by the shirt and pulled him into his face. "Right now I got other things to do. You take Jay's action like you take everybody else around here. I figure he owes you or you owe him so you know where he is. You get the message to him that we need to talk. I'll be back tonight and he better be here or your little concession stand goes down. You understand?"

O'Sullivan kicked back his chair loud enough to draw attention. When he was sure he had Tommy's attention and the attention of everyone around him he abruptly walked away leaving Tommy as the focus of stares. O'Sullivan had played the tough cop just as it had been described in the manual. Only in this instance he was not sure what he was doing. He was guessing that Jay had placed a bet with Tommy. He was guessing that Tommy knew where Jay was. If this long shot didn't pan out O'Sullivan had no choice but to arrest Tommy and draw the wrath of his colleagues in the precinct. His backup plan was to nab Brian tonight at the Troubadour Club when he made a delivery. It was a good chance that Brian knew where Jay was hiding. The obvious downside is that the action would sever his own supply of nose candy and create extreme animosity among his friends. Nevertheless, he was willing to do what he had to do in order to protect his wife who he suddenly discovered he really loved. Life had turned into a real bitch.

Tommy was taken back by the exchange with O'Sullivan. Many times in his long career he had been the target of a shake down by the local constabulary. This was new. Not so much in the approach but in the person. The cop asking for the action was a Narc who was generally disliked and not considered too swift. The word was out that O'Sullivan was going to be bounced for non-performance and some said he was hooked on dope. Uncertain about what was happening, Tommy decided get in touch with Jay and let things happen from there. Jay could decide if he wanted to talk with O'Sullivan. Tommy was just the messenger.

Within the hospital and among the staff there is little that is not known. Patient information is held in confidence only if the staff doesn't talk about it. Otherwise, everybody knows about everybody else. The records are circulated throughout the hospital, used for training, analyzed by coders and billing clerks, sent to insurance companies, and scrutinized by patient advocates, pastoral associates, nurse clinicians, dietitians, and quality assurance specialists to name just a few. If everybody keeps their mouth shut then the record remains confidential.

Tommy knew Jay was a patient in Psych. He had picked up the information from two Psych residents who were discussing Jay's diagnosis as they were looking at the point spread on the National League line. One had used Mr.

Marquart's name inadvertently but Tommy had heard it all. He and everyone else in the hospital knew that Jay Marquart was in Psych—not that they really cared. The Psych Unit was usually full so there were a lot of people to talk about if that was what you wanted to do. Generally no one wanted to discuss patient information—except O'Sullivan. If O'Sullivan had asked his wife he might have found it out—then again, he might not.

Tommy took a few extra minutes to write a note to his Doctor Psych Resident customer. He placed it an envelope with the doctor's name written on it and sealed it. Then he gave it to the cashier who he knew would be on duty when the good doctor arrived for lunch. The cashier had assisted Tommy for years in passing messages, results, and dunning notices. Tommy always saw that she had a Merry Christmas.

The doctor picked up his message at noon. It asked that he arrange for Jay to have cafeteria privileges this evening in order to handle a personal matter. The envelope also contained a sealed note for Jay. In other words, Tommy wanted to collect. The physician returned to the Unit and wrote the order as Tommy had requested. Then he visited Jay, delivered the note, and told him about the request from Tommy.

Jay had been making excellent clinical progress over the past several days. His condition was stable. Privileges to visit the chapel, cafeteria, and recreation lounge had been agreed to by staff that morning so the resident's order was not out of line. Actually, the staff was pleased to learn that Jay would have the benefit of companionship when he ventured off the unit for the first time since his admission. They reasoned that Tommy would be good therapy for Jay.

Jay waited until the resident had left before he opened the envelope. Inside were two five dollar bills and a note from Tommy. The money was the return on the bet Jay had made last week. The note explained that the Red Sox paid two to one. It also briefly explained that O'Sullivan wanted to talk to him this evening in the cafeteria. The final line boosted Jay's morale. It simply stated, "No sweat—if we want him we got him."

Jay left the unit promptly at five-thirty. He was dressed in slacks and shirt and except for his patient identification bracelet would hardly be recognized as a patient. The only money he had was the ten dollars from Tommy. He planned to give half of it to Susan when she visited him that night. He would use some of it to buy a sandwich and a soft drink and maybe a pack of cigarettes if he could stretch it that far. He noticed that signs posted in the corridors and elevators announced that St. Anslem's Hospital was a recycling hospital under a waste management program conducted by Action Waste Management. Recycling containers for paper, plastic and glass were prominently placed in the elevator lobbies and corridors. Jay's program was being implemented. He felt the sting of pride.

As he entered the cafeteria, Jay spotted Tommy at his usual table. Tommy saw Jay at the same time and waved Jay's attention to a corner table where O'-Sullivan sat waiting. Jay nodded at Tommy and walked to O'Sullivan. O'Sullivan saw Jay coming to the table and kicked a chair away from the table as a form of greeting.

Jay acknowledge by pulling the chair to the opposite side of the table and sitting down. Then he spoke. "You wanted to see me? What about?"

O'Sullivan leaned back in the chair and waved. "Yeah. We need to talk about a few things. Kristie is what I think you would have first in mind. You ain't been around to pick her up lately."

Jay sat across from O'Sullivan. He sensed immediate anger when the cop mentioned Kristie. He became defensive. "I been sick. I'll probably have her this coming weekend. She's no business of yours. This is between Cecile and me."

"Well, everything is sort of mixed up right now so suddenly Kristie gets caught up in it all. You understand?" O'Sullivan decided to play the good cop.

This is not the type of conversation that the doctors would have prescribed for Jay. With no small amount of irritation Jay fired back. "What I understand is that I got a legal right to my kid. We got joint custody. If you think you can change that because of my illness then you got a big ass fight on your hands, bro. I ain't gonna take any shit from you or Cecile. I'm protected by law."

O'Sullivan tried to smooth Jay's anger. "Look, I didn't ask to see you because I was looking for a fight. In fact, I want to make a little deal. We both want something and I think I can see an opportunity for both of us. You want to listen or do I just go ahead and bust you for being a user. Then you can have your sister explain it to the court one more time. Only this time I'll bet the hanging judge would see it different. You and Kristie are finished. I mean done, man. You want to talk?"

Jay sat silently and contemplated a response. He felt certain that O'Sullivan had never seen him use cocaine. All O'Sullivan had was hearsay from Cecile and possibly Brian. On the other hand, Jay had heard from Tommy that O'Sullivan was possibly a user. Tommy's note said, "If we want him, we got him." Jay decided to play trump.

"O'Sullivan, that user thing is a dangerous accusation. You got to have proof to make that stick. I would never say that about you unless I actually saw you take the stuff or knew somebody that saw you who would testify. That would be a tough rap for a cop to handle. You know, all that scandal would pass on to Cecile. Hell, she could get canned over that. Might even lose her license if the hospital figures she was involved in anyway. Shit, man, you got to watch what you say about people. Some things are better left unsaid. You following my drift?"

"How come you in this joint, Jay?" O'Sullivan tried to counter. "You got a bad case of sniffles, maybe? We can always discuss the user thing. Let's get back to Kristie. How would you like it if I arranged for Cecile to forget about kicking you out of joint custody? You can share Kristie as long as Kristie goes along with the deal. Someday the kid is gonna grow up and make up her own mind. How does that sound? You got to realize that Kristie loves her mother as much as she loves you. You harm her mother in any way and Kristie is gonna hate your guts for the rest of her life. That's how you'll lose her, my man. You mess with Cecil and you're messing with Kristie."

Jay tensed. "Who's messing with who, man? I didn't start this march to justice. Good old Cecile drug my ass to court and tried to get the judge to take Kristie away from me. You think Kristie wanted me out. No way. Cecile was out to nail my ass pure and simple. I think I owe her for that."

O'Sullivan smiled. He had Jay just about focused. "That's just the point, Jay. You two are fighting over the kid but the kid doesn't want you to fight. Think about it. Suppose you two declared peace on one another instead of war. It makes more sense that way. Everybody lives happily ever after."

"It takes two, man. Peace is a fragile thing. How do you put something like that together so it holds?"

Jay attempted to look disinterested by glancing out of the window.

"You create a bond, a partnership that has a lot to lose if either one messes up. Here it is. You are associated with drug users and suspected dealers." O'-Sullivan leaned forward, got well into Jay's face, and began to whisper. "I got just enough evidence to convince the court that you are not a suitable parent. You, on the other hand, have some information that implicates me with drug traffic. Cecile, in a different arena, is about to lose her nursing license and career. That's something that means a lot to her and is paramount to her life with Kristie. You have the power to preserve that. You help Cecile. I help you.

You help me. We go on the line for each other and Kristie has a happy life free of parental strife. How's it sound?"

Jay was almost thinking out loud. He wanted to understand what was being offered. "So the deal is that we stop pissing on each other. If one starts then the other blows the whistle so everybody goes down. It sounds like a suicide club."

"Look, we all have addictions." O'Sullivan leaned forward, put his arms on the table and continued to whisper. "Some are obvious and some are not. Yours and mine are very visible. Cecile is addicted to her work and nursing. Without that RN after her name she would be completely destroyed. We got to care for her, man. We have to take care of Cecile because I love her and you love Kristie. I'm begging you, man. If we bond ourselves we form a triangle that is strong. If one side gives way then everything collapses."

It sounded like something that made sense but Jay was being cautious. "That's some triangle—a junkie, a fag, and a nurse. You got to hand me more than a sermon. Cecile has to buy into this before I go along. If you can deliver her then I'm in. What do you want me to do?"

This was the moment O'Sullivan had worked for. Jay was ready to deal. He fired the last shot. "You get the hospital to back off this charge against Cecile on violating patient confidentiality. You can do it because you're the patient. Just tell them it ain't so."

Dr. Anderson was worried about the public relations impact of the impending hearing involving Nurse O'Sullivan. He knew that it could not be avoided but he wondered if it could be handled with less ceremony and dispensed quietly. His appeal to Dr. Sutton fell on deaf ears. Sutton was a stricter on process. Any deviation from due process was certainly subject to litigation. Litigation was the issue to be avoided. Therefore, the hearing process must follow defined steps clearly outlined in the hospital's procedure manual as prepared by the hospital's attorney.

Anderson knew that the hospital trustees authorized policy. That being the case they could also exempt policy. It seemed to him that the matter should be brought to the Board before the hearing in order for the Board to decide if and how the hearing should be conducted. With that in mind he hounded Joe Durant to call an emergency session of the Executive Committee of the Board of Trustees.

Joe was sympathetic to Anderson but for a different reason. He felt that the session was an opportunity to subject the great Folley to some criticism for his lack of attention to the quality of services in the SACAP. Folley liked the idea of an Executive Committee session because it gave him the opportunity to further embarrass Durant for the purchase of the stupid telephone system.

The only remaining opponent to calling a meeting of the Board Executive Committee was Dr. Sutton who finally agreed when Durant used Rod Weaver's expertise to explain that potential litigation of this magnitude could result in a qualified audit opinion. Sutton had no idea what a qualified audit opinion meant but since it sounded severe he went along with the request for a special meeting of the Executive Committee.

The Executive Committee of the Board consisted of Kevin Hardly, Thomas O'Shea, and Charles Patello—otherwise known as the terrific trinity. Bishop Hanks was an ex-officio member as was Joe Durant. All consented to attend a seven AM meeting the next morning to review the pending crisis involving Nurse O'Sullivan. Doctors Folley, Anderson, and Sutton were also scheduled to attend. Anderson also felt that Bob Markley should be present since he was witness to the alleged violation of patient confidentiality.

Joe Durant objected to Markley's attendance but Anderson invited him anyway and advised Durant that Markley was attending with or without his consent. Durant decided not to argue the point and simply moved the meeting from his office to the Hardly Board Room. He also ordered the usual style of Hardly breakfast to be served as a buffet without servers being present.

Bob Markley was uneasy about attending the Executive Committee meeting. He disliked the formality of such sessions and he especially disliked the plush extravagant surroundings of the Hardly Board Room. Being in the presence of such obnoxious splendor caused him to become cynical and very outspoken if not insulting. The terrific trinity were known to him only by reputation and he held a general dislike for them—a dislike that he tried to overcome with prayer for tolerance and reconciliation to God's mercy.

Markley prepared for the meeting by reviewing Jay's SACAP medical record coupled with a review of his current admission. If he was asked to say anything at the Executive Committee meeting, he intended to limit his remarks to pure objective fact. His preparation caused him to work overtime which was not unusual. He was sitting at the nurses Station in the Psychiatric Unit studying Jay's clinical notes for the day when Jay returned to the Unit following his meeting with Officer O'Sullivan. Markley was deeply involved reading the clinical summary that recommended discharge with continuing outpatient therapy when he heard Jay's voice.

Jay announced his presence. "Markley, you just the man I wanted to see. You got a few minutes to talk?"

Markley looked into Jay's somber face and recognized the serious nature of the request. He slowly returned the chart to the rack on the center table and faced Jay. "Sure, Jay, I've always got time for you. That's what I get paid for. You want to go to your room or sit in the lounge?"

The patient lounge was always occupied by somebody. It was usually filled with cigarette smoke and loud noise from the television. Sometimes patients found it to their benefit to discuss matters there with counselors. Retreat to the confines of their room sometime signaled a relapse to a paranoid state. Jay knew the significance of Markley's question.

"Let's take a walk, Bob. I'm cleared off the Unit. How about your place downstairs? You still have an office or someplace where we can talk?"

Markley consented. "Sure, Jay. Let's go. It's not the same as you remember it but it will do, I suppose."

SACAP had been undergoing a change over the past weeks. The furniture had been removed from all but two of the patient rooms. The reception area was still furnished with cast off equipment from other hospital units. The desk was the same but there was only a single place for a receptionist where in the past there had been three or four people busy coordinating patient care. The clean clinical odor was replaced by the smell of mildew from stacks of records piled against the wall. No night shift personnel were present.

Markley had to turn on the lights and they entered. Jay noticed a fresh sign hanging outside the door that read, "Chemical Addiction Treatment Program of the Boston Catholic Archdiocese.—St. Anslem's Unit."

Jay waited while Markley found two folding chairs that he placed in the center of the reception area. Then the two men sat facing each other.

Markley was the first to speak. "Okay, Jay, what can I do for you?"

Jay turned his chair around and sat with his arms folded across the top rungs of the back. He looked at Markley with a strong resolve. There was no doubt that he was in control of his senses. "Bob, what would you do if you were asked to get somebody off the hook by being nice to them and in return you got what you always wanted? Do I make sense?"

"I'm not sure you are making sense, Jay. You say that you are being asked to be nice to someone who in turn will give you what you want. Sounds like a no-brainer to me. What's the problem? Being nice isn't that hard. You ought to give it a try."

"Well, it ain't that easy, man." Jay stood up and began to pace. "The person is my ex-wife, Cecile, or more like her ol' man who wants me to cop out on nailing Cecile on that confidentiality thing that I got her on. You see, if I cop out on that, O'Sullivan gets her to lay off taking me to court on the custody rap. O'Sullivan says that Cecile is gonna lose her license on account of me and that will screw up her life and Kristie's too. Man, I don't want to cause that. If we could ease out of this with no pain I got to go with it. What do you think, man? Who do I have to talk to so this thing gets buried? You the man?"

Markley was blown away at the thought of Jay's compromise. He sat back in his chair and tried to hide his own excitement as he attempted to answer. "No, I'm not the man. In fact, you might be too late. The Nursing Ethics Committee has already decided that O'Sullivan violated her nursing ethics and the matter is going to the hospital Hearing Committee sometime tomorrow. Once they decide, it is reported to the State License Board who will most likely pull her license. The hospital Executive Committee is going to be briefed on the situation tomorrow morning at seven. I'm not supposed to be telling anybody about this. Did Cecile put her husband up to this? How do you know that she will live up to her promise?"

Jay pointed his finger at Markley signaling that the question was right on. He then raised both arms as if to underscore the doubt. "Bob, right now I'm not sure of anything except that I love Kristie more than anybody or anything else. Cecile can fry in hell for all I care about her but if Kristie loves her mom then I'll fight like hell to see that her mom isn't harmed. Cecile might rat out but she'll offend Kristie. She'll lose that way—the same way that I'll lose. The courts haven't got a thing to say about it. It's between Cecile and me with Kristie getting hit from both sides. That's got to stop. So how do I stop it?"

It was certain that Jay wanted to protect Cecile. Markley knew that this was a very important change in Jay's attitude and that it had significant clinical importance. He felt obligated to help Jay. Carefully he began to explore Jay's new behavior. "Jay, this is the first time since I met you that you are motivated by love for someone rather than hate or anger. I'm with you, man, but you have to hustle to get this done in time. See if you can get Cecile and yourself outside of the Hardly Board Room tomorrow by seven. I'll do what I can to get you in the meeting. Then it's up to you. I haven't the slightest idea about what you have to say to those eagles. Personally, I don't think they are wrapped too tight individually or collectively. One other thing, don't mention that I put you up to this. Okay?"

Jay was energized. "Yeah, okay. Uh, I got a couple of questions—who's gonna be there and where's the Hardly Board Room?"

Bob pointed as he talked. "It's that big room with the mahogany double doors just down the hall from Joe Durant's office. Durant will be there with Drs. Folley, Anderson and Sutton. The Board members that will be there are Mr. Hardly, Mr. O'Shea and Mr. Patello. They have me coming to represent the issue since I was there when you did your crazo. I'm not sure if there will be anybody from nursing or a secretary. That's about it I think."

Jay's eyes lit up. He nodded in confidence. "I know most of those guys. Durant and me have talked several times. Sutton is really interested in the waste management deal and Patello and I go way back. I'm in with the CEO, a doctor, and a big cheese on the Board. This could be easy. We'll be there at seven."

Jay stood and shook Markley's hand. Markley was happy for Jay although he knew that the morning would be time of tension that could trigger another of Jay's temper tantrums if all did not go well. He held Jay's hand for a few seconds and then instinctively gave him a hug as he congratulated him on his new life based on love. Bob Markley felt the charisma of another lost soul found.

The hug was unexpected. Jay accepted it with some embarrassment. Still he felt the warmth of a friend who seemed to care for him. Markley was truly a friend with whom Jay could share his joys and sorrows. Markley could be counted on tomorrow. He was genuine.

Jay wasn't sure about O'Sullivan. The weird cop had offered a deal that Jay had accepted without any collateral. He told O'Sullivan to get Cecile lined up and he would see what he could do. Now he had it arranged. Or at least he had an opportunity to get it arranged if he could persuade the hospital Executive Committee to back off.

The missing piece was Cecile. Would she go along and be with him in the morning. On his way back to the Psych Unit, he stopped at a lobby pay phone and used one of his few remaining dimes to call the O'Sullivan residence. Officer Michael O'Sullivan was preparing to go to the Troubadour for the evening when he answered the phone. Jay was excited and babbled about how he could pull off the deal if Cecile would join him in the morning and if she was willing to do as O'Sullivan said she would.

O'Sullivan was flabbergasted. He had not mentioned his conversation with Jay to Cecile except to say that he was working out a deal with the hospital. She was very depressed and had cried constantly during the time that her husband had been home. Regardless, O'Sullivan knew that she would do most anything to save her professional status. He was at the moment uncertain if that included making a truce with her ex-husband over the custody of Kristie. O'Sullivan tried to stall while he thought things out.

"Look, Jay, you got me at the wrong time. I mean we haven't really talked this out yet. You know what I mean. So, I think, I mean I know we got a deal but I got to make sure that Cecile understands is all. Can I get back to you later? I'm on my way out. How about around midnight?"

Jay felt the familiar surge of anger. He had been schooled in the last few weeks about controlling his temper. This was the supreme test. He took the obligatory three deep breaths and responded. "Officer O'Sullivan, when we talked this afternoon I had the distinct impression that your lovely wife was completely aware of what you were proposing. Now you tell me that you have yet to mention it to her. In view of the fact that her fate is going to be decided in less than twelve hours from now it seems appropriate that you mention it to her immediately and gain her complete cooperation. In fact, I'll hold the phone while you talk. I won't be available at midnight. So get this matter cleared up right now. You dig?"

O'Sullivan got the point. Jay waited as he heard him call for Cecile. The receiver was muffled as the two talked. Jay could not make out anything that was being said.

After about five minutes Cecile answered the phone. "Jay, what are you up to? Michael says that you are talking to the CEO tomorrow and you want me there. Why?"

Frustration mounted and Jay's temper began to flare as he answered, "Cecile, your good husband suggested to me this afternoon that we could make peace over the custody issue and Kristie if I could some way get you off the hook on the confidentiality charge they got you on. So, I pulled a few strings and got us set up to meet with the bigwigs tomorrow at seven. Now if you don't want to do this just say so cause it ain't my ass that's on the line. I can sleep in and be just as happy."

"My, you are elegant, Jay. Just exactly what do you have in mind?" Cecile's tone of voice was compromised.

Jay felt reinforced as he attempted to explain. "Well, when your old man talked to me, we realized that Kristie was the focus of our anger so why not make her the focus of our love. You can love her and continue to be a nurse. I'll go my way and continue to love her too. We don't fight over her anymore and she has our combined love rather than court bullshit. What way do you think is best?"

Cecile got the drift but she was reluctant to trust Jay. "Jay, I can keep the matter out of court on custody but I won't let you put her in danger or subject her to a drunken existence. You know that."

It was clear to Jay that he had to be sincere in selling the proposal. Carefully he attempted to form an alliance with his response. "Cel, I've spent a lot of time lately coming to the same conclusion. You know that I got a problem, always had, and always will. Hell, I admit it. That's the point I'm trying to make here. Kristie is important to my recovery. Without her I'll be a no good drunken son of a bitch. And you, my dear, will be a former nurse looking for a job in a nursing home. We can work together to avoid this misery simply by declaring peace on one another, as the fella said."

Cecile let Jay know that she was buying in. "I'm worn out. I'll try anything to get this thing settled. If you think you can pull off a miracle with the hospital administrator I'll go along with what you want. But, Jay, don't cross me."

"Trust me. See you tomorrow at seven outside of Durant's office."

Jay hung up the phone and leaned against the wall. He suddenly felt very fatigued. The pressure was mounting. He was in the middle of the deal of his life and he was all alone—at least he felt alone. There were no lawyers, no doctors, or no bosses backing his play. This time he carried the ball. He had no idea what or how he would talk to the hospital leaders in the morning. He would just have to wing it.

Susan came into the hospital lobby and walked toward the elevators on her way to the Psych Unit for her daily visit when she spotted Jay next to the pay telephones. He was looking somber with his eyes fixed on his shoes. She approached him and kissed him lightly on the cheek. "Penny for your thoughts, honey. You look kinda sad for a fellow that just got his walking papers from this place. The doctors tell me that I can take you home tomorrow. Discharge order has been signed and everything. You ready to go?"

With all that had been happening Jay had overlooked the fact that his discharge was set for the next morning after a discharge conference that was scheduled for eight A.M. No Psych patient could be discharged until the final counseling session or discharge conference was conducted. Susan was to be involved in the counseling session as she had been for the past two weeks. The therapy was designed to involve them both as a team in assisting Jay to build mental stability and control his addiction. The joint counseling had strengthened their bond and had practically dissolved the effect of the violent episode.

The prospect of being back from the Board Room session by eight seemed remote creating more pressure on Jay's fragile mental condition. He rubbed his temples as he thought about the complications and attempted to explain them to Susan. "Oh, yeah, my dear, I'm ready to go. But we have a little conflict that I'm gonna need your help on. You see, I got to straighten out the leadership of this place tomorrow at seven so I could be a little late for our counseling session at eight. If I'm not there on time you got to stall them till I get there. I think I can make it by eight-thirty."

At first Susan thought Jay was having some kind of an allusion. "Jay, who are you meeting with and why?"

"The President, Chairman of the Board, and the Chairman of Medicine to name a few. We gonna talk about Cecile and how it is that she's gonna get her job back as a nurse. I'm the guy who's gonna save her ass. Then Cecile and I quit fighting over Kristie and everything's cool from then on. How's it sound?"

Now Susan was convinced that Jay was hallucinating, "Sounds like you think you're Napoleon. I'm not sure they will let you out of here if they hear you talking like this. I'll stall them as long as I can but I'm not going to try to explain where you are. They might try to put me away. Can we talk about us for a few minutes? I don't want to screw up tomorrow."

Susan had been counseled about how important she was in the conduct of Jay's recovery. She was recognized as the support for her husband and as the foundation for the love that was necessary to maintain his composure. She was expected to assist him in avoiding those occasions that led him to excess consumption of substances that created his manic-depressive state. She felt the pressure that was directed to her by the counselor and as a consequence felt no small amount of guilt over the events that led to Jay's violent behavior and his attempted attack on her.

Jay led her to a quiet comer of the hospital's spacious lobby where they sat on a comfortable couch away from the ears of other visitors. After they were seated he tried to calm her fears. "Hell, sure, you ain't gonna screw up. What's bugging you?"

Susan let it out. "Well, I know that you got to stop getting high and all that. And I understand why, 'cause it puts you down and you lose it and all that. I know that I got to help you but you know that I can't quit. I haven't got a problem with booze, pot or coke so you know that I'm gonna take a little now and then. If they ask me if I'm gonna quit, I'll lie to get you out of here but, Jay, you know that I ain't gonna quit. You know that I love you and I'll help you but I got to be honest with you, honey. This is scary!"

Jay put his arm around her and tried to be consoling. "Suse, we are in this thing together. You got to help me but I got to help you too. I've had mine. I'm messed up and now I'm getting fixed. You do what you gotta do. We'll get along. We just got to be there for each other when we hit a crisis. It's gonna happen for you just like it's gonna happen for me. We just got to live one day at a tıme. We'll make out. Let's have a little faith and see where it takes us. I'm the last guy to tell somebody that they got to get off the stuff. That's a decision you got to make when you are ready. Believe me, you'll know when. Sooner or later everybody quits. I love you no matter what. Okay?"

Jay was a qualified expert on matters of substance abuse. He realized that Susan had taken a few snorts before coming to see him. He silently prayed that she would be sober in the morning. Rather than mention it he held her hand while the tears that she was shedding slowly moved down her cheeks. Across the hospital lobby was the Chapel entrance. Jay stared at the entrance for a while and then took Susan by the hand and led her into the quiet Chapel. His intent was to get her out of the view of the public but once inside he found the dark quiet, peaceful place to have a calming influence. They sat for a long-time in silence.

After a while, he spoke to her. "It's nice in here, isn't it?"

Susan had stopped crying. She sat silently and looked around before she answered Jay. "Yeah. Quiet. Kind of restful."

Jay was satisfied that he had taken Susan's mind off the matter of her drug use. He decided to approach another subject that had been on his mind. "It's neat that they made it so easy to get into. Having the entrance in the lobby is a good idea. I mean anybody can come in. That's neat."

“Yeah, I guess.” Susan remained anxious.

Jay posed the question. “Susan, I been thinking. Maybe we should start going to Church. The kids might like it. They never been to Church. I used to go when I was a kid. Even went to Catholic school. What do you think?”

Susan was taken back by the suggestion. She really wanted none of it. “Oh, golly, Jay, I don’t know. It kinda scares me to get into the hocus-pocus thing. It’s nice and quiet here but it’s the same way in the library. We could take them to the library and they would benefit more don’t you think? God doesn’t care if we come here or not.”

Jay was shocked. “The library! That’s not the same as church.”

“Well, I can’t see the difference except for the preacher.” She offered, “We can go the library for nothing. The church wants money and we can’t afford it. Without money you wouldn’t be welcome in church. We don’t have any money. We just wouldn’t be welcome there, Jay. We wouldn’t be welcome.”

It was more than obvious that Susan wasn’t buying the church bit so Jay dropped the subject. In fact, he dropped the conversation. They sat in silence enjoying the ambiance for another hour. Jay fell asleep. He awoke when Susan gave him a kiss on the cheek and announced that she had to get home to the kids. Jay returned the kiss and walked her to the Jeep. Then he returned to the Psych Unit for his last night in captivity.

Charlie Patello drove swiftly but carefully trough the dark rain slick streets of downtown Boston. The rush hour traffic had almost cleared as he pulled into the avenue leading to the freeway. He intended to avoid the usual delays by heading west on Mass Ave and then out to Arlington where he was scheduled to meet with Phil Mondi, Mario Capizzi and Tony Marone at the Vista Motel. He had been scheduled into the meeting by Uncle Frank who let it be known that this was a very important meet. Frank had briefed Charlie on the situation with Patriot and the Boston PD. Indeed, this was a very important meet.

The earlier call from Joe Durant’s office requesting an emergency session of the St. Anslem’s executive committee was now secondary except the idea of being at the hospital by seven in the morning remained an irritation to Patello considering the prospect that the meeting with the New York executives could go into the early morning hours. He arrived at the Vista a half-hour after the scheduled time that dinner was to be served. Phil Mondi had just arrived a few minutes earlier so no time was lost. Mario and Tony had used the time to have a few extra drinks.

The men ate in the dining room. Dinner conversation was pleasant without any mention of business. After dinner, the four adjourned to Mario's modest room that he had registered under a false name. They immediately got down to business without small talk or diversion. Mario led the conversion. He began by recounting the changes taking place in the drug distribution system.

"I know that Frank has filled Charlie and Phil in so I won't go over all the details except to say that pressure from the Boston authorities requires us to make some changes in our organization and methods of doing business. Patriot Transportation has been sold to a holding company in Boston who will operate it as an affiliate of *Portland Courier* but will remain a separate corporation. Patriot stays in business with its regular line but the side operation with the distribution is all handled by Portland. Portland delivers to special customers in Boston through its affiliation with Patriot. Patriot has no idea what's being shipped into Boston. To keep it clean we will replace Patriot's management with new people. Maybe move a few of the longtime folks up the ladder. Make 'em feel good and ask fewer questions. That will create a buffer between the Portland and Boston operations. Phil goes to Portland as the new President of *Portland Courier*. That guy Eddie, who was the Patriot dispatcher and handled the special accounts, will do the logistical stuff between Portland and Boston. Is that about it, Phil?"

Phil Mondi seemed eager to comment. "Yeah, that's about it except for my wife who is in Portland now looking for a house and wondering if I've lost my mind. I just keep telling her business is business and this is just one hell of an opportunity that I couldn't pass up. She can't believe that it had to be done this fast. Oh, yeah, I should mention that my Vice President who handled all operations except the special accounts is now the general manager of Patriot although he doesn't know it yet. We are telling the troops about all of this tomorrow. Another thing is that Eddie wants a kid that he had helping him in the special accounts to move into the dispatcher's job. This gives Eddie a tie into the distribution without involving the general manager. Keeps it clean so to speak. Eddie also thinks that a friend of Brian's, a guy named Jay Marquart, could do occasional delivery since he and Brian are sort of wired together. Keeps it under control sort of. Also, Eddie claims he can control Marquart through Marquart's wife who is one of his customers. I don't know if I like that or not."

Patello was impressed with the amount of detail that had already been implemented. It was obvious that his fears of a long meeting were not to be realized. He had made up his mind that he would just listen and not comment until he heard Jay Marquart's name mentioned.

"Mario, from what Phil has mentioned it seems that the special accounts now belong to Portland but are being delivered in the blind so to speak by Patriot. That's good. It also seems like the use of his former dispatcher, Eddie I think, is a good idea for liaison as long as he doesn't have any contact with the Patriot GM. So that speaks well for having the kid, Brian, in the dispatcher spot. So far so good. Now the guy mentioned for delivery is known to me. I recommended him to Meehan for a spot at Action. He's been involved with us for some time although he doesn't know anything about the big picture. What I'm saying is that he is sharp enough to add it all up if he gets a deep enough insight. My thought is that we don't want people who are too bright. They either get honest or greedy. What say you, Phil?"

Mondi seemed ready to agree. "I got similar vibes, Charlie. Marquart is an unknown and the unknown bothers me. But he is just a delivery boy. He really doesn't know what's in the packages. He just drops 'em off and gets the receipt. Somebody else collects. He doesn't even handle any money. He might not even want the job if he's making good money with Action."

Mario listened to the exchange until he became bored with the discussion about a delivery boy. Then he asserted himself into the conversation between Phil and Charlie. "Gentlemen, I realize that we need to pay attention to detail but the matter of the delivery person can be well attended to by our liaison man and his dispatcher. It's really not anything that we need be concerned about. Let it happen the way they want it to happen. We have to be concerned about the bigger picture. In that regard we are going to take a dive on the import process in the next week or so. You will know nothing about it until it happens and then your information will be from what you read in the papers and see on television. My point is that the dive part is being handled by our Navy. We aren't involved. Okay?"

It was a rare occasion when the brain machine of National Associated Investors missed a significant detail in planning. This was one of those occasions. Neither Mario Capizzi nor Tony Marone associated Jay Marquart as the user who was leading Officer Michael O'Sullivan of the Boston Police Department Narcotic Division up a blind alley seemingly away from the import and distribution process of Big Frank Patello's lucrative narcotic concession in the Northeastern United States. Unaware of the possible crack in the NAI armor, Patello simply shrugged in agreement of Mario's comments. Mondi nodded. With that the meeting ended. The men left the room one at a time so not to be noticed. Charlie was home and in bed by ten in plenty of time to be well rested for his seven A.M. session at St. Anslem's.

Jay was up very early. The night shift was just beginning to prepare their report for the incoming staff and almost missed Jay's departure from the Unit. His request to the duty nurse to punch the button to release the lock on the outer door startled her. Gamely he answered her question about where he was going by claiming that he wanted to get an early breakfast in the cafeteria since the food for the Unit usually arrived at seven-thirty and he had a discharge conference at eight. This made sense to the nurse who noted his departure and opened the door. Jay waved her his thanks and made for the elevator and then into the cafeteria for a cup of coffee which was all he could afford. To his surprise, Tommy was already at his post doing business with the off-duty night personnel. It was only six-fifteen.

Tommy saw Jay pass through the line and to the cashier. As Jay approached Tommy gave a quick wave to the cashier who then advised Jay that the coffee was paid for and that Mr. Tommy would like to talk to him. This was accomplished by a prearranged signal that Tommy had worked out with his friend, the cashier, whenever he wanted to speak to a client about payment.

Jay was pleasantly surprised and moved quickly to Tommy's table. "Hey, Tommy, thanks for the coffee. Oh, yeah, and thanks for the ten bucks. Man, that's all I got being off work for the last couple weeks. How's it goin'?"

Tommy was his usual self. "Well, Jay, well. How's by you? You getting out of here soon? You got cafeteria privileges usually means that you're about to get sprung."

"You got that right, man. I'm out of here today. Just as soon as I deal with the head man on the matter with my ex, then I'm gone. I appreciate you putting me on to her old man. We worked something out if I can get it to stick this morning. Hey, what did you mean when you said, 'We got him if we want him'? You after his ass about something? He owe you money?"

"He don't owe me, Jay. I just don't like the guy. He ain't so popular with my friends across the street in the Precinct. They protect my business and I help them in any way I can. I learn a lot from my customers that I pass on to the detectives and some of the undercover guys. We work together. I get a lot of information about patients that nobody is supposed to have. It helps when some of these characters they bring in here get back on the street. I guess that's why I been in business here so long. The hospital hasn't got a clue about any of this. I understand that you are the man doing this trash bag thing for the hospital, that right?"

"Yeah." Jay nodded. "Well, I was but it's been moving along without me while I been in the loony unit. I'm not sure I still got a job. I'll find out today. Why?"

Tommy seemed evasive. "Can't tell you much 'cause I don't know. All I know is that my contact wants to know about the trash deal and I figure you could fill me in some and maybe pick up some patient info that I need now and then. What I can do is slip you some cash for your trouble. You can always use a little extra, right? You're just doing a little consulting on the side. Nobody gets hurt. What do you say?"

"Right, man," Jay bought in. "I can always use a little extra. If I can answer your questions I will but you got to understand that I need my job. Actions been good to me and I think it's a good company. There's nothing going on with them that I see. What do you want to know?"

"Right now, nothing. The man will be by today and let me know what he wants. You stop by when you get back to work. Put down a bet. We'll talk then. Good chatting with ya, Jay. Oh, by the way, if anybody asks, I never heard of ya. You understand?"

Tommy always protected the confidence of his customers. It was apparent that no one was to It was apparent that the meeting with Tommy was over. Another customer was waiting and within ear shot. It was time for Jay to move. He selected a table in the rear. His coffee was only warm as he gulped it down and then ran into the corridor toward the mahogany doors of the elaborate Hardly Boardroom.

"Good morning, Jay. Are they ready for us yet?"

Her appearance startled Jay. It was the first time he had seen Cecile in her dress whites. She was very impressive. Jay gave her an excited greeting. "Hi,

Cecile. Boy, I hardly recognized you. You look like you're ready for battle. Nobody's shown yet except us and the food people. You think they will let us eat with 'em?"

Cecile rolled her eyes at the suggestion. "Don't hold your breath. What exactly is this meeting? My official hearing is supposed to be this afternoon. This better mean something because I'm not prepared with any kind of defense."

Jay gave an affirmative nod as he started to explain. "You know Bob Markley? Well, he said that the bigwigs were meeting this morning to decide about the hearing. Decide what I don't know. Anyway, when I told him I wanted to get you off, he said this might be the chance to do it—if he can get us in."

Cecile had thought that the meeting was set. The "if" word destroyed any confidence she had in the event. "My God, Jay, you mean they don't even know we are here!"

Jay's answer was interrupted as Joe Durant arrived. He had never met Cecile. The presence of a nurse outside of the Boardroom caused him to pause. He looked as if he was about to speak to her when he noticed Jay Marquart by her side. He greeted Jay with a good morning, nodded to the nurse and entered the Board Room without further comment.

Instead of checking the breakfast fair as was his custom Durant sat at the table and placed his head in his hands pondering the significance of the two people in the corridor. His thinking was interrupted by the sudden arrival of Kevin Hardly. Hardly was upset by the absence of staff to prepare his favorite omelet and he let Durant know his dissatisfaction. Joe accepted his criticism and tactfully led him over to the buffet, handed him a plate and served him some scrambled eggs. From that point on Kevin moved through the line serving himself generous portions of everything available. From there he moved to his place at the head of the table and began to eat. Joe attempted to explain the agenda for this special session and warn Kevin of the subjects in the hall but Kevin wanted only to eat and relax in the comfortable surroundings. He asked Joe to let him alone.

Dr. Sutton arrived with Dr. Anderson and Dr. Folley. Bob Markley followed them in a rather meek fashion. It was obvious to Durant that they had a pre-meeting and he was fairly certain it centered on the presence of the two people in the hall. Sutton waved to Durant to join them at the opposite end of the long table away from Kevin Hardly who hadn't notice their arrival. Joe moved quickly to join them.

Durant pressed for information. "Okay, so what the hell is going on? What's Mr. Marquart doing here?"

Dr. Sutton was quick to reply to Durant. "Apparently he wants to speak to us about the incident. He asked Markley about this late last night. I think it would be a mistake to let him into an official meeting like this. His lawyer would tear us apart in court."

Dr. Anderson shook his head negatively. "I disagree with you. This is really not an official meeting. It's informational. Hell, we could say that it is a meeting that didn't happen. Let's listen to the guy. We can use whatever he has to say to our advantage as much as his lawyer can. I don't see any lawyers around. Do you?"

Sutton ignored Anderson's question and looked to Durant for direction. Joe was uncertain about the situation. It was always considered best not to let the principals in a complaint meet with the authority of the hospital. That rule would dictate that Mr. Marquart and especially the nurse, that he assumed was Ms. O'Sullivan, not be allowed into the meeting. On the other hand this was not, as yet, an official meeting of the hospital Executive Committee. It would become one when the Board Chairman called it to order—if he called it to order. Joe looked at the other end of the table where Kevin Hardly was sipping some coffee and trying to put jam on a bagel. Kevin's unconscious stare gave Durant an idea.

"Let's do what Ron suggested. We can have a gathering without having a meeting. When O'Shea and Patello show I'll tell them that the official meeting of the Executive Committee has been canceled. Kevin doesn't know where he is anyway so I won't need to explain it to him. We can have some food and chat about things. Mr. Markley, you can invite the patient and Ms. O'Sullivan to come in for a bite. He can say what he wants. Nothing goes on the record. We listen. If we hear anything important we can meet about it in official session after they leave. Is that okay with you, Dr. Sutton? I think to ignore him would put us at a greater disadvantage."

"I don't think this will hold up under interrogatories, Joe." Sutton was skeptical. "If you want to listen to the patient you must accept the risk that our lawyer might not be able to build an adequate defense. The patient issued a formal complaint and that is cause to cut him off from official contact so the professionals can work out a settlement. This is a very risky move. I'm against it but I'll go along if everybody agrees. Remember we can't take notes or call this a meeting. If he makes demands for anything we are in a spot. I mean a big spot."

Bob Markley sat quietly and listened to the exchange. He was shocked at the apparent fear of the patient that the Chief Executive and Physicians had. The simple act of human communication was being restricted by legal policy and procedure in the hands of amateurs in personal skills who were expert professionals in the science of medicine. Worst yet, the distrust of the patient and a member of the nursing staff, who was considered guilty by predetermination, seemed to dominate the minds of leadership. Somehow trust, dignity and compassion had been set aside for the sake of process. He was about to explode with his own emotional input when, fortunately, Thomas O'Shea arrived followed in short order by Charlie Patello.

The two Board members looked confused as they saw Kevin Hardly alone at the head of the long table and the CEO and Doctors at the other end. Each moved to Kevin and greeted him. Kevin was cordial and pleased to see his friends and colleagues. He suggested that both men sit down. He proposed that the servers would take their order shortly and then they would get started as soon as Mr. Durant and the doctors arrived. Kevin complained that the meeting was late getting started and then resumed eating his breakfast.

O'Shea and Patello moved to the buffet table, picked up some breakfast and walked to the opposite end of the table to join the doctors. Hardly didn't seem to notice. As they began to eat, Dr. Folley asserted himself by expressing his in-depth knowledge of the situation and giving a rather succinct explanation of the incident and current situation the reason why this was a non-meeting. Patello became irritated that a matter of this relative insignificance caused him to rearrange a very busy schedule to attend a non-meeting at seven A.M. O'Shea constantly glanced at the head of the table to see if his boss, the distinguished Kevin Hardly, had returned to this planet

Bishop Hanks arrived suddenly and unexpectedly. His office had informed Durant's Executive Assistant that the Bishop would not be available because of a conflict. Apparently the conflict had been resolved. The Bishop looked irritated when he entered and became more so when he discovered that the meeting was totally disorganized. He sat next to Kevin Hardly and ignored the assembly at the other end of the table.

Joe Durant walked to the Bishop and greeted him. "Good morning, Bishop. We are glad that you could join us. As you can see we are not yet started. In fact, we have sort of decided that a formal meeting may not be in order. I would like to explain."

An explanation was very much in order for the Bishop. He was angry and fired back at Durant. "Mr. Durant, I find this whole thing to be very unusual. Mr. Hardly is left alone while you seem to plot something away from his attention. He is the Chairman of this Hospital's Board appointed by His Eminence and certainly deserving of your respect. I assure you that he has mine and I intend to see that he had yours as well."

Durant knew he was in trouble and tried to make amends. "Yes, Bishop. You are right. Mr. Hardly certainly deserves our respect. We were reviewing the situation surrounding this gathering and trying to formulate its conduct. You see, we have an employee involved and a patient who we think should be with us but because of possible legal complications we are trying not to make it a matter of record so to speak."

Bishop Hanks didn't buy it. "There's no reason to treat employees that way. The Church is very explicit about the rights of the working person. If you are referring to the two people out in the hall it seems to me that they are tired and have waited long enough while you play with this foolishness. Bring them in, or would you like me to invite them. I don't have all day and I'm sure the Cardinal will ask me about this embarrassment. I trust this is in no way leading to scandal."

Durant nodded and looked at the people at the opposite end of the table. They were watching the exchange. Although they could not hear everything that was being said they realized that the Bishop was resolving the matter with emphasis. They picked up their coffee and moved up the table around Kevin Hardly who simply smiled as they sat down.

Durant, intending to keep the session informal regardless, opened the doors and invited Jay and Cecile to join them. "Ms. O'Sullivan and Mr. Marquart, we apologize for keeping you waiting. Please join us. We are having some breakfast and would like you to partake as well. Please enjoy the buffet."

Jay gave Cecile a quick wink as they entered the Boardroom. Cecile was overwhelmed with the elaborate surroundings. Her professional confidence so well fortified in dealing with the sickest patients was shattered in this environment. The only thing she wanted at that moment was out. Jay, on the other hand, was determined to seize the moment. He was not one to be easily over powered by plush surroundings. He enjoyed playing the bull in the china shop. This was going to be fun if he didn't let his desire to perform overshadow the purpose of his presence.

Jay stepped to the buffet and filled a plate with everything in sight. Cecile walked behind him but took nothing. Together they sat at the table next to Joe Durant who, in correct fashion, allowed Bishop Hanks and Doctor Folley to flank Kevin Hardly. The other Board members and Doctors sat across the table. Bob Markley purposely sat directly across from Jay in excellent position to monitor the emotions of the patient. All were silent as Jay ate.

Finally, Kevin Hardly spoke. "Well, I see that the staff has arrived so now we can start the meeting. I seem to have forgotten my usual prayer. Bishop Hanks will you honor us with a prayer, please."

Nothing created formality like an opening prayer. Durant felt the pressure build. *What next?* he thought. *Maybe we could sing the National Anthem.*

The Bishop accepted Kevin's invitation and asked all to stand, join hands, and say the Lord's Prayer. Afterward the Bishop gave a brief homily about the dignity of work and preserving the dignity of the working person. Eventually he said "Amen" and all sat down.

Kevin Hardly thanked the Bishop and then gave a lengthily announcement about the upcoming investiture of the Knights of the Holy Cross to be conducted by His Eminence in the Cathedral on October fifteenth. Of course, everyone was invited. He made special mention that Mr. Durant and Mrs. Durant were among several others who were to be titled Sir and Lady of the Order of the Holy Cross. When it came to matters of the Knights Kevin Hardly always seemed to have his facts straight. Beyond that he seemed constantly confused. When he finished he paused then looked at Joe Durant.

"Mr. Durant, I'm not sure of our agenda this morning. I'll turn the proceedings over to you. Please conduct the meeting."

Durant was pleased to be in control. He intended to make things informal from this point on without affronting the Bishop who sat erect, hands folded, looking very formal. Carefully, he tested his lead by circling around the issue. "Thanks, Kevin. I believe everyone has finished their breakfast. It's nice that Ms. O'Sullivan, one of our Medical Intensive Care Nurses, could join us. I am also pleased to have Mr. Marquart drop in. This is really an opportunity to get together and chat about things in general. We have no particular agenda at this time. If an issue surfaces then naturally we'll discuss it."

Bishop Hanks was not in the mood for this sort of thing. He had rearranged his schedule for the day with great difficulty in order to attend a special meeting of the hospital's Executive Committee dealing with a matter of great urgency. Now he was being told that he was just eating breakfast. That was more than the Bishop could take. "Mr. Durant, excuse me, but I can't believe that you called a special session just to eat breakfast and chat. I really don't have time for this. Are we here for a reason or not?"

Durant knew he was caught. There was no way that he could bring the matter to the front as casual conversation. He decided to be direct. "Sure, Bishop. We are aware that Ms. O'Sullivan has been accused of violating hospital policy regarding the confidentiality of patient information. If such accusations are true then she could lose her license as a nurse. We saw this as a serious matter and wanted to clarify the situation in her best interest. Perhaps Ms. O'Sullivan would like to give us her side of the story. That's really the reason for the meeting."

Durant had succeeded in disarming the Bishop. Regardless of how he viewed the situation as a matter of importance the Bishop could not deny the employee an opportunity to speak after his emphatic commentary in support of the working person. He simply nodded to Durant and waved for continuation.

Durant turned toward Cecile. "Ms. O'Sullivan, you have had the incident reviewed by the Nursing Ethics Committee and this afternoon it will be heard by the Hearing Committee. All of this is formal process toward the determination of guilt or innocence. The meeting this morning is not part of the process but an opportunity for all of us to see if this is just. Please give us your point of view."

Cecile was not prepared for this. She had listened to the exchange between the hospital's CEO and the Bishop and could not decide who her friends were, if any, in the room. Now she was being called on to bare her soul about the whole mess. She knew she could not do it. Her emotions were running away with her thoughts and she was about to have another sobbing fit that had been characteristic since she had been relieved of duty.

Unconsciously, Cecile grabbed Jay's hand and squeezed it. Jay looked at Cecile and realized that this was his cue. "Mr. Durant, I think it would be best if I talked first since I'm the patient involved. You see, it's kinda like you said. There's not anything to this because what's supposed to have happened didn't happen. We can just forget about it. Okay?"

Durant was blindsided by Jay's comment. "What do you mean, 'didn't happen'?"

Jay saw Durant as a friend and tried to maintain control. "Well, like I said, I'm the patient and for her to violate my confidentiality I got to agree that she did it and I don't agree. She didn't do nothing. It never happened. It's just that simple."

Dr. Sutton looked skeptical. He leaned forward in his chair and stared directly into Jay's eyes. "Mr. Marquart, the medical record contains an incident report noting your anger that Ms. O'Sullivan knew about your admission and treatment. Do you say that the record is wrong? According to the report you were very upset."

Jay sat back, relaxed. "I don't know about the record. I've never seen my record. It's probably got a lot of things about me that I don't know about. I was sick. I even busted up the place a few times. That doesn't mean that some working stiff has to get canned. Everybody was just doing their jobs, man. Nothing else happened. You know."

Bishop Hanks became very interested. He addressed Jay in a friendly way. "Sir, as I understand what's said so far is that the nurse here was taking care of you and you became irritated with something she did or said. What was it?"

Jay smiled at the priest and gave him a friendly wave. "No, Your Worship, it wasn't anything like that. It's sort of a family matter between Cecile and me. We used to be married and we got a kid. Cecile knew I was sick and was just trying to make sure that Kristie, that's our kid, was okay. Nothing else. I didn't really understand what she was doing 'cause I was too sick to understand anything so I blew my top and busted things up a little. The folks in the Unit probably thought that Cecile caused it. She didn't. I just blew. Everything's cool now. It's no problem. Cecile can go back to work 'cause nobody got hurt."

Charlie Patello nervously looked at his watch. He was due in an important meeting on the bank merger in less than an hour. Tom O'Shea was to be included in that meeting. Patello decided to move this session to a close. "Bishop Hanks, I'm pleased to say that I have been acquainted with Mr. Marquart for several years. He is a man of integrity. If he states that no harm has been done then we should accept that and bring this matter to a close."

Durant stepped in before the Bishop could agree. "Charlie, the matter has other serious possibilities. If there is litigation on a matter such as this then the hospital could be subject to a restricted audit opinion. That would complicate our venture opportunities and affect our bond ratings. A clean opinion is essential to us at this critical time. We need to have the matter resolved in a formal way."

Patello looked at Jay. "Do you intend to sue us, Jay?"

Jay had always been straight with Patello. He intended to keep it that way. "Mr. Patello, I don't know much about the law. My sister, she's a lawyer, and does what I need done in court. Well, she taught me a long time ago that you can't sue without cause. I don't have cause. Again, nothing happened. Why would I sue?"

Patello simply nodded. "Okay, Jay. I believe you."

Patello also knew that Jay could be controlled by other ways—either by Action or by the pending opportunity with Patriot and the special accounts section of Portland *Courier*. Jay's intelligence was evident at this meeting. He certainly would be smart enough to understand the consequences of any act that would affront Patello's interest. Patello was ready to support Jay's statement and get on with the day.

Bishop Hanks was also ready to end the meeting. However, he remained concerned about the possible injustice to the employee, Ms. O'Sullivan. The good Bishop decided to penetrate the matter to his satisfaction. "Well, it's said that nothing has happened. But here is a nurse away from duty for some reason. Something has happened to cause this. Why is she even being subjected to this process if she has done nothing? You mentioned that she is subject of a hearing this afternoon with possible career-ending consequences. That sounds like a gross injustice. She would have cause to sue us then. That would be a major scandal that the Cardinal would not tolerate. I believe we should stop this immediately or else I'll have to report to His Eminence that he needs to become directly involved."

Doctor Folley saw an immediate opportunity for political advantage since it was evident that the matter was for all practical purposed resolved. "Bishop Hanks, your concerns are very well appreciated. This hospital is intent to serve the Church and its healing mission. Our employees are essential to that end. We must safeguard their dignity. To think that this Nurse would be subject to a process that denies her dignity and her profession is a major departure from the charge that is ours to protect. Acting as the Cardinal's representative on matters of health affairs consistent with the duty of the Office for Health Affairs of the Archdiocese, I recommend that Ms. O'Sullivan be returned to her duties immediately and the Hearing Committee Meeting scheduled for this afternoon be canceled."

Folley realized that his recommendation was being made in a quasi-informal way. Its implementation required executive action by Joe Durant. He alone would be responsible for the act good or bad. Furthermore, the manner in which Folley had made the recommendation left the incident as part of the record to be acted on in the future if appropriate. Cecile, unknowingly, would remain subject to the violation. Furthermore, her charge by the Nursing Ethics Committee of violating nursing ethics remained on the record of that Committee.

Bob Markley had been pleased with the process of the discussion. He was certain that Cecile was going to be rescued by Jay's heroics. When Dr. Folley made the recommendation to close the issue Markley felt immediately uncomfortable. His instincts told him that he suddenly had a hand in the matter beyond that of an innocent bystander. With a start, he remembered that he had filled out the incident report and brought it to the attention of his superior, Dr. Anderson. Markley was the source of the problem or non-problem as it was turning out to be. He felt obligated to clear the record.

Markley spoke. "Bishop, Mr. Durant, Dr. Folley, I am thankful to Mr. Marquart for clarifying a matter that has been troubling me ever since the time that the incident we are referring to occurred. I believe that I am possibly the cause of the confusion that existed and that Jay, Mr. Marquart, has now clarified. I was the one who observed Mr. Marquart's behavior and heard his comments after the telephone conversation with Ms. O'Sullivan. Obviously, I misinterpreted his actions. That was poor clinical practice from me. You pay me to be accurate in understanding the patient. I realize now that I made a mistake. I sincerely apologize to Mr. Marquart, Ms. O'Sullivan and to the Board of Directors. However, I have reviewed the clinical record of Mr. Marquart's admissions and believe them to be accurate. The incident report is the record in question and accordingly incident reports are not considered part of the clinical record. Therefore, I suggest that we dispose of the incident report. We could do that and leave the clinical findings intact."

Ron Anderson was not about to let Markley discredit himself is this discussion. He valued Markley's ability and wanted to avoid making him the fall guy. "Gentlemen, please don't allow Bob Markley to shoulder the blame for this matter. He is one of our most trusted counselors. You note that the incident occurred as a result of a telephone call that revealed the treatment location of the patient thus revealing his diagnosis by default. This is not a matter that Mr. Markley could control. If anything could be identified as the cause of this confusion it should be the technical problems with our telephone system. Dr. Folley has made that point on several occasions. We need to correct that problem but we also need to do as Bob suggests and dispose of the incident report. I also suggest that Nursing Administration be advised that the ethical matter brought to their attention was erroneous so their records can be corrected as well. Do you agree, Dr. Folley?"

Anderson realized that he had set Durant up for another of Folley's ranting about the incompetence of Administration and the stupid telephone system bought without the input of the medical staff. On the other hand, the Board members, including Bishop Hanks had heard it all before. It was an opportunity to get Markley off the hook and deliver the focus back to the Chief Executive where the ball belonged.

Folley took the bait. "That's not the only thing that Administration had done, Ron. You may have noticed the ugly trash cans all over the hospital. Well, our genius administrator brought in some wild outfit that's going to get us to recycle everything. It's an expensive and un-necessary. We need to have this matter reviewed by the full Board."

Patello had had it. Folley's shot at Action touched him off. "Bishop Hanks, this has gone on long enough. Folley's intention to have us listen to his short-sighted observations about matters that he knows little about is a waste of your valuable time. May I suggest that Mr. Durant make the necessary calls to settle this issue right now and then we can get the hell out of here. Pardon my language but I've really had it."

"Yes, I quite agree," stated the Bishop. "Mr. Durant, will you call nursing or whoever and see that this young lady gets back to work? We'll wait a few more minutes. Thank you, Charlie, for pushing us on. We all need to get to more important things."

Joe Durant was livid. He expected to get into a fight with Folley sometime in the meeting. He did not expect the blind side shot from Anderson. His anger was barely under control as he called the Vice President for Nursing and advised her that the matter with Nurse O'Sullivan had been resolved and that she was to be returned to duty immediately. He briefly explained that the incident report was in error and therefore all ethical charges should be dropped. He agreed to follow the conversation with a memorandum.

When he hung up the telephone Durant turned his attention to Cecile. "Ms. O'Sullivan, the Nursing Office understands that this matter is resolved.

You are authorized to return to duty. In fact the director of your Unit would like you to report immediately because there is a very heavy census this morning. They need all the help they can get. Thanks for your time and understanding."

Cecile could hardly talk. She uttered her thanks and asked to be excused so she could get to the Unit. The tears were evident and she stood to leave. Jay was far more eloquent. He held Cecile by the hand, not out of affection, but to keep her from getting away before he extracted a pound of her flesh. She had no choice but to wait while he took his parting shot.

Jay addressed the assembly. "You have been very kind to us today. I'm pleased that you realized that the patient is what counts in the end. This is a great Hospital but like everything else there is always room for improvement. I'm sorry to hear that some of you don't understand the waste management program. I would like to explain it to you so you would understand it better. It's really another way that this hospital is contributing to everybody's welfare. I'm proud to admit that I designed the program for St. Anslem's. I work for Action Waste Management and I'm proud to admit it. They are a great company. Dr. Sutton is working with us to install the program and I'm sure he can explain it to you some other time. Thanks again, we appreciated the breakfast."

Charlie Patello gave Jay a very approving grin that didn't go unnoticed by Durant. Jay reached across the table and shook Patello's hand. Then he walked Cecile out the door. Markley hurried to catch up. At Markley's urging the three moved rapidly away from the Boardroom toward stairway five where they would be alone.

O'Shea caught up with Patello and asked to ride with him to their meeting at the bank. Patello was pleased to accommodate him. Doctors Anderson and Sutton went their separate way. Bishop Hanks was delayed by Dr. Folley who talked at length about Durant's incompetence. Kevin Hardly listened to the conversation and uttered his agreement with the criticism of the CEO. Eventually the three walked to the lobby where Mrs. Hardly waited to drive her husband home.

Bob Markley, Jay, and Cecile paused on the landing of stairway five. It was deserted as usual. Markley knew that Dr. Anderson would be coming through soon as a shortcut to his office. He was hoping that the three of them could have a brief session with his boss before Cecile returned to duty. Jay was anxious to have a moment alone with Cecile so he attempted to cut short Bob's presence.

"Hey, Bob, that was great help. Thanks. We kicked ass, right. Man, that reverend guy was pissed at Durant. Look, I got to have some time with Cecile on a personal matter then I got to get up to Psych for a discharge conference. Susan's up there now, holding the fort. If we can cut this short I might just make it on time. What we got here, five minutes to eight. I'm due there at eight."

Markley caught on and cut his conversation short. "I understand, Jay. I'm supposed to be with you at your discharge conference. I guess we can talk more then. What I want to say is that Cecile, you dodged a bullet. Best you don't say anything about what happened in that meeting to the staff in Psych. The word will get out anyway but for your own good you best let management spin the story to their advantage. I'll probably take a little heat but that's okay because I'm not part of the establishment. Bishop Hanks is a friend of all of us. We don't have to worry from now on. Okay?"

Jay did not want to extend the conversation but Cecile had regained her composure and was interested in what Bob had said. "Mr. Markley, you know how the staff will react to this. They'll want to know the whole sordid tale. I can't tell them nothing? Why do you want me to keep mum?"

Markley knew that Jay wanted him to move on but he decided to take some time to explain the issue to Cecile. "Cecile, if you explain how screwed up the leadership of this hospital is and how indifferent they are to patient and staff if would start a further decline in morale that we cannot tolerate now. We have a complement of patients this morning with barely enough staff to care for them. People are stretched too thin. If they hear that the Board of Trustees is more concerned about the damned audit report than the quality of care, everything will be up for grabs. The patients will be the ones who suffer the most from lack of care. I figure that the CEO will send a memorandum to Nursing stating that the incident was a misinterpretation of the patient's comments by a member of the SACAP staff. It will fall short of any apology. Let's let it happen that way and avoid any further hassle. Somebody has to care, okay? You can do a lot for the patients by letting this whole solution look like an act of compassion. If we let it alone the staff will draw their own conclusions and in the absence of anything negative it will be positive and supportive to morale. What do you say?"

Cecile got the point. "You want me to provide cover for the Board of Trustees and Mr. Durant even though they were willing to throw me to the wolves. That's a tall order, Mr. Markley. I'll give it a shot. It's too bad that the staff doesn't get a chance to elect the Administrator. You would be a great candidate."

Jay was amused at Markley's concern about the administration. "Markley, you smooth talking son of a bitch, you just saved Durant from a lynch mob but I bet the reverend ties a can on him real soon. You wanna bet? Look, Cecile and me has gotta talk. You mind?"

Markley grabbed the opportunity to move on. "I understand, Jay. Thanks, Cecile. Jay, I'll see you upstairs."

Jay waited for Markley to exit from the stairway into the corridor. Then he turned to Cecile who was beginning to walk up the stairs to the Medical Intensive Care Unit. He grabbed her arm and pleasantly caused her to stop. "Cecile, I wanted to remind you that we had a deal here. I delivered. Okay? I mean you are off the hook and I'm the guy that got you off. They got nothing on you any more 'cause I said nothing happened. So, I delivered like I said I would. Now I want to be sure that you are willing to stick with our deal. No more hassle over Kristie. Is that right?"

Cecile knew that she was obligated to keep her end of the deal. Yet, her motherly instincts caused her to qualify her answer. "Jay, what happened this morning is just short of a miracle. I am relieved and very grateful to you for what you did. Yes, we have a deal. But you have to remember that I will not let Kristie be subjected to drugs or anything else that threatens her health, safety, or general wellbeing. I love her and I know that you do to. You are trying to do what's right and I commend you for that. But for our deal to hold up you have to continue to stay sober and protect her from negative influences. Do we understand each other?"

Jay realized that Cecile was making an indirect reference to Susan and their friends who he was sure Kristie had described to her mother on several occasions following the Saturday night rituals. "Yeah, Cecile, you made the point. You got to understand that the sword cuts two ways. You might have a problem on your side that I take exception to. Then we will have to be honest with each other and talk it out. That drug thing is serious stuff."

Cecile did not get the point of Jay's comments. She had no idea that her husband was a suspected user. She passed over Jay's comments with a parting wave. "Of course we will have to talk, Jay. The success of this new deal is how willing we both are in using open communication. I have to run. Thank you for what you did for me. I am grateful."

Jay watched her go. For an instant, he felt the romantic attraction for her that existed so many years ago. She was the mother of his child. She deserved to be loved. But no longer by him. His mind was beginning to wander back to the time of their marriage when he heard his name. It was Dr. Anderson now standing beside him. Anderson was speaking but Jay was not listening. Whatever Anderson said it was said with a smile and ended with a handshake. Then the doctor ran down the steps and disappeared. Jay left the stairway and Boarded an elevator for the Psychiatric Unit and his discharge conference.

Jay took the elevator to the Psych Unit. He was told that his discharge conference was in process in the small conference room adjacent to the nursing station. He knocked at the door and entered. Susan was seated at a table with the Psych resident, medical social worker, head nurse, and Bob Markley. Markley had already offered to the conference that Jay's recovery was adequate for discharge. The chief resident agreed noting that his progress was well documented on the record. The nurse and social worker supported his discharge noting that he had excellent home support from his wife that they had just There was no further comment. The attending psychiatrist walked over to Jay, shook his hand, and wished him well. He reminded Jay to call for assistance anytime he thought he needed it. There was a hot line set up in the Psych Unit to assist their graduates day or night. The rest of the attendees left the room leaving only Jay, Susan and Markley. Markley motioned Jay and Susan to sit down.

Markley took up where he and Jay had left off a few weeks back. "Jay, you and I have been here before. We both know that beyond this minute are many hours, days and years of temptation to try it again. We think we can control it. Yet we know that we can't. We need all the help we can get. We need help from a friend who will rescue us from that point of depression when we know a drink or a snort will be the answer. We need help from someone close, a spouse, who can understand our problems and give us comfort that we might otherwise try to find in a jug. We need the satisfaction of being loved and of loving others instead of placing our affections in a mindless substance. We have tremendous needs, Jay. You and I need each other to realize that we are dependent people. We have endless needs. But our salvation can be found in the realization that others need us. You proved that when you helped Cecile this morning at your own risk. We can care for them. Our love, our compassion, our caring nature will bring us what we need, Jay. Remember we are the ones who need to care. You ask me if I care. I'll tell you, man, I do. And so do you, you digging me?"

Jay nodded. He gave the right answer and then asked a question, "Yeah, man, I dig. But nobody answered my question."

"What question, Jay?" Markley was puzzled.

"Am I a crazy that got drunk or a drunk that got crazy?"

Part Three

Chapter Seventeen

Eddie was sometimes sentimental about things. Usually he couldn't care less but the Portland thing made him a little blue. He liked the idea of change when it served his ego. He had been promoted. That's what he was told but he didn't feel any different even though everything else was different.

Eddie was now the liaison man between two companies that had a big piece of the transport delivery and courier business in, around, and between the two metropolitan communities of Portland and Boston. His job, as it was explained to him, was to make sure that pickups and deliveries were exact and on time. He was also in charge of the special accounts. This is where the change was most noticeable. The special accounts were no longer an identified part of the Patriot operation and were held separate and distinct from the books of *Portland Courier*. Eddie was all alone when it came to special accounts. His contact man was not a part of either company. This made Eddie blue. He liked being a part of the identified business community. Now he was an independent agent serving two clients, Patriot Transport of Boston and *Portland Courier* in Maine. The special accounts were his, except for the collection that was now conducted by another agent unknown to Eddie. If there was a problem with collection Eddie was still "The Enforcer" which was part of his liaison duties. All of this was explained to him at a lengthy meeting with Mr. Mondi and a few people whose first names were only mentioned once and now forgotten.

No longer would Eddie go to his comfortable comer desk near the loading dock of the Patriot shipping area. He would operate for a few days out of his hot wheels pickup truck communicating with his clients and customers by cellular telephones. He had three. One was dedicated to Patriot, another to Portland, and the third for special accounts. They also gave him a list of code words to use for certain transactions in order to avoid communication in the clear that may tip off an eavesdropping constabulary.

One of the most frustrating parts of the change was when Eddie had to spend a day with a "security officer" from someplace in New York who schooled him in the use of the telephones and code. The security officer was a weird guy who wanted everything done by the numbers. He reminded Eddie of the strict army top sergeant that he had seen in television movies. Only the guy didn't look like a sergeant. He was short, round, not fat, and very, very strong. He drank a lot and smoked constantly. Those were traits that Eddie liked. When Eddie asked the security officer his name, the man said he was known as "Sam, the Security Man, but Eddie could call him Sir."

The security officer also told Eddie that his hot wheels pickup truck was too visible and allowed for an easy make. The truck had to go. In its place the "Company" provided a new Buick Century sedan. This part really made Eddie very blue. An offset to his doldrums was the money. Eddie was now making big bucks.

Each company sent him regular checks for his services. As an independent contractor Eddie was not subject to any withholding so he decided that the government could get along without his routine contribution until he inadvertently mentioned it to the security officer who immediately assigned Eddie to one of the special accountants. Eddie now found his account being dunned for quarterly payments to Massachusetts, Maine, and Uncle Sam.

The security officer found Eddie's lifestyle marginally acceptable for the duties he performed. His wild clothes and heavy necklaces made him look like a dealer and pimp. Eddie invited Sam the Security Man to engage in combat when he made the observation. However, the security officer performed a quick karate chop that destroyed a table causing Eddie to consider a diplomatic solution. The security officer had one ready. Eddie was given the name of a tailor who would provide Eddie with a complete "working wardrobe." An appointment was made for the same day. The "Company" would pay the expense.

The one thing that Sam the Security Man found acceptable was where Eddie lived. Eddie had acquired a one bedroom condominium in a high-end development in North Quincy on Dorchester Bay overlooking Boston Harbor.

The Unit was moderately valued on the third floor. A large marina was part of the complex with a Boardwalk, shops, restaurants, and bars. The area was frequented by yuppies and tourists looking for a good time and frequently a buy. Eddie lived in a place that was good for business. He spent many a night in the not so quiet confines of a back-door bar called the Shanty where he would make some contacts and, to his recreational delight, find a variety of ladies seeking companionship. Eddie liked that.

It was in the Shanty a few years earlier that Eddie first met the Sailor. The Sailor was known on the Boardwalk and the marina staff as a little weird. He worked in the boatyard, piloted tour boats, crewed on fishing boats, pumped gas as a dock hand, and drank. He drank a lot. The minute the clock hit five the Sailor hit the Shanty and stayed there until the midnight closing. Nobody was sure where he lived or knew his real name. He listed a Post Office box with the marina who refused to give his name out to those who inquired. He was simply "The Sailor," a likable sort who loved to talk with strangers.

All of the Sailor's conversations eventually turned to the prominent tattoo on his arm that was always exposed. The tattoo was of a Navy Patrol Boat with the initials PBR under it and under the initials the words "USN Riverine—Proud, Brave, Reliable." The tattoo took up most of the Sailor's upper right arm which prompted conversation. When you bought the Sailor a drink he would explain that he had served on a PBR in 1966 patrolling Vietnam's Mekong Delta. He would speak with reverence about his comrades and their bravery. Then he would ask his friends to drink a toast to the brave sailors who died patrolling the Delta. Of course, whoever paid for his drink also paid for the toast that included everyone in the joint. Regulars to the Shanty would spot the Sailor's latest prey and then huddle near the bar in expectation of the toast and resulting free drink.

The Sailor rarely if ever talked about himself. Consequently no one appreciated the fact that the Sailor was a decorated hero. He had received the Silver Star and the Purple Heart. His many commendations included several accounts of bravery under fire while exposing himself to enemy fire in order to save wounded comrades. But the commendations didn't include the time that the Sailor was severely wounded. His best friend pulled him to safety as their boat came under heavy fire. The Sailor's life was saved but his friend was blown apart by an incoming B40 rocket. The Sailor never talked about that. He wanted to forget the horror and, like so many veterans, resorted to trying to escape with booze and eventually drugs. The Sailor left Nam a junkie.

The Navy tried to rehabilitate him but eventually forced his retirement after twenty years of service. The Sailor had a pension and disability income, memories good and bad, and remarkable boat knowledge and handling skills with which he managed to scrape out a living.

After the bars closed the Sailor would stagger to the monument for Vietnam War Veterans in the middle of the Boardwalk. He would stand at attention, pause, and after a minute render a salute. Then he would stagger off to wherever he spent the night.

It wasn't long after Eddie moved into his Condo that he met the Sailor. Eddie was exploring the bars on the Boardwalk and entered the Shanty to find only the Sailor. It was early and the usual crowd had yet to arrive. The Sailor was friendly. Eddie bought the first drink and several drinks after that, eventually buying the usual toast for the house. In the days that followed Eddie would buy the Sailor his first drink but avoid lengthily conversations. In time they became better acquainted. The Sailor recognized that Eddie was doing some sort of business with selected people in the bar and he assumed rightly that drugs were either being bought or sold. Carefully he asked Eddie if he could make a buy. Eddie put him in contact with a neighborhood dealer who at Eddie's direction gave the Sailor a deal. This expanded their friendship.

Eddie recognized talent. He especially had an eye for talent that could be used in the business and who would work cheap. The Sailor fit. Pressure from the law had forced a radical change in the import system and it so happened that the business now required someone who was expert in small boat handling and capable of navigating high seas. The import system involved a pickup of the offshore drops in the lobster beds outside Boston Harbor in place of the over the road relay system. The underworld Navy would let Eddie know when the drop would be made and Eddie had to arrange for someone to make the pick up as far out as ten nautical miles from the harbor entrance. Often winds in excess of fifteen knots blowing from the northeast would create waves of six to eight feet. Only the best boat handlers could take a small boat into that sea. It also required a man who was a little crazy. The Sailor was qualified.

He was offered a hundred bucks for every trip and a constant supply of cocaine for his trouble. Eddie thought he had hit the motherlode. Two nights later the Sailor made his first trip in an old Sea Sprite that he bought for eight hundred and fifty dollars borrowed from Eddie.

After a few more successful imports Eddie reasoned that bringing the material to the Shanty was dangerous. The Sailor agreed and suggested that he would be less conspicuous running in and out of the Hingham Boat Dock which he allowed was closer to Eddie's desk at Patriot by taxi. Eddie also required that the Sailor use a different Cab Company every time in order to avoid suspicion. Payment for the Sailor's service would be returned to him by a special courier within twenty-four hours after the import.

Eddie selected Brian to connect with the Sailor since Brian was being used for the special accounts anyway. Brian always met the Sailor at the Hingham Dock. The Sailor was never late and very friendly. He liked Brian and the feeling was mutual. They developed a friendship. Sailor saw in Brian a similarity to his Vietnam buddy. He gave Brian many boat handling tips, fishing suggestions, and maintenance lessons. He even let Brian borrow the boat for Friday night fishing trips.

The Sailor continued to work at the North Quincy Marina. He met Eddie no more than once a week at the Shanty. At Eddie's suggestion, he cut back on his nocturnal socializing. The one meeting a week was when Eddie would give the Sailor the pickup schedule. They would meet on different days each week, have a drink, pass the information, and leave. It was no more than a half-hour. Afterwards, Eddie would walk out to the Boardwalk and then to an adjoining restaurant. The Sailor would hang around for another drink which he bought instead of mooching. Then he would leave for Hingham. An hour later Eddie would return and resume his hunt for the ladies. No one took special notice of the ritual since it was inconsistent as to time and day and always short.

The system worked well. However, the change of operations to Portland required a change in the import system. Eddie had incorrectly assumed when he was being informed about his own change of status that he would move the Sailor to Portland and do business as usual. However, in a following session with Sam the Security Man, Eddie was told that the Sailor was now expendable. He was scheduled to take a fall that Eddie would trigger when he passed the next schedule. The details were omitted. All Eddie knew was that he was to deliver a pickup schedule according to routine and give the Sailor specific instructions about moving the shipment Nothing was to be said about change except that the imported material would be picked up my a runner instead of transported to Patriot by taxi. The Runner was identified as a black man driving a blue BMW Convertible. He would walk to the dock from his car as the Sailor tied the boat to the pier. The Sailor was not to say anything—just give the sealed shipment in its waterproof pouch to the runner. Everything else would be the same as usual meaning that Brian would show up the next day with the payment.

Eddie was uncomfortable with the deception. The Sailor had been loyal. He didn't deserve to be screwed. But business was business and Eddie had to be concerned about his own welfare.

The details that Sam the Security Man had omitted from Eddie's briefing were known only to the New York Office and their Navy. NAI's operation in Queens had arranged by contact to sell shipments to the biggest dealers in Dorchester neighborhood of Boston for a reasonable price. Dorchester was the most notorious neighborhood in Boston. Drug dealers were on nearly every corner selling to junkies and high school kids from the block. Gangs fought for control of the lucrative trade. Drive-by shootings were common. Citizens demanded that the City take back the streets and put an end to the conduct.

Dorchester provided the perfect set up for NAI's sting operation. They arranged for a controlling dealer in Dorchester to pick up a shipment at the Hingham Dock from the Sailor who would be identified to them by the blue Sea Sprite. An appealing feature to the buyer was that payment was not required at delivery. After the merchandise was inspected and value determined, a representative from Queens would contact them for payment. At the point of delivery only the Sailor would be the seller's representative. He would simply hand the shipment to the Dorchester contact man. The Contact Man would get in his car and attempt to leave the scene. Everything after that was on automatic pilot.

In addition to arranging the import and the sale to the Dorchester connection, the New York Office of the Navy had also tipped the Boston Police, who tipped the Hingham Police and Massachusetts State Police that a buy was going to go down at the Hingham Dock. This was the tip that the Authorities were waiting for to cap their suspicion that the supply of drugs to the Boston area was by sea.

The Boston Police also tipped the media to be at the Hingham Dock to get the bust on film. The New York Office of Action's Navy had anticipated the publicity and had arranged the pick up at a time that would allow the Sailor to arrive at the Hingham Dock in plenty of time for the reporters to make the six o'clock news. The Sailor and the Dealer's man would get nailed and the Authorities would use them as proof certain that the biggest drug supply ring in Boston had been broken. The youth of the Boston Metropolitan area were again safe from the ravages of cocaine.

This plan was a winner for everyone but the Sailor and the hapless dealer from Dorchester. They were definitely expendable. No one would miss them as they did a twenty-year stretch. The Sailor could possibly implicate Eddie who could deny the whole thing. The legal staff for the company would put up a terrific defense that would acquit Eddie in trial. Eddie was at very low risk. Beyond Eddie little could be proven if they penetrated the protective cover. Eddie had no idea that he was at the slightest risk. The set up seemed perfect. However, the brain trust had failed to consider one small matter. The Sailor was no sucker.

The Sailor had survived Nam for three reasons: He was well trained; He had gained valuable experience in combat; and he always followed his instincts. When he entered the Shanty to get his pickup orders from Eddie, he had no idea that he was about to be set up for a fall. However, as Eddie explained the next import to him, the Sailor's instincts began to give off warning signals. They were the same type of feelings that the he used to have in the Delta when he sensed an ambush. He listened to Eddie without registering his concern. However, Eddie was not the same Eddie. He was nervous and seemed to be holding back something about the pickup. Eddie's eyes constantly glanced away from the Sailor. The new suit was not Eddie. There was too much change too soon. The Sailor smelled an ambush.

After Eddie left the Shanty, the Sailor had another drink and thought about the assignment. Eddie had always been fair and the two had conducted their business without any hassle. Eddie was not the enemy. But who was? Why was Eddie so different? He didn't look like Eddie. He didn't talk like Eddie. He didn't even smell like Eddie. He smelled more like the Suits. "Yeah, Eddie smells like the Suits and the Suits always fuck things up," he said to himself as he paid for his drink and walked out to the Boardwalk.

The Sailor was given the coordinates for the pick up as usual. The shipment was to be distributed in two lobster traps again as usual. However, the rest of the trip had some significant changes. The Sailor was told to pass the material to the contact man at the Hingham Dock tomorrow at one P.M. instead of the usual early morning time. The Sailor had always been warned by Eddie not to let a shipment in his possession for more than an hour. Consequently, the Sailor had always put the shipment in the hands of a courier within minutes after he returned from a pick up. The Sailor always tried to make his pickups at dawn when there was some cover from darkness and other lobster boats were moving about working their traps. He would move among them and gradually check the ones specified in the pickup order. Then he would remove the waterproof pouches, secure them under the deck in the bow, and make a routine run back to Hingham. When he arrived, he would go to the nearest pay phone and call a taxi. It always worked well. Within an hour after he tied up he had passed the shipment and was on his way to work at the North Quincy Marina.

Tomorrow's action would require him to skip work, make his run in broad daylight, arrive on target after most lobster boats had cleared their traps, and return to Hingham at a time when the daily recreational traffic was reaching a peak. Then, for the first time, the Sailor was expected to physically pass the shipment to a contact person described to him only as a black man in a BMW convertible. He concluded that this definitely was a set up that required modifications to the standard operational procedure in similar fashion as he had done in Nam when his instincts flashed caution. He was going to take evasive action.

The Sailor found the marina Security Guard in the marina Office Sipping coffee. He explained to the guard that he needed to get into the repair office to check a work order on a boat that was to be ready for hauling in the morning. The guard didn't want to leave the office so he gave the Sailor the master key to the marina facilities with the requirement that the key be returned and that the Repair Shop be locked after the Sailor finished. The Sailor thanked the man and moved with haste to the shop. Inside he went directly to the key Board and selected the keys for a twenty-eight-foot Grady White fishing boat that he knew had been left by its owner for hauling, cleaning, and winter storage. The boat presently was tied up in a transient slip away from public view and, most importantly, the view of the security guard. Eddie took the keys, locked up the repair office and returned the master key to the guard in the marina office. Then he walked to the transient slips and found the Grady White.

The Grady White was selected for several reasons not the least being the fact that the owner had left the boat that morning with instructions that it be hauled and stored for the winter because he was going to Florida on an afternoon plane. That meant that the owner would not suddenly appear to check the boat. Another attraction was that the Sailor had filled the gas tanks that afternoon. Most appealing was that the Grady White had a full bank of electronics that included a Marine radar and integrated Loran.

The Grady White was only twenty-eight feet in length but was built for offshore fishing and could take heavy seas. A NOAA weather check indicated that winds were calm but were expected to increase to twenty-five knots by early morning. Small craft warnings had been issued

The Sailor started the twin outboards and slowly moved out of the harbor into Dorchester Bay. He looked at his watch and noted the time of departure as seven forty-eight in the evening. Seas were calm allowing for good headway. An hour and twenty minutes later he arrived at the pickup point and wrote down the latitude and longitude coordinates on the Loran screen. Then he reentered the data into the Loran and designated the spot as a way point in the Loran's memory bank. He then set the radar on two-mile range and picked out a fishing area one mile toward shore from the pickup point.

With precision, the Sailor moved to the fishing area where it was common for boats to anchor and fish all night. He dropped anchor and waited. It was now after ten P.M. The Sailor figured that the drop would be made sometime between now and dawn.

He punched the Go-To button on the Loran and entered the way point number of the pickup area. The loran gave him a distance of one and two tenths mile to the target pick up point at a bearing of ninety-seven degrees. The radar accepted the data from the Loran and plotted the target on the screen in a circle one and two tenths mile from his position. The circle gave the Sailor an indication of any object entering and leaving the target area. He only had to wait for the boat making the drop and try to stay awake in the meantime. He also set the guard zone alarm on the radar to warn him if by chance he fell asleep. The alarm would wake him as soon as a boat entered the target area. He checked the radar screen and noticed that three other boats were within a mile of his location and appeared to be anchored. The Sailor concluded that they were fishing boats.

The easy rock of the calm seas caused him to doze. He slapped himself in an attempt to stay awake but eventually fell sound asleep. He awoke with a start as a cool rain started falling and the winds started picking up speed. The Grady White lived up to reputation and rocked casually in the growing waves.

Suddenly the Sailor heard the beep of the radar alarm. A boat of considerable size and speed was entering the target area. Immediately the Sailor set the plot and monitored the approaching vessel. It slowed and then appeared to stop. Fifteen minutes later it appeared to be underway but the Sailor couldn't be sure. The seas were building and the now severe rock of the boat made it difficult for the radar to keep electronic surveillance. The Sailor wanted to wait until he was sure that the vessel cleared the drop zone before he checked to see if the drop had been made. However, the increasing wind and waves required him to pull anchor and move rapidly to the spot.

He approached the first lobster trap marker and tried to tie on to the line in order to raise the trap. It was a difficult task for one man operating in good sea conditions but the raging surf now made it nearly impossible. His hands became cut and raw as he struggled with the lines. Finally, he managed to tie on to the bobbing marker. Then he attempted to raise the trap. Waves broke over the side and stern of the Grady White. Its bilge pumps wined as they tried to keep ahead of the seawater now rising to the floor Boards. The two idling outboards sputtered as the waves rolled over their cowlings. The port motor quit.

After about twenty minutes of constant struggle, the Sailor managed to pull the trap onto the transom and then let it fall into the boat. The trap sprung open when it hit the deck. The Sailor removed a large, heavy, waterproof box. He pushed it into the cuddy cabin without bothering to secure it. Then he returned to the helm to steer to his second mark.

The pickup order called for two traps to be used for the drop. The second trap marker was less than a quarter mile from the first. The Sailor was exhausted. Good sense and his instincts now told him that he should make for safe harbor and leave the other trap for a calmer day. In fact, the Sailor was wondering if he had overstayed his welcome on the ocean. Winds by his estimate were nearing gale force and seas were running at least six feet. They would be following him to shore which was to his benefit but that would only help if he could right the craft and turn her without capsizing.

Desperately, the Sailor slipped into the captain's chair and tried to start the port engine. It sputtered and then, to his relief, started. Then he picked a trough and made his turn before the following wave could roll him over. He had the sea at this back pushing him toward the rocks at Graves Light and beyond to the safety of Boston Harbor. The radar was no longer working. The loran gave him a compass heading that he tried to follow. The wind and surf constantly threw him off course. His corrections were blind and he worried that the rocks were to his port. Consequently he favored the drift to starboard that caused him to take the surf more on the beam.

The Grady White rolled and pitched, took water, and wallowed. Gradually the surf began to lessen. This signaled the Sailor that he had passed the Light and was in President's Roads behind the reef soon to be in the protected Boston Harbor. The lights of the City were completely obscured by the haze. Occasionally a navigation light gave an indication that the channel was ahead. Then the haze cleared somewhat and the City lights became visible. The Sailor had made it back. He steered into Dorchester Bay passed the Kennedy Library landmark and made direct for the North Quincy Marina entrance.

The Grady White was back in the transient slip by four-fifteen A.M. Its bilge pumps were still working at removing the seawater from when the Sailor made the final tie. Then he washed the boat down from stern to stem in order to remove the salt from her hull. He wasn't sure if the boat was damaged. That would be discovered when she was hauled in the morning. For now, it would be hard enough to move the box from the cabin, find transport, and take the shipment to his Blue Sea Sprite rocking on a mooring at Hingham Boat Dock.

With no small amount of effort, he pushed the box onto the pier. Then he wrestled it onto his shoulder and walked to a pay phone station. He called a taxi that he had used to transport the shipment to Patriot. The night dispatcher was reluctant to take the request but the Sailor remembered the driver's name who had helped him on an early morning delivery before. That convinced the dispatcher who sent the cab. Before the cab arrived, the Sailor went to the marina Office and put the keys on the desk of the security guard who was sleeping peacefully. The Sailor was on the Hingham Dock an hour later.

Darkness, high wind, and heavy rain prevented the Sailor from seeing his Sea Sprite that held to a mooring less than fifty yards from the pier. The Sailor had moved the Sea Sprite to the vacant mooring after the Dock master threatened to beach his boat.

Getting to the Sea Sprite was one problem. Starting its engine and bringing it to the pier was another. The Sailor was very tired. He sat on the pier and wondered if his luck had finally run out. Then he spotted a small dingy turned upside down on the sand. Its owner had prepared it for the storm by putting it on the beach and running a line to a tree. It was well above the tide line. The Sailor pushed his shipment box under the pier and crawled to the dinghy. As he rolled it over he found two oars underneath. He untied the line from the tree, pushed the dinghy into the bay where he thought the Sea Sprite was moored. He found it on the first try, climbed aBoard and let the dinghy float free into the pounding waves.

The Sea Sprite took a while to start but finally coughed to life. The Sailor made sure that the engine was idling smoothly before he slipped away from the mooring. The water began filling the hull. The Sailor made it to the pier just as the motor flooded out. Then the Sailor placed the shipment box under the front deck and secured it as if it had been brought in on the Sea Sprite. He didn't attempt to pump her out. Instead he thought it more realistic if he let the boat fill and possibly sink at the dock. Then he went to his pad, backed a duffel bag and left to find a different place to sleep for a couple of hours.

An hour earlier a sleek fifty-foot Bay Liner moved through the heavy surf into Salem Harbor fifteen miles north of Boston. The Skipper of the express-style high-speed craft moved skillfully past the moored boats and tied up at the transient dock of the Boston Yacht Club. After all lines were fast and the Yacht rigged for the night the Skipper placed a call to New York on his cellular phone. A female voice answered on the first ring.

"Security. This is Mary. How can I help you?"

The Skipper gave his friend a cheery greeting. "Mary, my dear, this is your best friend, Skip. How's the weather in the Big Apple?"

"Miserable, Skip. I trust all goes well with you."

"We're okay, honey. Just wanted to let you know that we made Boston on time and on target. We have a gale blowing now so we grabbed a slip at the Yacht Club in Salem. This weather is expected to be over by morning. Then we will get on with it. You best tell the folks up North that we might be running a half day late. Okay?"

"Sure, Skip. Anything else?" Mary scribbled on a notepad as she listened and talked.

"Yeah. When we approached our mark, we picked up a blip on radar that looked like a small boat laying a mile off. Unusual because seas were building and the fishermen had all gone home. Anyway, we dropped on the marks, resumed course, and watched the blip. It moved onto the mark when we were about a mile past. Then we lost it on radar because of weather conditions and it being so small. Anyway, it seems to me that whoever it was hit the traps. Probably wanted to clear them before the storm. That could be good or bad depending on who it was. So, I thought I would mention it in case the locals wanted to check. I'll call tomorrow when we get underway. Bye."

Mary disconnected the call from Skip and immediately pushed the speed dial for her boss. He listened to her report and then called Phil Mondi.

Mondi called Eddie. "Eddie, this is Phil Mondi. Sorry to wake you at this ungodly hour. Apparently, a delivery to our attention from New York may have gotten delayed or lost due to the storm. Can you check it out and let me know? It is very important to today's work."

Eddie was barely awake and his night's companion was apparently interested in the conversation. "Uh, yeah, sure, Mr. Mondi. I'll look into it and let you know. It may take me an hour or so to check it all out. Okay?"

"Sure, Eddie. Let me know as soon as you find out anything." Mondi discontinued the conversation and returned to his slumber.

Eddie was only half awake and wasn't sure just what it was that he was supposed to check out. He threw some water in his face and tried to remember what was special about today's work. The only thing that came to mind was the operations order that he had given to the Sailor last evening. That had to be it. The shipment that the Sailor was supposed to pick up got lost or something. Okay, so how would he find the Sailor? Eddie had always met him in the Shanty. No one was there at four-thirty in the morning. Then he remembered that Brian had delivered the payment pouch to the Sailor every week somewhere in Hingham. Brian knew the spot where the Sailor had his boat. He simply had to call Brian and have him drive to Hingham and check out the boat. That would be the first step in his review.

Brian's phone rang several times before Louise answered it. She was barely awake and slammed down the receiver when Eddie tried to joke with her. Eddie tried again and this time Brian answered it with a blast of profanity.

Eddie was determined not to lose the call. "Brian, please, it's too early in the morning for my delicate ears to listen to such talk. You are supposed to be a valued part of the Patriot management team. As their new dispatcher it behooves you to be kind to anyone calling. You awake enough to listen, asshole? This is Eddie."

Brian had received his promotion from the new general manager at Patriot earlier in the week. He had spent long hours since, learning the duties of the dispatcher. Eddie had moved out and left the desk to him. A desk that Brian had yet become accustomed to. It was actually a welcome relief to hear Eddie's familiar gruff voice.

"Eddie! Hey, man, it's good to hear ya. Man, I miss you. That dispatcher job is a bear. I'm doing okay but I got a lot to learn. How you doin'? Boss says that you gonna be around now and then. I guess we work together on special accounts. Right?"

A friendly chat was not what Eddie was all about. He let Brian down easy. "Yeah, Brian, I'm doin' fine. We got special accounts you and me. Patriot only delivers. We'll work it out. Look, right now I need you do make a special run. You still got the Chevy? I want you should go to Hingham and check on the Sailor. See if his boat is at the docks and let me know. You got my number?"

Brian couldn't believe what he was hearing. "You want me to go out now, Eddie? It's the middle of the night. The Customer ain't gonna be there. Hell, nobody's gonna be there. You want me to make a delivery at this hour? You sober?"

That did it. Eddie busted Brian's chops. "Brian, you asshole, I don't want no crap from you. Just do it, man. Get your butt in the car and go see if the Sailor's boat is tied up at the Hingham Dock. There's nothing to deliver. Mondi wanted me to check with the Sailor. If he ain't there, you call me and tell me about the boat. Is that too difficult?"

Brian caught the drift. "Don't get pissed, man. I'll do it. It will take me an hour at least to get there. Hey, man, it's raining like hell. Why would you want to think the Sailor would be out in this stuff?"

"Brian, just do it. I'm not in the mood to answer your stupid questions." Eddie slammed the receiver in Brian's ear.

Brian mumbled and got dressed. He told Louise that he had to check on a delivery and left. It took him forty-five minutes to drive to Hingham in the heavy rain. When he arrived at the dock he had to leave his car and walk to the pier to see if the Sea Sprite was there. He found it properly tied with spring lines holding it fast in the wind. The floor Boards were afloat as the boat without cover captured the rain. Brian stepped in and pushed the bilge pump switch. Gradually the bilge pump began to eliminate some of the water in the hull as more entered from the driving rain. If the heavy rain continued the Sea Sprite could sink at the dock in a few hours.

Brian wondered where his friend, the Customer, a.k.a. the Sailor, could be found. After a few minutes he switched off the pump and returned to his car.

Finding the Sailor at this point was not a big problem. Brian arrived at the dock at the same time that the Sailor was moving from his nearby pad. The Sailor noticed that the headlights from the car were pointed to the dock and that a person was walking onto the pier. Instinctively the Sailor moved closer but stayed in the shadows. He recognized Brian's car and carefully crawled into the back seat.

Brian returned from his inspection of the Sea Sprite and picked up his cellular phone. He had just been issued the device as part of the equipment that went with his new job. This was Brian's first attempt to use the phone. He turned on the car's interior lights and began to read the operating instructions in the telephone manual.

The Sailor made a fast move from the rear seat placing his left arm around Brian's neck holding him tight against the head rest. With his right arm he cut the car lights as he whispered in Brian's ear, "Don't say a word, man. Don't you even breathe. I'll snap your fucking neck. You understand?"

Brian was horrified. It was impossible for him to speak or even move with the hold that the Sailor had on him. Even without the hold Brian was too scared to utter a sound. He let out his remaining breath and expected to die. The Sailor felt him relax and loosened the pressure on his throat. Brian was able to swallow and realized that maybe he could survive. He tried to speak.

"Okay, man, okay. I ain't gonna yell. You can have my money. I ain't got much. Hey, I got insurance. Company insurance. They don't want anybody messing with me. That's it, man. What you want?"

The Sailor leaned forward so Brian could see his face. "Brian, what I want is a cup of hot coffee and some breakfast. You got enough for that. We got to move before somebody else gets here. What you doing here, anyway? What's with this company insurance shit?"

Brian felt the release of the grip. The Sailor removed his arm and Brian turned to the back seat. "Oh, Christ, Sailor, you the one I'm looking for. The boat's sinking man. We got to keep the bilge pump turned on."

The Sailor crawled into the front seat next to Brian and picked up the cellular phone. "Don't worry about the boat, man. She'll be fine. What you doin' here at this hour? Who you fixin' to call?"

Brian recovered. "Eddie, man. You know Eddie? He got me out of bed and tells me to get my ass down her and see if you and the boat is around. I don't know why, man. He wants me to give him a call, I guess I better do it. I just got a promotion. They shook up the whole company from top to bottom. We got a new owner. Everything's different."

Sailor nodded." Yeah, I know it's different, Brian. I think I better get outta here. Let's drive into Quincy and get some breakfast. Dunkin' Donuts is open. They got good coffee. You go ahead and give Eddie a call. Tell him the boat is here, tied to the pier where it's supposed to be. Don't tell him about me. Me and you got to talk some more. That okay with you? We been buddies. Okay?"

"Yeah, okay. I don't know how to use that thing." Brian pointed to the cellular phone in the Sailor's hand.

The Sailor pushed the on button and asked Brian for Eddie's number. Then he punched the number into the handset and handed it back to Brian.

"Brian, you see that button that says send, well, you just punch that button and listen. Eddie should answer."

The Sailor was right. Eddie answered almost as soon as Brian had pushed the send button. Eddie was pleased with Brian's report. The boat was where it should be. A little worse for wear having been out to sea during a gale. The Sailor was missing but certainly around. Eddie reasoned that the Sailor was protecting the Shipment. He reported the situation to Mr. Mondi who reported to Security in New York. New York made contact with the pickup man in Dorchester and informed him that in spite of the storm the shipment was safely waiting in a Blue Sea Sprite tied up at the Hingham Town Boat Dock.

Then Security again tipped Boston Police that the buy was going down. Boston alerted the Hingham town Marshall, County Sheriff, and State Police. They also tipped the media.

Brian had twenty dollars. More than enough to get breakfast for the Sailor and himself. They drove to Dunkin' Donuts on the south side of Quincy just across from the police station. The Sailor devoured two breakfast sandwiches and four donuts. He drank several cartons of juice and three containers of coffee. Brian sipped coffee and watched in amazement as his friend gobbled everything in sight.

Finally the Sailor stopped eating and spoke to Brian. "Brian, you and me are buddies, right? I got some trouble that I need a buddy to help me get out of. I got to rely on you to keep everything quiet. If you don't want to help say so and we split right here. It involves your company and all those changes you talked about. I don't know what's happening for sure but I think they are figuring me to take a fall. I ain't gonna do that. You understand?"

Brian had liked working with the Sailor. The Sailor had allowed Brian full access to his boat and had been generous with special favors like extra bait and a few beers left in the boat's cooler. He was a friend that Brian valued as he valued his friendship with Jay. The two were his brothers. He wanted their loyalty and he was willing to give them his. He had no thoughts about the risk of being loyal to his friend. Friends were very important to Brian. He sought friendship above status or financial rewards. He was, by most modern standards, a bit simple if not backwards.

Brian was quick to answer his friend. "Hey, Sailor, we been buddies. I'll help you as much as I can. You know that I ain't gonna rat on anybody. You gonna go on the lam?"

The Sailor was pleased and relieved at Brian's response. "No, I ain't gonna split until I'm sure what's happening. I figure that whatever is gonna happen is gonna happen soon. Maybe even today. What I need for now is a place to stay and get fed. They gonna be watching my pad and I can't go back to the marina. Eddie, I figure, is gonna be after my ass. I ain't done nothing to him that I know but he's got someone pulling his chain. If things don't go like they want then they are gonna send Eddie after me to find out why. You got to act like you don't know where I'm at. You ain't seen me. You dig? But I need you to tell me what you see. Then I can figure out if I need to lam out. You don't have to rat on anybody. Just answer my questions and keep me hid. Oh, yeah, I'm gonna need to stay fixed. You got to bring me a little stash. How about it?"

"Man, you don't want much, just a little stash and a place to hole up. Shit, Sailor, I don't run the underground. Give me a break," Brian recoiled.

The Sailor wasn't in the mood to be refused especially when the issue of his dope supply was involved. He reached across the small table and grabbed Brian. "Yeah, I could have given you a break an hour ago. I could have broken your fuckin" neck, old buddy. Think of that. Yeah, you could be under the dock fillin' with seawater if I had a mind to do it. But I thought you was a buddy that I could count on. I ain't askin' for much. You just too high up now with your fuckin" new job to care about my trouble. Shit, you don't want a buddy. You want to be a big man and screw the rest. There was a lot like you in Nam. I should have fragged all the bastards."

The mention of Nam only confused Brian. He wanted to help his buddy. "Sailor, you got my help as much as I can. But you got to be straight with me. If you done something to hurt the company then I can't get caught up in it. What's really happening here?"

"Man, I'm being straight with you." The Sailor slammed his fist on the table. "I don't know what's coming down! All I know is that it ain't the same. I think I was being set up to take a fall. I don't know why. I been loyal. Why is the company trying to screw me?"

"How do you know you're being set up?" Brian tried to offer sympathy and again appear to be the Sailor's friend.

"Christ, will you listen? I don't know anything for sure. I smell trouble. I baited the Sea Sprite. The shipment is in the bow—at least part of it. If something is coming down it should happen today when I'm supposed to make delivery to a pick up guy from Dorchester. Dorchester, man! Think of that. Why some dude from Dorchester? You never picked up. I always sent it in by cab. Now they want me to handle it and hand it over to some Dude from the neighborhoods. Hey, it's coming down I tell ya. Well, let it happen only I ain't gonna be there. We'll let the man pick it up without me handling it. If the Dude don't pick it up then everything is cool and I go back to work. Same if he picks it up and nothing falls. Everything's cool. I don't take anything that isn't mine or due to me. That's the way I got it figured. Now you know it all."

Brian seemed convinced. "Okay, man, as long as everything stays cool we got no sweat. Nobody told me about a shipment. I guess I'm out of that end of it. You want a place to stay? I guess maybe you could hang out at the Sister's. She don't ask questions. You just help her out in any way you can. She won't ask for help. You got to volunteer. Then she'll put you to work around the place fixing up and cleaning, serving food and stuff. Can you get over to St. Anslem's by noon? I got to pick up some food and deliver it to her at her place. You help me with the delivery and then I'll see if she can take you on. You can move out if it don't suit you. She don't ask questions. Take the T from Quincy. Red line it and transfer to the Green. Get off at Cambridge Street and walk up to the hospital. Be there by noon. Hang out in the cafeteria. I'll find you there. How's it sound?"

The Sailor tried to focus on the directions. He seemed satisfied. "Your Sister's. I guess it will do. You find out this afternoon what happens when the dude goes for the shipment. If everything is cool then I got to get to Eddie and explain a few things. I'll meet you at the hospital like you say."

Jay returned to his desk at Action with anticipation and fear that he had lost valuable time in the conduct of the St. Anslem's project. Ken Ryan met him as he arrived. A staff briefing on the St. Anslem's project coupled with an executive session on the Boston Hospital waste management program was the first thing on the schedule for the day. Jay joined the staff and management in the conference room. Mark Meehan sat at the head of the table. Next to him was the large bulk of Mr. Veto Celi, Action's crack waste management representative and foremost salesman.

Celi's unbuttoned collar and wide knot tie was barely visible under an abundance of chin that gave the impression of no neck. His comical appearance caused Jay to smile. Ken noticed Jay's expression and wondered what caused it until he caught view of Celi scratching his middle.

Ken made a comment to Jay that caused laughter. Jay replied and both men began to giggle noticeably. Meehan caught the juvenile conduct. He stared at the two until they recovered.

When all seemed in order, Meehan started the meeting. "Ladies and gentlemen, I am pleased to report that the implementation of the St. Anslem's project is now on schedule and should be completed by us over the next week. In that regard I want to welcome back Jay Marquart who designed the project. Jay, as you know, has been ill but is now ready to resume his duties, Welcome back, Jay. Our end is nearly finished. After that we will be maintaining the agreement by providing the hospital with the supplies for the project and doing continuing promotion and training of hospital personnel. Ken Ryan will supervise the contract and I understand Jay will do the foot work at the site. Is that right, Ken?"

Ryan responded with an emphatic nod. This was a relief to Jay who expected to be relegated to a minor job because of his absence. Ken looked at Jay with an encouraging smile.

Mark Meehan was moving into the next subject. "With St. Anslem's behind us we need to concentrate on the Boston Hospital design and implementation and on expanding our market base to other hospitals and healthcare institutions in the metropolitan area. One contract is not enough to support our activity as we have projected it to be. In that regard, now for the bad news, we are experiencing about a five percent deficit at this time when we had anticipated profits would be running about ten percent. Mr. Celi, as you know, is our marketing man and I've asked him to give a brief report for your information."

Everyone in the room knew Celi could barely speak his name. To think that he could give an intelligent report was ludicrous. To everyone's complete surprise Celi stood and moved to an overhead projector that he tried to turn on. Mr. Meehan's secretary, sitting next to the projector, casually assisted Celi in the task. Once the projector was ready the secretary stood and put on the first transparency. Celi stood in front of the screen blocking the view as he began his commentary.

"As youse can see, we ain't doin' what we want. So we got to get more business."

The secretary changed to the next transparency. A graph showing the intersecting lines of projected revenue and expense crossing at a point that revealed anticipated profit in months after the start of the waste management business line was evident. It was also evident that the expected profits were now noticeably behind schedule. Celi just waved at the transparency as if it was self-explanatory. Actually, it was, but Celi was incapable of explaining it in any case. Jay was tempted to ask Celi a question just to make him sweat. He thought better of it in view of the possibility that Celi might figure out that he was being had. Then there was the prospect of Celi rearranging Jay's anatomy. Having just been released from the hospital, Jay had no desire to return as a patient.

The secretary placed several more transparencies on the projector that were very demonstrative of the sorry status of the company's business plan. Celi stood in front of the screen and waved to each transparency as it appeared.

Following the last transparency, the secretary turned on the lights and Celi went back to his seat. Mr. Meehan thanked Celi for his comprehensive report, gave a little pep talk about economy and efficiency of effort, and then brought the brief meeting to a close.

Meehan was pleased with the meeting. He knew that Celi was the joke of the year. The staff openly criticized the company for having a disreputable clown representing their efforts. On the other side of the issue was the fact that Celi was the perfect fall guy. He could be easily blamed for the mounting deficits that were really attributable to the revenue skimming that was being taken by Park Environmental. In the New York office at Park One there was no concern about Action's profits even after the payoff to Mr. Muldoon and his man, Celi. Everything was going according to plan. At least everything had gone according to plan as far as they knew.

Under Secretary of Labor, Robert Cowan, was bored stiff. In the few months that he had been a part of the Federal Administration he had only once been in the limelight as a back drop to the secretary who made an official announcement about some damn thing that Cowan couldn't remember. He missed the action of the Boston City Council and ward politics. Cowan was a street fighter. He realized that his move to the big show in Washington was a move by his opponents in the party to simply get him out of sight. Carefully, he planned his triumphant return from exile. He still had a small army of supporters who would benefit from his return to power. These were people who had also been benched when Cowan was disposed.

Labor was not to be trusted but Cowan knew that some people in the administration of the Boston Workers Guild were looking to move Mr. Muldoon aside. Those people could be counted on to do the necessary undercover work so important to a politician's success. It was possible to assembly his army. Funds were difficult. That would require Party support and Party support was controlled by special interests.

Cowan needed to get special interest to push him into the Party's spotlight. Special interest supporting an incumbent was impossible to move to a challenger. Cowan required the support of a wealthy special interest currently on the outside looking for an opportunity to put "their man in office."

Robert Cowan was still a good ticket. He was still known to the electorate. He had media recognition. A back door news release would get him space in the Boston papers and time spot on the radio and TV news. The publicity would serve as an advertisement that Cowan was available and could be had by any organization that would like to sponsor his comeback. Somebody would certainly buy. He decided to give it a test run.

Staff reporters for the *Boston Globe*'s Washington office were routinely seen walking the halls of the administration buildings following leads, seeking interviews, and hustling staff. They would meet in the staff lunch rooms and stalk their prey. Cowan knew the routine. Purposely he took his lunch and sat alone at a table visible to all. The trap was set. In less than an hour he had a bite. A *Globe* reporter laboring through a slow news day spotted the Under Secretary, Former Mayor and moved in. Cowan acted surprised to see the reporter who he remembered from the press conferences in Boston. They exchanged small talk and eventually the Reporter asked him about his future plans. The question was really in context with the conversation that Cowan had carefully maneuvered to that point. The Under Secretary paused and then asked for the confidence of the reporter that was quick and easy in coming. With that said, Cowan confided that he had given some very preliminary thought of returning to the State and was considering making a run for the Party's nomination for Governor. Of course, this was only a thought and nothing had been done to further the idea so far. It was just a thought.

The reporter didn't even blink. He seemed to consider it a routine remark hardly worth following conversation. He changed the subject to the weather. Talked about sports for a few minutes and then wished the Under Secretary a good day. Cowan, the old campaigner, knew he had registered. The reporter was probably on the phone talking to the political editor in Boston with the scoop that Cowan was thinking about running for Governor. Now Cowan only had to wait for the reaction. The formal reaction would come from the incumbents who would say things like "no comment" and party leaders who would say that they "had not discussed this with Cowan and were in no position to confirm or deny the story." Informal reaction would come from former friends and supporters who would either encourage or discourage him. Hopefully, a wealthy person or organization would seek the opportunity to be his sponsor. That was the reaction he was looking for.

Jay sat with Ken Ryan for two hours after the staff meeting. Ryan filled him in on Meehan's experience at the St. Anslem's meeting where Action apparently took a shot. Meehan wanted the project on fast track. That was done while Jay was in Psych. Jay nodded his understanding. In response he explained to Ken that Dr. Sutton was the man to contact for the advancement of the project. Jay volunteered to contact Sutton immediately in order to ensure that everything was satisfactory. He decided not to mention to Ken that he had met with the Board's leadership on the matter with Cecile. That was personal. If his acquaintance with Patello, the Bishop, or even any of the doctors was necessary to help he would use it. For now, he would hold that in reserve. Ken gave Jay a list of items that had been installed at St. Anslem's during his absence. He suggested that Jay take the afternoon to tour the hospital and become familiar with the state of the program and chat with Dr. Sutton.

The last thing Jay wanted to do was to return to St. Anslem's. For the present he wanted to forget the place and put his life back together. On the other hand, he realized that St. Anslem's was very much a part of his life and would probably remain to be a part of it. A meeting with Sutton was called for and he also thought about Tommy the Tout's proposition to get the goods on Officer Kelly. If he was going to take advantage of Tommy's offer he would have to stay active in the Action project. For now, he was just relieved to know that he was still a member of the Action team and that his work was appreciated. Mr. Meehan's comments remained in his mind.

After Ken completed his briefing he left Jay alone. Jay's desk was piled high with inter office memorandums, policy statements, and various newsletters. He scanned them and placed a few in his out box for filing. The rest were thrown in the wastebasket A number of telephone messages were held by a large paper clip and hanging from the switch on his desk light. Jay fumbled through them. Most were over a week old. One mentioned that Donovan from the Union had called every day and wanted Jay to call at his earliest convenience.

Brian had also called every day looking for Jay and wanting to talk. However, there was one message on top of the stack that had come in early that morning. Brian wanted to talk to Jay on a very important matter. It was Thursday. Jay figured Brian wanted to check on this Friday's action. Jay wanted to go fishing but was determined to avoid hitting the sauce. Brian would have to help him stay sober. That was going to be the rule from now on. He picked up the phone and returned Brian's call.

Jay was surprised when a secretary answered the phone for the Dispatcher's desk. She stated that the Dispatcher was on another line and invited Jay to hold. Jay explained that he wanted to talk to Brian not the Dispatcher. The secretary informed Jay that Brian was the Dispatcher. Jay decided to hold. In less than a minute Brian answered. He excitedly explained to Jay about the new set up at Patriot. More importantly, he had to talk to Jay about some recent changes in things and about an opportunity he had come across for Jay to help with the Special Account deliveries. Brian explained that he had to make a pick up at St. Anslem's at noon and wondered if he could meet with Jay at the hospital. Jay agreed since he had to go to the hospital anyway. That ended the conversation.

Jay's head was spinning after the call to Brian. He could hardly imagine the bungling Brian as a dispatcher for Patriot Transport. It was difficult for Jay to think that a lame brain like Eddie could handle the job. Now Brian had stepped into the job. *No wonder the business got sold*, he thought.

Donovan's calls were numerous and all marked urgent Jay decided to place a call to him before leaving for the hospital. Donovan answered immediately.

"Hey, Donovan. Jay Marquart here. How can I help you? Sorry about not getting back to you sooner."

Donovan was pleased that Jay called but upset with the delayed reply. "Marquart, where in the hell have you been? You got one of those no show jobs like the politicians? Goddamn it, we got work to do. You in this Union or not, man?"

Jay felt the Donovan's sting. He gave a quick answer. "You want all of those questions answered? Well, I been sick in the hospital. No, I don't have a no show job like you guys in the Union and yeah, I'm still in the Union unless you threw me out. Anything else?"

"Sorry. Nobody told me you were in the hospital." Donovan true to his personality offered somewhat of an apology. "You okay? We got a contract finished with Action. All ratified and everything. No surprise I guess. We mailed out copies to everybody. Yours went to your house. Anyway, with that over you and I have to sit down and think about the members and how we are going to support them with grievances and all that. Can you give me some time tomorrow?"

Jay agreed to meet Donovan for lunch on Friday. He threw the rest of the messages away, turned out his desk light, and left for St. Anslem's, He arrived at the hospital around ten-thirty in the morning and began touring the halls looking for the many items on the list that Ken Ryan had provided. Most of the items were promotional waste containers in waiting areas, elevator lobbies, and main lobbies. Jay felt they were ugly displays that violated the otherwise sedate decor of the hospital. His idea was to use special containers that accommodated the decor instead of offending it. He made a note to complain to Ken about the containers.

The list also included special information guides for waste handling provided to the staff in the environmental and food services departments. As stated, the information was posted at prominent places but Jay noticed that the personnel from both departments ignored the directions. He tactfully asked a few of the employees about the signs. They all responded in similar fashion. Essentially the troops had no idea why the signs were posted and had received no direction in the conduct of waste handling. Jay remembered Mr. Mondi's comments about the project being nearly complete. From what he had observed the project was barely started.

Jay hung out in the office of the director of Environmental Services until noon. Finally, the director arrived for a brief few minutes to collect messages before returning to a nursing floor where he was filling in on a short staffed cleaning crew. He allowed Jay five minutes of interview during which Jay learned that the Environmental Services management had no knowledge about the recent status of the Waste Handling Project. The containers and posters around the hospital had been authorized by the President's office. Environmental Services emptied the containers daily and threw everything into the trash without regard to the recycling information. So far Action was batting near zero. Dr. Sutton was next on Jay's list but he remembered that he had promised to meet Brian in the cafeteria at noon.

Brian came to St. Anslem's to pick up the food and make the run to The Little Portion on Melina Cass Boulevard. He backed his Patriot Van up to the freight dock and explained to the clerk at the receiving desk that he had to go inside for a few minutes. The clerk was very courteous and explained to Brian that she would call the kitchen to bring the food to the dock and load it into the Van. She also told Brian that Mr. Durant wanted to be notified when the Van arrived. It was obvious even to Brian that he had best not keep Mr. Durant waiting. Brian knew that on previous trips it had taken Food Service at least fifteen minutes to a half-hour to get the food to the dock and loaded. He looked at his watch and made note of the time that he had to be back at the dock. Then he moved swiftly to the cafeteria.

The Sailor was sitting in a very prominent position at a table just in front of the cashier. He had three donuts on a plate and a very large container of coffee in front of him. His tattoo was very visible and he openly moved the arm to attract attention as people passed by. Many of then looked at the tattoo and smiled. He was in his glory.

Brian moved swiftly into the chair next to him. "Hey, Sailor, what you doin', man? You got everybody in this place lookin' at you. I thought you wanted to be on the lam."

The Sailor looked up at Brian but ignored his comments. He gave a broad smile and a wink to a passing nurse. He was very drunk. "Yeah, this is the place. Let me stay here. I'll die a happy man. Oh, my, but they got pretty ladies here. Yeah, this is the place."

Brian noticed that just about everyone was looking at the Sailor and commenting about his strange appearance. Brian tried to get the Sailor to shut up and move out. "Sailor, you can't stay here. I got a place all scoped out for you. We got to get there now 'cause I got to make a delivery. Come on!"

The mention of a delivery triggered a smile from the Sailor. He answered Brian in a loud voice. "A delivery, you say. You got a delivery for me? You promised me some stash. I need it. I got to have some stash. Where we goin', Brian?"

Brian managed to get an arm around the Sailor's midsection and raise him from the chair. Then he began to move him toward the exit. They were almost out of the cafeteria when Jay came in and saw them. He realized that Brian was apparently trying to help someone and moved to assist. Other hospital personnel were offering to help but Brian courteously declined their help. Jay came up from behind and took hold of the Sailor from the side opposite Brian. The Sailor looked at Jay and just smiled. He made no attempt to resist his exit.

Jay offered a greeting to Brian. "How's it goin', Brian? Sorry I'm a little late. Who we got here? Smells like a candidate for the hospital's tank. You into hospital work now?"

Brian looked at Jay. "Hi, Jay. No, man, this ain't no patient. This is the Customer. You know, the guy that owns the boat we use for fishin'. We got to help him outta some trouble. Can you take a ride with me on a delivery? I got a lot to talk about with you. "

Jay just shook his head in disbelief. "You're the dispatcher, man. You don't make deliveries. You gotta get yourself some good help. This stiff one of your recruits?"

The Sailor looked at Jay and gave him a drunken glare followed by a threatening smile. Jay saw the look and realized that he had better not kid around. The man that he held was indeed strong and when irritated possibly dangerous. When they arrived at the loading dock Joe Durant was waiting. He watched Brian and Jay awkwardly load the Sailor into the front seat. Jay exchanged a few words with Brian and then crawled into the cargo section with the food containers that the food service workers had just loaded. Brian secured the doors and walked over to Durant.

Brian offered Durant a greeting. "Afternoon, Mr. Durant. I guess we're ready to go. I got some extra help with me today. The company changed hands and I got a promotion. I'm gonna break in some new help on this run. As long as the new manager don't say nothing we can keep helping you out. Actually, he don't know about this yet. You going with us?"

This was the first that Joe Durant had heard about Patriot changing hands. He wondered if Phil Mondi was gone or still in town. He had worked out the delivery to Sister Celest with Mondi and now the driver told him that the deal was in place only because the new manager of Patriot didn't know about it. Durant had another five-thousand-dollar donation from St. Anslem's that he had intended for Brian to deliver with the food. Now things were different. He decided to follow the Van to the mission.

"Brian, I'll follow you in my car. You're full, I see. Do you know if Phil Mondi is in today? I could give him a call and straighten everything out."

"He's gone, Sir. I understand he bought a new business in Maine. Kind of sudden I guess but business is business they say. I'll see you downtown."

The metallic green BMW convertible with half-shade headlight lenses, high chrome wheel covers and chrome trim on the door edges moved gracefully into the parking lot at the Hingham Town Boat Dock. The driver looked over his dark glasses and surveyed the area before he opened the door. He was dressed in a light green suit with a white vest. His shirt collar was open displaying several gold chains around his slim neck. The white shoes were highly polished. As he lowered his arms several gold bracelets fell to his wrists. He was the man, on time, to make the pickup from a dude in a blue boat called a Sea Sprite. Since the deal had been cut he had made several trips to the Hingham Dock to case the area and learn where to expect the boat to be. As promised, the Blue Sea Sprite was visible at the pier.

Contrary to the plan, no one was at the boat. The contact looked all around for someone who might be the man to make the pass. One man sat fishing on the end of the pier. Another person in a Hingham Town working vest was picking up trash around the launch and picnic area. Across the street two men were working with a fishing boat on a trailer. None of them seemed to notice the Contact man as he walked onto the pier and looked at the Sea Sprite. It seemed to be nearly submerged. Water was visible above the floor Boards. Forward under the deck he noticed a large waterproof square container. This was obviously the shipment. Still there was no one to make the pass.

The Green Suit walked back to the BMW and made a telephone call. Then he waited in the car for nearly an hour. At two-fifteen, near the deadline for the six o'clock news, he got out of the car and walked onto the pier. Carefully he moved into the Sea Sprite and removed the water proof box. His shoes and pants were soaked up to the knees. He had ripped his suit coat on the rugged edge of the boat. Nevertheless, he had the shipment and proceeded to return to his car.

The fisherman came from behind. The man picking up trash came directly at him. The two men working on the boat trailer were running toward him. One was talking into a hand held radio. Sirens wailed. Blue lights on speeding police cars came from all directions. The Green Suit was cuffed. Vaguely he could hear someone reading his rights. He was photographed in the custody of the Sheriff and State Narcotic Agents. Then he was pushed into a police car to be taken to the Hingham Town Government Center and booked. Television Cameras recorded every minute. At the Government Center, a pre-planned news conference was held at which the Sheriff praised the unselfish cooperation of law enforcement agencies is breaking up the largest narcotic ring in this area. A spokesman for the Boston Police stated that the Harbor Patrol had been watching the boat that brought in the drugs for some time waiting for an opportunity to capture the perpetrators in the act. In response to a question planted by the State but asked by the *Globe*, the estimated street value of the shipment was nearly one million dollars. Video and photographs were taken of the shipment box containing bags of white powder.

Sister Celest was relieved when the Patriot Van parked in front of her door. The Little Portion was gaining in popularity, not in the least because of the quality of its food. Patrons were already lined up for the one o'clock serving. The food was late and some of the citizens were becoming restless. To her dismay the first item unloaded was not food but a rather large and very drunk person who Brian and a helper placed in a chair. Then without any explanation they brought in the food. Celest went immediately to the kitchen and began to prepare the food for service. As was her custom she placed Brian on the serving line. Jay only watched for an instant before Sister Celest ushered him to his station. With everyone ready the food line began to move.

The last person served was the Sailor who woke up just in time to get the last bite. He smiled his gratitude and tipped his dirty cap to Sister Celest. Then he returned to his chair, ate his meal, and went back to sleep. He had had a bad night.

Brian knew the routine almost as well as Sister Celest. He enjoyed helping her in the mission. Frequently he would stop by after evening deliveries and assist her with various jobs that needed doing. They had developed a friendship. He recognized her as a compassionate person. She was what the God thing was all about. He intended to introduce Jay to her today but things were now a bit complicated with the Sailor in the act. Rather than try to explain everything at once he decided to let the Sailor sleep it off while he and Jay worked on the cleanup.

Sister Celest had become acquainted enough with Brian to understand that behind his simple exterior and unfinished behavior was a loving person who wanted to do right. He often discussed his lifestyle and asked her opinions about the right and wrong of his relationship with Louise. He had never discussed his job. When Celest had attempted to question him about his night work with Patriot he changed the subject. About the only thing he ever mentioned was his trips to the Troubadour Lounge but he never mentioned why he went there. He had also mentioned his best friend, Jay, who he was very concerned about. He wanted Jay to be happy and free from some illness that Brian would not discuss. Now the compassionate Brian had arrived at her doorstep with two strangers. Sr. Celest was prepared to help Brian help them if that was what he wanted to do. She could wait for the explanation.

Her thoughts about Brian were interrupted as Joe Durant came into the mission and waved her to join him at a table in the comer of the dining room. She took off her apron, poured two cups of coffee and went to the table.

"Good afternoon, Sister." Joe Durant stood in proper Catholic grammar school fashion as the Sister came to the table. "It seems as though you are becoming a success in your venture to save the homeless." Then he handed her the envelope with the five-thousand-dollar check from St. Anslem's.

"Good afternoon to you, Mr. Durant. Please sit down. Thank you for this and for your continuing support to the food line." Celest sat across from Durant and patted his hand in gratitude. "We have some extra help today. Do I owe my thanks to you for that as well? I really didn't expect to see you today."

"No. Quite honestly I don't know how to explain this," Durant offered. "Brian and Jay are friends. Jay does contract work at the hospital for Action Waste Management. They were trying to get the big guy to walk when I met them. They just threw him in the truck and brought him here. I haven't the slightest idea who he is. I didn't expect to come today either. But Brian told me that Patriot has been sold and Phil Mondi is no longer with the company. This could affect our delivery deal since the new boss at Patriot apparently doesn't know about this. Brian is going to keep it going as long as he can. I guess we need to come up with a contingency plan."

Sister Celest was under control. She felt confident that her friend Brian would find a way to keep delivering the food from St. Anslem's. Her greater concern was Joe Durant's support. So far he had managed to keep The Little Portion in a positive cash position.

"Joe, your help is invaluable. These weekly checks are keeping me alive. Things are picking up though. The other day a guy from Hardly's bank suddenly showed up and gave me a thousand dollar gift from one of the bank's foundations. I don't know how he found out about us. Anyway, until those types of donations become frequent I'll need to have continuing support from good old St. Anslem's. Can you keep this up?"

Joe became pensive. "Celest, I'm not sure how long I'll be with St. Anslem's. The Board is trying to nail me and now the good Bishop is on my case about employee morale. Can you beat that? That pompous ass votes with the Hardly boys for layoffs and then gets miffed when the troops gripe. I tell you, I've about had it."

Sister Celest rolled her eyes in an understanding way. "You've got my prayers, Joe. You can always work here. I can't pay you but you will have at least one hot meal and a place to flop. Looks like the big guy is beginning to stir. I better find out from Brian what he wants me to do for his friend. Thanks, Joe. You know I'll help you any way I can. God bless you."

The Sailor had rolled off his chair and fell to the floor. He groaned once and then went back to sleep in a fetal position. Sister Celest stepped around him in a way that she had become accustomed to in accommodating her clients. Brian was putting cups back into the wooden cupboard while Jay sipped on a coffee cup. The good Sister gave him a friendly nod as she approached Brian.

"Thanks again, Brian. We really appreciate your help. Will I see you tonight?"

"I don't know, Sister. I got new duties now so I'll have somebody else make the night deliveries for me. My friend, Jay, here is the guy I think might do it."

Jay gave Brian a surprise look when he heard the comment. He stood up as Sister walked to him and extended her hand.

Celest was first to speak. "You are apparently, Jay. I'm very pleased to meet you and thankful for your help. Brian has become a very good friend. If he says you are the one to fill in then I know he has picked a very good man. I'll look forward to seeing you more often."

Jay took the Sister's hand and nodded with a smile. He was completely unaware of what Brian was talking about. His expression betrayed him. Sister Celest realized that he was confused but she decided to let it alone. Instead she turned her attention to the sleeping Sailor.

"Brian, you have blessed me with many gifts over the past few weeks. Pray tell what or more properly who is that lying on the floor? Is he another member of your staff?"

"That's the Sailor, Sister. He needs a place to stay for a while until some things work out," Brian explained. "He's a little drunk right now but he's a good guy and he'll help out. You can count on that. He's okay. I guess I better come in tonight and check on him when he wakes up."

Sister Celest felt some comfort in knowing that Brian would return to help her deal with her new client who at the moment was unconscious and obviously unaware of where he was. She wondered if he would stay in her care once he became aware that he was in a soup kitchen. Even the destitute maintained some sense of dignity that was offended by being dependent on the charity of her mission.

The Little Portion had emptied out after lunch but by evening her clients would begin filtering back for dinner and to take advantage of the beds in the run-down hotel now under her administration. The Sailor was destined to sign on and meet the crew.

Brian drove Jay back to St. Anslem's and on the way explained that he needed someone to make the deliveries to special accounts. Most of the deliveries were made late in the afternoon or in the early evening. Occasionally there was a late delivery like the once a week trip to the Troubadour Lounge. Brian reasoned that Jay could make the deliveries as special part time temporary hire of Patriot. He could do the work after he got off duty at Action. It was like a second part time job. He could also do the special delivery to The Little Portion on his lunch hour. The money was very generous. Jay agreed to give it a try.

When Jay returned to the hospital he wandered around the corridors and checked to see if the visitors and staff were properly using the recycling containers. As he suspected, the containers were being ignored. Trash was indiscriminately thrown in the stairways and elevators. Soft drink containers were left on banisters and ledges. Surgical booties and hair nets were abandoned at will. The place was a mess. Action Waste Management signs were there as an embarrassment for the public to behold. In disgust Jay returned to his office and proceeded to blast away at Ken Ryan about the sorry state of affairs.

Ken appeared to be very intent. He listened to Jay's every word. When he finished, Ken suggested that they get a cup of coffee and further discuss the matter. Instead of going to the employee lounge in the cafeteria Ken asked his secretary to bring the coffee to his desk. After she delivered the beverages, Ken excused her for the afternoon and closed the door for a private and confidential chat with Jay. Ken explained to Jay that as long as Mr. Mondi was of the opinion that the St. Anslem's project was okay then it was okay. Jay's opinion was not important nor was it important that the project continue to function. It was only important that the project be installed on time. The project had been installed. The hospital was responsible to see that it worked. Jay was to see that the hospital understood its end of the contract. Therefore Jay needed to discuss the problem with Mr. Durant and not bother Mr. Mondi with these details.

Jay felt betrayed. He had taken a lot of pride in designing the St. Anslem's project. He wanted it to work. He believed in the benefits of waste management and recycling. This was his contribution to a better world. He pounded his fist on Ken's desk and let his attitude be known.

"Goddamnit it, Ken, this thing is going to work if I have to clean up that hospital all by myself." Jay again slammed his hand on Ken's desk.

Ryan did not want to argue the point. "Keep it cool, Jay. This is just one account. We're going after a lot more. We'll go to school on this one and make the others work. Mondi doesn't care if this one bombs."

"Screw Mondi! St. Anslem's is my hospital." Jay stood and began to pace as he shouted, "I care about the place. No way am I gonna let the place get ripped off."

"Careful what you say, Jay. Word gets out that you're not working with the team and you're outside looking in. This is not just a one-horse company. It's part of a very big operation that can chew you up. You be careful."

Jay leaned forward on Ryan's desk and spoke into his face. "I'll be careful, man. But I still got my pride. I care about my work and I want to do something that has meaning. They taught me how important that was when I was in the goofy bin. Mondi has got to realize that we want this company to look good. Don't he want that?"

Ken didn't answer. His body language signaled to Jay that the conversation was over. That was fine. Jay turned without another word and marched back to his desk where he spent the rest of the day in a general funk. Ken let him pout. They had few disagreements in the time that they had worked together and this matter didn't deserve a breech in their usual compatible relationship. Besides if Jay wanted to do some patch up and maintenance work on the St. Anslem's implementation it couldn't hurt.

Just let him alone. He'll work it out in his mind eventually, was Ken's concluding thought.

Joe Durant left The Little Portion and returned to St. Anslem's. He liked to visit with Sister Celest. Her sincerity, compassion, and wonderful sense of humor were an inspiration to him especially in light of the depressing situation he faced at the hospital. However, when he arrived at his office the details of administering the complex institution were piled in front of him. Budgets, deficits, politics, arguments, complaints, all waited his miraculous resolutions. Failure to satisfy all involved generated criticism from the dissatisfied and not a word of gratitude from those supported. The two sides of every issue required a winner and a loser. There was no such thing as compromise among those who had to desperately compete for the favor of authority that dispensed increasingly scarce resources. Durant could only help some at the expense of others.

Every decision cost him prestige and loss of favor among his constituents. The days when he could solve the needs of others by applying more money, equipment, or personnel were over. He was locked in a bad news situation. It was nearly six in the evening when he turned out the lights in the office and began his drive home.

The Mass Pike was crowded and it took him nearly a half-hour to make the circle onto Interstate 93 toward Hingham. Another forty-five minutes found him on Route 3 just a few miles from the Hingham exit. It was at this point that he noticed the red low fuel light flashing prominently. The gas gauge registered below the empty mark Joe didn't need this hassle. Running out of gas on busy Route 3 would mean at least two hours waiting for help. Fortunately he made the exit and stopped at the Shell station located at the bottom of the ramp. The young attendant worked part time at the marina gas docks and recognized Joe. He was excited about the big drug bust that had taken place that afternoon and proceeded to dramatize the affair as he told Joe about it with his own enhancements of guns and fights at the scene.

Durant was fascinated with the story. It was the perfect diversion from his own problems. He raced home, greeted his wife with the news of the event, and settled into his favorite chair to watch the late edition news on television. Dinner could wait. As expected the lead story was about the success of the law enforcement agencies of the metropolitan area in breaking the largest drug ring in Boston. Several interviews with the smiling officers came onto the screen. A few shots of the captured offender were also shown. The backdrop for the entire report given by on the scene reporters was the Hingham Town Boat Dock. The Blue Sea Sprite was visible behind the reporters and was used as a concluding scene.

Joe came forward in his chair when he recognized the boat. Then the report switched to the Office of the Captain of the Boston Harbor Police. The Captain was complementing the cooperation of the various agencies involved and at the same time was taking credit for originating the investigation that led to the arrest of the suspect. This was followed by the department's file video of the Blue Sea Sprite crossing Hingham Bay. Durant thought he recognized Brian at the controls with Jay sitting next to him. The video was apparently taken in low light so the figures in the boat were not very clear on television. Nevertheless, Durant popped out of his chair to get a closer look. Too late. The report cut back to the reporter now in the Harbor Police Station that the estimated retail value of the confiscated drugs was in the neighborhood of one million dollars. The owner of the boat was being sought by Police for questioning.

Mark Meehan began watching the Boston Television stations at five when the first news reports were made. Radio had been reporting the event from the scene and on the hour since the bust had happened. After the eight o'clock newscast Meehan called the Security Office in New York. The Security Office had been monitoring the Boston media via satellite and was aware of the reports. Meehan was satisfied that the plan had succeeded. However, Security was more reserved. The Sam the Security Man was open in response to Mark's questions about the value of the confiscated drugs and added some comment that was not a part of the media reports.

"Mark, I guess we could say that we accomplished the mission. The Fuzz got their man and they got the shipment. That was enough to give them something to crow about and make the politicians look good. You can operate on the new routes beginning tomorrow. Now here's our concern. First of all the goods weren't worth a million. That's the cops making it look good. We packaged two loads that maybe had retail value over thou each. Our people at the scene only saw one box taken from the boat. Where's the other box? We know the cops don't have it and the pickup guy didn't get it. Okay. The next thing is that the boat guy, they call him the Sailor, didn't show for the bust. Why? Was he tipped? By who? Maybe Eddie? We got to find that out and we got to find that Sailor."

Meehan was concerned about Eddie. The Enforcer wasn't smart enough to pull a con but he was smart enough to know that you didn't cross the company. Besides, Eddie was very visible. Meehan tried to calm Security. "You don't have to worry about Eddie. He's easy to find. If you want I can have him call you in a few minutes. I always know where he is and he is loyal. If he has any answers to your questions you can have then in short order."

Sam liked the suggestion. "Okay, have him give me a call. Our Navy reported that their radar picked up a small boat on the drop mark within an hour after they passed. That means that the Sailor picked up the drop. So, it looks like maybe the Sailor cut himself in on half the load and took off. Now he ain't got much and it's not high grade so he isn't gonna do well if he thinks he is gonna go into business. He probably thinks he got the motherlode and is gonna use it for his own stash. Our point is that he apparently knew about the bust. How did he know? If we got a leak we got to fix it. This guy might be dangerous. He could cut a deal with the Fuzz. Maybe he's undercover. We got to find him and get some answers. Have Eddie call me."

Eddie was enjoying a beer and eyeing a cute young thing at the Shanty when his cellular phone made its disturbing ring. He moved away from the bar to a quiet corner and answered. Meehan gave Eddie a brief report of his conversation with Security and directed him to call the Security Office immediately. Eddie acknowledged, disconnected, walked out of the bar into the parking lot, and dialed Security.

The Sam the Security Man was blunt. He wanted the Sailor for questioning that he would personally conduct. Eddie's assignment was to find the Sailor, take him into his personal custody, and hold him until Sam could interrogate him. Sam advised Eddie that he would be in Boston in the morning. Eddie was expected to have the Sailor available and the other box? We know the cops don't have it and the pickup guy didn't get it. Okay. The next thing is that the boat guy, they call him the Sailor, didn't show for the bust. Why? Was he tipped? By who? Maybe Eddie? We got to find that out and we got to find that Sailor."

Eddie pushed the end button and called Brian. Brian's line was busy. He was talking to Jay who had seen the six o'clock news. Sea Sprite's prominence in the daily events was shocking but when the file video of Brian and Jay cruising across the bay came on the screen Jay let out a yell that scared Susan and the kids. They thought Dad was on another violent tear and went for the door. Instead of chasing them, Dad grabbed the phone and called his buddy. Susan and the kids came back into the house and started to eat dinner. Jay ranted and cursed at Brian. None of it made sense to Susan who, after the first few minutes, turned off her interest and the television.

At first Brian was confused. Jay was not making much sense yelling about the Sailor, the boat, a drug bust and about being involved in something that was on television. The whole thing was beyond Brian. Finally, after making Jay repeat himself several times Brian began to get the drift. Eddie's early morning call to go to the Hingham Dock, the Sailor's back seat attack on him, having breakfast with the Sailor, and hiding him at the Sister's. He remembered that the Sailor had said that something was coming down. Apparently, it did. He tried to calm Jay down and promised to call him back after he watched the news. He hung up the phone and tried to convince Louise to let him watch the news instead of *Jeopardy!*.

She argued to the contrary and before he could convince her the phone rang again. This time it was Eddie. "Brian, my main man, how you doin'? Hey, I got to talk to the Sailor. You seen him lately? Think you can find him and bring him to my place? We need to chat."

Brian realized that this was the call that the Sailor had predicted. "I ain't seen him lately, Eddie. I can look around. If he wants to, you want me to bring him over to North Quincy?"

Eddie agreed. "Yeah. But look if he don't want to come you just give me a call and I'll come to him. It's kinda important."

Brian didn't like the tone of Eddie's voice. He sounded like the Enforcer did when he went after a delinquent account. This meant that his friend was headed for trouble. Now Brian was in a fix. He didn't want to cross the company and he didn't want to endanger his friend. He knew where the Sailor was a few hours ago. But that was a few hours ago. If he was gone from that place when Brian looked there then he could honestly tell Eddie that he didn't know where the Sailor was. He returned the call to Jay.

"Jay, look, man, we got a problem. You know Eddie. Well, he wants the Sailor and he wants me to deliver him if I can find him. It's all tied into this television thing. Can you do me a favor and find the Sailor then stash him some place that I don't know about. I don't ask and you don't tell. Eddie won't think about you. I'm his man. Can you handle it, man? You get the Sailor out of the Sister's place so he ain't there when I check in an hour. I tell Eddie he ain't where I last saw him."

Jay was plenty miffed. He had agreed to help Brian with the food delivery to the Sister's but he hadn't bargained to become involved with another drunk. Why should he get involved? The Sailor was just another drunk—another drunk that needed help. Markley came to mind and he knew that Bob Markley would always step forward to help another drunk. Jay was about to have his inning in helping the helpless.

"Brian, I don't know why I'm getting into this. Hell, we made the six o'-clock news cruising in a boat that was busted for bringing in drugs and now you want me to help the guy who owns the boat. The cops are looking for him, man. Not just Eddie. What do you want from me, man?"

"Hey, Sailor didn't do nothing, man." Brian swiftly tried to defend his friend. "The cops want him they can find him. We don't mess with the law. The Sailor's got to have some time to figure what he wants to do. He might turn himself in. That's his decision. We got to help him make up his mind before Eddie splatters him. You dig?"

Jay understood Brian's attempt at being a friend. "I dig, man. I'll help the man because him and me belong to the same club. We're a couple of drunks. He was plenty soused last I saw him. I'll help him get sober if I can. Then he's yours and the cops if Eddie don't get to him first."

Susan listened to Jay explain in careful detail how he was doing some part time work helping Brian in the evenings and some weekends. Brian's call was asking for help on a business matter. He had to go downtown and check something out. Susan was worried that Jay would become involved in Eddie's business and its complications especially her own account with Eddie. Jay suspected that she had an arrangement but was not fully aware that she was using Eddie's support payment as a means of paying for her needs. This was not discussed as a family matter. She simply nodded her understanding of Jay's explanation, accepted his parting kiss, and warned him to be careful.

Jay drove his Jeep to The Little Portion. The place was spotless and nearly empty. A few people loitered around making half-hearted attempts to wipe tables and empty trash containers. Sister Celest was in the kitchen putting away a few serving items. The Sailor was not in view. Jay walked to the kitchen and greeted Sister Celest. She turned at the sound of his voice and appeared startled. Jay apologized for scaring her noting that he was looking for the Sailor. Sister moved away from the cupboard to a nearby table, sat down, and asked Jay to join her.

Sister explained to Jay that the Sailor had come out of his drunken stupor about an hour after he and Brian had left that afternoon. He was badly hung over but well behaved. Gradually he warmed up to his new environment. He asked Sister many questions about The Little Portion and the people who came in for food, lodging, and care. After Sister had answered his questions he asked if he could be of any help. She put him to work in the hotel section collecting blankets, turning mattresses, and doing minor repairs to blinds. Then he assisted with the preparation of the evening meal. When the clients began to arrive he turned his attention to them, greeting each one, and extending the hospitality of the house.

The Sailor had become an instant member of the staff Sister was surprised at his enthusiasm and curious about his motives. During the meal, he would move from person to person trading tales, talking of the past, and telling war stories. By the time the meal was completed the Sailor had collected a special group of friends who Sister believed to be Vietnam veterans. With the Sailor at the lead they formed up and marched away to some unknown objective. Sister was unsure if she would ever see the Sailor again.

Jay was grateful for the information. He was also relieved that the Sailor had solved the immediate problem by doing a disappearing act. All Jay had to do now was inform Brian that the Sailor was nowhere to be found. Brian could make that report to Eddie and everything would be cool. From this point the Sailor was on his own.

Sister Celest seemed to want to talk more. She asked Jay about himself and wondered if he would be interested in helping her out as a volunteer like Brian did. Jay was impressed with the kind attitude of the religious woman. He also noticed that her compassion toward her clients was real and not sugar coated with religious fervor. Her dress was very practical for the work she was doing. A religious symbol was on a chain around her neck and another like it was sewn on her blouse. No other religious symbolism was evident except for two small statues, one near the door and the other near the kitchen. The statue near the door, Jay recognized as Jesus Christ. Sister explained that it was there to reflect Christ's healing ministry and His love of the poor. She talked about the gospel story of the loaves and fishes and related that to the choosing of the name, The Little Portion. She also explained that the statue of St. Francis in the kitchen was there to remind all of the need to care for the poor, to be thankful to God for all the gifts that we receive, and to love one another. Sister felt that more was taught by action than words. She wanted Jay to be a teacher by his actions in caring for the poor and needy. His love and concern about his friend, Sailor, was evidence of his compassion.

Jay was blown away by her sincerity. He came close to explaining his real reason for trying to find the Sailor. Instead he decided to let it as she thought it to be. He simply replied that he would be glad to volunteer and with little thought he volunteered Susan to come in with him on occasion. Susan loved to cook and Jay offered to have her, Louise, and Brian all involved in providing a genuine home cookout for the clients. It would be a great substitute for the usual weekend bash. Jay desperately needed a substitute activity for the Saturday night fling. His mental health advisors had said so. This seemed like the thing to do.

Sister Celest was elated with the idea. She thanked Jay and asked when the event could be held. Jay thought by the following weekend he could persuade his wife and friends to participate. It would be good for the kids to join in, he thought. Sister was a little reserved about having children involved but on second thought decided that a few children might be good therapy for her clients.

Jay said his goodbye and started for the door. He stopped and asked Sister to give him a call if the Sailor returned. He wrote his home telephone number on a napkin and then added his work phone as well. He also explained that he was spending a lot of time at St. Anslem's so she might locate him there. Sister acknowledged that she was well acquainted with St. Anslem's and would look for him if necessary through Mr. Durant's office. Then Sister explained that she returned to her home every night around eleven. The door to The Little Portion was locked but the hotel remained open with a night clerk on duty. If the Sailor returned the night clerk would know but he was not reliable to make a call except to the police for assistance. Jay suggested that if the Sailor was in the house when Sister arrived in the morning that she should let him know.

It was past midnight when Jay returned home. Susan was asleep. Jay called Brian and reported on the Sailor. Then he finished the leftover coffee and went to bed. It was Friday morning, his second-favorite day.

The Sailor wasn't quite home but he was well within his element. With his new friends he had invaded the bars on the South side of Boston and in nearby Roxbury. The tattoo worked to perfection. Time and time again the bar would break into "Anchors Away," "The Marines Hymn," and occasionally "The Caissonss Go Rolling Along," although the Sailor barely tolerated the latter. He preferred a silent toast to the memories of his fallen comrades. However, he couldn't quibble as his new found friends hustled the patrons for a round or two in tribute to the fighting forces. By two A.M. they had been excused from every place in sight and had no other alternative but to find their way back to The Little Portion. When they finally arrived the door was locked. The night clerk at the hotel door refused to let the merry band of near violent drunks into to the lobby. Their threats were countered with his announcement that the police had been called. Where upon they moved back to the door of The Little Portion, lay down, and went to sleep. Sister Celest found the pile of humanity when she arrived to fix breakfast. One by one the Sailor's platoon of night riders came to and moved inside. Sister Celest fortified them with hot coffee, lots of bread, and a loud lecture. Each man took his medicine. A few managed to become helpful. Most simply ate and left to find a restful spot under the viaduct where they would spend the day wondering about their fate.

The Sailor remained motionless on the sidewalk. With the help of two of his comrades, Sister had him dragged inside and placed on a chair. His eyes rolled back as she tried to revive him. He was sick, very sick. Sister Celest had encountered this before in the brief time that her mission had been operating. Several times she had called 911 for the life support assistance followed by transport to Boston Hospital. This time she felt that another method was necessary. Instead of 911 she called Jay Marquart.

Jay was not very cordial when Sister called. He had only three hours of sleep. He also had to be at his desk in two hours and driving downtown to see a drunk at the Sister's was not to his liking. He announced this fact to Sister Celest who reminded him of their conversation of the prior evening. Jay knew he wasn't going to win. He told the Sister that he was on his way and got dressed. In less than an hour he was sitting next to the Sailor who was half unconscious and holding his head in his hands. The Sailor would only mumble in answer to Jay's questions.

Jay felt that the Sailor was in need of professional help so with Sister's help he pushed the Sailor into the Jeep, strapped him in, and made for St. Anslem's expertise in the person of Bob Markley.

Jay found a wheelchair at the hospital entrance and wheeled his drunken friend through the hospital lobby and back to the SACAP Unit. The lights were still off indicating that the Unit was not yet open for business. Jay opened the unlocked door, turned on the lights, and placed the Sailor in his wheelchair in a comer behind the reception desk. The Sailor seemed to want to respond to the rough treatment that Jay provided but his instability only allowed him to occasionally take a weak punch at Jay as he moved him about.

Bob Markley was the first to arrive. He entered the Unit surprised to find the lights on and shocked to see Jay behind the desk with a patient behind him. "Jay, what are you doing here and who is that with you?" The tone of Markley's voice was more of an admonition than a greeting.

Jay answered in a calm and friendly way. "Good morning, Mr. Markley. I bring to you a very important person in the eyes of many who, as you may have guessed, is in need of your excellent service. I give him to you."

"Okay, I'll call Admitting." Markley seemed very matter-of-fact.

"None of that bullshit, Markley." Jay held up his hand as a gesture of opposition. "As I said this is a very important patient. You take care of him. Sober him up. He don't need any of that crap from admitting. I'll pick him up this afternoon and take him back where I got him. Good St. Anslem's don't need to know that he was ever here. You told me that this wasn't run by the hospital any more.

Markley pleaded, "Jay, be reasonable. The man needs care. He may be injured. I need to have him evaluated and examined. We have to build a medical record on his care. You do want him cared for, don't you?"

Jay was not about to accept Markley's explanation. "Care is exactly what he needs, Bob. What you want to do is treat him and if your buddies are lucky one of them might even cure him. I doubt if they will care for him. I don't think anybody in this place except you knows the difference between caring and treating. They treat but they don't care. I brought this man here for care. Your care. That's the difference. He needs care, man. Keep the wolves away from him."

"Do you care, Jay?" Markley asked the question in a rhetorical way.

Jay had a ready answer. "You're damn right I do!"

"Why?" Markley shouted in his face.

"Because he's a goddamn drunk just like you and me. That's why."

Satisfied, Markley consented. "Okay—so do I. Check back with me around three."

Chapter Eighteen

Frank Patello was very mad. Boston was his dream. He wanted to move his entire operation to Boston and put his nephew in charge. He wanted to retire. The whole idea of creating a new cover for his operations by developing a nearly respectable banking business was predicated on his move and retirement. Now some jerks had seemingly loused up the whole thing. Frank Patello was mad, very mad.

Mario Capsize was scared. He had seen Big Frank lose his cool before but he had never seen him so mad. Frank had exploded in rage when Mario gave him the report from Sam the Security Man that the drug bust set up in Hingham had caused a glitch because the Sailor had been a no show and probably had half the shipment. The shipment meant that the Sailor had the goods to implicate their system and bring the Boston move to a quick halt. Sam wanted Big Frank to back off the Boston idea until the Sailor was found and appropriate corrections implemented. Big Frank said that Sam could go to hell. Mario Capsize was scared, very scared.

Charlie Patello was confused. He had called his uncle to tell him about a news item in the *Boston Globe* reporting that Robert Cowan, former Mayor and now Under Secretary of Labor, was contemplating returning to the State and running for Governor. Patello hated politicians, especially politicians that didn't stay bought. He screamed at Charlie to "pull the string on the bastard and make him eat shit." Uncle Frank had never screamed at him before. Charlie knew that he had to "pull the string" on the former Mayor. But he couldn't understand what caused Frank to start screaming. Charlie Patello was confused, very confused.

Tom Callahan was elated. He had great news. The medical staff of St. Ansley's Hospital had voted by a strong majority to form a Physicians' Organization as a for profit corporation. Dr. Foley had managed to have himself elected as the President of this new corporation that would now seek its startup and working capital from St. Ansley's. That would move the Physicians' Organization rapidly to the status of a Physician Hospital Organization. The new corporation would seek additional capital and Bay Area Health Maintenance Organization would be there to supply it. That would be the formation of the Keystone Management Services Organization to be run by a consortium of the three but in effect controlled by Park Bay/Area Health Care. The master plan was working. Target Boston Medical was on target. Callahan's call to give Mr. Patello the good news was left to be returned. Mr. Patella was on another call and had a very important meeting to follow. Tom Callahan didn't mind. He was elated, very elated.

Big Frank would listen no more. He had heard all he wanted to hear from Mr. Capsize about how Sam the Security Man wanted to back off and let the bank deal dissipate. He held up both hands as a signal that he had heard it all. When Mario stopped talking, Frank picked up the phone and dialed Sam the Security Man's private number. He blew past the secretary and right to Sam who was working the Boston project.

When Frank was sure that he had the right man, he became very explicit. "I have been told by Mr. Capizzi that you have fucked up the Boston transition. Now here is what we are going to do. You are going to Boston and find the Sailor and the missing half of the shipment. Then you are going to fix anything that is broken. I don't have to remind you that this whole caper was your idea. So fix it. We are going ahead as planned. You see that nothing goes wrong. I mean nothing. You understand?"

The person on the other end of the conversation must have understood. Big Frank simply grunted loudly and hung up. Then he turned to Mario. "This is enough for one day. You heard what I told him. He's gonna fix it. You better check in with Charlie. It seems that the former Mayor is on the loose. We gotta tie him down. You help Charlie get it done. I'll tell our friends at the Union."

Robert Cowan liked what was happening. No big supporters had called him as yet but several of his former staff members had called to volunteer for his campaign in return for appointments after he was elected. The Washington Post had made a following inquiry to the *Globe* report. Top party bigwigs had also called to verify his intention. Other gubernatorial hopefuls had rushed to comment on radio talk shows. The whole thing was gaining momentum just as he had planned. He decided a visit to Boston was in order just to be seen if not heard at some of the political watering holes. Another impromptu conversation with a reporter would add fuel to the growing flame. Once the matter became hot then he could determine the degree of support and opposition.

As yet the White House had made no comment. The Secretary of Labor, Cowan's boss, was obviously waiting for the issue to become prominent before making any inquiry. Protocol directed that the Under Secretary give the secretary plenty of notice before he officially declared his intention to run for public office. Cowan decided to wait for another week before he had a meeting with his boss.

Jay Marquart knew that Bob Markley could attend to the Sailor. Marquart was tired and hungry. He had to get to his desk at Action, meet with Donovan sometime this morning, and then get back to St. Anslem's to have a meeting with Dr. Sutton about the waste management project. For the moment he decided to go to the hospital cafeteria for a cup of black coffee and a donut to charge his batteries. As he was attempting to pay, the friendly cashier handed him a note and nodded to Tommy at his usual perch. Jay didn't have to read the note. He just accepted the obvious. Tommy wanted to see him. Jay moved to Tommy's table and sat down. Tommy sat back in a relaxed fashion and greeted Jay. Jay in turn nodded a good morning without saying a word. He busily pursued the donut and coffee while waiting for Tommy to speak.

Tommy took the advantage." You must be busy, Jay. Ain't seen ya around much since you been sprung. How's it going?"

Jay took a large gulp of his coffee and gave his buddy a quick response. "Okay, Tommy. I'm way behind on a lotta things. Right now I'm late getting to the office. Okay?"

Tommy gave him a friendly smile. "Sure, Jay. I won't keep you. Remember our deal about you talking to a few guys who might want to ask you about some things? Well, there's a guy who wants to have a meet. I told him I would make the arrangement. That okay? He'll give me a few bucks for the service and I pass some on to you."

The idea of a few bucks just to meet seemed like a good deal to Jay. "Yeah, I guess so. Who is it and what does he want to talk about?"

"I'm not sure but I'd bet he comes from the Attorney General's Office." Tommy shrugged his shoulders as if he was guessing. "Some sort of an investigator be my guess. My friends from the precinct put him on to me. Wants to know something about what's going on in your line of work. That's all I know."

"Tommy, I just do my job as I'm told to do it. I don't know much about the business." Jay stood to leave.

"Just meet the guy, Jay. He'll decide if you know anything about what he's after. What do you say?" Tommy insisted.

Jay consented. "Okay. I got a few irons in the fire right now. Think he can meet me here. I'll be back this afternoon."

"When you get back stop by the cashier. She'll have it for you. Thanks, Jay."

Jay made a fast exit and proceeded to Action. He excused his tardiness by explaining to Ken Ryan that he had made an impromptu visit to St. Anslem's on his way to work. He repeated his view of the following day pointing out that the project was having no effect. Ken accepted the excuse but did not want to hear the report. He again reminded Jay that this was a learning experience and to keep his criticism to a low level. When Jay finally made it to his desk Dave Donovan was waiting for him.

Donovan was fidgety and noticeably nervous. He seemed irritated that Jay was late arriving even though they had not specified a time for their meeting. It was very apparent to Jay that Donovan had something important on his mind. Jay's attempt to make small talk was bluntly rejected. Donovan wanted to get right to the point. He even took Jay by both arms as if he were trying to hold him down so he could talk without being interrupted and came on strong. "Marquart, I got to have an understanding with you. Do you believe in the Union? It's important that I know your exact sentiments. Are you in the Union or are you just paying dues?"

The strong arm of Donovan alarmed Jay. He let the Union leader know that he did not like the approach. "What's with you, Donovan? Christ, I been sick in the hospital. I'll do the job now that I'm out. I told you that when we talked a couple days ago. Gimme a break, man. I just got back to work and I got a lot of catching up to do. I'll get up to speed with the Union. Gimme time. What's buggin' you, man?"

Donovan backed off and even seemed to be apologetic "That's not what I mean, Jay. It's the Union. We got some trouble heading our way and we got to know who we can count on when it hits the fan. Are you Union or not?"

Jay tried to dismiss the idea of trouble. "What trouble? You got a contract. Everybody seems happy. The company likes the deal. The Union likes the deal I guess. So what trouble? Relax, man."

"No, here it is." Donovan was now insistent. "We got some internal things going on that could break up the Union. When it comes down we got to know who we can count on to help us recover. Some of our top guys are being looked at for maybe dipping in the till and doing some back-door stuff. If we try to stop it then the Union has a civil war thing. A lot of heads roll. Maybe some go to the slammer. That hurts us bad. The employees feel they ought to decertify and contracts are lost. Members fall out. The whole labor movement gets knocked back. Some of us got into this because we believe in the right of collective bargaining. We want a good clean Union that works for its members. Now we have to clean house and that could hurt. Where do you stand? You gonna cut and run when it happens? I figured I could talk to you about this because you're not tied to anyone who is maybe on the take. You got to keep this quiet."

Jay was confused. "Donovan, I haven't the slightest idea what the hell you are talking about. Somehow I got pushed into being the Steward for Action. You, Hart and Muldoon seemed to want it this way. Okay, so I ain't been always available 'cause I been sick. I read the manuals. I went to your meetings. I signed up the troops. That's it. I don't know anything about what's going on in the big office. You got to understand that the Union wasn't my idea. I don't know where in hell you guys came from. You just showed up one day and told me I was in the Union and then I was the Shop Steward. What else is there?"

Donovan stood up and walked to the window. He waited for a few minutes before returning to the table. He sat down and looked Jay in the eye. "There's a hell of a lot more. You been sick. Suppose you lose your health benefits. How you going to pay for that? Suppose the waste management contracts with the hospitals don't go over. Whose gonna protect you when the layoffs start? Those things could happen. If the Union and the company have a sweetheart deal, the members get the dirty end of the stick. We have to worry about that. If our top guys are in the tank then we got to get things straight fast. That's what I'm talking about."

As Donovan was talking Jay was reflecting on the severe morale decline at St. Anslem's when the cutbacks were implemented. Then he thought about the sorry state of the waste management project. Nobody seemed to care about the quality of the effort. The experience that he and Cecile had at the hospital's Executive Committee came to mind with the Bishop's lament that the administration seemed unconcerned about the people doing the work. The hospital somehow had lost its caring attitude. If that could happen to a hospital then it certainly could happen to a company like Action Waste Management. Donovan was silent now and looking into Jay's eyes for an answer. Jay remained silent and stared back into Donovan's eyes. He saw a look of despair.

Jay carefully reacted. "Donovan, I always thought that the Union thing was some kind of a skin game. Hell, what isn't? Everybody's on the take. Right? I'm not getting any so I make my moves to get on the inside. That's the way the game is played. Nobody takes anything serious except for what's in it for el numero uno."

Donovan sat back exasperated. "Marquart, the only redeeming quality that you have is your naive stupidity. I guess that's what made me think that I could maybe count on you to do the right thing. You paint everything the same color—only it's the wrong color. Think about it differently. Some of us care about what happens to others. If you care, and I still believe that behind that cold exterior you have a big soft heart, you will do the right thing. I'll have to give you time to think about it. We might not have a chance to talk about this again. Things are going to happen fast. You'll realize what I'm talking about when it happens. Hopefully we'll have the opportunity to be on the same team."

Donovan moved rapidly away from Jay's desk and out the door. Jay was left alone in a complete quandary about what the meeting was about. He realized that he was being called on to be supportive of something or someone that had to do with the Union hierarchy but he wasn't sure just what he was expected of rum. He regretted hurting Donovan with his abrupt reply. Donovan was, in Jay's mind, a sincere and honest man. Maybe that was the problem. Jay wasn't accustomed to dealing with business associates who were honest and sincere. His closest friends, Brian and Bob Markley were exceptions. Jay trusted them. Ken Ryan was also a loyal friend that Jay would trust in a pinch. He hadn't gotten to know Donovan that well but he was willing to trust him. If they did have another meeting like this one, Jay was determined to align with Donovan. He hoped for the meeting.

Markley had his hands full. The Sailor was belligerent and wanted to leave. He was still drunk and delirious. He had symptoms of emphysema punctuated by periods of severe coughing. He was in need of a physician but Markley could not officially request one since the patient was not officially a patient. Out of desperation he called Dr. Anderson and asked the good doctor if he could come to the Unit to see a walk-in patient. The request was not unusual except that Markley would normally call the resident or the attending on duty. The cuts had forced the elimination of the attending and the residents were now spread out over the entire medical service. Their response would sometimes take hours. Dr. Anderson realized that Mr. Markley required stat response since he had placed a direct call to him. He put on his white lab coat, grabbed his stethoscope, and ran to the Unit.

The Sailor came to attention when he saw Dr. Anderson enter the room.

Anderson looked at the Sailor and gave him a friendly nod. To Markley's surprise the Sailor responded with a hardy, "Good Morning, Sir." The sudden military bearing of the patient was at first disarming to Dr. Anderson. However, Anderson had encountered many veterans who had the instilled ability to react when an officer entered the room.

Dr. Anderson walked over to the Sailor and took careful note of the prominent tattoo. He made several complementary remarks about the U.S. Navy as he did a careful exam of the patient. All the while the Sailor held a rigid position in the wheel chair and cooperated with Dr. Anderson's every request.

When the exam was completed Anderson spoke to the Sailor. "Son, you have to start taking better care of yourself. You're in pretty bad shape but I think we can cure your problems. I'll order some medication and Mr. Markley will tell you what you need to do after that. I take it you like a drink now and then. Maybe more now than then. You ever thought about giving that up or cutting back? We ought to take some urine to see what else you might be on. You on drugs of any kind?"

"Sir, yes, Sir, I take a drink, Sir!" Sailor shouted.

Anderson gave the answer brief thought. "Uh-huh. Well, we'll look you over some more. Bob, give me the order sheet and we'll start some therapy."

This was the request that Markley had feared would come. "Dr. Anderson, we haven't registered this patient. He is a voluntary walk-in under the supervision of one of our program volunteers. I don't believe he would accept admission. Could you accept him as a private patient and write a prescription on your personal number? I'll do everything else that he needs or see that he gets good supervision."

Anderson looked at Markley as a parent does to a child. "Bob, you know that I can't do that. You admit him as an outpatient to the Archdiocese program. I'll write the script and orders and have a resident do the H&P. You keep your friend quiet."

Markley smiled at Anderson's direction. The Archdiocese did not have a license to accept patients. The chart that would be prepared for the Sailor's medical record would be to a program that didn't exist. However, the medications orders and therapy would be given by the hospital to the Archdiocese as a contractor. Consequently, the hospital would not have a patient record. Anderson had denied Markley's request but had done him one better by directing the patient's admission to the nonexistent program. It was illegal but efficient.

The Sailor was back to his belligerent attitude. He seemed to sneer as Dr. Anderson walked out of the room. "Damn officers! Always got to have this holier than thou thing. Shit. He knows I get stoned. So what? He ain't seen the shit I been in."

Markley wanted to defend Dr. Anderson. "He's seen it all, my friend. Don't sell him short. He did his time in Korea as a PFC. Went to medical school after he got out. He's been there."

The Sailor pounded his fist in his hand. "Korea, shit, man, Nam is where it happened. That's where I was. I don't know no Korea. I was scared stiff. You ever been so scared that you just hunkered down and cried. Couldn't move. I mean just really scared stiff. Couldn't move. Well, I been that scared, man. You ever been that scared?"

Markley shuttered at the thought of combat. He remembered the feeling. "Yeah, Sailor, I been there. I was scared too. Never got over it. I just got stoned and stayed that way. It didn't change things. I was still scared but I didn't give a damn if it happened. Just got drunk and stayed out of everybody's way. That helped I thought but it didn't."

The Sailor perked up at Markley's remark. "You was in Nam? Where? Hiding out in some slop house and pushing shot records around a Debark Station, I bet."

"Yeah, I pushed shot records." Markley seemed to be searching his memories. "The Navy had the mistaken impression that I could be a med. tech only after they made that decision they needed some corpsmen and I got reassigned. Suddenly I was in the mud with the Marines at Mai Xi Tai. We rode your damn PBR's up and down the river."

"Yeah! You was Navy?" The Sailor was excited to meet a comrade in arms. "Shit, bro, I was there. We shuttle your ass in and out on patrols all the time. Man, I was scared. Was you scared?"

"Like I said, I was scared. I tried to hide but somebody found me and took the time to try to straighten me out. He's still trying. He saved my life and kept me from screwing up real bad. God was good to me. I got out. You're still there. We got to get you out."

The mention of helping a buddy pushed the Sailor back into depression. "My buddy tried to help me. He got it. I just laid there too goddamn scared to move. He got it. Oh, shit, man, I got to have a fix. I got to get fixed. I can't handle it, man."

The Sailor put his head in his hands and began to sob. Occasionally he would roll off the chair and lay on the floor in a fetal position. Then he would crawl back on the chair and cry some more. Eventually he moved to a corner of the room and lay down. Sleep followed. Markley covered him with a blanket and let him alone.

Jay arrived at St. Anslem's in the early afternoon. He went to the cafeteria and checked with the cashier who handed him an envelope. Jay took it and left without opening it. He wanted to check in with Dr. Sutton and didn't want to be distracted by Tommy's note. It was bad enough trying to concentrate on his job after the disturbing encounter with Donovan. He had almost forgotten about his friend, the Sailor, now peaceably sleeping on the floor in the vacant SACAP unit under the watchful eye of Bob Markley. The Sailor came to mind as Jay passed the SACAP entrance. He forced himself to walk by rather than obey the impulse to check on the Sailor's progress. That would be another distraction from his assigned task of interviewing Dr. Sutton.

Dr. Sutton seemed genuinely pleased to see Jay. However, he seemed more intent on discussing the events that took place in the Executive Committee meeting rather than the Waste Management program. Jay listened patiently as Dr. Sutton detailed all the procedures involved in reviewing patient quality and protecting confidentiality. It seemed as though Dr. Sutton was intent on proving that Jay never had a legal case against the hospital. Jay said little, mostly because he wasn't given a chance to speak. Sutton was on a soap box and Jay was his audience. Eventually the doctor mentioned that he had asked the hospital attorney to review the entire matter and see that nothing was left undone. He asked Jay for the name of his attorney so the two lawyers could communicate.

Jay had not discussed the outcome of the Executive Committee with his sister and lawyer, Martha, and in fact had not even mentioned the deal he had cut with Cecile. He had accomplished the matter without involving lawyers and he was determined to keep it that way. Tactfully, he explained to Dr. Sutton that he had not involved a lawyer in the matter and did not intend to call one at this late date. As far as he was concerned the whole incident had been resolved with the understanding that nothing significant had happened.

Sutton was hard to convince. He countered Jay's point by explaining that the medical staff was very concerned that administration had placed patient confidentiality in jeopardy with the purchase of a telephone system that allowed a person receiving a call to know from where the call was being placed. Sutton wanted Jay to confirm that was the case but to do so would require Jay to admit that his confidentiality had been breached. Of course, this would place blame on the hospital but Jay could excuse the institution once the administration had been identified as the culprit. In response to Jay's question, Sutton admitted that Mr. Durant would be identified as the person responsible and therefore be terminated,

Jay recognized the set up. Durant was headed for a fall. Somebody wanted him out and Jay was being looked at to pull the trigger. It suddenly occurred to him that the Waste Management Program that was a point of criticism in the Executive Committee was another pawn in the game. It was not intended to succeed. Its failure would be another reason for Durant's professional demise. Sutton was not being at all subtle about what was going on. His direct statements about the administration and the intent of the medical staff were not at all like the Dr. Sutton that Jay had first met a few weeks earlier. It seemed to Jay that perhaps Sutton was trying to send a message to the outside world that St. Anslem's was under siege. He decided to give the doctor the benefit of the doubt.

"Doctor, I'm not sure what or where you want me to go with all of this. I won't involve an attorney to raise these accusations since I think the matter has been settled. But I will bring the matter regarding the waste management project to my boss who I'm sure will want to speak to somebody about the way the project is being received. Who leads the opposition?"

Dr. Sutton had a look of fear when he considered answering Jay's question. Instead of giving a direct answer he went into a detailed explanation of the medical staff organization followed by commentary about the new developments that involved the Archdiocese, a physician organization, and a new management services organization that Dr. Folley had brought into existence. The only name that Jay had heard in the entire response was Dr. Folley. He thought he had the answer to his question. The rest, in Jay's mind, was useless rhetoric.

Jay felt the impulse to care swelling in his emotions. Joe Durant had become a friend who cared for the less unfortunate just like the good Sister at The Little Portion. They used the hospital to deliver compassion. Jay knew that the hospital was a center of the compassion that was very much part of the healing process. Some force that he couldn't see or understand was gradually destroying the compassionate institution. He decided that he would attend to the hospital as he had attended to the Sailor and others who needed his help. Jay wanted to be a minister to the caring institution. The recycling project would succeed. It was part of the mission of caring.

After he left Dr. Sutton's office Jay stood in stairway five and opened the envelope from Tommy. It contained a simple handwritten message that said a Mr. Walker would call him at home this evening to arrange an appointment. Jay put the message in his pocket and walked to the SACAP Unit. It was after three o'clock and past the time that Markley had suggested that Jay return. The Sailor was up, scrubbed, and dressed in a set of hospital surgical blues. He looked almost professional as he nosed around the desk looking for anything that might capture his interest and that his interest capture for trade. On the desk were several plastic medication containers that Jay concluded were for the Sailor. Sailor jumped back from the desk as Jay entered. When he recognized Jay he went back to his scavenging without concern for Jay's presence.

Jay sat on a folding chair and watched the Sailor go through the desk with the precision of a thief. Everything was looked over and either put in a plastic bag or meticulously replaced. Nothing was ignored. After about fifteen minutes the Sailor had nearly exhausted all the drawers and was working on the door of a locked cabinet when Bob Markley entered the office. Markley saw the Sailor jump away from the cabinet and into a chair opposite the desk. Typically, Markley smiled at the Sailor while ignoring his actions that were obvious. Then he took the plastic bag with all the goodies that the Sailor was trying to hide behind his back and dumped the contents on the desk.

In a satirical way Markley proceeded to scold the Sailor. "Nice work, my friend. You have a good eye for things of value. This junk that you collected would probably bring enough for a bottle of very cheap wine."

The Sailor acted remorseful but seemed pleased with Markley's comments. "Yeah, well I could have traded up. Then maybe get enough for a line. Man, that's what I need is a line or two. I know where I can get it if I can get a boat. You know anybody that's got a boat I can use?"

Jay shook his head at the remark. "Hell, Sailor, you still got a snoot full. The way you got scrubbed up, I thought you was sober. With those surgical blues on you could get into surgery and suck up all that laughing gas. You wouldn't need a sniff after that—just the undertaker. Jesus, you are a dope head."

Markley saw the Sailor's anger flash at Jay's remarks. He moved quickly to avoid any conflict between his two clients. "Sailor, we got your clothes cleaned. They're in that cabinet that you seem so interested in. You have your medicine. Jay will drive you back to The Little Portion Mission as soon as you get dressed. It's important that you take the medicine and get some rest. Jay will pick you up in the morning and drive you back here. Dr. Anderson wants to do a complete work up on you tomorrow. Okay?"

The Sailor glared at Jay. "Yeah, that's okay. I get up early. He gonna pick me up early. He bugs me a little."

Jay smiled at the Sailor's comments. "Hell, man, you don't know early from late. It's all the same to a doper. You just be there when I get there. I won't have no time to look around the gutters for your miserable ass. We ready to go? I got things I got to do other than play taxi."

Markley opened the cabinet and gave the Sailor his clean clothes that the Sailor put on over his blues. He now had clean clothes and a set of surgical blues that would be very impressive to his friends under the Viaduct. The St. Anslem's name was very visible through his worn T-shirt.

As the Sailor finished buttoning his pants he growled at Jay. "You talk like a drunk. You act like a drunk. You think like a drunk. You even smell like a drunk. Hell, I bet you are a drunk. You are also a little short to go trash talkin' me, little man. So I gotta take your ride back to the Sister's but I don't have to like you. You keep mouthin' off and I might put you on the deck and over the side. You watch your smart ass mouth. Dig?"

Markley expected Jay to become angry and walk away leaving the Sailor as a problem for him to deal with. Instead, Jay smiled at the Sailor, fifteen years his senior, at least fifty pounds his better and a foot taller. Then he raised his right hand in a gesture of the high-five. The Sailor responded with a toothless smile and grasped the hand. The two exchanged a grip, did a fist to fist, then a high-five. The Sailor put his arm around Jay and guided him toward the door.

"Let's go, little buddy. You got other things to do than play taxi. Shit," chuckled the Sailor.

Jay guided the Sailor through the corridors and out the front entrance toward the hospital parking garage where the Jeep was waiting. As they entered the garage Joe Durant came in step with them. Durant greeted Jay and nodded to the Sailor who scowled at the fine suit. Jay and Joe entered into brief conversation about The Little Portion and the good work of the Sister.

The Sailor stood apart from the conversation until he heard Jay mention Joe's boat. Joe responded to Jay that he was planning to prepare the boat for winter storage this weekend. The Sailor moved immediately into the conversation offering to be of assistance to Durant in preparing the boat. He tried to establish his credibility as a first-class boat mechanic.

Durant listened intently to the Sailor. He liked the man's rough style and particularly his apparent knowledge about boats. But there was something about the man that seemed familiar in a very negative way. Suddenly Durant placed the face. The man was the stoned out, obnoxious boater that had made such a grand scene at the marina gas dock when Durant had accidentally bumped into his boat. Now this same aggressive person was trying to sell his ability as an expert boat mechanic. His personality was definitely different. Durant decided to believe that St. Anslem's had succeeded in treating the man and delivered another miracle cure.

The Sailor was close and speaking directly into Durant's face. "Sir, I happen to be one of the most experienced boat specialists in this part of New England. If you need someone to winterize your boat, I can do it fast and at a very reasonable cost. I got no overhead. You buy the material and give me what you think the job is worth. I'm a little down on my luck right now and will do you a good job. I could sure use the work. Jay, here, he can tell you that I'm okay."

Durant was very interested. "Well, I had hoped to get it done this weekend but the guys at the marina tell me they can't get to it until next month. They said if I could do it myself, they could do the shrink wrapping next week. I don't want to wait until the snow flies before the engines are winterized. Can you get to it this weekend?"

Jay stood in silence as Durant and the Sailor talked enthusiastically about boating and fishing in and around Boston Harbor. The Sailor became very convincing about his mechanical abilities and knowledge about winterizing a boat. Durant looked more and more like a man who had struck gold as he now seemed eager to employ the Sailor. The Sailor was being cautious and mentioned that it would be difficult to work Durant's boat into his very busy schedule. Finally the Sailor concluded that he could do it the first thing tomorrow morning. Durant agreed and offered to drive the Sailor to The Little Portion and pick him up first thing in the morning. The Sailor accepted the ride immediately and gave Jay a wave as the two walked toward Durant's car.

As they departed, Jay felt relieved from having to drive through the heavy rush hour traffic to Melina Cass Boulevard and back to Roslindale to pick up Kristie and then over to Waltham. It was Friday, his second-favorite day, and time to begin his modified weekend festivities without fishing, pot, coke, or booze. Regardless, he had Kristie, Susan, Benny and James. Brian and Louise would join them. They could get high. Jay would just enjoy the company, the food, and being free. Hopefully, he would enjoy the freedom. He would not be without the pressure to return to the clutch of abuse that had seemed to be the foundation for good times. He was free—or was he? Time would tell—minute by minute, hour by hour, day by day. Time would tell. He had forgotten his promise to bring the Sailor to St. Anslem's in the morning.

Being no longer responsible for the transport of the Sailor, Jay had extra time to drive to Roslindale and pick up Kristie. He arrived at her house over an hour ahead of his scheduled pick up time. Kristie and Cecile were out doing house hold errands. Officer O'Sullivan was preparing for his Friday night dinner with Cecile at a fine restaurant. Afterwards, they would return home and Cecile would retire early to get some extra rest following a hectic week in the MICU. Afterwards, Officer O'Sullivan would make a run to the Troubadour Lounge for some friendly conversation and a few lines of coke.

Kristie's weekend with her father was very accommodating to her mother and step father's schedules. O'Sullivan answered Jay's knock on the door and invited him in to have a cup of coffee while they waited for Cecile and Kristie to return. The two men talked at length about the outcome of the hospital's Executive Committee meeting. O'Sullivan was grateful to Jay for coming to Cecile's defense. He explained that it was very apparent that the hospital had changed its attitude toward Cecile. She had a very good week and had regained the respect of the nursing supervisor. All seemed right with the world.

Jay noticed that the officer was shaking and perspiring. The red eyes and runny nose indicated a cold or another problem that Jay could diagnose from experience. Officer O'Sullivan had a problem that sooner or later would get him into trouble.

Tommy the Tout had mentioned it and Brian had hinted at it. Now Jay saw it. O'Sullivan was hooked. Jay made a cautious attempt to engage O'Sullivan in the subject by mentioning his own problem and the process that he had experienced as a way of suggesting that O'Sullivan look in the mirror. It didn't work. O'Sullivan flat out stated that he didn't want to hear about junkies and drug deals. Then O'Sullivan described how had been berated by his superiors for not besting the Harbor Police in nabbing the import of drugs by small craft in Boston Harbor.

"It wasn't fair, Jay," the officer glibly stated, "that they had me chasing you instead of going after the main guys. It couldn't have been you doing the dealing. Christ, anybody could see that—anybody except the stupid ass that I work for. You and your buddy, Brian, just delivered the stuff. I could have nailed you the first night that you walked into the Troubadour. Hell, you sat there and looked at me like you had seen a ghost. If I had said boo you would have caved in. I knew that you didn't know squat about the operation. Brian doesn't either. He just delivers and I just buy. The goddamn water cops got lucky. They get the big bust and I get my ass chewed. I'll tell you this, there is just as much coke on the street now as before and I'm gonna get the next bust."

O'Sullivan wanted to talk and Jay just listened as the good Officer explained to Jay that he had been the subject of investigation that was a blind alley purposely contrived by the higher ups to allow the Brass to bypass Narcotics and get the glory of the big drug bust. O'Sullivan had been made the goat and was destined to pound a beat. For the first time Jay realized that he had also been in the center of the target.

Cecile and Kristie arrived in time to prevent Jay from going into complete shock. Cecile was very warm to Jay and the two sat and talked while Kristie got her things together for the weekend stay with her father. It was very apparent to Kristie that her parents were friendly and no longer fighting. She felt the warmth of their combined love. It was a natural feeling that gave her comfort. Before, she wanted to be with her father but didn't want to leave her mother. Now she felt as if she would be with both of them in love even though they were apart. She looked forward to the weekend of fun.

Jay and Kristie made it to Waltham in time for dinner. Susan had prepared her special pasta with a Caesar salad that was Jay's favorite. Usually Jay washed it down with several beers. This night he used iced tea. Susan drank a gin and grapefruit at first then switched to iced tea. The kids slurped the pasta and then moved outside to enjoy the cool evening. Jay gave Susan an affectionate pat on the fanny as she cleared the table and he moved into the living room to watch television. Just as he was about to sit down the telephone rang. He answered it with little emotion. The voice on the other end seemed less excited by contrast.

"Mr. Marquart? I'm Mr., uh, well, you don't know me. I called because well you might talk to me about uh well we need to maybe get together on some things that uh well you know, that we need to understand better. Can we meet someplace?"

Jay thought the caller was either drunk or crazy. "You want to meet me? Why? You selling insurance or what? Man, you got the wrong number."

"No, wait." The caller was insistent. "We or I mean you were suggested to me by the office. We are looking into a few things about the waste management thing. Your name came up because you're on the list as a technician and a shop steward. I can explain it all when we meet. You know Tommy? He said you would talk to me."

Jay remembered that Tommy had said someone would call. "Sure. We can talk but it's the weekend and I got the kids so I won't have any time until maybe Monday. You want to call me at the office?"

The caller was insistent. "How about Sunday? We can meet after Mass. There's a Dunkin' Donut on Mass Ave in the middle of Waltham. Bring the kids. I'll pop for the donuts. They can eat and we can talk. Won't take long."

"We don't go to Mass and we sleep late."

"Okay. Make it around noon. That's a good hour to eat donuts. What do you say?"

"I guess. You got a name? How do I find you?"

"My name is Wally. I'll find you. It's no problem. See you for donuts on Sunday."

If it hadn't been for Tommy and the prospect of a few bucks Jay would have told the caller to stick it in his ear. Now he was saddled with the enormous task of shepherding the family to Dunkin' Donuts on Sunday morning after their usual Saturday night party. The difference, he reminded himself, is that he would be sober and absent the usual hangover that incapacitated him on Sunday. He could make it. The next problem was explaining to Susan that the family had an invitation to Dunkin' Donuts on Sunday morning.

Susan was very concerned that Jay was trying to lure her and the kids into church.

Dunkin' Donuts was fine as long as someone else was paying but she was adamant that they would not be forced to go to church. Church was the one place where she knew that she and Jay would not be welcome.

This was a no-fishing Friday night. The Customer's boat had been confiscated by the Harbor police and the Customer was hiding from the mob and the police. Brian was maintaining a safe distance from the Customer, AKA the Sailor, in order to avoid compromising his friend and his boss, Eddie. Jay, committed to sobriety, had unwittingly become the coordinator of the promenade. He sat back in his recliner, watched Susan drink her after dinner grapefruit and gin, stared at the television for a few minutes and fell asleep.

The Commuter flight from Washington, as usual, was full and about an hour late. The pilot offered the customary explanations about traffic in and out of Logan airport as the cause. Then he reported that they were now over Providence and beginning the descent into Boston. Michael Cowan fastened his first-class seat belt as the attractive flight attendant walked by. She nodded her approval and moved on. Cowan gave her his best "vote for me" smile. Twenty minutes later the wheels of the Boeing 727 skimmed over the water of Dorchester Bay, cleared the Fort, and touched down on runway four.

Cowan was impatient. The plane was held on the taxi way until a gate could become available causing another fifteen-minute delay. When the plane finally approached the gate, Cowan got out of his seat and removed his carryon bag from the overhead compartment. This caused a chain reaction as everyone in the aisle seats followed his lead. The Flight Attendants demanded that everyone remain seated until the Captain had given the signal. By now the plane's congregation had had it with Captain Bligh and his flight crew. They remained in the aisle moaning their plight as the plane came to its final stop. When the doors were opened the passengers rushed to exit ignoring the gratuitous comments of the flight crew. It was a typical Washington to Boston flight.

Cowan was running late but he moved through the crowd at Logan at a slow pace in order to be recognized by the electorate. Several people recognized him and pointed. He acknowledged them with a wave and if close enough took the time to shake their hand. Cowan was a politician not a bureaucrat. He knew how to work a crowd. He still had visual recognition. It was time to reestablish the name. He needed media time. That was the purpose for his weekend jaunt to Boston—to be seen and then to be heard. His old friend, Mayor Alphonse Siro, had agreed to meet him for dinner at the Harvard Club at eight o'clock. That was the best time to be seen and the best place. The Harvard Club attracted the cream of the Boston business community who assembled around six for cocktails and dinner. Cowan's arrival at eight with the Mayor would be the highlight of the evening. Usually reporters from the Boston Business Journal were hanging around trying to pick up inside tips at the bar. They would flock to the Mayor and that would give Cowan his media opportunity. After dinner he would hold session in the Harvard Club bar until closing. Then he would retire to his family home in South Boston. On Saturday morning he would walk the talk in his old neighborhood and on Saturday afternoon he would visit the taverns and stump for the working man. Saturday night he would dine at the Allenton Club with the wealth of Boston. Sunday morning, he would Board the return flight to Washington. Then he would wait for the results.

Traffic was heavy as usual and the tunnel from Logan Airport into Boston was jammed. Mayor Siro had arranged for a City Limo to meet Cowan and with the aid of flashing blue lights it moved reasonably well around the toll gate and into the City. His arrival at the Harvard Club was a half-hour ahead of the time that the Mayor was expected to arrive so Cowan sat in the elaborate lobby and greeted old acquaintances as they came in. He was definitely in his element. To his very pleasant surprise many had seen the *Globe* report about him considering the nomination for Governor. They were all encouraging.

Mayor Siro arrived on time and the two were escorted to a center table in the packed main dining room. All eyes were on the two politicians as they nodded greetings to everyone. Gradually people began to stop by their table to say hello and chat. It was a perfect plan made even better when two reporters, one from the Boston Business Journal and the other from the *Globe* asked to join them. Siro seemed reluctant to have the reporters cover him on City business at this time and suggested that Cowan meet with them alone after dinner. The reporters acknowledged that they were interested primarily in Cowan at this time and agreed to wait until the two had finished dinner for an opportunity to interview Cowan. Mayor Siro seemed unusually willing to step out of the spotlight.

After dinner, Cowan walked into the bar and found the two reporters sitting at a corner table.

He joined them and ordered a round of drinks. The reporters were grateful and took advantage of the offer. Cowan sat back and invited their questions. To his dismay the first question asked by the *Globe* reporter centered on the issue of his campaign fund. According to the reporter, those who were opposed to his campaign for Governor had suggested that when he was Mayor he accepted money from special interests into his campaign and had also diverted considerable amounts into his personal accounts. It was also suggested that some of his closest aides had accepted bribes from special interest groups and individuals. The reporter asked Cowan to comment on these allegations.

Cowan had not expected to be assaulted. He was forced to go on the defensive contending that such allegations had no foundation and were contrived by the opposition who were using smear tactics to cover their own tracks. From that point on Cowan circled every question with general comments until the reporters left to meet their deadlines. Cowan took a taxi to his house in South Boston.

The Saturday morning issue of the *Boston Globe* carried a front page one-column file picture of former Mayor Cowan with a story headlined, "Cowan denies campaign fund charges." The story carried detailed accounts of the former Mayor's campaign spending, elaborated on his lifestyle, and concluded with an analysis of Cowan's property values in Boston and Washington. It suggested that a man of modest means elected to the office of Mayor had to have special help from wealthy supporters to conduct a successful campaign. It also pointed out that the salary of the Mayor was not sufficient to allow for the accumulation of wealth. If a poor man became Mayor and then became rich the obvious conclusion was that he had used campaign funds for his personal use and/or had accepted bribes while in office. The reader was given to draw a conclusion.

Former Mayor Cowan and now Under Secretary of Labor Cowan was from a modest or poor neighborhood and was living in luxury. The reporter included comments from the Attorney General that an investigation would be conducted and several of the former Mayor's close aides would be contacted.

Mayor Siro read the morning paper and felt pride in his expertise. He had carefully selected the *Globe* reporter from several who covered his office. The young man was ambitious and eager to win the favor of the editor. Siro had used the reporter's ambition on several occasions since he had become Mayor. Now he found the young man to be just the right person for a special assignment. Mayor Siro had talked to Charlie Patello right after Cowan had called to arrange the Harvard club meeting. Patello had asked for the set up. Siro had planted the question on campaign funds with the reporter. *The Globe* editor had accepted the story. It was perfect. Siro finished his coffee and telephoned Patello.

Patello had also read the paper and was elated. The string was being pulled on Cowan. He thanked Siro for the help and promised him that he had the gratitude and unlimited support of his "organization" in the future. After his conversation with Siro, Patello received a call from his man that was assigned to keep tabs on Cowan. Cowan had caught the ten-thirty plane back to Washington and was scheduled to arrive at noon. Patello dropped a dime to the *Washington Post* correspondent in Boston who in turn contacted the *Post* in Washington. A reporter was immediately dispatched to meet the plane and ask for comments about the *Globe* story from Cowan. The pressure was mounting. Patello had also contacted a private detective to follow Cowan when he arrived in Washington. The detective called Patello at one in the afternoon and reported that Cowan was in his Washington office. Patello dialed Cowan's number.

Cowan let the phone ring the required six times before voicemail answered. After the greeting concluded he heard Patello's voice. "Bob, this is Charlie. I know that you are in the office. You would be better off answering the phone. Pick up the receiver, Bob."

Cowan accepted the caller's advice. "Charlie, how nice to hear from you. You seem upset. What can I do for you?"

Patello was not fooled. "Forgive me for being direct, Robert, but I am disturbed that you didn't let me know that you were coming to town yesterday. Perhaps if you had contacted me some of the un-pleasantries might have been avoided. As it now stands you are pretty much on your own. We, of course, will cooperate with the public interest and inquires. We might also be in a position to help relieve some of your pain."

Cowan did not want the conversation to be on the record.

"Charlie, this conversation is being recorded as you know. Well," Patello continued, "it so happens that I will be in Washington tomorrow and would love to have a chat with you. Can you meet me tomorrow at National? I'll arrive at two on U.S. Air."

"Sure thing, Charlie. I'll pick you up at U.S. Air. See you tomorrow."

Cowan knew that his political career had just ended. He would be forced to sell out completely to the Patello interest which meant that he would have to crawl back into the Under Secretary barrel and stay there in complete oblivion. That was only the down payment. He would pay dearly to have the matter of campaign funds erased from the public interest and removed from the agenda of an ambitious attorney general.

Michael Logan enjoyed his brisk jog in the cool autumn breeze. He had completed his usual 6K run and was now showered dressed and settled down with coffee, juice, and the morning paper. The wife and kids were out for a walk. It seemed like the start of a perfect day until he read the *Globe*. Cowan had bungled it again. The man was a political disaster as far as tactics were concerned. Somehow, he had been trapped into the campaign funds issue. Had he used a team of advisors who could have developed a strategy this issue could have been avoided or at least dealt with in advance of a public inquiry by the press.

Besides damning the ignorance of his former boss, Logan realized that he could become the focus of the investigation. He felt he was innocent of any wrong doing but he did have information that could incriminate Cowan and himself. The circumstances surrounding his resignation as City Commissioner and appointment to the Office of Health Affairs for the Archdiocese would receive considerable scrutiny by the press. His reputation would be tarnished forever. He might even be convicted of a felony. He needed time to think. However, he could feel the inquiring press coming to his door. He decided to run. Quickly he packed a bag, grabbed all the available cash in the house, scribbled a note to his wife that he loved her and would contact her soon, and jumped his car. Canada was only eight hours away.

Big Frank Patello's direction to "fix it" did not go without response. The well-dressed muscular Sam the Security Man that had schooled Eddie in the proper conduct and dress of a drug dealer and engineered the sting arrest of the Dorchester dealer, left New York and drove with haste to Quincy, Massachusetts. He set up operations in a scuzzy motel next to the Neponset Bridge and began his search for the Sailor. His approach was to take Eddie by the back of the neck and threaten to pound him senseless if he did not produce the Sailor. Eddie, in turn, put the pressure on Brian to find his friend. Brian turned to Jay to keep the Sailor away from him, Hingham, and the North Quincy Marina where Eddie and his shadow spent most of their time.

The Sailor realized that the Boston Harbor Police and his former friend, Eddie, wanted to find him. He was more concerned about finding his next fix. Foremost in his mind was that a quantity of cocaine was waiting for him in a lobster trap just outside Boston Harbor. The lat/long coordinates were in his tattered billfold. All he needed was a boat. A boat would give him the access to enough stash to last more than a month, or longer, if he didn't have to share it. He saw his chance. Joe Durant was a typical boat owner. He knew what his boat required but he had no idea how to do the work. The Sailor easily convinced Durant that he could do the winter conditioning of his boat's engines. Durant, in turn, saw an opportunity to have the work completed without the hassle of high expense, long delays, and sloppy efforts by the marina staff. Durant picked the Sailor up early on Saturday and drove him first to the North Quincy Marina where the Sailor "borrowed" a set of tools and oil changing equipment from the maintenance shop. Then they drove to the Hingham Boat Club where Durant's thirty-foot Carver rested in its slip. Durant purchased the oil and filters from the Boat Store, gave the Sailor the keys to the boat, and left him to do the work. The Sailor explained to Durant that it would take most of the morning for him to condition the engines and do a final run up. He suggested that Durant pick him up around two in the afternoon.

It was the perfect con. The Sailor had his boat with a full tank of gas, radar, loran, and even a complete head and galley. Not that he needed the galley but the refrigerator did hold a six pack of Sam Adams that the Sailor guzzled en-route to the lobster trap. The seas were moderate with waves running three feet and a breeze blowing at ten knots from the Southwest. The Sailor felt good. Only the thought of a fix gave him increasing encouragement. Within an hour after he pulled out of the slip he tied onto the lobster trap. Twenty minutes later he had the shipment box on deck.

Carefully he dried the box before opening it. Using the carpenter knife from the tool box he opened one end of the shipment box and removed the case. Then he pried open the locks and counted the contents. Seventy small clear plastic bags of the delicious white powder were laid on the deck. He slit one open and fixed a couple of lines that he inhaled. Once again the world became peaceful. He had no fear. He had been reinforced. The open bag was placed inside a sandwich bag that he found in the galley. Then he put it and another two bags from the case into his pockets. He repacked the case and put it back in the waterproof box, slipped the lines, and set course back to the Hingham Boat Club.

Once inside Hingham Bay he made for the Hingham Town Boat Dock in order to fill the half-depleted fuel tanks. The gas attendant was pleased to see the Sailor who explained that he was conditioning the boat for winter. The Attendant knew that the Boat belonged to Joe Durant and was not surprised that the Sailor charged the fuel to Durant's account. The Sailor chatted with the attendant for a while and then returned to the Boat Club. He finished the conditioning process in the next two hours and was feeling no pain when Durant arrived at two P.M.

Durant gave the Sailor a hundred dollars cash for his good work and offered to drive him back to The Little Portion. At the Sailor's insistence, he drove instead to the North Quincy marina where the Sailor returned his borrowed tools. The Sailor thanked Durant for the money and insisted that he could find his own way back to the Mission. Durant knew that the Sailor was headed for a binge but felt powerless to do anything about it. The two men shook hands and parted.

The Sailor made his rounds on the Boardwalk eventually landing at the Shanty. He ordered a couple shots with a beer chaser and listened to the bartender explain that good Old Eddie and a friend had been in just an hour earlier. They had asked the bartender to call if the Sailor happened to drop in. The Sailor convinced the bartender with a twenty-dollar tip to give him a half-hour head start, bought two fifths of Early Times, and walked out. He stopped at the monument and paid solemn respects to the KIA's then walked a mile to the Red Line. Twenty minutes later he was under the Viaduct sharing the whiskey with his buddies.

Eddie got the call from the bartender exactly thirty minutes after the Sailor had left the Shanty. He and his now constant companion, Sam the Security Man, ran from Eddie's condo to the Shanty and listened to the bartender explain that the Sailor had been in for only a few minutes, bought a drink and left. He reported that he had no conversation with the Sailor but it looked like the Sailor had been working on the boats because his hands were covered with grease and his shirt was dirty. Eddie and his friend went immediately to the shops where they learned that the Sailor had requisitioned a few things earlier in the day that had been returned. It was obvious that he had been working on boats but they were certain that he had not been working on any boats at North Quincy. By the time that they left the shops it was nearly dark and a cold early fall rain was beginning, being blown by a brisk wind. The day was over. Eddie went back to the Shanty. Sam the Security Man went back to his dingy motel to think about the recent events.

Jay had started Saturday just as early as the Sailor. He got up unusually early for a Saturday. The kids were already up, finished with breakfast and looking for Dad to start the Saturday ritual of working in the yard. The grass needed mowing and the leaves were beginning to fall. The flowers that Susan planted in the spring had to be cut back and screens had to be moved from windows so storm windows could be put in place. Jay liked doing this kind of work. The kids would join in and between tasks they would get Jay to play a little football or tag. Kristie was an excellent blocker and tackler. This worried Jay but he just assumed she would gather more feminine traits as she grew older. He contemplated the day's work as he ate cereal and drank his coffee. After cereal he lit a cigarette and poured another cup. The cigarette was becoming more habitual and definitely replacing booze as a crutch. He looked at the burning tobacco and thought about the effects of nicotine. This triggered thoughts about St Anslem's that triggered thoughts about the Unit and suddenly he remembered that he was supposed to get the Sailor back to the hospital for his physical examination and treatment.

With a start he telephoned The Little Portion and asked for Sister Celest. Sister was busy with the clients. The person who answered the phone promised Jay that he would ask Sister to call him back. In less than a half-hour Sister Ce1est returned his call. She explained to Jay that the Sailor had left with Mr. Durant early to help Mr. Durant work on his boat. She expected the Sailor back sometime around noon or soon thereafter. Jay thanked the Sister and asked to be called when the Sailor returned. He made sure that Sister had his home telephone number. Sister thanked Jay for being concerned and promised to let him know when the Sailor returned.

Jay then called St. Anslem's SACAP Unit only to be connected to Bob Markley's voicemail that offered to accept a message unless it was an emergency in which case the caller was told to press one for an operator. Jay fired a blast of profanity after the tone and added his report on the whereabouts of the Sailor.

For the next several hours Jay worked without stop around the house. He, by his own estimate, drank several quarts of coffee during the time that he usually consumed seven or eight beers. His kidneys were functioning well which prompted several trips inside. The caffeine had him wired. His explosive energy and rapid movements were obvious in the footballs plays were he continually ran for touchdowns and chided Benny for missing tackles. He was astonished when a Patriot Van driven by Brian pulled into the driveway. It was only eleven-thirty. Brian and Louise weren't due for another six hours. Brian jumper out of the Van and caught the football that Jay fired at him.

Brian gave his buddy a Bronx cheer. "Nice pass, man. You could play for the Pats. They need help. That's what I need, man, help and you're the one who can deliver. We got to make the food run to the Sister's. We go now and be back in time to watch the game on the tube. You ready?"

Jay wasn't interested and he said so. "Brian, I'm busy with all this house stuff. I haven't got time to make the run. I couldn't care less about the damn football game on the tube. Who's playing?"

"BC and Pittsburgh. Should be a blowout next week they go to Notre Dame. The Irish will eat their lunch. Com'on, we gotta go."

Jay told the kids he would be back in a few hours, kissed Susan, and loaded himself into the Van. Brian drove in his usually crazy fashion and arrived at the hospital just as the food service staff were rolling the carts to the loading dock. The receiving desk was not manned on Saturday so the food was loaded without delay. Jay wondered why the desk was necessary and made a mental note to ask someone about it.

When they arrived at The Little Portion, Sister Celest helped unload. Brian and Jay reciprocated by working on the serving line. Brian kept looking around for the Sailor although his instincts told him he would be better off not seeing him. After the meal had been served and the carts were placed back on the truck Sister Celest mentioned to Jay that the Sailor was still missing.

Jay nodded and gave Brian a shoulder jab. "Nothing to worry about, man. You don't see the Sailor so you don't know where he is. Fact is I don't know where he is either. I guess that takes us both off the hook."

Brian said nothing but registered a look of concern for his friend. He feared that Eddie had found him and was extracting a pound or two of flesh.

Jay understood Brian's fear. "Hey, man, he's okay. Probably out on a binge. He'll show up. I'll take care of him when does. You don't have to sweat. He's gonna take care of himself. I'll help. Relax, man. Let's go watch the game."

Brian nodded but said nothing. The two men got into the Van and drove back to St. Anslem's where they unloaded the empty food carts. Then Brian drove Jay home. From there he drove back to Patriot picked up his Chevy and drove home to watch the BC game. The game started at three. At halftime Brian and Louise turned off the television and drove to Jay's for the usual Saturday night festivities. The wind had started to blow and the temperature had fallen into the forties. A light rain was falling. Everyone gathered inside while Jay prepared the fish on the grill outside. Brian sneaked into the living room with his beer and turned on the TV to watch the end of the game. BC was about to score its fifth touchdown when the cellular phone on Brian's belt made its screeching sound. Brian moved to the driveway and answered the phone next to where Jay was working the grill. Brian talked loud enough for Jay to hear.

"Yeah, okay, Eddie. If I see him I'll definitely give you a call. That's great, man. Yeah, I'll drive out to Hingham tomorrow and look around. I'll give you a call sometime tomorrow afternoon. See ya, Eddie. Have a good one, man."

Brian pushed the end button and placed the Cellular back on his belt. Jay was staring at him waiting for a report. "You got it, Jay. Good old Sailor was running around North Quincy this afternoon and the goons spotted him. Now they're on the scent. That goddamn Sailor's got a death wish. He's gotta be stoned outta his mind. You got any idea where he's headed? Don't tell me. Just find him and get him under wraps. Christ, I don't want to see a guy like him get snuffed."

Jay had no clue about the whereabouts of the Sailor. "Brian, I haven't got any idea where he's going. Hell, I haven't controlled any of his movements. He just takes off. The guy is something else. He'll take care of himself. My bet is that he shows up at the mission. When and if he does I'll give him whatever help he lets me give him. He's definitely in charge, man."

"Okay, Jay. You told me more than I want to know," quipped Brian. "Do your thing, man. When we gonna eat? I'm starved."

Eating inside was a definite downer. The kids were uncontrollable. Afterwards the kids went to the basement to play games. Susan and Louise retreated to the bedroom where they inhaled a few lines. Brian drank a lot of gin and then went to work on the depleted beer supply. Jay envied their consumption but drank coffee and Diet Pepsi. After the kids were in bed Jay assembled the adults around the kitchen table where they discussed next week's cookout at The Little Portion.

Susan's biggest concern was paying for all the food. Jay realized that they could not afford to buy the food but thought that Sister Celest could arrange for a donation from the hospital. Brian thought that was a great idea. He reasoned that a donation of uncooked food was a lot cheaper than cooked food. In his opinion, Durant should jump at the idea. Louise was uncomfortable with the idea of serving the people who frequented the mission. Jay laughed at her concern pointing out they that were no different than she. Louise missed the analogy. They all agreed to make at least two group visits to The Little Portion during the week to discuss and plan the event with Sister Celest. It was only eleven o'clock when the Saturday night party broke up.

Brian and Louise drove toward home but stopped at a few taverns en route. Jay was wired from the caffeine and watched television. Susan went back to the bedroom, inhaled a line, and went to sleep.

The Sailor also inhaled a few more lines, drank what was left of his whiskey, and lost consciousness. He laid at the edge of the Viaduct in the driving rain. Two of his companions pulled him under the shelter of the overpass. They went through his pockets and relieved him of the thirty-three dollars remaining from his morning labors. The cocaine that was tucked under his shirt armpit was overlooked after they covered him with his shirt and left him to sleep it off. They also took a few extra minutes to make sure that he was sufficiently camouflaged to avoid detection by the police patrols. The Sailor seemed to smile as they left. He wasn't scared.

Michael Logan was very scared. He made it to the outskirts of Montreal and took refuge in a small motel. He wanted to call his wife but feared that her phone lines would be tapped. He had no reason to think that way except his mind kept telling him that the inconsistent methods of former mayor Robert Cowan in administering campaign funds would reflect on him and, as things go, he would be the fall guy. Carefully, he thought over all his dealings with the Mayor's campaign funds. On several occasions, he was aware that the Mayor had used the fund for personal trips and possibly for family matters. None of that would reflect on him. The only thing he could think about was the so-called "signing bonus" he accepted when he resigned from the City and took the job with the Archdiocese. Something was wrong with the way that was handled. He suspected that the money was transferred from the Mayor's campaign fund to Logan's special account at the Hardly Security and Trust. In the past several months, Michael Logan had withdrawn money from the special account. Each time he was informed that the withdrawal was being given to an officer of the bank for approval. He vividly recalled the messenger telling him that a Mr. O'Shea wanted Mr. Logan to know that "the money, wherever it came from, was in his account." Now he suspected that it was Mr. O'Shea that was watching the account and giving the approval on transfers. That was his only clue and it made him scared enough to run and hide.

It was a slow news day in Boston. The usual drive by shootings had not taken place. The Governor was out of town. The Mayor was at peace with the City Council. The Red Sox were out of the pennant race as usual. The Patriots were expected to lose. Even the local college teams were having uneventful and predicted results. It was cold and raining so the reporters weren't walking the streets looking for human interest stuff. The only item worth beating to death was the *Globe* report about former Mayor Cowan's alleged misuse of campaign funds.

The cute beat reporter for Channel Seven met her sometime suitor from the *Globe* and worked him for more details about his story. He let it slip as he nuzzled her ear that he was tipped there was some hanky-panky with the funds but he had no facts. He had fired the question to Cowan as he had been paid to do and the Under Secretary of Labor and former Mayor went a little ballistic. She broke off the conversation, pushed his hand back where it belonged, and went back to her office where she began calling former City Council members and Commissioners in the Cowan administration. Her questions were uniformly answered with no comments. The last call she made was to the home of Michael Logan.

Mary Logan was experiencing pure panic. She could not understand why her husband left without telling her where he was going or why. She had spent the entire afternoon wondering if she should can the police or at least tell a relative or friend that Michael was missing. She decided to wait and see if he called or came home. When the telephone rang she was certain it was him. Her anxiety was obvious when she answered. "Michael, thank God. Where are you? I'm worried sick!"

The reporter picked up on Mary's panicked greeting and immediately pushed for information. "Oh, I'm sorry. Is this Mrs. Logan? Is it really true that Mr. Logan left town? Don't you know where he is or why he left? Can I help you find him?"

The offer to help caused Mary Logan to view the reporter as a friend. "Do I know you? Yes, I could use some help. Do you have any idea where Michael could have gone?"

The reporter moved in. "Mrs. Logan, I'm Nance Pritchard of Channel Seven News. I've spent most of the day following up on the possibility that Robert Cowan will seek the nomination for Governor. A report in the *Globe* gave some mention of impropriety in the use of Campaign funds by the former Mayor. Was Commissioner Logan involved or does he have knowledge about the campaign money? Is that why he left town? Can you comment? I will be willing to use my contacts to try to find him. May I come to see you?"

The caller seemed sincere in her offer to help. Mary needed help. She was alone and without anyone to talk to about this most unusual situation. She decided to accept the offer. "Yes, thank you. Are you coming soon?"

"Yes, Mrs. Logan. We should be there in an hour. If you hear from Michael in the meantime would you please call me on my mobile phone?"

Nancy Pritchard immediately called the News Director who gave her the green light to headline the story for the ten o'clock news. He assigned a cameraman and an assistant to go with her to the Logan household. In less than ten minutes the truck was on its way.

Mary Logan was now having second thoughts. Her husband had schooled her about the media. Her accommodation of Pritchard's request to come to the house was possibly a mistake. She began to think clearly and dialed her mother and father. They lived an hour away but immediately left to be with her. Then she called Michael's boss, Dr. Richard Folley. The Great One's answering service received her call and offered to contact the doctor. The service expected that he would return her call within the hour.

Richard Folley, M.D., wife and children were dining with his in-laws, Mr. and Mrs. Thomas O'Shea, at their plush home in Weston when the pager on Dr. Folley's belt began its piercing whine. Folley with his usual super important expression punched the silent button, excused himself with a duty calls air, and telephoned the St. Anslem's Physician Referral and Answering Service. The duty operator explained that a Mrs. Logan had requested that he call her immediately on an extremely urgent matter. The fact that the call was from Mrs. Logan and stated as urgent gave Folley the sense that Michael was either very ill or very dead. Hastily he dialed the number given to him by the operator.

Mrs. Logan answered immediately. She explained the circumstances about Michael's sudden and unexpected departure to parts unknown. Then she described how the Channel Seven reporter had offered to help and was on the way to her house. Finally she asked the good doctor to give his opinion and be with her as she faced the media. Folley in typical bed side fashion told Mary that everything was going to be all right and that she should be calm. He said that he would try to be with her within the next hour. In the meantime if the media had questions about Michael's position with the Archdiocese she should simply refer those questions to him and he would answer them when he arrived. Mary was reassured. Folley was scared, although you couldn't tell it.

The Great One was also a little confused. He wasn't sure if he should call the Chancery and report this matter in view of possible scandal or wait until he met with the media to decide. He also wondered what impact this event might have on his formation of the Medical Management Services Corporation that he with the help of Tom Callahan was going to spring on the St. Anslem's Medical Staff in the next week or so. Perhaps he should call Callahan and ask his advice. Next on his mind was his fellow trustees at the hospital. Should he report the matter to them? That was a no brainier. His Father in Law was, for all practical purposes, the brains of the hospital Board. He simply had to explain the matter to him and consider the hospital Board informed. Easy enough. He would talk to Father-in-Law Tom before he left for Logan's and let the rest wait. He and Tom then spent twenty minutes in the study going over the matter. Eventually, he kissed the wife and kids and cut out for Logan's and a date with Channel Seven. He liked that.

After Dr. Folley left, Tom O'Shea returned to his study and closed the double doors. He wanted to be alone to think about the events of the hour. He lowered the lights and sat in his comfortable leather recliner. It was happening. He expected something like this. Logan was set up by Patello and his associates to be a fall guy for Cowan. That's one theory, he thought. Another is that Logan was actually set up not to fall but to be the source of evidence if one was needed to cause Cowan to fall. That figured. Logan accepted funds from Cowan that Cowan took from the Campaign account. Logan would be an accomplice but Cowan would be the one guilty of the felony and do the time. Patello and his boys had the canceled check that had been deposited in Logan's special account to prove the point O'Shea also had the evidence to prove the scheme. He had made copies when the account was established and the original deposit was delivered by messenger. It was time to cash in.

He gave his old classmate and longtime friend, Charles Patello, a call. "Charlie, Tom O'Shea. Look, I heard from Dr. Folley that Channel Seven is going to break a story on the ten o'clock news that Michael Logan is somehow involved in the campaign fund mess of which Bob Cowan is accused. Richard is on his way now to meet with Michael's wife and the reporters. Seems that Michael has taken off and is apparently hiding out. This thing is going to get out of hand. Now I would like to meet with you tomorrow afternoon to discuss some things related to all of this."

Charles Patello was speechless. The last thing he expected was for the Cowan issue to break wide open before he had a chance to meet with Cowan and get him to back off. If the Channel Seven report was anything substantive then Cowan would turn State's evidence and implicate Patello and the whole operation. The bank merger would fall. Apparently his good friend, O'Shea, had some angle on this. He knew he had no choice but to meet and listen to him.

"Tom, you took me off guard and I might add you have me at a disadvantage since I'm not sure what in the hell you are talking about. Unfortunately, I'm scheduled to be out of town tomorrow. If it's real important we can meet tonight. You available?"

O'Shea was impressed at the cool attitude expressed by Patello. The man was well under control. He made the matter seem trivial yet O'Shea was positive that Patello was busting his gut.

O'Shea pressed forward. "Sure, I guess. The grand kids are here but the wife can see that they get home. How about meeting halfway? Someplace downtown. The Four Seasons sound okay? We can sit in the lounge or the lobby. If you can make it by nine we can watch the ten o'clock news from there after we talk."

"Sure, Tom, the Four Seasons is fine. It will take me about forty-five minutes. See you there," Patello agreed.

Patello dressed quickly into a business suit. The Four Seasons was not a place for casual dress. His drive into Boston from his home in Situate took all of the forty-five minutes that he said it would. En route, he tried several times to call Mario Capizzi. The Capizzi's were apparently out for the evening so all he could do was leave a message to call back at his earliest convenience. He added that the matter was urgent. He thought about calling Uncle Frank but decided against it in view of Frank's recent emotional outburst about the former Mayor. Best to get the complete story before bothering the top man with the problem whatever it was.

Tom O'Shea made the run to the Four Seasons in thirty minutes. He carefully scouted around for a quiet place to talk with Patello. A small table back in the corner of the lounge adjacent to the main dining room but out of sight seemed like the perfect place. He tipped the maître-d to hold the table and added another twenty dollars to keep the area vacant of other customers. Fortunately, the lounge area was not busy at this hour since most of the patrons had moved into the dining room and were in the process of being served. Having secured the spot, he went to the front lobby to wait for Patello to arrive.

Shortly thereafter O'Shea spotted Patello giving his car to the care of the Valet. He went to greet him and the two men walked to the reserved place in the lounge. A waiter moved quickly to take their order. O'Shea ordered a double Chevis on the rocks.

O'Shea looked into the eyes of his friend and spoke. "Charlie, I know you must think I'm a little crazy to get you to come to town on a Saturday night like this but I think things are about to explode around the Cowan run for Governor thing. Mary Logan, Michael's wife, called Dr. Robert an hour or so ago and said that he had skipped town or something like that and that the television reporters were coming to her house for a story to be on the ten o'clock news. She doesn't know anything about Michael's dealings with Cowan or anybody else I guess but I figured out a few things that might concern you so I thought we ought to talk before too much was made public. Robert went over to the Logan's to do what he could for Mary."

Charlie Patello thought at length before he replied. In fact, he delayed a response for so long that O'Shea was wondering if Patello had heard what he had said. Finally, Patello took a deep breath and spoke. "Tom, what in the hell are you driving at? I don't know anything about this Cowan thing and I sure as hell don't know anything about where Michael Logan could be spending the afternoon or night as the case may be. What's this got to do with us?"

The waiter arrived with the drinks and asked if the gentlemen would like to see a dinner menu or would just prefer to have hors d'oeuvres. Patello gave the waiter an angry look that O'Shea picked up as a signal that the super cool exterior was shielding a very hot interior. The waiter glanced over to O'Shea who thanked him and politely dismissed the waiter with the message that the drinks were adequate. Then he returned his attention to Patella's question.

"Charlie, the media has got the scent. They will blow this thing about Cowan into a major story that will cause the Attorney General to investigate if for no other reason to get himself reelected. It will be to everyone's interest to nail Cowan just to satisfy the crazy media. I have records about money that was laundered into Logan's account that you had deposited. If that gets out, you get headlines and the bank merger gets the trash can. We don't want that. We want to get this bank deal done fast I want you to know that I'm with you. I want to be a survivor in the merger. I can see that things go unnoticed. I help you and you help me. It's an age-old proposition. We've done it before. Back at BC. I got you hooked up with Hardly and good things happened for both of us. We can do it again. That's what I've got in mind. I wanted to offer you my help before things got so far downstream that the deal was lost."

"You're still double talking, Tom." Patello leaned in. "Hardly is over the hill. He and his family want out of the business. You know that. He isn't going to interfere. The Attorney General's office has approved the merger. It's all set except for the organization plan that we have to submit in the next few weeks. Cowan and Logan have nothing to do with the bank. What's your point?"

"Christ, Charlie, don't act so goddamn naïve." O'Shea twisted in his chair to demonstrate his contempt. "My point is that you and your goddamn friends from New York or wherever need the bank deal. I know that. You moved Logan out of the City administration so you could get a patsy like Megan to take over as Commissioner and give our friend Meehan a juicy deal. Hell, that thing at St. Anslem's is over ripe. It smells, my good friend. I got the records of the payments from the hospital. I got a copy of the contract. But what really tops it all off is the copy of the canceled check from the bank with his endorsement giving Logan ten grand to get lost. That's an illegal endorsement. I also have the dispatch record from Patriot that could even implicate our fellow hospital trustee, Phil Mondi, who suddenly cut a trail to Portland. So now Logan splits and the media wants to know what he's running from. Maybe I could tell them. Why should I do that?"

"You tell me, Tom." Patello had O'Shea locked in a cold stare. "Tell me why you should tell anybody anything. All I know so far is that you seem to be one hell of a file clerk. You have records but you seem to be a little short of facts and long on imagination. Listen, I have to catch a plane in the morning. Can we cut this short? Let me ask again. What's your point?"

O'Shea leaned back in his chair and seemed to relax. "This is a simple proposition, Charlie. I understand business and what's necessary for a venture to succeed. I don't want to interfere. I want to help. In other words, I want in. Cut me in, Charlie. You understand?"

Patello sat back. "You give me a lot of credit, Tom. You might not be talking to the right person. What do you mean, you want in? What's in? Help me a little so I can understand what it is you're trying to sell."

It was the right time to lay it on the line. O'Shea gave it his best shot. "CEO, Charlie. I want to be named the Chief Executive Officer of the merged banks. You can swing that. My loyalty deserves your consideration. Your organization plan requires that the corporate officers be named in the next week so you can get it approved by the secretary of State. You can convince the new

Board that I'm the guy for the CEO Job. We've been friends a long time. You know that I'm capable. It would never be questioned. My background is perfect for the job. Hell, you know that the chief exec selection in these deals is nothing but a beauty contest anyway. We got a deal? Say yes, my records get lost, and you can go home and get some rest for your trip tomorrow."

O'Shea rested his case and sat back with a friendly smile. He sipped his drink and remained relaxed. He had said his piece and felt that he was very convincing. The waiter looked over at the table and O'Shea waved for another round of drinks.

Patello saw the signal and reacted. "No more for me, thanks, Tom. I've got to get home. I got your message. I'll have to think about it and get back to you. You know that these kind decisions are not made by one person. I'm not as much in control as you think I am. Let me think about this."

"Sure, Charlie, I understand. It's almost ten. You want to watch the news? They have a television in the waiting area at the end of the lobby. It's probably vacant. We can take our drinks with us."

"Good suggestion, Tom. Then I've got to split."

The Great Richard Folley, M.D., had one admitted fault. He couldn't find his way at night. Michael Logan's address was in a part of the City that Folley was familiar with and in the daylight, he would have driven right to it. But it was dark and Folley was very prone to error in the dark. That was his little secret that he never revealed. His wife knew it all too well from many years of correcting his direction. Otherwise, his secret was safe. Unexpectedly, the well-lit house of Michael Logan appeared before him just as the Buick with Mary's parents arrived followed closely by the Channel Seven Van. The three vehicles actually competed for entrance to the driveway. Folley was first. Channel Seven was a very close second scraping the bumper of the Great One's Benz in the process.

While the doctor and the cameraman exchanged looks Mary's parents ran to the house followed by Nance Pritchard, crack news hound. Mary attempted to greet her parents who wanted to know what was happening. Nance Pritchard was struggling to move Mary into position for a live interview due to be on the air in less than twenty minutes. Folley was desperately trying to push his way into the varied conversations and the camera man was attempting to find the right angle and set up lights. The kids ran about shouting and the dog started barking.

Mary finally succeeded in getting everyone crowded into the small living room. Then she politely moved her parents into the kitchen where she attempted to explain that Michael had suddenly left town but had left a note promising to call her. She had no idea that the television crew would show up with the reporter who she thought was trying to help her find Michael. Mary's father was about to offer some advice when Nance Pritchard pushed into the kitchen with her notepad at the ready. Folley was working with the cameraman who was using the Great One to establish the lighting effect. Folley was posing for the camera. He was good at it.

The telephone rang and Mary answered it. Michael responded to her greeting. "Honey, I'm sorry about this. I was afraid that the reporters would be hounding us about Mayor Cowan and I needed time to think. I'm afraid that this could be trouble. Are you okay?"

The mass confusion and noise disappeared when the phone rang. All eyes were on Mary as she answered it. Immediately she grasped the realization that the last thing she should do was let the reporter know that Michael was calling. She also had to tip Michael that the media was in his kitchen. "Please, Sir, I have no information. Channel Seven is here now. I really have nothing to say. You might want to call back tomorrow. Goodbye."

Then she looked at Nance Pritchard. "Well, Ms. Pritchard, it seems as though your competition is also offering their help. Really this is all overwhelming. I don't have any information that I can give you."

Mary had done an excellent job in alerting Michael. He caught her message to call back and decided that three A.M. would be the best time. Nance Pritchard was not easily distracted. She noted the sudden mood change that Mary seemed to exhibit before the telephone call and after she hung up. Nance guessed that Michael was the caller.

She decided to push the point. "Mrs. Logan, your husband disappeared suddenly this morning. Was his disappearance in anyway connected to the allegation that his former boss, Michael Cowan, is accused of using campaign funds for his personal use?"

Mary had no idea how to answer the question. She looked at her father for help. He was not at all in a position to offer a response. Carefully, Mary gave the only answer that came to mind. "Please, I really have nothing to say."

Pritchard moved in for the kill."Mrs. Logan, did Michael have information that may incriminate Mayor Cowan? Is that why he fled?"

Mary tried to move out of the kitchen. Pritchard followed her into the living room where Folley was now doing sound takes with the cameraman. Pritchard repeated the question and the cameraman shouldered the camera for the take. Mary was caught in the flood light as she began to answer. "Let me restate that Mr. Logan is not at home. He left this morning on a business trip. I don't believe he has any idea about the allegations surrounding Mayor Cowan. Really, Ms. Pritchard, this is enough. We don't have anything to talk about."

Pritchard noted the response and looked at her watch. She only had a few minutes until her live report. With a signal she moved the cameraman onto the porch, made the link to the studio, and on cue from the anchor, began her report. "We are live at the home of Michael Logan, former Commissioner of Health in the Cowan administration. Logan suddenly left town this morning when allegations surfaced that the former Mayor used campaign funds for his personal use. His whereabouts are unknown. His family has desperately appealed for him to return. Channel Seven has also learned that the Commissioner had extensive information about Cowan's resources. It is also believed that the Commissioner was to be a key figure in the former Mayor's campaign for Governor. Just a few minutes ago we talked to Mrs. Logan who verified that her husband is indeed missing. With her at this time are her parents and a physician. Mrs. Logan has no idea what information her husband might have that would possibly prove Cowan's guilt."

The anchor thanked Ms. Pritchard for the report and then repeated the information contained in the *Globe* report. Leaving the viewers to draw their own conclusions, the newscast switched to weather and then to sports. Nance Pritchard put her notebook back in her bag. The cameraman carried his equipment back to the truck. They Boarded the truck, backed over the lawn, and drove off into the night.

Mary was happy to see them go. She walked back into the kitchen and prepared a pot of tea. Then she returned to the living room with cups and a plate of cookies. The kids were set at the kitchen table with milk and cookies while the adults talked in the living room. Mary introduced her parents to Dr. Folley who seemed a bit flustered at the brief report and rapid departure of the media.

Mary's father had taken special notice of Folley's cooperative spirit toward the media and pulled his daughter aside to caution her not to include the doctor in any confidential information. Mary's dad was suspicious that the good doctor was a media spy. As a result of her father's warning Mary talked only about her concern for her husband and hope that he would call soon. She promised to inform everyone when she heard anything. Folley seemed intent on staying for the night but Mary escorted him to the door, thanked him for coming, and bid him a good night. Folley did not realize that he had gotten the bum's rush. He was more intent on finding his way home in the dark.

Tom O'Shea and his buddy Charlie Patello sat in the bride's waiting room at the Four Seasons and watched the ten o'clock news. The story about former Mayor Cowan was next to the lead off about a car bombing in Palestine. The anchorman seemed to be delivering a sermon as he enhanced the story with incriminating looks and an all be damned delivery.

Patello realized that there was a complete lack of substance in the story. For some reason Logan had lost nerve and ran. That meant nothing unless he was found and cracked under pressure. If the story lost steam because Cowan backed off from the Governor's race all would be forgotten. The key to solving this mess was to get Cowan to back off. The trip to Washington was important to begin with and now was very important. O'Shea was now the real problem. He was attempting to shake down the establishment. Big Frank had to be informed.

Saturday was always a tough day for the clergy. For Bishop Hanks it had been especially difficult. He had met with the Cardinal at eight that morning to review a number of parishes that were very shorthanded. Hanks had tried to convince His Eminence that Priests in administrative posts outside of the parishes should be brought in and assigned to parishes. He contended that the central focus of the Church was its congregations. The Cardinal agreed but presented a very broad definition of a congregation that included missionary work and service in charitable institutions and programs. The Cardinal contended that a Priest serving as a counselor in a social service agency was serving a congregation.

Hanks tried desperately to explain his point by explaining that some of the large parishes were down to two priests and the smaller parishes in some parts of the Diocese only had a pastor. Lay deacons had been utilized but they were few in number. St. Anslem's Hospital had the benefit of two full-time priests serving as chaplains and directing the Pastoral Care Department. Hanks felt that they could be assigned to nearby parishes and continue to serve the hospital on an on call basis. The Cardinal felt that it was essential to the identity of a Catholic Hospital to have a priest available to the patients at all times.

After an hour and a half of intense discussion the Cardinal abruptly cut off the conversation, gave Hanks a number of administrative tasks, and left for the airport. Hanks spent the rest of the morning and most of the afternoon working in his office. At three-thirty he left the Chancery to go to a suburban parish where he assisted the Pastor by saying the five o'clock Mass. After that he traveled back to the City where he said the seven P.M. Spanish Mass at the Cathedral. He got home around nine-thirty, had a bite to eat, and sat down to watch the ten o'clock news. When he saw the report that the director of the Office of Health Affairs for the Boston Catholic Archdiocese had skipped town, he wept. He wondered what kind of identity the Catholic hospital would have under an Archdiocesan system directed by a felon. It was too late to call the Cardinal. He would try to reach him sometime Sunday afternoon after he had talked with Dr. Folley. The Cardinal would expect them to do everything possible to avoid scandal and would expect a very detailed report of their actions.

It was nearly midnight when Patello got home. He immediately took the Boston Area telephone book into his study and searched for Michael Logan's number. He was relieved to find it. Mary Logan answered quicker than he expected. She sounded nervous but controlled. Patella had never met her and was concerned about her reaction to his call. Carefully, he tried to explain his purpose without causing her additional anxiety.

"Mrs. Logan, my name is Charles Patello. I helped recruit your husband for the position at the Archdiocese. Let me say first of all that I'm very sorry for the undue pressure that you must be experiencing. I know Michael well enough to be certain that the reports have no substance. He is a very good man and certainly not involved with any improper activity."

Mary Logan had been constantly on the phone for the past two hours responding to well-wishers and those who wanted to condemn. She accepted Patello's call as just another from the curious. "Thank you for your concern, Sir. We are fine. I'll tell Michael that you called."

"Mrs. Logan, when you talk next to Michael will you please tell him that Mr. Patello is meeting with Mr. Cowan tomorrow in Washington? It would be beneficial to all concerned if Michael could join us. I will be arriving at National at two P.M. Please ask Michael to join us at the U.S. Air Club in the U.S. Air Terminal. Whatever he decides, ask him to telephone a message to the club. I'll pick it up and either look for him to show or know that I should continue without him. Is this clear enough?"

She answered with caution. "Yes, I think so. Could you please give me your name again? I don't know when I'll hear from Michael."

"The name is Patello, Charles Patello. Michael will know me. Thank you, Ms. Logan. I'm sure everything will be all right. Goodnight."

Chapter Nineteen

It was a beautiful day. The rain had passed and with the dawn came brilliant sunlight that warmed the air with every passing hour. It brought the Sailor out of his stupor. He wondered where he was. A look around didn't give him a clue. The dark gray concrete pillars supporting the viaduct planted deep in the dirt and mud embankment only further confused him. He heard the rumble of passing cars and trucks pounding the concrete slab only a few inches over his head. The noise was tremendous as it resonated in his senses. Around him was the debris left by his companions who had shared his whiskey and then in gratitude robbed him of his meager earnings. Carefully, the Sailor retrieved his tattered wallet from the dirt. In it he found his VA Card and retired military identification among other less important remembrances. His money was gone. No surprise. Cautiously, he reached under his arm. With great relief he found the remaining packs of cocaine. It had not been a complete loss.

The Sailor pushed aside the cardboard cartons that had covered him overnight and prevented his discovery by the Boston Police referred to by his associates as the blue bum patrol. He was soaking wet nevertheless and the cool morning air caused him to cough uncontrollably. Once on his feet he attempted to walk from under the viaduct but the steep decline caused him to lose his footing. He rolled down the embankment to the street below. He laid in the sunlight on the warming asphalt and waited for his strength to return. Pain shot through his lungs. He coughed up blood. He could not seem to catch a breath and he thought that he was going to pass out. The medication that Dr. Anderson had given him was back at The Little Portion in a cupboard that he had requisitioned for his personal use. He had no recollection of it. He felt the small pouch of cocaine tied to his shoulder and hung under his arm. He pulled the plastic pouch free and stared at it pondering its contents. Instinctively, he made a small opening in the top of the pouch and inhaled. Gradually, the pain began to disappear. He tried to stand but fell painfully into the gutter. He inhaled more cocaine and pushed the pouch into his pocket.

The sun had warmed the asphalt to the point that it was very comfortable. He laid there until he felt some strength and again tried to stand. This time he succeeded. A post holding a stop sign became his support. He held it tight and then turned his body to lean against it while he inhaled more of the white powder. The cool fall air entered his lungs caused him to have another uncontrollable coughing fit. He fell to his knees and then to all fours. Again the warm pavement gave him strength and he pulled himself up. This time he steadied and began to walk across the street. Traffic stopped to let him pass. When he reached the other side he sat on the curb exhausted. A driver of a small car called him a junkie. The Sailor gave him the finger.

Market estimates suggest that, while there are no definite figures, on Sunday more people frequent donut shops than go to church in the metropolitan Boston area. This is evidenced by the fact that the number of donut shops out number churches and are a close second to taverns. The taverns are generally prohibited from opening before noon, if at all, so the faithful have their choices limited to donuts or prayer. The Catholic Churches have attempted to counter the donut thing by offering free donuts and coffee after each Mass. It is unknown if the marketing ploy has had any impact.

Jay Marquart and his family had not participated in either Church or Donut. This Sunday was different. The Marquart family was going to Dunkin' Donuts. Susan had the kids up by ten and dressed. She fed them some cereal and juice and warned them not to spoil their appetites. Jay drank several cups of coffee. They left the house promptly at eleven-thirty and arrived at Dunkin' Donuts fifteen minutes later. Jay ushered the family into an open booth and told them they would have to wait until the mystery man and donut benefactor arrived.

The kids' sullen attitude was suddenly changed when a box of two dozed mixed variety gooey pastries complete with holes was unexpectedly placed in the middle of their table by a young, small slender man with thick rimmed glasses. He wore a plaid sport coat over a green cotton shirt with an olive drab tie and blue jeans. He nodded a greeting to Susan and extended his hand to Jay.

"Good morning, everybody. Isn't it a great day to hit the donuts? Enjoy! My name is Wally Wallace. Will you excuse your daddy and me while we go outside and talk? You eat all of those and Uncle Wally will see that you get more. Nice of you to make it, Jay. Can we talk?"

Jay shook Wally's hand and picked out a donut. "Sure, Wally. You must be a Harvard man."

"Well, actually I am, Mr. Marquart. Nice of you to notice. Class of '89. Went to BU Law. Let's go out to my car. There are a few notes that I have and I want to make sure that I get everything straight. You mind if I use a tape recorder?"

Jay wrapped his donut in a napkin and walked with Wally to a green Saab sedan parked over the line of two spaces. As soon as the two men entered his car, two other cars facing each other positioned themselves to occupy the parking spaces that they thought were about to be vacated. When Wally did not start the engine one of the waiting cars backed away. The other continued to wait. Wally opened a notebook and turned on his tape recorder. He began speaking into a small microphone

"Mr. Marquart, as I said I'm Wally Wallace. You can call me Wally. I'm a researcher with the State Attorney General. We have had some reason given for us to look into the nature of Union organization methods and labor agreements in the current year. You are a member of Local 936 and a shop steward employed with Action Waste Management. Is that correct?"

John looked at the tape recorder and then reasoned that he should look at Wally as he answered. "Yes. Say, Wally, if you're with the Attorney General and a lawyer and all maybe I should have my lawyer talk to you rather than me. What are you going to do with this stuff?"

"I know Martha quite well, Jay." Wally tried to put Jay at ease. "I would welcome the opportunity to talk to her but I don't think I'm her type. We have had one date. I'm only gathering information. None of what you tell me is directed at you. At the most you might be called on as a witness if anything ever comes of this. Relax."

"Okay. I just wanted to be sure. You know Martha? How did you know she was my lawyer?"

It was a question that Wally was pleased to answer. "She did campaign work for the AG. We worked together. That's when we had our date. She told me about your Union thing and when your name came up in the research I thought I should contact you. The guys over at the Brighton Precinct got your name from some guy that gives them tips now and then. That's it. Did you ever meet a guy named Bob Muldoon?"

"Yeah." Jay was now at ease. "Muldoon is the head guy with the Workers Guild. He helped organize Action and he gave me the once over when I was made the shop steward. He's a gruff old fart."

The driver from the waiting car came over to the Saab and tapped on the closed window. Wally opened it a couple of inches and stuck his nose toward the inquiring soul. "Can I help you?" he offered.

The red-faced heavyset blonde lady nodded in response. "Are you going to move? There are cars waiting for these spaces, you inconsiderate son of a bitch!"

Wally didn't reply. He rolled up the window and asked Jay his next question. "How about Veto Celi? Did you ever meet him? How does he fit in with Muldoon?"

Jay saw the blonde lady mouth the words "fuck you" as she went back to her car.

He tried to suppress a laugh and answer the question at the same time. "Celli works for Action in sales. I don't know how he ties with Muldoon if at all. I ain't never seen them together. Hey, Wally, fill me in. What's the beef? Muldoon got his hand in Celi's pocket?"

Wally had a ready reply. "I can't tell you much, Jay. We don't have much except a tip that some Union leaders are taking money from sources unknown for their personal use. Muldoon was one name that was given to us and Celi was another. We haven't been able to link them together. The way that these things sometimes work is that the original informer finds an innocent bystander to pass us information. That's because the informer is maybe too close to the guy who is on the take and might be discovered. We take that information and piece it together. Sometimes we have a case and sometimes we don't. The informer may have two or three people fingered to pass us information. Eventually he knows who he can trust by the way information is passed. Then we set up a communication chain and get our man. Until all this gets worked out we have to follow every bit of information and every lead. You are part of the process. This is just an introductory meeting to let you know that we are involved. If you are the carrier selected, you'll get contacted and we'll have a few more meetings."

The humor of the moment suddenly disappeared, Jay felt pressure. "Anybody ever get hurt doing this?"

Wally was less than reassuring. "Yeah, sometimes. It's been nice meeting you, Jay. Enjoy the donuts. You have a very nice family—a beautiful wife and three lovely kids. You're a rich man." Wally closed his notebook, turned off the tape recorder and started the Saab.

John got the message, thanked Wally for the donuts, and got out of the car. The blonde lady's car was parked over the line two spaces down.

The two dozen donuts were down to eight plain. Jay munched on one as he drove the family home. Susan was curious about Jay's friend who seemed to be such a gentleman. Jay gave simple answers to her questions. He was involved in his own thoughts about the conversation and reflecting on his meeting with Donovan on Friday. Donovan had mentioned that some bad things were coming down in the Union. He had asked Jay if he could be counted on. Donovan was definitely a player in whatever was happening. In his heart Jay felt another sting of concern. This was a matter of caring for what was right—Union or not. Who was wrong? What was right?

Michael Logan never missed Mass on Sunday. This Sunday he wouldn't make it. His wife gave him Patello's message to be in Washington by two. The direct flights from Montreal left in the afternoon. His only recourse was to catch a six A.M. Air Canada flight to Chicago and an eleven A.M. United to Washington. That would put him in around twelve-thirty if everything went according to schedule. The tough part was making the flight in Chicago since the hour time difference only gave him forty-five minutes to make the connection. Fortunately, he was traveling light. He parked his car at the Montreal Airport Long Term Parking area and caught the shuttle to the main terminal. It was five-fifteen when he approached the counter to buy his tickets. That was another problem. He had to use his credit card. Mary warned him last week that they were near their maximum limit and he should go easy until they had a chance to pay down on the debt.

So much for good intentions, he thought. The family budget was well blown.

Patello never went to Mass except on those rare occasions when the Knights assembled for induction, promotions, and such. That was scheduled for next Saturday at the Cathedral. Today he had to get it all together to fly to Washington for his showdown with Robert Cowan. Before he left home he called Uncle Frank. Frank Patello was a very devout Catholic who never missed Mass on Sunday. That's where he was when Charlie placed his call. Consequently, Charlie could only leave the message that he was on his way to Washington to meet with the Under Secretary but a very urgent matter had come up that he needed to discuss with him. Charlie concluded by promising to call again when he landed at National. Then he kissed his wife, gave her instructions about his return flight that evening, and began his drive to Logan Airport.

His Eminence, Francis Cardinal McMahon concelebrated Mass with other Bishops attending the United States Catholic Conference meeting in St. Louis. The Prince of the Church said Mass at the Old Cathedral on the River Front overlooking the Mississippi. He gave a very moving homily to the packed Church in which he emphasized the Church's obligation to assert its teachings in the mores of modern living. After Mass, he stood outside the entrance and greeted the laity as they departed. Then he got into his waiting limo and returned to his hotel to freshen up before the session. The message light on the telephone blinked his attention. There was a message to call Bishop Hanks at his earliest convenience. The Cardinal concluded that the Bishop would be in his office at the Chancery and dialed the number.

When his phone rang Bishop Stephen Hanks knew that it was the call he had been waiting for from Cardinal McMahon. His greeting to the boss reflected relief. "Your Eminence, Praise God, thanks for returning my call."

The Cardinal listened intently to the Bishop's explanation of the Channel Seven report concerning Michael Logan. Bishop Hanks also read the *Globe* story from Saturday and a copy story from the Sunday morning *Herald* to His Eminence. When the Bishop finished the Cardinal remained silent for a few seconds and then commented.

"Stephen, you said that the television reporter mentioned that there was a physician with Mrs. Logan last night. I wonder who it was. Perhaps Dr. Folley was there. Have you discussed this with him? Has he called you? It also occurs to me that this is more a media inquiry than any presentation of fact. I don't see that Michael has done anything according to what has been reported. It is interesting to me to see that we are not even mentioned in the reports. If Dr. Folley was there he obviously did an excellent job of keeping us out of the news. When he calls in please tell him that I am very grateful for the way that he is handling this. So far there is no scandal and I really don't expect any. You are doing a very good job. Please continue to keep me informed. Is everything else all right?"

Bishop Hanks realized that the Cardinal was not concerned. He also got the message that the good Dr. Folley was to be the Cardinal's man in this matter. Hanks was relegated to the status of messenger. He resented that but he was also an obedient servant. Carefully, he reacted without disclosing his feelings.

"Your Eminence, I will most certainly advise Dr. Folley that you are satisfied with the way he is handling this matter. If anything further comes of this, we will inform you immediately. When you return I would like to discuss the whole matter of the Healing Ministry in relationship to the new organizations being formed at the hospital. I wonder if they are consistent with our ministry."

Cardinal McMahon was also concerned about the direction that the ministry was taking. He regarded it as the work of the Holy Spirit and maintained good faith that whatever happened would be for the good of the Church. However, he knew that he had to remain vigilant and attentive to the concerns of his staff. He quickly agreed with the Bishop.

"Of course, Stephen. There is a lot of change taking place in the health field in Boston. We are in the middle of it and need to continue to be very prominent in the new systems just as we have been in the past. I think Dr. Folley has us positioned to be a major provider. I look forward to having a chat with you about this. It might be well to have Dr. Folley join us."

Bishop Hanks realized that he was not about to get the idea across that Dr. Folley was his concern. The Good Doctor was established as the Cardinal's man in healthcare. There was no way around that. Obediently, he accepted the Cardinal's direction and gave his goodbye. "Thank you, Your Eminence. I look forward to your return."

Robert Cowan had to be very careful. He thought he spotted a beat reporter from the Washington Post sitting in a car down the street from his Georgetown townhouse. Since the neighborhood was filled with Government functionaries, it wasn't certain who the reporter might be staking out. Nevertheless, Cowan sneaked out the backdoor and walked unnoticed over to the next street where he hailed a cab for National Airport. He arrived an hour ahead of the time that Patello was scheduled to arrive. The U.S. Air Terminal was another caution zone for him. Reporters were always there waiting for arrivals and departures of VIP's. Cowan moved cautiously through the terminal lobby and the security scan. Then he rode the escalator to the departure area. No reporters were evident so he moved into the food service area where he decided to have a couple of donuts and a cup of black coffee. Patello's flight was listed as on time and due in forty-five minutes.

Logan's worst fears were realized. The flight from Montreal arrived at Chicago O'Hare on time but was delayed getting into the gate. It seemed that it took forever for the door to be opened. Then he pushed his way off the plane and ran to the United Terminal where he had to stand in line to clear security. He repeatedly set the alarm off and was finally given the electric wand treatment by a security guard who seemed to take delight in passing the instrument over his body at least three times before he was waved through. When he arrived at the departure gate the doors were being closed. At first, the gate agents refused to reopen and let him Board since standbys had already been given the remaining seats. At the last moment the last vacant seat was discovered and he was allowed to Board the plane. It took off an hour after scheduled time for departure which was par for Chicago.

An hour and a half later the pilot reported that they were beginning their initial descent into the Washington area and a few minutes after that reported they had been placed in a holding pattern in order to let departing traffic clear. When the wheels touched down at National, ninety minutes late, Logan was in a sweat. It was only one-thirty, giving him thirty minutes to spare, but he still had to get from the old main terminal to the U.S. Air Terminal nearly a half mile away. He ran through the concourse, out into the street and jogged to U.S. Air.

Patello's flight had arrived on time at gate ten just opposite the U.S. Air Club. Cowan watched for the passengers to begin to exit. Then he moved into the club to wait for Patello to arrive. It wasn't good tactic to greet him in the open lobby where they might be spotted. Within minutes Patello walked into the club and checked in at the desk. Cowan waited for him to turn around before he greeted him. The two men shook hands, exchanged comments about health, and moved immediately to a small conference room that Patello had reserved. They each poured a cup of coffee from the thermos and sat down to begin their conversation when a sweating Michael Logan entered the room. Cowan looked shocked.

Patello was amused at Cowan's facial expression. He offered an explanation to the Under Secretary as Logan slumped into a chair. "Robert, I asked Michael to join us since what I have to say involves both of you. You may have heard that Michael left Boston before the media could pin him down on the allegations that you may have confiscated some campaign funds. It has flamed suspicion that you two are conspirators. For Michael it's a clear case of guilt by association."

Cowan knew he had purposely been put on the defensive. He tried to regain an advantage. "You understand, Charlie, that I haven't any intention to push this matter. There is no basis to those allegations. Of course, I will have to fight to prove my innocence." Cowan seemed adamant as he stared at Logan. "Have some coffee, Michael."

Patello pointed to the thermos next to him and opposite Cowan. Logan nervously poured a cup and nodded his thanks to Patello. Patello then resumed the conversation with Logan.

"Let's assume for purpose of discussion that there was some proof that you had used those funds for your personal benefit. Even if you got away with a slap on the wrist, the Party would never let you have the nomination. Even if they did, no significant contributor would want to be associated with your campaign. You would be finished. What's more likely, though, is that you would be fined and maybe serve a sentence. I can imagine that Michael, here, would be compromised to tell whatever he could about your crime. That would get him probation if he had the right lawyer."

"You miss a major point, Charlie." Cowan leaned forward and pointed a finger at Patello. "Let's also assume for purposes of discussion that the funds I used were given to me by a contributor who knew that I was going to use the funds for myself and in fact gave me the money especially for that reason. That puts the contributor on the line. I might even have evidence of certain contracts and kickbacks that went along with the deal. Now we wouldn't want that to surface, would we?"

Logan looked very pale. He thought he was going to faint. The sweat was running down his face and dripped from his nose. Patello pushed a box of tissues toward him and continued the banter with Cowan.

"Of course not, Robert. Someone always gets hurt when that happens. We wouldn't want anyone to get hurt over this. Would we? The pain that a person might experience from something like that is often worse than going to prison especially when a family suffers as well. It would be best if we could just make this thing go away. Don't you agree?"

The pain that Patello referred to was the message that Cowan had expected to hear. He wanted to make sure that the muscle was backing Patello before he started to back down. Now he knew that he had to work out a deal. "It's not necessary for anyone to be hurt, Charlie. I'm sure that good reason will offer us a method to dispel any false allegations. What do you think?"

Cowan leaned back on the legs of the chair. He crossed his hands over his middle as if he were playing out a poker hand and contemplating a raise to back a bluff. Before Patello could say what he thought, Cowan added another point. "You know, Charlie, the Governor could help a lot of people with contracts and concessions. It might be worth it to see that I get elected."

Patello was thinking that Cowan was ready to compromise but his suggestion that he could still be Governor caused Patello to want to give it to him straight. "Not a chance, Robert. You're through. Add it up. You were put down here by the people who got you elected because they wanted to get you out of the way. That's fairly clear. Now you have crossed them by threatening to come back into the forum. That's not smart, my friend. They can take the hit of public scrutiny a hell of lot better than you. Remember you will be all alone in paying for a defense. You won't have a dime of support."

Michael Logan had to go to the bathroom. His kidneys were about to burst. The conversation that he was listening to only aggravated the problem. He wanted to raise his hand and ask permission but he was afraid of missing something. This was like watching a scene from the Godfather. He decided to pee his pants. Patello saw him squirm and noticed the pained expression on his face.

"Something bothering you, Michael?"

"Yes, Sir, a couple of things. One is I wonder what I'm doing here and another is I desperately need a break. Can we take a few minutes for me to get refreshed and then resume. I want to be sure that I understand what it is you gentlemen want from me."

Patello agreed on a break. Michael ran as best he could without losing control to the men's room. Charlie went to the desk to check on his return flight. Cowan sat alone in the room and contemplated his fate. When Patello saw Logan return he immediately went back and resumed the conversation.

"Robert, I'm simply a messenger and your advisor. The message is that you had better forget about running for Governor and my advice is that you had better forget about running for Governor. Am I being clear?"

Cowan realized that the meeting was coming to a close. "Sure, Charlie. I understand. The message is clear and I accept your advice. Is that all we have to talk about?"

Patello leaned into Cowan. "Not quite. You sent up a trial balloon when you blabbed to the press about your aspirations. Now we have to reel it in nice and easy. That's where I think Michael can help. We also have to have an understanding about all of this so we don't have to repeat ourselves in the future. We'll work it out this way. Michael will return to Boston and meet with the press to report that he met with you to discuss your candidacy for Governor. He will tell the press that the two of you recognized the problem with certain funds that Michael felt may have been misplaced in your account. Michael will point to a ten-thousand-dollar deposit that was made to your campaign that was erroneously deposited in your Washington account. Michael will show the press a ten-thousand-dollar check from your personal account that you have made payable to your campaign fund as restoration of the amount taken in error. The balance of your campaign fund will be turned over to the Party for their use. Everything is square. Michael also announces that you have informed him that you have decided not to run for Governor and intend to retire from politics when the President's term is complete. When the press contacts you, you simply verify what Michael has said. Simple enough?"

Cowan's chair was sitting on all four legs. He was also erect with his hands placed on the table. "It sounds simple, Charlie, except that I don't have ten thousand dollars in my account. A phony check won't convince anybody. You got to do better than that."

Patello waved his hand as if there was no problem. "You just write the check, Robert. Michael will cover it out of his special account at the Hardly Security and Trust. That's where the error was made. Somehow one of your checks got deposited to his account. That kind of puts you both in the soup unless you admit the error and correct it. The timing is not too bad."

The sting was apparent. Michael Logan now better understood what was happening. His so-called "signing bonus" with the Archdiocese from anonymous donors was a slush fund for the Mayor. He blushed at the embarrassment and reacted. “Mr. Patello, how in the hell can I cover that check? I’ve used at least three thousand dollars of that money. You told me it was mine. It was supposed to be a signing bonus.”

“It is yours, Michael.” Patello knew he had things under control. “As it now turns out you owe that money to Mr. Cowan, here. What I can do is loan you the amount to cover it. Your check will clear by the time it is deposited. We can see to that. Do you have your checkbook with you? Good. Write a check to Robert for ten thousand dollars. You’ll need to transfer the money first thing in the morning. That will close the special account at Boston Security. Robert, write a check for ten grand to your campaign fund and give it to Michael. That way the pot is right. What might happen is that the State will want to investigate further. I think that can be handled by the lawyers. After Monday, the press is out of it. Do we all agree?”

Michael Logan shook his head in disbelief. “Agree! Agree to what? I came here because you asked me to and it cost me ten thousand dollars. Cowan started this mess and it doesn’t cost him a dime. Why do I get screwed? Hell no, I don’t agree.”

Patello sat back in his chair and gave the young Mr. Logan a fatherly stare. “Michael, this is an investment in your future. Trust me. This will be made up to you in many ways. Right now, it seems like a gross injustice but it is better than some sort of entanglement. Remember, you are the one who ran from the media. They smell blood. This will take them off the scent. It’s the best way.”

“I agree with Charlie, Michael. You’re better off this way,” Cowan echoed.

Patello seemed to relax. He felt that he was off the hook.

“Now, Robert,” Patello exposed a fatherly grin as he turned toward him, “there is the matter of your account here in Washington that we don’t want to have investigated, do we? That has other funds in it I’m sure. What do we need to do to protect that? We need to arrange to have the balances covered by a second mortgage instrument that eliminates your net worth. That way you’re just another poor man in public service. I’ll arrange to have the papers brought to you the first part of the week. They’ll be back dated. You’ll be flat broke by Wednesday. Don’t worry. If you need cash it can be arranged as long as you are a good boy.”

The message was very clear. All the money that had been paid to Cowan and Logan a few months earlier to assist them in their transition from City government was being reclaimed. Cowan's ambition and ego was responsible. His gains from prior dealings with supporters were also being confiscated. He was being put on the hook for the balance of his net worth. That would keep him honest, so to speak, by preventing him from speaking out on political issues or again running for office. He belonged to his creditors. From this time forward, his life depended on maintaining their favor.

Patello asked if either man had any questions. Neither responded. Logan was shocked at the polite way that Patello had destroyed Cowan. Cowan held his head high but his moist eyes betrayed his true emotion.

The meeting adjourned without further comment. Patello escorted Logan to the desk and had the clerk arrange for a direct flight to Montreal. Logan would arrive at six-thirty. Then he would begin the long drive back to Boston. Hopefully he would arrive before dawn, grab a few hours of sleep, and be in his office by eight-thirty. Patello told him that a reporter from the *Globe* would be contacting him before noon.

Cowan left in a rush. His temper was under control but he had a large lump in his throat. He threw caution to the wind. Let the damn reporters find him. He had nothing to say.

Logan Boarded his flight to Montreal an hour before Patello was scheduled to return to Boston. When Patello was sure that Logan was in the air he returned to the U.S. Air Club and phoned Uncle Frank. He gave the good news to his favorite uncle.

"Frank, I'm pleased to report that our friend, Robert, has seen the error of his ways and wants to make it all up to his friends. He understands that his net worth is to be covered by a mortgage loan. I don't think Boston Security should handle this. Can you have a shark from Washington or Baltimore take care of this? Robert expects to sign the papers by the middle of the week."

Frank was most pleased with the report. It was refreshing to realize that his nephew had learned tactics so well. Frank deplored violent methods. "Of course, Charlie! We'll take care of it. No problem. Our associates in Baltimore will be happy to accommodate the man. Tell me, how did it go with the young man from Boston? You mentioned in your message that you had asked him to join you. I expect that he made it. I also suppose he was somewhat taken back by the penalty that you had to impose. That's usually the way with youth. You also said that you had another urgent matter to discuss. What's up?"

"It's Tom O'Shea, Frank. He's at it again. It seems that he figured out what we are attempting to do with the bank deal and he is guessing that Action's deal with St. Anslem's is tied in. Basically, he's on target but he hasn't got it all pieced together. So far he hasn't stumbled onto the Target Boston Medical thing. My guess is that he will put that piece into the puzzle when Callahan tries to get capital from the hospital. What he wants is to be cut in. He thinks that he should be named CEO of the merged banks. That's all. He wants to be a part of the action. He is holding out the copy of the records on Logan's money in the special account as his ticket. By the way that account will be closed sometime tomorrow."

Big Frank paused for a moment before he responded. "Logan, that's his name. I couldn't remember the young fellow's name. Good thing that you're closing the account. O'Shea will still have the record but it means less when the account don't exist anymore. You say that this guy O'Shea wants to be the CEO. Okay, tell him he's got it."

"Frank, for Christ's sake, you can't be serious!" Patello was shocked at Big Frank's reply, "O'Shea will get his nose under the tent and will try to steal everything in sight. The guy is a crook. I've known him too long. We got to do something else. You can't let this guy inside."

"Charlie, my boy, you got to trust your Uncle Frank." Frank was reassuring. "I know what's best. You got a lot to do up there in Boston. You fill out those papers for the secretary of State and you put Mr. O'Shea's name in as the Chief Executive Officer. It'll be okay. Trust me. Okay? Hey, you don't want to miss your plane. Go on home and get some rest. Tell Mr. O'Shea tomorrow that he's gonna be named on the paper as the new boss but he's got to keep his mouth shut about it until the secretary of State returns the paper. Then it's official but not before that. If something should happen to our new executive, God forbid, we'll have to send in amended papers. I know how that works from some of our other deals. You okay with that?"

Patello wasn't certain what the old man was thinking but if he wanted to have O'Shea's name submitted in the organization plan as the Chief Executive Officer it was okay with him. "Uncle Frank, you always know what you are doing. I'll take care of it as you suggest."

It was getting late in the afternoon when Frank finished his phone conversation with Patello. He was very tempted to wait until after the Giants game before following up on Patello's call. The Forty-Niners were ahead by twenty-three points so the outcome of the game was obvious. He decided to get busy. First order was to summon Capizzi and Marone to his plush office for an after-dinner business meeting. This was most unusual for a Sunday night. Both men realized that it had to be urgent. Both would be there. Then he called the special telephone number of the Sam the Security Man that he had dispatched to Boston to find the Sailor and the missing half of the shipment. The number was to a cellular phone that the Sam the Security Man always carried.

Sam the Security Man answered in appropriate code using the generic name of an agent on dispatch. "This is Wanderer. How may I help you?"

Big Frank responded using the code name for top brass, "Wanderer, this is Heavy. Call me on a code 3 at seven-thirty tonight. It's urgent."

"Okay, Heavy. Will do." The conversation abruptly ended.

Code 3 meant that the Sam the Security Man should call from a public phone away from observation and eavesdropping surveillance. It also meant that the call was top security and should be placed to a special number that Sam the Security Man had forwarded to Patello's office when the Boston sting was set up. After the security call was completed, Sam the Security Man became very nervous and concerned that the Sailor had somehow managed to get to Frank for a payoff. This would mean that Big Frank would be very upset.

The Sailor had not managed to get to Big Frank. In fact, the Sailor had only managed to cover about three blocks the entire day. He inhaled cocaine as he sometimes crawled and sometimes walked from one telephone pole to another. Then he would sit for an hour and let the sun warm his shivering body. The Little Portion mission was his intended port of call but he wasn't sure he was headed in the right direction. He had no navigational electronics to guide his path as he did on the boats. He was attempting to steer himself by dead reckoning and he was almost dead. The sun disappeared as it usually did in the early evening and the Sailor dropped his anchor next to a telephone pole too exhausted to continue his journey. In his foggy mind he heard someone talking to him.

"Sailor, get up and get inside. You can't sleep out there. Where have you been? I've been worried sick about you." Sister Celest pulled at his nearly lifeless form but couldn't get him to move. Then she tried to pry his hands apart that were gripping the sign post on the curb in front of The Little Portion.

The Sailor had made it to port but was not as yet safely in a berth. He wouldn't cooperate. The rolled-back eyes, semi-consciousness state, and bloodstained filthy clothes were qualities of his dehydrated body that convulsed repeatedly. His only sound was a low growling cough that occasionally elevated to a loud bark followed by a bloody expectorant that flowed involuntarily.

In desperation, Sister Celest abandoned her single effort and went inside to the food line where she volunteered four of the half-starved customers to pull the Sailor into the Mission. They placed him on a chair and went back to their pursuit of the finer things of life. Sister first checked to see that the line was moving and the food was being properly distributed by her other volunteers. Satisfied that the process was in order she returned to the Sailor and tried to bring him to a state of consciousness. This time she had moderate success as he accepted a small cup of soup that he held in his hands without tasting. His eyes were open but not focused.

The Marquart family had a wonderful Fall Sunday afternoon. After arriving home from Dunkin' Donuts the kids convinced Susan that the remaining donuts needed to be consumed. Jay helped. After he took a nap they piled into the Jeep and drove along Interstate 95 to look at the colors beginning to form on the trees. Once back home, Susan prepared a pasta feast complete with meatballs. Jay consumed more than his share, grabbed his cigarettes, and moved to his worn recliner to watch the Dolphins devour the hapless Patriots. The two-minute warning brought the seemingly endless and tasteless commercials on the screen that placed Jay in a trance suddenly broken by the telephone's ring. He answered with a bland, "Hello."

Sister Celest's voice was pitched. "Mr. Marquart, Jay, oh, thank God you're home. I need your help."

At first Jay was uncertain who would be calling and especially who would be calling for his help. In a second he realized who was on the other end of the line. "Hey, Sister, how you doin'? You need my help now? What's the matter—maybe Brian didn't get the food down to ya? I can give him a call."

"No, Jay. We have the food. That parts all right. It's your friend the Sailor. He's very sick. I think he's in serious trouble and needs to go to the hospital. I usually call the City and they pick my people up and take them to Boston Hospital. I thought that you might want to help him and maybe take him to St. Anslem's. I found his medicine in the food cabinet and understand that Dr. Anderson has been treating him. We have to act, Jay. I'm afraid that the man could die."

The last thing Jay wanted to do was drive downtown to The Little Portion. On the other hand, the Sister was calling for help. She wanted to help the Sailor. Jay knew he was obligated. "Oh, yeah, Sister, I'll try to help. If he's sober enough to get in my car I'll drive him in and see that he gets into the tank. Only they don't operate like they used to. He could end up in the looney bin. We don't want him there I don't think. Can we maybe stash him in one of your hotel rooms and I'll see if I can get good old Bob Markley to make a house call. You think that could work?"

Sr. Celest was frustrated. "Jay, someday in the not-too-distant future I will have an infirmary here and a volunteer medical staff to care for these people but for now I have to get them to wherever the care is available. The Sailor needs medical care not just treatment for substance abuse. I think he is suffering from something serious like TB or pneumonia. He needs to be seen by a physician. Do you want me to send him over to Boston Hospital?"

Jay knew that Boston Hospital would cross check with the Police. That would put the Sailor in more danger. "Okay, you win, Sister. It'll take me about a half-hour to forty-five minutes to get there. Keep him alive in the meantime. Jesus!"

After he completed his conversation with Sister Celest, Jay called St. Anslem's in an attempt to find Bob Markley. The operator was courteous but only offered to connect him with the Emergency Department. Mr. Markley was not on call and was not available. In desperation Jay accepted the transfer to the ER where a clerk informed him that new patients to the program had to wait until regular business hours on Monday to be admitted. In the meantime if it was an emergency the patient should be brought to the Emergency Room where doctors would treat the patient. Jay knew what that meant. He had that treatment. But Sister Celest mentioned that she thought the Sailor was suffering from a medical condition that justified medical care.

When Jay arrived at The Little Portion the kitchen was closed and the patrons had migrated to the hotel or back to the streets. Sister Celest sat alone in the dining area with the Sailor. He was still alive and conscious thanks to the good Sister's efforts to give him nourishment and keep him warm. He sat in a wooden arm chair with his feet propped on a small step stool Sister sat next to him with a cup of hot broth that she attempted to spoon into his mouth between coughs. She looked very tired and her age that Jay had never noticed before was very apparent. It was also apparent that most of the refreshing liquid had been rejected onto the Sailors filthy shirt and covering blanket. Jay picked up the man's disgusting smell a long distance from where he sat. Sister's ability to sit next to the Sailor and give him care was remarkable. Jay who in his mind knew that she was far more compassionate than he thought he could ever be. Yet he also realized that it was his turn to step in and continue the care that Sister had started. Her part was finished. Jay was now the man that was expected, by whom only God knows, to carry the Sailor through this crisis and restore the Sailor's pride and personality.

How in the hell did I get into this, he thought and actually mouthed the words. "Sister, the cavalry has arrived."

Sister exclaimed, "Jay! Oh, thank God. He needs get to St. A's as soon as possible."

The Sailor seemed to recognize Jay and managed a weak wave from his wrist.

Sister motioned for Jay to move to the right side of the Sailor while she held him on the left. They moved the Sailor out the door and into the Jeep. Jay found the seat belt coiled under the seat where Susan had kicked it. He fastened in around the Sailor and gave him a reassuring pat. The Sailor looked at Jay and seemed to give him a smile. Sister Celest gave Jay a hug. Then she reached into the packet of her slacks and produced a tattered bag that contained a small amount of white powder.

"Jay, I think this is the snake that bit him. The hospital might need to know about this. He was trying to inhale some while my back was turned. It fell out of his hand when he started to cough. I picked it up and kept it away from him. I don't think he knows that I have it."

The thought of the good Sister holding a bag of cocaine in her slacks caused Jay to break out in a broad smile. "Sure, Sister. You sure that ain't a little something that you had for the rest of the boys. You dealing?"

"It's nothing to laugh at, Jay." Sister missed the humor. "You want me to keep this here? Is it a problem for you to carry it? I can just flush it down the sink. Maybe that's best."

She pushed the bag back into her pocket and moved to close the car door next to the Sailor. The Sailor looked at her with a grateful stare. Painfully he raised his hand and put it over hers. She gave him a tender touch on his arm with her other hand and slowly closed the car door.

Jay moved behind the wheel and started the engine. He turned on the heater in the Jeep and kept the fan on high. One reason was to keep the Sailor warm but the other reason, more prominent in Jay's mind, was to keep the air moving and reduce the odor. He had the driver's side window open about an inch to let the air circulate. It was almost bearable. The Sailor's cough seemed to be somewhat diminished.

Surprisingly he started to talk. "Thanks for coming along, little buddy. We goin' to see the corpsman? He's gonna get me out. I gotta get out. He said he could get me out."

"Hey, you relax, Sailor. We're goin' to get that cough taken care of. Who's the corpsman?"

The Sailor didn't answer. He had other things on his mind. "The lady kept my stash. Hell, I got plenty. She can have it. I got plenty."

Jay looked at the Sailor who had a sincere and determined look on his face. He held one hand in a tight fist and placed it in the other as if to make a statement. Remarkably the Sailor straightened his back as if he were getting ready to fight. Jay attempted to get him to relax.

"Hey, Sailor, don't get your back up over a little stash. You got plenty? That's okay, man. You got more on you? They'll take it away from you at the hospital. You want to give it to me for safekeeping?"

Suddenly the Sailor began to cough uncontrollably. He doubled over with pain and then raised his head and spit at the closed window. Jay watched helplessly. The traffic prevented him from rendering any kind of assistance without stopping. Instead Jay accelerated. He wanted to get to St. A's as fast as he could. The Sailor remained doubled over but tried to speak.

"I ain't got no stash on me you asshole. No way they gonna take it away from me. That bastard Eddie. He's gonna finger me. Fuck him. I got it outta the way on the Suit's boat. He don't know it. It's safe for when I want it. Shit! We going to see the corpsman. He's gonna get me out. Christ, I hurt. Get me to the corpsman, little buddy. You gotta hurry. I'm messed up big time. Man, you gotta get me to the corpsman."

Jay tried to reassure the Sailor. "Yeah, we ain't got far to go. You'll get help. Try to relax. You talk and that coughing starts. Christ, you messed up that window. Who's the fuckin' corpsman?"

The Sailor didn't answer. He had passed out. Jay looked at him and wondered if he had died. He pulled into the St. A's Emergency area and parked in the ambulance space. A hospital security guard immediately rushed over and demanded that he move the Jeep. Jay demanded that the guard get a gurney and help take the Sailor into the Emergency Room. The shouting attracted the attention of the nurse supervisor who brought a gurney and two attendants who rapidly moved the Sailor into the ER leaving Jay and the guard blasting each other with profanity. Jay was far more expert in such exchanges resulting in the Security guard's withdrawal. After he walked away Jay moved the Jeep to a public parking area. Then he went into the ER to find the Sailor.

The Sailor had been taken far into the recesses of the Emergency Department and was placed in a trauma room. He was now surrounded by a team of doctors and nurses who were busy taking all kinds of vital signs and debating the need to call the cardio-pulmonary resuscitation team. The Sailor was in deep trouble. A clerk met Jay as he came into the ER lobby. She asked him to sit down at the desk where she placed herself behind a computer keyboard and began to ask the identifying questions. Jay couldn't satisfy her when she asked for the patient's name. His response that the patient was known as the Sailor was rejected by the computer. Jay didn't know the patient's address. He had no knowledge about next of kin and he certainly didn't know anything about his insurance.

When Jay explained that he voluntarily brought the Sailor to St. A's from The Little Portion on Melina Cass Boulevard the clerk explained that people from that part of town usually went to Boston Hospital. She also announced that after the patient was stabilized they would arrange for the transfer to Boston Hospital. Jay didn't want to inform the clerk that the Sailor was known to Bob Markley for fear that the Sailor would be sent to the psychiatric unit. As a last resort Jay mentioned that the Sailor was a patient of Dr. Anderson's and that is why the Sailor wanted to be brought to St. A's. That seemed to push the magic button. The clerk got up from the desk and immediately went into the sanctum.

Jay continued to sit at the desk. Fifteen minutes later a nurse came out and asked Jay to join her in a small office. As he moved to join the nurse, the clerk returned to her post at the computer keyboard. The young attractive nurse had a very pleasant personality. She immediately placed Jay at ease and extracted his complete cooperation. She seemed like a fun person. In fact, she was well trained at her job as the triage nurse for the ER. She explained to Jay that they had contacted Dr. Anderson who verified that he had prescribed medicine for the patient a few days ago and had done a preliminary examination. The patient had failed to show for a complete physical examination that had been scheduled for Saturday.

Dr. Anderson was not surprised that the patient was now in serious trouble. He ordered that the patient be admitted and if necessary be placed in the medical intensive care unit. The ER physicians were still evaluating the patient and would be in consultation with Dr. Anderson. It was also her understanding that Mr. Markley was coming in to see the patient.

The triage nurse concluded her report by asking Jay if he could give her information about the type and amount of drugs that the patient might have taken in the past twenty-four hours. Jay told her that the only thing he was aware of was the cocaine that the Sister had found. He had no idea about how much the Sailor had inhaled. She thanked Jay for the information. She assured him that the Sailor was in good hands.

It was obvious to Jay that he was not essential to forwarding the care of the Sailor. Dr. Anderson was directing things from this point on. Nevertheless, Jay decided to hang around for a while to see what was happening and hopefully to have a chance to chat with Markley when and if he showed up. He told the triage nurse of his intentions and asked her to inform Mr. Markley that he would be in the waiting room. The nurse agreed to tell Mr. Markley and also said that she would keep Jay informed about the status of the patient from time to time. Jay thanked her and retreated to the ER lobby.

Markley was not hard to find. Dr. Anderson knew his routine well. Sunday was totally devoted to God and the Church that Markley loved. Markley spent Sunday in Church or Churches doing the work of the Lord. By evening he had moved to doing missionary work at the support sessions for religious and priests struggling with the ravages of alcoholism. Dr. Anderson had started him on this crusade many years ago. The sessions that Markley conducted on Sunday night were the same ones that Anderson conducted for a long time before Markley came along to relieve him. His deal with Anderson was that he did not take call or work on Sunday at St. Anslem's in return for his dedication to the Sunday night sessions. Anderson had always kept the bargain except on rare occasions. Tonight was one of those exceptions.

Markley realized the need to respond when Anderson called. He arrived at the ER while Jay was talking to the triage nurse. The Sailor was unconscious. A respirator and several IV's were attached to his body. The physicians were waiting for stat lab reports pending a diagnosis. The nurses were attending to the patient. Markley sat at the nursing station and reviewed the preliminary findings. He talked to the doctor in charge and then called Dr. Anderson. Afterward he walked to the lobby and greeted Jay.

"Good work, Mr. Marquart. You got him here in time. He's very sick and will probably be admitted to medical ICU. It's going to be touch and go for a couple of days. We'll have to pray for the best."

Jay was relieved that Markley was on the scene and taking personal care of the Sailor. "Christ, Bob, I didn't know that the guy was about to croak. I thought he was just loaded. The Sister knew he needed help. She called me. Otherwise, he would have landed on the Boston junk pile. Hell, I don't even know his name. Ain't that something? I couldn't tell the admitting clerk the guy's name. She looked at me like I was on something."

"You know his name, Jay." Markley was holding the Sailor's chart that he used for reference. "It's Saylor, Albert Saylor. He had a birth certificate in his wallet. He was born in Fort Wayne, Indiana at St. Joseph's Hospital on August thirteenth, nineteen-forty-five. There's no record of next of kin. He also had a Veterans card. Was in the Navy from sixty-two to eighty-three. Honorable discharge and decorations. We'll check with the VA tomorrow and get everything he needs. The VA will take care of him and we'll see that they do."

"Yeah." Suddenly Jay remembered his conversation with the Sailor on the way to the hospital. "Hey, Bob, when I was drivin' him in he kept asking me if we was goin' to see the corpsman. He said the corpsman would get him out. I asked who the corpsman was but he didn't say. You know what he was talking about?"

Robert Markley's eyes filled with tears. He tried to speak but was choked with emotion. Jay watched and waited while Markley turned away. After a few minutes he seemed recomposed. "Yeah, Jay, I know what he was talking about." Then Markley walked back into the ER.

Jay went home.

At precisely seven-thirty P.M. the telephone on the credenza in back of Frank Patello's desk made a buzz indicating an incoming call. Frank waited for the repeat buzz then answered, "This is Heavy."

The caller was cramped in his car with the pay phone from the drive up pulled to its maximum stretch. Traffic in and out of the Merit Gas station was constant so Sam the Security Man had to raise the window to near the closed position to hear. When he heard Frank's greeting he flipped his cigarette out the small opening at the top of the window.

It didn't clear and the burning tobacco landed on the car seat. "Oh, god-damn it—shit—wait, Frank, I got a problem. Ouch! Shit! Jesus!"

Frank had switched the receiver to a speaker so Mario Capizzi and Tony Marone could participate in the conversation. The two trusted lieutenants looked at each other bewildered at the profanity flowing from the caller. Frank put his hand to his forehead and looked to the heavens. Sam the Security Man had a reputation for being very profane and reputation was deserved.

Security answered, "Heavy, sorry about that. Everything's under control. Please convey your message."

"Okay, Security. Here it is," said Frank. "With me are Light-heavy-one and Light-heavy-two. We have information that a major breach of our security exists. Person Thomas O'Shea at the Hardly Security and Trust in Boston is principal and alone in this. We conclude that we have no recourse. I repeat no recourse. Do you understand?"

Sam the Security Man repeated the message as acknowledgment that he understood. "Heavy, I understand that we have no recourse to correct our breach. Thomas O'Shea at Hardly Security and Trust is principal and alone. I will respond. Anything else?"

Frank looked at Tony and Mario. They both shook their heads from side to side. Frank nodded his agreement to their silence. "Security, you have it. Do you have anything to report on our previous matter?"

This was the question that Sam the Security Man had expected from Heavy and feared. He had very little to report on the whereabouts of the Sailor and the missing half of the shipment from the bungled sting operation. Sam the Security Man needed to look good and get more time to recapture his diminishing reputation. "Yeah, the search process turned up our man on Saturday doing work around the docks. We have him under surveillance. I expect that he will lead us to the missing shipment. My plan is to wrap all this up next weekend. Everything is under control."

Mario and Tony were all smiles when they heard the report. Frank didn't have the same attitude. He had lost confidence in Sam the Security Man and began to have doubts about the cover of the import process move to Portland. He concluded the conversation and hung up the phone.

Afterwards the three men discussed the current status of the move. Mario had Tony explain all the details of the operation. Everything had gone well. The shipments were coming in regularly. The demand was being met. The Boston special accounts were increasing. Revenue was up. The only glitch had been the cover plan to throw the cops off the scent.

Sam the Security Man had managed to push the burning embers on to the floor carpet where it continued to smolder. He crushed it into the floor and brushed the burn on the cuff of his expensive suede jacket. Getting the Boston Police off the scent was his only glitch. Even that worked except for the relatively minor problem of the Sailor and half of the cover shipment that was now floating around someplace. Security had it under control. The Sailor and the shipment matter would be resolved in a few days. No problem.

Sam the Security Man was very upset. He realized that Frank Patello, the number-one heavy, was doubting his ability. Frank hadn't said so but his tone and expression conveyed the sentiment. The matter with this Thomas O'Shea would be dispatched. That was one thing but the Sailor was beginning to bug the expert in security. He wanted the Sailor and he wanted him soon.

When the conversation with Big Frank ended Sam the Security Man threw the receiver out his car window and drove from the Merit Gas Station on Neponset Drive to the North Quincy Marina. The marina and the Boardwalk were nearly deserted on the cool fall evening. It was dusk and only a few people were strolling around. Only two of the ten or so bars and restaurants were open. One was the Shanty. Eddie the Enforcer was at his usual spot eyeing the football game on television and the girls at the table in the corner. He didn't see the Sam the Security Man walk in and sit at the bar next to him.

Sam ordered a beer and gave Eddie a quick jab in the ribs. "You been sitting here all day, my friend?" Sam asked.

Eddie turned abruptly rubbing the spot where he had been punched. "Christ, man, you are a friendly sort. I been here about an hour. I thought you took Sunday off and went to church. Why you here?"

"We got to talk. Finish your drink and let's go outside where it's quiet. The girls will be here when you get back. You won't score any way."

Sam the Security Man let Eddie take another sip of his drink and then pulled him off the stool and out the door. The bartender was about to serve the beer ordered by the Sam when he noticed the two going out the door. He simply added the price of the beer to Eddie's tab.

Once outside, Sam the Security Man grabbed Eddie by both arms and forced him in back of the dumpsters placed across from the bar. Then he punched Eddie in the stomach and straightened him up with a wicked upper cut that snapped Eddie's head against the dumpster. Eddie fell forward on his knees. Blood dripped on his jacket from a cut on his chin. Sam waited for Eddie to shake his head clear of the fog from the beating then he pulled Eddie to an upright position and slapped him across the face. Eddie blinked at the pointed finger that was pushed into his face. The security officer now had Eddie's full attention. It was the right moment to begin the promised conversation.

Sam let Eddie hear it. "Now you listen well, you son of a bitch. I want the Sailor. You get him to me you understand. I don't give a shit how you get him. Just do it. He don't show in the next couple of days and you can expect that what you got tonight is just a down payment of what you got coming in full. You understand?"

Eddie nodded his understanding. Sam the Security Man let him fall next to the dumpster. Eddie said nothing. Sam walked away. The conversation was ended.

Sam the Security Man strolled over to the Boardwalk. He paused to look out over beautiful Boston Harbor. Sunday, the Lord's Day, ended with a beautiful sunset followed by a full moon shining over Dorchester Bay. Sam the Security Man felt good. He was making progress.

Chapter Twenty

Rod Weaver was dumbfounded. In his many years of financial management that included ten years in public accounting and thirteen years of hospital financial management he had not encountered a proposal seemingly as asinine as the one that Mitch Daly had put before him. It contained a long litany of reasons why the St. Anslem's physicians should become joined in a professional physicians' organization to be served by a management services organization. The management services organization would manage their practices and most importantly would acquire and manage contracts with Health Maintenance Organizations and manage care companies.

The document that Daly set in front of Weaver had been well crafted by Tom Callahan. It concluded that the success of the venture required extensive startup capital and a partnership between the hospital and the doctors that gave the doctors equity and majority control over the new entity. The plan proposed that the Physicians' Organization capitalized by a three-thousand-dollar investment by each member physician would then buy into the Management Services Organization. The Management Services Organization would be held sixty percent by the physicians and forty percent by the hospital.

Callahan had estimated that the capital required by the Management Services Organization would be in the neighborhood of seventy-five million dollars for openers. According to Callahan, the hospital would be expected to provide all but three hundred thousand dollars of the capital. The doctors would put up the three hundred thousand and would obligate the physicians' organization to the exclusive use of St. Anslem's Hospital in return for their equity. The hospital would put up seventy four million seven hundred thousand dollars for forty percent equity in the management company. All revenues from payers would be paid to the management services organization that would in effect buy hospital service from St. Anslem's. St. Anslem's would be relegated to the status of a cost center in the new complex.

Daly had brought the plan to Weaver for comment after Weaver had collared him for information about the physicians' organization that the medical staff had voted to form. Daly was also concerned about the concept when it was mentioned that Park/Bay Area Health Care was a possible source of additional capital if needed. The report contained a letter signed by Joseph Bauman, President of Park/Bay attesting to the interest of his company in a possible joint venture. Daly reasoned that the new partner would bring its own administration into the organization forcing him out of a job. It was time to ally with his old enemy, Weaver, in a conspiracy to save himself unless he could find a way to work into the arms of Park/Bay Weaver's violent reaction to Callahan's plan was what Daly had expected. Now he needed to fan the flames of opposition from Weaver. If Weaver became the opponent then Daly could play both sides until he discovered which benefited him the most.

Weaver needed no encouragement from Daly. He was livid. The proposal was a big rip off that was spearheaded by the great Dr. Folley who had become the President of the Physicians' Organization. It was also very evident to Weaver that Folley would be the kingpin in the management services deal. Folley was trying to steal the hospital. There was nothing subtle about it. It seemed like a case of being mugged and held up in broad daylight. He intended to yell like hell for help.

Tom Callahan had convinced Dr. Folley to arrange a meeting on Monday with Joe Durant and his executive team to bring them up to speed with the medical staff developments. Folley was against the idea. He thought the best approach was to organize the physicians and then meet with the hospital's Board of Trustees on the capital issue. Durant and his band of flunkies seemed like a wasted step to Folley.

Michael Logan, before his disappearance over the weekend, had been listening to Mitch Daly's appeal to include the executives prior to the Board as a matter of courtesy. Logan was a man of peace. He finally persuaded Folley who called Callahan with a change of heart.

The meeting was scheduled for ten A.M. in Durant's office. Daly had been prompting Weaver since seven-thirty. Folley and Callahan arrived exactly on the hour. Daly and Weaver had preceded them. Durant was waiting for all of them. Logan was late. When he arrived, nearly a half-hour after the starting time, his suit was badly wrinkled and he looked like he had been up all night. In fact, he had. Folley had not expected Logan to be present. He thought the young man was still on the lam.

Durant brought the meeting to order but Callahan took over. He passed out the master plan for the organization of the St. Anslem's Health Services Organization that included a proprietary company held forty percent by St. Anslem's Hospital and sixty percent by the St. Anslem's Physicians' Organization both of whom were investors in the company. The proprietary company was known as the BCA Medical Management Services Company. BCA was the abbreviation for Boston Catholic Archdiocese. The St. Anslem's Health Services organization was an umbrella organization that consisted of an overseeing agency currently known as the Archdiocesan Office for Health Affairs. The elimination of specific identification with the Church gave better market potential according to Callahan. It also served as the holding company for St. Anslem's Hospital and allowed for the preservation of the religious ethical issues in the hospital but sheltered the physicians and others from the application of those rules in the conduct of their private medical practice.

The concept had been used elsewhere and had been approved by several Bishops across the country. Callahan demonstrated each point with flowcharts, diagrams, and organization charts that carried the logo of Park, Inc. of New York on the bottom margin. After forty-five minutes of uninterrupted presentation he rested his case.

Joe Durant looked very pensive as Callahan concluded. Durant fingered the many papers that had been placed in front of him. The lump in his throat prohibited him from speaking. Daly looked at Durant and then a glance to Weaver as if to give him his cue. Weaver was ready. Without invitation he let his emotions fly.

"This sucks, I mean it really sucks. Where in the hell do you get off stealing the hospital equity and keeping the profit? That's the worst con I've ever seen. The James brothers got nothing on you bastards. There's no way I'm going to let you get away with this. His Eminence needs to be advised about this rip off. You boys ought to be in jail."

Callahan flushed at Weaver's remarks. Folley pushed his bulk in front of Weaver and responded, "Mr. Weaver, you must have missed our point. The purpose of this effort is to save the hospital not to cause it harm. Mr. Callahan has proposed a plan that will bring the physicians and the hospital together to meet growing competition and at the same time preserve the hospital's mission. It's unfortunate that you misinterpret our intent. Let me assure you, His Eminence will be very supportive of this plan. I have that on very good authority. You can be of great help by assisting the Board with accurate reports divorced of any creative methods that may distort the hospital's financial position. I mean, what we need at this point is objective data not emotionalism. Our purpose in explaining this to you was for that reason. Certainly no one in this room will make any decisions. That's for others to decide."

Weaver was not convinced. He wanted to fight. "Horseshit, Dick! You set this thing up for your own benefit. This is contrived to kill the hospital not save it. You are being set up. Who's pulling your chain? You must be on the take or they got something big on you. Don't give me that holy, holy, shit. Joe, do you see what they are doing?"

Durant was both panicked and grateful for Weaver's reaction. Yet he agreed that it was misplaced. They were wasting time and energy arguing with these experts. He felt the best tactic was to withdraw and regroup.

"Rod, Dr. Folley makes a very good point. We are not going to be the ones who accept or reject this plan. It is a Board decision. I'm sure that the Cardinal will review it very closely. Let's take it for what it is and react later. Okay? What do you say, Mitch?"

Daly had not intended to comment but now he had no choice. He was satisfied that Weaver had committed professional suicide with his outburst and he was determined not to make the same mistake.

"Well, Joe, I think that we need to do some major reorganization to compete in this market. The big teaching hospitals downtown have already done similar things. We need to act soon or we can get left behind."

Durant nodded and looked toward Logan who he expected to comment. Michael Logan was sound asleep. Folley also noticed that his number-one was in slumber. He properly concluded that Michael had driven all night to make it to work. If Durant was aware that Michael had been among the missing over the weekend he was doing a good job of ignoring it. In fact, Durant, Daly, Weaver and Callahan were well aware of the intrigue of the Mayor's Campaign

Fund and the disappearance of Michael Logan. His sudden arrival at the meeting had been a shocker but since he was only a half-hour late nothing was said. It was just generally accepted that the prodigal son had returned. The gossip would follow in good time.

Folley took Michael by the arm and led him out of Durant's office. The meeting was over. Callahan asked if he could answer any additional questions. None were forthcoming. He took the hint and left.

Daly sat back down expecting a post mortem. Durant did likewise. Both looked at Weaver who took the cue and began to rant about the ridiculous train robbery and the robbers attempting to abscond with the entire fund balance of the hospital. His two colleagues listened but said nothing. Weaver shouted and pounded the glass table. He turned red and nearly fell as he kicked at the waste basket. Finally, exhausted, Weaver flopped into a chair and put his head in his hands.

Durant remained silent but in his mind he felt exactly like Weaver. The outward expression of anger and frustration about the hospital's transition had passed him some time ago. Now the Chief Executive appeared apathetic while inwardly he screamed with resentment.

Daly was looking for survival. It was apparent that he would not find it working for Durant. He chose not to comment but made up his mind to get off the sinking ship.

Charlie Patello called Tom O'Shea early in the morning. O'Shea was in the shower. Patello waited for the new chief executive officer of the largest banks in the Northeast and one of the top ten largest in the Nation to dry himself. O'Shea seemed chipper as he greeted Patello.

"Hello, Charlie. My, you are up early this fine day. I hope you are calling with good news."

Patello took a sip of his coffee before answering. "As a matter of fact, I do have some news as far as you're concerned, my friend. I have been instructed to enter your name as the chief executive on the organization plan going to the secretary of State's Office in the next few days."

"That's excellent, Charlie. I'm delighted." Actually, O'Shea could hardly contain himself. "When do I meet with the Board and work out the contract?"

"Probably next week, Tom. They asked me to remind you that nothing is official until the secretary of State gives the okay on the organization. You understand. In the meantime it's best that you don't say anything to anybody about this. The business journals will want to do a big spread about the bank and its new CEO. We don't want to do anything that might preempt the publicity. We want to milk this for everything we can, okay? Oh, one other thing, I understand that some expert from a PR firm will be contacting you today or tomorrow. He's working for us."

"Sure, Charlie. Anything else?" O'Shea gave his regal response.

Now Patello had his opening. "Yeah. The deal with Cowan is settled. He isn't running for Governor. Michael Logan talked him out of it. Michael will be closing his special account this morning early. Could you make sure that it's done without a delay? It's very important that there are no glitches. Why don't you call the data center and remove the cash restrictions so his withdrawal and transfer clears from the ATM. You going to do that?"

O'Shea was delighted. "Right away, Charlie, just as soon as we hang up. Anything else I should know about this."

"No. You have the whole story. Have a good day, Tom." Patello wanted to puke. He detested O'Shea now more than ever. He wished that he had argued more with Uncle Frank about appointing O'Shea to the top post. Frank seemed to be at peace with the appointment and whatever it might bring so Charlie tried again to accept it. He still wanted to puke.

The Great Dr. Folley had Michael Logan under the arm and the back of his collar. He hustled the half sleeping Logan through his outer office and into his plush suite where he threw him on the couch. Logan didn't notice the rough treatment. He was too tired. Folley wasn't irritated as much as he was curious.

"Where in the hell have you been, Michael? You had us all worried sick. Your poor wife needed my care to calm her nerves. The press hounded her until she was nearly out of her mind. It was a miracle that I got there in time to prevent a major scandal. We'll have to report this whole affair to the Cardinal."

Michael sat up on the couch and rubbed his eyes. "Doctor, do you have any coffee in this museum? I've been up all night and I expect a reporter to meet me at the desk in the SACAP in about a half-hour. I'm sorry that I was late for the meeting but I had to stop at the bank and do a little early morning banking. Everything's fine. Does the Cardinal want my resignation?"

The reply threw the doctor's timing offbeat. "Coffee? No, I don't have any. You'll have to get some in the cafeteria. You ought to change clothes before you talk to the press. They notice poor grooming. I'll join you to answer their questions about the Archdiocese. We must avoid scandal you know. Michael, I'm absolutely shocked at what you did. How can I explain this to the Cardinal? He's very concerned I'm sure. My whole reputation with the clergy is at stake. The SACAP won't do. You'll meet them here in my office. I'll get a long lab coat for you. It will cover your dirty clothes and make you look very professional. Yes, that's it. We'll make you look very professional. The press always believes anybody in a long white lab coat. Try on one of mine. There's a clean one in the closet."

St. Anslem's Chemical Abuse Program (SACAP) was for the most part dissolved. The inpatient unit was closed. Outpatient services had been cut way back. Counselors were seeing patients in their homes and support group sessions were being conducted in nearby churches. There was nothing left except the space with a sign on the door that read SACAP—A program of the Arch Diocese Health Services—St. Anslem's Unit.

A reporter from the *Boston Globe* pushed open the door and met the silence. He turned to leave when Bob Markley came in and offered to be of assistance. The reporter asked to see Michael Logan and explained that the two had agreed to meet in this office because Mr. Logan thought it would be "out of the way" Apparently Mrs. Logan had been the go between the reporter and her husband since early this morning.

Markley was attempting to explain that Logan was not usually in the Unit when to his surprise Michael Logan appeared in the doorway wearing a very large long white lab coat that drooped over his shoulders and covered both of his hands. He looked like a Norman Rockwell creation. Behind him was a breathless Dr. Folley who pushed past Michael and welcomed the stranger who, he assumed, was the reporter.

The reporter shook Dr. Folley's hand and turned to Michael who was placing a couple of chairs next to a small table. The reporter took the hint and sat down. Michael sat across from him. Dr. Folley was left to find his own chair. The reporter explained to Michael that he had been the one who wrote the story for the Saturday edition and his editor had asked him to follow up on the matter. He was tipped that Michael's disappearance was actually a secret trip to Washington to confer with Robert Cowan.

Michael confirmed that to be true. He went on to explain to the reporter that he had convinced Secretary Cowan not to run for Governor and to do the necessary things to correct the unfortunate errors in the accounting of his campaign fund. Those errors, Michael explained, were based on inappropriate personal expenses that had been put on his expense account by member of the clerical staff. That expense voucher had not been audited. Had it been audited the items would have been disallowed and no discrepancies would have existed. The rumor about the fund began when an internal audit report somehow was leaked to one of the former Mayor's political opponents. Mr. Cowan has refunded the amount given to him in error and the Campaign Fund is now correct. However, Mr. Cowan also feels that the time is not right for him to return to elected office and, because of his advancing age, has decided to remain as the Under Secretary of Labor until his retirement. Michael suggested that the reporter might want to verify this with Secretary Cowan.

The reporter took notes, asked a few obligatory questions, shook Michael's hand and started to leave. He stood up just as Dr. Folley pushed his chair in place and sat down. Folley grabbed the reporter's arm and offered to answer any and all questions about the Office of Health Affairs for the Boston Catholic Archdiocese of which he was the Director of Health Affairs. He offered the reporter his card. The reporter took the card out of courtesy, said his goodbye and left. The meeting lasted less than a quarter of an hour. Michael Logan walked out of SACAP to the cafeteria where he purchased a much-needed cup of black coffee.

Bob Markley had about as much sleep as Michael Logan. He had spent the night in the Medical Intensive Care Unit watching over the Sailor. Dr. Anderson came in at eleven P.M. to check on his patient. Anderson tried to convince Markley that he should go home and get some rest since the Sailor was doing as well as expected. He was in critical condition but resting easy. Consultations in cardiology and pulmonary were ordered. Still Markley refused to leave. He stood next to the Sailor's bed and waited. Occasionally he would rub the Sailor's hand and speak to him. There was no response. Markley would assist the nurses and move around the Unit doing whatever he could to help with other patients then he would move back to the Sailor's bed and repeat his ritual. He was even given some routine assignments. At seven A.M., he stepped out of the Unit, cleaned up, and walked to what was left of the SACAP. On the way, he stopped in the Chapel, attended Mass, and prayed for the Sailor, his comrade in arms that he had promised to "get out" of the hell that captured him to the memories of Vietnam.

After the *Globe* reporter walked out of the SACAP followed by Michael Logan, Bob Markley sat next to the bewildered Dr. Folley and asked if there was anything else he could do for him. Folley waved his hand in the negative. Markley without further comment got up and went into the men's shower room. The great Dr. Folley had moved his thoughts away from Michael Logan and was now reflecting on the proceedings of the earlier meeting that included the shouting Mr. Weaver. Folley concluded that Weaver's attitude could spread to some of the less committed such as Bishop Hanks and Sister Elizabeth. They might be able to persuade the Cardinal to have second thoughts on the Management Services organization. In fact, the Cardinal had not yet had first thoughts on the subject since Folley had not yet pushed the capitalization plan to the Chancery.

Folley realized that he needed to communicate with Bishop Hanks to predetermine a positive resolution. Michael Logan's safe return would be a good overture followed by a rapid and positive verbal outline of all the good things to come. That would make the Bishop's day who in turn would make the Cardinal's day. That accomplished, Folley would then move to implement the professional executions of Rod Weaver and Joe Durant. He slapped his knee with excitement, got out of the uncomfortable folding chair and left the deserted SACAP for the comfort of his office.

The telephone call from Dr. Folley was welcomed by Bishop Hanks. The Cardinal was expecting a call about the Michael Logan matter this morning and obviously Dr. Folley was calling with the latest information. This was good. Bishop Hanks could report an accurate account. He greeted the doctor warmly and got less in return.

Folley, as usual, came on strong. "Bishop Hanks, good morning to you. I believe I should talk to His Eminence as soon as possible about our situation here. Can you tell me where he is and how I can contact him? I believe it's imperative that we talk."

Hanks was offended by the approach but true to his charitable inclinations he gave a courteous reply. "Yes, Doctor, I know where His Eminence is. I would be pleased to tell him that you need to speak to him. Can I tell him the nature of your call? I'm sure he will ask."

It was suddenly obvious to Dr. Folley that he had made a tactical blunder; his message would be delivered by Bishop Hanks who always acted as the dutiful Vicar General. Folley was only the Archdiocesan Secretary for Health Affairs who had been just put back in place by the Bishop. He changed his approach.

The good doctor tried again. "Bishop, I would appreciate and actually prefer to speak to you about all of this. You have excellent comprehension about these temporal matters and can explain them to the Cardinal much better than I. I know how busy you are and I thought it would be impertinent of me to assume your valuable time but if you can assist me I would be most grateful."

Bishop Hanks enjoyed listening to Folley crawl out of the hole he had dug. "Dr. Folley, I expect to speak to the Cardinal in a few hours. What is it you would like to have me tell him? He is aware of the matter with Mr. Logan and would appreciate knowing what is happening. Do you have any information for him?"

"Certainly, Bishop. You may tell His Eminence that I met with the reporter from the *Globe* this morning and I believe I successfully brought the matter to resolution. Michael has returned. He was in Washington meeting with Mr. Cowan who has decided not to run for political office. Michael has corrected some accounting problems that the former Mayor had in his campaign fund. Everything is fine. Michael is back on the job this morning. It was really nothing, I'm pleased to report. Can we talk about another more serious matter?"

Bishop Hanks was not easily convinced that the matter with Logan was resolved. "Richard, His Eminence is very concerned that no scandal applicable to the Church results from this. I trust your conversation with the press avoided any matter that might be considered scandalous."

"Bishop, I assure you that I said nothing that could in any way be scandalous." Folley was positive.

Bishop Hanks pushed on. "His Eminence will be very pleased to hear that, Richard. What else do you have to report?"

Finally, Dr. Folley was able to change the subject. "Yes. It's about an opportunity to significantly expand our healing ministry. The focus of the new ministry incorporates the physicians with the hospital. We can become one of the most prominent healing components in the community. It would truly be the integration of the physicians' healing skills, science, technology, and capital combined to foster the Ministry as Christ had intended. I'm very excited about the prospect of this and wanted to share this with His Eminence. He will be elated. It's what he wanted the Ministry to accomplish. We have had the institutional component of the Ministry for over a century with St. Anslem's but this opportunity brings the physicians into the fold as well. They have always been independent of the Ministry although somewhat aligned in practice. Do I make myself clear? I'm so excited about this I tend to ramble and pass over the fine points."

It seemed to Bishop Hanks that Folley was intent on running the Church's ministry of healing. He resented the doctor's intrusion into clerical affairs. "Richard, His Eminence mentioned to me yesterday that when he returns on Wednesday he would like to meet with you and me to discuss the very thing you mentioned. I know he will be pleased to hear that you are making such excellent progress with the Ministry. Shall we plan to have lunch Wednesday? Let's say noon. I'll confirm that and let you know but I believe it will be fine with the Cardinal. Anything else, Richard?"

The Great Dr. Folley was overjoyed. He felt that he had Bishop Hanks Action to convince the Cardinal that the Management Services organization was truly an extension of the Healing Ministry. That done, he now had to take care of the rebellious Rod Weaver and the devious Joe Durant. He began the execution with a call to his Father in Law and CEO to be of the arising banking empire, Mr. Thomas O'Shea.

O'Shea had been on cloud nine since his early morning conversation with Charles Patello. He could hardly contain himself as he sat behind his desk and dreamed about the power and wealth waiting for him. He had hinted to his secretary that bigger and better things were headed her way. She had guessed what was on his mind but he denied it in a way that allowed her to hold the thought. Now his son-in-law was to be given a hint—just a little hint. He answered the phone with a special greeting. "Richard, I'm so glad you called. You need to know that you are talking to an experienced banking executive who has the opportunity to become one of the most powerful persons in the Area and possibly in the Country. How does that sound?"

Folley wasn't used to being overshadowed in the ego department. His father-in-law's boastful comment caught him completely off guard. "My goodness, Dad. You sound like you have taken over the financial empire of the universe. What inspires this enthusiasm?"

O'Shea decided to leak it slowly. "Well, I can't tell you the whole story since it won't be official for a couple of days. Haven't even told the Mrs. or your wife. I'm number one to be the new CEO when banks merge. Got the message today. Please keep this under your hat. I thought you ought to know since your status and mine combined will be a powerful force around town. We can control a lot of what goes on around here and more importantly who does what. This has been a long time coming."

Folley was disturbed by the thought of sharing the limelight with his father-in-law. Nevertheless, he gave the opposite impression. "This is wonderful, Dad. I'm certain that a lot of celebration is in order. I'll be most pleased to witness your ascension to the ranks of the ordained and dignified. This is just wonderful. We need to form our plans for the new society. Can we begin with a matter concerning the leadership of St. Anslem's? Rod Weaver is very negative on reorganization and especially the capitalization plan for our new entity. You recall that the Board was very enthused about the plan. Now Weaver is suggesting that ulterior motives are in place and that our plan is dishonest. I believe that he should be removed."

O'Shea was pondering Folley's comment about ascension to the ranks of the ordained and dignified. He heard little between that and the part about Weaver being removed. "Right you are, Richard. I told that goddamn Durant to fire him a long time ago. We probably ought to can both of them. I'll call a few people and get it done."

It occurred to Folley that the Cardinal had to approve Durant's dismissal under the reserved powers of the Board. That would give Durant an audience to explain the more complicated and somewhat negative features of the grand scheme. It would be best to eliminate Weaver and let Durant dry on the vine when the new organization essentially eliminated his position. Quickly, he decided to dissuade O'Shea from going after Durant. "Dad, I think Weaver is the problem. Let's eliminate him. Durant will take care of himself in time."

"Let me handle this, Richard." O'Shea was wanting the kill. "I think I know best how to get it done. Durant won't fire Weaver unless his own ass is on the line. We need to give him an ultimatum. He cans Weaver or we can him. It's that simple. Durant will see the light. Weaver is as good as gone. Trust the old man. I know how executives think. Loyalty is to their own career first and others after that. Durant is a pro. He'll cover his own ass."

Folley didn't like the idea but he knew that O'Shea was determined. He agreed to the plan and left it in the good hands of his Father in Law. O'Shea would normally put the matter to the Chairman of the hospital's Board, Kevin

Hardly, but poor Kevin was not available. His dementia had progressed to the point that his comprehension was frequently affected. He no longer came to the office. He maintained his interest in his many Church and civic activities with the assistance of his loving wife who drove him to meetings and prompted him on matters put before him.

O'Shea easily convinced Patello, his friend and ally in the bank, to jointly sign a letter to Joe Durant requesting that Mr. Weaver be discharged because of his inappropriate behavior and failure to support the mission of the hospital. The letter strongly implied that failure to comply with the request would seriously affect the Board's continuing confidence in the executive leadership of the hospital. O'Shea dictated the letter to his Secretary and instructed her to hold it for Patello's signature. Patello usually came to the bank on Tuesday. After it was signed, O'Shea intended to deliver it personally to Durant. The feeling of ultimate power was thrilling. O'Shea loved it and he hadn't even started yet.

Action Waste Management and Recycling Company as it was now named had its usual Monday morning staff meeting. Jay Marquart was on time for a change but his attention was on many other things than the rah-rah speech being given by Mr. Meehan. He constantly had the Sailor in mind since he had left St. Anslem's the night before. Markley had tried to persuade him that the Sailor was resting and comfortable. Jay knew from his experience at the hospital that when a patient was referred to as comfortable it meant the patient was in big trouble but in no pain. Markley was with the Sailor. That was good. He would see that Sailor got what he needed. Jay knew that he was in good hands. Yet he continued to be concerned. He asked himself why but couldn't come up with an answer other than he cared.

Jay also thought about Wally and the donuts. That brought on another question. What was the deal with the Union? Why worry about it? He liked Donovan and he cared about whatever was bugging him. Then there was St. Anslem's. The place was screwed up big time and Action was ripping them off. Should he bother with that? Just do his job and let the hospital take its lumps. No. He knew that the hospital could be better if it had a good environment and waste handling was a big piece. He wanted to see it happen. He cared about the quality of his work and he cared about how the institution was served. He also cared about his buddy, Brian, who was getting in deeper with the Patriot special accounts. Brian asked Jay to help and Jay said he would because he thought he should but was he doing the right thing? He didn't know the answer.

Jay cared about his precious Kristie. Her love was very important to him and now he understood how important her love for her mother was to maintaining their relationship. Now in place of hate he nursed a concern for the welfare of Kristie's total family that included Cecile, Officer O'Sullivan, Susan, Benny and James. That was a lot to care for and about. O'Sullivan and Susan were hooked and needed redirection. That was a big job. Finally, his thoughts moved to his new friend, Sister Celest, and The Little Portion. All things considered, Jay Marquart had a lot to care about.

Jay's eyes were fixed in a stare. Kevin Ryan was worried that Mr. Meehan would notice the lack of attention that Jay was exhibiting as Veto Celi moved to the podium and explained that several hospitals had signed letters of intent with Action. Celi waved the letters and prompted everyone to prepare to work long hours in the preparation of a service plan for the new accounts.

Celi's portly frame was bathed in the sunlight causing an image of a large balloon standing on end. This caught Jay's attention.

Suddenly he stood and fired a question at the huge man. "Hey, Celi, screw the new accounts. What about the old ones? What are we gonna do for them?"

Celi was blown away by the question. Not only did he not understand it, he had no idea what to do when someone asked him a question. This was not part of the script. He glared at Jay, so did everybody else in the room. Kevin Ryan wanted to hide under a chair.

After a brief period of silence, Mark Meehan moved back to the podium and gently moved Celi's bulk to the side. "Mr. Marquart, I don't believe we fully understand your question. Mr. Celi was pointing out that we need to tool up to take on more business."

Jay again stood up and interrupted the Boss. "That's what my question was all about, Mr. Meehan. Why are we taking on more business when we aren't doing a good job with the accounts that we have. The St. Anslem's job sucks. It needs a lot of work and we go running off doing other hospitals. It seems to me that if we do one job right then we got reason to do others. If we can't do one job right then we ought to take some time to find out why. That's my question."

Meehan acted noticeably upset with Jay's comments. "Mr. Marquart, the St. Anslem's project is your design. If it is less than adequate I suggest that you determine why. I trust you can do that. The information that we have is that the project is progressing very well. They are making full payment. Mr. Celi assures me that the hospital is cooperating fully. I think you are out of order with your criticism except as it applies to yourself. I suggest that we continue with the meeting. Mr. Celi, please continue."

Celi returned to the podium and began to recite the words on the page in his hand. The room was very quiet. Ryan stared at Jay in amazement. Jay glared at Mark Meehan. Meehan sat on a wooden chair with his legs crossed and glared back at Jay.

When the meeting ended Ryan ushered Jay out to the parking lot where they could talk and where he knew that Meehan would not look. Ryan was certain that Jay had cooked his goose. His hope was that he could keep Jay out of Meehan's sight long enough for the boss to get involved in other things and eventually mellow out. Jay, in the meantime, had to be put under wraps until Ryan could figure a way to square it with Meehan.

Ryan moved Jay behind a row of cars and started to crawl his frame. "Damnit, Jay, you had to shoot your mouth off and draw attention. Now the boss has reason to look at your record and give you the heave-ho. You're the one that screwed up the St. Anslem's deal by getting sick and letting it go to seed. Nobody worked the account until I went over there and set up the superficial things like the collection boxes. The truth is, the hospital doesn't give a damn about the project. They are just paying off like everybody else. You got to keep your mouth shut. Be grateful that you got a job—if you still do."

Jay wanted to ignore Ryan but his last statement caught Jay's interest. "What do you mean, 'paying off'? You telling me that Meehan is shaking down? Gimme a break."

"Add it up." Ryan decided to give Jay a lesson in reality. "Celi didn't go to Harvard Business School. Meehan did. So how did a jerk like Celi get a job in marketing? He's muscle that's all. I think he's busting heads to get those letters from the hospitals. They pay up and we haul trash. The rest is just window dressing. They don't want that waste management recycling crap. You and me, we, are just a couple of slobs getting paid to paint the picture. Don't make waves. Okay, so it might be a con but we just do our job and let Meehan do his. We still get paid. Chill out. You might also get lost until I can get Meehan off your case. Go back over to St. Anslem's and look busy."

Jay's feelings were hurt. He thought that he was making a contribution to a beneficial service. Now he was told that he was just a bit player in a con game. All sense of loyalty to the company was lost. He pointed the Jeep toward Waltham where he intended to go home and get some sleep but at the last moment he turned the comer onto Cambridge Street and drove to St. A's.

The hospital was picking up momentum after the weekend slow down. The surgery schedule was heavy for Tuesday which meant that patients were arriving for their work ups. Some were being admitted but most were getting their pre-operative testing on an outpatient basis thanks to new managed care rules. Ambulances from area nursing homes were lined up in the parking area waiting to discharge patients for therapy. Vendors were arriving to introduce the latest gadgets designed to save life and reduce suffering. The parking garage was jammed so Jay drove to the opposite side of the hospital and parked next to the loading zone at the freight dock. This was usually available to maintenance and repair companies making service calls. Jay reasoned that he was making a service call. To prove his point, he placed a makeshift sign in the windshield that said "Action Waste Management and Recycling Company." He desperately wished that he could take pride in the company but for now he felt disgust. His anger began to peak.

The main purpose of his trip to the hospital was to visit Joe Durant and ask for a donation of food or cash to support the dinner that Jay and friends were planning to prepare for the clients of Sister Celest's Little Portion mission on Saturday. As he walked in he suddenly thought of Tommy who would be winding up his morning hours in the cafeteria. It would be a good time to see The Tout and explore the thing with Wally the Donut King. Then there was the Sailor in the Medical Intensive Care Unit. Jay wondered if he was still alive.

His caring instinct put the Sailor as a first priority. Jay turned to the SACAP to find Markley for the latest information on the Sailor's condition. As he walked down the corridor toward SACAP he passed the Great Doctor Folley walking briskly in the opposite direction. Jay nodded a greeting that was ignored by the distinguished Folley as he took notice of Jay's identification badge with its prominent logo of Action Waste Management and Recycling Company. Jay felt the snub and once again his anger accelerated. He slammed the door behind him as he entered the SACAP.

Bob Markley had just stepped out of the shower and was nearly dressed when he heard the door slam. It was either Folley returning for something or a client charging in to vent frustration and trash the place. Either way Markley reacted and bounced out of the men's shower room. He was fully dressed except for his shoes and socks that he held in his hands.

Jay looked at Markley standing in bare feet with his uncombed hair. It was a bit of comic relief that eased Jay's anger only slightly when he greeted his friend and mentor. "Mr. Markley, I see that the cutbacks have forced you to work without shoes. It's a nice touch. Very becoming."

Markley was pleased to see Jay. The impromptu press conference in the Unit an hour ago had blown his mind. Now with Jay's unscheduled visit he once again became focused on the Unit and the clients it supported. He waved at Jay to sit in one of the chairs next to the table where Logan and the *Globe* reporter had been. Markley sat in the other and began to put on his shoes and socks.

"Good to see you, Jay. Thanks for coming by. Excuse the bare feet. I just got cleaned up. We spent most of the night with the Sailor. Dr. Anderson came in around eleven. Sailor's not doing well. How you doing?"

"Okay, kinda." Jay's depression was obvious. "You know I got one hell of an urge to get blasted. Damn, I think I'm going to do it. The whole goddamn world sucks. Why in the hell should I worry about anything when nobody else gives a damn? The Sailor comfortable? You going back to see him?"

Markley gave a positive nod. "Sure. I haven't got any appointments until this afternoon. They're making rounds this morning and the consults are being done. I thought I would drop into the MICU in about an hour from now and see what's being done. You want to come along? I can get you in for about a ten-minute visit. He may not be conscious. He was out all last night. What's this about getting blasted?"

Jay slapped his knee for emphasis. "Bob, goddamn it, every time I try to do something right I get in some sort of a mess. I tried to get this Hospital to improve the waste management program and Dr. Sutton tells me that the doctors don't want the program so I try to tell Meeham, the big cheese at Action, that we have to do a better job at the hospital and he tells me that I should dummy up. All he wants is the money. He couldn't care less about what we are trying to do. I bust my ass to set up a good program and nobody wants anything to do with it. The goofy hospital just throws money around to buy off Action for some reason and screws you and the rest of the employees. So, what the hell. Why should I worry about it? I worried less when I was drunk and stoned. Being sober is one hell of a drag, man. If I get blasted then I won't worry about this shit. It's the only way, man."

Markley tried to act unimpressed. "Did you come in here to tell me that or to check on the Sailor?"

"No, man, I came in to see about the Sailor." Jay drew back. "I saw that damn Folley guy in the hall and all of a sudden I decided that I was gonna get me a couple of drinks. That's all, I just feel like hittin' it hard."

"What you feel like doing is not that unusual." Markley finished tying his shoes and looked at Jay. "You've done that for a long time. You don't have to explain it to me. I know exactly how you feel. You know I have the same problem as you. Hitting the jug is something I think about often. The urge is overpowering. It's easy to cross that line. I know from my own experience. It doesn't help. It only makes things worse when you have to piece everything back together after a binge. The staff at your discharge conference explained the effects that a binge would have on you. You know that you can't handle it anymore. You'll end up in the Psych Unit again or worse. Give it some more thought. Maybe you ought to spend the day here and if you still feel the same by tonight I can arrange to stay with you until you feel better."

Jay reacted. "Bob, when I get pissed I feel like drinking and taking a snort. So now I'm pissed. It helps talking to you. I've got to hang around here and see a few people. Hell, I don't know if I'll change my mind by tonight. What's the difference? Drunk or sober, life sucks, man. Who cares? Nobody cares, I mean, nobody."

"Do you care, Jay?" Markley brought back the all-too-familiar question.

"Man, you always ask me that. Ask me if I care. Yeah, I guess I do. Why else would I get pissed? Ain't that a crock?"

Markley didn't react. He accepted Jay's answer as matter-of-fact. "Get back here in an hour and we'll go check on the Sailor."

The morning traffic in the cafeteria was down to a trickle. The night shift had long gone. Day shift had been through on first break. Residents and attending had moved away from table conferences to bedside. Tommy the Tout had his bets and was preparing to leave when he spotted Jay at the coffee urn. He waited for him to clear the cash register. As Jay turned away from the register he spotted Tommy who waved him to the chair at his table.

Jay caught the wave and moved promptly to the table. "Hey, Tommy, I met with your man, Wally, on Sunday. He's a piece of work. What the hell is all this about? He don't make much sense. "

Tommy was not sure how to respond. He gave it his best shot. "I never ask what it's about, Jay. I really don't care. I got twenty bucks for you and a message. Here's the double sawbuck. The message is that you're the guy. He said that you would understand. He's gonna call you for another meet. I'm the agent and will slip you the cash when he gives it to me. Sometimes I'll tell you where and how to contact him. When he tells me, I will tell you. That's it."

Jay took the twenty-dollar bill and held it in his hand. He said nothing while he thought about the entire matter. He remembered Wally's question about Celi and it dawned on him that maybe he could do some good by using Wally to put pressure on Action to improve its quality of work. It was a positive feeling. He began to experience a change of attitude. The money was something that Jay desperately needed but it reminded him of Meehan who only did things for money. Jay wanted to do something for the good feeling that it gave him. He sensed that it was the same feeling he got from going on a binge. Maybe doing good things was just as intoxicating and money was the unfortunate addiction that stimulated deceptive effort and false gains. The twenty-dollar bill was a symbol that Jay didn't want. He didn't want to be paid for doing nothing. He preferred to be paid as a reward and in recognition for a valuable contribution. So far he hadn't made any effort that justified the twenty dollars that he held in his hand. He also knew that if he didn't accept the money it would go back into Tommy's pocket.

Suddenly he had an inspiration. "I'm gonna let this twenty ride, Tommy. You got any long shots?"

"You know I love a sport, Jay." Tommy's eyes widened/ "How long you wanna go? I got some odds out to ten and a few longer but they are really out there 'cause they don't carry a chance. Real sucker bets. You don't want them. You wanna shoot for something in reason, Right?"

Jay shook his head from side to side. "Gimme the longest you got, Tommy. It don't have to make sense."

"You're the customer. I can give you Boston College over Notre Dame. They play Saturday. The Irish are twenty-one point favorites and that's being charitable. Some say that BC could go down by forty. You want to play the spread or maybe an over/under shot? BC to win pays long at twenty to one on this morning's line."

Those were the kind of odds that Jay was looking for. "Twenty bucks at twenty-to-one says BC wins. I like it, Tommy. Write it down and hold the twenty."

Jay liked the idea of bucking the odds. He was betting money that he didn't earn on a long shot. If the long shot happened then he had earned the reward because he took a chance. That's what a business man does. He also reasoned that the reward had to be shared with others to justify his good feeling and satisfaction. He intended to give Sister Celest half of the winnings. If he lost the bet then he had actually lost nothing and done no harm but if he won he would do a good deed by giving some to Sister Celest and keeping the rest as his just reward. He walked away from Tommy with a smile on his face and a renewed spirit. Tommy was also smiling.

It was pure luck that Jay met Joe Durant in the corridor. Durant had walked across the hall to the restroom and was returning to his office when Jay turned the corner and almost collided with the hospital executive. Jay imposed himself in such a way that Durant was powerless to do anything but listen as Jay explained the Saturday bash planned for The Little Portion. Durant was fascinated and agreed to provide the food for preparation by Jay's friends. He declined Jay's invitation to participate since he was already scheduled to be installed as a Knight in the Order of the Holy Cross on Saturday.

Jay was pleased that Mr. Durant was willing to support the effort and that he wanted a list of the requested food by Wednesday. When Jay attempted to press his good fortune by bringing up the state of the Waste Management program, Durant became suddenly irritated and cut off the conversation with the comment that Jay should "ask Mr. Cell about it."

Jay felt good. His meetings with Tommy and the hospital's CEO had been positive. He felt he was on a roll. It was time to head back to SACAP, hook up with buddy Markley, and go see the Sailor. For the time being he had forgotten about going on a binge. Markley was waiting and the two went promptly to the Medical Intensive Care Unit. Markley ushered Jay into the ICU visitors' lounge while he went into the Unit to arrange the visit. Jay sat patiently with others waiting for time to visit. The small windowless room was crowded with anxious relatives of patients. The drab off white walls were punctuated with landscape paintings that some interior decorator decided would give a more spacious impression. It didn't work.

Other than the small paintings, the walls had typed signs pasted on with surgical tape. One sign on the wall in large type listed official visiting times as every hour on the hour. Visiting time was limited to ten minutes and subject to other restrictions as may apply from time to time depending on the patient's condition. Exceptions to visiting time and length of visit could also be made as necessary and appropriate when the patient's condition so warranted.

Jay noticed that some of the people waiting were sleeping. Others were apparently praying. One person nervously fingered a rosary. A very kind hospital volunteer came into the lounge from time to time and delivered written messages or information for people in the MICU. She also maintained the pot of coffee and hot water, removed used cups, put clean ones in place, and gave instructions about hospital procedure. A tray of cookies sat untouched next to the coffee. Jay took two of the cookies and began to nibble when Markley returned and motioned for him to follow.

The medical intensive care unit was familiar to Jay. When he was an EKG technician at St. A's several years back he had made many trips to the unit. That was before the super sophisticated monitoring equipment had been installed. Now the patient's condition was constantly monitored with space age technology. The computerized panels at the nursing station reminded Jay of the television scenes he had seen of NASA. The Sailor was wired to the monitors and was being watched by the ever-vigilant staff who took no notice of Jay as Markley ushered him to the Sailor's small compact room.

Sailor was awake but looked very tired. Different from when Jay saw him last, he was clean. His dirty clothes were nowhere in sight. Markley gave the Sailor a reassuring pat, checked his bed, and left Jay alone with the patient. The Sailor's eyes met Jay's and they smiled at each other.

Jay took the Sailor's hand and gave it a gentle masculine squeeze. "You look good, Sailor. Man, we got to get you outta here."

The Sailor looked at Jay. His eyes were moist. He attempted to swallow and speak. "No way I'm gonna get out. Thanks for gettin' me here. The corpsman, he's taking care of me."

"Okay, Sailor." Jay could agree now that he knew Markley was the corpsman. "Hey, man, don't try to talk. Yeah, man, the corpsman is the best. You rest easy. Things are gonna be fine. I'll be back and we can talk more when you feel better."

The Sailor seemed suddenly irritated. His eyes opened wide and he tried to raise his head. When that effort failed he gripped Jay's arm as hard as he could and pulled Jay toward him. He labored to talk in a raspy whisper. "Little buddy, you got to move my stash. I hid it on the Suit's boat—in the engine room. Back deck. Pull the center hatch. It's fixed to the bulkhead forward on the main beam, ahead of the Batteries. You got to get it outta there."

Jay didn't understand the terminology but he got the message. The Sailor had hid his cocaine on Markley's boat in the engine room and he wanted it moved. "Okay, man, I'll get it for you. Where you want me to stash it? It'll be waiting for you to get sprung."

The Sailor leaned back and seemed to relax. He looked at Jay and offered him a gift. "It's yours, little buddy. I'm getting out. The corpsman's getting me out. You take it."

No more was said. The Sailor closed his eyes and seemed relaxed. Jay was speechless. He had been given a gift that just a month earlier would have seemed like a million bucks. Now he had been offered a stash of cocaine that he was reluctant to accept. He had no choice. It was on Joe Durant's boat and Durant was unaware that he was committing a felony of the worst order. Boaters who smuggle drugs into Boston Harbor were the focus of the Police. Durant was set up to take a very big fall. Jay had to remove the cocaine. Then he could decide to keep it in case he went on a binge, share it with Susan, Louise, and Brian next Saturday or flush it. He was calculating the various options when Markley came next to the Sailor's bed.

Carefully, Markley said, "He's sleeping, Jay. It's a good time to leave. Did he say anything?"

Jay was reserved. "Yeah, but it wasn't anything. He thanked me for bringing him in. Says you're gonna get him out. I think maybe he's sorta giving up. That's bad, ain't it?"

Markley wasn't sure if the Sailor would recover. Yet, he was reassuring to Jay. "Maybe not. He's got a pretty good chance of pulling through. Once he's out of Intensive Care then we can start our work. He wants to kick the habit. That's what he means by getting out. It ties back to his days in Nam. He had a tough life. Was raised by the Nuns in an orphanage in Indiana. Went to high school in Ft. Wayne. When the orphanage closed he was placed in foster homes by the Diocese. No parents. Joined the Navy right out of high school. That was his home until he retired. We got the history from the Veterans Administration. The VA has agreed to take over when we get him back on his feet. They'll take him now if we can stabilize him enough for transfer. We'll see."

Jay was tempted to tell Markley about the Sailor's involvement with the drug ring and his attempt to escape from further involvement. The bit about the stash of cocaine would remain with Jay for now. That point didn't merit broad discussion until Jay decided when and how he would retrieve the package from Durant's boat.

Markley again interrupted Jay's thoughts. "Jay, there's one other thing you need to know. I arranged your visit with the Sailor by putting your name on his chart as the responsible party. That gives you access to him in emergencies and on the regular visitation schedule. You can take advantage of that as you like. If he gets into trouble the hospital is likely to call you. I'll be with him too but you are likely to get called. Okay?"

Jay made no comment. He simply nodded in agreement. He had no idea at the time what the role of Responsible Party meant. The two men walked back to the SACAP. Several people were in the waiting area. Markley greeted each one by name. Jay knew it was time to leave. With a wave he left. The rest of the day was spent wandering the halls of St. Anslem's asking employees about recycling. Surprisingly he received many favorable comments about the concept but nothing positive about the program. Most of the employees were aware of the receptacles in the corridors and lobbies but they had no understanding that the hospital was involved in a special effort. It was another downer.

He left in the late afternoon as depressed as when he had arrived. Once home he loaded up his shotgun and drove into the hills where he stalked birds until dusk. It was dark when he arrived home at quarter past six. Susan had dinner waiting. Also waiting for him was a message from Brian asking Jay to call him as soon as possible.

Chapter Twenty-one

Patriot Transportion and Courier Service had been exceptionally busy. Brian had not had a break all day. He was watching the clock in the late afternoon hoping to pack it in for the day when he received a call from Eddie. There were some special accounts to be delivered that evening. Contrary to the usual practice, Eddie was bringing the merchandise to Patriot himself and wanted Brian and whoever was helping with the special deliveries to meet him. Brian had no choice. He was required to stay. Jay, on the other hand was an extra that Brian had used on a cash basis. He was not obligated to attend Eddie's special meeting. But Eddie was aware that Jay had been on some assignments.

Brian gave Jay a call. By the time Jay returned the call, Eddie was already at Patriot. Jay listened to Brian's desperate request for him to come in. He left in a rush leaving Susan wondering and worrying about his pending encounter with Eddie, her former husband and current supplier.

When Jay arrived at Patriot he found Eddie sitting at his old desk and Brian standing to the side. Eddie's face was a mess. His lip was split and his nose looked like it had been broken. There was a bandage on his chin. One eye was discolored.

Someone had beaten the shit out of the Enforcer. It wasn't Brian. Brian had taken a shot himself that Jay immediately realized had been delivered by Eddie. Brian held a handkerchief to his nose to stem the bleeding. Tears flowed from his eyes. Brian was in some pain. Jay intended to avoid having the same inflicted on himself. Cautiously he gave a greeting to the two.

"Hi, Eddie, Brian. Sorry I'm late, I think. If I'm interrupting anything I can come back."

Eddie growled at Jay. "Get in here, asshole. You took your goddamn time. We got to talk. Have I got your undivided attention or do I slap you up like Brian here. You ready to listen, dumbshit?"

Jay moved inside and away from Eddie's reach. "Yeah, Eddie. Don't get pissed, man. I'm all ears. What's up? You okay, Brian?"

Eddie stood up and walked to Jay. "He's fine, asshole. I do the talking. You listen. When I want you to talk I will tell you. Okay. Here's what it is. We got to have the Sailor by tomorrow. You see what I got. Well, if you two don't find the Sailor by tomorrow night then I get my ass kicked again only this time it will really hurt. Now before that happens you two are gonna get yours because I'm gonna let the muscle know that you two are hiding the man. They play rough as you can see so don't mess with this. You dig?"

Brian realized that Eddie was about to give Jay a shot to the face. He moved in front of Eddie blocking Jay from any harm. "Yeah, Eddie, we can deliver I guess. Jay, I told Eddie that I didn't know where the Sailor was but you might have some idea. He gave me a shot just to let me know that he's serious. You know where the Sailor is? You tell Eddie. He's the man. We got to bring the Sailor in."

Eddie smiled at Brian's cooperation. "The Sailor and the shipment is what is wanted. He's got some coke that belongs to the man and it's got to be returned. You see to it. If you get the Sailor you make sure he brings the goods. He don't cut it emptyhanded. You understand the problem, assholes?"

Jay took a deep breath and tried a response. "Eddie, man, the Sailor's gone. I mean, I saw him right before Brian told me you was looking for him. I went back and looked for him but he's gone, man. I don't know where. Man, he's gone. Disappeared, you know."

Eddie didn't buy it. "What I know is that you coke heads would sell your mothers for a fix. You and those dopers you live with are sniffing the stash that the Sailor copped. That's the way it comes off. Now you want to avoid the hurt you get it up by tomorrow night. That's it."

Jay knew he was captured to Eddie's anger. Instinctively he decided to try another tact. "Eddie, it seems we all got the same problem. Some muscle is gonna bust our heads if we don't get the Sailor and the stuff. Seems to me that the first thing we got to do is make sure that we don't get hurt and the muscle gets what he needs, a good ass kicking. Can we talk about that?"

A good ass kicking was what Brian expected to happen to Jay when he dared to infer that Eddie would be anything but loyal to his assignment. Jay's suggestion that the three conspire to mutual protection was heresy for which one pays with physical pain.

Eddie, to Brian's amazement, seemed more curious than angry. Eddie strolled around Brian and Jay with his hands low but relaxed. His eyes moved from Jay to Brian and back to Jay. He squinted his eyes and licked his wounded lips. Finally, he pushed Brian away from Jay and stepped in front of him.

"What you got in mind, asshole? How do you intend to pull this off without getting your head handed to you?"

Neither Brian nor Jay realized how much Eddie hated the Sam the Security Man, who made him wear clothes he didn't like, drive a car instead of his hot wheels pick up, pay income tax, change his screwing habits, and pounded him senseless which in Eddie's case was redundant. Eddie was confronting Brian and Jay out of desperation, not confidence. Eddie wanted an answer to the Sam the Security Man's mandate that Eddie produce the Sailor or else. Eddie wanted to avoid the or else. The idea of turning the table on Sam the Security Man was very appealing but it had to be a very good plan. Jay had managed to hit a very special chord.

Jay didn't have a clue about what to do next. Eddie was on one hook but Jay had managed to get himself on another. Eddie wanted to know how Jay was "going to pull it off" but Jay was uncertain what "it" was. Quickly he mentally added his currency. He knew where the Sailor was. He also knew where the cocaine was. At the moment he was the only one to have those answers. It was best that he maintained that advantage. On the opposite side he did not know who was pulling Eddie's chain. To develop his plan he needed to know who the mark was. Jay decided to explore further.

"Well, look, Eddie, ain't no reason for anybody to get hurt. What I was saying was that if we somehow got the Sailor and his coke for whoever wants it without going through this muscle then he looks bad and you look good. That's kinda it. We help you and you help us and we sorta eliminate the middle man. Who is this guy that's on your case? Can we go around him? I mean if you can point him out to me then maybe I can work out an angle. I know a lot of guys downtown. It don't take much to get help. Hell, we got a lot of guys we do business with here that might come up with the where with all. You know what I mean?"

Brian was flabbergasted at Jay's attempt to double talk Eddie. He was also shocked at how Eddie was being taken in. The Enforcer was rubbing his fists and nodding his head up and down while walking in circles around Jay. He sat back down at Brian's desk and seemed to be in deep thought. The old desk chair seemed to creak in resentment as Eddie leaned back and placed his greasy head against the dirty wall. He pointed his stubby finger at Jay

"You make sense, asshole. Here's what we can do. He's got this very special package comin' to him." Eddie held out a small package from his pocket. "It's got to be delivered tomorrow exactly at noon. I was gonna give it to my man, Brian, here so he could make it tomorrow. Okay, what we'll do is have you deliver it. That way you get the make on the guy. We get together after that and you can explain the rest. That gives you the rest of the day to come up with a play that keeps you from getting greased. How's it sound, asshole? You know where Hardly Security and Trust is? Well, the man is gonna be waiting for you in the lobby tomorrow at noon. You deliver the package to a Mr. Sam Wells. I don't think that's his real name but that don't matter. You'll see the guy then."

Eddie put the small package on Brian's desk. It wasn't more than a couple inches square, wrapped in plain brown paper, and addressed to Mr. Sam Wells. No other identification was on the wrapping. Then Eddie stood up. He gave Brian a light slap, did the same to Jay and walked out. Brian sat down at the desk and fingered the package. Neither person spoke. Finally, Brian broke the silence.

"Hell, Jay, how you gonna do this? You meet the goon at noon and come out with a deal. Shit, it ain't possible. He'll eat you alive. What we gonna do, man? Who do you know downtown that's gonna do us any good? Man, we are in it good."

Jay was satisfied with escaping a beating for the moment. He had no idea what to do next. He looked at Brian with confidence. "Hey, man, we got a minute we got a life. Something will happen. Who do I know downtown? Let's see. I got all those leading citizens at Sister's mission. We could get the bum club to do a sit in on the muscle's head. Then there's your connection at the Troubadour Lounge, we could...yeah...why not? Hey, Brian, we got a shipment for the Troubadour tonight? Let me take it. That might be it. Yeah, shit, that's it!"

Brian was lost. Jay's mental wandering was confusing. "Sure, we make the Troubadour nearly every night now. I usually take it when I go home. It's late now. They'll be looking for it. You better go now. What you got in mind?"

Jay was excited. "I'm not sure, Brian. Right now, I'm winging it. I got a few ideas that I'll try to work out after the Troubadour. The shipment ready?"

Brian wanted to go with Jay but Jay insisted on making the delivery by himself.

Less than an hour after his encounter with Eddie, Jay walked into the Troubadour Lounge. The bouncer recognized the package in Jay's hands and motioned him toward a back booth where Officer O'Sullivan and his friends sat. When Jay approach the booth O'Sullivan stood, grabbed him by the arm and pulled him to a vacant area in the rear of the club. Jay feigned a protest at the treatment.

"Jesus, Sully, people will get the wrong idea. What's with the rough stuff? You're actin' just like a cop I used to know."

Officer Sullivan was indignant. "I am a cop, Marquart, and I don't need you reminding me. Where's Brian? You got no business coming here. Give me the delivery and get the hell out of here. We shouldn't be seen together. Some of these people work at the hospital."

It never occurred to Jay that hospital employees would be the type to frequent the Troubadour Lounge. He made a quick look around for a familiar face. No one was recognized. Then he returned his attention to Officer O'-Sullivan. "You're right, Sully, I shouldn't be here and neither should you. You see this package? Well, I just decided that this place is a hot zone and I ain't gonna deliver it. The addressee ain't here, man. I got to return this to Patriot. I don't know the guy listed here."

O'Sullivan was more indignant. "What the hell are you talking about? I know the guy who the package is for. Give it to me. That's what Brian always does. I'll take it and you blow out of here. Come on."

Jay had the cop where he wanted him, begging. "Hey, Sully, you ever hear of a guy named Wally who works for the Attorney General?"

"Yeah. He's a wimp that does research or investigation. So what?"

Jay sat back and relaxed. "Nothin' much except he's been asking me questions lately about the drug scene. He says some snitch is pointin' out cops on the take. You figure they know about you?"

O'Sullivan's attitude changed. Fear was very apparent as he heard Jay's comments. He sat down at a table and wiped the perspiration from his brow and hands. "Jay, what do you know? I mean, what does he know about us I mean me? I got a habit I admit but I'm not on the take. Christ, I'm clean. You can tell him that. Right?"

It was working. O'Sullivan was taking the bait.

Jay carefully played out more lines. "I can't tell him what I don't know. He asks questions and I answer. That's all. See, if I give you this package and he asks me if I gave it to you, then I got to say that I did. It don't make no difference what's in it. He gets that information from someone else then just puts it all together, I guess. It's like doing a puzzle."

Sully was exasperated. "I know how investigations are done, Jay. I'm a cop with a degree in Criminal Justice. We have to throw him off the scent."

Jay made his play. "Well, what I was thinkin', Sully, is maybe we put him on the scent of some one that really smells. Maybe if you made a big bust he would have to find something else to investigate. Hell, they don't worry about the heroes, do they?"

"No. What in the hell are you talking about?" Sully wanted the fact.

Jay sat down next O'Sullivan and carefully looked around the club. No one seemed to care about the two sitting close at a table in the dimly lit area. "Sully, you let it slip last week when we was talking that I was under your special surveillance as a suspect in the drug import system for Boston. That was a wild goose chase that made you look like a sucker when the water cops pulled off that bust in Hingham. Shit, you know that I'm just a user like you. They really suckered you just to take you off the hunt. So now I got an angle on a guy who is the big import guy. I give you the lead and then you get the bust and be a hero. You're a real cop again. You might even kick the coke. Give it some thought only we ain't got much time to pull this off cause the guy we want is gonna go back under wraps."

Sullivan came up. "You know something about a shipment, Jay? You better tell me. I could sure use a big collar right now. Sure, they suckered me and I got plenty upset. I don't know right now if I want to stay in law enforcement. There's too much damned politics. I'm not one of the chosen few. If I could bring in a top collar the Narcotic Chief would have to give me a promotion. Then I could decide to stay or leave on my own terms. Give me the name. I'll check it out. Thanks."

"Sully, we got to work together on this." Jay held up a hand. "It's gonna take some undercover stuff. You know more about that than me. So, can you meet me tomorrow at eleven-thirty outside of the Hardly Security and Trust? Make it on the corner so the people in the lobby don't make us together. You game?"

Sully was in. "Yeah, I guess. What's the drill? What are we up against? Do I need back up? There's certain procedures that I have to follow when I make a bust. The shift commander will have to be briefed and the area will have to be secured."

"Shit, Sully, this ain't gonna work if you call out the National Guard. This has got to be done nice and easy, man. Look, we ain't gonna make any bust tomorrow. What's gonna happen is that you meet the man and arrange for him to get some goods that he's lookin' for. I see to it that the rest gets set up. You got to trust me on this. For now it's just you and me. Keep the brass out of it. Okay?"

Sully accepted. "Okay, Jay, I'll take the next step as you call it. You got to have an angle. What's in this for you? I can arrange a payoff for you from the Intelligence Section. You'll go on the list as an informer. We could be a good team."

"Will you get off this super dick shit?" Jay had the deal. "Tell you what. We pull this off and you agree to meet another guy that knows about users. He'll work on you to get rid of the monkey. You agree to that? I got to get going. This package has got to go back to Patriot. Too bad the addressee ain't around. I might have gotten a nice tip. As it is you're the one who got tipped. Hey, man, see you tomorrow downtown."

Jay felt good about his conversation with Officer O'Sullivan. It looked like a good sting depending on O'Sullivan's ability to convince the Muscle that a deal was in the offering on the Sailor and the shipment. He didn't intend to give O'Sullivan any information on the whereabouts of either. All he wanted to do at the meeting tomorrow was gain time until he could figure out the next step. He was playing it by ear.

The undelivered package for the Troubadour party was sitting on the seat of the Jeep next to him with the small package that was to be delivered to Sam Wells at the bank tomorrow. Jay pulled into his driveway and went into the house leaving the precious cargo in the unlocked vehicle. He had no worries.

By Tuesday morning the rumor mill had spread the word that Thomas O'Shea was the number-one prospect for the CEO position of New England Trust or NET as prompted by the flashy logo. His office was badgered with telephone calls of well-wishers who mentioned their availability and sent their resumes via fax. Tom acted as the gentle giant, accepting the accolades but not confirming or denying his appointment. He had just finished a telephone conversation with Charles Patello who announced that he was coming over to sign the letter to Durant, when his secretary informed him that a Mr. Wells from a public relations firm wanted to speak to him on a personal matter.

O'Shea knew that was the call he was waiting for from the promotion firm that was going to prepare the various news releases and conferences that would be forth coming. He grabbed the phone and told his secretary that he wanted no more calls and no interruptions. Mr. Wells was a priority call.

Mr. Wells was soft spoken but had a bit of a New York accent that seemed to be of the Brooklyn variety. O'Shea found it humorous that a Brooklynite would be representing a sophisticated public relations firm. It just seemed reasonable that the whole promotion would be coordinated by one of the best firms and the best was always out of New York and Madison Avenue. Okay, so Madison Ave used a kid from Brooklyn.

Wells was very adamant that no publicity be leaked before the right time. He needed to do the initial preparation for O'Shea and wanted to meet and get some background. He suggested that the two have lunch and offered to pick O'Shea up at twelve-thirty in the bank's lobby. He did not want to come to O'Shea's office because he didn't want to draw any attention. He also advised O'Shea not to tell his secretary about the luncheon appointment because the business press was beginning to pick up the story and might want to follow them. Everything had to be very well protected. O'Shea agreed.

Patello arrived about an hour after O'Shea had made his date with the mysterious Mr. Wells. He told Patello that he had been contacted by the public relations firm and that he was going to meet the representative for lunch. Patello looked pleased that the process was moving and told O'Shea to keep the matter confidential. O'Shea readily agreed. Patello read the letter to Durant and after a few minutes of thought signed it. He handed the letter to O'Shea who immediately signed in the signature block under Patello's and gave it to the secretary who placed it an envelope addressed to Mr. Joseph Durant. The envelope was marked delivered by hand. O'Shea winked at Patello as he placed it in his inner coat pocket.

"I'm going to hand this to Joe this afternoon. I've got a luncheon appointment then I'll go to the hospital, meet with Doctor Richard, and then we'll go see Durant. I don't think he is expecting this. Do you?"

Patello looked at O'Shea as if he were a fool. "Tom, he would have to be brain dead to not expect this. The Board has been beating him around the head for the past several months. The whole thing with the formation of the Archdiocesan Office for Health Affairs was a very loud message. Yes, I think Mr. Durant is expecting something like this and won't be the least bit surprised. I certainly wouldn't be. I wish we could do this some other way." Then he waved at O'Shea and walked out of his office.

Jay called Ken Ryan early to check on the climate around Action. Ken told him to stay around the hospital for the morning and check into the office in the afternoon. Meehan was scheduled to be out of the office most of the day and Ryan was anxious for him to be away by the time Jay made an appearance. That was fine with Jay. He had an appointment downtown with Officer O'Sullivan and he didn't want to be delayed by anything as insignificant as his job.

The Sailor was sleeping when Jay paid him a brief visit. That was adequate. He had done his duty. Then he checked in with buddy Markley to let him know that he had been in to see the Sailor. After that he drove to Patriot and returned the undelivered package to Brian and gave him a report. Brian listened with little comprehension as Jay described his conversation of the night before with Michael O'Sullivan. Between answering telephone calls, assigning drivers to various deliveries, and listening to Jay, Brian was becoming very confused.

He finally put everything else aside and tried to concentrate on what Jay was trying to explain. "Man, you got to help me understand this. You're gonna have O'Sullivan meet the Muscle at noon? Why? I mean what the hell is O'Sullivan gonna do? He don't know where the Sailor is and he don't have the stash. The Muscle is gonna get pissed and break his head. Then what? I mean this don't add up to nothin'. Geez! What am I gonna tell Eddie about the delivery that you brought back? He'll give me another shot to the head for sure.

Com'on, Jay, gimme a break here. What are you trying to do besides gettin' us both busted up, man? Eddie's probably got a collector knocking on O'Sullivan's door this morning. He don't collect and Eddie call's me about it—bang! I get another slap aside the head."

Jay tried to calm Brian. "I got it covered, man. O'Sullivan thinks that the Troubadour is staked out. He'll tell Eddie that he ain't buyin' no more until the heats off. Eddie can't argue that. So, I have O'Sullivan meet the muscle and the muscle sees that he's a user delivering a message. The message is from the Sailor that it will take a couple of days for the Sailor to get back into town. That's it. We got us a couple of days to figure out what to do next. All I'm trying to do here is get us some time to find the Sailor and get him to do what he has to do. The Sailor gets back on the street or wherever and squares it. End of story. Time, man, is what we need. You dig? Trust me. I got to get downtown."

Jay left Brian in a quandary and drove to the financial district. He parked his Jeep two blocks from the Hardly Security and Trust building and walked to the corner adjacent to the bank's main entrance. Michael O'Sullivan was standing on the opposite corner as Jay approached. O'Sullivan walked across the street against the light and met Jay. Carefully, Jay pulled him around the comer out of sight. He produced the small a package and shoved it into O'-Sullivan's hand.

"This is your ticket, Sully. Just hold it so it can be seen. This guy, Wells, will come to you when he spots the package in your hand. He knows what to look for, I guess. If he asks you anything you say you don't know nothing except that you was paid a few bucks to bring him this box. Then you tell him you also got a message. The message is that the Sailor is gonna be around on Thursday and that a meet can be arranged. Then ask where he can be contacted about the time and place. That's it. Oh, yeah, if he offers you a tip take it, man. We got to make this look real. Okay? Make sure he don't think that you know anything. You just deliverin' the message. He wants to know more you say that you don't know nothing. Just deliverin' that's all."

Officer O'Sullivan was not in the same condition as the night before. He was in full control of his emotions and intellect. "Yeah, Jay, I understand. What I don't understand is where this is leading me. I deliver this goofy message to some mark along with this little box that couldn't hold an ounce. I've got nothing that suggests he's dealing. You said last night that this would put me onto a deal. How? I've got nothing. Unless you can give me something to chew on, you can forget this little act. Deliver this yourself." O'Sullivan shoved the package into Jay's hand and began to walk away.

Jay grabbed O'Sullivan by the arm and dragged him into the bank's side entrance. "Sully, for Christ's sake, listen. I explained it all last night. Wally, you know the guy from the D A's office, he's on to something. We got to get him thinking that you're a good cop staking out a bust. Okay. So this Wells guy has got to be connected. I hear this from guys that are in the know that I deliver to. Yeah, he's in town to see that a shipment gets through."

O'Sullivan wasn't buying it. "Jay, you are full of it. Either you haven't got a clue about what's going on or you know a hell of a lot more than you are telling me. I don't like being used. You fill me in with the whole story or I'm out of here."

Jay realized he was cornered. The situation called for a little truth, very little. "Sully, you got to realize that I'm just an innocent bystander that happened to be in the right place at the wrong time. You see, when that sting went down in Hingham the boat where the guy got the dope was the one me and a buddy had used for fishing. We didn't know the guy that owned it was running stuff. Anyway, he stiffed the operation. The guy the cops nabbed only had half the load. Our friend took half and split. This guy, Sam Wells, is in town looking for him and the shipment. The guy that owns the boat wants out. He tells me that he'll deliver the stuff to the law if the law takes the muscle off his back. I was supposed to deliver the message to Wells to make the pickup but I got no way to get to the law except when I saw you I got the idea that you could be the man. You could use a collar with Wally and all that. Everybody wins here. So this is what it is. You make Wells and he agrees to meet for the pickup. When he gets the stuff you grab him. How's it sound?"

O'Sullivan was nearly convinced. "Why do we have to wait until Thursday? Why not this afternoon or even Wednesday? This thing could come apart the longer it takes. Where is the boat guy? They got a warrant out on him. If he shows I'll have to take him too. You know that. You could be implicated in all of this."

"Hey, Sully, I'm giving you a tip, man." Jay raised his hands in protest. "I got nothin' to do with this. You never saw me. Where you got your information is for you to know and others to wonder about. No way you gonna implicate me in this mess. I'm an innocent citizen trying to help the law. The boat guy is outta town. I don't know where. He calls a buddy of his who gives me the info. I never see anybody. It's the same as the way Wally works it for the DA. You know. Now here's the fuckin' box, you gonna do this or what?"

O'Sullivan took the small package without saying another word. He walked around the comer into the bank's main lobby and stood by the security and information counter with the package in the palm of his hand so that it was well exposed to view. To his surprise, Jay came into the bank and walked over to the main bank of elevators and began to stare at the building directory. O'Sullivan noticed that Jay was watching him out of the corner of his eye.

After a few minutes, a small portly gentleman that had been in the lobby when O'Sullivan came in, walked over to the information desk. He stood next to O'Sullivan for a few minutes and then spoke. "I think you have a package for me. My name is Wells."

O'Sullivan promptly handed the package to the gentleman like it was a hot potato. "Sure. I also have a message."

Sam the Security Man Wells was trained to beware of major variations of procedure. The transfer of the package was a simple act with a purpose. Simplicity avoids errors. Now a message was tied to the delivery. This was not part of the authorized procedure. He turned to walk. "You got a message for me? Maybe you should just send me a letter. I got no time for messages."

Wells started to walk away. O'Sullivan grabbed him by the arm and talked fast. "The Hingham bust! A guy wants to return his half. He can get it to you by Thursday. Where can he meet you?"

Sam the Security Man paused and without turning replied, "I'll be having lunch at the Shanty at the North Quincy Marina. If he's around he can meet me there." Then he walked away from O'Sullivan and toward another gentleman who came off the elevator.

Thomas O'Shea looked very dapper. He was wearing a new tailor-made suit. He had also managed to get a barber to come to his office and give him a trim. O'Shea stepped off the elevator and collided with Jay Marquart who was blocking the way while appearing to review the directory. Jay remembered O'Shea from the hospital executive committee meeting. O'Shea gave Jay a disgusted look and seemed not to remember him. Then O'Shea moved quickly to the lobby where he was warmly greeted by Sam the Security Man Wells dubbing as a PR man from Manhattan. The two did a fast exit out the front door. Jay ran around the bank of elevators to the side exit. O'Sullivan was standing on the curb just outside the side door.

Jay was breathless with excitement. "Hey, Sully, you did great, man. What did the dude say?"

Officer O'Sullivan was well composed. He had the look of a policeman as he thought about the encounter. "It was short and sweet, Jay. He seemed upset with the fact that I had a message for him. I expect that he has been trained to be suspicious of anything like that. He's a pro. You better be very careful what you do. He said that he could be reached at the Shanty in North Quincy at the Marina around lunchtime on Thursday. Let me know what the boat guy is going to do. If I don't hear from you by tomorrow afternoon I'll be all over you like a dirty shirt. You don't want me collaring you for harboring a felon, I'm sure."

"Sully, goddamn it, I'm on your side," Jay pleaded. "You're in, man. I'll get to you just as soon as I get the word. Hell, you can find me anytime you want. If you need me in a hurry just call your buddy, Wally, over at the DA's office. Me and Wally talk all the time."

O'Shea was excited. He chatted continuously as he walked with Mr. Wells Wells suddenly stopped at a car parked on a meter about a block from the bank. He unlocked the door and ushered O'Shea into the front right seat. O'Shea stopped talking long enough for Wells to walk around the care and slip into the driver's seat. Wells pointed the car toward the Mass Pike and then headed west.

Once on the Pike, O'Shea resumed his banter. "Where we going? Cambridge? That's convenient. I've got an appointment at St. Anslem's after lunch. My Son in Law is the boss there. I help him in the administration and I'm on the Board. That's something you might want to play up in the press releases. Do you want copies of my resume? I didn't bring a copy but my secretary has one updated and ready. Let me know where to send it."

Sam the Security Man looked at O'Shea. He hardly knew how to answer the barrage of questions and comments that were flowing from O'Shea. Finally, he held up his hand as a gesture for silence. O'Shea got the message. When the Mass Pike intersected with Interstate 95, Wells took the South exit onto 95 and then the first exit right to the fashionable Pillar House Restaurant.

O'Shea was impressed with the selection. They parked close to the door and entered. Wells didn't have a reservation since he wanted to maintain complete anonymity. Fortunately, there was plenty of space. They were seated in a small comfortable room that, at the moment, was vacant of other guests.

Wells ordered double martinis for openers. The drink helped to settle O'Shea down. He became friendly although slightly giggly.

Wells felt he had gained the opportunity to advance his agenda. "Tom, our firm is very pleased that we have been selected to do this bit. You are an excellent subject. We aim to execute this with a maximum result. What we'll require is your complete cooperation as we put things together. You need to be prepared. This is going to be your finest hour. Just let us do the work and you reap the benefits. For now, let's drink it up and have a good meal. One never knows when it will be the last. I love Martinis. How about another?"

O'Shea was content to slosh martinis. Conversation was light and little was asked. It was time to celebrate and let it all hang out. He had wanted to cut loose since Patello had told him he was the CEO. He had several drinks and became very drunk. Lunch was served and the table cleared. O'Shea didn't realize that he had been fed. He continually found a fresh drink in front of him. This was the best meeting he had attended in years. It was also a celebration of his ascension and he was taking full advantage of it.

Wells was also satisfied. He was careful to only take a sip of every drink and pour the rest secretly into an empty water glass that he kept at the ready. He was cold sober. The moment Wells was waiting for came suddenly when O'Shea announced in a rather loud voice that he "had to pee" and staggered toward the restroom.

Wells ordered fresh drinks that arrived shortly before O'Shea found his way back to the table. In the interim Wells had removed the wrapping from the package that had been delivered to him at the bank. Inside was the small round tablet that he was expecting. He placed the tablet in O'Shea's drink and stirred it until the tablet dissolved. When O'Shea returned, Wells announced that it was time for him to leave. He stood and proposed a toast to the success of New England Trust. O'Shea got to his feet with difficulty and raised his martini. Together they drained their glasses.

O'Shea was too drunk to walk but Wells maneuvered him without incident to the parking lot and into his car. O'Shea was jabbering continuously. His head was weaving back and forth. He slobbered on his tie and peed his expensive pants. Wells knew what was due. The man would become sick and vomit. Then he would convulse. Eventually he would ease into a comma. Mr. O'Shea had been given an overdose known on the street as a speedball that combined with alcohol was strong enough to kill. He could die but the intent was to cause brain damage that would render him incapable of maintaining executive function. This was the standard prescription when there was no alternative to a problem. O'Shea had been the designated problem for which there was no alternative. Sam the Security Man had completed his task.

Wells drove to the entrance of St. Anslem's and opened the car door for O'Shea who was still conscious and mumbling about his appointment at the hospital. O'Shea seemed to realize where he was and pulled himself out of the car. Then he staggered into the lobby and slumped into a chair. Wells pulled carefully away so not to attract any attention. O'Shea tried to get out of the chair but repeatedly fell back. The receptionist watched carefully and concluded that the man was drunk. She called the hospital's security office who dispatched an officer to investigate.

The security officer listened to O'Shea's irrational blabbering about a meeting and finally concluded that the drunk man was trying to contact Dr. Folley. He called Dr. Folley's office. The Great One was not in at the moment but his secretary had Mr. O'Shea scheduled for an appointment. Immediately she and another clerk from the Department of Medicine went to the lobby where they met the distinguished and apparently very drunk Mr. O'Shea. With the aid of the security officer and the receptionist the two ladies managed to place him in a wheel chair and wheel him to Dr. Folley's office. Then they placed an urgent page for the doctor.

It took only a few minutes from the time that Dr. Folley got the page for him to call his office. His secretary told him that his Father in Law was in the office either very sick or very drunk. She didn't feel qualified to make a definitive diagnosis. Folley broke off his conversation with Dr. Anderson and ran to his office. He found Thomas O'Shea in his office sitting in a wheel chair and unconscious. His pulse was very weak and he would not respond to Folley's shouts. Instantly, Folley called for the secretary to summon the cardiac crash team while he attempted CPR. The hospital's audible page repeated the message that there was a code three in the Department of Medicine. Team members from throughout the hospital rushed to the department. The first to arrive was the Physician Fellow in Cardiology who relieved Dr. Folley.

Folley realized that O'Shea's problem was not just a cardiac arrest. He went to the phone and summoned the hospital's foremost authority on substance abuse and toxic overdose, Dr. Anderson.

The patient was still alive when Anderson arrived at Folley's office. O'Shea was nevertheless still unconscious and had a very weak pulse. It was too early for the Crash Team to declare a save. Anderson consulted with senior cardiologist leading the team. The two decided that O'Shea should be admitted directly to the Medical Intensive Care Unit. With dispatch he was placed on a gurney and rushed to the Unit where he received full life-saving attention.

Dr. Folley recovered from the shock and called his wife who called her mother. Within an hour the two women arrived at Dr. Folley's office. Folley and Dr. Anderson gave them an up to the minute account of Thomas O'Shea's condition and then escorted every monitoring device known to medical science but was reported to be resting comfortably.

Mrs. O'Shea asked Dr. Folley to call the secretary at Hardly Security and Trust with the information about Thomas. Dr. Folley did as his mother-in-law requested. He also called Bishop Hanks and reported that Mr. O'Shea was in intensive care at St. Anslem's and was very ill. O'Shea's secretary was very upset after she talked to Dr. Folley. Somehow, she managed to sob the information to Hardly's office. The clerical staff then busied themselves with the task of alerting the entire organization of Hardly Security and Trust that the key executive had been stricken with a heart attack and was near death.

Kevin Hardly's office called Charlie Patello's office with the information. Patello called Uncle Frank. Frank directed Charlie to change the name of the CEO on the proposed organization plan for New England Trust and send the plan to the secretary of State. The name that Uncle Frank wanted on the form was Charles Patello. Charlie did as Uncle Frank directed.

Dr. Folley felt that all the necessary people had been informed. Then he remembered the hospital's Board of Trustees. Instinctively, he directed his secretary to call all the members of the Board who had not as yet been informed of Mr. O'Shea's illness. She did as directed until she came to the very last name on the list, Mr. Joseph Durant. She had been directed by Folley that standard procedure required her to check with him before making any contact with the hospital's chief executive officer. Obediently she advised Dr. Folley that she had contacted everyone on the list except Mr. Durant. She asked his direction. Folley thought for a moment realizing that O'Shea had set up an appointment with Durant the purpose of which was to give the CEO an ultimatum in writing to fire Weaver or quit.

Folley was scheduled to accompany his Father in Law at the meeting. That mission had to be accomplished. Quickly he checked the MICU visitors lounge and talked with his mother-in-law who had been given the contents of O'Shea's clothes. She had the letter addressed to Mr. Durant along with other valuables belonging to the patient. Folley dispatched his secretary to rescue the letter. Then he called Durant and announced that he was coming to see him.

St. Anslem's Hospital had specific procedures for the admission of a patient. The Director of the Admitting Office was adamant that those procedures be followed to the letter. She was continuously frustrated with emergency admissions causing certain shortcuts in the process that forced her staff to reconstruct and correct. When she was informed by the MICU that they were accepting an emergency admit of a visitor with suspected cardiac arrest she immediately began crossing the T's and dotting the I's as her staff collected the information to properly fill out the details on the required admitting form. One of those details was to cross check the name of the patient against a VIP list that administration had provided. Thomas O'Shea's name was on the list as a member of the hospital's Board of Trustees. As required, the Admitting Director telephoned Mr. Durant's office with the report about the VIP that had been an emergency admit. Durant was reviewing the admitting report when Dr. Folley barged into his office. He had been expecting the doctor's rude arrival.

Durant greeted Folley with respect. "Good afternoon, Doctor. I'm very sorry about Mr. O'Shea. How is he doing? Is there anything we can do for Mrs. O'Shea?"

Folley was taken by surprise at Joe's greeting. He thought he and Anderson were the only two who knew about O'Shea's admission. "He's very sick, Joe. Resting comfortably. He's in good hands. I've seen to it that Mrs. O'Shea is being taken care of. The MICU is an excellent Unit. Probably the best we have. They deserve much more than we give them. You need to be more interested in that department and spend less time worrying about things that don't matter. That's why I've come. I wanted to deliver this letter that Thomas was bringing to you when he took sick."

Durant took the sealed letter and opened it. After he read the letter he placed it on the credenza in back of his desk. He offered no comment and looked at Folley as if to ask if he had anything else on his mind. Folley was upset with the lack of response. He stared at Durant waiting for an answer. When none was forthcoming he offered his own comment.

"Joe, I'm somewhat aware of what was in that letter. Mr. O'Shea confided in me about what he was going to ask you to do about Mr. Weaver. I assume you will do what is expected."

Durant was angry but determined not to let Folley see his resentment. "Doctor, you must have Mr. O'Shea very much on your mind right now. I could hardly expect to burden you with these Durant matters now. Please see that Thomas is well cared for. I will consider the letter and let the Board know. Mr. Patello also signed the letter so whatever I decide will be conveyed to him in time. Thank you for delivering this. I really need to get to my next meeting. Let me know how Tom is doing."

St. Anslem's was very well organized to treat the seriously ill. One whole floor was devoted to intensive care. There were three distinct Units, a surgical intensive care unit, a coronary intensive care unit, and a medical intensive care unit. Nurses trained in coronary care were cross trained in medical intensive care and rotated assignments between the two units.

Cecile had completed her rotation in Coronary and was back in the MICU. She noticed that Jay was on the approved visitor list and had missed him on his visits to the Sailor but was intent on catching up with him on his next trip to the Unit. For the moment she had been put on a one on one special assignment to a recent admit that was in bad shape. Thomas O'Shea was not aware that Cecile was carefully watching his vital signs and adjusting the IV's attached to his withering body. She, on the other hand, did not remember him as being present at the hospital's Executive Committee meeting where she and Jay had made an appearance.

Jay had followed Wells and O'Shea out of curiosity until they got into a car. Jay wanted to make sure that he had a good look at Wells and that he could recognize him again especially at a distance since he was determined not to get to close to the gentleman. Then he went back to his Jeep and drove back to St. Anslem's. When he arrived he placed a call to Ken Ryan as he had been directed to do. Ryan reported that Meehan had returned but was busy doing other things and seemed to have forgotten about Jay's insubordination. Ryan suggested that Jay stay out of sight for the day and report back to his desk tomorrow.

Jay spent a couple of hours walking around the hospital and chatting with the environmental services people until three-thirty when the shift ended. Then he sat in the cafeteria and began to plot the next move for the Sailor and Brian. He hoped that the Sailor would be conscious enough to understand the situation and give some direction. He wanted to talk to the Sailor and then fill Brian in later that evening. He expected that Brian would get some word from Eddie if the Muscle, a.k.a. Sam the Security Man, reported about the message that O'Sullivan had delivered. After about a half-hour he left the cafeteria and checked in with the Volunteer at the desk in the MICU visitor lounge. He was early and had to wait for the ten minute authorized visiting period.

The Sailor was having difficulty breathing. Every breath was painful. His tear-filled eyes could not focus at the young physician checking him over. A very pretty nurse stood next to the bed and worked with the doctor. Sailor liked the fresh scent of the nurse who seemed to be smiling at him. He wasn't sure. The pain seemed to be getting worse and he struggled to get his breath. The monitor would make a warning sound every time that it was connected. Nothing was going right. The doctor called a technician who checked the equipment and then checked the way it was attached. The oxygen tube in the Sailor's nose was irritating his nostrils that were dry and sore. With what little strength he had the Sailor pulled it out but the pretty nurse put it back in place.

He decided not to contest the pretty nurse. She smiled at his cooperation. Then the technician left, the doctor followed, and finally the pretty smiling nurse walked out. He stared at the figure coming into the room and recognized his little buddy.

Jay put his hand on the Sailor's arm. Sailor's eyes were filled with tears that flowed down his cheeks onto the small pillow under his head. Jay could not speak. He looked at the Sailor and tried to gain enough composure to begin a report about what had happened. The Sailor was in no condition to listen to anything that Jay was going to say. His breathing became very rapid and the pain intensified. Suddenly he convulsed and began to suffocate. The alarms all sounded in unison. Staff rushed into the room and pushed Jay aside as they applied life-sustaining measures. Technicians and physicians seemed to appear from all sections of the unit. The Sailor had drawn a large crowd.

Jay was left alone. He walked over to the nursing station and waited. He leaned against the counter and looked around. All the patients looked alike covered with the white linen and attached to a variety of equipment. There were no distinguishing characteristics such as sex, race, age, or economic status. They were barely recognized as human in this dehumanized environment. The people treating them were expertly trained and experienced. The process made Jay think about the complicated video games where the objective was to avoid the ultimate catastrophe. This was no game. This was a real life and death struggle that the staff wanted to win. He wondered why they tried so hard. What was the motivation? Did they care about the person or were just trying to score a win for their professional satisfaction? He felt guilty for questioning their motives.

Most of the nursing staff had gone to the Sailor's room to do what they could in support of the life-saving effort. Some nurses remained with other patients per assignment. Jay noticed them and wondered about the patients they were covering. He glanced around from room to room and suddenly spotted Cecil working feverishly with a patient who Jay estimated to be in a very bad way. Carefully he walked to the room and waited for Cecile to have a moment to catch her breath.

When she finally backed away from the patient, Jay announced his presence. "Hi, Ceel. Looks like you got a tough one. How's he doin'?"

Cecile was surprised at Jay's sudden appearance. She stepped away from the patient and moved to the door but maintained close observation of her charge. "Jay! You startled me. I see your friend is having difficulty. They'll take good care of him. Those people are the best and very committed. I saw your name on the chart as the responsible party. Is Mr. Saylor a close friend or relative? I don't remember him."

"He's a friend, Ceel. Poor guy is all alone. I met him through Bob Markley. Bob's helping him with a problem like mine. I think the guy is in bigger trouble than I ever was in. I guess I'll be the one to work with him when he gets outta here. If he does. Who you got there?"

Cele became protective. "Jay, you know I can't tell you that. He's in very bad shape. Drug overdose we suspect. We see too many of these. Most are addicts and some are attempted suicides. You can see what that stuff does. Please take care of yourself."

Jay did not respond to Cecile's comment. He had been distracted by her patient who Jay suddenly recognized as Thomas O'Shea. The same Thomas O'Shea that he had bumped into at the bank just a few hours ago. He was about to say something to Cecile when Bob Markley appeared at this side. Bob gave Cecile a nod and pulled Jay toward the nursing station. He pushed Jay into a chair and sat next to him.

Markley had a very serious look on his face as he and began to speak. "Jay, the Sailor is in very serious condition. The staff feels that he won't live much longer. They doubt that he will regain consciousness. They'll keep him on life support for the next twenty-four hours. If he doesn't respond then we will have to deal with a very difficult decision."

Jay wasn't sure what the difficult decision was but he had a pretty good inclination. "Hey, man, what decision? I don't make no decisions. He's a friend that's all. I'll help him anyway I can, man, but I don't make decisions. No way. What kind of decision?"

Markley held Jay by the hand in good clinical manner. "The decision to remove him from Life Support is what I'm talking about, Jay. The Sailor has no living relative. We're all he's got. You and me. I put your name on the chart as the responsible party. The hospital will bring the question to you when the time is right. I'll be with you and will help you but I wanted you to be aware of what's coming. The doctor will want to talk to you about this in a few minutes. I told him I would prepare you for this. You understand?"

Jay was shocked. "Christ, Markley, I don't want to make that decision. My God! Get somebody else. Geez, I'm not the one to say that he's got to die. What the hell is this, man?"

Markley tried again. "Jay, the Sailor knows when it's time for him to die. His life will come to its natural end. You are simply an agent that represents him after his death. You will be the one who realizes on the Sailor's behalf that the life support system is just artificially causing his body to function without the qualities of life. The hospital will only ask your permission to discontinue the artificial mechanisms that are temporarily replacing his natural function. You aren't making a life or death decision. God made that decision. Do you understand?"

Jay was not convinced. "Hell, Bob, the hospital put that damn thing on him without asking me. Why can't they take it off without asking? This is a bummer, man."

Markley leaned away from Jay. He knew that he had to explain it all. "Well, actually they can but only with permission of the court. What happens is that the hospital petitions the court for a guardian who is authorized by the court to make the decision. It will be some stranger who never met the Sailor.

I thought that you would be better since you are his friend. We'll get you appointed guardian this afternoon."

That was a line that Jay did not want to cross. "Hold it, man. What's with the court shit? I ain't goin' to court. Man, I assure you that the Sailor does not want his name brought to no judge. No way!"

"Jay, what's bugging you?" Markley was surprised at Jay's attitude. "This is a simple procedure. The hospital's Social Service Office will have you sign the official forms that petition the court. You don't have to appear. The hospital takes care of everything. The Sailor's name and yours will only appear in the court records. Neither of you will be placed under any investigation. Are you two in some kind of trouble with the law? Are you hiding from something?"

There wasn't time to respond to Markley's question. Fortunately, Dr. Anderson motioned to Bob to bring Jay into a small conference room in the Medical Intensive Care Unit. The three men sat at round table. Dr. Anderson explained in no small detail that the Sailor's physical condition was very serious and that he was expected to die. He repeated what Markley had said about guardianship and the need to have a responsible party make the decision to discontinue the life support system if it became necessary.

Jay was passive as Anderson spoke. His mind was completely focused on Mr. Wells, the small package, and Mr. O'Shea. He wondered what the connection was between Mr. Wells, Mr. O'Shea, the Sailor and the stash so well hidden in Mr. Durant's boat.

When Dr. Anderson asked Jay if he would consent to be the guardian for the Sailor, Jay simply nodded in the affirmative. A social service worker was summoned and Jay signed the petition. It was taken to the judge less than an hour later. The decision was rendered and Jay was named guardian for Albert Saylor, Orphan—Vietnam Hero—Expert Seaman—Junkie, Fugitive—and one hell of a Great Guy. An entry was made on the Sailor's chart that a Mr. Marquart, responsible party was now appointed guardian. Jay was unaware of the honor. He had left the hospital and drove to Patriot Transportion and Courier Service where he sought a conference with Brian.

It was five-fifteen in the afternoon when Jay left St. Anslem's and began the drive to Patriot. Daylight had changed to dusk in the October afternoon. The cloudy skies accelerated the oncoming dark night and a light cold mist covered the windshield. The shaggy top of the Jeep gave way easily to the dampness. Jay shivered as he impatiently waited for the aged car heater to send its warmth. He was unusually patient in the traffic snarls that collected in the streets as he continued to ponder the circumstance regarding the Sailor, Mr. O'Shea, and the interesting Mr. Wells. He wondered if the small package had been an instrument in the sudden loss of health experienced by O'Shea. If so what was the legal status of Officer O'Sullivan in the act since he unknowingly passed the instrument to Mr. Wells. Jay speculated that at this point he was not involved in any illegal activity since he had only passed information to the law through O'Sullivan.

O'Sullivan was acting on his own when he gave the item to Wells. Or was he? Could O'Sullivan implicate him? Would a court find Jay an accomplice to whatever crime had been committed on poor Mr. O'Shea? Then again Jay was only guessing that O'Shea had been victimized by Wells. O'Shea may have tried suicide or he might have had some kind of an accidental poisoning. O'Shea would provide answers to the lot of questions as he regained consciousness. Jay could only wait. It was foolish to speculate about the outcome. The Sailor, the cocaine in Mr. Durant's boat, Eddie, and Mr. Wells and expectation that Thursday would bring it all together were the more pressing issues that he began to think about as he parked in the visitor space at Patriot Transportion and Courier Service.

Brian's day had been boring. The deliveries were few in number and he had sent the drivers home early. When Jay arrived, Brian was playing with his small radio and chewing on a pencil. The usual call in for a special delivery to the Troubadour Lounge had not come in but Brian was determined to wait until six o'clock before leaving just in case. He was very relieved to see his friend, Jay.

"Hey, Jay. Man, I'm glad you got here. There ain't nothin' goin' on. I'm ready to bust out. You wanna get a drink down at the tavern? Oh, shit, man, I'm sorry! No way you want a drink. What's happening? We off the hook with Eddie?"

"Well, I tell ya, Brian, I sure could use a belt right now." Jay was tired. "Shit, man, this day has been a gas. I mean a real gas. Hell, I don't know where we are with Eddie. My guess is that we got us some breathing room at least until Thursday. Then I don't know what's gonna happen. I put O'Sullivan on to the Muscle like I said I was gonna do. It came off smooth. He takes the package that Eddie gives us last night and hands it to the Muscle with a message that the Sailor is gonna come across. So, the Muscle says that the Sailor can contact him at the Shanty at the North Quincy marina on Thursday around lunchtime. That's it, man, end of story I guess. You heard anything from Eddie?"

Brian gave a nod. "Nothin', Jay. I ain't heard nothin' from Eddie. Christ! You put O'Sullivan on to the Muscle. You said that was what you was gonna do but I thought you was kiddin'. Okay, so now you got to get the Sailor to meet the Muscle and square it all up. You gonna do that? Then what you gonna do with O'Sullivan? Is he still in or did you give him the brush?"

Jay wasn't sure how to answer Brian. He wanted to take his friend into his confidence and tell him about the Sailor and O'Shea but he wasn't sure what to say or how to explain it so Brian could understand it. He decided to let it ride.

"Brian, you gotta believe me when I say that the Sailor is gone. I mean gone. There's no way that he's gonna make a meeting with the Muscle by Thursday. Hey, I wonder if the Muscle got the stash he would forget about the Sailor?"

"No way, Jay. Eddie says he's gonna rap me alongside the head again if the Sailor don't show with the stash. Remember? He said that one don't cut it. It's gotta be the Sailor with the stash. How you gonna do it, Jay?"

Jay couldn't answer Brian. He was giving thought to a reply when the large figure of Eddie the Enforcer appeared before them. Eddie glared at Brian and then turned to Jay. "Okay, asshole, who was the apple ass user that passed the goods to Wells? You had some junkie deliver the shit for you! Man! What's this shit about the Sailor goin' to show on Thursday? He bringin' the shipment too? It better happen, you asshole, or else I get the shit beat outta me and then you get yours. You bought your self an extra day. Don't fuck it up."

Brian moved out of harm's way in back of the small desk. Jay tried to move out of Eddie's reach but hit the wall and knocked over a waste basket. Clumsily, he regained his balance and held out his hand to Eddie as if making a friendly gesture. "It's cool, Eddie. Yeah, you see we got to get this set up just right. See, the Sailor, he's still outta town but he knows about the meetin' for Thursday. The user, well he ain't really no user. He takes a sniff now and then but he's some muscle that hangs around and does some head bustin' on contract. He's the Sailor's buddy and he'll gang the Wells motherfucker when Sailor says. It's all gettin' set up. The guy who made the pass today to Wells, well he's the guy who's been deliverin the word from the Sailor. He's the Sailor's buddy like I said. I don't know what's gonna happen but I could see a bunch of guys show up at the Shanty and drag this Wells guy out and beat his ass. Then the Sailor, he shows and gives you the stuff. Afterwards, he disappears and you hand the bag back to whoever wants it. How's that grab ya?"

The Enforcer had a smile on his face as Jay stumbled through his explanation. He gave Brian a look and grabbed Jay by the shirt forcing him against the wall. "That's fine, asshole, except this Wells guy wants me to be with him on Thursday. That means that any fight that starts will require me to stand with Wells. I get beat up either way. That means that you lose big time. You come up with something else, asshole."

"Okay, sure, Eddie. I can do that." Jay fell back. "We'll get this Wells guy off by himself somehow. You can count on it comin' down on him. The Sailor can fix it. No sweat, man."

Eddie was smiling. He relaxed his grip on Jay's shirt and gave him a slap on his face. "Yeah, I like that the Troubadour is a little hot so we won't be makin' any deliveries there for a while. It's like you said. Some sort of bird-dog got his eyes on the joint. We'll stay out till it clears. You get any calls from there act like you don't know what it's about. You dig?"

Brian nodded his understanding. Eddie gave a friendly wave and disappeared back into the night. Jay sat on the floor and put his head in his hands. The day had been too much for him to handle. He looked up at his buddy, "Hey, Brian, let's go get that drink."

Brian was shocked. He looked at Jay and saw that he was serious. Without another word, he closed the Dispatcher's desk and turned out the lights. Brian and Jay then drove their own cars to the nearest tavern where Brian ordered a beer and Jay demanded a double Diet Pepsi on the rocks. Neither said a word as they sipped their drinks. Finally, Brian broke the silence.

"Jay, I'm glad you didn't get drunk. Man, you shouldn't drink. You get bad. I mean really bad. I hope you never take another drop. I'll help you, man. You're my buddy. You got to stay sober. We'll work this out. Eddie won't hurt us. You tell Sailor that I'm still his friend."

The sincerity and simplicity of Brian's comments caused Jay's eyes to tear. He gave the thumbs up sign to Brian. "Brian, goddamn it, I sure am lucky to have a buddy like you. We are in a mess. You set me up with the Sailor. He's your friend more than he's mine. You should know. He's gonna die I guess. He's been at St. A's for the past couple of days in intensive care. They told me today that he's not gonna make it. They think that I'm his only friend. Hell, man, you should be with him, not me. We got to keep those goons from finding out. You can't tell them. Please, Brian, help me keep those bastards away from him. I got an idea but you got to help. You got to get in the act and help steer those sons of bitches off course. Okay?"

Chapter Twenty-two

Cardinal McMahon was up at five A.M. He said a private Mass in the Chapel and, after a light breakfast, went to his office in the Chancery. It was unusual that no ceremonial visits or events were on the calendar. This was to be a very busy day catching up on the many details of running the Boston Catholic Archdiocese. He had been away for the previous seven days. Many letters, reports, and telephone messages were neatly stacked on his desk. He had a brief two hours to review then before a parade of staff started the march to his office. Scheduled first was the Vicar General, Bishop Hanks, who always had an endless list. Of special significance was the luncheon appointment that Bishop Hanks had arranged with Doctor Folley, Archdiocesan Director for the Office of Health Affairs, to discuss the rapid changes taking place in the Health Ministry.

After the Cardinal had been brought up to speed by the respective members of his staff he planned to schedule a general staff conference late in the afternoon so all the news of the various sections and components of the Archdiocesan operation could be shared with the entire staff. Later in the day the Cardinal planned to summon his driver and spend the evening visiting the hospitals, funeral homes, and charities. He expected to return back to his residence around ten, spend an hour in meditation and prayer, catch the eleven o'clock news, and retire around midnight. To have a Wednesday with a relatively flexible schedule was very appealing. His Eminence was looking forward to the day.

At precisely eight A.M., Bishop Hanks entered the Cardinal's office. Instead of the usual commentary about how nice it was to have the Boss back at his desk, Bishop Hanks delivered the shocking news that Mr. O'Shea was seriously ill and in the intensive care unit at St. Anslem's. Cardinal McMahon made an on the spot adjustment to his schedule. He directed the Bishop to immediately inform Dr. Folley that they were coming to the hospital to visit Mr. O'Shea. Then if conditions so warranted they could have their discussion about the Health Ministry in Dr. Folley's office.

Bishop Hanks left the Cardinal's office to make the arrangements as requested by the Cardinal. He also called Mr. Durant's office to inform the CEO that the Cardinal was coming to the hospital to visit Mr. O'Shea. He instructed Durant to meet the Cardinal's car and escort him into the hospital. As a final note he directed that the hospital's CEO be ready to provide any additional assistance that may be required. He emphasized that "this was not a drill."

Dr. Folley was on his way to the hospital when he received a call on his cellular phone his office advising him that the Cardinal was coming to visit Mr. O'Shea. Folley moved at flank speed to St. A's. En route he called his office back and alerted them to notify the Medical Intensive Care Unit. All patient linens were to be changed. The hospital Chaplain was to be in the Unit. Dr. Anderson was to be summoned. The Chief Resident was to be in place. All personnel were to be issued clean ICU Blues. Environmental Services was to be dispatched to clean the Unit and all areas adjacent to the Unit. Lobby and elevators were to be policed. Security Officers were to be ready to greet the Cardinal's car and escort him to the MICU.

Joe Durant had not slept well the night before. He arrived at the hospital an hour ahead of usual and spent the time mulling over the demand that he fire Rod Weaver. He intended to meet with Weaver later in the morning and discuss the situation. The call from Bishop Hanks about the Cardinal's pending visit was just another irritation. He simply directed his Executive Assistant to initiate the Cardinal Visiting Procedure that included all of the things that Dr. Folley had started but was broadened to make sure that all corridors and elevators were clean since the Cardinal was a stickler for good housekeeping. Durant also made sure that the light above the Cardinal's picture in the lobby was turned on and working. Bishop Hanks had been very critical on a previous visit by the Cardinal when the light had not been shining. With the procedure enacted Durant moved to the main lobby to meet and greet His Eminence.

The Environmental Services Office was understaffed and very busy with routine cleaning when the direction came to drop everything and prepare for the Cardinal's visit. Personnel were immediately pulled from the patient units, surgery, and administrative areas to concentrate on the arrival of the Cardinal. The few supervisors still on duty and staff grabbed mops, buckets, and carts and headed for the first floor to guard the elevators, and lobbies from being violated by some inconsiderate visitor or uninformed employee.

Jay Marquart had just wandered into the Environmental Services Office when the Cardinal alarm sounded. He thought that it was one of the hospital's prescribed disaster drills or perhaps a real disaster. His offer to assist in the MICU preparation was gratefully accepted by a beleaguered supervisor who was at least three people short in the Unit anyway. Jay was thrown a set of housekeeping MICU blues and sent to help with the Unit preparation. He walked into the Unit with a squad of housekeepers who set about putting the always clean Unit into better order by emptying wastebaskets, dispensing the soiled linen, setting equipment in its proper place, and wiping down gurneys, wheelchairs, and anything that moved. It seemed to Jay that the Unit was already overcrowded with staff and more arriving every minute. In spite of the commotion, the patients were well protected and cared for by the nurses who stood guard over their every charge. The Sailor and Mr. O'Shea seemed to be resting comfortably.

Cardinal McMahon's black Ford Crown Victoria piloted by his arrogant Master of Ceremonies arrived at the hospital's main entrance. A security officer stepped to the car door but was brushed aside by the Master of Ceremonies who ran from the driver's side to the right rear door and obediently opened the door. The Cardinal slowly exited. Then he moved to the security officer and thanked him for his kindness. Meanwhile, Bishop Hanks exited the car from the left rear door and positioned himself next to the Cardinal blocking the Master of Ceremonies who the Cardinal directed to park the car. The hospital security officer motioned the Master of Ceremonies to park in a nearby space reserved for the handicapped.

Joe Durant met the Cardinal as he entered the Lobby. The Cardinal shook Joe's hand and commented how much he appreciated the clean neat appearance of the hospital. Then he suggested to Durant that the signs around the hospital were badly in need of repainting and that he had made the suggestion they be replaced at least three times before. His final comment to Joe was to ask why he couldn't get the signs fixed. Bishop Hanks made a note of the Cardinal's irritation. Joe attempted to answer the Cardinal but was brushed aside by His Eminence as Mrs. O'Shea came to greet him. The Cardinal gave her a blessing and then took her by the arm as they moved through the hospital to the Medical Intensive Care Unit. En route the Cardinal greeted the visitors and employees by giving them a special blessing that the faithful gratefully accepted from the Holy Man.

The Medical Intensive Care Unit was ready for the Cardinal's visit. The VIP procedure had been fully implemented by the time His Eminence arrived. The standard white walls seemed to be extra white and bright. The gray tile floor sparkled. Lights had been turned on high. The usually cluttered desk at the nursing station was absent of papers and reports that waited filing. Patient chart covers were neatly placed in their round holders. Personnel in clean uniforms stood at attention close to the patient cubicles as if waiting orders. The disciplined silence of the Unit was only disturbed by the low whine of equipment, hissing of oxygen, and occasional beep from monitors. MICU stood ready for inspection. The patients were also very quiet. Those who were conscious wondered about the lack of commotion. The others rested comfortably.

Dr. Folley was the first to greet the Cardinal when the entourage entered the Unit. He presented Dr. Anderson who introduced the Chief Resident and the remaining physicians in training. The Vice President for Nursing introduced her Supervisor who in turn introduced the Head Nurse who introduced the nurses on special duty with Mr. O'Shea, the patient. With Dr. Folley in the lead they proceeded to Mr. O'Shea's little room where the hospital Chaplain dressed in vestments waited patiently to assist the Cardinal in the administration of the Sacrament of the Sick.

Bob Markley was also in the MICU but not in O'Shea's room. He stood outside the Sailor's room that was next to Mr. O'Shea. The Cardinal saw Markley and moved quickly to him. They exchanged a greeting and embrace. A few words were also exchanged that no one could hear. Markley seemed to nod and smile as the conversation came to an end. Then the Cardinal entered Thomas O'Shea's room, distinguished from the others in MICU only by the numbers of people crowded into the limited space. O'Shea was still unconscious and was not improving. Anderson whispered to the Cardinal that his recovery was doubtful. The Cardinal noticed that Mrs. O'Shea was apparently resigned to the inevitable.

In the room next to O'Shea, Jay Marquart had kept a vigil on his friend. The hospital had called him at five A.M. and requested that he come in. When he arrived the resident took Jay into the small conference room and explained that the Sailor was expected to die shortly. The Sailor's electroencephalogram was very weak and was expected to be flat in the next few hours. Then the test would be repeated a few hours later. Consultants would each review the results of the tests. If they concurred that the patient was brain dead, the attending physician, Dr. Anderson, would recommend to Jay that the life support system be removed. Jay dreaded the decision that was being forced on him. He hadn't bargained to be in the position of making this kind of call. He only knew the Sailor for a few weeks.

This is unfair, he thought. *Why me? What did I do to get into this mess?* Then he realized that he had known the Sailor for years even though they were never formally introduced. The Sailor represented Jay's future as a junkie. He also represented Jay's destiny as he breathed his last moments. Jay was there to learn from this experience. This was Jay's birth, his wake-up call, as it was the Sailor's death. Jay was the beneficiary of the Sailor's experience. He had to repay the Sailor for the lesson of life and death. He leaned back and accepted his duty to help the Sailor. He began to understand and he began to care about the Sailor's death and his own life. When the conference ended Jay went to the Sailor and waited. Bob Markley came in a few minutes later and the two men sat quietly with the Sailor. After an hour Markley suggested to Jay that he go to the cafeteria for breakfast and then check back from time to time. Markley promised Jay that he would maintain the vigil.

Jay accepted Bob's suggestion. The cafeteria coffee seemed to revive him. He called Ryan and reported that he was working the St. A's account. Ryan was pleased and told Jay to stick with it. This prompted Jay to go to the Environmental Services Office to see if he could expand the knowledge of the housekeeping staff on waste management. He was about to deliver his oratory to the Supervisor when the word came in that the Cardinal was on his way to visit the Medical Intensive Care Unit. Jay's offer to assist was accepted and as a consequence he was dressed in MICU housekeeping blues and standing in the MICU when the Cardinal made a grand entrance.

The Cardinal's greeting to Bob Markley did not go unnoticed by Jay. Jay was impressed by their apparent acquaintance. But he was more shocked when the Cardinal came out of Mr. O'Shea's room and went into the Sailor's. At that point Markley stuck his head out of the Sailor's room and motioned for Jay to come in. The rest of the Cardinal's friends stood by. Only the Chaplain and

Bishop Hanks joined the Cardinal as he visited the Sailor with Bob Markley and Jay. Quickly Dr. Folley and Dr. Anderson pushed themselves into the room. Folley pulled Anderson to the front next to the Sailor where in hushed tones Folley explained to the Cardinal that the patient was under the care of Dr. Anderson. This was Anderson's cue to introduce the patient and explain to the Cardinal that this was an indigent patient not expected to recover from pneumonia.

Folley added that the care of this patient was an example of the hospital's mission to care without regard for the patient's ability to pay.

The Cardinal listened politely but seemed to want to move next to the Sailor. Anderson moved aside to let the Cardinal come closer. When he was next to the Sailor, the Cardinal put his hand on the man's forehead and prayed. Then he beckoned to the Chaplain who assisted in the administration of the Sacrament of the Sick. Bishop Hanks began to usher everyone out of the Sailor's room except the Cardinal and Bob Markley. Markley held Jay by the arm so that he wouldn't leave. The Cardinal held the Sailor's hand and after saying a prayer that was joined by Markley, he left the room.

"Dr. Folley, Mr. Marquart has informed me about the hospital's program in recycling and waste management. This is a very impressive effort and in the best interest of the community. It is a true example of what Catholic hospitals should be doing to support community health. Please see that the program gets every bit of support. Bishop Hanks will also convey my sentiment about this to Mr. Durant but you might do so as well. This is something that merits emphasis. Don't you agree?"

Folley was at first disarmed but true to his political ability he recovered quickly. "Your Eminence, the recycling program is one of very special interest to the medical staff. You can be certain that we will do what is necessary to bring it to a proper conclusion."

Cardinal McMahon smiled and winked at Jay as he let go of his hand. "Thank you, Dr. Folley. I know that you will give this matter the attention that it deserves. Now should we go to your office and discuss other matters. Please see that Mrs. O'Shea is comfortable. Is someone staying with her?"

Then the Cardinal shook Jay's hand and proceeded down the corridor. Jay and Bob Markley went back to the Sailor who seemed to be resting comfortably.

Jay couldn't control his exuberance as he chatted with Markley. "Hey, man, you set that up, right? Oh, man, did that Dr. Folley guy eat grass. I mean the Big Cheese in red socks tells him that the way it is, is that recycling is it, man.

Holy, shit did you see the look on his face? Man, you had to set that up. You did that right. Markley, you are one hell of a good buddy. You in big with the man! Right?"

Markley attempted to defuse Jay's excitement. "Jay, the Cardinal has a real interest in these kinds of good works. He was sincere in directing support for what you are attempting to do. I simply asked him to encourage you in your efforts. He had no idea that you were experiencing any opposition. He likes you and he appreciates what you are doing to help the Sailor."

Jay was excited. "Yeah, he prayed for Sailor. That's nice, man."

Dr. Folley's office was clean and at the ready for the conference with Cardinal McMahon and Bishop Hanks. Tom Callahan and Michael Logan were in a nearby office should they be needed to support the discussion with their slides and transparencies. Even Mitch Daly had been put on alert to supply background data if it was needed to fill a gap in the presentation. The office was divorced of the usual stacks of paper that the Great One used to support his self-inflicted prominence. His many pictures and plaques now hung straight and had been dusted. All this preparation had been accomplished in less than an hour from the time that his office had received the word that the Cardinal was coming. The secretary stood at attention as the trio entered. She accepted the Cardinal's blessing with a slight curtsy and closed the door after the trio entered Folley's sanctum.

Bishop Hanks began the meeting by explaining he had suggested that a discussion be held regarding the future of Catholic Healthcare in the Archdiocese in view of the many changes taking place. He pointed out that the Cardinal was most appreciative of the suggestion and had asked that Dr. Folley lead the discussion.

Folley seized the opportunity. "Thank you, Bishop. I am very pleased to begin. For background, we all know that health services have been established in the Archdiocese for well over a century. The ministry has been represented in its many programs by the presence of an institution, a hospital that captured the attention and attracted people in need of treatment. Health professionals came to the institution to practice because that was the central focus of healthcare."

Folley continued to pontificate. "The Healing Ministry has always been identified by the Catholic hospital as distinct from the provision of care by physicians and nurses who practice within the hospital and therefore within the Ministry. The institution served as the anchor for the Ministry. Today, as things change in the modern format, the provision of health services is beginning to concentrate away from the institution and center on the provider. The principal provider of healthcare is the physician. Therefore, the future of the Catholic Healthcare Ministry is with the physician and no longer will be concentrated on the institution. The institution will only be an instrument in the total process of care. The Catholic Healing Ministry must develop a new central focus. What we are suggesting is that the new central focus be a conglomeration of physicians, health professionals, institutions and fiscal resources that collectively hold a Catholic identity. That will ensure the continuation of the Healing Ministry."

Bishop Hanks looked at Cardinal McMahon and assumed permission to speak. "Your Eminence, if I may, Doctor Folley makes a very good point about the fact that the institution is not the human side of the Healing Ministry. Certainly, we need professional and religious people to give the Ministry true life. Initially the institution was punctuated with the presence of Women religious who gave the institution its identity and advanced the Mission. We no longer have the religious but we have dedicated laypeople who have done well to continue the spiritual as well as the physical dimension of the Healing Ministry. The brick and mortar of the institution serves as a fortress for the defense of the ethical directives. If we abandon the fort then I believe that we will be defenseless when we try to uphold our ethical positions. I cannot imagine that a conglomerate such as Dr. Folley describes would be tolerant or controlled in a way that would preserve our identity and ethics."

The Cardinal noticed that both men were adamant in their respective positions. He looked for a middle ground on which to development agreement. "Bishop. I believe that you and Dr. Folley agree that our Ministry is people not things such as buildings. We care for the people. It is the people who give the care. The question for the continuation of the Ministry is how can we best serve the people, those giving care and those receiving it? There is no question about the preservation of the Church's teachings. That is an absolute that you both accept. So, we agree on two major points, the ethical religious directives and the human quality of the Healing Ministry."

Again, Folley moved to speak. "Absolutely, Your Eminence, this is a service to humanity of which we speak. There is a bonding agent if you will that holds the service in tact as we expand our Ministry. That agent is wealth or more properly capital. We are blessed with resources that require our stewardship. As good stewards, we must place our resources in a position to grow, not to decline. Without a margin, there is no mission. That's been well proven."

"Doctor, I don't understand your point if you have one." Bishop Hanks was restless and visibly irritated at the Great One's rambling. "We are discussing the Ministry not money. On the other hand, I'm not surprised that you would confuse the two. History points out that the good Sisters that started St. Anslem's had no money but managed to give compassionate care just the same. If we concentrate on money as essential to mission we are distorting the mission. That is very wrong!"

Dr. Folley was at a disadvantage and struggled to recover. "Excuse me, Bishop. I meant to explain that we are obligated to care for the wealth that supports the Ministry just as we are obligated to care for the Ministry. That's our stewardship. You cannot have one without the other. The Church requires funds to function. Am I right, Your Eminence?"

Cardinal McMahon was not ready to get into the conversation. Carefully, he fielded the question. "Money is one important factor, Doctor. Another that requires judicious use is time and I am about out of both. Could we come to the point of this discussion? I have to get back to the Chancery."

Folley realized that he was about to lose the moment if he did not press the point. "Yes, Your Eminence. We have the opportunity to expand our ministry by incorporating the doctors with the hospital in a mega corporation. The doctors would become very real partners in the Ministry just as the Church would become associated with the professional in the provision of care. What is needed to bring that about is the assignment of the hospital's fiscal reserves to this endeavor. Otherwise, the funds become dormant and eventually erode as the Ministry evolves to a proprietary system. This is our chance to establish a Catholic network of health services. I wish to request that the Church through His Eminence's authority give permission to advance this system. The hospital Board has given their support."

The Cardinal felt the pressure and tried to move to a controlled position. "Doctor Folley, I pray that you will understand if I don't give you carte blanche to spend the hospital's funds on a venture with which I am not familiar. Your point is nevertheless well made that we need to invest in the future. How much money is required to initiate this corporate relationship with the physicians?"

Folley was pressed to respond. He wanted the whole investment portfolio of sixty-five million dollars. Less than that would signal that the Cardinal was hedging. "Your Eminence, I would like to be conservative but as you mentioned earlier, time is of the essence. We need to make the change as soon as possible in order to squeeze through a small window of opportunity. The major teaching hospitals downtown have already set up their physician organizations. They are rapidly increasing market share. One or two major proprietary chains have purchased hospitals in the suburbs and are now acquiring physician practices. These are Practices that used to refer to St. Anslem's. We need to commit no less than fifty million to the project. It would be better to have sixty-five. Look at this way. We simply change St. Anslem's corporation from a Hospital to a Medical Services Organization. The doctors provide some capital as well and become of the corporation. The hospital remains but subordinate to the MSO. The same Hospital Board plus an equal of physicians form the new corporation and under the Ethical and religious Guidelines and Canon Law conduct healthcare in its wider scope. The funds remain under the control of the Church but are spent as appropriate in the new and expanded venture. From your position, fiscally nothing changes, except the capacity of the Ministry to serve experiences a dramatic increase."

Bishop Hanks was visibly upset with the idea of placing millions of Church dollars at the disposal of the terrific trinity and especially, Dr. Folley. He pleaded with the Cardinal to deny the proposition. When it appeared that the Cardinal was leaning favorably toward Folley's idea, Hanks became desperate. He again sounded the need for the Cardinal to attend to the Parish ministry and forego the healing ministry's avarice demands. Hanks contended that the true ministry was with the people in need and they were best served by the parish priest.

"If need be," pleaded Bishop Hanks, "it would be best to sell the hospital to the doctors and use the money to educate religious and the laity in other forms of ministry that would reach the poor and underserved. Your Eminence, again I ask that you put all available priests into parishes. We are not intended to be in the big business of medical Services. Our mission is to serve and to care for the people of God. Dr. Folley is a business man. He should get his capital from the bank, not the Church."

Cardinal McMahon listened attentively to Bishop Hank's disjointed arguments. He was grateful for the intense loyalty that the Bishop exhibited in defending the Parish Ministry but was upset with the embarrassing manner that the Bishop used to make his point. The Cardinal felt he was being publicly scolded by his Vicar. The two men debated the relative merits of the Church's various ministries at length while Dr. Folley sat behind his desk and fidgeted.

After an hour and a half of very broad reaching discussion, The Cardinal accepted Folley's point but wanted to reserve some control as required by Canon Law. "Dr. Folley, as long as the funds are not removed from the control of the Church and as long as those funds remain within the control of the Board that I appoint then I can go along your suggestion for reorganization. Who is going to direct this new corporation?"

Folley sensed victory and eagerly moved to demonstrate confidence. "We have a management structure already in place, Your Eminence. I will serve as the Chief Executive consistent with my position as Secretary of Health Affairs for the Archdiocese. Mr. Logan will be my Vice President. We will hire a physician to deal with practice acquisition. Management of payer contracts will at first be administered by a consulting company, Park Medical, and we will have the benefit of corporate consultation provided to me by Mr. Tom Callahan associated with the consulting company of Debur and Tandy. Everything is ready for your approval. Mr. Callahan and Mr. Logan are here if you would like to talk to them about any of this."

The Cardinal waved his hand as a gesture of surrender more than approval.

"Bishop Hanks, it seems that what is being proposed is a not so much a new structure as a revised structure of our existing Hospital corporation. The funds simply transfer with the adjustments but remain very much under Church control. I have no reason to object. You, of course, will remain a part of the new structure as my personal representative just as you are at the hospital. I have no time now to meet Mr. Callahan. How is Mr. Logan after his ordeal? I am very grateful, Doctor, for the way in which you handled the whole affair."

The Cardinal didn't wait for an answer to his question about Logan. He stood to leave. Folley had won a qualified victory. The organization was approved but the spending remained under the control of the Board and the Terrific Trinity. Kevin Hardly was in another world most of the time. Thomas O'Shea was near death. Charles Patello was alive and well. Unknown to the Cardinal, Bishop Hanks, or Dr. Folley, Mr. Charles Patello was the big winner and he hadn't even attended the meeting or was even aware that it was happening.

Cardinal McMahon walked back to the lobby with Bishop Hanks where they met the Master of Ceremonies. The car was brought to the entrance. The Cardinal blessed the receptionists, got into the car, and returned to the Chancery. Back in the Medical Intensive Care Unit the residents, for the rest of the day, greeted each other with a wave simulating the sign of the Cross. The nurses generally ignored their childish and irreverent prank. Otherwise, Mr. O'Shea and the Sailor continued to rest comfortably.

Joe Durant had not followed the Cardinal around the hospital. He felt the Holy Man's rebuke when he was admonished for not painting the signs. He took that as a notice to get lost. Consequently, Joe returned to his office to resume a normal schedule such as it was. The letter from O'Shea and Patello demanding Weaver's dismissal was the item for the day. Weaver was sitting across from Durant getting informed about the missal from on high when Durant's executive assistant interrupted to advise Joe that the Cardinal was about to leave. Joe thanked her tor the information and resumed his conversation with Weaver.

"Rod, the Board in the persons of O'Shea and Patello have demanded that I ask for your resignation. Apparently, they are upset over your attitude. I don't agree but they don't give me a voice in these things obviously."

Weaver appeared angry but he wanted to plead for some consideration. "Joe, you know that I need to keep my job. I've got two kids in college and one in high school. Hell, I can't afford to be on welfare. Do they offer any kind of settlement?"

"They don't mention that, Rod. Actually, they want me to terminate you which suggests that you would be fired without benefits. I think that sucks. I can probably work something out that would go unnoticed by them. O'Shea won't be active for a while if ever. He's a sick cookie. "

"That leaves Patello," commented Weaver. "He can get Hardly to back his play whenever he wants. Can I talk to Patello and try to work something out?"

Durant shook his head from side to side. "Look, Rod, there is an option that I want to consider first. Let's keep this thing on hold for a while. O'Shea isn't going to make any waves in his present condition. Folley might get on our case but he's pretty much involved sticking his head up the Cardinal's ass for the money to conduct the Physician Organization. If you stay out of sight and keep your mouth shut for a while I'll see if I can come up with something that will be suitable. Okay?"

Weaver was uncomfortable leaving his fate entirely in the hands of Joe Durant who was a marked man as well. Reluctantly, he agreed to put it on hold but he also intended to do some politicking in his own behalf as opportunity presented itself. Durant, on the other hand, was considering the option of resigning himself rather than discharging Weaver. He reasoned that he could probably expose the suspected fraud being perpetrated by Folley better than Weaver but he would be expendable in the process. Once the matter was brought to the surface the Board would be hard pressed to discharge Weaver for attempting to protect the hospital's assets.

At this point Durant was completely unaware that the Cardinal had given Folley tacit approval to create the Medical Services Organization that effectively subordinated closed his door and began to carefully pen a proposal to the Board of Directors of St. Anslem's Hospital. Durant simply proposed that his position as the Chief Executive Officer of St. Anslem's Hospital be eliminated. The Executive Director of the MSO, if there was to be one, could administer both organizations. Furthermore, according to Durant, the administrative staff of both organizations could be integrated thus minimizing expense and avoiding duplication and conflict in decision making. He pointed out that the finance function would require stability during the transition and, therefore, Mr. Weaver should be retained as the corporate fiscal officer of the holding company. He also suggested that Mitch Daly would be an excellent strategic planner.

In consideration for his willing and cooperative attitude toward the formation of the MSO, Durant asked for a severance agreement that provided him income and benefits for four years until his normal retirement age of sixty-five. He read the draft several times and when comfortable with the content he asked his executive secretary to type the letter that was addressed to Charles Patello with a copy to Thomas O'Shea and Bishop Hanks. When the letter was prepared he signed it and sent it on its way.

The Great Doctor Richard Folley sat at his desk in a massive quandary. He had the permission to proceed with the Medical Services Organization but he wasn't sure that he had established himself in full authority. The Cardinal seemed to place Bishop Hanks in a blocking position to Folley having absolute authority. The question concerning Joe Durant also remained. Folley wanted to get the authority to can the whole administrative staff. He intended to use the waste management project as a club to subdue Durant. Now the Cardinal had adopted it as a personal project and had actually directed its completion under Durant. That caused Folley to look for another item to clobber Durant. The telephone system was the only object left but it had been exonerated by that bumpkin, Jay Whatshisface, who excused the nurse and in the process excused the telephone system. It was all that Folley had at the moment until something else came along. He decided to go after Durant's professional demise based on his decision to buy a new telephone system.

Rod Weaver returned to his office and thought about his conversation with Joe Durant. Durant was going to get his sooner or later. Weaver knew that and he needed to find a new protector. Folley was definitely the person with power. If he could ally with Folley then he would be protected when Durant was rousted. Weaver had at hand the club that Folley could use to get Durant. The Internal Auditor had reported on excessive food purchases that had been authorized by Durant for distribution to an outside source. The auditor at first thought that Durant was supporting a catering service but when excessive cash disbursements to a soup kitchen named The Little Portion surfaced on the ledger a connection was made and brought to the attention of the Vice President for Finance. Weaver remembered that this was the reason that Sr. Celest was discharged. It could also be the basis for the discharge of Durant. What Weaver was unsure of was how he could use this information to save himself. He thought about it for several hours and then came to a conclusion that it was every man for himself. He picked up the phone and called Dr. Folley for an appointment.

The last thing Folley needed at the moment was a face to face meeting with Rod Weaver who he held in about the same amount of contempt as Durant. When Weaver mentioned that he had information about some fiscal discrepancies of administration, Folley immediately found time for Weaver. The hospital's Chief Fiscal Officer was in Folley's office in less than a quarter of an hour. Folley greeted him with warmth and placed him in a chair looking at the Great Man as he sat in his large padded chair behind his ornate large mahogany desk.

At Folley's invitation Weaver began his explanation. "Dr. Folley, you may be aware that the Executive Committee has become increasingly focused on the fiscal condition of the hospital. This is certainly a matter of importance to you as you develop your new venture. My reaction to this activity was negative and I must admit a bit out of order. I apologize for that."

Folley didn't comment. He simply waved his hand as a signal for Weaver to continue.

Weaver picked up the signal and continued. "Doctor, my concern is for the mission of the hospital. As the hospital's Fiscal Officer, I'm obligated to protect the fiscal state of the institution. If that mission changes then I'm certainly prepared to change with it. I believe that I work for the hospital Board and directly for the hospital's Treasurer, Mr. O'Shea. My operational relationship is with the CEO but I'm required to watch the use of funds and see that any improper use is reported to the Board. The information that I bring to you is what I intended to give to Mr. O'Shea before he got sick. Since you are the Cardinal's representative I believe that I should give it to you."

Folley was warming to the conversation. He still held Weaver in contempt and was suspicious that he was about to be victimized by some plot that Durant had conceived with Weaver. He decided to give it a shot.

"Okay, Rod, get to the point. Somebody got their hand in the cookie jar?"

"To be direct, yes, Sir. Joe Durant has been spending Hospital funds in support of an activity not approved by the hospital's Board. I warned him about this but he seemed to think it was okay. He is sending food and cash to a mission down on Melina Cass Boulevard. It's the same problem that the Board had with the former President, Sister Celest. Your recall the Executive Committee requested her resignation."

Folley had been instrumental is convincing the Terrific Trinity that St. Celest should be terminated. Now he had the same opportunity to can Durant for cause. The thought was delicious.

"Rod, you are doing the hospital a great service. Let me have the information and I'll take care of it. Thanks for being so alert."

Weaver was not about to surrender the information without something in return. "Well, Doctor, I have to put it all together. The problem is that I've been given notice by Mr. Durant that the Board has requested my resignation. I've got to arrange interviews, get my resume updated, and start networking. Those things are time consuming and Mr. Durant has told me that I should concentrate on them. He essentially said that my job was to find a job. You know what I mean?"

The drift was apparent to Folley who was a master at the subtle shakedown.

Weaver was selling out on Durant and the price was a job. He decided to buy. "Rod, I understand where you are coming from. It's not easy to find a job although I've never been in that position myself. Tell you what I think we can do here. I'll explain to Mr. Hardly and Mr. Patello that you have agreed to work with the Medical Services Organization as its fiscal officer. We can satisfy their direction that you leave St. Anslem's by transferring you to the Archdiocesan Office for Health Affairs. I'll tell Michael that you are coming on Board. You can transfer out of the hospital tomorrow. When can I have the stuff on Durant?"

It was that easy. Weaver had bought a job with Durant's blood. "Uh, yeah, thanks, Doctor. I can have it for you first thing in the morning. Yeah, thanks. Do I get a contract?"

Tom Callahan was elated with the report that Dr. Folley gave about his meeting with the Cardinal and Bishop Hanks. Immediately after he left the hospital, Callahan called Tony Marone of Park Consulting in New York and advised him that he was preparing a multi-million-dollar contract for Park to do organizational planning and operational consulting for the Medical Services Organization as yet to be named. The contract would require a two-hundred-thousand-dollar payment up front and a two hundred thousand dollar retainer fee paid each quarter for a two-year period plus additional payments for administrative fees that were to be no less than two hundred and fifty thousand dollars every six months. This allowed for a million and a half dollars to be paid to Park Consulting. Target Boston Medical was now alive. Dr. Folley had agreed to the terms and would sign the contract as soon as it was prepared. Marone related the good news to Mario Capizzi who sent the word to Big Frank.

Michael Logan sat down with Rod Weaver and worked out a letter of employment. Then Weaver prepared a transfer of one million dollars from the hospital's investment fund to the Archdiocesan Office for Health Affairs account at Hardly Security and Trust. Logan informed Folley that the money was in the bank. Folley informed Callahan that the check was in the mail.

Big Frank and Mario Capizzi sat in Frank's office and took stock of the situation. The drug import and distribution business had been successfully reorganized and was back in full swing. The matter with the Sailor and half of the sting shipment remained unresolved although the Sam the Security Man had promised progress by tomorrow, Thursday. The Waste Management project was in its fourth month and was stagnate. Revenues were slightly less than expected and new business was slow in coming even with the persuasive Mr. Celi heading the marketing efforts. Target Boston Medical had moved through its organization phase and was now beginning to produce revenue in big bunches. The formation of the mega bank was over its last hurdle and was expected to be operative in the next few weeks.

Apparently, the question about its Chief Executive Officer had been worked out by Sam the Security Man. The way was now prepared for the transfer of National Associated Investors headquarters to Boston. Big Frank was ready to retire and name his nephew, Charlie Patello, as the new man in charge of NAI as well. The news was good.

All things considered the executive brains of National Associated Investors reasoned that it was the right time for a modification and expansion program in the waste management business to offset the sagging momentum. Big Frank and some of his mid-western associates had been discussing the combination of waste management with other institutional services to include environmental management, nutrition, and maintenance as a combined contract to their current contracts and new prospects. To accomplish the merger of the various companies a gradual buyout of the necessary organizations had begun. It was agreed that since the waste management companies had become the subject of concern by various States' Attorneys, they would be sold to parent organizations currently providing housekeeping and food service to institutional clients. This would bury the waste management business under the cover of the other two services and divert any open activity that could give cause for an investigation.

Big Frank had directed Mario Capizzi who in turn directed Tony Marone to inform Mark Meehan to prepare Action Waste Management for sale to a Chicago firm that operated under a national trademark as Universal Services. It was agreed that Universal Services would own twenty-five percent of Park Medical in addition to full ownership of Action. Universal Services would be owned sixty percent by National Associated Investors.

The Chicago people insisted that before the daisy chain could be linked it would be necessary that the deal with Muldoon and Celi be eliminated. Meehan agreed to give Muldoon the ax. He began a subtle method of discrediting the Union leader by secretly giving out information to other members of the Union hierarchy about Muldoon's and Celi's extraordinary income. Martin Hart, President of the Service Workers Local 936, was one of the first to receive an anonymous note about Mr. Muldoon. The contents didn't surprise him but he saw it as an opportunity to unseat Muldoon from the Presidency of the Boston Workers' Guild and gain the position for himself He selected Dave Donovan to pursue the matter through investigation.

Donovan was a Union loyalist who had no ulterior motives and truly cared about the plight of the employee. He contacted an acquaintance in the State Attorney General's Office who had the matter assigned to a research associate, Mr. Walter Wallace. Mr. Wallace began to review the background of Muldoon and the process of organization that took place at Action. This investigation brought him to the shop steward, Mr. Marquart, who he was told could best be contacted at St. Anslem's. In order to avoid suspicion Walter arranged for a Police informant, Tommy the Tout, to set Mr. Marquart up for a meeting.

Meanwhile, Meehan continued to pass out information on the QT and to set up Celi for a big fall. The Universal people were anxious to move in but for the time being the sale of Action was held as a corporate secret.

The old Jeep wouldn't start. It had been sitting in the hospital's open parking spot behind the receiving dock since early morning. When the temperature dropped after sunset the moisture in the air formed ice on the windshield. Jay had to scrape it off with his fingers having lost his ice scrapper. Then he tried to start the motor only to get a light moan and a clunk. The battery was dead. With the help of the security officer he managed to get a jumpstart. Now with the motor running, he waited for the battery to charge before turning on the lights and starting to move. He feared that the battery was shot. He couldn't afford to replace it but he had no alternative. The volt meter on the indicated that the battery was taking some charge but was definitely weak.

Jay resolved himself to the obvious. Somehow he would have to find the money out of their tight family budget to buy another battery. The engine was beginning to warm up so Jay turned on the heater before the lights. The warm air entering the car made him sleepy. He wanted to go home but he had to see

Brian and work out a plan for tomorrow. Mr. Wells would be expecting the Sailor for lunch.

Brian sat patiently at his desk waiting for Jay. He feared that Eddie might show up instead. Brian was at a loss for answers to questions that Eddie would pose for tomorrow's meeting between the Sailor and Wells. Brian was very relieved when Jay's old Jeep pulled into the parking lot outside of his office. Jay would have all the answers. He always had answers.

When Jay walked into the Patriot Dispatch Center, he looked like a man with more problems than solutions. With a dejected state, he greeted his friend. "Sorry I'm late, Brian. That fuggin' Jeep wouldn't start. Got to get me a battery. Hey, man, you been givin' any thought to what we gonna do tomorrow?"

Jay's question threw Brian into shock. He was unable to speak. All he could do was stare at Jay with his mouth wide open. Jay laughed at Brian's incapacity and then began to answer his own question.

"Yeah, look, Brian, we got to make some moves. The Sailor is still alive but barely. He's out of it. We could tell 'em that but then we get our asses kicked for not tellin' 'em that sooner. Besides I don't like that Wells guy much and Eddie is a real prick. What we got to do is stick it to 'em. I got an idea how we goin' to do that but I better keep it to myself in case you and Eddie get tangled up. You dig?"

Brian was disappointed that Jay was not going to include him. "Jay, hey, I got to know what's comin' down. It ain't gonna do if Eddie comes by and asks questions. He'll kick my ass. You gotta tell me somethin', man. What can I say?"

Jay waved his hand in the air as a sign of agreement. "Okay, man. If Eddie asks you tell him that the Sailor ain't gonna show. You tell him that somebody's gonna call the Shanty tomorrow with a message about the stash. It will be a message for Wells."

"That's it!" Brian was blown away. "Shit, man, I ain't about to tell Eddie that. Eddie will stomp me into dust. A goddamn telephone call won't keep us alive, man. Wells will feed us to the fish before the sun sets. You got to do better, Jay. Christ!"

Jay seemed to regain his confidence. He became boastful about his plan to destroy Eddie. "Yeah! You think I'm gonna let that slime ball get me? No way, man. I'm gonna dust his ass. You want some protection? Okay! I'll cut you in on the action but you gotta stick to the plan. You can't let Eddie scare you off. Okay? We gotta do this for the Sailor. Let's go down to the Troubadour tonight. O'Sullivan has got to be a part of this or we are in deep shit."

Brian agreed to pick Jay up at his house around nine. They knew that O'-Sullivan usually arrived at the Troubadour between nine and ten. They planned to arrive around nine-thirty. Jay intended to have the three of them plot the next day's activity at the same table in the dark corner where he first convinced O'Sullivan to make the bank delivery to Wells. Jay waited for Brian to close the dispatcher's office for fear that Eddie would suddenly appear. When the office was dark the two men went their separate ways. Brian rushed home to Louise and ate a very fast dinner. Afterwards the two departed for the shopping mall where he intended to hide out from Eddie. Jay luckily got the Jeep to start and drove to Waltham for a relaxed meal with Susan, Benny and James. After dinner, he helped the kids with homework and waited for Brian to arrive.

Brian arrived at Jay's in his old pickup truck at a few minutes after nine. They drove downtown and arrived at the Troubadour Lounge twenty minutes later. The place was crowded. All of the tables were occupied including the one where Jay had expected to meet with O'Sullivan. To make matters worse, O'Sullivan was not in his usual booth with his usual friends.

Brian looked at Jay half in fear and half in doubt. "Christ, Jay, there's no room in this joint and O'Sullivan ain't around. What we gonna do now? You said that O'Sullivan had the plan."

"Cool it, Brian." Jay was slightly irritated at the fears exhibited by his buddy. "What I said was that O'Sullivan was the key. I got the plan. You go on over to the three ferries in the booth where O'Sullivan hangs out and ask them if he's gonna show. Hell, they probably think you bringin' some snuff. Go on over and see."

Brian accepted Jay's direction. The three people in the booth welcomed him. Jay sat at the bar and watched as Brian exchanged high-fives while engaging in animated discussion. The bartender tapped Jay on the arm and asked for his order. Jay unconsciously ordered a beer that the bartender promptly served with a tab for payment. Jay was concentrating on Brian and without thinking took a long draw on the beer. The bartender waited for payment. Jay didn't have a dime. He suddenly realized that he was drinking a beer and that he couldn't pay.

With a calm expression, he directed the bartender to run a tab that he hoped Brian could pay. Meanwhile, he reasoned that the beer was there and he had begun to drink it so he reasoned that it was best for him to finish it. It tasted delicious. He took another long sip and felt a sudden jerk on his arm.

"I thought you were off the booze, Mr. Marquart. Why don't you pay the man and get the hell out of here before you get into some serious trouble?" O'Sullivan was angry and very sober. He intended to throw Jay out of the bar.

Jay was shocked at O'Sullivan's attitude and very obvious anger. Typically, he tried to create a friendly response. "Hey, Sully, good to see you, man. I was just sipping a beer that was put here by mistake. I ain't gonna have no more. You're the reason I'm here. Yeah, me and Brian, he's over at the booth, we got to talk to you. You know about the drop and the thing at the bank and all. You got some time? We need to get to a place where we can be private. How you doin'?"

O'Sullivan was being very official. "Jay, my time is available to you only in my capacity as an officer of the law. If you have something to tell me then you need to know that I will regard it as information that may lead to an arrest of a person or persons engaged in an unlawful activity."

"Yeah, right, Sully," Jay reacted. "This joint ain't no police station. I suppose you hang out here in an official capacity and those gentlemen in that booth are a trio of undercover fags. What is this shit, man? You gettin' a little bitchy, bro."

O'Sullivan was not about to take any of Jay's smart mouth. "Jay, I made a drop for you the other day and got nothing. I mean nothing that would be of any help. You claim that the guy who took the drop is going to make a pickup of the shipment that was supposed to be in the arrest that the sea scouts made. Well, this time you produce or you are going downtown for trafficking. Am I making myself understood? Don't bother giving me any of that stuff about you and Mr. Wallace. Wally and I had a conversation earlier today about another matter. He claimed he didn't know you."

Jay was disturbed that Wally and Officer O'Sullivan had apparently discussed his wellbeing. Nevertheless, he tried another con. "Shit, Sully, no way is Wally gonna tell you about what me and him got goin'. Okay, you want to get some real stuff. Well, that's why I'm here, man. Me and Brian over there with your buddies, we got to talk and we got to talk now. How about we go out to your car? Hey, can you pay the tab here? I'm a little short."

O'Sullivan nodded to the bartender and threw three dollars on the bar. The bartender glared at Jay but accepted the payment. Jay didn't notice. He was busy giving Brian the "hi" sign. Brian caught the signal and moved away from the booth toward Jay. He recognized O'Sullivan next to Jay and quickened his pace. When Brian came close Jay slipped off the barstool and proceeded to the door followed by O'Sullivan.

Outside Jay stopped and let O'Sullivan lead them to his unmarked police car. O'Sullivan slipped behind the wheel. Jay sat in the right front and Brian in the rear. Being in a police car bothered Brian.

Jay tried not to let it affect him but he had to comment. "Wow, Sully, you got the company car tonight. That's cool. Can I take it for a spin with lights and siren? Always wanted to do that. How come you driven this?"

"Because I'm on duty, Marquart." O'Sullivan maintained an official attitude. "I told the boss that I had a lead on some cocaine coming in so he gave me a car, extra time, and a back-up. Now I'm ready to do business. What have you got? Remember, I need a bust and you either give it to me or you go down. What's it going to be?"

The remark threw Jay off guard. His recovery was clumsy. "Yeah, well, look, Sully. I need to ask you a few questions so I know how to set this up. If you saw a guy give Wells some stuff what would you do? I mean like if I set him up with the stuff do you got to arrest me?"

"Sure, Jay. We arrest both the buyer and seller." Sully gave no quarter.

Jay remained calm. "Okay. So, suppose you get the stuff and give it to Wells. Then all you do is arrest him. Right?"

"No good, Jay. That's entrapment. His lawyer would beat the hell out of us. Do you have the shipment?"

O'Sullivan began to zero in and Jay tried desperately to avoid being tied to an answer, "No way, man. I'm just trying to figure out how to advise a friend who says that he knows a guy who might want to unload. You know. What I think we can do is this. Tomorrow I'll arrange for Wells to get the stuff. When we find out where and when, we tip you off so you can make the bust. You got to keep us out of it. Okay?"

"Jay, if you are there when the bust goes down, you go with it. I can't make any exceptions. Their lawyer would have a field day with that. Remember, we have to make it stick. Wells has to have it in his possession. How are you going to arrange it?"

Jay gave his assurance. "Can't tell you that, Sully. Here's what we'll do. Brian here will give you a call with the info when things are set. You got a mobile and so does he. So give him your number. I guess it will go down sometime tomorrow afternoon. Can you make a bust outside the City or does it have to happen in town?"

"I can do it out of town, Jay, but procedure requires that I have assistance and a backup from the local jurisdiction. It would be better for me if it can happen in the City. I might add that it would be better for you too if you get my drift."

Jay nodded. The conversation was over. O'Sullivan was primed and ready. Now all Jay needed to do was arrange for the cocaine in Joe Durant's boat to somehow get to Wells without getting Brian or himself involved. Brian was also aware that only part of the plan had been arranged. As he drove Jay home he asked him about the next important moves. Jay tried to answer Brian's questions in a reassuring way but his vague responses were demoralizing. By the time they arrived at Jay's house Brian was a nervous wreck. He was afraid to go home so Jay let him sleep on the living room couch. Susan found him there in the morning.

Durant's boat, The Jubilee, sat in its berth at the Hingham Marina. It was shrink-wrapped and winterized. The cold New England winter would try to give the thirty-foot Carver a damaging impact but thanks to the efforts of the Sailor, Joe Durant's yacht sat well protected. Marina dock hands checked the boats daily and owners usually dropped by on the weekends. Some of the boats had access panels put into the Shrink wrap so the owners could periodically check the cabin and engine room. Joe Durant felt that was an unnecessary expense. Once his boat was prepared for winter he left its fate to nature and the marina staff. He didn't check on it until late March or April when the effect of a long winter gave him his usual case of cabin fever. Then he would go to the marina on Sunday afternoon, cut an access hole in the shrink wrap, and begin to putter around in the cabin. Late October was the time that he put his favorite hobby aside. The Jubilee was resting comfortably and with it rested the waterproof package of cocaine tucked securely in the engine room against the forward bulkhead.

Not resting comfortably was Joe Durant. He had a sleepless night wondering and worrying about his own career and that of Rod Weaver. His wife had realized several weeks earlier that their time in Boston was approaching an end. She tried to console Joe that it was time to leave the rat race to the rats. She continuously took advertisements from the newspapers about retirement property in Florida, Georgia, and South Carolina and put them in front of him. Joe would glance at them and occasionally place a call to a developer. He seemed to be nearly convinced. His announcement about his intent to negotiate a termination agreement signaled to his loving wife that it was time to contact an agent to sell their house. Joe couldn't focus on leaving yet. He had to settle things for Weaver, Daly, and his own reputation. When he arrived at the office on Thursday, Rod was waiting for him.

Weaver was nervous. The black circles around his red eyes, stooped shoulders, and unbuttoned collar revealed extreme tension. For the first time in their long association, Durant noticed that Rod couldn't look him in the eye. The two men exchanged a morning greeting but didn't engage in the usual conversation about family, sports, or other small talk. Instead they walked silently into Durant's office. Durant opted to sit at his round conference table and motioned Weaver to do the same. Weaver sat down and then put his head in his hands as if he was saying a silent prayer. Then he raised his head and looked at Joe. He began to speak in hushed tones as in the confessional.

"Joe, I don't know just how to explain what I've done. I hope you'll understand. I had to save my job. With the kids in school and my wife only working part time I just had to take the action to keep it together. You got to understand that if I was better situated, I would have done things differently. You understand?"

Durant realized that Weaver had sold out but he wasn't sure to whom or for what. He felt angry and sad. "Rod, I don't understand anything. What are you trying to say?"

"Joe, I'm resigning from St. A's and taking a job with the Archdiocese in the Health Services Office as the CFO. Dr. Folley gave me the job. He's my boss now and I work with Logan. I start today. I'll continue to do the finances here because Folley says that the Archdiocese is taking over the hospital's administration. You see, that's why I did it. We're finished and I guess that includes you. You understand?"

The message was becoming very clear to Durant. "Yeah. You copped out. What did you give him?"

Weaver knew that he had achieved open communication. "Okay. Your head on a silver platter. Christ, I feel like a Judas."

"Skip the biblical reference, Rod. It doesn't seem appropriate. Just how did you manage to serve me up to that scuzz?"

"It was the Mission thing, Joe. You know, that money you been sending downtown. The internal auditor spotted that and the extra food purchases. It was in her report that I have to give to the Board. They would have had you by next month anyway I thought that since you were going to get nabbed for unauthorized spending I would take the benefit of turning you in now and get something in return. If I kept my mouth shut they would have cause to can me without any termination benefits. This way I keep my professional reputation and have a job. I just had to do it. You understand? I really had no choice."

Durant understood but he didn't want to believe it. "How did Folley react when you gave him the information?"

"He doesn't have the hard copy yet. It's being prepared in final this morning. He'll get it this afternoon. My guess is that he'll try to string you up tomorrow. You ought to get ready. Maybe get yourself a good lawyer to negotiate an out."

"Yeah, right. Any other good advice?" Now Durant was angry.

"Well, if you are going to try to deal your way out, I suggest, now that you know the jig is up, you don't compound the problem by continuing to give the mission money or food. You ought to shut that down right now," Rod thought aloud.

"I guess I don't understand what difference it makes," responded Durant in question. "I gave the money to the Mission because I thought it was the right thing to do. Just because some damned money cruncher finds out about it is no reason to suddenly stop it. It was the right thing to do, Rod. Why should I stop it?"

Weaver assumed the posture of authority. "Morality isn't the issue, Joe. The issue is authority, your authority. You had the trust of the Board of Directors to safeguard the assets of this hospital. You had limits of authority that were consistent with that trust. When you overstepped your authority in making unauthorized disbursements you violated your trust. Justice has nothing to do with this. You can only try to reestablish the trust so that you can work out a deal for yourself. If you continue to spend then you are flaunting it to the Board. Then they stick it to you. I'll see that the information going to

Folley is soft so that maybe Bishop Hanks and Sister Elizabeth will back you on a severance deal. That's the least I can do."

"Sure, you do that, old buddy. Make it good and soft." Durant closed the conversation.

Jay tried to explain to Susan why Brian was spread eagled on the couch but it was obvious that he wasn't getting through. Finally he gave up and just gathered Brian up, fed him some cornflakes and coffee, and pointed him out the door. Fortunately Jay left the house with Brian because the Jeep battery was dead. Attempts to jumpstart the car failed so Brian gave Jay a lift to the hospital.

Jay telephoned Ken Ryan from the hospital and learned that a Mr. Wallace had been trying to reach him. Ryan felt that Mr. Wallace would be trying to contact him at the hospital. Ryan also told Jay there was a rumor the company was being sold or expanded. Talk was being circulated that Celi was going to resign. Everybody was nervous. As a parting comment, Ryan also mentioned that Donovan from the Union was looking for Jay. Ryan instructed Jay to come back to Action by noon and take care of several matters on his desk.

The pressure was on. Jay had to get a ride to Action, get the cocaine out of Durant's boat, and come up with a story to hand to Wells about how the stash was going to be delivered. Next he had to deliver the stash. Then he had to arrange for O'Sullivan to make the bust. He also had to figure out a way to buy a replacement battery for the Jeep, get in contact with Wally, return Donovan's call and, if that was not enough, he had a list of food items that Susan and Sister Celest had prepared for The Little Portion cookout on Saturday that he was supposed to deliver to Durant so he could arrange for the donation.

Jay's plan was to check on the Sailor first, then talk to Markley about when or if the Sailor was going to die, and then see Durant with the food list and at that time find out where Durant's boat was located. Of all the things on his list it seemed his visit to Durant was key. After he finished his call to Ryan he headed for the SACAP.

Markley was there but busy. Jay simply waved and turned to leave. Markley motioned for him to wait and excused himself from his client. Then he approached Jay and the two walked into the corridor. Markley seemed anxious to talk.

"Jay, the Sailor is expected to die in the next twenty-four hours. The MICU knows to call me when the time comes. I'll be with him. I'll call you. You'll have to come in to sign the consent to discontinue treatment. Are you okay with that?"

"Bob, I'll do it because you say it's the thing to do," Jay responded, "but I gotta tell you I ain't right with it. I mean it just don't seem right that I'm the guy who does this. This is what family is for. Right?"

Markley didn't answer. He didn't have to. Jay knew the answer. He was the Sailor's family and so was Markley. They had a definite relationship. Jay walked away and headed for Durant's office.

Durant wasn't happy to see Jay, to say the least. His reaction to the list Jay presented was near violent. He gave out with a blast of profanity that nearly made Jay blush. Then he tore up Jay's list and threw the pieces on the floor. Jay stood quietly as the hospital's chief executive officer went through his tantrum. Exhausted, Durant slumped into his chair and looked out the window.

Jay looked around the room half expecting someone else to be present. Then he tried to comment. "Mr. Durant, is this a bad time? I mean if you want me to come back later I will. You seem upset. If we asked for too much food then I'm sure that the Sister and Susan can cut it back. I mean what's buggin you, man? You don't have to get so pissed, uh, I mean upset. We can work this out. What do I have to do?"

Joe Durant turned away from the window and looked at Jay. "Mr. Marquart, due to circumstances beyond my control, St. Anslem's is no longer able to furnish food or any other support to The Little Portion. I'll call Sister Celest with this message in a few minutes. You came in to see me just after I had been informed of the necessity to discontinue our support. I regret that I cannot honor your request. Please leave me alone."

It was very obvious to Jay that Durant was under great emotional distress. His normal reflex was to care for the man in some way. How was a mystery since he was not sure of Durant's issue. He decided to try to find out. "Mr. Durant, I'll certainly leave you alone. You obviously have greater things to deal with at this time. But let me offer to help. Can I take you home or get someone to help you? You sick?"

Jay's kind offer to help moved Durant. He had not received a kind word or offer of concern from anyone at the hospital in the past few weeks. Now a contractor's representative stood before him with a hand sincerely outstretched, not to receive, but to give compassion. Durant wanted and needed a friend who he could trust and believe. Jay had demonstrated that he was trustworthy with his frankness, as crude as it was. Durant put his hands together as if he were about to pray. He seemed to be thinking about something. Then he slapped the top of his desk and gave Jay a big smile as he commented.

"Hell yes! It can be done, my friend, and you can do it even though I can't."

"Uh, do what, Sir?" Jay was taken by surprise and backed away from the desk as if he expected to be attacked.

Durant jumped up. "The food, man! You can get the food and deliver it. You'll have to steal it but what the hell, that's what they think I did. Besides Action is good at this sort of thing. So before they lock everything up you can take what you need. Yeah, only you will have to move fast. Do you have anything on your schedule this morning?"

"Yes, Sir. This is kinda a bad day." Jay was reserved. "I got to get over to our office and then I have to make some calls and I have a personal matter downtown to deal with before noon, and I don't have a car cause my battery is dead. Maybe Patriot can help. This is not a good time. Why? I don't understand that bit about the food. I got to steal it? Why? I mean how come we just don't have food service put it on the dock and we load it up like we always do?"

"Sure. Let me explain." Durant was returning to normal. "The hospital, I mean the hospital auditors, think that the food that has been going to The Little Portion is being stolen so they are going to put controls in place that prevent any more food going out. I have to order that those controls go into place immediately. Now if I delay giving that order for let's say another hour, you could collect what you need from food stores, load it into the truck and be out of here before anyone's the wiser. Do you understand? Can you remember what it is that was on your list? I'm sorry that I tore it up."

"Most of it, I guess. It was all stuff that would keep except for the steaks. We wanted a lot of beef. That might be hard to get out of the food lockers. How am I going to do that?"

Durant was exhausted. "I don't know. You are on your own. You figure it out. I'll call Sister Celest with the bad news that I have to cut her off. When are you going downtown? Do you have anything else on your mind?"

For a brief minute Jay thought he: saw an opportunity to bring up another subject that he could relate to The Little Portion food matter. He was about to speak but then thought better of it.

Durant noticed his hesitation. "Jay, you have something else. What is it?"

Jay saw his chance. "Well, Sir, there is a matter about a patient here in the MICU that I brought in from The Little Portion. He's the guy that worked on your boat. They tell me he's dying. Anyway, he told me he left something on your boat that he wants me to get for him before he dies. Some tools or something that he thinks is important. Anyway, I promised that I would get it and I think he's gonna die maybe today or tomorrow. Could you let me go on your boat and see if I can find his stuff? He said that he thinks that he left it by the engine."

Durant knew that he could not honor Jay's request yet he wanted to help. "Jay, the boat is shrink-wrapped. There's no way that you can get in. Tell you what I can do. I'll call the marina and ask them to put an access panel in the shrink-wrap. Then I'll get the tools when I check the boat over the weekend and bring them to you probably on Monday. Okay?"

Jay shook his head. "No good, Sir. The Sailor won't last that long. Can I get on the boat this afternoon after we deliver the food to The Little Portion?" Jay appeared to be pleading.

Durant felt Jay's compassion to honor the wish of a dying friend. He decided to try to help. "Look, Jay, I can't allow you to go on my boat. It's technically under the control of the marina. I'll do this. I'll call and ask them to cut open the shrink wrap, remove the tools, and hold them for me. I can drive out there this morning and pick the tools up and on my way back stop at the mission and give Sister the bad news first hand. That's better than a telephone call. You can pick up the tools at the Mission. Will that do?"

Jay felt that he was suddenly on a roll. He decided to try to parlay his advantage. "Hey, that's great, Sir. Could I ask one additional favor? You see, the Sailor, he wants to give the tools to a friend of his and he wanted me to see that they got delivered. I don't have a car and have no way of getting them where he wants them to go. Anyway, what I was wondering is if you could, on your way to the Mission, maybe drop off the tools to a guy at the North Quincy Marina? He expects the stuff, uh, I mean the tools, around noon. See, he eats lunch at a place called the Shanty. Could you take the stuff there? It would sure be nice."

"This is getting complicated, Jay." Joe had many questions. "What should I tell the marina to look for? Where is it on the boat? Who do I deliver it to and where is the Shanty? You write it out. I'll get the marina on the phone and you tell them what it is they are to find on the boat. If they can have it for me by ten-thirty I should be able to be at the North Quincy Marina by eleven. I want to see Sister Celest before noon. Okay?"

Jay simply nodded. Inside he was jumping for joy. Joe Durant immediately called his marina and asked for the dock master by name. He explained the nature of the call and seemed satisfied that the invasion of his boat could be accomplished by ten-thirty. Then he handed the telephone to Jay and directed him to tell the dock master what to look for and where to find it.

Jay tried to describe the location of the package as best he could from what little the Sailor had told him. The dock master seemed less than enthused but apparently understood that he was to look for a "package" stored in the engine room against the forward bulkhead. The dock master asked to speak to Durant and concluded the conversation about how much this favor would cost especially the repair of the shrink-wrap. Durant accepted the charge and made a mental note to put it all on his expense account since it was being done for the benefit of a patient.

Jay found the Shanty listed in the telephone book. He wrote the address on a piece of paper and gave it to Durant. He also made a note of the telephone number for his own use. He then told Durant to deliver the package to the Shanty and give it to the bartender with the instruction that it was to be given to Mr. Wells and nobody else. Jay was concerned that the bartender might give the package to Eddie instead so he repeated several times that only Wells was to be the recipient.

Durant became bored and a little irritated with Jay's admonition. "Look here, Mr. Marquart. I've got a few other things on my mind today. I'll deliver this, whatever it is, to the bartender at the Shanty as you request but after that I'm gone. I don't have the time or interest to hold the bartender's hand until he delivers it to this Mr. Wells. Please understand that this is about all I can do for you."

It was the end of the line for Jay's meeting with Durant. He had accomplished far more than he had expected. To press further could cause a reversal of his good luck. It was time to retreat. "Mr. Durant, I very much appreciate what you are doing for the Sailor. This is his dying wish. I thank God that there are people like you. Thanks for this. I'll take care of everything. It's great knowing an honest man like you. Right now, I better get busy and steal the food like you say."

The pressure was still on but Jay felt relieved nevertheless. He had the beginning. Durant was the delivery man. Now he had to make sure that the bartender at the Shanty was reliable enough to deliver the goods to Wells. He also had to tip O'Sullivan that Wells was going to receive the stuff at the Shanty around noon. There was also the matter about stealing generous amounts of foodstuffs from the hospital's pantry and meat locker before Durant issued his security watch order. This triggered the need to get transportation for his contraband from St. Anslem's to The Little Portion. Brian would have to help. Ken Ryan also expected Jay back at Action Waste Management by early afternoon. The pressure was definitely on.

Jay found an empty desk with a telephone in the Environmental Services Office. The secretary just nodded at Jay's greeting. She was accustomed to him being in the office now and accepted his presence as she did the department director. Jay was one of the diminishing family. He called Brian and explained briefly that he had things under control but needed him to help make a food run to The Little Portion. Jay promised Brian that he would explain everything in detail when they were taking the food downtown. Brian agreed to meet Jay at the loading dock in an hour. Then Jay called O'Sullivan at his home.

The policeman was eating a late breakfast before resuming his undercover assignments. O'Sullivan seemed displeased with Jay's intrusion. Jay, on the other hand, ignored O'Sullivan's grumpy greeting and went immediately into the purpose of his call.

"Sully, look, man it's coming down. This guy Wells that you made the drop to is going to get the goods around noon at the Shanty Bar at the Quincy Marina. The way it's gonna work is that the drop will be made to the bartender who will be instructed to give it to Wells. When Wells takes it from the bartender, you got your man. The bartender won't know what's in the package and the guy deliverin' it hasn't got a clue. I don't know when it's gonna get there. The bartender might already have it. Anyway, all you got to do is nab Wells with the stuff. Right?"

O'Sullivan choked down his bagel and tried to sound casual. "I got it, Jay. The Shanty in North Quincy around noon. I'll have to have the Quincy PD back up the bust. It can be arranged. This better happen or else you're the one who's going to fill my dance card. You got that?"

"Trust me, Sully. This is one you can take to the bank. No pun intended."

Next, Jay dialed the Shanty's telephone number. He let it ring for nearly a minute before a very unhappy person answered. It was still early and the bar was just being readied for the day's business. The bartender who also served as the day manager was occupied with inventory, stocks, lunch menus, and a wide variety of tasks that he was expected to accomplish without any assistance. A waitress was expected in an hour but until she arrived the bartender was required to do it all. Jay's telephone call was a major interruption and a large irritation. When Jay explained that he wanted the bartender to accept a package and deliver it to a customer, Mr. Wells, the bartender explained to Jay that he should call Federal Express and slammed down the receiver. Jay tried again. When the bartender finally answered and heard Jay's greeting he slammed the receiver after shouting a list of profanities.

Jay felt the rejection. The thought that the unhappy bartender might throw Durant and the package into the dumpster caused Jay to consider a very risky maneuver. He again called Brian and this time explained that he had arranged for the delivery but he was faced with an uncooperative bartender at the Shanty. He asked Brian to call Eddie and explain that the delivery was on its way. Jay hoped that Eddie could use his influence to convince the bartender to accept the package for Wells. Jay instructed Brian to tell Eddie that the Sailor had called and specifically directed that the goods be returned in this way.

The assignment caused Brian to break into a nervous sweat. He had called Eddie many times on business matters pertaining to the special accounts but this was very different. Eddie always inhibited Brian. Now Brian was expected to deliver a message that the Sailor had called and arranged to return the missing merchandise. If Eddie asked questions Brian was very sure that he could not give convincing answers. Jay insisted that the call had to be made immediately since the delivery process was already in motion. Brian had time to worry but he didn't have time to think. He had to act. With a shaking hand he dialed Eddie's coded cellular telephone. Eddie answered with a cordial greeting that put Brian more at ease.

Eddie listened to Brian's explanation about the Sailor's call and the delivery instructions. There was a very long pause before Brian got a response. "Brian, you tell me the Sailor ain't gonna show but the stash is gonna be at the Shanty. Who's bringin' it in, man? That asshole, Marquart, know about this? He and the Sailor got something goin'? How do we know that the package is gonna have the stuff? Tell you what. It don't make any difference. We either get the stuff or you and that asshole buddy of yours are gonna get yours. Now here it is; I see that the guy at the Shanty goes along with this. I'll call you tonight about this deal. If it goes okay then we got to talk about how we find the Sailor. I got to meet Wells for lunch so I'll know if it happens. This better be square, man."

Brian was relieved that Eddie chose not to pursue answers to his questions. Eddie's threats to Brian's life were a welcome alternative. He thanked Eddie and tried to break off the conversation. Eddie kept blasting away at Brian with a litany of injuries that he was prepared to apply to Brian and Jay. Brain would utter an occasional sound in acknowledgment. Finally, Eddie seemed to tire of the one sided conversation and abruptly hung up. Brian called Jay and informed him that Eddie was going to take care of the matter with the bartender at the Shanty. At least he thought Eddie was going to cooperate. He omitted telling Jay about Eddie's determination to render them both to scrap.

Joe Druant drove slowly along the Mass Pike and onto the south bound lanes of Interstate 93. He wondered out loud why he had agreed to make this stupid and pointless run. He answered his own question with the realization that he was motivated by the pressure of the day. Weaver had blown his mind with the announcement that he had sold out to Folley. Durant wanted to escape and the best escape he had was his boat. Even if it meant only a brief visit in the cold of winter it would relax him and give him renewed strength. Marquart had provided him with an excuse to drive to the Hingham Marina and look at his precious Jubilee resting comfortably in its berth and dressed for the ravages of winter. Yes, this trip would do him good. He turned onto Route 3 and then took the first exit through Hingham to the marina.

The Jubilee looked cold. Her canvas had been removed and the antennas had been lowered. The shrink-wrap stretched over the supporting framework made the craft look like a sea going pregnant elephant. A cut had been made in the shrink wrap tied to the swim platform where the dock hand had apparently Boarded her to search for the package that Marquart said contained tools. Durant found the scene more depressing. The uplift he had hoped for was not there. He walked away toward the marina office where he expected the package to be found.

The dock master saw him coming and when he entered presented him with a large package wrapped in mysterious waterproof packing that had been opened and resealed. The dock master assured Durant that they had not opened the package and had no knowledge of the contents except to point out that the weight and consistency of the container suggested that it contained anything but tools. He looked at Durant with a degree of suspicion that Joe ignored. A work order for the search and repair was presented for signature. Durant glanced at the paper and promptly signed it without asking price. Then he departed for North Quincy and the Shanty.

Eddie called Sam the Security Man Wells after he hung up on Brian. Wells was nursing a gigantic hang over. He listened to Eddie babble about the delivery and the connection and the Sailor and a few other things of lesser importance. Finally, he broke into Eddie's commentary to ask if there was any change to the meeting time. Eddie answered that all was still on the noon schedule. Wells hung up and went back to bed for another half-hour.

Eddie left his comfortable condo and walked to the Shanty. It was just past eleven and the waitress had arrived. The doors were opened but the kitchen was not yet ready to begin serving lunch. The waitress suggested to Eddie that he might want to come back in a half-hour. Eddie called her an uncomplimentary name and walked into the kitchen where he found the bartender talking to the short order cook. The bartender recognized Eddie and moved to the corner that Eddie beckoned him into. There Eddie explained that he needed the bartender's cooperation in accepting an incoming package. He held out a fifty-dollar bill and asked if he could pose as an assistant bartender to accept the delivery. The bartender was most willing to cooperate. Eddie found an apron, took off his suit coat, and positioned himself in back of the bar in a relatively inconspicuous spot.

At eleven-thirty customers began to arrive. The waitress took their orders and brought drink requests to Eddie who told her to get lost. She moved to the real bartender who told the waitress to stay away from Eddie. He gave her a five dollar bill to soothe her ruffled feathers.

Durant arrived as the Shanty was beginning get crowded. He elbowed his way to the bar and put the package on the counter. Eddie spotted it immediately and moved to greet Durant. Durant explained his mission and gave definite instructions that the package was to be delivered to a Mr. Wells. Eddie was very kind with his response pointing out that he was well acquainted with Mr. Wells and knew that he was due very soon. He assured Durant that the package would be delivered as requested. Durant thanked Eddie the Bartender and dropped a dollar on the bar. After Durant left, Eddie brushed the dollar on the floor and moved the package to the end of the bar where he stationed himself.

Three customers in New England Bell Telephone coveralls sat at an elevated table in the center of the dining area. One faced the bar. Another faced the door. The third watched the movement in and out of the kitchen and around the bar. Officer O'Sullivan was the one watching the bar. He saw Durant place the package on the bar and he saw Eddie accept it. He watched carefully as Eddie placed it at the end of the bar out of sight. O'Sullivan gave a slight kick to the undercover Quincy cop who watched Durant walk out. The drop had been made. It was evident to the experienced officers that they stand in the corner until Durant arrived with the package. This was definitely the mark.

The three officers were discussing how they were going to make their move and put the bust on Eddie when Wells walked into the Shanty. Wells stood just inside the door and surveyed the crowd. Eddie saw him and gave the "hi" sign followed by the okay signal. Wells nodded and proceeded to the bar when he noticed the three bell telephone men. In the middle chair was a very familiar face. O'Sullivan made eye contact with Wells. The two men stared at each other for what seemed to O'Sullivan to be an eternity. Wells gave a slight nod in the direction of O'Sullivan and moved to where Eddie was standing. O'Sullivan was not certain if his cover had been blown. He could not explain to the other officers that he had met Wells on another drop that he had made. He would be compromised and even implicated. It was too late to back away. The drop had been made and his colleagues expected to make the bust. The only thing to do was to follow through.

Sam the Security Man Wells was impressed by the Sailor's methods. The first pass to Eddie was very clean. Eddie had the goods so Wells reasoned that the three jerks in telephone suits were the muscle that the Sailor had sent to back up the deal and to cover the second pass to him. In Wells' mind, the Sailor was one cool dude. He knew how to make a pass and he was obviously going to be a force to be reckoned with in the future. Wells reasoned that this whole affair was a very clever and subtle message sent by the Sailor for Wells to take back to New York when he returned the goods. The nod that Wells had given to O'Sullivan was a simple acknowledgment that the message had been received. No more needed to be done or said. He simply had to take the shipment and depart. The Sailor's disciples could be expected to give him escort but he knewthat they would not attempt to recover the shipment. That would be a violation of their professional ethics. Wells would leave the Shanty, get in his car, and drive post haste to New York. Mission completed.

The Police team wanted to grab Eddie before he ran for the side door. O'Sullivan held them back. In hushed tones he explained that he thought the guy in the tailored blue suit was going to take the shipment. He counseled his colleagues that the bartender was not involved in the pass although his actions betrayed that fact Eddie looked more like a goon than a bartender. The Quincy cop was not convinced. He told O'Sullivan that the delivery man was not a professional in drug trafficking since his methods were clumsy and very evident. They decided not to signal any pursuit of the delivery man.

Durant was in the clear and now driving toward The Little Portion. Eddie, on the other hand, seemed to be very much a part of the delivery process. He was dressed like a bartender but in the time that O'Sullivan had been observing him, Eddie had done nothing. The Quincy cop was going to make his move on Eddie. Fortunately, Eddie handed the shipment to Wells just as the Quincy cop got off the stool. Wells took the shipment and walked rapidly to the door. O'Sullivan moved just as fast. The two collided in the parking lot where O'-Sullivan made the arrest and confiscated the shipment.

Wells was in the bag. No one in the Shanty was aware of what happened except Eddie who saw the three telephone men rush out the door and grab Wells. Eddie knew that the Sailor had delivered, "just like that asshole, Marquart, said he would."

Jay could only hope for the best. The entire matter was now out of his control. He was depending on Brian to make the arrangement with Eddie and he had to hope that O'Sullivan would be there to make the bust. Jay just had to wait for the results. In the meantime, he had to do as Durant had suggested and steal all the food from the hospital that he could carry before the new security rules went into effect. Time was short. He had to have his contraband on the loading dock in less than an hour when Brian was expected to arrive with a truck that they would use to haul the loot to The Little Portion.

To begin his caper, Jay went to the laundry storage area and borrowed a food service white uniform. Then he walked into the kitchen where he found a large food cart. In the back of the food preparation area were three large refrigerated food lockers that held the hospital's meat supply. Jay opened the door to the first locker and removed all the pre-cut portioned steaks that he could carry. Then he pushed the cart to the next locker and removed trays of hamburgers. In the third locker he found frozen food. Bags of French fires, mixed vegetables, and frozen desserts were piled high on the cart. Then he pushed the cart into the locker in order to keep things fresh until he found another cart to load with staples from the large pantry at the other end of the food preparation room.

A large cart was not available in the kitchen so Jay went back to the main hospital store room and borrowed an electric cargo handler complete with pallet. He maneuvered the clumsy equipment into the kitchen where he raided the pantry. Several employees in the kitchen watched him remove the food but no one questioned him. Fortunately, the supervisors were attending an in-service training session so no one was available to challenge his requisitions. He then piloted the cargo handler to the loading dock where he parked it in anticipation of Brian's arrival. He asked a security guard to watch the pallet while he went back to the lockers for his collection of refrigerated items. He returned with the over loaded cart in fifteen minutes. Brian arrived five minutes after that and they proceeded to load the Patriot van. The hospital security guard helped.

The Little Portion was crowded with the noon diners. Sister Celest moved from one serving station to another giving direction and assistance to her guests and clients that she had enlisted to serve. Things were going smoothly until Joe Durant arrived and asked her for a moment to discuss an important matter. The Sister, usually a very strong person with excellent emotional control, was reduced to tears as Joe explained that the hospital was no longer going to be her source of support. She replied that she had some support from other organizations but it was only a small amount compared to what the hospital had been providing. She was certain that the Mission would be forced to close.

Durant could only shake his head and hold her trembling hand. They were sitting at a table staring out the front window when the Patriot van parked in front of the fire plug by the front door. Jay popped through the door carrying a large case of bread and buns. Brian followed. It took the two men nearly an hour to empty the truck and store all the items borrowed from the hospital. Durant offered to help but Jay, acting as his lawyer, suggested that he should not be involved since he was the person thought responsible to safeguard the hospital's property.

Sister Celest didn't fully understand what was going on but accepted the donation without any question. Although she constantly asked questions during the time that the van was being unloaded, no explanation was forthcoming from either party. When the process was complete Jay gave the Sister a hug and announced that he thought that they were ready for the Saturday afternoon cookout. Sister wiped back her tears and agreed.

The three men excused themselves from Sister and went to a corner table in the dining room where they huddled. Jay was anxious to hear from both Brian and Durant about their respective encounters with the passing of the stash. Brian reported how he had convinced Eddie to convince the bartender to cooperate with the pass. Joe didn't know who Eddie was and seemed irritated that the two were obviously not letting him in on the full story but concluded in his own mind that he was probably better off not knowing what this whole matter was really about. He then described to Jay how the marina people had found the box and brought it to the office. He mentioned that the box had been opened and the people at the marina felt that the content was something other than tools.

Jay did not comment. Brian just looked at the ceiling and remained silent. Joe continued to report that he delivered the box to a bartender who he thought was rather rude. After that he left and drove to The Little Portion. End of story. Joe Durant left the two sitting at the table. He gave Sister Celest a parting hug and drove back to St. Anslem's.

Neither Jay nor Brian wanted to call Eddie to see if the bust had gone down. Jay thought about giving O'Sullivan a call but was worried that if it didn't happen O'Sullivan would be looking for him. Jay decided that it was best to wait it out and see if anything turned up on the evening news. Brian drove Jay to Action Waste Management. He offered to pick him up at five-thirty and drive him home where they could watch the six o'clock news. Jay accepted the offer, gave Brian a reassuring pat on the shoulder and went back to work.

The mood of the employees at Action was beginning to get depressed. Rumors about the sale of the company had been circulating since early morning when the waste handling personnel arrived and found people inspecting their vehicles, reviewing records, and checking inventories. Meehan was in his office meeting with strangers. His secretary moved in and out of his office with files but would say nothing to other members of the clerical staff. Management staff had expected a meeting to be called but so far nothing had been scheduled.

Jay checked in with Ken Ryan who could only fill him in on the rumors. Together they went to Jay's desk where various messages and memos were piled. Ken and Jay reviewed each one and decided on appropriate replies. Then Jay sat at his keyboard and typed out the messages on his word processor. In two hours, he had cleared the desk. Now it was time to answer phone calls. On top of the list was Dave Donovan.

Donovan was pleased to receive Jay's call. "You must be a very busy man, Mr. Marquart. I've been expecting your call for some time. Are you alone? Can you talk without others hearing?"

"Sure, Donovan. I been pretty occupied the last couple days. Sorry about not getting back to you. What's up?"

Donovan picked up that Jay did not comment..

"Mr. Donovan, I'm willing to help you any way that I can. Please understand that I won't do anything that might be considered illegal. I have my own reputation to be concerned about and I don't want to be involved in any improper activities."

"Of course, Jay." Donovan was reassuring. "This isn't illegal. In fact, what we are doing is helping the law. Your reputation can only be enhanced by doing this. Now, when you meet with Mr. Wallace this Sunday you tell him when he asks that Mr. Muldoon owns a Condo in Fort Meyers and another in New Hampshire. You will have the addresses and collateral information for him in a couple of days. Also tell him that Mr. Celi is employed by the Workers Guild as a special assistant to Mr. Muldoon. We have pay records to substantiate that. Have you got that?"

"Hey, Donovan, I thought Celi worked for Action. He work for the Guild too? Man, that's crazy."

"Jay, that's enough for now. I'll call you again with more. Don't mention this to anybody. Especially don't say anything to your boss or Meehan. You got that?"

The plot was beginning to thicken. The Union was setting Muldoon up for a fall.

Celi seemed to be a target as well. Jay realized that he was just as Wally had said, "A messenger boy." That was okay with him. He had no stake in the Union thing. He had to be more concerned about what might happen if the company was sold. He began to get the jitters. Anxiety was contagious.

Brian picked Jay up at five-thirty and, as planned, they drove to Jay's house to watch the six o'clock news. Susan's concern was that Brian was going to spend the night but Jay put her fears to rest. He cleared the living room by sending the kids down to the basement to play. Then he switched to Channel Seven. The lead story centered on a drive by shooting in Dorchester, followed by a series of muggings in Chelsea, and a fire in Maulden. After a commercial the Anchor reported that the Quincy Police operating in conjunction with the Narcotics Division of the Boston Police Department had made an arrest of a suspected drug supplier at a marina in North Quincy. More details would be reported soon.

Chapter Twenty-three

Death is a natural thing. Nevertheless, when a patient dies it is difficult for the care givers to accept the loss. Physicians, nurses, technicians, and hospital staff all unite in a constant effort to heal the person and prevent suffering and death. They know full well that death is inevitable. Still they use all the knowledge, skill, and resources available to them to forestall it. They are generally saddened but sometime thankful that the patient no longer suffers. The most difficult patient death for the medical professional to accept is the sudden unexpected crash that occurs often without warning when a patient is seemingly making good progress toward recovery. By comparison the patient who has no chance of recovery is made comfortable, kept free of pain, and watched over until the moment of death. Even then the staff responds to ensure that life is given every chance to continue. Orders to "Do not resuscitate" or to "not use heroic means" are reluctantly obeyed by professionals. They give support to the spouse, children, relatives, or appointed guardians who, with the physician's counsel, decide in the patient's behalf that only so much could be done. It is inevitable. Death is a natural thing.

The Medical Intensive Care Unit of St. Anslem's Hospital was occupied by patients on the brink. Death occurred frequently but the staff took pride in the high percentage of "saves" that they produced in responding to the life-threatening crisis experienced by many of the patients entrusted to their care. That was what the Intensive Care Unit staff was trained to do. Many times, they seemed to produce a miracle. That was their trademark. They were expected to perform miracles.

This was one Friday when they fell short of the mark. Cecile O'Sullivan, RN had just returned from taking report at the beginning of the seven A.M. shift. She was assigned as a special care nurse for one on one care to VIP Thomas O'Shea. Mr. O'Shea's vital signs had been steady and improved over the night. He seemed to respond to touch. The doctors were optimistic. Dr. Anderson had been encouraging to Mrs. O'Shea the prior evening. Otherwise, the patient was reported to be resting comfortably.

Cecile began a routine check of Mr. O'Shea as she entered his small room crowded with monitoring equipment. As she began her check of the vital signs flashing on the small screen the patient suddenly convulsed followed by a rapid drop in blood pressure. The monitor alarms started to sound. Cecile immediately pushed the panic button on the wall adjacent to the bed. O'Shea was experiencing a cardiac arrest. Cecile knew what was happening and actually beat the equipment in signaling the crash. Residents and nursing staff attending in the MICU rushed to assist. The hospital's crash team members from around the hospital rushed to the scene as the code was announced by the hospital's communication center.

Dr. Anderson was attending a faculty meeting of the Department of Medicine when he heard the code for the MICU. He suspected the worst and went to find Dr. Folley. Folley also heard the alarm and met Anderson in the corridor. Together they raced down stairway five to the MICU. By the time the two physicians arrived the entire response team was present and attending to Mr. O'Shea. Anderson stepped in to assist and give direction but little was required by the experienced assembly. Folley stood back and waited for the outcome. He knew that his father-in-law was receiving the very best care available. Forty-five minutes later the team cleared the code. It was no use. Thomas O'Shea had died.

Through the previous night the MICU staff had awaited the decision to discontinue the life support system that maintained Albert Saylor's biological function. They knew that he was already dead but the attending physician, Dr. Anderson, had to make the final determination. It was only a matter of time. Anderson had promised the staff that he would write the order to discontinue treatment in the morning when he made rounds in the MICU. It was expected that he would be in the Unit around eight AM after he attended the faculty meeting. Mr. Saylor had been prepared. Little else could be accomplished. Occasionally a nurse or resident checked the equipment and noted the consistent results on the chart. Albert Saylor, also known as the Sailor, was dead. His time of death was to be determined.

As requested, the Chief Resident in the MICU telephoned Bob Markley at six AM to report on the Sailor's status. Markley knew that Anderson would discontinue treatment in a couple of hours. He dressed and rushed to the hospital just to be with the Sailor during the final hours. After he arrived he gave Jay a call and informed him that the Sailor would be pronounced dead around eight o'clock. He asked Jay to come to the hospital and be available to sign the permission to discontinue treatment form as required by hospital procedure. Jay had to call Brian to give him a ride to the hospital. They were both waiting in the MICU Visitors' Lounge when the code alert was sounded. Markley was with the Sailor. He prayed for him and waited.

The excitement in the next room as hordes of people tried to rescue Thomas O'Shea was watched by Markley. He kept his vigil with the Sailor but also prayed for the other patient. He prayed for the staff who were experiencing the loss of their efforts and he prayed for the loved ones of Thomas O'Shea who would undergo the shock of grief. Markley understood death as he understood life. His own life had been difficult and filled with grief. He was now dedicated to the physical and the spiritual wellbeing of humanity. He understood and he prayed. Albert Saylor and Thomas O'Shea had died. They were at peace. They had not died alone. People who cared for them were by their side.

Dr. Anderson was unnerved by O'Shea's death. He knew that it was a strong possibility but it was unexpected. He tried to prepare himself for the eventual explanation that he would give to Mrs. O'Shea. Dr. Folley was in shock. He sat at the nurses' station and tried to assemble the words that he would use to tell his wife and mother-in-law. The hospital Chaplain and the Social Service Director were by his side waiting to assist. They knew that he was facing a very difficult task. Anderson wanted to stay with Folley and help him as best he could. Both physicians sat at the nurses' station in silence as if waiting for something to happen. Folley paged through Mr. O'Shea's medical record that was placed on the desk by the resident. It seemed that Folley was intent on finding something in the record.

Finally, a nurse supervisor asked Dr. Anderson to move away from the station so she could ask him a question. Anderson nodded and followed the nurse to a small conference room. The nurse did not sit down and Anderson realized that she intended for the conversation to be brief. In her hand was Albert Saylor's chart. She asked Dr. Anderson to write the order to discontinue treatment. Anderson nodded in the affirmative and scribbled the order.

The nurse supervisor thanked Dr. Anderson. She moved directly to the chief resident who found the attending nurse and another resident. They went to the Sailor's room and turned off the life support equipment, unplugged it, and moved it out of the room. Markley watched them leave. Then he waited for Albert Saylor to come to final rest and the nursing staff to prepare the body for removal. It would be awhile. The nurses were busy in the next room. The chief resident returned and asked Markley if he could locate Mr. Marquart so that the permission form could be completed. Markley explained that Jay was waiting in the visitors' lounge. He offered to take the form to Jay for signature. The resident was pleased to have Markley's assistance.

Jay sat silently and listened as Bob Markley explained the form and talked about the Sailor's death. He told Jay and Brian how he had been with the Sailor and had prayed for him. Jay took the form and pen from Markley and nervously wrote his name in the blank marked with an X. Brian stood and paced around the room. Tears were in his eyes. Jay watched Brian. Tears began to form in his eyes as well. He did not expect this emotion. He felt unusual. Markley saw their emotion and waited with them. Finally, Jay choked back his grief.

"Bob, what happens now? I mean who takes care of Sailor? He's got to be buried and prayed for and all that. Who does that? Do I do that? I don't know nothing about this sort of thing. What's gonna happen, man?"

Markley looked at Jay with true compassion for his emotion. "Don't worry about that, Jay. We contacted the Veteran's Administration. They are waiting for us to notify them. They will take care of all the arrangements. Sailor will be buried with full military honors at a Military Cemetery. I'll go with him and see that the spiritual matters are properly attended to. Do you want to attend the funeral? I'm sure that we can arrange that."

"I don't think so, man." Jay spoke in a reverent whisper. "I haven't got wheels and it's gonna be a busy weekend with the cookout at the mission and an appointment I got on Sunday. Things are happining at work so I better not take any time off. You understand?"

"Sure, Jay, I understand." Markley was reassuring in his reply.

Jay looked at Brian and then turned back to Markley with a question. "You think it's okay if maybe I sat in the Chapel and gave Sailor some thought? It's nice and quiet in there. I can think a lot better in a place like that. It's real nice and I would like to be alone to kinda give some things some thought. You want to come along, Brian? Then maybe you can drive me over to Action."

The three men sat quietly in the visitors' lounge. Markley patiently waited for Jay and Brian to make the first move. Finally, Jay stood and motioned for Brian to follow. They shook hands with Markley. As a parting comment Jay mentioned that he knew of a person who he thought Markley could help. He stated that he would introduce Markley to his friend, O'Sullivan, next week. Then Jay and Brian took the elevator to the main floor, walked to the lobby and into the Chapel.

The Chapel was deserted and very quiet. The blond oak pews setting on dark green carpet contrasted by the off-white walls punctuated with religious art. The modem impressions of the Stations of the Cross reflected in the multi colors of a large stained-glass window behind the altar. The decor assisted the peaceful atmosphere.

Jay sat in a back pew and seemed to relax. Brian was uncomfortable. He stood at the back for a while then began to walk around. He inspected the small altar, looked into the Sanctuary, turned lights on and off, scanned the Mass books and felt the holy water. His constant movement irritated Jay who was about to calm him down when a group of people suddenly entered the Chapel. Brian seemed to run for cover as he darted into the pew with Jay. An older woman was being helped by a younger one. Both were crying. Jay recognized Dr. Folley who walked behind the women and helped them into a front pew. A Priest who was with them seemed to be giving console to the three. They knelt together and began to chant prayers that the Priest led. The older woman clutched rosary beads. Her sobs were audible to Jay and Brian.

Brian sat next to Jay but continued to be fidgety. He had to comment, "Hey, Jay, let's blow this place, man. They're gonna have a funeral or somethin'. Man, we don't belong here. This ain't a place for us. Let's go, man."

Jay gave Brian a quick elbow in the ribs. "Bullshit, Brian. Everybody can use this place. This is what it's for, man. Those people just lost someone. So did we. Okay. So now we can think about it and say what a good guy the Sailor was just like they are. We belong here, man. Just cool it for a while."

Brian seemed to reflect. "Yeah, well, the Sailor was my customer and a great guy, man. He let us use his boat and we had a blast fishing and boozin'.

Hell, that's what I remember. I don't need to cry about that. He was a great guy, man. Why they cryin'? Maybe their guy wasn't so great?"

"Get off that shit, Brian. I bet you cried when your old man croaked."

Brian looked sad. "Not really. He was never around. I cried for my mom. Maybe they lost their mom."

Jay decided to ignore Brian. He closed his eyes and tried to think about what had happened. The Sailor was dead but he and Brian were the only two outside of the hospital who knew about it. Eddie thought that the Sailor was on the lam and perhaps serving as an informer. Wells was in the slammer. Eddie also thought the Sailor was still alive and active. Both Eddie and Wells thought Jay and Brian were the Sailor's contact to the action. This put both of them in the middle as far as Wells and Eddie were concerned but actually Jay and Brian were free agents protected by the Sailor's legacy. They could walk away from the action without being threatened by Eddie because they had the Sailor who would protect them from harm. It was the perfect out. Jay decided to try to explain the opportunity to Brian.

"Brian, I been thinkin", what if we quit the deliverin' thing for Patriot? You could get another job. Eddie ain't gonna bother us as long as he thinks that the Sailor might rat on the operation. The mob, or whoever, they are gonna go nuts trying to find the Sailor. We can get out of this and go do somethin' else. What do you think?"

Brian looked confused. He was about to try to answer when Cecile walked past their pew and went to the group in the front. She gave each woman a hug and nodded to Dr. Folley. The Priest stood and watched. They chatted briefly and then Cecile seemed to join them in prayer. Then she began to leave. As she walked toward the chapel door she spotted Jay and Brian and stopped to talk.

"Jay, I want to say that I'm very sorry about the loss of your friend. He had a peaceful death. We will remember him in our prayers. It's nice to see you in here. You too, Brian."

It was the first time Brian could ever remember that Cecile talked to him in a kind voice. He didn't know how to handle it.

Jay, on the other hand, was quick to respond. "Thanks, Cecile. Me and Brian just stopped in here to collect our thoughts. Nothin' spiritual or anything like that. This is a nice place to kinda put it all together. You know what I mean. You know those people with Dr. Folley?"

"Yes, I was doing special duty for Mr. O'Shea. He died suddenly this morning about two hours ago. Very unexpected. Mr. O'Shea is Dr. Folley's father-in-law. Mrs. O'Shea and Dr. Folley's wife are here with the Chaplin. She's having a hard time. I came in to express my sympathy and say a prayer. Mr. O'Shea was on the hospital's Board. He was at the meeting that you and I attended. I don't know if you remember him. He was a top man with the bank."

Jay nodded. He remembered Thomas O'Shea not only from the Executive Committee meeting of the St. Anslem's Board but as the mark who Wells met after Cecile's junkie cop husband dropped him a package. Sully delivered the goods that Wells used to bomb O'Shea. It figured, but Jay was at a loss to know why Wells hit O'Shea. It didn't matter. He would simply tuck the facts away in his mind for future reference.

Jay offered little comment. "Yeah, Cecile. I seem to remember him. Too bad. Hey, did Sully get in on that bust yesterday. I see where the cops made a score in North Quincy. Sully get in on the action?"

Cecile straightened up to leave. "We don't discuss those things, Jay. He was very elated last night. He had to work late but from what he said I guess he was the man who made the arrest. I really worry about him getting hurt. I wish he would find another line of work. Take care, Jay, I have to get back to the Unit. Are you picking up Kristie this weekend?"

Jay nodded. "Sure. We're taking the kids with us to help out with a picnic for some poor people. Should be a blast. I'll pick her up tonight around six if I can borrow some wheels from Brian. My Jeep is on the fritz."

Suddenly Jay realized that today was Friday, his second-favorite day, and it was a "bummer."

Dr. Sutton was very mad. He stormed into Durant's office and pushed his way past the Executive Assistant. Durant had been notified that O'Shea had passed away. He was attempting to find Dr. Anderson for more information when Sutton, red faced and angry, suddenly appeared. Durant put down the phone in order to listen to Sutton who, aside from his anger, was speaking in hushed tones.

"It's illegal, Joe. He can't do this. It's not professional. I tell you he is violating the law. You have to put a stop to this."

Durant put up both hands as a signal for Dr. Sutton to slow down. "What are you babbling about, Dr. Sutton? Slow down and explain it to me. Who is breaking what law?"

Dr. Sutton stopped talking and sat down. He took a deep breath and began again.

"Folley! Folley is breaking the law and Anderson won't stop him. They have pulled all the toxicology reports off Mr. O'Shea's medical record. That's not legal. I am certain that Mr. O'Shea died of complications following an overdose and that makes it a coroner's case. I know! I followed his care every day. The man overdosed, I tell you. Folley refuses to allow an autopsy and pulled the lab records. That's illegal. You have got to stop him before the body is released to the undertaker. It's your duty as the CEO to see that the law is upheld."

Durant became angry at Sutton's insistent behavior. "I know my responsibilities, Dr. Sutton. What's the problem? Whatever complications that may have figured in Mr. O'Shea's death should have been recognized early and if necessary reported to the authorities for investigation. I can't believe that he took an overdose. This isn't necessarily a breach of justice."

Sutton just shook his head in the negative. "It is against the law. And it is based on pride. That family is too proud to admit that O'Shea may have had a problem. They are willing to break the law to cover it up. Well, my job is to recognize these things and see that they are properly reported. If someone is selling drugs illegally then the authorities need to be informed that a death had occurred. That's also true of suicide. These things are reportable by law. We could lose our license. You have to talk to Dr. Folley about this now before it's too late."

Dr. Sutton left Durant's office as abruptly as he had entered leaving Joe to ponder the matter. Joe Durant was not concerned about the issue that Sutton reported. He couldn't care less if O'Shea doped out. He intended to have a talk with Folley about the matter but in conjunction with his own problem. Sutton had given Durant the ammunition to force a deal. What Durant pondered was the timing of his conference. In all probability Folley would be unavailable until after the funeral. That meant nearly four days and by that time the issue brought to the front by Sutton would be buried with the corpse. In spite of all that had happened now was the right time for a conference with Dr. Folley. Durant picked up the telephone and speed dialed the Great One's page.

Dr. Folley was in the Chapel when he got the page. He recognized Durant's extension and moved into the Chaplains office to answer. Durant expressed his sympathy and then mentioned that there was a very important matter to discuss before he could authorize the release of Mr. O'Shea's body. Folley immediately realized he was about to be had again. First Weaver put the bite on him and now it seemed likely that Durant had an angle. Without hesitation, he agreed to meet him but insisted that Durant come to his office where he intended to put Durant on the defensive. The incriminating material provided by Mr. Weaver was at hand. His Wife and Mother in Law were in the care of others now and he felt it appropriate to attend to a few matters before rejoining them in grief.

The telephone was ringing constantly in Dr. Folley's office as news of O'Shea's death was spread throughout Boston. He directed his secretary to accept messages of sympathy and to prepare a list for return calls. She was busy doing that when Durant arrived. Folley had preceded him and was waiting in his office. The secretary simply waved Durant toward the Great One's door. Inside, Durant found Folley postured behind his large desk in a prominent state of authority. He did not offer Durant a seat. Instead he attempted to have him stand before the desk as a humble servant. Durant recognized the tactic and pulled a chair from across the room taking a very informal and relaxed tact. Folley was offended but held his status. Durant leaned forward in his chair, placed his elbows on the desk and held his head in his hands before he spoke.

"Well, Doctor, this had been a very difficult morning for you. We are all saddened at Mr. O'Shea's death. But it seems we have a problem with his medical record. Apparently, you have altered the record, removed lab reports, and refused to allow a questionable death report to be sent to the medical examiner. This, I believe, could be considered a crime. Now I don't want to make it more difficult for Mrs. O'Shea but we need to come to an understanding before I can authorize the release of the body. You understand how this works. Normally, there is no delay but when Dr. Sutton refused to approve the release then it gets bucked up to me. Dr. Sutton has given the matter to my attention. He thinks that you are doing something illegal. Are you?"

Folley's list of professional assassinations was getting very long. He realized that as long as he was knocking off the dreaded lay administration he would be supported by the medical staff. Now he was in a position of having to punish Dr. Sutton, a respected and revered member of the medical fraternity. He could blow by Durant but then he would have to face Sutton in a medical staff show down. Sutton would win if the matter was subjected to a medical and scientific review. That would be embarrassing and bad politics. He realized that the better course would be to deal with Durant and gain the release of his father-in-law's body to the undertaker. He immediately changed his attitude toward Durant.

"Joe, this has indeed been a most difficult morning. We are in shock. Dad was a wonderful person, well respected, and a leader in the Church. He would have been delighted to welcome you as a Knight of the Holy Cross. I understand that you are being inducted tomorrow. I would very much enjoy being there with you but events of this morning have changed all that. Let me congratulate you now and say how pleased I am to have you as a brother Knight. We have a wonderful comradeship under the flag of the Holy Cross. You will hear wonderful things about how we support one another in the name of the Church. You will be my brother. This matter that Dr. Sutton alludes to is unfortunate. We, Dr. Anderson and I, feel that the amount of lab tests performed were inappropriately ordered by the resident staff. They will be denied as a matter of reimbursement anyway. We have already spoken to the residents about this. They understand. So, Dr. Anderson and I felt it appropriate to remove those excessive lab reports from the record. They proved nothing. Dr. Sutton seems to want to go through a review that would be pointless and only place further grief on my family. We would be very appreciative if you would release the body."

Durant felt he had gained the advantage but he thought he better use it carefully. "Well, Dick, as you have so often reminded me, I don't have any business questioning the decisions of a physician pertaining to the care of the patient. I assure you that I have no intention of questioning the appropriateness of those lab tests. If you and Dr. Anderson say that they were inappropriate and non-conclusive then I can only accept that. But I have another physician who sees the matter differently. That puts me in the middle. My only recourse is to make an administrative decision. How I make that decision depends on the administrative facts. I'll needtime to figure this out. It's like a physician trying to interpret financial reports. The physician often seeks the advice of a fiscal expert. Sometimes the data needs careful interpretation by an expert before the physician can make a proper conclusion. The same holds true for me in trying to determine the medical importance of the lab tests. Perhaps I should seek the assistance of a medical consultant. I don't want to question your medical judgment. As a brother Knight, I'm sure you don't want to question my administrative judgment."

Folley caught the drift and offered a counter. "You make a very good point, Joe. I have some information here that suggests that a crime may have been made in the disbursement of funds and use of material from this hospital for an unauthorized purpose. That could be serious and serve to destroy the reputation of the person responsible. The Board would expect the hospital to prosecute or at least effect termination for cause. That could mean a loss of pension and other benefits. But maybe I don't really understand the situation. I should refer the matter to someone schooled and experienced in administration."

"Dick, here we are talking about crime as if we were the police. Wouldn't it be better if we just resolved these matters as gentlemen?" Durant stood up, moved behind his chair, and leaned against the back looking down at Folley.

Folley sensed that Durant's body language signaled concession. "I certainly agree, Joe. How do we go about that?

Durant pressed on. "Dick, we cannot undo what's happened. Tom O'Shea is dead." Durant moved back into the chair and pointed a finger at the Great One. "Let's let him rest in peace. I'm tired of administration. I had thought about retiring. Even wrote the Board a letter suggesting a way out for me. Did you happen to see it? I offered to retire and suggested that you could run the Archdiocese health system and St. Anslem's. It would save a bundle of money. I even suggested that Weaver work for you. I see that has already happened. Well, my thought is that when I retire you could be the CEO and then everything we talked about this morning becomes mute. That's one way of getting this done." The deal was proposed.

Folley was quick to accept. "Joe, I believe we can arrange for your retirement. We should do this now. I'll arrange for a Board meeting the day after the funeral and you can step down then with honor. We'll have an employee reception, and a medical staff party in your honor. The Board will give you a going-away bash. We'll bring in the media and have a press conference like they do when they replace the Red Sox manager. All the things that a loyal hardworking executive deserves will be done."

Durant leaned back in the chair and relaxed. "Thanks, Dick. I appreciate your kind thoughts. We need to work out a severance agreement. I think we should have our lawyers do the word smithing just in case. In the meantime, if you can get me a memo under your signature as the Secretary of Health Affairs for the Archdiocese accepting my retirement, like we said, then I can take care of authorizing the release of Mr. O'Shea's body. We ought to have this cleared up in an hour. Don't you think?"

"Sure, Joe. I'll dictate the memo now. You'll have it in less than an hour. It's nice to be able to work things out in brotherhood." Dr. Folley flashed a forced smile as Durant extended his hand to seal the deal.

Frank Patello damned the day that he decided to send Sam the Security Man Wells to Boston. It seemed that everything Wells tried to do turned into a disaster. Now the clown had managed get arrested with a package of cocaine in his possession that was originally intended as bait for the Dorchester crowd. Fortunately, the Quincy police who held Wells in custody had no idea that they had the person who could expose the entire drug traffic system for the entire East Coast. In addition, Wells was the man who made a hit on the bank executive that was attempting to shake down Portello's major money laundering program and the big bank merger. Wells had to be disciplined before he was discovered by more competent authority like the DEA.

Mario Capizzi, Tony Marone, and an army of "corporate" lawyers called in by Big Frank met through the night to devise a defense. After many hours of consultation without result the usually quiet and reserved Tony Marone suggested a plan. He proposed that Wells be given a very large raise in pay and a bonus as a sign of the confidence the company had in him and as a sign that they were going to take care of him—one way or another. He also suggested that Wells should cooperate with the Police and inform them about the drug trafficking system in the Quincy, Milton, and Dorchester area. Wells would be supplied the names of key operatives in those neighborhoods that were not part of Patello's operation. These unfortunate designates would be the beneficiary of Wells' cooperative attitude. The diversion would cause the police to center on areas away from the Patriot business.

As a consequence of being an informer, Wells would bring down a lot of small dealers doing business on street comers, high schools, and low-income neighborhoods. This is where the politicians wanted to show effort in drug enforcement. Wells would be viewed as a supplier of the small timer, be allowed to cop a plea, serve a light sentence, and be out in a couple of years, max. After his release, and as a reward for his loyalty, National Associated Investors would transfer him to Las Vegas and give him a job parking cars.

Capizzi endorsed the idea. He offered that the alternative of wasting Wells would heighten the interest of law enforcement and would also cause a decline in morale within their organization. Big Frank listened with interest and then nodded his approval. The legal defense team went into action. A local Quincy attorney who was willing to work on a cash basis as the front for the defense team was selected to defend Wells and in addition give him the information that he was to give the Quincy Police.

Wells was contacted by the Quincy attorney early Friday morning. By noon Wells was delivering a wealth of information to the Quincy, Milton, and Boston narcotic squads.

Big Frank was relieved but also reserved. He was certain that the Sailor was obviously waiting to put the squeeze on the organization. When he surfaced, Frank intended to pay him off and if possible get him to work for NA. The Sailor was the kind of man that Frank liked.

Frank also wanted to proceed with the bank merger as fast as possible before the Wells matter could blow up in his face. Once the banks were merged it was unlikely that any connection could be made that would disrupt business. However, if Wells somehow let it leak that he was connected to a prime investor in the merger then it would be delayed by the Secretary of State's office until the matter was clarified. Big Frank called his favorite nephew and urged him to proceed immediately with the merger.

Charlie Patello was very pleased that Big Frank wanted to move fast. The Secretary of State had approved the merger documents and the organization plan. Charlie Patello was now the Chairman and Chief Executive Officer of New England Trust or NET as the flashy trademark prompted. The formal announcement would be made Monday or Tuesday at a press conference following Tom O'Shea's funeral. Charlie loved the poetry.

It was a cold but sunny Saturday morning. Jay had Benny, James and Kristie out of bed and fed before Susan managed to get showered and dressed. Susan and Louise had finished Susan's stash the night before while Jay and Brian put the final touches on their plan for the cookout at the mission.

Susan had been on the telephone with Sister Celest several times on Friday. The two of them had the menu and food preparation well decided. Susan also informed Louise not to worry about the details that the men were trying to determine. Instead the two women moved to the bedroom where they inhaled some coke. Jay suspected what the girls were up to but decided to ignore it.

The kids were excited about the picnic with older people but didn't understand that it was not going to be in a park or in the backyard where picnics were supposed to be held. Jay explained several times that the people were poor and older folks that wanted to be inside when they had a meal. He suggested to the kids that they could help serve and clear tables like big people. It was to be a fun day.

Bob Markley rode in the front seat of the hearse carrying the Sailor from the undertaker to the Military Cemetery located thirty miles north of Boston on the Hamilton Military Reservation. The Veterans Administration had arranged for a brief ceremony to take place before internment.

Bob and the hospital Chaplain offered the early Mass that morning for the Sailor. The Chaplain had also administered the Rites before the body had been removed from St. Anslem's on Friday afternoon.

As the hearse maneuvered along the winding New England roads, Markley thought about the Sailor and prayed for the repose of his soul. He remembered doing the same thing twenty-five years earlier as a young navy corpsman who was awarded the Navy Cross for bravery. He returned from many sorties into the waterways of Vietnam and had to transfer wounded marines to the hospital and the dead to the care of Graves Registration. The pressure of combat and constantly attending to the wounded and dying had its effect. Markley spent his off-duty time in a drunken stupor. He smoked pot and did whatever he could to avoid going out on detail. He hated the war and he hated the bureaucracy responsible for it. He wanted to run. He got drunk on duty, screwed up, and was thrown in the brig.

The Catholic Chaplain came to his rescue and had him reassigned as a chaplain's assistant. The Chaplain became his friend and advisor. After the war

Markley followed his Chaplain friend into the ministry of healing. Often, the Chaplain came to his rescue as Markley struggled to free himself from addiction. But now Markley feared it was payback time. He was scheduled to meet with Cardinal McMahon that afternoon after he returned from taking the Sailor to his final resting place. The Cardinal had been very emphatic that Markley meet with him before the Cardinal had to conduct the installation of the newly appointed Knights of the Holy Cross.

The men and ladies to be inducted into the Knights of the Holy Cross arrived at the Sheraton Hotel at ten A.M. They registered and went to an orientation meeting where Sir Kevin Hardly, First Leading Knight of the Order of the Holy Cross, and his gracious wife, Lady Ann, greeted each one. The inductees were given instruction about the induction ceremony from the Third Leading Knight. This task was usually done by the Second Leading Knight, a position held by deceased Thomas O'Shea.

Kevin introduced the Third Leading Knight and asked for a prayer and a moment of silence for Sir Thomas. Then the Third Leading Knight explained that in ceremony the Knights processed cloaked in ceremonial capes in a column of twos to the front rows of the Cathedral. Men to be inducted into the Knights would follow carrying their ceremonial white capes over their left arms and take the pews in back of the installed Knights. Ladies of the Knights then followed in a column of twos. They wore simple black robes and a mantilla of black lace. Ladies to be inducted followed carrying their capes over their arms as well but wearing the mantilla. Mrs. Durant seemed upset with the arrangement but remained humble and subservient.

Following the orientation, the candidate Knight and Ladies listened to an inspirational speech given by a Priest from Jerusalem who explained that the purpose of the Knights was to give financial support to the Church. Pledge cards were distributed that contained an explanation on how promotion in the Knights was based on contributions. After an hour, the inductees were given a break before having to reassemble for lunch and listen to another speaker who kept them glued to their seats until it was time to Board the busses for the Cathedral and the installation ceremony.

The hearse passed through the Military cemetery gate and proceeded to the office. A military retiree in a VFW Cap greeted them. A young man behind the desk beckoned the undertaker to sign the necessary forms for internment. Markley noticed the Graves Registration title on his name tag. He felt the urge to jump back into the hearse and take the Sailor to another resting place but he realized that the military was the Sailor's home. The Sailor was home now. May he rest in peace.

The young man in Graves Registration explained that the grave site would not be prepared until Monday so the body would be held in a vault until then. The VFW would provide an honor guard at the grave site when the ceremony finally took place. He asked how many people would be attending the ceremony and who would receive the flag covering the casket. Markley explained that the Sailor had no family and that no one would be attending the ceremony. He asked the gentleman from VFW to accept the flag and place it prominently in their Hall of Honor. The gentleman gave an affirmative reply and saluted. Markley inadvertently returned the salute.

Brian's beat up pickup truck was loaded with the Jay's picnic table, benches, and the Webber grill. Jay thought it would be "cool" to set the picnic table and grill on the sidewalk in front of The Little Portion as advertisement for the event. He intended to cook hamburgers on the grill, pass them out to people passing by, and ask for donations from those who looked like they could afford one.

Louise, Susan and the kids followed the pickup in Louise's little Toyota. The convoy arrived at The Little Portion at ten-thirty. Sister Celest had already begun the food preparation. Susan and Louise joined her in the kitchen. Jay, Brian, and the kids set up the table, benches and grill. Brian pulled a radio/tape player boom box from the truck and turned it on full volume. Heavy metal music penetrated the standard noise of Melina Cass Boulevard. The games had begun. For the next five hours, The Little Portion was filled with patrons seeking nourishment. They ate hamburgers that Jay cooked and then went inside for a full meal. Portions were generous. There was no rationing. All of St. Anslem's food was being consumed by the hungry. Brian's boom box played the same tape over and over until the batteries failed. Then he brought it inside and plugged it into the electric socket. Jay followed him in since the hamburger supply needed to be replenished.

Before Brian could insert the tape the radio announced the opening kick-off of the Boston College vs. Notre Dame Game. Jay suddenly remembered that he had a twenty-dollar bet on Boston College that could produce four hundred. He noted the place on the dial where he could check the score now and then.

Brian pushed the tape player button and heavy metal music filled the dining room.

Some of the patrons left with their plates in hand to sit at the benches on the sidewalk. When Brian walked out to help Jay, Sister Celest turned the radio off, removed the tape, and put it in her apron pocket. The sudden silence was deafening.

The music in the ancient Cathedral was very loud. Trumpets combined with the large pipe organ herald the procession of exalted Knights of the Holy Cross. They processed up the center aisle in grand fashion. Arranged by rank, Kevin Hardly led the Knights down the aisle but was preceded by an altar boy carrying the cross flanked by two acolytes. Knights, serving as ushers, moved the Knights, Knight candidates, Ladies, and Lady Candidates into the proper pews. Then the noise level of the Cathedral increased as the trumpets, organ, and choir joined to announce the procession of the clergy and eventually, His Eminence, Francis Cardinal McMahon.

Joe Durant stood at his assigned place with his cape over his left arm. Mrs. Durant was somewhere in back with the other ladies obediently waiting for their men to be honored so they could be given to His service. Joe knew that his loving wife would not let him hear the end of this humiliation that she was now enduring. Joe's wife had always helped him in his career. They worked as a team. Joe often told her he could not do his work without her. They were very devoted to each other. Now he was in front wearing the pure white cape of a Knight. She was in the back adorned in black waiting to be titled a Lady. He was not going to hear the end of this. He had explained to her last night that they were almost retired. No longer did they have to tolerate the insults of Folley. Their life was theirs to enjoy beginning next Tuesday or Wednesday.

This Saturday they had to put up with the Church thing for a couple of hours. It was just a matter of business not to be taken seriously.

When the Cardinal finally arrived on the altar and took his place on the throne, Kevin Hardly moved to the lectern and announced the opening of the induction ceremonies. He welcomed all present, expressed his gratitude to Cardinal McMahon, and then proceeded to eulogize the deceased Second Knight. Thomas O'Shea. Kevin referred to O'Shea as "The Silent Knight," causing some of the Knighted wags to softly hum the Christmas Carol.

It was then that Durant realized that not everyone was taking the ceremony seriously. Miniature earphones were obvious on many and hand-held television sets were in nearly every pew. Those without equipment huddled close to those who did. The score was relayed among the faithful. Boston College was leading Notre Dame by ten points.

After several prayers, a couple of spiritual readings, and a deafening musical interlude, the inductees were led one by one to the Cardinal's throne where the Third Leading Knight read the name of the inductee, the Cardinal presented the badge of rank, gave a personal blessing, and read the Commission of Knighthood from the Pope. Then the new Knight was adorned in his ceremonial Cape and returned to his pew in time for the second half kickoff.

By the time the ladies had been through the process the game was in the fourth quarter and Boston College was clinging to a five-point lead. Notre Dame had a first down on the BC eighteen yard line when the Cardinal began his closing remarks. The Irish scored five minutes into the Cardinal's homily and held a two-point lead with slightly over a minute to play. BC had all of its time outs left and the Cardinal was coming to a conclusion. Three plays and two time-outs later, the Cardinal raised his hand to give a final blessing as the Eagles lined up for the winning field goal. "May the peace of Christ be with you," he said. The snap was high but the holder managed to get the ball down. "And also with you," cheered the faithful. The kick looked wide right but hooked to the left and split the uprights. The Cardinal raised his arms. BC had defeated top ranked Notre Dame. The recessional began with loud trumpets and the organ blaring with what sounded suspiciously like the Boston College Fight Song. The Knights hugged their brothers and gave high-fives as they walked up the aisle. Victory was theirs.

Cleaning up proved to be very difficult. The Little Portion's kitchen was filled with dirty pots, pans, utensils, and plates. The dining room was cluttered with food scrapes and spilled drinks. Benny, James, and Kristie had tired of the day and were busy fighting with one another. Several junkies had tried to steal the Webber grill and the picnic table from the sidewalk. Everyone was tired. Jay took care of the kids while Brian fought off the junkies. Susan and Louise worked with Sister Celest on the kitchen detail. When Jay had the kids settled down he attempted to pick up the trash in the dining room. To keep the kids diverted he turned on the radio to get some tunes that might calm them down. Instead he caught the last play of the game. At first, he was silent and then he erupted in a loud shout. He was four hundred dollars richer. He knew it would be Monday before he could get to Tommy the Tout for a payoff but with Tommy it was as good as money in the bank. He had hit it big.

Everyone was happy for Jay's good fortune. It seemed to give them the boost to get the work done. Two hours later the truck was loaded and the kids were packed into the Toyota. Sister Celest gave each one a hug and thanked them for what they had done for her mission. Susan promised that she would come back and help cook on weekends. Louise only nodded when Susan volunteered her as well.

A few minutes later the caravan was headed back to Waltham for their own Saturday night bash. Jay felt like celebrating. He had Brian stop at a supermarket where he bought all kinds of goodies including beer and a bottle of Jameson's. He used his charge card to pay even though it was near its limit. Come Monday Jay would pay down on a number of debts. Tonight, it was time to cut loose. He hadn't felt like this for weeks.

Twenty minutes later the merry band pulled into the driveway of the Marquart Waltham estate. They unloaded the truck and went inside. Susan and Louise prepared a spread of delectable items on the kitchen table. The kids were already into the chips and Pepsi. Jay grabbed a beer, made a large sandwich and joined Brian who was watching an SEC football game on the living room television. Brian was drinking a boilermaker. He watched Jay gulp down the beer and bite into the sandwich before he commented.

"You gonna get drunk, Jay?"

Jay was trying to relax. He didn't need to be hassled. "Fuck you, Brian. I'm havin' a beer. Okay? Get off my case, man. Who's playin'?"

Brian looked back at the television as an apology. "Sure, man. Just wanted to know. Don't get sore. It's cool. Couple of those foreign teams from down South goin' at it. Looks like a good game. You wanna watch?"

The kids romped around for a while and then went to bed without a whimper or argument. Jay and Brian watched the game and nursed beers. Brian hit the Jameson now and then and was working up a good jag. Jay was envious. He thought he could handle it and was strongly considering having a double shot. Susan and Louise were into the gin and grapefruit and feeling no pain. It was a mellow feeling. He could handle it. A few more drinks wouldn't hurt. He had been a good boy. It was time to let it loose.

The telephone rang four times before Susan realized that Jay was not about to get out of his chair to answer it. She had a little trouble finding the telephone buried under a stack of paper bags that had contained the goodies Jay had brought home. A strange voice responded to her greeting asking for "Jay Marty Quor or something like that." Susan instructed the caller in a somewhat rude manner that he had reached the residence of Jay Marquart.

"Fine," said the caller. "Put his nibs on."

Susan interrupted Jay's thought about Jack Daniels and handed him the phone.

Jay looked at her in disgust and spoke a greeting. "This is Jay Marquart. Can I help you?"

The caller seemed indignant. "Yeah, you can help. I been trying to find you for over an hour. I got a guy here who says that you can help him so he wants me to get you to come get him. You gonna do that?"

Jay was in no mood for this. "Who is this? Man, you got a problem? Who needs my help and where in the hell are you?" He looked at Susan as if she had been responsible for the call.

The caller took a deep breath in exasperation. "Look, buddy, I don't like this any more than you. I'm Tony from Tony's Tavern on Brighton Ave. We got a guy in here who wants you to come and get him. Says he needs your help. I think he does. His name is Markley or something like that. He's been buggin me to call you for a couple of hours. I'm tired of this jerk. You come and get him or I throw him out of here on his drunken ass. Okay?"

Jay was shocked. He thought for a minute before he replied. "Okay, Tony. Keep cool. Tell Markley that I'm on my way. You say you're on Brighton—where?"

Jay scribbled down the address as Tony dictated it. When he hung up he poured his beer into the kitchen sink. Then he asked Brian if he could borrow his truck for a couple of hours to take care of a sick friend. Brian handed him the keys without question. Jay gave Susan a kiss and told her that Markley needed him to help with a problem. He thought it would only be a few hours before he got back. He waved to Louise, gave Susan a peck on the cheek, and left.

Twenty minutes later Jay found Tony's Tavern but it took another fifteen minutes before he found a parking place in a dumpster loading zone.

Tony's was a one-bartender tavern that catered to the working man on his way home. The dirty large plate glass windows displayed faded gold lettering announcing Tony's. The door was recessed about three feet from the sidewalk. A varied collection of litter had been positioned by the wind so it could be tracked inside. Beyond the entrance was a few ancient round tables with hard-wood chairs. The wall opposite the long bar had three booths awkwardly spaced between wall beams. The dismal tavern thrived during the week from three to nine. On weekends, it was virtually deserted except for the hardcore drunk that kept Tony solvent and absent from his nagging wife.

Tony was an ex-minor leaguer who also ran numbers and an independent loan sharking business. He was a middle-aged heavy weight with a bulging midsection. He carried his two hundred and fifty-six pounds with some difficulty but he had the strength of a bull. Jay walked into Tony's with an attitude that he rapidly changed when he saw Tony standing behind the bar.

At the far end of the bar, away from the door, Bob Markley was slumped over, apparently sleeping. Jay walked carefully to position himself in front of Tony but in a way that Markley would not be disturbed. In a guarded whisper, he opened conversation with Tony.

"You Tony? Hi. I'm Jay Marquart. You called about Mr. Markley. Is he okay? I'm here to help."

Tony leaned across the bar and held Jay by the lapel of his jacket. "Markley is fuckin' drunk. I want you should get his ass out of here. That shouldn't be too hard to understand. He's been hangin' around here for three maybe four hours. You pay up and he's all yours."

Jay pulled away and stepped back from the bar. "What's this payin' up shit, man? I don't owe you nothin'."

Tony's face flushed at Jay's comment as he extended a clenched fist. "Markley's been runnin' a tab since he got here. He said you would pay up so you pay up. He's into me for seventy-three bucks. That's a lot of booze and he drank it all. Gimme the dough."

Jay took another step back from Tony and held up both hands. "Look, man, I ain't gonna pay you nothin'. You poured the drinks. You got the problem."

Tony pushed his bulky frame across the bar and with what resembled a round house right, renewed his grasp on Jay's jacket. "Wrong, shithead. You got the drunk here. You got the problem. Now one of you bastards is gonna come up with the dough or I start bustin' heads. What's it gonna be?"

Jay was contemplating poking the giant bartender in the eye and making a break for the door when his thoughts were interrupted by Markley who reached out and grabbed him by the arm. "Good evening, Mr. Marquart. Awfully glad you could join us. My friend, Tony, is a bit mercenary but underneath all that flab is an otherwise totally unlikeable character. Why don't you pay this Neanderthal and we can adjourn to more accommodating surroundings where the whiskey isn't watered down?"

Jay was watching Tony for fear that the large man was about to become violent. When he heard Markley's voice, he turned to respond while remaining in the clutches of Tony. "Bob, what is this shit? I can't pay this guy. Seventy-three bucks is a lot of bread and, I might add, a hell of a lot of booze. Man, you really fell out of the tree. Christ!"

Markley straightened himself up and took an indignant posture. He pushed himself off the barstool and staggered toward Jay and the attached bartender. When he was close enough, Markley put his face to Jay's.

"Mr. Marquart, I'll thank you and Dumbo here to stop using profanity and the Lord's name in vain. It's offensive and in very poor taste."

Jay pulled out of the bartender's grip and attempted to square up to Markley. "Bob, don't try that holy-holy shit on me. I got to—"

Before Jay could say another word Markley brought a haymaker from the left that caught Jay below the right eye. Jay went down like a rock and sprawled onto the dirty floor. Dazed, Jay tried to recover. He could only see the blur as Markley jumped on top of him screaming about profanity and the Lord's name. Jay felt another blow to his head and was now half unconscious. He tried to grab Markley's arms and fend off the continuing blows to his head and body. He was about to get Markley in a clinch when he felt the crushing weight of Tony pilling on top. Then everything became a blur.

Jay could hear Markley shouting and Tony the bartender cussing but he could not clear his vision. He had trouble breathing with the combined weight of Markley and the Bartender on top of him. He lost consciousness for what seemed like only a minute. Suddenly he felt himself being lifted onto a chair. He struggled to stay on the chair and to regain clear vision. The first color that he perceived was a flashing blue light that seemed to dominate the entire room. He shook his head and felt the piercing pain from the blows to his face. Gradually he began to see things better. Markley was across the room sitting on a barstool. The fat bartender was holding him with Markley's arms pinned behind his back. Another person was standing next to Jay looking down at him. Jay noticed the badge on his blue uniform. Sometime in the past minutes when Jay was struggling with regaining consciousness the party had been joined by an officer of the law,

The policeman put his face next to Jay's and offered a greeting. "You okay, son? Can we talk about this? I need to know your name and a few other things. What's your name, son?"

Jay looked at Markley who was trying to break the bartender's hold. Markley's lip was bleeding and Jay wondered if he or the bartender had landed the blow. With his eyes fixed on his friend, Jay tried to answer the policeman.

"Yeah, man, I can talk. The name is Jay Marquart and I don't have the slightest idea what happened. I think Fatso over there belted me. I'm willing to forget the whole thing. Tell him to let that guy alone."

The policeman looked at Markley held fast by the bartender and then in slight sympathy offered to explain the situation to Jay. "Well, Mr. Marquart, it seems that Fatso, as you call him, has a different point of view and he isn't willing to forget it. According to Tony, you and your friend started a brawl, busted up the place, and are trying to beat him out of a seventy-three-dollar bar tab. Now, those things will be settled in time. For now, you and your friend will have to go with us to the station. Your friend is being booked for disorderly conduct and public intoxication. I suspect vagrancy and creating a disturbance will be your end of the proceedings. So, if you can walk, we will go outside to the car where my partner and I will escort you to your next stop. You ready to go? I hope you aren't going to resist."

Jay was in no condition to resist arrest even if he wanted to. The officer politely escorted the cooperative Mr. Marquart and the combative Mr. Markley out of the tavern to the waiting police car. Markley and Jay waited while the policemen talked to one another and then seemed to discuss something with someone over their radio. When they finished Jay was placed in the back seat with one of the officers. Markley was placed up front next to the driver. Tony stood in the doorway of his tavern with a somber attitude. He didn't even wave goodbye. The ride to the police station took less than ten minutes. Markley and the driver seemed to be engaged in what Jay observed to be a friendly discussion. When they arrived at the station, Jay was told to sit at an empty desk and wait. Markley was taken into a small office where he continued to have an animated and friendly discussion with a man who seemed to be in charge.

Jay couldn't be sure what was happening. His right eye was closed and the pain in his face and upper body was intense. He thought that he might have bruised or broken ribs. At his request, he was given some aspirin and a glass of water. After a few minutes, he put his head down on the desk and fell asleep.

The Brother Knights had celebrated the occasion of the Induction with great enthusiasm. They spent the time between the Cathedral ceremony and the concluding formal banquet in the watering holes of the Sheraton Hotel talking to their new comrades and drinking toasts to the victorious Boston College Eagles. By the time of the dinner hour the assembled were well nourished, feeling no pain, and half asleep.

Following dinner, custom required the First Leading Knight to give a report of the past year, renew the commitment of the Knights, and pledge their unyielding support to the Cardinal. Kevin Hardly was experienced at this sort of thing. He read his report with great eloquence. The assembled slept quietly, except for the ladies who looked at each other and chatted in hushed tones about fashions and shopping discounts. When Kevin finished his lengthily statement about the Knights loyalty he rushed into his patronizing commentary about the Cardinal. His intent was to announce the intent of the Knights to be true to the Church's position on abortion.

Kevin's tongue was a little too thick and his mind a little to fogged for the occasion when he concluded, "And Your Eminence, you may be sure that the Knights will always respect life. We have only to remember that the fetus is alive. We were all fetus at one time. You were feces, I am feces. And the entire Order of the Holy Cross is feces."

Joe Durant and his lovely wife had had it with the overbearing ceremony. They wanted to go home and leave the Knighted ones with their noses in the lettuce. Besides, no one was listening to Hardly's speech except Joe and his wife who both heard the shocking change in words emitted by Hardly. Durant looked around the room for the reaction. He saw none. No one seemed to have heard the slip of the tongue. Durant made a quick look at the Cardinal who sat emotionless, listening to Hardly's every word. The Cardinal didn't blink. If he heard the mistake he had enough class not to react. He waited for Hardly to finish and issue him an invitation to respond.

Durant was now wide awake. He wondered how the Cardinal would react to having been called a piece of shit. The Cardinal rose to speak. The assembly stood and gave him a standing ovation. When they settled back down the Cardinal gave a very brief talk, thanking Kevin and the Knights for their continuing support and loyalty. He remarked about how the deceased Thomas O'Shea had served the Church and was an example of the dedicated servant. Then he gave a final blessing. Once again, the Knights stood. This time to accept the blessing and give the Cardinal a rousing "send-off." Then they struggled to get to their cars and go home. It had been a long day in the service of the Church.

The Cardinal made a quick exit out the back of the banquet hall and down the elevator to his waiting car. He, too, had enough of the Knighting ceremony. He had tolerated Kevin Hardly's day long program because he felt that Kevin deserved the recognition. Tonight, had convinced him that Kevin had to go. The man was becoming a major embarrassment. He thought about Kevin's slip of the tongue and found it difficult to muster forgiveness only to realize that Kevin would never intentionally make such comment. Kevin's dementia was the cause most certain. The Cardinal decided to forget the matter but intended to suggest to Mrs. Hardly that Kevin should take life easier and resign from some of his high-level positions.

As His Eminence stepped into the right front seat of his car, the young priest that had volunteered to drive him this evening handed him a message received on the Cellular phone. Bob Markley had done it again.

When Jay awoke, Markley was lying on a bench across the room, sound asleep. The policeman that had been in charge was gone and another man was in his place. The arresting officers were nowhere in sight. The pain in Jay's head and body had subsided but he still felt the effects of the beating. He desperately had to go to the bathroom. Carefully he got out of his chair and started to search for a restroom. The officer saw him move and shot out of his office. He shouted at Jay like a traffic cop.

"Where do you think you're goin', Mac?"

Jay turned and pleaded, "Man, I got to pee. You got a john in this place or do I use a dry corner?"

The cop gave a wave. "Don't be wise. It's over there, second door. Don't try to leave."

"Okay. Hey, do I need a lawyer?" Jay decided to try to make a friend. "Am I under arrest or what? How come I'm just sittin' around? Ain't I supposed to be in a cell or something? How about my rights? Can I make a phone call?"

The young cop was not interested in conversation. "Yeah, right. Take your leak and go back to sleep. Someone is coming to pick you up. Don't ask any questions because I don't have any answers. All I have is orders and my orders are to have you guys wait for your ride. Don't give me a hard time. Okay?"

Jay turned away and spoke to the wall. "Sure, somebody is gonna pick me up. That's cool, only nobody knows where I am. How in the hell is somebody gonna find me?"

The policeman didn't answer. Jay found the restroom. He cleaned up and tried to wash the dried blood from his swollen face. He hardly recognized himself. After a few minutes, he returned to his place at the desk and tried to go back to sleep. Markley had rolled off the bench and was sleeping soundly on the floor. Jay had to smile at the respectable Bob Markley in his drunken snoring slumber.

The fix took all night. Cardinal McMahon called a friend who called a friend who went to see Tony. Tony took the money that was offered but refused to drop the charges. Finally, a lawyer that the Cardinal had picked because of his very discreet nature manage to explain to Tony that once he took money for damages he had no cause to prosecute. Tony backed down when the lawyer revealed his real connections. Then the Cardinal had to use more influence to see that no arrest record was made. That required some contact with the top man in the Police Department who let it trickle down that the dynamic duo in custody were not to be charged. Then the Cardinal asked that the two men not be allowed out of the station until he could get to them. It was after five in the morning before everything was fixed.

Bob Markley was awake and sitting up when the Cardinal walked into the station. The two men greeted each other warmly and walked together into the small office where the Policeman in charge sat. Jay watched as the three chatted for a while. Some papers were exchanged, they shook hands, and walked out of the room. The Cardinal walked toward the door with Markley following.

Suddenly, Markley stopped and spoke to Jay. "You coming, Jay? It's time to go. Our ride is here."

Jay recognized the Cardinal from their first meeting when His Eminence had prayed for the Sailor. The Cardinal was dressed in standard clerical dress this time rather than the vestments he wore the first time but his large athletic form was unmistakable Jay pushed himself up and started for the door as he answered Markley. "Sure thing, Bob. I been ready to be sprung for hours. The Good Shepherd gettin' us out?"

"You got it right, Jay. I thought you would recognize him. That's His Eminence, Francis, Cardinal, McMahon. My protector. He got us out of this mess. I'm sorry for what I did to you. That's a hell of a black eye. Honestly, I don't remember doing that."

Jay simply nodded and walked toward the door. Cardinal McMahon greeted Jay warmly, opened the door to the front seat, and invited Jay to sit next to his designated driver. The young priest looked at Jay and gave him a high-five. The Cardinal and Markley got into the back seat. The driver moved the car into the early morning traffic.

It was apparent that the Cardinal's good nature had reached its limits. He began to tie into Markley like a father to a son. Jay could not help but hear the scolding although he was not certain what exactly was being said.

Markley was trying to be apologetic and respectful. "Your Eminence, I, once again, am very thankful for your help. You have pulled me out of these situations too many times. I'm sorry. I promise that I'll do everything I can to avoid getting into this kind of a mess again. You know what caused it, I'm sure."

The Cardinal was shouting at Markley. "If you are referring to our talk this afternoon, Bob, I refuse to let you use that as an excuse. It's time that you face up to the demands of your vocation. You are needed now in the Church."

Markley spoke in hushed tones and glanced back and forth from Jay to the Cardinal as if he was trying to block the sound of his voice from Jay. "Your Eminence, I have always thought that my mission with the addicted was a mission of the Church. It's a very important service. I guess when you suggested that I was not in concert with the work of the Church and my vocation I lost my will to resist my own problems. In a word, I got stinking drunk."

"Yes, Bob, your certainly did," the Cardinal replied. "Just as you have done so many times before when the pressure was on. Do you think you are the only person on earth with pressure? We all want to run but God intended us to face up to these challenges and persist. It is the will of God that we overcome our own temptations and help others overcome theirs. You know that. You have done very well with the addicted. We all appreciate that. But the Church needs you now in another cause. You have to accept that just as I have to accept the task of assigning you to it."

No more was said. They rode in silence. It seemed like a long ride and Jay was not sure where they were going. After the Cardinal and Markley ended their conversation Jay dozed for a few minutes. Then he woke and looked out of the window. They were on the Interstate moving South. Then they took the familiar exit onto Route 3 and headed for Hingham. They made a few turns onto roads that Jay had not traveled and suddenly they stopped in front of a Church. The sign in front read St. Francis by the Sea Catholic Church. Masses: Saturday 5:00 P.M.—Sundays 7:00 A.M.—8:30 A.M.—10:00 A.M. Confessions: Saturday 4 to 5 P.M.

Cardinal McMahon spoke with authority in loud tones. "Father Markley, this is your Parish effective in two weeks. The parishioners have been told that their new pastor will say the seven o'clock Mass today and greet them at the other Masses this morning. Make no mistake about it. The Church needs you here. Your days of free-wheeling it have come to an end. We all have to double up in our efforts. The Church is desperately short of Priests. This is your mission. You will care for the spiritual, emotional, and temporal needs of these people. You will, drunk or sober, say Mass for them every day on schedule. And you can be damn sure that I will see that you do. Do I make myself perfectly clear?"

Markley stepped out of the car and stood erect. "Yes, Sir, Your Eminence, I understand my mission and will carry it out to the very best of my ability. Thank you, Your Eminence." He raised his arm as if he were going to salute but then recovered.

Cardinal McMahon waited for Jay to crawl out of the front seat. Then he gave a parting shot to Markley. "Very good, Father Markley. Now if you and your friend will excuse me, I have a few other matters to attend to this morning. God bless you."

Jay stood next to Father Markley. They watched the Cardinal's car drive away.

Then Father took Jay by the arm and led him into the Church. A few of the parishioners were beginning to arrive. Jay had a ton of questions that he could not seem to figure out how to ask. Markley was in no mood to answer them anyway. He ushered Jay into a back seat and disappeared.

The faithful began to arrive in increasing numbers as seven o'clock neared. The ushers looked at Jay with contempt since he was occupying their reserved pew. Jay looked back at them with his one eye and nursed the pain and fatigue that dominated his body.

Someone in the front of the Church asked everyone to stand and sing the opening hymn. As the music began the altar girls and the lay ministers started processing from the back. Jay was almost asleep when he saw Father Bob Markley, fully vested, at the rear of the column now marching down the center aisle of the small Church. Father Markley looked clean, refreshed and very much a priest except for a swollen left cheek, a mouse under his eye, and bruised knuckles on both hands. Bob Markley looked at Jay as he passed the pew and gave him a quick blessing. Jay stood up with his mouth wide open. Markley grinned and moved on.

Joe Durant had somehow managed to convince his wife that the best way to overcome the effects of the Saturday night banquet with the Knights and Ladies was to go to an early Mass and quickly return to the normal ritual of the Church. They got up early to go to seven o'clock Mass but not early enough. They were late in arriving at St. Francis by the Sea. The Priest had given the opening blessing and the first readings were being read by a lecture. Joe stood in the back of the church and surveyed the available seats. He preferred something to the side and to the rear to allow for an easy exit thus avoiding the handshaking with the Priest after Mass. As he looked left he noticed the sleeping beat up Jay Marquart in the back pew. Then he glanced to the Altar and recognized the vested Bob Markley looking pensive as the readings were being presented. Joe thought he was dreaming. He wife had already proceeded into a pew. She turned to look for him and then beckoned him to join her. He did so with the expectation that Dr. Folley would suddenly descend from the Cross.

Jay heard some of the homily. Father Markley was a smooth talker. He explained his new assignment to his parishioners and invited them all to become active members of the Parish. When he gave special praise to the retiring pastor the people stood and applauded the elderly Priest who was waiting to assist Father Markley with the distribution of Holy Communion.

Jay fell back to sleep until the loud music of the recessional brought him out of his slumber. As Father Markley processed by he gave Jay a sign to stay in the pew. Then Markley went outside on the steps and greeted the people who stood in line to meet him. Mrs. Durant insisted that Joe join her in welcoming the new Priest. Joe embraced Father Markley and wished him the very best in his new job. Markley returned the affection and wished Joe the very best.

At that point, Father Markley became the first of the St. Anslem's staff to hear about the retirement of the hospital's Chief Executive. Joe explained that he had decided to hang it up. Both men were now beginning another phase of their lives.

An usher tapped Jay on the shoulder and told him that Father Markley was waiting for him. The usher then escorted Jay back to the vestry where Father Bob as he was rapidly becoming known was changing into some clean clothes that the retiring pastor had provided.

Father Markley gave Jay a hug and held him by outstretched arms. "Jay, we have had quite a night. Thanks for all your help. I suppose all this is a bit of a shock. It is for me. The boss set me off when he told me I had to take this job. Well, you were a help in getting me back on track. We need to keep in touch. We have a good reason to stay in contact. We'll need each other from time to time. You consider St. Francis as a place where you are always welcome. Please bring the family to see us."

Jay didn't know how to respond. He was blown away by the fact that the man with whom he had argued, cursed, fought, and spent the night in the slammer was standing before him as a full-blown Priest. "Yeah, sure, Bob. Man, you really caught me off guard. Looks like you got a good deal here. When you get settled in, I'll bring the family out. The kids will think it's cool that I know a Priest. Hey, man, how do I get home?"

Father Markley pointed to a small man waiting at the door of the Church. "Mr. Murphy will drive you to wherever you need to go, Jay. He's the man that woke you up and brought you in here. God bless, buddy."

Mr. Murphy said very little as he drove Jay into the City. Jay was not very talkative either except for trying to explain to the driver where he thought he had parked Brian's truck the night before. Murphy obediently followed Jay's instructions that took them over and over the same territory. Finally, Jay spotted a side street next to Tony's Tavern where the truck sat. Murphy left Jay out and departed without acknowledging Jay's expression of gratitude. Jay got into the pickup and drove home.

It was close to ten A.M. when Jay walked into the house. Susan was up and trying to look unconcerned as she characteristically tided up the kitchen. She looked at Jay's black eye and bruised face as he entered and gave her a quick kiss on the cheek. Then she gave him a hug.

"Jay, we were very worried. Is everything all right? Where have you been? The kids expect to go out for donuts this morning. Should we still do that? Oh, honey, we love you."

Jay held Susan close to him. He felt the pain of his bruised ribs but her warm affection made the pain worth it. He gave her another kiss and thought about how to answer her questions. The kids and the donut thing registered first in his mind. He had promised Wally that he would bring the message that Donovan had given him. He tried to remember exactly what it was and thought he could recite it correctly.

"Yeah, hon, we're goin' to get some donuts. We all got to squeeze in Brian's truck. I'm fine, just a little bruised from a fight. That's all."

Susan looked into his swollen face. "From a fight! Oh, Jay, where were you this morning?"

"I went to Mass, Susan,"

"Who gave you the black eye?"

Jay gave a low reply. "The Priest."

Susan was shocked. "Oh, Jay, I told you we were not welcome there."

Chapter Twenty-four

Susan left Jay alone although she wanted to ask more about his encounter with the Priest who gave him the punch in the eye. Actually, she was afraid that if she displayed too much interest in the matter, Jay would interpret it as an interest in the church thing. That she didn't need. Benny and James, on the other hand, had no such inhibitions. They looked at Jay's black eye and asked questions about the other guy. Jay would give brief answers. He tried to ignore the kids by acting as if he were sleeping. It didn't work. Mercifully, the time to drive to Dunkin' Donuts arrived. When Susan informed Jay of the hour, Benny and James were instantaneously diverted into thoughts about jelly filled donuts. Jay's black eye was put aside for another time.

Jay managed to overcome his pain, pack the five of them into the cab of Brian's cluttered truck, and drive to the crowded Donut Shop where the faithful had assembled. Wally was waiting with a large box of the gooey kind that were the kids' favorites. He placed it in front of the boys. After a quick greeting to Susan, Wally hastily pulled Jay and into his Saab. The motor was still running and the car was stifling hot. Jay felt like he was going to barf but managed to control it after he found the button to open the window.

Wally sat in the driver's seat with his hands gripping the steering wheel as if he were driving a race. He looked straight ahead and said nothing but seemed to be contemplating his next remark. Jay waited for something to happen.

After a few minutes Wally opened the conversation. "We got what we want almost, Jay. Just a few more pieces and it all goes down. You're a big help. What have you got for me?"

It amused Jay that the little bit of seemingly useless information relayed in the last meeting was apparently so useful to whatever Wally was trying to do. The little runt from the Attorney General's office reminded Jay of an insect trying to devour a horse. He put his hand to his painful battered eye and tried to give Wally's ego a boost. "Well, you know, man, you are really on to something, I bet. Donovan is as nervous as a whore in church. I guess he don't care much for Muldoon. Anyway, he says that it is happening and he gave me some more poop. You want it straight or do you want to bullshit for a while?"

Wally didn't want to waste time. He seemed to be in some sort of a hurry. "Give it to me straight, Jay. I've got to get back to the office and put it all together. Who busted you in the eye?"

Jay ignored the question and relayed the message from Donovan about Muldoon's condo in Florida and all the rest. Wally scribbled in a small notepad as Jay was talking. When Jay finished, Wally put the notebook into his shirt pocket and without comment opened the door and stepped out of the car. Jay got out the other side. Then the two men walked back into the Donut Shop where they rejoined Susan and the kids. Wally stood next to the booth and placed his hands on the table. He smiled at the kids and gave Susan a quick kiss on the forehead as he attempted to say his goodbye. "Well, my friends, your daddy has been a great help to me. I hope you enjoyed the donuts. I've got to go back to work now. Enjoy your day and see that Daddy gets his rest. It looks like he needs it."

Again, Jay ignored Wally's reference to his black eye. He simply thanked Wally for the donuts, and proceeded to help Susan and the kids finished their bounty. Wally gave the kids a hug and told them they should call him Uncle Wally.

Susan thought Wally was a true gentleman. She talked with Wally while Jay gulped coffee and donuts. Jay wanted to go home. Eventually Wally got around to saying a final goodbye but before leaving bought another dozen donuts for the road. Wally had won the hearts and minds of the Marquart family.

Back home, Jay called Brian and arranged to use the truck to go to St. Anslem's on Monday. As usual, he had formulated an impromptu plan for the next morning. The first step was a quick trip to see Tommy the Tout to pick up his winnings. Once he had the money in hand he would pick up Brian. Then Jay would talk Brian into driving him to the auto parts store where he would purchase a new battery. Following that, the two would retreat to Jay's home so they could install the battery and get the Jeep running. This would unravel the complicated transportation web that had plagued Jay for the past few days.

Brian was still in bed recovering from Saturday's activities when Jay called to reveal the Monday morning action plan. Louise managed to roust him to accept Jay's call. Brian seemed to understand the schedule that Jay presented. He moaned agreement and hung up. Jay smiled as he placed the telephone receiver down, confident that his life would return to normal, so to speak. Somehow the trauma of the past two days passed from mind as he finally laid down to rest. He slept from two Sunday afternoon until five A.M. Monday.

The coffee was hot and the donuts fresh. It was just after six A.M. St. Anslem's cafeteria was being prepared for the morning rush. Tommy the Tout arrived promptly at six-twenty. He was at his table and prepared to do business ten minutes later. Monday morning was an important and busy time for Tommy. Bets that covered the weekend activity had to be settled. Tommy had taken a large hit as a result of the BC upset over Notre Dame. Most of the winners had played the spread so the payout was significant. The big winner, in fact one of the largest payoffs ever, was to Jay who was the only person that bet on Boston College to win.

Marquart was waiting for Tommy to open his stand. Tommy tried to convince Jay to let the four hundred bucks ride on a sure thing that had Boston College knocking off West Virginia next Saturday. Tommy was certain that the momentum would easily carry BC past favored WVU. Jay acted interested only to placate Tommy. After what seemed like careful consideration he took the money but promised Tommy that he would place a bet later in the week when the odds were fine tuned. Jay shook Tommy's hand and moved away from the table. Several other customers were waiting.

Jay was very hungry and decided to treat himself to a full breakfast that he offered to pay for with one of the eight fifty dollar bills given to him by Tommy. The cashier didn't have change so she waved Jay past at no charge. Jay figured he was on a roll. His black eye was a good luck sign.

The delicious breakfast caused Jay to relax and reflect for the first time on the weird events of the weekend that began with the Sailor's death and came to a climax in a seedy bar where he duked it out with his good friend Father

Markley. The title "Father" stuck in his mind. He should have known all along that Markley was more than he seemed to be. The guy was close to perfect. It figured that he had to have a few other fine qualities other than just being a drunk. Being a Priest was the opposite dimension that escaped Jay's imagination. Father Markley was a friend that Jay valued now as he valued Brian and his boss, Ken. He also thought about Joe Durant and how dedicated he was to helping The Little Portion. Durant took a big chance when he encouraged Jay to "borrow" the generous quantity of food for the cookout at the Mission. Durant was a genuine person that, aside from being a suit, as the Sailor would say, was also down to earth. That reflection moved Jay to decide to drop into Durant's office and offer a hundred dollars of his winnings as some payment to the hospital for the borrowed food.

Joe Durant was not in his office. His day began promptly at seven A.M. Dr. Folley had called him at home on Sunday to advise that the Board had accepted his offer to retire in principle but that the details had to be determined first thing on Monday morning because Mr. O'Shea's funeral was scheduled for ten-thirty. Folley explained that he would start the meeting and then leave to attend to his Family and the funeral. An attorney for the Archdiocese would negotiate a settlement with Durant. It was expected that the entire day would be required to come to a final conclusion. Folley announced his intention to return to the discussions by mid-afternoon. It was obvious to Durant that the Great One was determined to put more than Tom O'Shea to rest on this day.

Dr. Folley was waiting when Durant arrived. The Attorney for the Archdiocese was seated with him in back of the desk. A long folding table had been placed in the office with eight chairs. It reminded Durant of the setting for the Paris Peace talks. Folley directed Durant to sit at the long table. The attorney then moved to the table and sat on the opposite side at the far end leaving the places directly opposite Durant vacant. Folley came around his desk and stood at the head of the long table. He then proceeded to pontificate.

"Joe, what we will do this morning is work out the basic details of your severance. When we have things in general agreement our attorney will put it into a contract. You may want to have your lawyer look over the agreement. Hopefully we can come to an understanding by this afternoon. Later today I have a PR firm scheduled to come in and prepare a statement for the press. We'll have an emergency meeting of the Board at seven tomorrow when I'll inform them about the change in the executive structure. We'll follow that with a meeting with medical staff leadership, an executive staff meeting, a general management meeting, and finally a press conference. By tomorrow night everything should be concluded."

The expediency of the process amused Durant. Folley's desire to anoint himself as the head of the hospital in addition to his position as Secretary of Health for the Archdiocese was overwhelming. The Great One was acting like a kid at Christmas. His ego subordinated his grief-stricken family. Folley had confused ambition and dedication to the extent that he no longer could tell them apart. This realization caused Durant to abandon the humor of the moment in exchange for some anger but more of compassion for Dr. Folley who had no idea how to operate the hospital.

A knock on the table by the Great One brought Joe back to focus on the remarks that were being made. Folley stated that the matter regarding inappropriate use of hospital funds was being held in file as a confidential matter. It would not be a factor in the negotiations. However, the matter of unilateral decision making by the hospital's Chief Executive Officer was to be stated in the agreement with very specific reference to the acquisition of a telephone system that complicated hospital operations. The fact that the system was purchased and installed without the advice and consent of the medical staff was the main reason that Mr. Durant's resignation and retirement was being accepted by the hospital's Board of Trustees. The bottom line was that Joe Durant was being retired for cause, not for meritorious service to the healing ministry. He had blown it by installing a state of the art communication system.

In fact, the Great Dr. Folley, once his father-in-law's remains were passed to the undertaker, had reneged on his agreement with Durant. Durant was trapped into a forced resignation. There was little recourse to the situation that faced him. Durant either accepted the retirement offer with its reservations or withdraw and await execution by Folley and the Board of Directors' firing squad.

Tom O'Shea's remains were waiting a Christian burial. Durant had allowed the body to be taken by the undertaker for preparation and he had ignored Dr. Sutton's plea to restore the medical record. Folley now held the best hand. Durant was out of trump. This was the moment for Joseph Durant's professional demise.

Tactfully Joe reacted. "Dr. Folley, I'll go along with this as long as I am not publicly disgraced and I have continuing income of some kind until my normal retirement."Folley tried to act compassionate but failed. "Joe, the Board wanted me to remind you that you are in no position to dictate terms. We have an offer for you that will be explained by our attorney. You can make changes but only within the general context of the offer. When I get back I hope that we have reached an agreement so we can proceed with the other matters on the agenda."

That was the end of the conversation. Folley took off his tailored full-length white lab coat and put on the coat to his very expensive tailored Sunday go to meeting and funeral suit coat. Then he walked out of the office leaving Durant and the stoic attorney for the Archdiocese. The attorney opened his briefcase and took out an official looking document marked "draft" and presented it to Durant. The document was a severance agreement that allowed for a one time lump sum payment equal to two years' salary. It also mentioned that Durant would hold no malice toward the Archdiocese and would forego any claim for any action against the Archdiocese from the beginning of time forward.

Durant read the brief document and handed it back to the attorney. Then he explained that the lump sum settlement as proposed would be subject to excessive tax penalty. He asked for a payout over time. The two men discussed the proposed agreement for several hours. It was a very trying experience for Durant.

The emotion caused him to become angry and begin to shout at the attorney who by contrast remained calm. Joe would take a break and return the office when he had recomposed himself Then they would begin again. Eventually, they agreed to an arrangement whereby Durant would be paid two years' salary over four years. During the four years he would remain an employee of St. Anslem's and be given full benefits including pension credits. His position would be as a consultant to the Office of Health Affairs for the Archdiocese. He would not be expected to be present on a day to day basis but would be subject to call by Dr. Folley. If Durant earned any money from any other source, that amount would be returned to the Archdiocese. Each year it was required that Folley and Durant would meet and review Durant's Federal

Income Tax Return to determine if any rebate was due to the hospital. After the lengthily negotiation Durant went back to his office and told his executive assistant that he had retired effective tomorrow. Then he began to clean out his desk.

The Archdiocesan attorney dictated the final agreement and gave the tape to Dr. Folley's secretary to prepare. An hour latter Dr. Folley returned from the funeral. With him were three people from a public relations firm that represented the Red Sox when they fired their manager a month earlier. Within the hour, three additional people arrived from another PR firm that Kevin Hardly's Office had recommended. Additionally, three people from the hospital's public relations office were summoned. The crowd of spin doctors piled into Folley's office joined by Durant and the attorney for the Archdiocese. The lawyer huddled with Folley at one end of the room and discussed each word in the severance agreement. The spin doctors huddled at the other end of the room and discussed the media presentation.

Durant sat alone and watched. By six-thirty in the evening the severance agreement had been signed. It took until ten-thirty for the team of Public Relations specialists to formulate a press release and prepare details of the presentation at the scheduled management meetings and press conferences. Durant went home that night a free man to contemplate his future. He and Mrs. Durant sat up until two A.M. discussing the events and wondering about Divine Providence.

Providence was foremost in Big Frank Patello's mind as well. Only it was Providence, Rhode Island, instead of the Divine variety. More correctly, Big Frank was concentrating on his luxurious home in adjacent Newport where he intended to move on a permanent basis as soon as the Boston bank mergers were announced and his nephew took charge. Then the One Park Avenue venue lease would be canceled and National Associated Investors would relocate to plush accommodations in the downtown Boston financial district.

Big Frank had things moving. A reorganization had already been implemented. Mario Capizzi was made the President of a new holding company named Atlantic Ventures that on paper held Park Medical Consulting as a subsidiary. Atlantic Ventures was headquartered in Philadelphia where Mario could oversee the entire operation of Big Frank's importing business. In addition, Atlantic Ventures acquired a majority interest in Universal Services that had purchased Action Waste Management and Recycling Company. Tony Marone was named Executive Vice President of Atlantic Ventures. Mark Meeham, deposed chief executive of Action, was named the President of the Eastern Region for Universal Services. Universal selected Hartford, Connecticut for its base and new home for Mondi. Park Medical Consulting had established its headquarters in Lexington, Massachusetts in a very expensive and elaborate high-rise office suite overlooking Interstate 95. Tom Callahan was convinced by Marone to accept the Chief Executive Officer position. Callahan left Debur and Tandy under threat of litigation since it appeared that he removed NAI from their client list for his own benefit. Marone assured Callahan that the matter would be resolved. Leaving the D&T issue to Marone, Callahan concentrated on the fulfillment of the Target Boston Medical project that was advancing well under the naive leadership of Doctor Richard Folley and the impressionable, unconscious Mr. Joseph Bauman, President of Park/Bay Area Health Care, a Health Maintenance Organization now owned by Park Medical Consulting.

Big Frank was very satisfied. He completed reading the report on the status of the reorganization and placed it in his briefcase. Then he turned out the lights in his office.

He was on his way to retirement. From now on Charlie Patello could oversee the complex operation from his lofty position as Chief Executive Officer of New England Trust (NET). Big Frank and his favorite nephew were only an hour apart by automobile. It would be a very easy commute.

The lights from the television cameras were blinding but they generated some heat in the cool auditorium. Several hundred people had crammed into the conference center at the Hardly Security and Bank Trust which was now the headquarters for the New England Trust. The news conference to formally announce the beginning of NET was scheduled for two PM on Monday. The selected time cramped the media for the six o'clock television news but allowed sufficient time for the dignitaries to return from Thomas O'Shea's funeral.

Some black bunting in O'Shea's memory was still evident in the building but it was well covered by the high-profile promotion that was part of the news conference. Charlie Patello welcomed everyone and introduced himself as President of NET. He read the prepared news release that contained a list of the NET Board members. Kevin Hardly and his cousin were on the list. They were also present and sitting at opposite ends of the table from which Charlie addressed the assembly. Charlie paid tribute to the Hardly boys, praising them for their years of success and complimenting them for their combined wisdom to form this new organization that would serve the financial interest of the Boston Community for years to come. Kevin and his cousin each read a brief statement and returned to their respective positions at opposite ends which was indeed reflective of their association.

After announcing the names of the NET officers and introducing each one, Charlie Patello made a surprise announcement. The Board of Trustees of New England Trust had agreed to establish a New England Trust Foundation with the primary purpose of supporting the people of New England by providing grants and financial assistance to deserving charities. Boston's Mayor Siro was sitting at the head table next to where Patello was speaking. When Patello announced the Foundation, Mayor Siro, on cue, rose and shook Patello's hand. Then Patello yielded the platform to the Mayor who waxed eloquent about the formation of NET, the stewardship of Patello, the Hardly family, and the many people who worked to better the Boston Community. He concluded by reading a proclamation from the City Council that applauded the formation of NET and the NET Foundation.

Patello thanked the Mayor for his generous support and for his courageous leadership. After the Mayor returned to his seat, Patello made another announcement that, while surprising to some, was generally unnoticed by the Media. The Director of the New England Trust Foundation, proclaimed a proud Charlie Patello, was Michael Logan, a well-known advocate for the poor and disadvantaged.

Logan was in the audience. He rose and waved when Patello made the announcement but he purposely did not attempt to garner any additional attention. He had not discussed the matter about accepting a new position with Dr. Folley. In fact, he had tried to see Folley on several occasions during the past week but it seemed that the Great One was occupied with the declining health of his father-in-law and obsessed with the execution of Joe Durant. It was the Durant matter that convinced Logan that he would be better served working for Patello.

Logan had figured out Patello. He knew a crook when he saw one. Folley was just as easy to describe but far more difficult to predict. Folley was an egomaniac who harbored no mercy for any person or thing that shadowed his perceived eminence. In Logan's mind Folley was more dangerous by far than any corporate thief. Logan's letter of resignation from the Office of Health Affairs of the Boston Catholic Archdiocese sat unopened in the large stack of mail on Doctor Folley's desk.

Patello had promised Logan a reward for assisting with the Robert Cowan fiasco. Patello always lived up to his word. The Foundation was a suggestion of the NET accountants who saw it as a way of laundering cash but Patello and Uncle Frank immediately realized that it could also serve as a form of political action committee where politicians could be bribed and bought. Logan was a natural for the job since he was acquainted with politics and had a reputation of supporting the public good. Logan had reviewed the boiler plate documents that formed the Foundation and accepted the position without question. Mayor Siro was the first to recognize the good works of the Foundation. Siro was an easy buy.

The funeral Mass for Thomas O'Shea had been said at his Parish church in Weston. The Cardinal said the Mass concelebrated by the Pastor. Afterwards, the Cardinal eulogized O'Shea. The procession to the cemetery was one of the longest in recent time. State Police provided an honor guard and assisted with traffic control at all major intersections. At the grave site, the Family surrounded the casket while the Cardinal gave the last blessing before it was lowered to a final rest. Kevin Hardly held a place of honor with the O'Shea family. Charlie Patello was relegated to the background which gave him an opportunity to leave early for the NET News Conference. Charlie had assigned a young assistant to drive Hardly's limousine and to see that Kevin Hardly left the grave site and went directly to the News Conference. Mrs. Hardly had been briefed and carried Kevin's prepared speech in her purse.

The other members of the St. Anslem's Hospital Board of Trustees were also at the grave site. Bishop Hanks wore vestments and stood ready to assist the Cardinal. Sister Elizabeth moved next to Charlie Patello, chatted briefly, and inquired about the purpose of the emergency Board meeting that Dr. Folley had called for the next morning. She seemed to be little concerned about O'Shea's passing but was appropriately respectful of the proceedings. Philip Mondi, yielding to Patello's suggestion, drove to Boston from his new home in Portland to attend the funeral. Standing next to him was Mark Meehan. The two men were not very attentive or respectful. Mondi was harboring very insecure feelings because of the matter regarding Sam the Security man and the Sailor. Meehan had to rush from the funeral for an important meeting with the management and staff of Action where he was to announce that the company was now a part of Universal Services.

Jay paid eighty dollars for the new battery sitting in a box on the front seat of Brian's truck. He drove the beat-up pickup recklessly through early morning traffic and arrived at Brian's crummy apartment before Brian had recovered from the night's slumber. Somehow Jay managed to get Brian to adjust to the morning light. Then he pushed Brian, still struggling with his shoes and shirt, into his truck. With a half-awake Brian at the wheel they drove back to Waltham where the two struggled to remove the old battery and install the new one. After the third try the ancient Jeep started. Jay put the old battery in the back of Brian's truck. Brian knew an excellent place to throw it out on the way to Patriot. Jay waved to his buddy and pointed the recovered Jeep toward Action Waste Management arriving in plenty of time before the start of the scheduled management and staff meeting.

David Donovan was waiting in the parking lot greeting the employees as they arrived. Small groups would form around him as he explained that the Union would force management to uphold the terms of their contract even though it was widely rumored that the company had been sold. Donovan collared Jay immediately and had him help with getting the protective message out to the arriving people. After everyone was inside, Donovan asked Jay to sit with him in the front seat of his car. Donovan looked at Jay's black eye but did not ask about it. Instead he began to talk to Jay about the Action sale and the Workers' Guild.

"Jay, the rumor is for certain that Action is sold. I guess you're gonna hear all about it this afternoon. Now we are going to make sure that our contract goes to the new owner. The only problem is that Muldoon caved in and let Action off the hook. We understand he waved the continuation clause on the final agreement. What that means is that we are going to have to organize the new company all over again. We don't want the members to know that just yet. As soon as we find out who owns Action, then we'll go for it."

Jay was not interested. "Donovan, it's been a rough weekend. I'm not up to all this organization crap. You point me in the direction you want me to go and I'll do what you ask. Man, just don't ask me to try to think. I ain't up to it anymore. Hey, I did meet with Wally on Sunday and gave him your message. What's with this, anyway?"

"It all ties into the Muldoon thing," Donovan replied. "Right now our great leader is winging it to Florida, leaving us in this mess. I suspect that he's on his way out of office. At least that's what we are trying to do. Wally is looking at what's happened and trying to figure if Muldoon is due a legal rap. If he is, we can get him ousted and maybe sent to the slam. Your buddy, Celi, seems to figure in but we aren't sure how it all ties together."

Jay suddenly became very attentive. "Man, you ratted on Muldoon. Ain't that against your code or something?"

"We didn't rat, Jay," insisted Donovan. "Wally came to us looking for some answers. He told us how to set up a relay system that kept us clean from being a direct informer. That's where you come in. You don't rat. You just give information that somebody else gives you. You have no idea what it means. Neither do we."

Mark Meehan knew what the information meant. He had planted information about Muldoon with the Attorney General's office several weeks before the actual sale of the company to Universal Services took place. He also paid a cash bonus to Muldoon to wave the continuation clause and plan to get lost. The involvement of the State Attorney General's office was the back up in case Muldoon decided to stay around and milk the operation.

Muldoon had greased Celi who was already pursuing other interests. Through special influence, Celi received some vocational training and was certified and qualified to hold a red flag at highway construction sites.

Donovan and Jay chatted for a few more minutes. Suddenly Donovan noticed that most of the employees were inside. He excused Jay with the request that Jay get to him as soon as the announcement about the official change of ownership was made to the employees.

It was several hours before the staff meeting but everybody seemed to know what was going to be announced. Everyone believed that there would be a major reduction in the work force. Donovan's assurance that they received in the parking lot seemed meaningless. The employees expected very bad news. Jay caught the feeling as well and became depressed. His conversation with Donovan added to the depression. As he approached his desk, Ken Ryan was seated in the chair waiting for him. This caused Jay to conclude that Ryan was there to deliver the bad news. Some valued members of management had been given advanced information in confidence because of the new status that they would personally have. One of those so selected was Ken Ryan.

Jay was in no mood for any soft soap. He hit Ryan with a direct statement. "Ryan, you gotta do what you gotta do. Say it and get it over with."

Ryan looked at the battered face and noted Jay's slumped posture, "Geez, you got the hell beat out of you. What happened to the other guy?"

"I guess he's got a high place in heaven coming to him. What's up?" Jay smiled at the thought.

Ryan accepted Jay's smile as a greeting. "Yeah, well, I wanted to talk with you before the meeting. Everybody seems to know what's coming. There are some changes that are going to happen that affects me and maybe you if you're interested. Meehan talked to me on Friday and said that maybe I should talk to you today before the meeting. The new company, Universal Services, does a lot more than Action. They do housekeeping, food management, general maintenance, repair and maintenance of technical equipment, purchasing, warehousing, engineering, laboratory services and waste management. The whole nine yards. They even have mobile stuff for x-rays and junk like that. What they want to do is get a quick account where they can expand their services and set up a beta site in New England. They are sending in a guy from Chicago to manage the transition and he has asked me to work with him as an assistant manager.

"I have to go to Chicago for about a month of technical training. We need somebody to manage the Beta site and I recommended you. You know St. Anslem's and have got a good grip on what's happening there. You told me about the thing with the Cardinal last week and how he liked what we were doing. You still have an in with him?"

Jay thought about the Sunday morning experience as he answered, "I guess so, Ken, me and the Cardinal had a chance to chat briefly over the weekend."

Ryan swung his fist in the air. "Great! What do you say, Jay? You want to join the new management team? I know it's a bit of a flyer because I haven't the slightest idea about money and all that but at least you have an option if you want it. If you don't like what happens then you can bail out. The way it works is that we set you up with an office at St. Anslem's and a desk here. You do most of your work at St. A's. That's where you spend most of your time now. You come in here when called or when we have management meetings and the like. The desk here will be for you to do work on projects or accounts other than St. A's. Oh, yeah, as a member of management you get out of belonging to the Union. How about it?"

Jay liked the idea although he had some second thoughts about leaving the Union. He acted like he was giving the matter a lot of thought before he answered. After circling the desk a couple of times, and starring at the ceiling, he gave his response. "Yeah, Ken. Why not? I'll give it a go."

Brian drove slowly along the back road to Patriot Courier and Transport. He waited until the traffic passed and then he quickly pulled to the side of the road, jumped out of the cab, ran to the back of the truck, picked up Jay's dead battery, and tossed it into the drainage ditch. Then he jumped back into the cab and drove at his usual high-speed, reckless way to the Patriot yard. Eddie's big wheel pickup truck was parked right in front of the door to the Dispatcher's Office. Brian, fearing the worse, parked his truck at the far end of the row and slowly walked to the door. He could see Eddie sitting at the desk with his feet propped against the file cabinet as he always did when he was doing the job. Brian sensed that he was being replaced.

Eddie was quick to confirm his suspicions as soon as Brian entered the office. "Brian, guess what. You're history as the dispatcher. The man thinks that I should do the dispatchin' so we have better coordination or something like that. So I'm back and I'm gonna give you a choice. You can have your old job back running special accounts if you bring in the Sailor or you can hit the road. It's your choice. What's it gonna be, asshole?"

Brian was not accustomed to making decisions when talking to Eddie. He really had no choice but Eddie didn't know that. The only thing Brian could do at this point was hit the road. It wasn't the choice that Eddie wanted him to make. In fact, it was not the acceptable choice since it was Eddie's idea that Brian would be anxious to save his job by telling where the Sailor could be found. Brian didn't realize that. All Brian could think about was that he had no choice. The Sailor was dead and Jay had explained how important it was for their continuing safety that Eddie never found out.

Brian, as carefully as he could, tried to respond. "Eddie, I been meaning for some time to tell you that I'm gonna leave. I ain't good at this business. This is the time to go, I guess. It's good to see you back. I couldn't handle the dispatcher thing. Too complicated."

Eddie shook his head in disbelief. "Don't give me that shit! Where's the Sailor?" He got out of his chair and walked toward Brian. "I got to see him about somethin' important. You know where he's hangin' out. Tell me or I'll bust you alongside the head with a fuckin' club."

Brian backed against the wall and braced for the inevitable blow to his head. "Eddie, I swear to God that I don't know. Yeah, that's it, man. Only God knows where he is. I suppose I'll find out someday and you will too I guess. For now, we just got to wait until somethin' happens and we get the word. I'm sorry that I can't help you, man. I'll leave here and try to find another job. Hey, it's been good workin' for ya." Brian was so impressed with his own response that he forgot about Eddie's threat to hit him with a club. He stepped forward and extended his hand to Eddie in a friendly parting gesture.

The sincerity of Brian's comment caught Eddie off guard. Eddie was taken back at Brian's unexpected courage and confidence. Acting on reflex, he shook Brian's hand and the two men parted. Not another word was said.

The Waltham Tap and Keg was, as always, crowded with the working class. Brian had called Jay at Action after the management meeting. Jay was exuberant about his new position while Brian was depressed over the loss of his. The two agreed to meet at their favorite place and discuss the situation. Brian got there ahead of Jay and proceeded to get very drunk. Jay found him sleeping in a booth when he arrived. Brian eventually woke up in response to Jay's repeating jobs to the shoulder. Jay, at Brian's request, went to the bar and bought Brian a beer and a coke for himself. When he returned to the booth with the drinks, Brian had disappeared to the men's room. It seemed like an eternity before Brian returned to the booth, seemingly refreshed. He slumped into the booth across from Jay and grabbed the waiting beer. After taking a long drink, he expressed his gratitude to his silent buddy.

"Thanks for the beer, Jay. Guess you're stayin' sober tonight, that's cool, man."

Jay sported an air of wealth and importance. "Yeah, man. I got my payoff from Tommy and I want to take it home and show Susan. We can get a few things paid off with this. Being sober is where it's at, man. You ought to try it sometime. "

Brian was visibly insulted at Jay's reference. "I ain't no drunk or junkie, Jay. I use but I don't abuse. You know that. Hell, man, I ain't had the trouble you had. You had to quit or die. None of that for me. I get that bad then I'm gonna quit like you. I got to stay sober and find me a new job. Eddie, he canned my ass this morning because I couldn't tell him about the Sailor."

Jay gave his friend a pat on the arm. "Eddie done you a favor, man. You're out of it, man. You can do a job now and not worry about some sonna bitch crackin' your head. Think about it, man. You can do what you want to do. The Sailor's takin' care of us, man. What you gonna do?"

Brian didn't answer. The two friends sat in silence sipping their drinks. Brian's eyes were teary. Jay felt sorry for his friend but knew that Brian had turned a very important corner in his life. Brian had escaped.

What was left of the St. Anslem's Board of Trustees met in the Hardly Board Room on Tuesday at seven A.M. Dr. Folley had made all the arrangements through his secretary. The usual lavish breakfast was replaced with a routine breakfast buffet. No food service personnel were present to wait on the members or prepare special omelets. The administrative vice presidents were absent except for Rod Weaver who attended in his new role as Chief Fiscal Officer for the Office of Health Affairs.

Michael Logan was present but looking very sheepish since the media had well publicized the NET Foundation and his new position as Director. He stayed very close to Charlie Patello who was busy accepting the congratulations of the others in attendance.

Kevin Hardly had arrived early, as was his custom, but was not met as usual by Joe Durant. Durant had been instructed by Folley to remain in his former office until the meeting concluded. Hardly roamed about looking for someone to fix him breakfast. Folley eventually noticed him and ushered him through the buffet and sat him down at a chair where he would be out of the way. Bishop Hanks arrived very early and spent considerable time bending Patello's ear about the needs of the Archdiocese Charities. Sister Elizabeth seemed very demur, said nothing, and constantly bit her lip as she waited for the meeting to start. Meehan arrived exactly at seven and gave his letter of resignation to Hardly who quickly handed it unopened to Folley. Phil Mondi's office had notified Durant's office late Monday that he would not be able to attend the meeting. He also faxed a resignation letter to Durant that Joe had given to Folley.

Folley carefully moved to the head to the table. Before calling the meeting to order he made a quick assessment. The Terrific Trinity was now reduced to one. Kevin Hardly was mentally disabled, Tom O'Shea was deceased. Only Charles Patello remained and he was the king of clout in Boston. Folley knew that he had to give Patello a lot of status. Bishop Hanks, the Cardinal's personal representative, was uncomfortable with the changes in organization that Folley was introducing. Folley had to be sure that the Bishop was made comfortable. Sister Elizabeth appeared to be trouble. She had been placated once before by giving her the lead in the strategic planning committee efforts by the hospital and the Archdiocesan Office of Health Affairs. Folley could not remember if the Planning Committee had ever met Indeed, Sister Elizabeth looked like trouble.

Sister Elizabeth was troubled but not about St. Anslem's or the Archdiocese. Sister Elizabeth's term as the religious leader of the Poor Sisters of Charity was at an end. At a Sisters' Chapter meeting that weekend her religious community had decided that Sister Celest was to be Sister Elizabeth's successor. Sister Celest was reluctant to accept the honor but when it was mentioned that she would automatically become a member of the St. Anslem's Board of Trustees she immediately accepted with the provision that the Sisters would continue to support and operate The Little Portion Mission. Sister Elizabeth was very concerned with the provision and now worried how the obligation could be fulfilled. The letter to Cardinal McMahon announcing the Sisters' choice of a new leader had been sent by Patriot courier yesterday. Sister wondered if Bishop Hanks had been briefed. She was concentrating on the matter when Dr. Folley called the St. Anslem's Board meeting to order.

Folley greeted all with a redundant good morning and asked Bishop Hanks to bless the assembly with prayer. The Bishop accommodated the request with an extemporaneous expression, forgetting the Hardly Prayer that usually was read from the Chair. When everyone was seated, the Great Richard Folley, M.D., began his explanation for the emergency meeting. He explained that several changes in the executive leadership of the hospital were necessary to better accommodate the implementation of the Medical Services Organization which was the cornerstone of the Catholic Health Services Network that the Board had recommended and the Cardinal had now approved. He explained in detail how the hospital now became a cost center in the operation of the big scheme.

"In fact," Folley explained, "the hospital was a subsidiary of the Catholic Health Services Network that was governed by the Cardinal, Bishop Hanks, and myself. The Board of Directors for St. Anslem's is dissolved."

He made a big point of thanking everyone for their unselfish participation and made special mention of Sister Elizabeth and the excellent contributions made by the Sisters over the past years. Folley was on a roll. He spoke down to the people with an eloquence that mesmerized everyone except Sister Elizabeth. Without hesitation she raised her hand and began to speak without waiting for formal recognition.

"Dr. Folley, you mentioned that the hospital's Board is now dissolved and that the Network is governed by you, Bishop Hanks and His Eminence. I have a problem with that. The Sisters, as you mentioned, have given their lives to the Health Ministry in this Diocese. We deserve to be a part of the Network governance. I must insist that the person in leadership of the Poor Sisters of Charity be given a seat on the Board and I assure you that I will take this matter to His Eminence immediately."

Sister Elizabeth had fired a broadside that Folley had expected. He used his abundance of political skills to accommodate and placate her. "Sister Elizabeth, you make a very valid point. I intended to request that others join us in the governance structure. Indeed, the Poor Sisters of Charity deserve to be represented. We will be most pleased to have you as a continuing member on the governing Board. Bylaws are being prepared and I will assure you that the Sisters will continue to serve. Thank you for bringing that to our attention."

Folley looked at Bishop Hanks who nodded in agreement. Satisfied that he had made the proper comprise, he delivered the next point. "In order to retain the continuity of the St. Anslem's Corporation with the Network, I also ask that Mr. Patello accept membership on the new Board. With Mr. Patello will be representatives of the medical staff and others perhaps from the major payers with whom we establish affiliations."

Charlie Patello gave a very slight nod to Folley but made no other indication of acceptance. He was intent on staying in the background. Sister Elizabeth looked directly at him when he made the gesture. Seeing it, she turned abruptly back to Folley and fired her next salvo.

"Doctor Folley, you seem to be the one appointing people to the Board. As I recall the appointments are reserved for the Cardinal along with the other reserved powers established by Canon Law. Are you forgetting about that?"

Doctor Folley pulled himself up to his maximum height and looked down at Sister Elizabeth. He paused long enough for her to get the impact of his authority. Then he delivered an emphatic reply. "Sister, please remember that when I was appointed to this office I was delegated the Reserve Powers and in fact represent the Cardinal in these decisions. I am in charge. Do you agree, Bishop Hanks?"

The Bishop was very uncomfortable with the question and more uncomfortable with his own reply. "Yes, Doctor, the Cardinal did delegate the function of the reserve powers to you within reason and as long as the decisions produce no scandal and are not in direct conflict with Canon Law. The appointment of trustees and executives are in line with your delegations. You are free to appointment who you wish as long as the people you appoint give no scandal."

Folley confidently folded his arms across his chest and continued. "Thank you, Bishop. That brings us to the next order of business. Mr. Durant has requested early retirement. Our attorney has prepared a document that specifies the terms of his resignation that is to some degree for cause. You will note that actually Mr. Durant steps down as the chief executive officer of St. Anslem's in order to allow for the new organization. We continue to retain him as a consultant for four years but he does not perform any service to our Network unless I request it. Actually, I expect him to move out of the area. I would appreciate your acceptance of this document and so move."

As if on cue, Kevin Hardly seconded the motion. No one offered any comments. Folley called for the vote. Sister Elizabeth cast the only negative vote. Durant was now officially retired.

Folley was about to move to another matter when Sister Elizabeth again raised her hand. "Doctor Folley, while we are on the subject of resignations are we going to vote on Michael Logan? You haven't mentioned his resignation."

The reason Folley didn't mention Logan's resignation is that he didn't know anything about it. He was the only person in the room, other than Hardly, who wasn't aware that Logan had been announced as the new head of the NET Foundation. Folley could only stare at Logan with his mouth wide open.

It was the moment that Logan knew would come but the one he dreaded the most. Logan stood and thanked Sister Elizabeth for being so considerate. Then he politely informed everyone that he was indeed working for Charles Patello and the NET Foundation. He explained that the decision was made over the past two weeks and that his repeated attempts to inform Doctor Folley had been overshadowed by the untimely death of Mr. O'Shea.

The explanation given by Logan allowed Doctor Folley time to recover from the shock. He sat while Logan talked but as soon as he finished, Folley sprang to his feet and gave Logan a hug. Then he waxed eloquent about the fine job that Mr. Logan had done in helping to get the Catholic Health Services Network initiated. Finally he asked for a unanimous vote of gratitude for Mr. Logan. This time Sister Elizabeth voted with the others. Michael Logan thanked them for their kindness, wished them well, and left the meeting.

As a final announcement, Doctor Folley informed those present that in order to maintain fiscal continuity he had decided to employ Ron Weaver as the chief fiscal officer for the Catholic Health Services Network. Weaver nodded but said nothing.

It was the right moment for Mark Meehan to speak, something he did very seldom in the Board meetings. Meehan explained that his company had been sold to a very prosperous, successful, company that was dedicated to providing the very best support service to institutions, especially healthcare and hospitals. That company, he explained, would now be supporting St. Anslem's and he hoped the entire Network of health service offered by the Archdiocese. Then he pointed to his letter of resignation in Folley's hand, explained the contents, and wished everybody well.

Doctor Folley thanked Meehan for his very loyal service and mentioned that "the Cardinal was especially pleased with the work done by the Action Waste Management Company." He added that he would welcome the new services offered by Universal.

Charles Patello mentioned that Phil Mondi had also resigned. It was Patello's suggestion that a resolution be passed that expressed the gratitude of the Board for the fine service of the retiring Board members. Sister Elizabeth suggested that Mr. Durant be included in the resolution but Doctor Folley reminded her that Durant's retirement had not been entirely voluntary. Following that discussion Doctor Folley adjourned the meeting.

The Saint Anslem's Chemical Abuse Program (SACAP) was history. It had once been a very active program within the hospital's complement of services primarily because Doctor Anderson had pioneered its success. Anderson had hand-picked the talented nurses and support staff for the program as it grew. Among them was Robert Markley. Anderson was the only one on the hospital staff who knew that Markley was an ordained Priest. The Cardinal, himself, had referred the troubled Priest to Anderson who had helped other priests and religious. Markley was all that the Cardinal had said he was. He was very caring, professional, talented, addicted, and especially tolerant of the afflicted. Markley became the essence of the program.

Markley sat in the small waiting room outside Dr. Anderson's office. He was there to present his official resignation to his boss. While waiting, Markley's thoughts reflected the route that brought him to this moment. He had screwed up in Vietnam and Chaplain McMahon, USMC, picked him out of the scrap heap, counseled him, trained him as a chaplain's assistant, and after the war, guided him into the ministry of caring. Soon he discovered his true vocation, entered the seminary and was ordained. Ordained, he thought, to care for those with the curse of substance abuse. His own problem caused him to fail at his ministry but, once again, McMahon found him and guided him to Dr. Anderson. Anderson not only treated Markley's affliction but trained him in the art and science of helping others. Together they built the St. Anslem's Chemical Abuse Program.

As Dr. Anderson's called for him to enter his office, Father Markley abandoned his thoughts about the past and entered the office to meet with his mentor. Markley was the only one left after the extensive cutbacks and now he stood at Anderson's desk in black clerical attire with roman collar to present his resignation. He had been called to another mission, the Parish Ministry.

Doctor Anderson sat silently listening to Father Markley explain that his services were now being directed to the Parish Ministry. Anderson was only half listening. He was more reflective of the changes in his own career since the decision by Doctor Folley to create the Catholic Health Services Network. Anderson was now the administrator of the Medical Practice Group within the network. His new duties prevented him from saving the SACAP. He had some hope that it would survive under Markley's leadership but that prospect was now gone. The addicted would find another cure from another caring agent but who and when? Anderson shook his head from side to side when Markley stopped talking. He wiped tears from his eyes and embraced his friend.

Markley promised to continue the effort to serve the addicted with some program in his Parish. Anderson beamed at the prospect and offered to be a volunteer. Maybe there was still some hope.

There was no hope for Mitch Daly. The little man with unlimited energy was caught in the middle. He had stepped away from supporting Durant because he figured rightly that Durant was a loser. Logan was a sure winner in his mind so he made a play to be prominent on the Archdiocesan staff as a planner. Now Logan had moved out and was on Patello's staff. Daly's arch enemy, Rod Weaver, had bailed out of Durant's camp and bought his way into favor and a high place by handing Durant's head to Folley. Weaver was the key executive pro-tem in the Archdiocese and well situated to block Daly's survival.

Weaver had already told Daly to get lost. Daly met with Durant as the Board was meeting and asked for a severance agreement. Durant suggested that he try Folley. Instead Daly decided to wait for Folley to find him and then work out a severance deal. In the meantime, he decided to take Weaver's advice and get lost in the confusion of transition. He figured he had at least six months of continuing employment before anyone realized that he still existed.

It was a very busy day for Doctor Folley, the self-proclaimed head of the Catholic Health Services Network, Secretary and Director of Health Affairs for the Archdiocese, and now chief executive of what was left of St. Anslem's Hospital. He went directly from the Board meeting to Durant's office and announced to him that the deal was done. Then he collected Durant and pulled him into a meeting with the leadership of the Medical Staff where the new order was explained. The physicians listened in silence. After the meeting, they individually wished Durant well.

The next meeting was with the entire management staff of St. Anslem's. Durant was not very well appreciated by this group since he had authorized the extensive layoffs. Less respected, however, was the arrogant Doctor Folley. Consequently, the message given by Folley and echoed by Durant was received with mixed emotions. Durant had a hard time talking to the assembly because he realized that his hospital administration career of thirty-five years was effectively ending at this meeting. His voice broke several times and he had to wait for his emotions to subside before continuing. The room was silent as he labored through his farewell.

The Piece de Resistance for this great day was the press conference. Doctor Folley had arranged to have the event in the hospital's auditorium that would seat two hundred people in chairs arranged theater style. Folley sacrificed at least fifty seats in order to allow for a press row with tables. Another fifty chairs were removed so the television cameras could be stationed in the center aisle and in the side aisles with an unrestricted view of the podium. A team of six press agents from two different communication specialist companies and another three people from the hospital's Press Relations office occupied seats behind press row. They were equipped with copies of news releases about the Catholic Health Services Network and a bio sketch of Dr. Folley. Their job was to prompt the media on significant details and arrange for photo opportunities and special interviews.

The first press release, however, announced Joe Durant's retirement as the Chief Executive Officer of St. Anslem's. It was planned that Durant would be the item to gather the press. Then the announcement of the Network would be presented in tandem. Folley had calculated that he would easily upstage the event. As it happened, Doctor Folley completely dominated the entire affair because only one representative from the media attended. He was from the Archdiocesan newspaper. The rest of the people present, aside from the hospital shills, were members of the hospital staff who sneaked in to sample the lavish refreshments that were in place in the back of the auditorium. Folley waited for a half-hour after the announced start time and then, acting on the advice of his appointed press agent, conducted the event for the benefit of the lone reporter. The reporter watched Folley go through his antics and then left after picking through the refreshments. Durant said nothing. He sat to the side with a boyish grin. After an hour of the failed press conference, Folley called the event over. Durant went home.

Mitch Daly was right. It took six months for anyone to remember that he was around. As expected, Weaver brought the matter of executive expense to the attention of Folley who then directed Anderson to arrange for a severance deal for Daly. What Daly was offered was out placement service and three months' salary and benefits. Daly took the deal and used his own funds to establish a consulting firm specializing in hospital re-engineering. He found several clients among Catholic hospitals in the Boston Catholic Archdiocese.

The Catholic Health Services Network for the Boston Catholic Archdiocese gained momentum over the same period. It was given extensive press as Hospitals throughout the Boston area pointed to the Network as an also ran in the Boston area hospitals' frantic race to seek affiliations with the emerging health conglomerates. The Cardinal, at Doctor Folley's request, admonished Catholic hospitals for being reserved in joining the Archdiocesan network. Eventually, several did join after Folley agreed to absorb their debt and cover the renovation expense. With the institutions beginning to fall into line, Folley began to concentrate on bringing the physicians into the network Dr. Anderson proved to be invaluable in this process. His steady reassuring manner convinced many that the Network was a sensible organization that allowed the physician to best control his or her destiny.

Backing Anderson was the tireless effort of the Park Medical Consulting firm with Tom Callahan in the lead. Callahan met personally with every physician who joined the Network and the Medical Services Organization. He adjusted their office practices and established arrangements with major payers in order to stabilize the physician's market and revenue.

The negative feature of the Catholic Health Services Network was that it reported a seven percent operating deficit for the first six months with negative cash flow. Hospital funds reserved for equipment replacement were being committed to cover the cash shortfall. Rod Weaver explained that the financial problem was caused by initial organization expense. Eventually the Network, according to Weaver, was projected to break even.

Proprietary national health services conglomerates saw the prospect of market share and positioned for the takeover. NAI courted their interest and waited. Park Medical Consulting was doing very well by comparison. It was generating revenues through consulting contracts with hospitals, physicians, Independent Practice Associations, Physician Hospital Organizations, and the Medical Service Organization of the Catholic Health Services Network. The standard contract with each client was predicated on three percent of the client's gross revenues.

Additionally, Park Medical Consulting had a special arrangement with Park/Bay Area Health Maintenance Organization in which it directed the marketing of its products and its acquisition of other health benefit and service organizations. Several of the acquisitions were hospitals that competed with the institutions in the Catholic Health Services Network but Park Medical saw that not as a conflict but as the opportunity to monopolize the market place. The rapid success of Park/Bay Area caught the attention of the national press following stories in the *Boston Business Journal.*

USA Today carried a front-page feature story about the company that featured Joseph Bauman. Bauman was pictured standing in front of the HMO's headquarters clutching a briefcase. He was quoted as saying that every hospital would soon be in a proprietary conglomerate and every professional provider would be employed in corporate medicine. According to Bauman, the ex-cop, ex-hospital administrator, and new expert on healthcare reform, health service was the new hot item on Wall Street. "Health services was now managed to provide the maximum value per share," exclaimed the expert health executive and wealthy Joseph Bauman.

The Wall Street Journal did a few inside stories and eventually had to give Bauman some space on page one. They agreed with his predictions. Callahan enjoyed maneuvering Bauman into the spotlight. The clumsy ex-cop did what he was told and made an almost acceptable presentation.

Folley was far less predictable and was constantly pushing for more public exposure. Callahan arranged for the Great one to be given a feature about his Christian nature and charitable attitude which supported the Healing Ministry thing. Callahan wanted desperately to keep the Cardinal comfortable until the whole transition could be completed. Otherwise, Folley was stroked but kept out of sight as much as possible.

Big Frank and Charlie Patello met routinely with Callahan and listened to his reports. Within the first six months, Park Medical Consulting, on the point for Target Boston Medical, had acquired access to fifteen percent of the gross dollars paid by the purchasers of health insurance to the Health

Maintenance Organization, ten percent of the gross paid by the HMO to the physicians and the hospitals, and now was beginning to extract another twenty percent of the expenses for support services within the institutions through the implementation of the contracts by Universal Services. As planned, the money was coming off the top of the health dollar. Frank and Charlie were very pleased.

The Narcotic Division of the Boston Police Department reported record arrests of drug dealers in Dorchester over the six-month period following the arrest of Mr. Wells who now rested comfortably under special protection in a country club prison. The Captain of the Narcotic Division was pictured in the press and on television each time a bust was made. His popularity was considered comparable to the Mayor who also appeared frequently on the scene when a raid took place.

Officer O'Sullivan was never pictured and his name was never mentioned in any of the media reports. O'Sullivan, although given credit for making the initial arrest that triggered the crack-down, was confined to desk duty as he sweat it out in a drug rehabilitation program selected by him after his introduction to Father Markley.

Markley, through Jay's efforts, became a friend of O'Sullivan and convinced him that he belonged in rehab. O'Sullivan then sought the help of the Assistance Program offered by the Fraternal Order of Police who also assisted him in reporting his problem to the proper authorities. O'Sullivan made excellent progress.

Cecile O'Sullivan was determined to help her husband through his rehabilitation. Their marriage of convenience had evolved into a relationship of true friendship and love. It was nevertheless surprising to both of them when Cecile became pregnant. Again, a difficult pregnancy was forecast and a baby girl was expected. Cecile cut back on her hours at St. Anslem's. Her time at home contributed to the family atmosphere that Kristie enjoyed. Kristie was overjoyed at the prospect of a baby sister to complement her two brothers that she shared with her Father and Susan, who she also liked very much. Kristie sensed the peace that now existed between her mother and her father just as she had sensed the hate that prevailed in the past. Even though they lived apart, had different families, and continued to compete for her affection she had their individual love. She had the best of both worlds. Kristie was content with her young life.

Jay was also content with his life although he continued to seek diversions from the self-inflicted pressures of the routine. He managed to become a popular figure at St. Anslem's and was constantly representing the state of the working class to the new management that shifted in under Doctor Folley's command. Folley saw that Jay, the Universal Services contract manager at St. Anslem's, had diplomatic privilege since he seemed to be in favor with the Cardinal. As a consequence, supervisors throughout St. Anslem's would use Jay as a sounding Board for their problems.

Jay enjoyed the popularity but disliked the responsibility of having to solve every problem. He looked forward to Friday, his second-favorite day, and the warm spring weather when he and Brian would set out on their fishing trip. On Saturday Jay would work in the yard and play with the kids while Susan prepared the fine food that would be served at the fish fry Saturday night and again on Sunday when they would visit Father Markley and help with the Substance Abuse Encounter Sessions (SAES) that were held Sunday evening in the basement of St. Francis by the Sea Church. Susan participated in the program but had a long way to go. Brian and Louise occasionally extended the Saturday night session to Sunday evening at St. Francis by the Sea.

Pepsi Cola was not Brian's favorite drink by far but he was very contented driving a route truck and delivering the beverage for the enjoyment of others. The money wasn't bad either. Somehow, he had managed to buy an antiquated eighteen foot Rinker runabout boat complete with a hundred and twenty-five horsepower outboard motor and trailer. Jay put up three hundred dollars for equipment that included a used VHF radio that worked. They named it "Sailor's Return." Every Friday evening, weather permitting, they launched at the Hingham Town boat ramp to fish the Bay until early Saturday morning. It was a perfect diversion but loaded with temptation that occasionally bested Jay. Brian served as his guardian angel and steered him to Markley for repair.

Father Markley needed a little direction himself from time to time. The good Priest had a tough time adjusting to the pressure of Parish life and the all too frequent dictates of the Chancery. He bolted on a few occasions but each time had the presence of mind to call his buddy, Jay, who got him home and cleaned up before the good people of the Parish discovered that their

Pastor was on a bender. The Cardinal was not as easily fooled. On one occasion, he was waiting when Jay brought Markley home. They both received a strong lecture and a blessing. Then the Cardinal gave Jay a special telephone number to call if he ever needed assistance with Markley in the future. Cardinal McMahon, Father Markley, Doctor Anderson, and Jay eventually became a team ministry of its own.

Those critical of leadership often find after their own ascension to responsibility a shocking revelation of the hard facts that dictate hard decisions. Sister Celest had often damned her religious leaders for their apparent inaction in responding to the needs of the poor. That was her reason for specifying that the Poor Sisters of Charity maintain The Little Portion Mission as a condition for her acceptance as the new religious leader. She was given that promise.

The acceptance of The Little Portion by the Poor Sisters of Charity was only half the battle. The first time that Sister Celest attended a Board meeting of the Health Services Network of the Boston Catholic Archdiocese, she introduced a formal resolution from the Sisters that requested the Network provide on-going financial support to The Little Portion. Sister Celest read the resolution and then made the motion that it be accepted. Dr. Folley was red with anger and then white with fear.

Bishop Hanks unexpectedly came to Folley's rescue by suggesting that The Little Portion should be placed under the guidance of Catholic Charities that was being very well supported by the NET foundation. Folley took the opportunity to follow the Bishop's lead by declaring the motion dead for the lack of a second.

Sister Celest was faced with the reality that The Little Portion was destined to close or face a worse fate as part of the bureaucratic Archdiocesan male-dominated Catholic Charities. She decided to protest as she had done many times before in her religious life. Using the authority of her position as religious leader of the Poor Sisters of Charity, she organized the few Sisters who were in reasonable good health. Early on a Monday morning they marched through St. Anslem's lobby and into the Chapel. When the Sisters were comfortable in their pews, Sister Celest sent an E-Mail message on the hospital's net from the computer in the Chaplain's office to Dr. Folley's office announcing that the Poor Sisters of Charity had taken over the Chapel in protest of his administration until he either resigned or provided fiscal support for The Little Portion.

Folley tried to enlist Bishop Hanks as a mediator but the good Bishop was not interested in getting into the fray. He had just received notice that he was to be the next Bishop of the Diocese of Springfield in Illinois. The transition to his new assignment took all of his time. He politely bucked the problem to Cardinal McMahon where it belonged. Cardinal McMahon persuaded his friend, Jay Marquart, to convince the Sisters that communication was important in order to solve the matter.

Jay brought a cellular telephone to Sister Celest. He also set up a deal to provide the Sisters with food and drink while they maintained their control of the Chapel. The telephone conversation with the Cardinal didn't cut it and late that afternoon the Cardinal found himself outside the locked Chapel door pleading with the resolute Sister Celest. Sister accepted the Cardinal's position that the Sisters' conduct was disrespectful to the Blessed Sacrament on the Chapel Alter. The siege was broken and the Cardinal agreed to the demands of the Sisters. Celest had won.

The media had a field day with the event and its outcome. Off camera, however, the Cardinal gave Sister Celest a very strong denunciation with a requirement that she resign as the Sisters' religious leader and return to the House of Prayer. Celest considered the outcome a victory and retired with a smile on her face.

Dr. Folley was unaware of the pound of flesh that the Cardinal had extracted from Sister Celest for her canonical misbehavior. The Great One thought that he had won the fight strictly on his strong perseverance. Consequently, the support for The Little Portion was not authorized by his office. Jay Marquart, on the other hand, had been informed about the settlement by Sister Celest. Consequently, Marquart used his own initiative to supply The Little Portion from hospital stores as he had done in the past.

In spite of all the effort by the Sisters and Marquart, the final blow bringing about the demise of The Little Portion came when a Special Commission on Services to the Poor appointed by Mayor Siro and chaired by Michael Logan, Director of the NET Foundation, recommended consolidation and merger of the many Charitable not for profit agencies located on Melina Cass Boulevard. The NET Foundation agreed to provide support for the consolidation of the agencies into no more than four Neighborhood Health Centers to be strategically located along the Boulevard. The Little Portion was to be absorbed.

Ironically, a politician did what Sister Celest thought a politician would never do. Mayor Siro ordered The Little Portion to merge with another mission or lose its license to operate. The Sisters opted to close rather than dilute the special qualities of The Little Portion.

Joe Durant kept in close contact with Sister Celest after he retired. He met with her frequently at the Motherhouse and discussed St. Anslem's, Doctor Folley, the Archdiocesan Health Services Network and tons of gossip about the players. Then in April he managed to sell his house and buy a retirement home on Hilton Head Island in South Carolina. He and his wife moved their possessions to their new home and a week later Joe returned to the Hingham Marina where he boarded his beloved Jubilee and pointed her South toward Hilton Head. Ten days later he arrived at the Island having been delayed en route three times by the Coast Guard who, for some reason that he could not understand, searched his boat for contraband. Joe was convinced that the War on Drugs was being taken to measures beyond reason. A few years later, reflecting on his tenure at St. Anslem's, he wrote a book but classified it as fiction since the whole experience was unbeliveable.

The Political Action Committee of the NET Foundation was very pleased with its current position. They sent a report to Charles Patello describing how the Executive Branch of the City of Boston was positively controlled by Mayor Siro who was beholding to the Foundation. In addition, the Legislative Branch of the City Government, represented by the City Council, had the majority of the members elected by NET support. The Judicial Branch was waiting for the NET. Appended to the report was a long list of local attorneys wanting to become judges and known to be supportive of the NET issues. Patello scanned the list looking for familiar names. His eye caught the name of Martha Marquart. He circled the name and continued to look through the list.

When he finished he went back over it again this time stopping to reflect on Marquart. He remembered young Jay who helped him with the Party business as a courier and how that same person kept reappearing at Action Waste

Management and then at St. Anslem's. Jay Marquart had always been supportive without being compromised. He seemed to be loyal.

Patello wondered if the attorney on the list was related to Jay. He decided to find out. On a whim, he picked up the phone and dialed St. Anslem's where he knew Jay was working. The telephone was answered on the first ring. A pleasant female voice gave a recorded greeting and message.

"Thank you for calling St. Anslem's Medical Services Center, an agency of the Health Services Network of the Boston Catholic Archdiocese and an affiliate of the Park/Bay Area Medical Conglomerate, Our President is Richard Folley, M.D. We are available seven days a week, twenty-four hours a day to serve your every medical need in a personalized cost-efficient environment. Please be aware that your call is being recorded for possible training purposes. If you know your party's extension and are calling from a touch tone telephone, enter it now. If this is an emergency, press one and a registrar in the Emergency Services Center will answer. If you wish to speak to the Department of Medicine, press two. If you wish to speak to the Department of Surgery, press three. If you wish to speak to the Department of Psychiatry, press four. If you wish to speak to the Department of Obstetrics press five. If you wish to speak to the Department of Pediatrics, press six. If you wish to speak to the Department of Anesthesiology, press seven. If you are unsure of your health problem press zero and the operator will help you with your diagnosis. Otherwise, remain on the line and your call will be answered in the order in which it was received."

Prognosis

Over the next year St. Anslem's continued to struggle financially. Deficits were mounting as the year progressed. Dr. Folley, as suspected, had no ability to coordinate the hospital's administration. Capital requirements were ignored. Supply distribution was inconsistent. Employee recruitment and retention were nonexistent. Middle and first line management had little or no direction. Folley was oblivious to the operational confusion. He languished in his elevated status as the Director of Health Services for the Archdiocese. His self-established salary of $2,000,000 a year was the highest paid health administrator in Boston and certainly the highest paid member ever on the Cardinal's staff. This soon became an item of interest in the *Boston Globe* and the Catholic population.

Cardinal McMahon and the Church were scandalized by the St. Anslem situation. He sought the counsel of his good friend, Father Markley, to remedy the situation. Father Markley offered that the healing ministry was far more than just a tertiary care hospital. He suggested that the solution was to discontinue the sponsorship of St. Anslem's Hospital and reorganize the health ministry of the Archdiocese to meet the needs of all people of God. The Cardinal accepted Father Markley's suggestion and appointed him Health Ministry Coordinator for the Archdiocese in addition to Father Markley's assignment as Pastor of St. Francis by the Sea Parish.

At Father Markley's request, Cardinal McMahon met with Charles Patello, CEO of New England Trust, who was considered the leading financial expert in Boston and a highly respected friend of the Church. The Cardinal asked Patello if he could help arrange the sale of St. Anslem's Hospital.

Patello said he "knew a guy" who might be interested. Within a matter of a few weeks St. Anslem's was purchased by Bay Area HMO. The hospital was reclassified as a proprietary institution. Boston Medical was in full swing. Frank Patello was elated

Father Markley met with Dr. Folley and informed him of the changes taking place. The Archdiocese Office of Health Services was dissolved and Dr. Folley was no longer on the Cardinal's cabinet. Rod Weaver, in his professional capacity as a Certified Public Accountant (CPA) assisted the Archdiocese with the financial procedures of selling St. Anslem's to Bay Area HMO. Following the sale he was retained by the Archdiocese as an accountant.

Frank Bauman, CEO of Bay Area HMO and famous for the original St. Anslem's Chapel door incident, informed Dr. Folley that he was no longer in charge of St. Anslem's and his salary of $2,000,000 a year was discontinued.

Dr. Folley resigned as a member of the St. Anslem's medical staff and as a consequence of his considerable donations to his medical school alma mater was given an emeritus professorship position. He gained international acclaim for his publication on Medical Ego-nomics.

The Archdiocesan Health Ministry was reformed to provide care to all people of God in need. Services included home nursing, counseling, alcohol and drug rehabilitation, hospice care, pregnancy services, and many others. The Poor Sisters of Charity were also involved. They remodeled their Motherhouse, with the aid of the Archdiocese, to become an assisted nursing facility. Lay women were also invited to become associates of the religious Order and assist in their ministries.

Brian remained a route vendor for Pepsi Cola. He was very good at it. He perfected his boating and fishing skills that enhanced his trips with Jay on weekends.

Jay Marquart became project manager for Universal Services that succeeded Action Waste Management. This new position involved Jay with Universal Services' many customers in all aspects of institutional management. He was successful and very well accepted. He also maintained a close relationship with Father Markley but came up short of joining the Church in respect for his loving wife who felt that "they would not be welcome there." Instead Jay, while sitting on the bow of Brian's boat late at night, would look up at the sky and give praise with gratitude to God for the wonderful gifts of life that he had been given.